WHAT'S DONE IN THE DARK

ALWAYS COMES TO LIGHT

THE ORIGIN PROPHECY
THE COMPLETE TRILOGY

SHIRE-HILL PUBLICATIONS
UNITED KINGDOM

ISBN: 978-1-914483-26-4

THE ORIGIN PROPHECY

THE COMPLETE TRILOGY

M.A. PHIPPS

REBECCA JAYCOX

SHIRE-HILL
PUBLICATIONS

LIGHT ACADEMIES

ᚷᚢᚦᚨᚱᚲᚠᚾᚷᛚᛗᛈᛉᛊᛏ

The Serapeum
EGYPT
Gabriel

Mount Nebo
JORDAN
Remiel

Petra
JORDAN
Serathiel

Mount Sinai
EGYPT
Raphael

Sidon
LEBANON
Amenadiel

Mount Zion
ISRAEL
Uriel

Qumran
ISRAEL
Azrael

DARK ACADEMIES

Megiddo
ISRAEL
Lucifer

The Tower of Babel
IRAQ
Asmodeus

Sodom
ISRAEL
Leviathan

Gomorrah
ISRAEL
Belphegor

Ashkelon
ISRAEL
Beelzebub

Tyre
LEBANON
Mammon

Machaerus
JORDAN
Abaddon

LIGHTFALL

BOOK ONE

"Abashed the Devil stood, and felt how awful goodness is,
and saw Virtue in her shape how lovely; saw, and pined his loss."

JOHN MILTON. PARADISE LOST

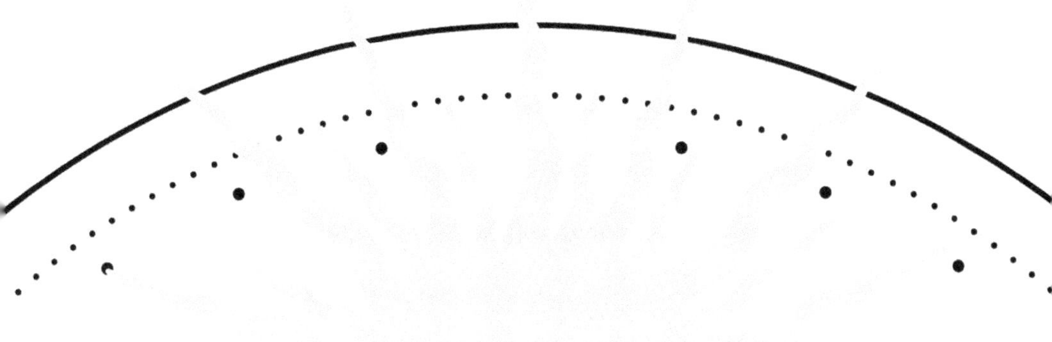

PROLOGUE

THE WORLD BELOW BURNED. Gabriel perched on the mountain peak like a giant bird of prey, wings folded into her body, her long, black hair snapping in the strong breeze like a flag. She watched the flames wind like rivers of fire through the fragile land. Humans scurried like ants, running from the blaze and the angels battling across the landscape, destroying everything in their path. The earth shook with the force of their rage. How had it come to this?

They were supposed to be brothers and sisters in arms, loyal to one another, and above all to the Creator. Now, they tore into each other like primitive beasts, grooving out lines of destruction in the ground. The newly made humans they were supposed to protect and shepherd were reduced to mere casualties of angelic rage.

Heat built behind her eyes and she blinked, furious. Gabriel couldn't remember tears before humans, before all these conflicting emotions inside her. Before her lover had decided to wage war on the heavens and his fellow angels—all in the name of free will. Her chest heaved as she regarded the chaos below her. If this was free will, the price was too high.

Tensing, Gabriel prepared to leap off and join the fray when a shadow hovered over her. Whipping her head up, she watched as her lover glided overhead, great ivory wings flapping before landing beside her.

The Morningstar. One of the most beautiful angels in Heaven. He turned to her, hair the color of antique gold, eyes the deep blue of the sea rimmed in citrine. His gaze was hungry when it roamed over her face, and she desperately wanted to touch him as she never should have. As if sensing her need, he fisted her long hair, the motion lightning fast, and kissed her. Despite the violence raging around them, despite the pain in her heart, she kissed him back, opening her lips and letting him inside.

He was Gabriel's forbidden fruit, her slippery slide into the seductive world of emotion. Her lust and want and need all wore his name. And her love. Her love for him rivaled her love for the Creator, and she couldn't allow that. Free will was a beautiful dream, an idea that *seemed* to be good and right. But who were they to disobey the Creator? They had a higher allegiance and purpose than indulging here on Earth. Her indulgence in Lucifer had helped lead to this. The death of humans who were so young and just finding their footing in this new world.

But despite knowing what must be done, she clung to him, memorizing his taste and scent, knowing this would be the last time she'd have him like this. She either had to convince him to stop this madness, or leave him forever and join her fellow angels in squashing the rebellion. Gabriel tore her mouth away, gasping. Leaning her forehead against his, she steeled herself for what she must say, what she must do.

Lucifer tipped her chin up, and she wanted to drown in the blue of his eyes, give in to his temptation and never leave him. But she couldn't—she wouldn't. She beseeched the Creator that she could find the strength to change one of His favorite children's minds.

Lucifer stood, taking her with him, balancing on the icy rock of the mountain. "Look, my love, soon we will be free. Soon, we will make our *own* choices. I will never have to be ashamed again for loving you, for wanting you. For being envious of them and what they are allowed to have that we are not." He flung his arm out in a sweeping motion, and Gabriel regarded the war scarring the land below.

She grasped his hand and brought it to her lips, only then allowing a single tear to escape. He tracked that tear, like a predator honing in on prey. He met her eyes, his expression confused, with a smudge of suspicion forming. Swallowing hard, Gabriel tried to find the words to tell him his dream was impossible, to make him understand they had a higher purpose—no matter how much she loved him. No matter how her heart was rent asunder.

"I love you," she told him, another tear falling. "I love you more than I should, more than *anything*." The confession weighed heavily upon her. Despite her tears, Lucifer relaxed at her words, only to tense again as she said, "And I… I've come to realize how dangerous that is. Don't you see? Look at what we've done." She tasted the ash on the wind and her heart ached.

Lucifer jerked away from her as if she'd struck him. "What have we done, exactly? Love each other? Want more from life than blind obedience and servitude?" he growled.

"We haven't just loved each other, have we? We created a rift in Heaven. I regret my...selfishness," Gabriel said, ashamed she helped cause so much suffering.

"Selfishness? Is that what love is to you? Nothing more than a whim you indulged in?" Fury rode his voice and colored his cheekbones ruddy. "Do you regret me? *Us*?"

His words crushed her. "No, no, I love you. I could never regret you. I regret the destruction we've caused, the death. We've turned on each other—angels fighting angels! We're hurting each other and killing them." Gabriel pointed to the terrified humans, made clear by her raptor vision.

"Them." His voice held quiet venom. "The Creator's new favorites, unbound by blind obedience. Given a choice, while we—superior beings—are slaves to duty, not allowed to love another, to experience the delights of this world. How is that fair or just?"

Gabriel pushed past her pain, reaching for him, but he dodged her hand. "We *are* superior beings," she said, desperate for him to see. "That means we have a higher purpose and calling. We are their protectors, this world's protectors. We owe our allegiance and obedience to the Creator. We owe Him our love, not our betrayal."

The Morningstar sneered at her, eyes filled with hurt and hatred, and her breath stuttered in her chest. "Yes, I know all about betrayal, my love. And it cuts deep."

"Lucifer, please," she begged. "Please understand, I don't want to hurt you—"

"But you are. You are choosing the Creator over me."

Gabriel winced. "No, I'm choosing a higher purpose. We—"

"We deserve to make our own choices. And if you choose to betray me, then that means we're enemies."

She felt like he'd taken his golden sword and skewered her. "No, we don't have to be enemies. It doesn't have to be this way, please—"

Lucifer's voice was like ice. "You've made your choice. You've chosen to break me." With one final look at her, he dove off the mountain toward the battle below.

Gabriel clutched her middle, pain lancing through her. Pain and regret and horror at what she'd done to him. For a precious few moments, she allowed herself to mourn their love. Then straightening, she shoved all that emotion down and somehow found her calm center. Her sword sang as she freed it from her scabbard and leaped off the cliff.

LUNA

*S*CREAMS FLOOD THE CRAMPED *room, growing alongside the flames, the writhing tentacles of fire thrashing in every direction, devouring the creaky metal bed frames and mattresses—reaching out to punish everyone present but me. I know in my heart the fire is my friend. It protects me when everything else wants to hurt me.*

It saves me even when the screams make me cry.

My eyelids jerk apart as I'm jolted awake by the jarring impact of the plane landing. The tires skid against the runway, the hissing of rubber on tarmac uncomfortably loud in my just-woken—and still drowsy—state, the remnants of my nightmare fading like the dying tings of an echo.

Weird, I don't remember falling asleep.

As the plane slows to a stop and the engines cut off, the overhead speakers crackle to life. A male voice makes an announcement in Arabic, followed by what I presume to be the same message in English. *"Ladies and gentlemen, welcome to Borg El Arab International Airport. The local time is 9:40 a.m. and the temperature is 28°C. For your safety and comfort, please remain seated…"*

I yawn a few times until my ears pop, releasing the pressure building up in my head. As the pilot's voice drones on through the cabin, I turn my gaze to the small window beside me. A hazy blue sky and stretch of sand patched with weeds await on the other side of the thick glass, offering a first glimpse at my new home.

Alexandria.

I press my fingertips to the warm glass. Despite the strange sense of calm overwhelming my body, I'm not entirely sure how I got here. I didn't even own a passport before yesterday, and the events of the last thirty or so hours are reeling through my head in a muddled fog surrounded by half-answered questions. Questions, which are strangely lacking in fear. All I know is that less than two days ago, I was in a psychiatric ward in central Maine, isolated with no hope of ever seeing beyond the blank gray walls of my cage. Dorothy in my own eternal Kansas.

But now…

My eyes snap to the tall, brunette man a few inches to my left, in the next seat over. He's handsome and on the younger side—no older than mid-twenties if I had to guess—and while he's familiar, I can't recall his name, only that he's my guardian on this trip, which should alarm me but, for some reason, doesn't. I *want* it to bother me. For all I know, he's abducted me and no one knows where I am. Something tells me that isn't the case, but still, why don't I feel afraid? Or more anxious about my first time on a plane? And why can't I bring myself to ask the questions anyone else would in my position? It's as if there's a fog pressing down on my mind, preventing that part of my brain from working.

Sensing my lingering stare, he looks over at me. His amber eyes seem to glow as he speaks.

"How did you sleep?" he asks in a lilting voice as a gentle smile curves the line of his lips. I can't pinpoint where his accent is from. He's definitely not American. If anything, his way of speaking is a strange amalgamation of several different accents, confusing me nearly as much as how I wound up in Egypt. And why.

"F-Fine," I choke out, my answer garbled from the grainy texture coating my tongue from the dry plane air. I must've been sleeping with my mouth open. Clearing my throat, I try again. "Fine."

"Good." His smile deepens as he drags the brown leather briefcase on the floor by his feet up onto his lap. As he opens it and gathers our travel documents, I search his sharp, angular face for answers regarding the muddled hours of the last two days. My efforts cease mid-thought when his fair complexion shimmers with something otherworldly, a halo of golden tendrils slithering across the surface of his skin like thousands of small whips of light.

As my eyes widen, taking in his inexplicable glow, the memory of his deep voice stirs in my ears, drawing forth a flicker of a past conversation between us. I was in that cramped, empty room at the hospital, curled up in a trembling ball on the icy floor, and he was crouched in front of me, speaking in gentle whispers.

"Luna, do you know why I'm here? I'm taking you away from this place."

His hand grazed my shoulder then, but I didn't jerk away from his touch—not like

I have with every other person who has tried to get close to me since the incidents began. I wasn't sure what, but there was something about him—something that set him apart from the other doctors who had long since cast me off as a lost cause unworthy of their time or attention. A patient incapable of being helped. That something made me want to trust him.

When I asked him why he wanted to help me, he answered with only three words. *"Because you're special."*

Special. That word rings again in my head, although I still don't know what he meant by it. If by special, he meant completely deranged, then sure. I'm definitely special, all right.

The light indicating for everyone to keep their seat belts fastened abruptly shuts off with a resounding ding, and in a flurry of movement, the passengers on the plane all climb to their feet, preparing to disembark. My chaperone follows suit, yanking the faded blue backpack full of my few meager belongings from the overhead storage compartment.

"Ready?" He gestures behind him, holding out his arm in the unoccupied space in the narrow aisle to keep it open for me.

Despite the questions beating against the wall of my skull, I nod and reach out to take my bag from his hand, although I'm not sure I'm ready at all. Every moment since I left the hospital has been like some sort of bizarre dream that I'm sleepwalking my way through, only half aware of what's happening. I can't even remember stepping foot on this plane. Maybe I was drugged. It wouldn't be the first time pharmaceuticals were shoved down my throat in the hope of suppressing whatever inner demons make me do the terrible things that I've done. By now, I'm used to feeling nothing, and that's probably for the best. Every time I start feeling, I only end up having to face what I am.

Dangerous.

If I weren't, I wouldn't have been isolated in a padded room for the past year. Last I heard, the doctors hadn't made any significant breakthroughs regarding my unhinged mental state, so why was I discharged from the ward? And why can't I clearly remember agreeing to leave with this man or bring myself to question him about where he's taking me?

How can I be ready when I don't know where I'm going?

A strange wave of calm washes over me again, dulling my senses and easing my uncertainty and desire for answers, as well as pushing down the fear creeping to the surface like bile rising in my throat. Sedated, I silently trail the man off the plane, letting him guide my steps without question or hesitation like a dog on a leash. As we walk, my gaze drags across the shining white floors and seemingly endless walls of windows, glancing anywhere but at the people around me. I already know what I'll find on their faces. How normal they'll look, their eyes unburdened by guilt.

How I wish I could know what that feels like.

The corridors we progress through are muggy and hot, even with the air conditioners thrumming on full blast through the airport. When we finally reach the line for border control, the heat in the room becomes sweltering as dozens of bodies press in close on each side of us, encroaching on my much-needed personal space. Perspiration beads along my skin, sticking my hair to the back of my neck and drenching my T-shirt and jeans with sweat. God, what I wouldn't give for a shower.

My fingers fumble with the blonde locks that now feel like a heavy curtain draped across my back, bundling them on top of my head and holding them there as I let out a breath. As if reading my thoughts, my chaperone offers me a rubber band to tie my hair up.

At the hospital, we weren't allowed simple luxuries like hair elastics. Most of the residents had their hair shorn short to avoid them finding unique ways to use it as a weapon to harm themselves or others. My own golden tresses were left alone, thankfully, but I know that's only because none of the staff wanted to risk becoming my next victim by forcibly shaving my head.

What the doctors failed to understand is that I never *wanted* to hurt anyone. The incidents… They just sort of happened—like the madness was leaking out of my body and simply latched onto the first available target. I couldn't stop the demons from lashing out, no matter how hard I tried to keep them at bay.

The people who get close to me always suffer.

I fling my hair into a ponytail as the line inches forward one trudging step at a time. With every passing moment, my racing heart picks up speed until my pulse is throbbing in my veins like a physical presence trying to break out of my flesh. When I inhale, the dank air—filled with the chaotic hum of dozens of voices all speaking over each other in different languages—presses down on my lungs, suffocating my already irregular breaths and making me feel even more out of place.

Closing my eyes, I breathe in through my nose and out through my mouth like the counselor at the hospital taught me to do when things begin to get…overwhelming. I can't recall the last time I was around so many people or cooped up in such a crowded space, and the pandemonium of it all is too much to endure. An irrepressible desire to be outside in the fresh air tickles across my skin like an itch.

But then, that peculiar sense of calm courses through me again, and gradually my heart rate slows, and my breathing steadies to a normal pace. When my eyes flutter open, I'm surprised to find myself standing at the front of the line. Strange. I could've sworn we were much farther back. I peek up at the graceful form of the man beside me who grins when I meet his gaze, as if he somehow knows what I'm thinking.

My lips part to speak, but he grabs my arm and escorts me forward before I can utter a word. Clamping my mouth shut, I let him lead me toward the immigration officer beckoning for us to approach her.

The woman, an attractive middle-aged Egyptian wearing a burgundy hijab, holds out an expectant hand for our travel documents. The man offers them to her with an amiable smile.

She glances at my companion's passport first, and as she stamps it, I catch a brief glimpse of his name. Alaric Walsh.

That's right, I remember now. He introduced himself at the hospital.

Another recollection breaks free from the fog in my head.

"Are you a doctor?" I asked, looking him up and down with raised brows. He didn't seem like the other doctors who had all tried and failed to help me since I was committed.

"Yes," he answered in a soothing voice. "But more than that, I'm a friend. You don't belong here, Luna. These people don't understand you."

"There's a problem with these documents." The immigration officer's curt tone shakes my attention away from the memory. She looks at me, her expression stern. "I can see you have an entry visa, but without evidence of a return flight, I cannot admit you. There's also the matter of your Letter of Consent… As you are a minor traveling internationally with an adult who is of no relation to you, it needs to be signed by your legal guardian. This hospital release form is not recognized consent."

My heart drops into my stomach at the thought of what this setback could mean for me. I don't have a legal guardian who can permit me to travel. I'm a child of the state, and Dr. Walsh—*"Call me Alaric,"* I remember him saying now—was my one ticket to freedom from who knows how many more years in that padded room. If I can't enter Alexandria as he intended, does that mean I'll have to return to Maine or be admitted to some other psychiatric ward back in the States? And if I am allowed into Egypt as planned, what alternative awaits me here?

Which path should I be more afraid of?

Either way, I know one thing for certain. I would rather die than go back to a hospital, and if it comes down to the choice between freedom or captivity, I'll make a break for it. I'll run as far and as fast as I can to avoid wasting away in a cage.

"Please," Alaric urges, placing his hand on the smooth, gleaming surface of the black counter. The mischievous glint in his gaze unnerves me. "Could you check the documents again?"

Out of the corner of my eye, I notice his forefinger lift a few inches and hang there, suspended in the air, as if he's pointing at something. His smile, which I had assumed was a permanent fixture, has vanished, leaving his lips set in a serious line.

"That..." The immigration officer trails off, her dark brow furrowing in confusion. "That's odd," she continues after a pause. "I could've sworn it said—"

Alaric's finger drops back to the counter. "As you can see, our documents are in order."

"Y-Yes." The woman looks up at him with wide ocher eyes then directs her gaze back down to the bundle of documents laid out before her. In the space of a few seconds, her dubious expression melts into one of indifferent acceptance. "Of course," she mutters, stamping the pages. "Welcome to Egypt, Mr. Walsh. I hope you and your daughter have a pleasant stay."

I balk at her casual—and wildly incorrect—statement.

Daughter?

Alaric's careful smile returns as we slip away from the counter and continue past the luggage carousel, through customs, and finally toward the exit, following the overhead signs written in English and Arabic to sweet liberation from the stifling confines of the crowded building. The sliding doors swish open at our approach, welcoming us into the dry morning heat. Although there's no breeze, a faint salty aroma hangs in the air, indicating that we're close to the water.

Excitement buzzes through me. I've never seen the sea in person before.

The minutes pass by without either of us speaking as we stand at the taxi rank outside, waiting for the next available cab. Gradually—perhaps thanks to the fresh air in my lungs—that curious fog lifts off my brain. As it fades, freeing me of that invisible restraint, I blurt out, "Why did she suddenly think I'm your daughter?" My stomach twists at the thought of a family—the one thing I've never had the luxury of and can't imagine ever having. As much as I crave a father, this man is a stranger to me, so him feigning the part has me flustered, regardless of how kind he's been since we met. The mere notion of it doesn't make any sense either. Alaric doesn't look remotely old enough to be the parent of a seventeen-year-old—a fact the immigration officer should have noted.

A thousand other questions spiral through my head, but I'm too afraid to ask them. Asking questions never did anything good for me. Silence was always safest around doctors and social workers, even though they were meant to protect me.

"A simple mistake, I'm sure." His tone is innocent, but he keeps his eyes fixed ahead on the bright yellow horizon, avoiding my questioning gaze.

"I'm not buying that," I force out, despite my reservations. "She had two reasons for refusing to admit me, and one simple ask from you and she swung the gates of Egypt wide open."

Maybe Alaric does magic tricks as a hobby or side gig to make extra money. From what I've heard, illusionists are good at sleight of hand. Why else would the immigration officer let me through after stating my documents weren't in order unless she thought she read the provided information wrong? Which Alaric and I both know she didn't.

He considers me for a moment, averting his gaze when a battered black and yellow taxi approaches. As it rolls up beside us, he opens the back door and offers me a nonchalant shrug. "Let's just say I used my incredible powers of persuasion."

I climb into the taxi and sink into the seat with his cryptic answer swirling through my brain. Alaric slides into the backseat next to me, slamming the door shut behind him. "Serapeum, *min fadlik*," he instructs the driver.

The man in front of me, who smells strongly of tobacco and garlic, grunts and takes off at a breakneck speed that sends my stomach lurching.

Stewing in my own confusion and annoyance at Alaric's lack of a proper answer, I stare out the window, watching the city—a mesh of ancient and modern—whip past in a dizzying, sand-colored blur. Occasionally, I spot the Mediterranean Sea peeking back at me through the staggered gaps in the buildings, but it, too, flashes by before I can get a good look at the sparkling surface reflecting the sun. Disappointment rises in me, extinguishing what little excitement had managed to break through my shroud of doubt and unease. Nothing new there. My life has been a constant shift from one place to another like I'm nothing more than a piece on a chessboard—a pawn surrendered to an invisible enemy in a game I never asked to play. Why should my move here be any different? I've never had any say in what happens to me, which is why I don't waste my breath questioning these things anymore. Others will always dictate my fate.

But what fate does Alaric have planned for me? And why did he let that lady believe I'm his daughter?

I roll my teeth over my lower lip, considering the nagging thought biting at me like a mosquito in the heavy heat of the summers in New England. "Back at the hospital…you said they didn't understand me." Although I don't turn to look at Alaric, I can sense his perceptive eyes watching me.

"Few can."

"Because I'm crazy?" My voice catches on that word. I've always hated it. I hate how it's come to define who I am.

Warm fingers wrap around my shoulder, comforting me much like the same action did two days ago when we met—the bright-eyed doctor and the broken girl.

"You aren't crazy, Luna. You just don't know what you are."

What I am?

This question scratches at the seam of my lips, but I can't find the courage inside me to ask it. My voice wobbles when another thought pushes through in its place. A dangerous thought. A thought that terrifies me to my core. "Where are you taking me?"

"Someplace where you will be among others like you. Someplace where you will be safe."

Safe from what? From myself?

Nausea churns my stomach as I gauge the deeper meaning behind his statement. "So, another hospital," I realize with dread.

His soft voice fills my ears as his slender fingers squeeze my shoulder again. "No, not another hospital," he promises.

The cab comes to a screeching halt, throwing me forward. The seat belt locks, and I wince when the rough fabric strains against my chest, cutting into my neck. Beside me, Alaric's posture is poised and eerily still, as if the sudden stop hasn't had an effect on him.

"We're here," he says in a buoyant tone, offering me an encouraging smile.

My brows knit together as I glance between his bright, joyous expression and the mound of rubble waiting outside. The only elements still intact that I can see from the taxi are a statue of a sphinx and a random pillar, but even those don't provide any clues or context that would suggest this could possibly be our destination.

I wrinkle my nose. "These are ruins. There's nothing here."

With a low chuckle, Alaric pushes open the door. "Just because you can't see something doesn't mean it isn't there. Come on."

He slides out of the taxi, and I follow closely behind despite my hesitation, standing off to one side of the road as he pays the driver, who takes off in a burst of speed a moment later without a second glance back at us. When Alaric appears beside me, I narrow my eyes at him, trying to figure out what he's up to and whether or not I should be afraid. He laughs again at the disgruntled look on my face.

"Now..." He leans in until his mouth is right next to my ear. "Look closely. See beyond the ruins before you. Only then will you understand why we're here."

I cock an eyebrow, unsure what he means. "See beyond?"

See beyond it how?

"Just trust me," he murmurs, his tone pleading.

With a sigh, I relax my shoulders, relenting. Focusing, I skim my gaze across every rock and every broken stretch of wall. As I take it all in, the air in front of me ripples, warping like a mirage in the heat until the ruins before me vanish behind the distortion. In their place stands a magnificent cream and gold-colored building towering at least one hundred feet above me—a conglomerate of pillars, decorative arches, and domes, which cripple the surrounding landscape with their beauty.

I stumble back in awe and trip over a rock, the ground rushing upward to meet me. Alaric catches me with a hand on my arm before I land flat on my ass. "How did you do that?" I gasp.

Smirking, he sets me back on my feet before proceeding up the staircase where only moments ago there was nothing but sand. He pauses halfway up the steps to glance back at me. "I didn't unmask it. *You* did, Luna. You just had to want to see it."

"See what? What is this place?"

The amber eyes watching me flick upward toward the ornate doors at the top of the staircase. "A school. For special people like you."

There's that word again.

"Special how?" *What are you talking about?* I want to scream. *A school for what?* My hands ball into fists at my sides, my palms hot and slick with sweat. The one question I couldn't bring myself to ask before tumbles from my quivering lips in a whisper. "What am I?"

Alaric gives me a careful smile then turns, continuing his slow ascent up the stairs. As the doors at the top swing open at his arrival, his voice echoes down the slope of steps and burrows in my ears, touching the deepest depths of my soul, like a hand carefully shaking me awake from a dream.

Disbelief ignites in my gut like a flame as a single word sets my world on fire.

"Nephilim."

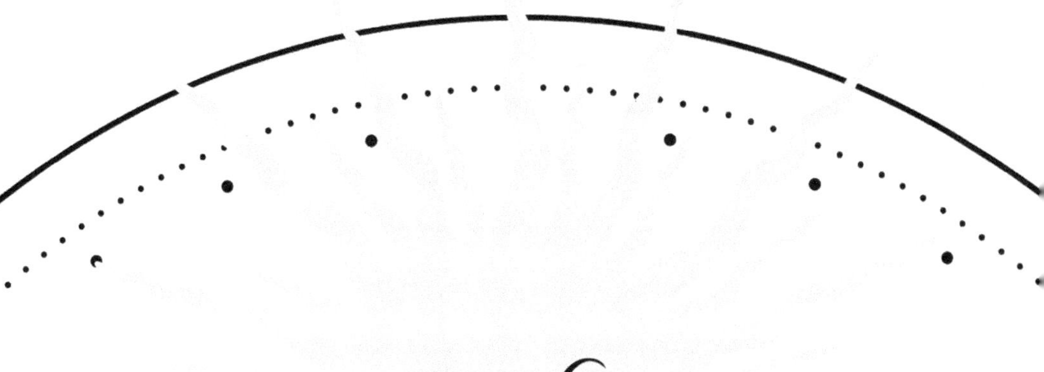

TWO

CALEB

THE CLEAN SCENT OF citrus trees in full bloom surrounds me as I stroll through the lush Hanging Gardens. I've always loved the Gardens. The jewel-bright colors both stimulate and soothe my senses. I wander here when I need a break from my friends or my latest hookup. Or when I've been surrounded by humans and their special brand of chaos and need to recharge.

The Tower of Babel looms over the scattered ruins. To the human eye, Babylon is nothing more than a rotting husk from an ancient civilization adjacent to Hilla, a small city never able to achieve the wonders of Babylonia. Archaeologists constructed a fake gate of Ishtar for tourists, even though the real gate stands next to it, flawless in its navy-blue beauty, although invisible to the mortal eye. Its alternating rows of bulls and dragons are etched with breathtaking detail. The one they display in a mortal museum is a well-crafted copy. I never grow tired of looking at the real one, this stunning ode to the goddess of love and war made by human hands.

Carefully concealed with angelic magic, the Tower has been preserved, perfect and untouched by time, along with other parts of the city. Like a handful of other ancient sites around the world, it houses one of the seven academies for Dark Nephilim, children of the Fallen bloodlines.

The midday sun floods the Gardens with heat, despite the pools of water nurturing the fruit trees. I step out of a puddle of shade into bright sunshine, my bronze skin absorbing the rays. With a lazy hand, I push back my black hair. It's grown a bit shaggy, but I find that women like to run their hands through it. And shit, I like it a little messy. What's the point of being a rebel if you don't enjoy looking the part?

A stunning woman captures my attention in a grove of trees to my left. She stretches her long-limbed figure to pluck a tangerine from a branch. Her white dress clings to dangerous curves. I stop, giving her a wary stare. Her presence here can't be a coincidence. Damn it.

Ishtar turns toward me, her scarlet lips curving into a slow smile that makes me want to step back. To mortal eyes, she appears as the epitome of seduction. But she hasn't earned her immortal reputation as a goddess of love and war by accident. She is the academy's professor of persuasion, teaching the Dark students how to wield their mental powers with precision and responsibility—although she does that last part begrudgingly. Even she has to follow the rules.

Raising my hand in a brief salute, I hope to pass her by. As a first generation Nephilim, Ishtar's power is strong. She's almost achieved immortality through her Fallen blood—almost. It may take another thousand years but she'll die. A fact I know that she resents. Hell, I resent it, too. My father was a second generation Nephilim and my mother human. Although my powers rival a second generation's, I'm a third. That means I'll live a long damn time, but I won't get forever. Despite all the power I possess, I'll eventually wither and die just like my mother.

"Darling Caleb," Ishtar calls to me, voice husky and sweet. I shiver at the sound and the way it kisses my skin. I hate that she can affect me, but she affects everyone, so I don't feel like too much of a chump. "I'll walk with you. I'm ready to return, anyway."

I pause, like the obedient student I am. Well, the Dark teachers don't encourage blind obedience, but they do demand respect. And only a fool disrespects Ishtar. I offer her a warm smile.

"It's always a delight to be in your company," I say as she draws up beside me.

She's chosen Babylonian-style attire today, the gauzy white fabric of her dress draped and folded around her lush figure, and held securely at one shoulder with a beaten gold pin, emphasizing the time period in which she flourished.

"Liar," she scolds, musical voice teasing as she slips her hand into the crook of my proffered arm. "I make you want to piss yourself."

I scowl. "No one but Lucifer could make me piss myself." Then I give her a genuine grin. "But you come pretty damn close."

A surprised laugh escapes her lips. "To compare me to the Morningstar is a compliment indeed." Her onyx eyes search mine, her brown skin gleaming in the strong sun. Her blue-black hair cascades down her back in gentle waves. "You've been to see your mother?"

I stiffen. Her question is innocent enough, but I know she disapproves. Not that

I give a shit. She may be a badass bitch, but even she doesn't get to interfere in my relationship with my mom.

"New York was fun," I reply, keeping my pace steady. "Mom's got a new job. And Queens is surprisingly cool. So many gorgeous ladies to play with." And play I did.

"Practice your mind tricks, did you?" Ishtar asks, amused.

"No, I don't need mind tricks to get laid. I'm a smokeshow. And like all the Darks, I believe in free will. Human or not, I'm not robbing anyone of theirs." My anger overrides my respect and cautious fear of the woman beside me for a moment.

Instead of the rebuke I expect, she pats my hand. "Spoken like a true Dark. I may hate the rules preventing me from showing the world how truly powerful I am, from keeping me from ruling over these lesser mortals, but to rob someone of their choice is to go against everything the Fallen stand for."

Not that we Darks aren't above manipulating human minds when we need to—like when mortals see something they shouldn't. And I know some feel it's fair game to mess with humans when it doesn't directly involve them. That's a fine line that will lead to punishment if you land on the wrong side, though. And punishment sucks. Yeah, I heal fast, but it still doesn't mean broken bones feel good. Or the lash of a whip.

And of course, it's always fun to play with the Lights. Stuck-up assholes.

I'm beginning to relax when Ishtar says, "When are you going to give up this unhealthy relationship with your mother?"

I bite my lip hard, straining not to resort to violence. I could get some good jabs in, make her bleed, but in the end, she'd break my spine to teach me a lesson. I glare at her. She's tall, but at a couple inches over six feet, I'm taller.

"Never," I say flatly. "I love her. She took care of me when my dad didn't give a shit. He was happy to play and then just ran off. I'm not going to abandon her." Mom knew exactly who she was raising, and instead of dumping me in the nearest orphanage because she couldn't handle it, she loved me. She prepared me. And when the Dark Nephilim came to take me to my primary academy, she let them. Not because she didn't care, but because she knew it was best for me.

"She'll die long before you. Don't you want to spare yourself pain?" Ishtar counters. "This attachment anchors you too strongly to the mortal world."

My laugh is bitter. "I'm part mortal and so are you." Her eyes cut into me and I flinch, but continue, "I'm anchored whether I like it or not."

She digs sharp nails into my arm and jerks my chin down to meet her eyes with her free hand. Her black eyes are fierce. "You're better than humans. Remember that. *We're* better."

"I *like* humans," I say and it's the truth. I love their messiness and their creativity. I even love their pain. They're like mayflies, trying to make the most of their short lives.

We resume walking and Ishtar snorts. "I like them, too, but they're not my equals. Never forget that you're superior to them, no matter how much they amuse you. Remember your bloodline."

"As if I could forget," I say, resentful. I never forget my bloodline.

Alexander the Great. My grandfather. He's also a first generation Dark Nephilim. After he tried to conquer the world, the Lights entombed him somewhere. Since he's like Ishtar, he would still be alive. But we brokered a truce with the Lights to avoid another war, and he's not coming back. That's what you get when you try to take over the world and go against the original agreement between the angels and the Fallen. Alexander had a good run, though, he almost made it. I wish I knew him. Maybe he wouldn't be a dick like my dad.

We walk past the stone lion tourists flock to. There are a couple of them out this morning, although with the political situation in Iraq, they're rare. Ishtar and I remain invisible to their eyes with a simple illusion that renders us as nothing more than part of the landscape. The lion stands tall and proud, and I trail my fingers over the smooth rock.

The Tower sprouts up ahead, shaped like a round, tiered cake built of fired brick that grows narrower as it reaches for the heavens. The masonry work is intricate, the carvings detailed. It's a stunning achievement, even if it is Nimrod's middle finger to the Creator. Nimrod might be a first generation Dark Nephilim, but he's also a bit of an asshole.

Ishtar speaks again, breaking our silence. "As you might already know, tensions are running high between us and our Light brethren."

I chuckle. "Aren't tensions always high between us and those goody-goody pricks?"

She arches an imperious brow. "This is different, Caleb. Some of us tire of hiding. We've chosen Earth as home, and we'd like to be completely free here."

I look at her, slightly alarmed. Yeah, total freedom sounds like a blast. To be able to show my powers and just walk around letting it all hang out, but I don't like the idea of humans getting hurt. My mom getting hurt. And if the Lights and Darks go to war, that's what will come out of it.

"What's happened?" I demand. I was only gone for two weeks. Did my entire world go to shit in that time?

Ishtar's smile is sly. "Nothing. Yet."

My unease grows as we climb stone steps worn smooth by thousands of years and thousands of pairs of feet.

"I hope you understand that I'd never condone harming humans," she says, and my brow raises. "They serve their purpose, and they are endlessly entertaining, but despite all their advancements, they're still like children. Greedy, only thinking of the now. Gold and war and destruction. Look at what they've done to their own lands?" She makes a sweeping gesture with an elegant hand.

Beyond our little oasis is a region torn by years of war and strife and terror. I can't argue with that, so I remain silent, waiting for her to get to the point. My gut churns.

She tosses her silky mane back, and I catch a whiff of honeysuckle. It's intoxicating like her, but she's too scary to ever let my mind wander down that path. She'd eat me for breakfast and pick her teeth with my bones.

And though you'd have to drive a spike in her eye to get her to admit it, I think Ishtar is still hung up on that Light jerk, Gilgamesh. I was accidentally in a room with them once, and the pheromones were flying so fast, even I wanted to smoke a cigarette.

"We were made to rule them," Ishtar continues, bringing me back to the here and now with a hard bump to my shoulder. "They need a firm hand to show them their folly. We could stop this foolish hiding, take our rightful place as lords of the Earth, and all prosper."

"That's a great dream, but the Lights won't ever agree to that. You're talking war. How do you plan to win without killing half the planet?" Shit, humans have no issue offing themselves now in conflicts. I can't imagine a global-wide slaughter. No matter how appealing freedom is.

Her smile turns triumphant. "Alexander the Great."

The enormous wood doors before us swing open of their own accord, spanning at least two-stories high, and the ringing voices and bustle of the academy spill out around us, but I might as well be deaf to it, my attention wholly focused on the goddess next to me.

I sneer. "Um, isn't he entombed somewhere, trapped, basically rotting away until death pays him a visit? I don't think he's going to win this one for us."

Rage shivers along the corners of her mouth, and it takes everything in me not to step back. Okay, so I might have been too much of a dick with that statement, but I get tired of bitter Darks talking about waging a war against the Lights. And yeah, if Alexander were around, he might succeed—he almost did before. But he's not.

Ishtar snarls, "Foolish child! Do you think you know everything? In your eighteen years, have you accumulated the wisdom I possess? Do you proclaim to know more than *me*?"

Each statement is like a slap I deserve. A few Nephilim exit the cavernous doorway, giving us a wide berth, as if they can smell the tension. I ignore them as does the furious woman staring me down, eyes like chipped stone. Without thinking, I move into a defensive stance, setting my feet wider apart. If she comes after me, I'll be ready.

I keep my voice calm as I say, "No, I don't claim to know shit, but I've been told my whole life that my grandfather is lost to us. *You've* told me that."

Her face shutters, the rage vanishes, and she shrugs. "I have the wisdom to admit I was wrong."

I startle, my own anger subsiding. "What do you mean you were wrong?"

Ishtar reaches for me again, slipping her warm hand back through the crook of my arm. We cross the threshold into the cool interior of the Tower. It's crowded here, the ground level housing classes for first-year students as well as the administration offices. The ancient architecture has received an update with some creature comforts and modern technology, but the ornate style is still stamped on everything.

Narrow, tall, arched windows allow sunlight to spill over the gray marble floor shot through with silver veins. Just like the rings of a tree, the first ring around the academy is a wide corridor with doors leading into the second ring, where classrooms are found, and the administration offices await in the third ring. The surface of the stone walls are painted a bright blue with mythical creatures marching in rows across its surface. Above the painted wall runs a stone relief, carved in meticulous detail, depicting the Fall and the war between the angels.

My brow arches as I wait for Ishtar to continue when she surprises me yet again. "The Lights have suggested an exchange program to help ease the tensions between our people and bridge a better understanding of each other."

My mind spins as I stare at her, confused. "What? An exchange program?"

Ishtar nods, a slow and satisfied grin curving her lips. "Yes, a Dark Nephilim will spend a year at a Light Nephilim school. We get to choose the school and the student, of course. And Asmodeus has already approved my selection."

A sinking feeling drags at the pit of my stomach. Although I already know the answer, I ask, "And who's the sucker you've chosen?"

Genuine mirth colors her laugh. "You do have a unique way of describing a wonderful opportunity, lovely boy."

"Getting treated like shit by a bunch of stuck-up Lights is an opportunity? Pass."

Her black gaze clashes with mine, and I still at the predatory gleam reflected there. "You'll not only embrace this opportunity, child, you'll thank me for it."

I scowl, both dreading and anticipating her answer. "Why?"

"Because I'm sending you to the academy at Alexandria, and guess who we've discovered is imprisoned deep within the bowels of the Serapeum?"

"Alexander," I breathe, stunned.

"Yes, and you're going to help us free him."

THREE

LUNA

Y EYES LOCK ON Alaric's back, his tall figure enveloped by that peculiar golden glow that seems to descend from the cloudless sky and wrap around his lithe body. As he steps through the doors, which hang open to welcome us, the answer he gave me vibrates through my head.

"Nephilim."

A few years before I was committed, I took a *History of Religion* class at a Catholic school I was enrolled in during a brief stint with a foster family in Boston. My guardians at the time thought force-feeding me Bible verses would help to suppress my inner demons, like some weird, new-age exorcism. Unlike with the other classes I had to take at that school—and at every other school I ever attended—everything the teacher told us resonated with me like I had heard it somewhere before, a distant memory I couldn't quite bring into focus. My teacher's lessons plunged me into a constant state of déjà vu, and yet I couldn't explain my fascination with the subject matter.

Especially any part about angels.

From what I remember, the Nephilim were the offspring of angels and humans and were viewed as an abomination by God. But rather than punish the angels for their deviancy, God chose to punish the humans by inflicting them with the worst penalty He could think of.

Mortality.

Or so the stories said. I never had cause to believe any of it was true...until now.

But do I believe it, even after what I've just seen? Maybe this is all a fantasy I've concocted, and the reality is that I'm still at the hospital, living out some grand delusion in my head from the confines of my padded cell. That's the only explanation that makes any sense.

Alaric disappears into the depths of the school, and the imposing doors remain open behind him, as if urging me to follow. The soles of my worn sneakers smack against the cream-colored stone as I race up the wide steps after him.

At the top of the stairs, my feet slow to a stop, and my eyes crawl over the towering entryway. The gilded doors, which stand several stories high, are decorated with protruding shapes depicting an image of angels engaging in battle. Carved clouds separate them into two groups—one above and the other below—and every angel wields a weapon as the world beneath them is consumed by an eddy of swirls my gut tells me is fire.

I glance at each of the angels in turn, but my attention is drawn to one face more than the others. The beauty of the Fallen angel emanates from the shimmering golden surface, and for a moment, I'm hypnotized by his gaze, which looks up at the heavens with rage and remorse. The pain driving his actions seems to leak from the metal, tempting my fingertips to touch his sculpted cheekbones. As my skin grazes the hard interpretation of his, there's a split second where I almost understand what he's feeling.

A gasp parts my lips as the echo of receding footsteps reaches for me through the still open doorway, dragging my thoughts back to my pursuit of Alaric. A long hallway with a high, vaulted ceiling stretches before me, and at the distant end, I spot him.

"Wait!" I yell out, sprinting over the threshold. My hurried steps resound off pristine white tiles cut through with streaks of gold that sparkle in the midday sun filtering in through the narrow stained glass windows lining the walls. The panes channel the light into starbursts of color on the floor. As I race forward, closing the distance between us, I catch glimpses of the statues situated on each side of the path. Seven made of white marble on my right, seven made of black on my left—facing one another across the wide path like opposing chess pieces. Fourteen in total. The statues are angels, some male, others female, but they're all vastly different in their portrayal, with such incredible detail I can't help wondering if they represent real people.

Not people. Angels, I correct myself. Assuming what Alaric has said about this place is true, and I haven't jumped off the metaphorical cliff into full-blown hallucinations.

Alaric glances back over his shoulder and smiles at me with a look that suggests he knew I wouldn't be able to resist following him. He waits patiently at the far end of the corridor, allowing me a chance to catch up.

Once I'm standing beside him, my natural tendency to not question anything in my life fades away. To hell with keeping quiet. None of this, from why I'm here to the mere existence of this place, makes any sense, once again forcing me to doubt if I'm not actually back in the hospital and all of this is just some figment of my imagination. I'm not sure which I'd prefer—the comforting but disappointing notion that I'm normal but crazy or the idea that there's something more to what I am. That, although my entire life might be a lie, there's also some answer as to why I've done the horrible things I've done.

"This is…all…some sort…of joke…right?" Every word escapes me in a pant as I bend over, my hands on my knees, out of breath. Spending a year in a psychiatric ward certainly hasn't done me any favors with fitness. "You don't…*really* think…I'm a—"

He shakes his head. "I *think* nothing, Luna. I *know*. Just like I knew from the second I saw you that you weren't disturbed like all those ignorant mortals believe."

"Mortals?" I straighten, arching a dubious brow at him as a choked laugh escapes me. "You say that like you aren't one."

An amused, crooked grin forms an endearing dimple in his left cheek. "Half actually. Like all our Nephilim brethren unless we want to get technical with percentages. Our life spans only differ depending on what generation we are. The more diluted the blood, the weaker the ancestral link, and the farther from immortality one is. Of course, anyone with angelic blood will still portray powers. It's merely the strength and lifespan that will differ."

I draw in a faltering breath then push it out through my nose. "Is this some kind of weird test to check my mental state or something? You're not making any sense."

"With time, everything will," he assures me with a chuckle. "Right now, you're in shock, and your body is coming down off the Calm. It's to be expected that this would all seem disorienting."

More like batshit crazy.

I'm debating whether Alaric is as off-his-rocker-bonkers as I am, but I keep those thoughts in check. Clearly, this guy believes what he's spewing.

"Calm?" I ask, wariness creeping into my voice.

Alaric averts his gaze and gestures toward a steepled wooden door behind his right shoulder. Beyond it lies a manicured courtyard filled with species of flowers I've never seen before in my life, in person or in any book. Petals of glimmering gold and silver surround us while others burn with the flaming color of fire. I take it all in as we walk side by side, staying under the cover of the encompassing cloister.

Several moments pass before Alaric breaks the silence. "When we landed in Alexandria, did you feel peculiar at all? As if you'd been asleep for a while and like everything was sort of hazy?"

I think back to when I woke up on the plane, remembering how fuzzy my memories of the previous two days were, and how everything felt like some sort of strange dream I was wading my way through, as if I was waist deep in muddy water. It wasn't the first time I'd experienced such a sensation given how medicated I was at the hospital, and yet, the apprehension that normally went hand in hand with the experience wasn't there this time. Despite the disorientation that muddled my head during the journey here, I wasn't afraid, even though the logical side of me kept insisting I should be. The worst I felt was a grating uncertainty.

"That's called Calm," he explains, clamping a hand on my shoulder. "It helps make the transition process to an academy less daunting for new students, especially those who've had no previous experience being around other Nephilim or were raised to believe they were human, like yourself. It takes away that initial fear. This is, after all, quite the revelation, and yet, it's not as surprising to you as it should be, is it?"

My mouth opens and closes again. He's...not wrong. If he had told me all of this back at the hospital, I probably would've thought he was as crazy as I am. But now, with that instinctual terror and doubt stripped away, I'm not finding what he's said as inconceivable as I should. Could it really be possible? Could I be a Nephilim? Or am I so desperate for an answer to explain why I am the way I am that I'll believe anything at this point?

I shake my head. Good intentions or not, I can't ignore the sting of betrayal I feel at his words. "So, you drugged me?"

Shrugging away from his touch, I stop walking and stare up at him, the accusation written all over my face. He's been kind, and because of that, I wanted to believe he was different. I *needed* to believe he wasn't like all the doctors who viewed shoving pills down my throat as the only cure for my condition...whatever the hell that is. I don't know anything for sure anymore.

"No," he murmurs, "but I understand why you'd think that. It's more like I used my powers of persuasion to alleviate any worries or anxieties you had."

It occurs to me this is the second time he's used that phrase: *"powers of persuasion."*

"Like how you made that woman at border control think I'm your daughter?" I knew he did something to convince the immigration officer to let us pass. I just didn't know what, or how exactly, he managed to do it.

He nods. "Just like that. I can make others see what I want them to see, and I can make them feel whatever I want them to feel. All Nephilim have their own special abilities. Those happen to be some of mine."

His words tumble through my thoughts as I consider the idea of what he's explaining to me. Every syllable presses against the walls of my brain, offering only one explanation I'm able to process.

"So…it *is* like magic." My suspicion that he dabbled in tricks of illusion wasn't too far off track after all.

Alaric chuckles. "Something like that. In time, you'll discover how it works for yourself."

He turns and carries on down the stone path, past rows of vibrantly colored flowers and manicured shrubbery. I watch him go, debating if I should follow. Wondering if I even have a choice in the matter.

Pausing at the turn ahead where the cobbled walkway veers off to the right, Alaric waves a hand in beckoning. "Come. There's someone here you should meet."

My chest swells with doubt, but behind it, I sense an overriding calm that I now know Alaric planted there for…what, exactly? To make me believe him? To help with my integration here? To make sure I wouldn't have another outburst that could endanger someone like what happened with my last foster family and the countless others before them? To avoid a repeat of my past incidents? Considering where Alaric found me, he must know that much about my life.

The thought of my past surfaces in the back of my mind, but I push it away before it can choke me. If only Alaric could take away those dark memories, then I'd accept his weird sorcery, no questions asked. Who knows, maybe this place could teach me how to do that. He said it himself—all Nephilim have their own special power.

Maybe mine could help me forget.

Driven by that hope, I trail Alaric through the cloister into a long-stretching corridor of an adjacent building. At least half a dozen wooden doors branch off from this hallway into what I assume must be classrooms. The bits and pieces I catch from the booming voices on the other side of each one confirm that suspicion.

Ornate, carved pillars stand at the end of the passage, framing a set of glass doors leading into what appears to be a surprisingly modern administration office given the aesthetic of the rest of this place. Considering how many times I've transferred schools, I've gotten a vibe for what these offices look like—even if this academy exceeds all expectations of what I've come to expect from even the stuffiest private establishment.

A woman with gleaming chestnut hair twisted into a fashionable braid smiles as we step into the office. Like Alaric, a golden light outlines her body.

"Morning, Evangeline. Is she in?" Alaric jerks his thumb toward a black door in the corner bearing a silver crest of a G in the middle of a shield with wings extended out to each side. Inscribed into the wood around the emblem are tiny feathers, which seem to drift to the floor.

The woman behind the desk—Evangeline—beams up at Alaric with longing in her sapphire eyes. A faint blush stains her cheeks, coloring them a flattering shade of pink as she practically sings, "She sure is."

I cast a sidelong glance at Alaric, wondering if he notices how obviously in love with him this woman is. I've been locked up for the past year and suck at even the most basic social encounter, and even I'm able to see it.

"Great." Pressing a hand to my back, he crosses the office, guiding me toward the black door. The fingers of his free hand curl into a fist as he raps his knuckles three times against the polished, dark wood.

From the other side, I hear a muffled, "Enter."

Alaric inches open the door and pokes his head through the gap. "Headmistress."

"Ah, Alaric," a coy feminine voice says. "I was wondering when you'd turn up again. What news from the outside world?"

"I actually have a new student for you." He pushes the door open the rest of the way to reveal a pristine, spacious office. The furnishings are elegant but sparse—clean and organized with everything in its rightful place—and in the middle of the floor stands a large, wooden desk lined with gold trim, just like everything else I've seen here. Behind the desk, a youthful woman stares at me with wide brown eyes so dark they almost appear black. Only when the light from the window catches her face do I notice the caramel tint to her irises.

"Luna," Alaric continues as the woman rises from her seat, "this is Gabriel. She's the headmistress of this academy."

Gabriel? As in the angel from the Bible?

I gape in disbelief at the statuesque woman before me, my eyes trailing from her long, ebony hair to the light burning across her ivory skin like a sweeping mass of golden flames. Her features are severe, as if they've been cut from glass, but she's beautiful—more stunning and regal than anyone I've ever seen before in my life. She reminds me of the statues I glimpsed in the entry hall, and despite the fact that she's likely been around longer than the entirety of the human race, she looks to be no older than her late twenties, trapped forever in eternal youth.

I stare at her, unable to tear my gaze away even as her brilliance sears into my retinas. How anyone can stand to look at her blinding radiance for more than a few seconds is baffling.

The flutter in my stomach only grows wilder when she takes a step toward me.

"H-Hi," I stammer, unsure what else to say. How are you meant to greet a renowned angel who's been alive for thousands of years?

Her lips pinch into a tight, reserved smile—an expression I've come to expect from school principals. "Welcome to Alexandria." Her hawk-like eyes turn from my face to Alaric's. "Alaric, may I have a word?"

Gabriel struts toward the window on the right side of her office, which overlooks another lush, vibrant garden. After so long cooped up in my room at the hospital, I'm drawn to the idea of exploring the outdoor spaces offered at this school. Assuming I don't mess things up, get expelled, and end up right back where I started.

When Alaric approaches Gabriel, she grabs his arm and pulls him close to her side.

"Where did you find her?" She says the words under her breath, but I hear every one as clearly as if I'm standing beside them and involved in their conversation instead of being the subject of it. Her gaze burns orange in the light streaming in through the window.

"A psychiatric hospital for adolescents in Maine. Everything you need to know about her is in here." Alaric opens his briefcase and hands Gabriel a large brown envelope containing my medical records, transcripts, and, if I had to guess, a detailed account of my incidents.

"Just…be gentle with her," he whispers. "She's not had the most stable upbringing."

I bristle at the cautious edge to his tone.

"Duly noted." Gabriel takes the envelope from his hand and tosses it across the room onto her desk with a lazy flick of her wrist. Clearing her throat, she fixes the full brunt of her gaze on my face again.

I tremble under the weight of her stare, which narrows the longer she takes me in. When she finally breaks her hold on me, it's as if all the air has been sucked from my lungs, leaving me breathless and lost for words.

Is this her special power? To intimidate her victims to the point of them nearly losing consciousness?

"I'll have a class syllabus prepared for you, which you can fetch from my assistant, Evangeline, in the morning, along with your uniform and textbooks." Gabriel's voice is a languid monotone. "In the meantime, perhaps Alaric could show you to the dorms."

Her raven hair falls in a curtain across half of her face as she returns to her desk and pulls something from the top drawer, sliding it across a stack of papers. As soon as Alaric retrieves the object, she shuffles the stack with an agitated vigor. When he picks it up, I note it's a small golden key. Taking her silence as our cue to leave, Alaric pushes me through the open doorway. "Come on, Luna," he mutters. Then, in a slightly louder voice, "Gabriel, until next time."

Evangeline offers a polite wave as we leave, but Alaric doesn't seem to notice. Poor girl. With one hand on my back, he ferries me out of the office and into the hallway beyond, continuing back the way we came until we reach the end of the corridor where we hook a right toward another set of ancient-looking wooden doors. We pass through them into yet another courtyard that leads us into yet another building.

Just how big is this place?

"You seem on edge," Alaric notes as he directs me toward an immense split staircase at the end of our current path, taking the side branching off to the left, and then up a smaller, tucked away set of spiraling marble steps a bit farther down the passage. "What's on your mind? I *am* a doctor. You can tell me anything, and it will stay between us. Doctor-patient confidentiality and all that."

Oh, I don't know. How about this is a lot to take in and all seems absolutely insane? And I would know. I am insane.

I glance back in the direction we came from. "Was that who I think it was?"

"That depends. If you're asking me if the Gabriel you just met is one of the seven Archangels and the Messenger of God, then yes. She is who you think she is."

"Huh. I thought Gabriel was male."

A sigh breaks the rising silence between us. "Religious texts are not always accurate. Have you ever heard of Chinese whispers? Every time a story is told, the details are altered until the original is barely present in the latest telling. Besides, the texts were all written by men, and I'll be the first to admit, we tend to have fragile egos. My gender has a terrible tendency to paint itself as the superior and prominent half of our species. As such, all angels were depicted as male."

"Oh." Another question occurs to me then. "Where are her wings?"

Alaric coughs into his fist to mask a laugh. "Hidden. But I assure you, she has them." His reaction makes me wonder if it's not polite to ask about such things, especially when he says nothing else on the matter.

When we reach the top of the stairs, he leads me down a long hallway, then down another, before turning a corner and signaling to a door a few feet away on the left with the number 317 carved into the rich mahogany surface in gold.

"Here we are. It will take some time to adjust, but this school really is the best place for you. People out there… Let's just say, it's not safe for our kind to be alone and exposed among mortals."

Exposed. The thought forms a lump in my throat.

Alaric fishes out the key Gabriel gave him from his pocket and shoves it into the embellished brass lock. A few seconds pass with his hand on the key, but he doesn't turn it, instead glancing at me out of the corner of his eye.

"I understand this is a lot to accept." His voice is soft and low. Calming. Is he using his gift on me now? Is he robbing me of feeling the full extent of everything I would otherwise be experiencing given the absurdity of what he's telling me? "You've been through so much in your short life already that couldn't be explained by rational thought. But you lived through those traumatizing events, and more than that, you *survived* them. Now, it's time for you to thrive."

Tears blur the edges of my vision as the inescapable hand of shame tightens around my throat. "If you're talking about what I did—"

"None of that was your fault. Everything you did was an unfortunate side effect of not knowing what you are. This place will help you figure out who that is."

He rotates the key, unbolting the door. My gaze sweeps over the bright interior of my new home—the room furnished and complete with all the essentials I'll need, like bedding and an alarm clock on the side table—before darting to Alaric's retreating figure. He quietly heads back the way we came without so much as saying goodbye.

"Are you leaving?" Panic makes my voice unsteady.

"I'm afraid I have to," he says. Although he's stopped walking, he keeps his back to me. "My job entails that I leave for varying stretches of time, but I'll be back before you know it. And when I am, you can tell me all about how you're getting on here. Sound good?"

"Okay," I whisper, although I'm not sure how I feel about him abandoning me. I'd hate to think that Gabriel will be the only familiar face I'll have in this place.

She might be an angel—as weird as that is to admit—but there's something about the way she acted during our meeting that doesn't sit well with me. Her behavior was too reminiscent of the doctors who were so quick to declare me mentally unfit for life around other people.

"What *is* your job, anyway?"

Alaric's gaze drifts over his shoulder to me. "I travel the world in search of possible Nephilim."

"Like me." It's the first time I've said it aloud. The first time I've dared to believe this could all really be happening.

"Yes," he says with a cautious smile, his eyes glowing with an emotion resembling sadness. Or fear. "Just like you, Luna."

FOUR

CALEB

ISHTAR LEADS ME TO her office in silence, opening the iron door for me, which was once black, but is now green with age. I sink into the gold embossed settee she's placed for students. Along one wall, books cover the entire surface. Books written on vellum and papyrus. Books human scholars would kill to possess. Along the other wall, sickle-shaped swords and spears crafted from iron hang over a wooden shelf displaying ancient pottery and miniature carved figures that are hand-painted.

My eyes snag on a figure of Ishtar herself. Ha! The artist got her expression wrong. I've never seen Ishtar look that serene.

The Mesopotamian goddess seats herself behind a modern desk complete with a sleek laptop. Her eyes clash with mine and she grins.

"You've been good long enough," she muses. "Ask." She waves an imperious hand.

"Are you sure he's really there?" I demand, my mind reeling. "How do you know? How can I free him?"

I don't think the headmistress of the Serapeum, Gabriel, will allow me free rein of her academy to search for one of their greatest enemies. *Oh, hey, pardon me, has anyone seen my gramps? You know, the guy who almost conquered Earth? Oh, he's under there. Why, thank you. Maybe you're not a total prick.* Yeah. Not.

She nods. "We're certain."

"Who's we?" I ask, craving more information. That's part of what we're taught here in the Tower. Ask, ask, and then ask some more.

Ishtar tilts her head, her expression carefully blank. "What is that delightful phrase mortals use? Oh, yes. It's above your pay grade."

Unease flickers through me once more, stronger this time. That's not a very Dark answer to give and leads me to believe an Archdemon has a hand in this. There are seven Archdemons who rule the Fallen and the Dark Nephilim, and they're all powerful, but Lucifer still runs the show. The Morningstar is content with his place on Earth, but not all the Archdemons are. Some resent the ban from their birthplace. And some Nephilim, like the goddess in front of me, also resent their secret, shadowy existence. Asmodeus is the head of our academy, her beauty as fiery as her temper. She's never outright preached rebellion—well, she has already participated in the biggest rebellion in history—but she and Ishtar do get along like thorns on roses.

But if Lucifer isn't on board with this plan, then I shouldn't be either. Ishtar observes me under hooded lids, but I don't let my discomfort show, hoping my silence will prod her into revealing more information.

A heavy sigh escapes her lips. "Darling boy, stop worrying. You trouble yourself for no reason. As Alexander's grandson, do you think I'd put you in harm's way? You know how we value bloodlines here, and his is strong as are you." Her stare is flinty. "And besides, Alexander was a friend of mine. He almost did what I could not, what I dreamed of. I wouldn't dishonor him by treating his kin like a lamb to be sent to slaughter."

I hear the truth in her words, but how much truth? Yes, the Dark and Light Nephilim prize bloodlines, no matter how diluted. And yes, she's a regular fangirl for my gramps. She might even secretly have his name tattooed on her ass, but I know she's not being open with me. She's already admitted it.

Her voice turns low and rich, like dark chocolate melting over strawberries. "Don't you want to know him, Caleb? Don't you want to learn from him? Think of all the things he could teach you." Her mouth twists into a scowl as she spits the last words, "He would never be so careless with you the way your cursed father is with his offspring."

I feel like she's sucker punched me. Ishtar rarely criticizes my father, although she doesn't think much of him, believing he hasn't lived up to the legend of Alexander and is rather useless, other than as a sperm donor. I know I have a trail of brothers and sisters out there, but I don't know who they are. Apparently, that's a condition my pops made with the Archdemons, a deal they only honor to avoid us creating our own little army and accidentally exposing all angelkind to the humans. Secrecy above all and what not. When his children are brought to one of the seven Dark academies, they aren't to be told they have family at any of the schools. Our blood doesn't sing to one another because the Archdemons put a blood bind on us, so we can't identify our family. In fact, the bind repels us from one another, so we don't accidentally get horizontal with a sibling. That would be disturbing. Of course, I only know this because Ishtar once let it slip that dear old Dad didn't want his kids to unite against him and hunt him down. Yeah, he should be afraid. I'd love a family reunion where I could take a turn beating his ass.

Whatever Ishtar's truth may be, my truth is I do want to know my grandfather. I *long* for it. And yeah, maybe Ishtar is playing me like a prized violin, but I don't think even she's crazy enough to go against the Morningstar, despite her extremist views. The Lights and Darks have both done shitty things to each other. Why should Alexander be punished his entire life? Sure, he tried to take over the world, but he's suffered enough for his folly.

Giving a slow nod, I say, "Okay, I'll do it. But how do you expect me to find him? No one in that place is going to volunteer info, and I doubt the student body even knows he's there. They're too busy stroking each others' harps and dreaming about their wings. And if they know I'm Alexander's grandson, I doubt they'll let me within ten feet of that school."

A huff of laughter slips past Ishtar's lips. "I do so love the colorful way you put things. Stroking each others' harps, indeed." Her face grows serious once more. "Caleb, you should know we don't give bloodline information to the Lights. They have no idea who you are. You have many gifts, lovely boy, like all the Nephilim, but you have a very special gift that you wield with precision. One that will be very useful in this mission."

I grin. "Oh, you want me to break into people's minds." Now that I think about it, that *is* the obvious answer, and I'm very good at it. My smile fades. "I got mad skills, but I don't know if I can break into a first generation's mind or an Archangel's," I admit, thinking of Gabriel, who runs the academy in Alexandria. From what I hear, she's an ice queen who is more than capable of taking your head with her sword. A total badass.

Ishtar braids her hands together on top of her desk. "I have faith in you, Caleb. And besides, you don't necessarily need to break into an angel's mind. All you need to do is plant the seed of curiosity in a vulnerable student and tend the seed and see what grows."

I chuckle. "That's easy. And fun," I add. Normally, I'm pretty responsible with my powers, but against Lights, I don't really feel the need to hold back. They've never exactly thrown kindness my way.

Ishtar stands and I follow. "Good. Now that that's settled, go pack your things and say goodbye to your friends. Meet me in the Hanging Gardens in one hour. Don't be late.”

I hurry to the door when she throws out, “Oh, they’re going to make you wear a uniform.”

Whirling around, I stare at her. “Are you kidding me?” I glance down at my faded jeans and soft, black T-shirt and scuffed boots.

“Sheep dress alike, darling,” she says, grinning, and I groan.

Ugh, Lights. Assholes.

I fist bump my best friend, Rafe, with one hand while I adjust my backpack on my shoulder. Then I grip a small roller suitcase. I have a lot more stuff, but I don’t know how long this goodwill exchange program will last. Best to pack light.

“Man, you’re really going into a Light school? With those holier-than-the-Creator little shits?” Rafe asks, scowling. His bright green eyes fill with disbelief as he shakes his head.

Rolling my luggage across the main foyer, I shrug. “Yup, keeping the peace and all that. Good will to all the little Nephilim.”

Rafe snorts. “Fuck that,” he says. “It’ll be boring as hell here without you. I’ll have no one to compete with for the top spot.”

I can’t suppress my smug grin. I’m not just a pretty boy—I’ve got a brain and plenty of talent. I share the top spot at the Tower of Babel Academy with Rafe and my friend, Shalina. All three of us occupy that position at different times as if we’re all in an endless game of musical chairs.

“I’m counting on Shalina to kick your ass to Heaven and back,” I counter, surprised when a slight flush creeps up his neck. “Dude, you and Shalina?” Shalina is my friend but she isn’t Rafe’s. They share a healthy loathing for each other—or at least I thought they did. Well, I guess all that tension had to go somewhere.

“Shut it,” Rafe snarls. Then he pretends to look at his watch and grins. “You better hurry, or you’ll be late, and Ishtar will kick your ass.”

I flip him off and he chuckles. “Later,” I say.

Rafe’s expression sobers. “Be careful, Caleb. I don’t trust those Lights.”

I nod. “Will do.” We bump knuckles one more time, and I walk through the massive front doors and down the long trail of stone steps, my suitcase bouncing behind me.

The afternoon sun sizzles and I squint, cursing myself for not wearing my sunglasses. I trod across ancient, uneven stone until I reach the Hanging Gardens and the sweet, fresh air there. Ishtar isn't alone. The tall, severe figure of Hammurabi stands next to her. He looks every inch the Babylonian king this morning, despite his modern clothing. His black beard hangs in neat curls, and he wears a capped turban around his head banded by a circlet of gold. His hawkish features are harsh, but I know more than a few females in the academy who lust for him. He's a goddamn honey pot. In all honesty, he plays by the rules, so I'm always taken by surprise he's on team Fallen. He and Ishtar have locked horns more than once because of her "I deserve to take over the world" views. But he's a total warrior and I admire him. Between training with him and Ishtar, my combat skills are well-honed.

He nods at me. "Caleb, Ishtar tells me you are to be our representative in this… diplomatic endeavor."

I wink at Ishtar. "She picked me because of my charm."

Hammurabi crosses his arms over his massive chest, frowning, but I just flash a grin. "Caleb, this is a serious matter. Tensions are high between our factions, and the fact that they've offered this olive branch means a great deal."

I grow serious. "Yeah, I know. I won't let the Tower of Babel Academy down. I'll do you all proud."

"I'd whip you within an inch of your life if you let us down," he says casually, and I hide my flinch. Did I mention Hammurabi is old school? I mean read his code of laws.

"I hardly think that will be necessary, old friend," Ishtar counters, rolling her eyes.

Hammurabi glares at her before shifting his gaze back to me. "You're a very bright boy, Caleb. So while you will do your best to succeed on this diplomatic mission, you'll keep your eyes and ears open, yes? This may be a genuine offer from the Archangels to soothe tensions, but just in case there's treachery afoot, you are to remain vigilant and report anything suspicious you see or hear. Understood?"

I dart Ishtar a quick look under my lashes, but her face remains blank. Hmm, I doubt the Babylonian king knows about Alexander. That's not a super comforting thought. Then again, he's not exactly Ishtar's main confidant.

I nod. "Yes, sir."

One big hand slides into a sheath hanging at his hip, and he pulls a dagger free and holds it out to me. My eyes narrow as I take in the beauty of the weapon. The hilt consists of gold with patterns of mythical creatures engraved upon it, their eyes decorated with jewels such as lapis lazuli, carnelian, and jasper. But that's not the most fantastic thing about the dagger. Etched into the gleaming steel is Enochian script. I can recognize it, but I can't read it. Both the Archangels and Archdemons keep their native tongue guarded like the Mona Lisa, unwilling to share it with us

Nephilim. Eyes widening, I stare at Hammurabi. My mind blanks as I search for words. He can't be offering me this, can he? Shit.

A grin breaks his fierce exterior. "So, you do know what this is?"

"I…uh…yes," I fumble. This dagger is a weapon from the Fall. They're forbidden now, locked away or destroyed, so I have no idea where Hammurabi got his hands on one. "But why—do you think I'll need that?" I glance at Ishtar for explanation, but she stares at the knife, her lips twisted in a sneer.

"I still can't believe this was in the museum at Babel this whole time, and I didn't know," she says, shaking her head as if to clear it.

Hammurabi's smile disappears, his face smoothing into an expressionless mask at her words. His stillness at her casual comment makes me uneasy, but then he focuses on me, his mouth flattening. "I hope you won't need it. This is a last resort. No one must discover you have this—no one, Caleb. Understood?"

I give a frantic nod, still shell-shocked. I take the dagger from him, a near silent hum emanating from the metal and invading my ears. It's light and agile, but it feels as heavy as iron shackles around my soul. This weapon can harm an angel, Dark or Light. I mean, if I punch an angel hard enough in the face, I might hurt them, but they won't bleed. But this? This will make them bleed like a mortal. This dagger will cause serious damage. I swallow hard.

"Not to sound like a dumbass, but where am I going to hide this thing?" I ask. "If I'm caught with this, the Lights will execute me for sure, peacekeeping efforts be damned."

Hammurabi nods toward Ishtar and says tersely, "Show him."

Ishtar bristles at the command but takes out a black silk drawstring bag from the pocket in her gown. "Give it to me." With almost relief, I hand over the dagger. She slips it into the bag and draws the string shut, only now I can't see the bag at all.

Shaking my head, I blink rapidly. Ishtar holds her palm open, as if she balances something, but all I see is empty air. I reach out for her hand, and my fingers brush against silk. Startled, I yank my hand back and they both laugh.

"Concealment spells," Ishtar says, smiling. "This bag takes on the exact appearance of its environment and suppresses the power of whatever object it carries."

"This is the shit," I say, and Hammurabi frowns at me, but I ignore him. With careful hands, I place the dagger in the folds of clothes in my roll-on luggage. After I finish, I look at Ishtar.

"It's time," she says.

"Until we meet again, Caleb." Hammurabi gives a shallow bow and marches in the direction of the Tower.

"So, um, you sure you want to take me? I can totally get there on my own. I mean, *he's*—"

Ishtar's glower shrivels everything below my belt, and my jaw snaps shut with an audible click.

I can almost see frost form in the air when she speaks. "He is of no concern. As your teacher, it is my duty to see you to Alexandria."

She marches farther into the shadows of a fruit tree and holds out an elegant hand. I step into the deep puddle of shade and grasp her fingers. And then we step *into* the shadows.

The Shadow Road swallows us whole, and we land on a dirt path, our surroundings smeared, like charcoal drawings. The Road ahead and behind us is barren and desolate and cold. I suppress a shiver as I walk beside Ishtar. We pass marker after marker, all identical to each other—if you don't know what you're looking for. To travel the Shadow Road is a Fallen gift, although not all of us can access it. If the bloodline is too diluted, the Road does not recognize you. When training to use it, I accidentally ended up on the Great Wall of China. I don't know who was more shocked, me or the tourists when I popped out of thin air.

Ishtar finds the marker she's searching for, and we step off the Road into the scorching sun of Alexandria, directly in front of the Serapeum. I raise my eyebrows as I observe the opulent academy, its cream-colored, marble exterior gleaming against the azure sky. It's blinding in its purity. I snort.

"Do you think it needs a touch of white? Subtle, aren't they?" I ask Ishtar.

A cruel smile plays upon her lips. "Subtlety was never their strong suit."

We make our way up the steps when the gilded, towering doors open, and a tall man strides out. People say Gilgamesh looks like those statues the Greeks used to make celebrating male perfection or some shit. I don't know about that, but he moves like an athlete, and I bet he packs a mean punch. He smiles at me in greeting, a friendly gesture that morphs into something unreadable as he turns to Ishtar.

I glance at Ishtar and have to stop my tongue from rolling out of my mouth. I thought she'd be all warrior goddess, but she's emitting seductress like it's a homing beacon for any male in a hundred-mile radius. Her scarlet lips are pouted, and an artful hand on her hip pushes out her rather amazing rack. However much he may not want to be affected, Gilgamesh is not immune. I see heat flash in his eyes before he shuts it down. The tension and silence stretches and stretches between them until I'm in desperate need of a cold shower. Ugh, I'm stuck at a Light school where I'll never get laid, and these two decide to eye fuck in front of me. I hate them both.

I clear my throat, not caring if I piss off Ishtar, just desperate to get away. "Um, I'll just leave you to it," I say, hooking a thumb toward the academy's entrance. "Gilgamesh, take your time with…*catching* up. I'll just be up there. Waiting."

I give a furious Ishtar a salute and hurry up the stairs, not caring whether Gilgamesh follows, or the two of them tear each other's clothes off or just tear into each other. It could go either way. I just got here, and I'm already sick of the drama between the Darks and the Lights because I know this will be my daily life with the Light students, well, minus the sexual tension. I just have to think of Alexander. My grandfather is what matters. Freeing him is my focus.

I hear Gilgamesh's voice behind me, calling out for me to stop. I turn and put my game face on. He wears a look of apology, and Ishtar is nowhere in sight. Man, I'll probably catch hell for that stunt later.

"I apologize, Caleb," he rumbles. "That was…unfortunate. And unprofessional, frankly. Welcome to the Serapeum Academy. We're so happy to have you join us." He holds out a hand.

Happy, ha! I glance at his hand warily, like it's a snake waiting to bite me. Finally, I sigh and shake it. Welcome to the Serapeum Academy, indeed, Caleb. Not. It's going to be a long year.

FIVE

LUNA

MY FINGERS TUG AT the starchy collar hugging my throat before moving to the tie hanging around my neck like a noose. The silky material is the same red as blood—*"A symbol of our celestial bloodlines,"* Evangeline told me when I went to pick up my schedule from the office this morning. Along with my schedule and the textbooks I would need for my classes, she provided me with a bundle of new day-to-day clothes and the uniform I'm expected to wear during school hours: a crisp, white button-up shirt, ruby skirt, and matching tie embroidered with the insignia of the school.

This isn't the first time I've had to wear a uniform, but as I glare at myself in the full-length mirror fixed to the back of my dorm room door, I struggle to recognize the person looking back at me. For so long, I've avoided mirrors out of shame and refusal to face my deep-seated trauma, afraid to face the monster I knew I'd find staring back. Seeing the guilt in my eyes only makes the horrors of my life that much more real.

Swallowing, I glance away from my reflection, my gaze catching on the small white box on my desk. My teeth sink into my lower lip as the memory of my encounter with Evangeline earlier comes rushing back.

After collecting my textbooks and uniform—and after muttering a soft "thank you" to the older Nephilim—I set off back in the direction of the dorms to prepare for my first lesson of the day. I barely made it halfway down the adjoining hallway when Evangeline burst out of the office, shouting, "Luna, wait!"

Startled, I turned back to face her, noting the small white box clenched within the cage of her fingers.

"I almost forgot," she said, rolling her eyes as she bopped herself in the forehead with the palm of her free hand. She then held out the box, which I eyed suspiciously. "From Alaric. He dropped it off this morning."

Confusion marred my brow. "I thought he had already left Alexandria," I muttered.

Grinning, she shrugged a delicate shoulder. "So did I. But there he was at the crack of dawn, sitting on the edge of my desk, waiting for me." A dreamy look passed over her face at the recollection, and a lovelorn sigh parted her lips. Blushing under my scrutiny, she offered me a bashful smile before clearing her throat. "Anyway, he insisted that I get this to you."

"What is it?" Frowning, I took the box from her hands, handling it with the care of a bomb disposal technician.

"I'm not sure. He just said that he thought you might need it."

My heart hammered against my ribcage as I carefully pulled the lid off the box and peered inside, my left eyebrow hooking upward at the sight of the cell phone nestled within, lying in a bed of red and white tissue paper. A folded note was tucked in beside it.

Luna,

I know how lonely this must all be for you, so if you ever feel the urge to talk or need to vent about something, I'm here. You can call or text me anytime, day or night. I've programmed my cell number into the contacts. I hope to hear from you soon.

Affectionately,
Alaric

As I slip out of the memory, I consider his offer. I've never had someone to talk to before, not really. Not when all the adults in my life up to this point abandoned me the moment they realized I was trouble. But Alaric—he knows what I am. He knows about my past, every dark, awful detail, and has reached out to me in spite of it all. Maybe he will be different, like I first felt at the hospital, even if I'm too afraid to hope for as much.

Maybe I should give him a call later…to thank him for the phone.

A quick glance at the phone reaffirms my decision when the screen lights up, buzzing with a text notification. Plucking it from the box, I swipe my thumb over the screen and peer hesitantly down at the message.

Good luck with your first day of classes. -A

My chest tightens, and a smile tempts the edges of my lips. I don't think anyone's ever wished me luck before. I nod to myself, resolved. I definitely need to call him. But right now, I have to get to class or I'll be late. Placing the phone back in the box, I collect the pile of leather-bound books from my desk and head for the door, stepping out into the empty hallway, prepared as much as I can be for my first day as a student of the Serapeum Academy for Light Nephilim.

It's still so unbelievable to me. When I woke up this morning, I half-expected everything, from the plane ride to meeting Gabriel, to be nothing more than a dream. A vivid dream, but a dream. On some level, I suppose I still do, like I'm waiting for the other shoe to drop.

Perhaps because I don't really know what it means to be a Nephilim, or what this school expects from me. All I can hope is that this place will teach me how to control whatever impulses have led me to do the terrible things I've done. And who knows? Maybe, in the process, I'll find the one thing I ever really wanted.

A home.

I follow the spiraling steps nearest my room to the bottom floor of the girls' wing of the dormitory, retracing my path from yesterday and this morning. The student residences intersect at a massive split staircase, which I hurry down before continuing onward through one of the academy's many courtyards to the building of classrooms, which luckily isn't too far given the vast size of this place. The door to my first class, *History of the Fall 101*, is the second to last on my right. *An introductory class,* I realize with dread, double-checking my schedule with a pained wince. Great. I might as well wear a sign on my head that reads *Newbie Nephilim* in large letters.

The space on the other side of the heavy wooden door is modern like the office, which is surprising considering the rest of the school looks like the inside of a centuries old cathedral or temple. Twenty desks are arranged in four rows of five, facing a dry erase board, which spans most of the wall situated at the front of the room. Beside it stands a tall, muscular man with broad shoulders who looks like he could be the poster boy for the Olympics. His sleeves are rolled up to his elbows, exposing the rich golden skin of his sculpted forearms, which strain as he writes in a book propped against the crook of his opposite elbow. Dark umber eyes scan the room, flicking from the students down to the book, as his mouth, framed by neatly trimmed ebony facial hair, soundlessly mutters every name.

Like Alaric and Evangeline, this man has a strange golden glow vibrating around his body like an outline of pulsing light. It's nowhere near as strong as Gabriel's, but still bright enough I'm tempted to hold up my hand to shield my eyes from his glory.

Palms sweating, I cross the room, tightly gripping my books, which threaten to slip from my grasp at any moment. My meek voice barely penetrates my trembling lips.

"Excuse me."

The man looks up at me, flashing pearly white teeth. "Ah, you must be Luna. I'm Gilgamesh. I'll be your teacher for *History of the Fall*."

He holds out a hand for me to shake, but I can't bring myself to take it. At least the few times Alaric touched my shoulder or back, he never encouraged me to reciprocate the gesture. If these people know what's good for them, they won't expect me to, either.

Gilgamesh lowers his hand and offers me a kindhearted look that seems to say, *Don't worry about it.* He then breaks my gaze and waves his hand at the desks. "Just sit anywhere. Oh, and try not to be too anxious. We're all here to help one another."

Keeping my head down, I make my way toward the back of the room where I spot two empty seats. The other desks are already occupied—I must be one of the last to arrive—and although Alaric insisted the other students are just like me, I can't find the nerve to lift my eyes and confirm that. I've been through the whole new school thing enough times to know that I never fit in.

My skin burns as I walk toward the empty desks. I can sense it—the other students staring at me. They don't mask their curiosity or even attempt to lower their voices. At least the kids at my other schools had the decency to pretend they weren't talking about me.

"Hey, is that her?" one girl says to her friend in a British accent as I shuffle past. Out of the corner of my eye, I glimpse yellow-blonde hair.

"Must be," the other girl answers in a deep Southern twang. An American, like me. "I'd steer clear," she adds in a tone of indifference, as if she finds the whole mystery of who I am to be unworthy of her time. "Yasmin told me she overheard a few of the teachers talking about her, and one of them straight up said she's crazy."

The hair on the back of my neck bristles when she utters that word—that awful, hateful word. Sinking my teeth into my lower lip, I hug my books even tighter to keep a hold on my emotions. I can't lose it, not now. Not when I only just got here.

I fix my gaze on one of the two unoccupied desks in the back row and slide into the empty chair. As I place my books on the floor under my seat, I glance up to find the two girls staring at me like I'm an animal in a zoo. They're both pretty in that airbrushed, magazine cover kind of way, but look a few years younger than me. As

I glance around the room, I note that I seem to be the oldest student in this class. Wonderful. There's nothing quite like being surrounded by a bunch of immature gossips who all think they're better than you. As I shift my focus back to the duo, I realize that, like everyone else I've seen in this place, their skin beams with noticeable outlines of light.

I turn my hand over on top of my desk and peer down at my own non-glowing skin. If I'm a Nephilim, then why don't I have an aura like they do?

"Really?" My eyes flick upward, settling on the blonde girl's pinched face. Her lips purse as she tilts her head. "She looks normal enough to me."

"Yeah." The other girl, the American, flicks a loose lock of rusty brunette hair over her shoulder. "Apparently, she killed a few mortals and burned down a building and a bunch of other crazy shit. They even tried to have her exorcized."

Sucking in a sharp breath, I fist my hands into my lap and look back down at my desk.

Block them out, I urge myself. But I can't. Every word they say reaches my ears with ease—cutting at the threads holding together my already questionable sanity. They chat as if the subject of their conversation isn't sitting only a few seats away.

"No way." The shock is apparent in the British girl's voice.

As is the scathing disdain in the brunette's.

"Yup." I can almost hear the smile in her tone, as if she's taking pleasure in my discomfort.

My jaw tenses as I fight the temptation to scream out that she doesn't know what she's talking about. She doesn't have a clue what it's like to be me.

"All right, everyone." Gilgamesh claps his hands, silencing the students' chatter and drawing everyone's attention to the front of the room. "Eyes on me. Ellie and Lisbeth, that means you, too."

The two girls whip around in their seats, but not before the brunette sneaks in a venomous sneer at me. I crumple beneath her leering gaze.

"First, we have a new student joining our ranks, so let's all do our best to make her feel welcome." Gilgamesh gives me a slight nod of acknowledgment but doesn't bother introducing me to the class. It strikes me as odd, considering what it's been like every other time I started at a new school. Then again, he's probably aware of my history and knows I don't do well with being put on the spot.

Hey, maybe being the crazy girl can work to my advantage this time and get me out of any mandatory class participation.

Gilgamesh turns his back to us and grabs a marker from the tray at the base of the dry erase board. Ripping off the cap, he writes the word *Recap* in large, elegant script.

"Today, I'm going to backpedal a bit and go through what we've learned so far about the Fall. This is a good opportunity for those of you who haven't been taking notes as this *will* be on the midterm." He casts a knowing glance over his shoulder at a deeply tanned male student sitting in the second row by the windows. "I'm looking at you, Jared," he says, arching a thick eyebrow.

The boy hunches his shoulders and sinks into his seat as the other students laugh at his expense. Gilgamesh seems to take no notice as he hastily scribbles a word on the board. My lungs tighten as my eyes rake over each letter.

Creator

"In the early days of humanity, all the angels lived in Heaven under the rule of the Creator. They were charged with protecting the newly made humans, for the Creator loved them dearly. Almost as much, if not more so, than the angels themselves."

A few students sitting in front of me yawn, and the wisps of their auras flatten into a lethargic slumber, their visible boredom suggesting they've heard this lecture a thousand times before. Their indifference agitates me as I cling to Gilgamesh's every word, entranced by the story of their ancestors. *My* ancestors. He paces in front of the board, recounting the details of a time I always thought was fiction.

"This angered one angel in particular who envied the humans for having free will and desired the same freedom for himself and his brethren. Can anyone tell me who that angel was?" His dark eyes jump from student to student until someone finally raises their hand.

Gilgamesh points to a red-headed girl in the front row.

"Lucifer Morningstar," she answers.

"Correct." Gilgamesh spins back toward the board and quickly scrawls a few more keywords for the class. Although I know I should be taking notes, I'm too transfixed by his story to move.

Looks like Jared and I will be failing the midterm together.

"So," Gilgamesh continues, "Lucifer rebelled against the Creator, and that rebellion led to what we know as the Fall. Now, just before the Fall, during the Great Battle of Heaven, the angels became divided into those who followed Lucifer in his quest for free will, commonly known as the Fallen, and those who sided with the Creator, who we all know as the Faithful. When the battle ended with the Fall, the two groups' differing desires led to their abilities and wings transforming to reflect either the darkness or light, with their bloodlines carrying on that change as a permanent reflection of their choice. Thus, one race was torn into two, with angels loyal to the Light and demons to the Dark.

"*But…*" He enunciates the word, his voice dropping an octave. "Despite their differences, the angels and demons still had one thing in common. Regardless of which side they chose, they all spent a significant amount of time on Earth—the Fallen reveling in their new freedom while the Faithful continued doing the Creator's bidding and looking over the newborn human race as intended. On both sides, many even went so far as to mate with the humans during that period, creating a new race of creatures known as the Nephilim, who were predisposed to favor the darkness or the light depending on their bloodlines."

My ears prick up at the mention of Nephilim. Gilgamesh meets my gaze across the room, flashing me a quick, hooded look, as if to say, *Yes, Luna. This is your history. It's real. Embrace it.*

"These offspring were half-mortal but incredibly powerful due to the celestial blood in their veins. However, many didn't know how to wield it, and since the humans who mothered and fathered the Nephilim were unaware of the existence of angels and demons, they incorrectly assumed their mates and their resulting children were like them: ordinary. As such, they were completely unprepared for the reality of raising a Nephilim child—a task made infinitely harder for many when the Creator called the Faithful back to Heaven and forbade them from having any direct involvement with their children. The Creator also proclaimed that all Nephilim would reside here on Earth and that they would be bound by the limitations of their mortal blood, regardless of their parentage. Their lives would be long, but they would one day expire. This was the punishment for the angels' intimacy with the humans they were charged to look after, which the Creator viewed as a threat to their loyalty and love for Him. If so many had not already been lost to the Fall, the Creator might have even cast the guilty out of Heaven. Instead, He chose to be merciful, imparting a new law on his Faithful children. From that point on, any physical union between the Faithful and humans was forbidden.

"And so, the ignorant humans were left to care for and subsequently grew to fear their half-angel offspring. The Fallen, who remained on Earth, did their best to hide their own children from human eyes, but exposure was inevitable and left them all open to persecution. In those days, due to their notable differences to the humans, the Nephilim were either revered as gods or put to death, an impressive feat considering these were first generations who, as we all know, can't be easily killed." An amused grin tugs at his lips at this comment, and the class lets out a collective chuckle, as if they're in on a joke that's flown over my head. If I had to guess, I'd say, based on the boastful look on his face and his renowned role in early human history, Gilgamesh is probably a first generation, which means he was there when all these horrors occurred.

No, he wasn't just there. He survived it.

A shudder rolls over my skin when his gaze darkens and his voice takes on a solemn note. "This went on for many long years, and it's said the Fallen and Faithful wept for seven days every time one of their children was burned alive or beheaded."

Tears blur the edges of my vision as Gilgamesh's narrative takes a familiar shape in my head. As an orphan, I know what it's like to be cast aside, like many of those Nephilim were. The only difference is, nowadays, they don't murder you for having a problem that defies rational thought, as Alaric phrased it. They just lock you up in a loony bin where life passes you by as you waste away.

Alone and forgotten.

I blink the moisture from my eyes and watch as Gilgamesh writes the number seven on the dry erase board. He circles it twice—once in black marker and then again in gold.

"Out of love for their children and concern for their safety, both sides eventually agreed to a truce. With the Creator's blessing, seven of His favored Faithful were allowed to return to Earth and work with seven powerful Fallen to oversee the fledgling Nephilim and establish fourteen schools as safe harbor—seven of Light, seven of Dark. Together, they formed a council of Archangels and Archdemons, and each became responsible for one of the schools, built with the help of the eldest Nephilim with the intent of training the future generations and keeping them safe from the humans who would seek to destroy them out of fear. And thus, the angels' and demons' focus turned away from war and settled on the measures needed to avoid the exposure and destruction of our kind. Now"—he spins on his heel again, facing the class—"can anyone tell me where the seven schools of Light are located?"

The brunette who sneered at me raises her hand. "We have the primary academies at Mount Nebo and Petra, then the secondary academies at Mount Sinai, Mount Zion, Qumran, Sidon, and here, at the Serapeum in Alexandria."

"Very good, Lisbeth," Gilgamesh praises. "Any volunteers who can tell me where the Dark academies are located? How about you, Jared? Let's see how well you've been paying attention."

Jared jerks upright in his seat. "Uhh…" He hesitates then slowly counts off on his fingers in French before answering in perfect English. "The primary academies are in

Sodom and Gomorrah. Then there's the secondary academy at Megiddo…"

"That's right, keep going," Gilgamesh urges with an encouraging nod.

"Ashkelon," Jared mutters. "Tyre, uhh… Machaerus, and—"

"The Tower of Babel," a deep voice finishes from the hallway.

A sharp inhale fills the silence in the room as all eyes fall on the boy at the door. He's dressed in the same uniform the rest of us wear, but where our shirts are white, his shirt and pants are as black as the obsidian hair crowning his head.

He stands propped against the door frame with his arms crossed—shirt sleeves pushed up to his elbows—and a gloating smile twisting his lips. The overhead lights bounce off his bronze skin as dark mischievous eyes scan the room. Whispers erupt around me, but I don't take note of a single word the other Lights say. All I can focus on is the aura enveloping the newcomer's body—the rich shades of dark blue and purple entwined with black, like tiny wisps of shadow reaching out to entice me.

Gilgamesh lifts his chin and snorts. "I see you've finally decided to join us. Come in and take a seat."

The boy straightens and struts into the room as if he doesn't have a single care in the world. He looks a bit older than the other students in this class—probably closer in age to me, seventeen or eighteen by the looks of him—and as he walks, he leans into each step with a confidence I can only dream of. He certainly doesn't have any of the new student awkwardness I always seem to exude. Even the mutterings of the students around us don't seem to faze him.

"Is he…" Ellie whispers.

"Oh, my God," Lisbeth gasps.

Gilgamesh claps in an effort to draw the class's attention back to him. "Everyone, this is Caleb, and he's coming to us from the Tower of Babel Academy. He'll be spending the year with us."

Lisbeth jumps up from her seat and slams her hands down on her desk. "But he's a *Dark*," she hisses with a vehemence in her voice I don't quite understand.

My mind wanders back through Gilgamesh's lesson, remembering what he said about the angels taking sides during the Great Battle of Heaven and how that choice carried on through their bloodlines after the Fall. This new student must be one of these Dark Nephilim he mentioned.

And so what if he is? What's the big deal? Surely, by now, after so many years, the Darks and Lights have learned to co-exist.

"That's enough." Gilgamesh's booming voice makes Lisbeth shiver, and she falls back into her seat as if her legs have been swept out from under her. "We are welcoming

Caleb to our school in the spirit of friendship. I expect you all to treat him with the same civility you would impart on each other. Now, let's move on."

The lecture, which had me captivated before, fails to hold my focus once the transfer student—Caleb—sits down. The only empty desk stands less than three feet to my left.

Swallowing, I peek at him out of the corner of my eye, bewitched by the shadows licking over his skin. They're eerie and haunting but astonishing. Beautiful. Unlike with the Light Nephilim, I don't feel an overwhelming need to look away, like I'll be blinded by his aura if I don't. If anything, my eyes want to linger on his face and devour that darkness forever.

Caleb looks over at me, and my cheeks flush with heat once I realize he's caught me staring at him. A sly grin hitches up the corners of his mouth as he angles himself across the side of his desk. Holding up a finger, he signals for me to lean in—like he wants to tell me something. Entranced, I do as he beckons, closing the distance between us.

When our faces are only a few inches apart, he looks me up and down with disgust.

"Take a picture," he scoffs. "It'll last longer, *Light*."

I blink, stunned by his scathing tone and the venomous way he spits that last word, hurling it like an insult. Embarrassed, I turn my gaze to the front of the classroom. But no matter how hard I try to concentrate, I fail to take in any new information for the rest of the lesson.

All I can think about is the Dark Nephilim boy beside me and his beguiling aura.

SIX

CALEB

MY EYES SLIDE TO the gorgeous blonde beside me. And she is gorgeous, despite being a Light. Her hair is an unusual shade of gold, not ditzy blonde like the hostile girl sitting in front of me who keeps trying to shoot daggers out of her eyes at me. Bring it, little girl. I'll tear your mind into pieces.

Goldilocks doesn't seem hostile, but she was staring at me like bacteria under a microscope. I feel a little guilty about my snarky comment. I'm not usually an asshole to women, and she appears…fragile, for lack of a better word, like I genuinely wounded her with my words. Ha! Like a stuck-up Light would give a shit about what I have to say.

Gilgamesh drones on and on about basic Nephilim stuff—why am I even in this class?—when honest-to-Lucifer bells chime, the sound clear and sweet. This place is such overkill. I miss the clear, aggressive war horns at the Tower of Babel. That sound said move your ass or be punished for being late.

Goldilocks stands up, the motion slow and hesitant. Despite my harsh words, she kept peeking at me the entire class as if she couldn't help herself. Hmm. Time to use that curiosity against her. I stretch to my feet, ignoring the scowls and glares thrown my way, my laser focus on my prey.

I follow her into the hall. "Hey," I call, and she pivots on one foot, surprise on her pretty face. "Sorry I was a dick before." I tug at my scarlet tie. Ugh, I'm wearing a bloody tie. At least my pants and shirt are black, unlike the red and white freak show going on around me. Thank God for small miracles.

Her hazel eyes widen. "Um, th-that's okay," she stammers. Her smile is sheepish. "I didn't mean to stare. I just… I'm new here, too."

It's my turn to be surprised. A Light apologizing? That's a first. Maybe the apocalypse really is coming. As I study her, I realize she's too old to be a first-year. I'm eighteen, and she's got to be close to that. She should be in my grade or maybe one lower. All Nephilim—Dark or Light—are assigned a primary academy at the age of seven to learn the initial steps of control then a secondary academy at fourteen where we hone our skills and figure out our special abilities. Before that, it's up to our parents to keep us in line so we don't go kaboom. But because of assholes like my old man, there are a string of orphans dotting the globe, placed in group homes run by the older, more experienced Nephilim who aren't teaching at the academies. There, the young Nephilim are watched over until they're of age to go to school. But I'm getting the vibe none of this applies to Goldilocks, so, why has she been enrolled so late? What's her deal?

I wave a dismissive hand. "Don't worry about it. Sucks to be new, right? So, you know my name, but I don't know yours. Doesn't seem fair."

She shuffles her feet. "Luna," she says, her voice so low I strain to hear it. "It's kind of nice not being the only new person."

Is she for real? My eyes narrow, seeking deception, but she radiates sincerity. "Yeah, but you're a Light. I'm sure everyone is falling all over themselves to be your friend. Getting ready for Ascension and all that." I scoff.

She frowns as if she's confused by my words. "Ascension?"

Stunned, I study her for a moment, but either Luna is the best actress in the world, or she has no fucking clue what Ascension means to Lights. "Are you serious?" Try as I might, I can't quite keep the bite from my voice. Luna flinches, ducking her head, and I give myself a swift mental kick. "And there I go, being a dick again. I didn't realize how shiny and new you really are."

Luna bites her full lower lip. Lucky lip. "Does…everyone know about Ascension?" She doesn't specifically say Dark Nephilim, but she doesn't have to. I bristle for a moment before she hastily adds, "I don't mean to offend you. No one's really explained anything to me."

Relaxing, I assess her. There's something so appealing about her. I'm not sure if it's her shy sincerity or the uncertainty that marks her every move. But it makes me want to be her friend, protect her. Suspicion creeps in, and that cynical, survival part of my brain wonders if this is a trap. Gabriel picks a hot blonde to follow me around and keep tabs on me. Maybe gets me to confess Dark secrets against those kissable lips. I'm a lot of things, but I'm not a sucker.

I send my powers toward her, like black, smoky threads unwinding from a spool. If she's working for the headmistress, I'll know it soon enough, and maybe I can plant a few suggestions in that vulnerable mind of hers. Finding the shield of her mind, I try to push through, but I am abruptly shut out, like a steel door slamming down. It jars me, and I shake my head. What the hell? I try again, this time forgoing subtlety for force, and once more hit an impenetrable barrier. *Shit.* How in Lucifer's name is Luna doing this?

My eyes dart to her, standing there, fidgeting, and I realize I've been quiet too long. "Yeah, everyone knows about Ascension. When all the good little Light Nephilim get their wings."

Her eyes grow impossibly huge. "Wings…"

The reverence in her voice makes me want to roll my eyes. "If you believe that line."

Confusion mars her smooth brow. "There's so much I don't know about all… this." She gestures vaguely to our surroundings. "Could you…" A blush stains Luna's cheeks and my brow raises. "Could you, maybe…help me? No one else has bothered to speak to me, not…"

She trails off, and I hear what she isn't saying in the silence. *Not like you have.*

I try one last attempt to break into her mind and test her truthfulness, but it might as well be the Vatican vault for how well it's fortified. She seems to tremble as she waits for my answer, hope shining in her eyes. God, I want to help. I want to tell her all the dirty secrets the Lights hide away from her. But I can't. I don't trust this feeling. I don't trust her.

Suddenly, her innocence seems manufactured and the hopeful look in her eyes calculating. Anger bursts through me. I refuse to be manipulated by a Light. Or allow one to spy on me. I sneer at her, and she withers like a dying flower.

"I don't think so. Best stick to your own kind," I say. Ignoring the hurt on her face, I push past her and make my way down the hall.

Why couldn't I crack her mind? It doesn't make sense. Has Gabriel placed a protection spell on her? I guess she could be a second generation and unusually strong, but that doesn't seem to fit. It's more likely she's been sent to spy on me. I take a sharp turn down the corridor and enter a cloister—one of many here. They need more cloisters like they need more touches of gold. Overkill.

To my left, the lush garden shows brilliant green under the hot sun with bursts of violet and pink and blue blossoms. Marble benches are placed in strategic positions under fig trees. It makes me miss the Hanging Gardens at Babel, but I crush that encroaching homesickness like the destructive weed it is.

Light students flow around me like I'm a boulder in the middle of a stream, and they might sully themselves if they crash into me. God, I hate these assholes, but they do provide ample opportunity to test my theory. I hop up on one of the low walls and lean against an arch, one knee drawn up to my chest and close my eyes. Taking a deep breath, I cast my net wide. Thoughts and distant mutterings flit by me.

Can you believe they let a Dark in here? He's disgusting…

Think Gabriel will take him hostage?

Guys, we should get together later and beat his ass…

I can't believe I had to sit near a Dark. Now, we have two freaks in class…

Relieved my powers still work, I hone in on that last thought. My lids flicker open as I seek out the source of that voice. It's that bitchy brunette from class. Oh, little girl, you mess with the wolf… A predatory grin spreads across my face as I slip into her mind and plant a small suggestion.

As she talks to her bottle-blonde friend, she begins scratching her side, discomfort growing on her face. She digs her nails harder and harder into her skin until the blonde clutches her hand, face askance. "Lisbeth, what the hell is wrong with you?"

Lisbeth looks positively panicked, and I squash my growing smile. "I don't know." She lifts up her shirt and squeals. "God, look at this rash! What is it? It itches so badly." She jerks her wrist from the blonde's grip and digs her nails into her smooth, unblemished skin.

"There's nothing there, Lis," her friend says, trying to grab her wrist again.

Those stupid bells chime, and the brunette takes off down the hall, her friend at her side, trying to calm her hysteria. I wait until the sound of students hurrying by dissipates before I allow a slow, satisfied grin to cross my face. I haven't lost my touch after all. That was easy.

I slide my feet to the ground, making my way to my next class, not in any particular hurry. It's my first day and I'm a Dark. I bet all my teachers' opinions are already properly low of me, so I'm sure they don't expect me to be able to find my way or give a shit about being on time. They'd be right about the latter. Though Hammurabi's words about representing the Dark Nephilim the right way puts a little spring in my step.

My thoughts drift to Luna and my glee evaporates. Why couldn't I read her thoughts like the other students? Is Gabriel interfering, or is it something else? And what had the bitchy brunette thought before? That there were *two* freaks in class. As I push open the door to my next class, I wonder who the other freak was she mentioned.

SEVEN

LUNA

THE FIRST FEW WEEKS of the fall term at the Serapeum pass by without incident. Unless you count Lisbeth and Ellie and their minions doing everything in their power to make my life hell. Those girls are only freshmen by normal high school standards, but they're veterans when it comes to mental warfare. They put mortal bullies to shame.

I've tried my best to ignore their attempts to get under my skin, but the effort is exhausting. Not to mention, it's an unwanted distraction from figuring out what my powers are—a goal that has consumed me throughout the month I've been here and with which I've made absolutely zero progress.

After calling Alaric to thank him for the gift, I realized how easy the Nephilim is to talk to and, despite the distance, we've formed a friendship of sorts, texting on a near daily basis and catching up over the phone at least once a week. But whenever I press him for more information about when I'll learn what my own special talent might be, he simply urges me to give it time. That I'll learn who I am through my lessons here. I want to believe him, but so far, my classes have mostly just been lectures about our history as Nephilim and what we're not allowed to do—not what we can. Sure, what I'm learning is interesting, but on a personal level, every day I feel a bit more disconnected from the subject matter, like I'm back in a mortal classroom where this is all fiction and none of it applies to me. It'd be easier to believe Alaric's repeated assurances about what I did before I was committed if I actually understood what I was capable of.

Even Ascension—which I've been curious about ever since Caleb mentioned it—

doesn't hold the same draw for me as it seems to for everyone else. Granted, I haven't spent my whole life daydreaming about gaining my wings, like some of these students clearly have based on the way they constantly harp on about it. My perspective on the idea is that of an outsider.

On the rare occasion our teachers do discuss Ascension, they merely preach that devotion to the light will lead to entry into Heaven and full angel status granted by the Creator Himself, where the Nephilim will finally be able to join their Faithful ancestors and achieve immortality. Of course, they always clam up when the students ask for specific examples of when this has actually happened, as if the act itself is private and not to be spoken about in any real detail. Add to that the fact that all our teachers are first generation Nephilim—not to mention some of the most prominent figures from history—and have yet to Ascend themselves, and it makes the whole concept seem questionable. If I'm honest, the whole notion sounds like propaganda—an incentive to convince the Lights to behave the way the Archangels in charge want them to. Even Alaric couldn't give me any real details when I asked him about it one night over text, claiming the experience is personal and unique to each Nephilim, not unlike mortal spirituality. As much as I like him and feel a certain growing kinship between us, his answer felt rehearsed, like he's merely regurgitating what he's been told.

Who knows if any of it is true?

Classes aside, the Serapeum Academy has been like most of my other schools, isolating and lonely. Friendless. Most of the time, I rush out of class before Lisbeth or Ellie can find new ways to torment me or convince one of the older Nephilim students to do the job for them. It never takes much convincing. Despite us all having celestial blood, to everyone here, I'm an outcast. A freak of nature—an imperfection in their otherwise perfect world.

And here I had assumed Lights were supposed to be good.

I haven't spoken to Caleb again, although I desperately want to. Every day, we sit next to each other in the few classes we share—no one else wants to sit next to the Dark or the crazy girl, forcing us to occupy the sole remaining seats—but he never looks at me, even though I'm always sneaking glances at him whenever I think he's not looking. I'm not sure what it is, but there's something behind his standoffish exterior that makes me sense we're the same, despite him being a Dark. And not just because we're both pariahs by the Lights' social standards, but because there's something about the shadows lapping over his skin that I recognize within myself. That I *feel* in the buried, unreachable depths of my own soul.

Not that it matters. What I think or feel is irrelevant if he refuses to talk to me. *"Best stick to your own kind,"* that's what he said. I don't fully grasp this feud between the Darks and the Lights, but if sticking with my own kind means turning into someone like Lisbeth or Ellie, I'll pass.

I'd rather be alone than be anything like them.

My fingers curl around the spines of my textbooks, hugging the heavy bundle close to my chest. On weekends, there's not a whole lot to do here, and it's not like I have any friends to pass the time with, so I spend those free days alone in my room or exploring the school, which is never-ending in its vastness. An unsent text on my phone awkwardly asks Alaric to come visit one weekend, but I've yet to work up the courage to send it, so today, I'm on the hunt for the library, which my teachers have claimed is legendary. According to my lessons, the Library of Alexandria was believed to have burned down centuries ago, the treasures within lost to flame, when in reality, unbeknownst to humans, the Archangels moved what they could salvage here—to the Serapeum where it would be protected by magical barriers, hidden away, and kept safe from the reckless destruction of mortals.

The teachers at this school—all first generations—never pass up any opportunity to moan about how rash and irresponsible mortals are, as if they aren't half-human themselves. I've yet to catch the snobbery running rampant among the other Lights, which only fuels the doubts I've had since Alaric told me the truth about what I am. I certainly haven't seen any evidence that would suggest I'm unlike the very same mortals the Nephilim here seem to detest. It's as if they believe themselves to be a superior species, which is illogical considering everyone here, aside from Gabriel, has at least one mortal ancestor somewhere in their bloodline. Even a child born of an angel and a Nephilim would still be part mortal—a first generation and powerful sure, but mortal, their blood watered down by the human connection through their Nephilim parent. Without humans, we wouldn't exist at all, not that the other Lights would ever admit that, especially when they make it a point to keep to our own kind to avoid further dilution of our celestial roots. Based on what I've heard in class and in passing, it was inevitable some notion of supremacy among the Lights would form over time, pitting them against the inferior humans who they see as responsible for their weakening bloodlines. From that viewpoint, I suppose it's easy to buy into an idea like Ascension when you already have an inflated opinion about yourself and where you belong in the world.

The hallways are empty as I search for the library. Many of the students who know and have healthy relationships with their parents, human or Nephilim, have gone home for the weekend—an escape I won't be partaking in any time soon. It's kind of hard to go home for a weekend when you don't have a home to go back to.

Considering where the school is located and that many of the Nephilim hail from the other side of the world, I was surprised to hear that any of them go home at all, apart from when the academic terms end and classes break up for holidays. I mean, who wants to take a flight lasting who knows how many hours only to then make the lengthy return trip to school less than two days later? Sounds tiring and not at all worth the effort.

At least, that's what I thought until I heard about the Blessed Road. That's one good thing about being an outcast—no one seems to take any notice when you're eavesdropping on their conversations.

Per my new knowledge, Nephilim, Light and Dark alike, have methods of traveling that are beyond the scope and understanding of mortals. I'm not really sure how the Blessed Road works, but when I asked Alaric for details about it, he compared the Road to a highway with exit points scattered across the planet. It's hard for me to imagine, but apparently it's faster than traveling by plane or any other form of human transport. When I then pressed him about why he didn't just use the Blessed Road to bring me to Alexandria instead of flying, he said the Road will only open for those who are aware of what they are, which, at the time, I wasn't. He had also muttered something about the possibility of my brain imploding if I saw something like that without having the proper time to process my being a Nephilim, and that statement was enough to shut me up on the matter.

The sun beats down on me as I pass into one of the courtyards sprinkled across the academy grounds. Although the light is warm, a shiver crosses my skin, leaving me cold and feeling exposed and alone. I can't stop thinking about how nice it would be to have someone to traverse this new landscape with—someone to help me make sense of what I am and this bewildering world I find myself in. While Alaric has been a source of comfort and is always available to lend a friendly ear, he isn't physically here. He has responsibilities that keep him busy.

But Caleb… I was foolish enough to think he might be that person, a friend even, but clearly, my first impression of him was sorely misguided. He's as disgusted by my existence as everyone else in this school, although his rejection of me is more painful somehow. Perhaps because I've made it a point not to get close to anyone since… well, the first incident that threw my life into disarray. He was the exception—the one person my own age I was ever tempted to try to get close to.

And not just because he's nice to look at—a fact my inconvenient teenage hormones have taken notice of—but because there's something there, in the billowing indigo and violet shadow outlining his body, that speaks to me in a way the brilliant radiance of the Lights hasn't yet.

Ironic, considering I'm supposed to be one of them.

I finally stumble across my destination in one of the western annexes. Immense, wooden doors framed by glimmering golden symbols lead the way into an extravagant room spanning the height of at least four stories. The walls are covered in tall, arching windows, and shelves full of books stretch from the floor up to the sky-scraping ceiling, which is painted to look as if Heaven itself gazes down on the library below with shining approval.

The structure is mesmerizing—like a painting brought to life—made all the more enchanting by the white marble floor, which reflects the details of my surroundings in its glistening surface.

At least twenty round tables fill the room, clustered around several rows of free-standing bookcases, which section off the space and create cozy patches of darkness I'm tempted to lose myself in. As I weave between them, I wince at the thunderous echo of my steps on the marble. My heart catches at the thought of drawing unwanted attention, but thankfully, the library is empty, apart from a few seemingly studious Nephilim, who make it a point to ignore me as I lumber past.

I make a beeline for a door in the corner, intrigued by the sign hanging over it printed with a single ornate word in gold leaf. *Exhibits.* I flatten my palm against the brass push plate and lean my weight into the wood, nudging it open. The hinges creak as if protesting my entry.

Behind me, the door swings shut as a breath of quiet awe rushes out of my lungs. The space is poorly lit—there are no windows in this room—and the minimal light from the low burning lamps ignites the dust particles in the air like floating embers suspended in time. Glass cases stand in clean rows like sentinels awaiting their orders, housing relics showcasing the history of the Nephilims' past.

I abandon my books on a small accent table beside the door and approach a miniature sculpture of the library that sits in one of the nearby cases. According to the placard, the model represents what the original structure looked like from the outside before it burned down all those years ago and its contents became a part of the school at the Serapeum. In another case, metal ornaments resembling skeletal wings fill the full breadth of the display, framing a shining golden breastplate. It's only when I glance down at the placard that I realize what I'm looking at is armor that was worn during the Great Battle of Heaven that led to the segregation of the angels and subsequent birth of the Lights and the Darks. Beside it lies a sword brandished with a familiar symbol I'm certain I've seen somewhere before. When the connection registers, it dawns on me which angel this sword and armor belonged to.

Gabriel.

The long, steel blade extends into a bronze hilt, the guard crafted to resemble two outstretched wings identical to the silver insignia branded on the door to her office. A glowing gem lies embedded in the pommel, matching the brilliant golden aura that shrouded her body the one and only time we crossed paths.

A low hum permeates the air, like the vibrations of a tuning fork, and I blink, breaking my gaze on the sword. Turning from the case, I move onto the next one. This display contains hundreds of preserved moths—all of the same species, size, and brown coloring. My eyes skim across the collection then fall to the sign beneath the glass, tracing over the accompanying epitaph.

To protect our children from human wrath,
the Dark and Light shall come together to offer salvation.
And with the lives saved, we will remember those lost.
The precious ones we build this for.

"For the moth will eat them like a garment,
And the grub will eat them like wool.
But My righteousness will be forever,
And My salvation to all generations."
ISAIAH 51:8

Beneath the inscription and Bible verse is a long list of names and dates spanning back thousands of years. Comprehension darkens my thoughts as I remember Gilgamesh's lesson about the Nephilim who were murdered in the early years of our species. Each of these moths must represent one of those lost children—a tragedy that served as the foundation for which the schools of Light and Dark were established.

The case is cool to the touch as I press my fingertips to the front of the glass. My eyes narrow, honing in on one of the moths, noting the different shades of brown interlaced with black and white adorning the arrow-sharp line of its body. Its wings are stretched out to the sides with the stiff precision of an airplane in flight.

My nails drum against the glass—*tap, tap, tap*—as if coaxing the moth to wake from the slumber of death. The longer I stare at it, the more I can envision it moving—its frail body returning to life and escaping the cage of this glass mausoleum.

An unexpected urgency twists my gut, and I find myself silently begging the moth to shake free from the confines of the pins holding it still. Maybe because I feel as trapped as that moth—imprisoned by the horrors of my past.

My fingernail taps again. A faint flicker. No, it was just a trick of the eye.

As I stare into the case, the whisper of a deep, masculine voice rises out of the hush and begins whispering nonsensical words in my ear. I whip around, tearing my gaze from the moth, a breath catching in my throat, but no one stands behind me. No one else is here. The room is empty.

I'm still alone.

Swallowing, I turn back toward the display. The instant my eyes return to the moth, the voice resumes its echoing hiss, this time in my head, filling my entire skull with its presence. The sound seems to simultaneously cut through and surround me, bouncing off every surface in the large space, while also lingering impossibly close.

"Anastēson auton. Ho skotos dia sou diarreitō."

My eyes snap closed at these words, and my palm flattens against the glass. A shiver crosses my skin as the voice purrs again.

"Anastēson auton. Ho skotos dia sou diarreitō."

I nod, driven by its unknown direction. Hearing a disembodied voice would shake any normal person, but for me, it's just another sign that I'm as deranged as everyone thinks.

The voice speaks once more, but this time, there's no mistaking its meaning. I don't know how I can suddenly understand what it's saying, but every word is clear, like the voice is translating on my behalf, so I can comprehend what it wants.

"Resurrect it. Let the darkness run through you."

A shudder of apprehension rolls over my body as my fingers press against the case, led by something outside myself I can't control. The voice speaks again, reassuring me.

Calming me.

"I am a friend. Trust me. You have the power."

Silence falls like a curtain at the end of a stage production, suffocating all sound apart from a faint flutter on the edge of hearing—like wings beating in the distance. Eyes flitting open, I peek down at the moth, both stunned and unsurprised to find it alive. It struggles against the pins for a moment, then breaks free, hunting for an escape. The glass crypt offers none.

A loud bang to my right tears my focus from the display, and blinking, I meet the gaze of a third-year Nephilim girl I vaguely recognize as one of Lisbeth's friends. She stands in front of the door, gaping at me with a hand clamped over her open mouth. The books she was carrying lie scattered across the floor by her feet.

"Y-You…" The girl stumbles back a few steps, her vibrant, seafoam-green eyes wide with fear.

I furrow my brow, bemused by her terror, as she glances between my face and the glass case beside me. When I follow her line of sight to the display, I notice the moth is no longer moving. The poor thing has returned to its grave.

"Blasphemy…" The word penetrates her lips in a faltering breath, just loud enough to draw my gaze again. Her pale, stricken face twists and she glares at me with disgust, as if I am a Biblical plague on this earth. "Blasphemy!" the girl says again, shouting this time.

"Wha—" A single step toward the girl sends her barreling from the room before I can get the full word out.

The door to *Exhibits* whips back and forth behind her like a white flag waving in surrender, each swing as furious as the glowering expression she wore, her visible revulsion seared into my mind. Between each swing, I catch a glimpse of the girl racing through the spacious room beyond, clutching a cell phone to her ear.

"Great," I mutter. *Just what I need.*

Sighing, I trudge toward the door, stepping over the abandoned books on the floor and collecting my own pile from the small table with a lazy swipe of my hand. The cavalry is probably already on its way—I should leave while there's still a chance to enjoy the rest of my weekend harassment-free.

Stalling, I cast a glance over my shoulder at the case where, for a fleeting moment, I was able to give that moth life.

Alaric was right, I realize with a laugh. Bitchy, high-school diplomacy aside, I do belong in this world. It wasn't a mistake.

I really am a Nephilim.

A thrill rushes through me at the thought, and as I push open the door, that voice returns for the briefest of moments, following me in my shock and glee. It caresses my shoulder like a pat on the back, offering its congratulations.

"Well done," it murmurs.

With a smile stretching across my face, I walk from the shadowed museum back into the warm glow of the main room of the library, for once in my life feeling powerful instead of weak and afraid of what I am.

EIGHT

CALEB

SHOVING MY HANDS IN my pockets, I head toward the famous Library of Alexandria, or what the Serapeum Academy managed to salvage from the great fire, which is actually most of it, unbeknownst to humans. They moved the library here to be safe and away from the stupidity of mortals. It's the one place in the academy I admire, vast stores of knowledge throughout the ages at my fingertips. The Nephilim are an ancient race, and I love spotting us in texts when the concept of civilization was brand new, and humanity was just discovering their full potential. The library also offers shadowy alcoves to read in, providing relief from all this white and gold. Today, I want to read everything I can get my hands on regarding Alexander the Great. I might find some clue, even amongst mortal accounts.

Frustration knots me. I know it's only been a month, but I've learned depressingly little about where my grandfather could possibly be. Mind surfing the Light students has yielded zero results and has been mind-numbingly boring. A lot of hatred for yours truly, the usual school gossip of who's sleeping with whom, and of course, every Light's obsession: Ascension.

And to my surprise, a lot of these Lights have a disdain for humans in the same way Ishtar does, although they'd never admit they share a common ideal with a Dark. They might not want to subjugate humans, but they sure do believe they're superior, despite their mortal blood.

And then there's lovely Luna. That's a nut I still haven't been able to crack. We sit next to each other in the handful of classes we share, and in each one I feel her eyes on me when she thinks I'm not looking. I hate to admit it, but I want to look back, and not just because she's a smokeshow. Yeah, I'm still convinced that something shady is going on there, but I can't be certain she's Gabriel's puppet, either. She seems so… lonely. Lost. From what I can tell, she doesn't have any friends. She hurries from class the moment it ends, and from what I've observed, those little first-years—Lisbeth and Ellie—have fun tormenting her. For the life of me, I can't figure out why. Is this all real or part of an act? Aren't Lights supposed to be all goody-goody and shit? At least to each other, I mean.

They have no problem being total dicks to the Dark Nephilim. And I have no problem dishing it back to them. Spoiler alert—I'm going to win that battle. I'll give them visions that will make them tear their eyes out if they push me too far. I hate bullies.

I put a little swagger in my step as I stroll down the endless corridors, stretching out my powers to catch any piece of conversation that might prove to be useful. But I don't have high hopes. I'm going to have to up my game and start targeting teachers, and that'll take a bit more finesse. And a bit more time.

As it is, every time I'm out and about, Light students avoid me, giving me a wide berth and looks full of loathing. Even after the teachers have preached about togetherness, there has been zero change in attitude. Shocking. As thoughts flood my way, my eyes narrow. This isn't exactly what I've been searching for but it *is* interesting.

I can't believe what she did in the library…

I didn't know Lights could do that. That's Dark shit…

I knew she was a freak. All those stories and now this…

Holy shit, Luna performed a resurrection. That's forbidden…

She doesn't belong here—she's jeopardizing our chance at Ascension…

Luna needs to be taught a lesson, crazy bitch…

I stumble at these thoughts, my feet slowing. Luna performed a resurrection? Raising something from the dead is strictly forbidden among the Lights because only the Creator has the right to wield that power. Only He has the right to creation. Resurrection is a Dark trait. And even then, we *don't* do it. We have no business meddling with life and death. Breathing life into inanimate objects doesn't count, although the Lights still look at it as creation. Oh, the blasphemy. My heart speeds up. What *is* Luna? And why would she be so foolish as to bring something back to life in front of witnesses? She can't be that naive, can she?

Then that last thought catches me like a punch to the gut. *Luna needs to be taught a lesson, crazy bitch…* My eyes scan the hallway as I pick up speed once more. There, up ahead, I see Lisbeth and Ellie and two guys I haven't seen before—or maybe I have, and I just haven't been paying attention. Making friends hasn't been my goal, after all. They're big dudes, and anger simmers in my chest. Four people to teach one girl who's a buck twenty a lesson? They're real brave, these pathetic excuses for Nephilim.

They hurry around a corner, and I resist the urge to break into a run. There are too many people around, and I'm outnumbered by Lights who would have no problem attacking me if they thought I was going after one of their own. The last thing I need is mob mentality kicking in. I consider myself a grade-A badass, but taking on more than five Nephilim at a time would be a struggle, even for me. Inside my head, I hear Hammurabi scoff, declaring he could take on ten Nephilim and not break a sweat.

I round the corner, but the dumbass quartet are nowhere in sight. Shit. The long hallway is nearly empty. I guess the library isn't a super popular place to be, so I throw caution to the wind and sprint. The few Lights I pass all shoot me wary looks bordering on frightened. It's not a bad thing being feared, as my classmates are about to discover.

Guilt nags at me as I run. Guilt that I rejected Luna and failed to notice the extent of how badly she was being treated. She's not my responsibility—I'm not her protector—but still, the guilt sloshes in my stomach like acid. I've been so focused on Alexander I didn't even pick up the signs that my Goldilocks is hiding some serious Dark powers. Ishtar would kick my ass if she knew how blind I've been. Luna isn't my mission, but I should have been paying attention.

I hit the corridor in front of the library, my boots thumping on the marble floor, the sound echoing to the tops of the tall ceiling. I pass the great library doors, and I see them not too far off, for once thankful for my bright ivory surroundings that make it difficult to hide. Luna's burnished gold hair is hard to spot, as she's surrounded by Lisbeth and Ellie and the two hulking boys. The anger that has been simmering boils over into full-blown rage when I watch as the spiteful brunette shoves Luna against the wall and delivers a backhanded blow to her face. The rest of them descend on her like wolves, and my vision washes in red.

I'm almost upon them when one of the guys looks up, a shocked expression on his face, as he finally realizes there's a bigger predator in their midst. My elbow finds his nose with a satisfying crunch, and I slam his head into the stone wall with a sickening thud. He slides to the floor, out cold. Dumb, dumber, and dumbest all freeze for a moment as Luna gazes up at me, stunned. I take precious seconds to see if they've hurt her, but aside from her dazed expression, she doesn't appear to be injured.

"You," Lisbeth hisses, bringing me back to the here and now.

"Me," I snarl, barely avoiding the blow her other male companion aims my way. I grin. Now, it's time for the real fun to begin.

My power lashes out of me like dark whips, wrapping around the minds of my victims with vengeful glee.

Ellie hops up and down screaming, "Get them off, get them off me! Oh, God!" She yanks at her clothing like a madwoman, and I step around her. Blondie then drops on the floor, rolling around.

Lisbeth screeches, "Why am I bleeding?" She swipes her hands under her eyes, holding them out in front of her, wailing, "It's coming out of my eyes. Out of my eyes. I can't see!" She sobs.

I smile and then focus on the last man standing. He falls to his knees, his eyes distant on some faraway horror. Suddenly, he curls in on himself like a baby. I step over him, finally reaching Luna.

Her eyes blink up at me, impossibly huge in her face. It's like she sees me, but she's still stuck in her own nightmare, and this one isn't an illusion. I keep my movements slow and deliberate as I bend down, making sure she can see my hands. I don't want to freak her out more than she already is.

"Hey, Goldilocks," I say, keeping my voice soft and even, but loud enough she can hear me over the screams and cries of the three asshats behind me. "You're safe now. I won't let them hurt you, but we need to get out of here, okay? I have to release them at some point."

A small headache nags me, reminding me of how much power I'm expending to keep three Nephilim trapped in a loop of terrors. I don't mind the pain. After what they tried to do, a splitting migraine would be totally worth it.

Luna blinks up at me. "Goldilocks?"

Her bewildered and unexpected reply startles a laugh from me. I wrap one finger around a strand of her silky hair and show it to her. "Yep, you can't deny who you are. I'm going to help you up, okay?"

"I… Yes," she says, allowing me to take her hands.

I lift her to her feet with ease and keep one of her hands tightly clasped within my own. Her skin is soft and smooth, and I run my thumb over hers, hoping that small gesture of comfort helps. I take her back to the library, knowing we can get lost in the shadows there.

When we enter, it appears mostly empty, but I don't plan on staying out in the open. I hurry past towering rows upon rows of books, the smell musty with knowledge, to my favorite secluded spot that features two deep amethyst velvet armchairs in a dim nook. This is the philosophy section, and for whatever reason, students avoid this area. Maybe it's because I've claimed it as my spot, but I wonder if the Lights don't like to read about morality too much. They might have to question their choices and beliefs. Oh, the horror.

With gentle hands, I sit Luna down before I collapse onto my own seat. Sweat beads on my forehead. I've been steadily sending illusions to those three idiots, and it's wearing on me like sandpaper. Closing my eyes, I snap the tethers connecting my power to their minds. Relief floods through me and I sigh. When I open my eyes, I find Luna studying me as she so often does in class when she thinks I don't notice.

Her eyes dart away, and a flush sweeps up her neck and along her cheekbones. I suppress a grin. When I notice her slight tremble, my grin morphs into a frown. "Are you okay?" A bitter laugh escapes me. "Well, four assholes just tried to jump you, so that's a stupid question, but they didn't hurt you, did they?"

She shakes her head, gazing at the floor. "Thank you…for helping." Her voice is so soft I barely catch her words. "I know this doesn't mean anything. I don't expect you to change your mind about…"

She trails off, and guilt claws at me as I remember what I said when we met. *Best stick to your own kind."*

Shit, she's killing me. I scoot my chair around, scraping the mahogany legs against the marble. Luna glances up, eyes rounded. I take her cold hands in mine, trying to warm them. She stares at my fingers as if she's never held hands with a guy before. Hell, maybe she hasn't.

"Look, I'm sorry I've been such an ass. It's just that—Lights—my experiences with Lights have been pretty shit. And I know that's not your fault, but when you tried to be nice to me…" I release another heavy sigh. "I thought you were playing me. And that pissed me off. I thought this whole thing you've got going on was an act, and you were trying to lure me into some sort of trap."

Shaking her head again, she whispers, "Thing I have going on?"

I wince at the confusion in her voice, hating myself a little. "The innocent, new girl thing. I mean, you're kinda old to be a new student, so it threw me off." I shrug. "Everything about you threw me off."

Her eyes rise to meet mine, and the unexpected anger I find takes me by surprise. "I can't fit in anywhere."

I grip her fingers harder, my own anger bubbling to the surface. "Hey, if people treat you like shit here for no reason, you don't want to fit in." My eyes bore into hers, and she drops her gaze.

Releasing one of her hands, I lightly grasp her chin, forcing her to look up at me. This close, I notice the ring of gold around the hazel of her irises. "I don't fit in here, either. Everyone hates me, and I haven't done a damn thing to deserve it but exist. Everyone hates me but you, that is. Know what I say?" I ask, and she shakes her head for a third time. "Screw 'em."

A giggle escapes her, making me smile. "Screw 'em," she repeats.

"Now you're learning," I say, letting go of her chin, my hand clasping her free one once more. "Luna, do you want to tell me what happened?" I know what happened, but I want her to open up to me. I want my suspicions confirmed.

She glances away, biting her lip and then turns to me, shrugging. "I don't know. They've been like this since I got here. They think I'm a freak." She gives me a helpless look. "So much for hoping this school would be different."

The mournful note in her last words catches at me, and I decide not to press her further. She's just been traumatized, and I want her to trust me. And I honestly don't think she understands the implications of what she's done, which is even more intriguing. If she's displaying Dark tendencies, how did she end up at a Light school?

Luna is a mystery I desperately want to solve, but she's not my reason for being here. Alexander is. But that doesn't mean I can't use an ally. I genuinely like her, and I can't toss her back to the wolves after saving her. That's not my way.

"Well," I say, "you've got me. That is, if you still want to be friends after I was such an ass."

She gifts me with that timid, sweet smile. "I'd like that." Then curiosity reflects in her expression. "What did you do to them?"

My lips curve into a satisfied smile. "Nothing they didn't deserve." I rise to my feet, pulling her up with me. "Come on, Goldilocks. I'll walk you to your room."

NINE

LUNA

A GROAN ESCAPES MY lips when my alarm goes off first thing Monday morning, each blaring beep like a drill bit cutting into my temples, carving a path straight to my brain. My hand smacks down on the clock, hitting the snooze button. I'm still drained from what happened this weekend—the only saving grace of the whole ordeal being my newly born friendship with Caleb.

I'm not sure what I would have done if he hadn't turned up. When Lisbeth and Ellie cornered me with their friends, it was as if I suddenly forgot how to move. My feet were rooted to the spot as my mind was pulled back to every other time I'd been accused of doing something terrible.

That's the part I still can't figure out. Why were they so upset by the fact I brought a stupid moth back to life? I'm sure the other Nephilim at this school can do far more impressive things than revive a dead insect for less than a minute. And yet, the way that girl looked at me in the library museum before running off to find her friends… There was an unmistakable fear and repugnance in her eyes, like I had just personally wronged the Creator.

I sit up, running a hand through my hair. Yesterday, just after I resurrected the moth, there was a moment when I finally believed I fit in here. That I wasn't possessed by evil like I'd always been told, and that I really was born with some greater power that made me different. Special, just like Alaric said when we met.

But my encounter with the other Nephilim has made it clear that my life is a pendulum, always swinging back and forth between the hope I belong and the grim reality that I never will.

Swiping my phone off the bedside table, I click on the screen and open the messaging app, bringing up my conversation with Alaric. The message I typed last night stares back at me, judging me, from where it sits in the text box, unsent.

Have you ever resurrected something?

Frowning, I tap the delete button, erasing the words.

A knock on my bedroom door makes me jump, and I bolt from the bed, my heart racing as I inch toward the threshold. Are Lisbeth and Ellie waiting on the other side, here to finish what they started? I cast a wary peek through the peephole to find a brown eye blinking back at me. A breath of relief fills my chest as the eye pulls away to reveal Caleb's face.

"Knock, knock, Goldilocks. We're gonna be late," he calls through the wood in a sing-song voice.

I unlock the door, crack it open a few inches, and poke my startled face through the gap.

A grin tugs up one corner of Caleb's mouth as he gives me a quick glance up and down. "Love the hair."

My hand flies to my head, still mussed from sleep, the golden strands sticking up in wild disarray.

My cheeks flush as I slam the door in his face. "I… I'll be out in a minute."

Stumbling toward my dresser, I pull out a fresh uniform then race to the bathroom where I tame my wild mane of sleep-tangled hair and scrub my teeth. Thank God all the rooms in this place come with private en suites. Sharing a bathroom with a judgmental psycho like Lisbeth or Ellie is just about the last thing I need.

Once I've freshened up, I grab my books off my desk and throw open the door to find Caleb waiting in the hallway, lounging against the beige stone wall directly opposite my room. His eyes find mine, making me blush again. The downside of being a pariah? I've not had much experience being social with boys. Or anyone for that matter, at least not my age. My only interactions lately have been with Alaric—and always only via phone call or text—but I haven't wanted to burden him with what's been going on here or make him worry, hence my growing habit of deleting my messages to him before I hit send. He got me out of the hospital, and for that, I'll always be grateful, but he's an adult with a life far away from this school. What I desperately want is a friend. Someone my age, *here*, who understands me the way only another teenager can.

"G-Good morning," I stammer, swallowing the dry lump in my throat.

Great start, Luna. Way to stay awkward.

Caleb stands upright, his lips curled into a lopsided smile that leaves me a little weak in the knees. The aura surrounding him pulses, the tendrils of shadow reaching out in warm greeting. My pulse quickens. He must be happy to see me.

"Ready to head to class?" he asks.

I fall into step beside him as we walk down the corridor, taking the fastest route to the large staircase marking the meeting point of the boys' and girls' dormitories. The other students stare as we pass, grimacing and shooting us both equally dirty looks, which I brush off and try my best to ignore. From the hushed whispers filling the halls, I gather word of what happened at the library this weekend has spread. I'm not surprised. I've been enrolled in enough schools to know how quickly rumors can travel, especially when the student body is smaller. And, in this case, when intent on their hatred.

As we follow the white marble stairs down to the ground floor and carry on through the adjoining courtyard, sticking to the cool shadows of the cloister, I risk a glance at Caleb. I'm no stranger to being at the center of rumors and bullying, but what about him? He seems incredibly level-headed and calm about all of this, but he also grew up in this world, aware of what he is. Before transferring here, he probably had more friends than enemies.

Now, he only has me. Me, the broken girl who's spent her whole life drifting from one foster home to another, socially isolated and unaware of my heritage. What kind of friendship can I realistically give him? I don't even know what friendship is.

"You don't have to walk with me, you know. I mean…if you don't want to."

Caleb raises his eyebrows. "I said I wanted to be friends, didn't I? Well, here I am, being friendly."

I want to believe him, but the part of me that's so used to being alone isn't sure if I can. Or if I should.

We continue for a moment in silence until he nudges my shoulder with his. "It's okay if you're worried. But, just so you know, you don't need to be. Those assholes won't bother you again. I'll make sure of it."

I shudder at the memory of my attackers, cowering on the floor, lost in some terrible hallucination Caleb inflicted on their minds—a Dark ability, I'd wager, based on their confused reactions. As awful as it was to watch, I don't feel any pity for their pain. If anything, seeing Caleb defend me like that only strengthened my desire to trust him.

At least I don't have to worry about either of us getting punished for whatever he did to them. If Lisbeth or Ellie went to a teacher or the headmistress, there would be questions about how the fight started, and I've been the victim of enough bullies to know the last thing they'd do is purposely get themselves into trouble. Especially since Gabriel seems like the type to suss out the truth and then punish the liars for their attempted deception.

"What about you?" I blink, looking up at him.

His dark eyes fix on mine. "What about me?"

"The things they say about you…" I trail off, clamping my teeth down hard on the inside of my lower lip. Surely, he must hear what the other Nephilim whisper about him in class when they aren't talking about me. I shake my head. "I'm not the only one they're terrible to."

Caleb stops dead in his tracks once we reach the academic building and signals for me to follow him into an empty classroom. As the door shuts behind us, his gaze slides to my face.

"Listen, I've grown up with this prejudice. I'm used to it. And believe it or not, it goes both ways. This segregation between the Darks and the Lights is old news." He waves a hand between us, as if to illustrate his point.

"I don't understand it," I mutter.

His biting laugh cuts through the room, making me shiver. "What, you mean the preachy, self-righteous lectures in *History of the Fall* haven't made it abundantly clear to you how much the Darks and Lights hate each other? Color me shocked."

As Caleb rolls his eyes, the darkness around him vibrates, projecting what he's feeling. Anger. Irritation. Injustice. I'm tempted to reach out and soothe the shadows—soothe *him*—but I don't know the first thing about comforting anyone. Hell, I don't even know how to comfort myself.

Besides, he knows and understands the rules of our kind far better than I do. Caleb and the other Nephilim seem to view our existence in black and white—two separate sides with their own ideas of what's right or wrong. Despite being a Light, I feel trapped in the middle, where all I'm aware of are muddied shades of gray. Nothing about this world makes sense or resonates with me the way I'm guessing it should.

"I don't know. It's just…I'm a Light, right?" The words escape me in a strangled breath.

Caleb hesitates. "Yeah? And?"

"So"—I shrug—"as a Light, shouldn't I feel some sort of divine devotion to their cause or something?"

How can I ever belong anywhere if I don't even know what to believe?

He worries his lower lip between his teeth, scanning my face as he considers my question. "It's more complicated than that. We aren't born with these prejudices against each other—they're learned. Because every new generation is exposed to these opinions, it's easy to see why there's still a divide, but being one or another—Light or Dark—doesn't automatically brainwash you into those ideologies or force your loyalty. Take the Darks, for example. We're all about thinking for ourselves. We'd never pressure anyone into doing something they don't want to do or to fight for an idea they don't believe in."

"And the Lights?" My voice is a tremulous whisper.

"Have different views than we do, and the academies do a damn good job of ensuring we all stay on our respective sides. They keep us apart to avoid sparking another war. Not that Darks and Lights ever want to play nicely."

And yet, Caleb is here. Enrolled at a Light school.

"If that's true, then why leave the Tower of Babel?"

A smirk warps his lips, and he reels back, impressed. "Someone was listening my first day of class."

A flush creeps up my neck. "I just mean…why would you come here if you knew the Lights would treat you this way?"

The smile slips from his lips, and for a long moment, he stares at me, saying nothing. Leaning back against the nearest wall, he crosses his arms. "From what my teachers told me back at the Tower, this whole exchange program is just a political move. Tensions are high, as they always are,"—he mutters that last part under his breath—"and the Lights want it to look like they're doing everything in their power to keep the peace."

That would explain why even the teachers don't seem too thrilled about Caleb's enrollment at the Serapeum. They're civil enough to him—more so than the students, at least—but it hasn't escaped my notice how on edge they always are in his presence, like they're waiting for him to cause some sort of problem. I guess it's hard for me *not* to notice when people have looked at me that way my whole life.

"You didn't answer my question." The accusation in my tone takes us both by surprise, and Caleb gapes at me, his eyes wide.

"I don't know," he says. "Boredom, I guess? Morbid curiosity? They needed someone, and I have thick skin. I knew what I was walking into. Although…" He pauses, clearing his throat. "Certain aspects of this place are definitely better than others."

The smile returns to his lips and he winks.

Oh. He means me, I realize.

My cheeks burn with the heat of a thousand suns as I shift my weight from one foot to the other, embarrassed.

As silence floods the room, it occurs to me that, although there's no physical barrier between us, I can sense the divide Caleb spoke of. I've seen it in the glances of the other Light students when they look at him like he's less than they are, even though he's so much more. It was there today, and it will continue to be there every time someone gossips about us in passing, even though I don't care what they think.

Regardless of how much I like Caleb or how much he likes me, the world and our history wants to keep us apart.

A tightness grips my chest at the thought. "Does that mean we're breaking some kind of unspoken rule by not hating each other?"

This friendship between us might be new, but I don't want to lose Caleb because of some stupid societal rule that says we shouldn't be mixing.

The darkness brimming along his skin expands outward like ghostly appendages reaching out to embrace me.

His smile deepens. "Maybe," he says, his tone mischievous. "But you know, I've never been big on following the rules."

TEN

CALEB

I LEAVE THE EMPTY classroom and then stroll into *Nephilim Powers 100* across the hall, Luna trailing in my wake. Not because I'm a sexist bastard, but because I want to take the brunt of the venomous glares. I can handle it better. And unlike lovely Luna, I couldn't give two shits if I don't belong here. Goldilocks is all the friend I need, and she was quite an unexpected and unplanned for friend.

My first assessment of her was spot on. She is totally innocent about this world, and that makes me fear for her. She didn't seem to understand why Lights would freak out about her resurrection trick, which leaves her underbelly exposed for attack. Luna can't protect herself if she doesn't know the rules.

As I slide into a chair behind a long, high table, I silently vow to do my best to give her the basics so she can build some defense. I can't be with her twenty-four seven, and I have my own mission to contend with.

Luna slips into the chair next to mine, causing a collective wave of silent hatred to roll over us. I just smirk at my fellow classmates, daring them to start something. I won't lie—I'm itching for a fight. Not so much for me, but for Goldilocks.

The door swings open, and our teacher for *Nephilim Powers 100* steps in. Lucifer's sake, they have me in a 100 class. Like I can't run laps around everyone in here. When I briefly met with Gabriel, she explained it was so I could gain a deeper understanding of Light powers and so her younger students could understand Dark powers better. Whatever. Mostly, I feel like a zoo exhibit.

Vesta—otherwise known as the Roman goddess of fire—steps in front of the classroom and smiles at us, a perfect, welcoming, practiced smile. I'm always surprised she's a Nephilim; she's so subdued, even for a Light. Her copper hair is pulled back in a neat twist, and she wears a lab coat, which strikes me as absurdly funny.

"Children," she begins as she always does. I guess we are children to her given how long she's been around. "Today, we are going to focus on something basic. Something that reveals our essence as Nephilim."

I feel Luna perk up beside me, and I suppress a grin at her eagerness. Damn, she's cute. I know what's coming, and I'm a lot less excited, but I enjoy her enthusiasm. This is literally a whole new world to her.

I was lucky. Yeah, my deadbeat dad bailed, but Mom knew what I was. I was never afraid of my powers or how I didn't quite fit in with the other humans. Mom told me what she could of my heritage, promising me that one day I'd go and be with my own kind. As a kid, that terrified me, and I remember crying a lot, not wanting to leave her. But as I grew older, I longed to go to an academy, and while Gomorrah was a great primary school, the Tower of Babel proved to be everything I ever wanted. It also helped me strike a balance between belonging to the Darks and the mortal world—to Mom.

I glance at Luna's face, shining with curiosity. She never got any of that from what it sounds like. And she deserves a hell of a lot more than the experience she's getting here. This should be a time of wonder and celebration for her, not bullying and distrust and cruelty. My Goldilocks deserves more than that. It makes me want to try to talk Ishtar into having her visit Babel.

Vesta's lilting voice interrupts my thoughts from treading down that dangerous path. "Today, we are going to create flame. All Nephilim carry the fire of creation inside them, whether Light or Dark." She gives me a pointed look, and I resist the urge to roll my eyes. "Caleb's fire will look different than yours," she says to the rest of the class, "but that doesn't make it any less beautiful, as it is all gifted by the Creator."

I arch a brow. Huh, Vesta just told these Light kids that my flame is as beautiful as theirs. I don't know whether to applaud her audacity or scoff at her bullshit. Not that my fire isn't scorching, but I doubt Vesta believes it's anywhere near as good as a Light's flame.

Luna gazes at me under her lashes. "As much as I'm dreading this, I'm also looking forward to seeing your other powers. I bet your fire's amazing," she offers, voice bashful. She waves her hand at me, as if tracing an invisible outline. "Everything else is." Those last words are so soft I barely hear them, but I do hear them, and I can't help the wide grin spreading across my lips.

"So brazen, Goldilocks," I murmur. "I knew you thought I was hot." I grin harder as a dark flush rises from the collar of her shirt to sweep over her face.

"Th-that's not what I meant! I…" She bites her lip, looking mortified.

I tilt my head, leaning a little closer. "So you don't think I'm hot?" Luna grows even more flustered, and I enjoy every moment of her blushes. I wink. "It's okay. I think you're hot, too."

Luna's mouth drops, and Vesta clears her throat. I glance back at the front of the class and shrug at my teacher. I'm a rebel. Duh.

"Now that everyone is paying attention," Vesta says, and I ignore the wrathful looks of my classmates. "Search deep inside, find that spark, the essence that makes a Nephilim. Your bloodline. Find your fire there." She looks at me once more. "Caleb, since you're an advanced student, why don't you go first? Demonstrate to the others how it's done, hmm?"

Huh, I didn't expect her to trot me out like a show pony. I better perform.

"My pleasure," I say. I whirl my fingers and flick out my wrist, exposing my palm. Heat singes my blood, building and begging to be set free. Ebony fire laced with the deepest purple bursts to life about two inches from my skin. The flames grow taller and split, until two figures writhe above my palm, dancing to a beat only I can hear. Luna gasps, and although her face is pale from nerves, I see her lace her fingers tightly together to keep from reaching out to touch my fire. My eyes move back to Vesta, and I flash a shit-eating grin.

To my surprise, I see her hide a smile. "Do you see, class? How the color of his fire marks his Dark bloodline? Now, you try it."

One by one, the Light students produce white and silver flames. All except Goldilocks. She fidgets in her chair and frowns, unease in her eyes as she stares at her palm. Vesta gives her a kind smile and produces a gold flame—like it literally looks like liquid gold—pushing it toward Luna until it hovers in front of her face. Luna flinches back and studies it, her full lips flattened in a straight line. Her discomfort is palpable. Sympathy flashes through me as I see how new and batshit crazy this must all seem to her.

"To be a Light is to serve," Vesta tells her. "To please the Creator until we can Ascend. Find that tranquil part of yourself and let it warm you, and you'll find your fire."

I resist the urge to projectile vomit. Servitude sounds fun. Not. Plus, none of these little angel wannabes are pure, kind, or particularly humble in their "service." Their treatment of Luna proves that.

Goldilocks focuses on Vesta's words but nothing happens. A few snickers ripple across the room, and she shrinks into herself. Dark flame crowns my head and I snarl, eyes searching for the laughing little fuckers. Shock descends upon the crowd as the Lights observe my skill with fire.

Vesta says in a calm voice, "Class, Caleb is very advanced. One day, you will all be able to have his control. Very nice, Caleb. You can put the fire away now."

I raise a sardonic brow at my teacher, and she inclines her head. I extinguish the flames and turn to regard Luna.

"I-I'm afraid," Luna admits, and I want to hug her.

"If you're afraid your fire is volatile, it will comfort you to know servitude to the Creator will give you the ability to control your powers. You have a higher purpose—"

I give a derisive snort. "Fire isn't tranquility," I counter, my eyes meeting Luna's fearful ones. "It's powerful and destructive and life-saving, at times. But it's *your* power, Luna, not the Creator's. A force you can master and bend to your will. Think of that first moment you felt a connection to your Nephilim nature. That's where you'll find your fire. And when you find it, take control of it. It's yours to wield as you will. Don't be afraid of it."

Luna swallows hard but obeys, brows dipped in concentration.

For the first time, Vesta frowns at me in disapproval. "Caleb, that may be how a Dark connects—"

A startled squeal escapes Luna as fire bursts above her palm, hovering in the air. My jaw falls open as I stare at her flame, and a collective gasp echoes throughout the room. Her fire is ruby red. Blood red. I have never seen anything like it, and judging from Vesta's stunned expression, neither has she.

Holy shit. What exactly is Luna?

ELEVEN

LUNA

Y HEART POUNDS IN my ears as a surge of blood rushes straight to my head, making me dizzy. Everyone is staring at me, even Caleb. His eyes betray the shock his face is trying to mask, his lips set in a tight, thin line. No one else bothers to try to hide theirs.

I peer down at the flame hovering over my palm, red just like the fire that changed my life the fateful day of my first incident. My past has chased me for as long as I can remember, the tormenting reminder of this willful evil inside me always lingering at the edge of my thoughts. Yet, like when I resurrected the moth in the library, I'm somehow in control of it at this moment. It's not lashing out on its own—it's been summoned, proving that I *do* have power. That I'm a Nephilim, and I belong here as much as the other students, despite how much they torment me for being different. It's proof that Caleb and I…that there's a greater power beyond explanation we share in common, regardless of the divide between the Lights and the Darks. Above all, it's proof that the horrors of my past—the incidents that led to my time in the hospital— really were accidents beyond my comprehension. I didn't *want* to hurt anyone. Fear was always my catalyst, my panicked reactions the puppeteer pulling my strings. But now, thanks to Caleb, I've taken the first step in conquering that weakness, in reclaiming dominance of myself. Like he said, it's *my* power, and only I can choose to wield it the way it was intended. Maybe, if I do learn how to fully control it, I'll never hurt anyone again.

And yet…something about my flame isn't right. I can tell as much by the way everyone is looking at me, especially Vesta. She gapes at my fire, as if I've somehow offended her.

"Enough!" she shouts.

I startle at the booming sound of her voice, and the flame dangling over my hand disappears.

"Class is over," she announces to the other students, her wary gaze never once leaving my face. A sharp breath catches in my chest when she crosses the room and slams a hand down on the table in front of me. "You. Come with me, *right now*."

I shift my gaze to Caleb, desperate to understand what I did wrong, but he looks as stunned as I feel. Vesta is normally so calm and collected—the perfect picture of control. Right now, her aura is anything but, as it trembles around her in a furious spasm, sizzling across her skin like an egg in a frying pan, the white light burning molten gold.

I don't understand her reaction. How could I, an inexperienced Nephilim, rattle someone as ancient as Vesta? Someone who was perceived as so *other*, so powerful by mortals who didn't know what she really was that they thought only to call her a goddess?

Swallowing, I push back my chair and hang my head to avoid the questioning stares of my classmates. I don't even spare Caleb a second glance as I follow Vesta out of the room.

As we step into the corridor, I expect my classmates to flock to the door to watch as I'm carted off to who knows where, but when I peek over my shoulder, the doorway to *Nephilim Powers* is empty. The other students don't dare to leave the room after us, despite Vesta dismissing them for the day.

My classmates' reactions are burnt into my head. They were terrified—but not of Vesta, even though her uncharacteristic outburst clearly unsettled them all. No, the fear in their eyes was for me. I recognize it, having seen that same expression on the faces of the people around me whenever I had one of my incidents. Considering what I did...well, I understand why my foster families were so afraid. Hell, I was afraid of me, too, until Alaric told me what I am.

But this? Why would a first generation Nephilim like Vesta have any need to fear an untrained student's flame?

Vesta quickens her pace through the hallway, her high heels clip-clopping along the long stretch of white marble like hooves. Her lab coat swishes around her knees.

"W-Where are we going?" I stammer, racing to keep up.

A lock of her burnt orange hair falls free from the neat twist of her updo. Nostrils flaring, she brushes it back into place. "To see the headmistress."

At the mention of Gabriel, my breath hitches and my thundering heart bangs into my ribcage. Seriously? I'm being sent to the principal's office? Sure, my fire looked a bit different when compared to the other Lights' flames—less like starlight and a lot more like blood, which yeah, I can see how that might be unnerving to a group of people who thrive on uniformity. But what do the teachers at this place expect from me? I'm new to this, and I'm trying my best. With time and practice, I'm sure my flame will be just as bright and pure as everyone else's.

Unless there's something wrong with me.

I shake off that thought and focus on the back of Vesta's white coat as she leads me down the corridor to the office. I haven't seen Gabriel since the day Alaric brought me here, but the memory of what I felt when we met is fresh, as if our encounter only just happened. I remember the awe consuming me in her presence…the way my heart seemed to seize at the sight of her…the terror when she fixed her hawk-like eyes on my face…

I'm not sure I'm ready to go through that volatile wave of emotions again so soon.

My breaths constrict as the office draws closer, and sweat forms on my palms as I clench and unclench my hands. Vesta doesn't seem to notice the anxiety radiating from my body like heat—if she does, she fails to show any remorse for her part in causing my growing distress. I've never been one to play the blame game, unless the person I'm blaming for something is me, but surely Vesta must be aware that her cryptic silence is pushing me toward an unstable precipice. I already live my life on the brink. Considering where Alaric found me, I suppose I hoped the teachers at this academy would make it a point to pull me back whenever I get too close to that edge.

Vesta peers at me over her shoulder then pushes open one of the glass office doors. Evangeline sits at her desk in reception, blinking once…twice…three times in surprise. Her large cobalt eyes drift back and forth between Vesta and an ornate grandfather clock positioned in front of the opposite wall.

"Vesta," she drawls in a condescending tone, "aren't you supposed to be teaching right now?"

With a delicate sniff, the goddess of fire plants her hands on her hips and jerks her chin toward Gabriel's door. "Is she busy?"

Tension ripples in the air, almost tangible, as I glance between the two Nephilim. It doesn't take a genius to surmise they don't get along.

As I wonder why, Evangeline's face contorts into a mocking, apologetic smile. "I'm afraid Gabriel's rather tied up at the moment—"

The aura of light around Vesta burns white hot and shivers with impatience. "This is important."

Grabbing my arm, she tugs me toward the closed black door in the corner, ignoring Evangeline's protests. Her hold on me is firm, her hand scorching through my shirt, as if the fire she's known for is leaping off her skin, intent on burning me.

Is this what it was like for the unknowing mortals unlucky enough to be around me during one of my incidents? Vesta is the epitome of control, but thanks to my display in class, she's on the verge of absolutely losing her shit. If she, of all people, is struggling to rein herself in, then no wonder I couldn't prevent all the terrible things I did before coming here. I didn't even know I had powers, let alone how the hell to restrain them.

Vesta throws open Gabriel's door without knocking then flashes a warning glare at me that freezes my steps on the other side of the threshold.

"Headmistress."

Gabriel looks up from an antique jeweled tome splayed open across her desk. "Vesta?" she says, scrunching her brow. Her eyes flash to mine, and her face immediately darkens. "Luna. What's the meaning of this?"

"Sit." Vesta signals for me to enter the room and gestures toward the chair intended for visitors facing Gabriel's desk.

Gabriel's narrowing gaze sweeps between us. "I'd like one of you to answer me. *Now.*"

Vesta steps forward obediently, arms pinned to her sides. "In my class just now, she produced a red flame. *Red*, Gabriel!" she shrieks. Her eyes are wild as she shakes her head vehemently. "Having her here has clearly displeased the Creator. It isn't natur—"

"Lower your voice," the Archangel snaps, "and be very careful what else you say." Her dark eyes flash with warning and threat.

Vesta flinches and lowers her gaze as she shuffles backward, cowering in the corner like a puppy who's been kicked by its owner. I wasn't the one Gabriel scolded, and yet, I'm mortified by the Archangel's anger. The displeasure of a greater power is almost painful to behold—like sharpened claws scratching into my soul. I'd hate to actually bear the brunt of her wrath.

If I feel this way about upsetting an angel, then I can only imagine how the Faithful must've mourned disobeying the Creator when He called them back to Heaven for mating with humans. Right now, I'd give anything to quell Gabriel's rage, so who knows what the Nephilim here are willing to do to get in the Creator's good graces.

No wonder they're all so desperate to Ascend. Ascension, to them, must mean forgiveness for their ancestors' misdeeds.

That thought doesn't sit well with me—the notion that everyone at this school was a product of someone else's bad judgment. Does that mean the Faithful viewed their Nephilim children as mistakes or just regretted the choices that led to them?

Do they resent our existence?

Gabriel adjusts the cuffs of her blue, button-up blouse and carefully closes the time-worn book. Folding her hands on top of the leather-bound cover, she fixes her gaze on my face. "Luna, why don't you tell me what happened?"

My chest tightens, and I hear Vesta's shrill voice in my head again. Except this time, I hear the rest of what she didn't get to finish saying before. The partially spoken sentiment wraps around my thoughts like a snake trapping me in its coil. *"It isn't natural."*

I'm not natural.

Something is very wrong with me.

"Am I in trouble?" I manage in a meek voice.

Gabriel smiles, and a weight lifts off my lungs, but it returns the instant I realize she didn't say that I *wasn't* in trouble. My stomach turns. "Just tell us exactly what happened in class. What was on your mind when you conjured your flame?"

"W-Well…" I hesitate, thinking back to that moment. "I tried what Vesta instructed but it didn't work. So, I-I did what Caleb suggested," I stammer.

"Which was?" Her lips twitch at the corners.

I look down at her hands. The knuckles are white from the strain of her fingers lacing together.

A lump rises in my throat, but I force myself to swallow it and keep talking. "He told me fire is a force I can bend to my will and to think…" I swallow again. "To think of the first moment I really felt like a Nephilim. When I did—"

"You produced a red flame," Gabriel finishes. "Tell me, Luna…" She rises from her chair and walks over to the window overlooking the colorful garden beyond. In the glass, I can just about make out her reflection in the bright morning light. "What moment came to mind?"

"I…"

Something feels wrong about this—like Gabriel's invading my privacy by asking. Why does it matter what I was thinking about? They should just be thankful I was able to conjure a flame without setting the building on fire.

The silence stretches on for too long, and I realize any answer I give now will likely seem manufactured. Suspicion ignites in Gabriel's eyes as she turns to face me, although that reassuring smile is still firmly in place.

"It's okay," she urges. "I'm here to help you."

My thoughts drift to Caleb. What would he do?

Based on what he thought of me when we met, I've gathered he's not a big fan of dishonesty. So, I'm going to take a leaf from his book. I'll be honest, if only to get out of this office and away from the Archangel's leering stare. And because I think Gabriel will know if I lie.

"The other day in the library, I…resurrected one of the moths in the exhibit room."

Vesta emits a screeching sound that reminds me of a dinosaur movie I saw with my last foster family a few months before I was committed. The pterodactyls in it made similar noises.

"Blasphemy!" she hisses, her face crimson with rage.

"*Vesta.*" Shadows drown the room as if the sheer boom of Gabriel's voice has sucked all the light out of the world. I shudder in my chair as Vesta presses her back to the wall.

Clearing her throat, Gabriel crosses the room toward me and perches herself on the edge of her desk.

"Luna, allow me to be frank with you. There are certain forces that we, as Lights, have no business playing with. Those are for the Creator alone to control. Life and death are two such forces."

Her reprimand sinks into my skin, striking me like the thrash of a belt on naked flesh. Tears spring into my eyes, blurring the room.

"I…I'm sorry. I didn't know—"

She holds up a slender hand, silencing me. My voice cuts off with a tiny whimper.

"I think, for your own well-being and the safety of the other students at this academy, it would be best if I put you on academic probation for now. You are to continue attending your classes but you are also to report here every Saturday morning. We will discuss any further developments as they arise."

A frown weighs heavily on my lips. I've been placed on academic probation before, although that's usually meant suspension from classes rather than whatever this is. One of my incidents even got me expelled, and yet, somehow, this seems so much worse. Maybe it's the way Gabriel says it, or maybe it's because I'm convinced I haven't done anything wrong. For once, I was actually in control of my emotions, and now I'm being punished for it.

As if reading my mind, Gabriel adds, "I want to reiterate that this is not a punishment, Luna. I'm doing this for your own well-being."

There's that word again. *Well-being.*

I bite back the temptation to scowl.

Standing, Gabriel skirts around the large wooden desk and gracefully sinks back into the seat behind it. Her long, deft fingers open the book to resume whatever research we interrupted.

"Gabriel—" Vesta pleads, pushing away from the wall.

Gabriel points at the door, which I suddenly realize has been wide open throughout our conversation. Evangeline sits at her desk at the other end of the office, looking just about everywhere else but at us, pretending she hasn't been listening. The heaving of her chest gives her away.

"But—" Vesta protests.

Gabriel's voice is a threatening snarl. "My decision is final."

Vesta shepherds me out of my seat and through the door, having the good sense to close it behind us before the Archangel can dole out any more reprimands. Neither one of us utters a sound as we step into the sanctuary of the reception area of the office. Even Evangeline remains silent.

The shame of disappointing Gabriel is an assault on my senses. I can barely see or breathe past its weight on my heart, and beside me, surprisingly, Vesta seems just as afflicted—the goddess of fire sniffling into her sleeve like a child, once confident but now knocked down by fear. Considering how long she's been alive and how deeply entrenched she is in this world, her reaction stuns me even if I think she deserves it. After all, she's the one who acted like I did something wrong and decided to bring me to Gabriel. Neither of us would be feeling this way if she had just left me alone.

That thought circles through my head as I finally risk a glance at my teacher's face. Glistening lines of moisture carve over her cheekbones as she steers me toward the closed doors to the hallway, and beyond the tears, I note something in her bereft gaze that makes me feel sick to my stomach. It's the same emotion I saw in the eyes of every other student in class today, including Caleb. I think I might've even glimpsed it in Gabriel's face when Vesta said I produced a red flame.

My chest constricts. No matter what I do or where I go...

Fear will always follow.

TWELVE

CALEB

I PACE BACK AND forth in the corridor, waiting for Luna. She's still in the office, and she's been in there for a while now. I glance down the length of the hallway, but the doors remain closed.

Frowning, I think back to class. Luna's flame was blood *red*. What does that mean? Nothing about Goldilocks quite adds up. First the resurrection and now this. I don't know what she is. Yes, she displays Dark characteristics, but I can't swear she's wholly Dark, either. Can a Nephilim be somewhere in the middle? I was told that was impossible. I mean, even if Ishtar and Gilgamesh took a roll in the sheets, I doubt they'd be stupid enough to have a kid come out of their affair.

I have a strong suspicion both Lights and Darks—despite their hatred—go slumming sometimes, just for the rush and the secret bragging rights, but a kid? One that was both Dark and Light would be thought of as an abomination and a total admission of forbidden sexing. Thanks to the schools, I know humans don't kill Nephilim children anymore—these days, they don't even know we exist—but a child born from both factions might be in serious danger from our kind. The Creator sure as shit wouldn't approve, and that might lead to the Lights eliminating the threat on His behalf. Hell, the Darks could go murderous, too, to ensure the divide.

But it's another thing I can't be entirely sure of, which brings me back to my Goldilocks.

Luna is an anomaly—and a dangerous distraction. So far, I've had nothing to report back to Ishtar about Alexander. It's true I haven't been here that long, but impatience trickles into my gut like acid, a constant burning. The student population has proven to be utterly useless, at least on the surface.

It's time to start planting suggestions and spies, but if I don't get it just right, I will raise all kinds of suspicions. And let's be honest, the only person who'd be interested in Alexander's whereabouts in this school is yours truly. I can't have that. I can't be sent back to the Tower before I find my grandfather.

One of the glass doors swings open, grabbing my attention as a distraught Luna spills out into the corridor. Vesta is beside her, and the ancient Nephilim's face is streaked with tears, shocking the hell out of me. Vesta says something to Goldilocks then heads off in the opposite direction. When I see Luna's face, I forget all about my mission for a moment. She looks terrified, and her eyes are haunted. What the hell did Gabriel say to her?

Anger rushes through my veins, but I keep my face calm as Luna's eyes find mine. She stumbles down the hallway toward me, and I resist the urge to hurry to her and take her into my arms. Ever since I rescued her, I've been careful not to touch her too much. I can't afford to get too attached, and she's someone I could easily get attached to. I genuinely like her and that's a problem.

She reaches me, and I notice she's trembling. Shit.

"What happened?" I ask gently, clenching my fists at my side, so I don't reach for her.

"I shouldn't be here," Luna says, anguish coloring her voice. "I don't belong with the Lights. I don't belong anywhere."

Oh, fuck it. I clasp her icy hands, trying to warm them. "What the hell are you talking about? Of course, you belong here. You're a Nephilim. That makes you special."

Shaking her head, she tries to pull away from me, but I won't let her. I'm pissed that Gabriel has made her feel this way.

"I'm a freak. I'll always be a freak," she insists, tears springing from her eyes and trailing down her cheeks. "And Gabriel..." She shudders from head to toe.

"Is that what Gabriel told you? That's such bullshit." I sneer. "Please, Goldilocks, tell me exactly what happened."

She takes great, gulping breaths, trying to calm down, and I pull her into a nearby cluster of shadows, allowing her a little privacy to get it together. "She's..." She hesitates, swallowing hard. "She's putting me on academic probation. I have to report to her once a week."

The gears in my head whir. "Oh-kay, that doesn't sound so horrible," I say cautiously, not wanting to upset her further. And I'm a little ashamed to admit that the calculating part of my brain is on red alert, pointing out this is an ideal opportunity to spy on the headmistress.

Luna gazes up at me, and her devastated expression feels like a punch to the crotch. "You don't understand. My powers—they aren't right. There's something wrong with me. That's why she wants to watch me. She and Vesta…they're worried about what I might do. Even here, everyone is afraid of me."

The bleakness in her voice shreds my heart, and I get into her face, forcing her to meet my fierce gaze. "That's the problem with these Light assholes," I say. "Anything that doesn't fit in their cookie-cutter mold is *wrong*. There ain't nothing wrong with you, Luna. I promise you that. Dark Nephilim celebrate our differences. We thrive on them. Fuck Gabriel. Fuck this entire place." Luna flinches at the venom in my voice. I take a deep breath and soften my tone, so I don't scare her. "Let me help you."

Hope creeps into her expression. "You think you can?"

I nod. "Look, our skill sets aren't identical, but we share basic things in common—all Nephilim do. I can help you get better and figure out what you can do. And we can practice away from judgmental eyes."

And in the meantime, I can figure out what she is. I know she's holding back on me, and I need her to trust me if she's going to open up. The awful, dragging anchor of guilt wraps around me, whispering I'm no better than the abusive Lights. At least they're honest in their cruelty. They're not trying to use her to get to Gabriel.

She blinks those big, hazel eyes at me and gifts me with a heartbreaking smile, and I feel like the biggest piece of shit on the planet. "Thank you, Caleb."

Her sincerity makes me want to lash out at her, to tell her not to be so trusting, so soft, but I bite back the words. Clearing my throat, I say, "You're welcome. Let's get out of here."

As I steer her toward the dorms, I stamp down my anger, reasoning that I'm not setting out to hurt her. That I can be her friend and use her to spy on Gabriel. I *like* Luna. I'm honestly outraged at how the other Lights treat her. My offer to help her was an honest one and she needs help. I can help Luna and find Alexander. What she doesn't know won't hurt her. I can do this. I can walk this tightrope.

And I won't fall.

THIRTEEN

LUNA

I DON'T KNOW WHAT I would do without Caleb. Ever since that awful day in Vesta's class a few weeks ago, he's barely left my side. In many ways, he's become my lifeline—the one person keeping me afloat in the waters of sanity when everything else here seems determined to drown me. Without him, I'm not sure I would be able to weather the constant looks and whispers that echo what Vesta said to Gabriel when she brought me to the Archangel's office—that my being here has somehow displeased the Creator. I've been the target of cruel rumors before, but something about what the Lights are saying is worse.

Without Caleb, I'm also not sure I would have the strength to survive my required interactions with Gabriel. Every session, she interrogates me, prompting me with bewildering questions to divulge every single little thing I did that week, right down to how I felt when I woke up that morning. As I talk, I expect her to interrupt and finally explain what these meetings are for—meetings that feel an awful lot like my mandatory therapy sessions back when I was committed—but instead, she just sits at her desk like a statue, staring at me with those predatory eyes. I can never tell what she's thinking. To be honest, I'm not sure I want to know.

I haven't mentioned any of this to Alaric—only that I've made a friend, which he seemed pleased about, even if I was sparse on the details. While he doesn't strike me as the bigoted type, I don't want to risk finding out that he is and lose all trust in and liking I have for the only adult who's ever been in my corner. Maybe that's why I didn't inform him about my academic probation either. Our conversations are a welcome reprieve from the tension of living among the Lights, and I don't want him to blame himself for putting me in this situation…or end up afraid of me like everyone else seems to be since I revealed my flame. I'd rather pretend everything is okay than sabotage one of the only good relationships I've ever had.

Thankfully, I have Caleb to confide in, not that I ever say a whole lot about my meetings with Gabriel since mentioning the headmistress tends to sour my mood, and I don't want to put a damper on the time we spend together, which has doubled over the last three weeks. On top of the few classes we share, we've been meeting after curfew every night—in a tucked away nook in the library, far from any potential prying eyes and ears. More than anything, the Lights value order, and their innate need to please has served us well, since no one is ever roaming the halls after lights out, which makes sneaking off in the darkness of night that much easier. Even the teachers don't bother to check if anyone is out of their rooms when they shouldn't be. They know the teen Lights will follow the rules rather than risk losing any points they've possibly earned toward Ascension. The students here are obedient—except, of course, when it comes to harassing me, although in their twisted minds, I'm sure they believe their actions are justified. Hell, for all I know, they've convinced themselves they're doing the Creator's bidding.

I haven't told Gabriel about how the other Lights treat me. I guess I fail to see the point. With my luck, she'd just turn it all back on me and somehow make their behavior my fault. If she knew more trouble was brewing with me at its center, I'd only be giving her another reason to view me as a blight on this school—the first reason being my friendship with Caleb, not that she's ever used those words, or any words at all, to express her displeasure. While she's never said it, I can tell she doesn't approve, which is why, although I don't hide my public outings with him, I don't dare tell her about our meet-ups after hours. I fill those blanks in my schedule with lies. She doesn't need to know he's been helping me with basic things that every Nephilim our age should be able to do, from how to twist my flame into different shapes to simple techniques like the best way to focus. I even managed to restore a dying plant the other day. Not for long—the leaves quickly wilted again—but it was a good start, although I failed to see the difference between that and what I did with the moth. Caleb explained that restoration is a Light gift and on a separate, more acceptable level to resurrection, but it's all the same to me. All I care about is that I'm finally starting to really feel in touch with my Nephilim nature, and the progress I've made is all thanks to Caleb. Considering it was his advice and not Vesta's that helped me conjure my flame at will, I'm more inclined to listen to him than I am to anyone else—even a terrifying Archangel like Gabriel. Caleb is accepting of the strange nature of my abilities while the Lights here all see me as defective. Even our teachers seem wary of me now and have sidelined me from participating in further class demonstrations. Possibly only out of fear of what I might do, although it's more likely Gabriel gave the order to forbid my inclusion after Vesta acted as if having a red flame was somehow heresy against the Creator.

Their reactions that day still plague my thoughts. It's as if being a Light means we have to all be the same. No one is allowed to be unique—we must all be as uniform as the matching clothes we wear, symbolizing our place at this school. I don't know how I feel about that. I've obviously had my fair share of standing out from the crowd, but that doesn't mean I want to be invisible, either.

Still, despite my frustration with classes and how the other Lights continue to ostracize me, I have zero desire to leave the Serapeum. Mostly because of Caleb, but also because, for the first time in my life, the events of my past are beginning to make some semblance of sense and have an explanation beyond some invisible demons pulling at the strings in my head, as if I'm an unwilling marionette. Whether I'm eventually expelled or I depart this academy of my own volition, I don't want to leave until I more fully understand this mystifying power inside me.

For years, I was branded as a danger to myself and others. Broken. Criminally insane. Unredeemable. Looking back, I can't blame the mortals for feeling that way. I thought it, too, and most days, even now—despite knowing what I know—I still do. Guilt is a tough habit to break, and the horrors I've caused will always find a way to haunt me. But lately, I've found myself wondering how much of what I actually did was my fault, and how much was the fault of the parents who discarded me to suffer through those horrors alone? What did they think would happen to a Nephilim child isolated in a human world? My powers were bound to manifest in some way, with or without someone in the know to guide me. It just so happened the way they came out unfortunately hurt so many people.

Ever since my first day of classes when Gilgamesh talked about our ancestors in relation to the Fall, I kept the notion of my own heritage at a safe distance. I could embrace the thought of a relative who lived thousands of years ago—our only link our connection through blood. But if I dared to draw the line between that past and my birth, I'd be forced to face the questions I've been avoiding ever since I learned I'm a Nephilim.

Who were my parents? Which one had angelic blood? What generation am I? Are they still alive? But above all, why…

Why didn't they want me?

If they hadn't abandoned me—if they had just taken the time to at least leave me with people who knew what I was—then maybe all the pain I've inflicted could have been avoided. Maybe then I wouldn't be this anomaly with powers no one else can seem to make sense of. Maybe then I wouldn't be left with this aching hole in my chest from so many years without someone to love me.

I hug my books close to my chest and lean my back against the stone wall next to my dorm room door. Caleb always meets me here, his knock a welcome interruption to sleep, which I haven't been doing a whole lot of lately. Despite the progress we've made, our midnight meetings and constant attempts to unearth the full extent of my powers are taking their toll on me—I have the bags under my eyes to prove it. I'm exhausted so sleep should come easy, and yet, I could barely sleep a wink last night, or the night before that, or the night before that, my head dizzy with a flurry of thoughts.

Last week, I realized we're halfway through the term, which means it won't be long until Caleb is forced to abandon the Serapeum and return to the Tower of Babel. He's only here for one year, and our time together is moving too quickly. When he leaves, I'll be without an ally in a school full of people who despise me. When he leaves, I'll be alone again.

Just like I always am.

My stomach clenches at the echo of footsteps, drawing my gaze to the nearby corner of the dimly lit hallway where the path diverts, continuing to the right in another long corridor—the only natural light seeping in through a stained glass window embedded in the wall facing me, which illuminates the tall figure standing in front of it. A crooked smile tugs at Caleb's cheeks when he sees me.

"Morning, Goldilocks. You're up early."

"Couldn't sleep." I shrug. No need to tell him my fear of him leaving me to go back to his own kind was the underlying cause of my insomnia.

"Bad dream?" he asks, taking my books from my hands. He piles them on top of his own, holding the load easily in the crook of his left elbow. The Lights can say what they want about the Darks, but Caleb has better manners than they do.

"Something like that."

A flirtatious smirk crosses his lips. "Well, you're still smokin' hot to me, dark circles and all."

Warmth spreads across my face when he winks.

We walk, side by side, ignoring the usual probing gazes of the other students, as we make our way to *History of the Fall*. Although he tries to hide it, I can sense

Caleb's disdain for this class. I see it in the way his aura quivers when we step into the classroom, the darkness striking out in every direction like hundreds of tiny whips in search of bare flesh to cut into. They continue to flail, even as we take our usual seats in the back of the room.

"Good morning, class." Gilgamesh bows in greeting and gestures to the whiteboard with a wide sweep of his arm where "Dark" and "Light" are scrawled in large letters, separated by a bold, black line. "Today, I want to dive into the separation existing between the Darks and the Lights, why that divide was born, and why it continues to thrive to this day, thousands of years after the Fall."

Caleb lets out a soft groan beside me. I glance at him out of the corner of my eye, noting the way his mouth is pinched at the corners, as if he's holding back some choice words on the subject. It must be hard for him—being the only Dark in this school. I'm a Light, and it's hard for *me* to listen to all the reasons why we're different. Or rather, why we're supposed to be different.

In reality, I seem to have more in common with Caleb than I'm sure I ever will with the Lights. Although she hasn't said it, I know that's part of the reason why Gabriel insisted on our weekly meetings. I glimpsed the unease in her eyes when I explained how Caleb helped me with my flame that day in *Nephilim Powers*. She doesn't like that he's succeeded where all the Lights have failed to guide me.

Gilgamesh's deep, soothing voice pulls my gaze back to the front of the classroom.

"At the dawn of time, Darks and Lights were the same. They were all angels under the rule of the Creator, but that changed when Lucifer Morningstar sparked the rebellion that led to the Great Battle of Heaven. As a result, a divide was born with Lucifer's followers on one side and those who resisted him on the other."

Gilgamesh peers down the aisle, his eyes flicking between my desk and Caleb's. Maybe I'm imagining things—it wouldn't be the first time—but I could've sworn that last sentence was directed at us. As if he's trying to tell us our friendship is dangerous. That we need to stay on our separate sides, as dictated by our bloodlines. To respect the divide.

As if to warn us Darks and Lights have no business mixing.

I look over at Caleb again to see if he noticed it, but he's doodling instead of paying attention to the lesson. He's hunched over in his seat, focusing on a caricature of Gilgamesh he's drawn across the top right corner of his desk. Once that doodle is perfected, he moves onto another—this one of a beautiful woman shooting lightning bolts straight into Gilgamesh's ass.

"The angels who fell alongside Lucifer believed in his fight for free will while those who remained loyal to Heaven believed solely in their duty to the Creator. Over the millennia, these views haven't changed. The Lights continue to swear their fealty to the only being truly worthy of our love while the Darks indulge in the freedoms on Earth that were never meant to be theirs. To this day, they're as blinded by their lust for a 'human experience' as the angels who followed Lucifer were by his betrayal. This is why Light Nephilim are encouraged to only reproduce with other Lights, although we aren't bound by the same rules as the angels in regards to our relations with humans. Still, in the eyes of the Creator, a union between Lights is the only way to slow down dilution and keep our bloodlines as close to their pure, Ascension-ready forms as possible. Meanwhile, Darks carry on their transgressions with mortals—"

Gilgamesh stops speaking when I thrust my hand in the air, a question forming in the crease of his brow. I wouldn't normally interrupt a lesson, but everything he's saying feels weighted to one side, like he's only telling us half of the truth. There are always two sides to every story—I would know. I don't think I'm a bad person, but I've done terrible things. I'm a Light, and yet, I empathize with the Darks.

If a Light can be filled with such darkness, then surely, a Dark can also reach for the light.

"Yes, Luna?" Gilgamesh asks, his tone cautious.

Caleb looks up at the sound of my name and meets my gaze across the aisle.

I draw in a breath. "Has a Dark ever Ascended?"

A collective gasp swamps the room as the auras of the Lights all flicker and twitch with disgust. Lisbeth and Ellie shoot dirty glares back at me, whispering behind their hands to each other. Even Caleb looks stunned by my question.

"I, uh…" Gilgamesh lets out a shaky laugh and runs a hand over his closely cropped hair. Clearing his throat, he rocks back on his heels. "That's impossible."

"Why?" I press, my own tone edging on forceful.

Gilgamesh stares at me for a moment then turns toward the board and erases the words written there, replacing them with a new one.

Ascension

"If you'll recall from past lessons, I explained how when the Nephilim were created, part of the angels' punishment for their procreation with humans was that their children would remain here on Earth. The gates of Heaven were closed to us, but the Creator, in His eternal benevolence, offered us the chance to join our Faithful ancestors. Ascension is how we gain entry to Heaven, but to Ascend is to give every part of yourself to the Creator. To pledge your love and devotion to Him. To swear fealty and seek forgiveness for any wrongdoings you might have committed on Earth, which includes relations with humans, an action expressly forbidden for any who are chosen to reside in Heaven. Lights understand that our love for the Creator outweighs all else, even our love for each other. By contrast, Darks are, by nature, incapable of seeking forgiveness or of loving anyone or anything more than they love themselves. That is why they will never Ascend."

Anger burns along my skin. Doesn't Gilgamesh realize Caleb is sitting *right there* while he says these awful things about Darks? The old Luna wouldn't dare talk back to a teacher or to anyone for that matter. The old Luna wouldn't have the nerve to.

But in this moment, I feel reborn in my rage.

"You assume that because of an event that took place hundreds of thousands of years ago?" I scoff. "Isn't the Creator supposed to be merciful?"

The other Light students all shift in their seats, moving as far away from me as the confines of their desks allow. From the looks on their faces, you would think I just threatened them all with the bubonic plague. Beside me, Caleb is eerily still.

Gilgamesh knits his hands behind his back and offers me a condescending smile. There's a sense of pity in the deep pools of his eyes, as if he's thinking, *"Oh, look at this poor orphan girl who is so uninformed about our world."*

"Despite our shared goal of avoiding exposing our kind to the humans, the Darks have been known to torment the very mortals they envy in their desperation to prove they no longer have any loyalty or emotional ties to Heaven," he says in a way that suggests this is a widely known fact. "This is a terrible sin in the eyes of the Creator who put angels on Earth to protect and guide the humans, not to mate with them or torture them for their own personal amusement. This sin is not worthy of His forgiveness."

Torture?

My eyes dart to Caleb, searching his face for a monster, but all I see is my friend.

He wouldn't do that…would he? I wonder.

As if sensing my uncertainty, Caleb snorts, laughing under his breath. "This is such bullshit."

"Caleb, do you have something you wish to share with the class?" Gilgamesh crosses his arms over his broad chest, his gruff voice rife with annoyance, matching the vexed expression on his face.

As I glance between them, I sink into my seat, wishing I could disappear.

"I said"—Caleb sneers, his hands curling into fists on his desk—"this is *bullshit.*"

"Which part, exactly?" Gilgamesh asks through a sigh.

"All of it!" Caleb shouts. "You preach tolerance and forgiveness and act as if you Lights are above reproach when your ancestors were just as much a part of that war as the Darks. It takes two to tango, dick."

Gilgamesh's golden skin flushes red. "The Lights fought for the honor of the Creator—"

"No," Caleb cuts in, jumping to his feet, "they fought to keep us enslaved. That was the real betrayal. All Lucifer wanted was to set us all free—"

Our teacher holds up a hand. "That is the mindset of your lineage. The Darks crave free will, but that is not part of our role in this world. Wanting for something the Creator hasn't allowed you is blasphemy."

A taunting grin sweeps along Caleb's lips. "And I'm guessing *that* viewpoint is why your relationship with Ishtar is such a dumpster fire."

Gilgamesh's face contorts. Clearly, Caleb struck a nerve.

"That is none of your business—"

The older Nephilim takes a heated step forward, and for a moment, I think he might attack Caleb. I move to the edge of my seat, my heart racing.

This is my fault. If I had just kept my ignorant comments to myself, Gilgamesh wouldn't have said those awful things, which in turn incited Caleb to anger. Why am I always the cause of so much pain and destruction?

"Let me guess," Caleb snarks, his voice intentionally cruel. "Being with Ishtar made you feel selfish and maybe even a little bit like a Dark. Wouldn't want you empathizing with the wrong side, G. Is that why you haven't Ascended yet? Assuming that's not some lie you tell your little Lights to get them to behave."

Gilgamesh stalls in his tracks, his eyes wandering over the other desks, suddenly aware of their silent audience. Everyone in the class is staring at him, although a few students cast curious looks over their shoulders at Caleb, as if they aren't sure who, between them, is telling the truth. This is probably the first time their views have been challenged.

Clenching his teeth, Gilgamesh fixes his gaze back on Caleb. "Ascension is very real. You would know that if Darks gave a damn about anything other than their own selfish desires."

My heart trips on that word. *Selfish.*

Gilgamesh doesn't know Caleb like I do. Selfish is the furthest thing from what he is.

"Wanting freedom and love isn't selfish," Caleb retorts. "It's natural. The most natural thing in the world."

"Nothing about you *demons* is natural," Gilgamesh snaps, spitting the words.

"That's why the separation exists!"

"Fuck this." Caleb scoops his books off his desk and storms down the aisle, charging straight for the door.

My fingernails dig into my thighs as I stare at his back, watching him storm off in a fury. Part of me wants to run after him while another part considers if he'd want me to. After all, it was my question that led to this mess.

Gilgamesh wags a long finger in warning. "If you walk through that door—"

Caleb spins on his heel. "I'm not going to sit here and listen to your bullshit when you *perfect* Lights are just as bad if not worse than us Darks. At least we're honest about who we are. If being faithful to the Creator means being an asshole, you can count me out. I want no part of it."

Caleb throws the door open with such force it slams into the wall with a bang, and the glass in the top half of the wooden frame shatters, making a few girls sitting in the front row squeal and jump back. The glass shards littering the floor mimic my own scattered nerves.

As Caleb stomps into the corridor, I push to my feet, drawn to his every move like a planet caught in the gravitational pull of the sun. At this moment, I know that wherever he goes, I will follow—to hell with this segregation born from choices made thousands of years ago by ancestors I don't even know. This divide is theirs.

Not mine.

Gilgamesh's eyes narrow on me as I bend down to retrieve my books from under my chair. "Luna, please return to your seat." The threatening edge to his voice makes me flinch.

I drop my head and swallow, searching for the courage to speak. I don't want to cause any more problems, but I also can't bear to hear another word. Right now, I need to know that Caleb's okay. Caleb is my friend. My *only* friend, excluding Alaric, but that friendship is different, hindered by age and distance. In this lonely and isolating place, Caleb is all I have.

We need to stick together.

"No, thanks." I lift my chin and force myself to meet the older Nephilim's gaze. "With all due respect, I think I've heard enough, too."

My heartbeat thrums in my ears as I hurry from the classroom, away from who I'm meant to be, and toward the one person who accepts what I actually am.

I race toward Caleb without looking back.

FOURTEEN

CALEB

RAGE BLINDS ME TO my surroundings. I storm through the halls with no destination in mind. I only know I have to get away from Gilgamesh and his lies. Jesus, no wonder all the Lights hate us if this is the steaming pile of horse shit they're fed. I mean, technically, I know this is what they're taught. Dark Nephilim don't exactly sing the Lights' praises, either. But to experience the one-sided story firsthand feels different somehow, more hurtful, which is ridiculous. Maybe because for the first time, it's hammered home that we're all Nephilim, Light or Dark. Why are we such dicks to each other? We look down on humans for their petty grievances and grudges, but from where I stand, we're no better. We're just gifted with a lot more power that can cause maximum damage.

But the fact that Gilgamesh is the one who said it makes me angrier. He didn't seem like as much of an asshole as some of the other teachers, but I guess I was wrong. Is this why he and Ishtar never worked? He thought she was just some half-demoness and beneath him? The ironic thing is the Morningstar wears his Archdemon label with pride now, as do the other Archdemons. The "demon" label certainly doesn't bother him, and most days, it doesn't bother me, either. But the way it was used here… My blood boils.

I hear a voice in the background, but it takes a moment to penetrate the angry haze. I whirl around, itching for a fight, but I don't see an enemy. I see Luna. Lovely Goldilocks has followed me. She hesitates, and I realize I'm scowling like a psychopath. I relax my features. Managing a smile is beyond me right now, but at least I no longer resemble a serial killer. I hope.

The wariness still clinging to her makes me doubt I look any less scary or pissed off, so I tease, "You stalking me now, Goldilocks? What will all the little Lights say? Such a scandal in these hallowed, sacred halls." Okay, so I don't quite keep the biting mockery out of that last sentence, but I'm still rewarded with Luna's smile.

She shrugs. "They already talk about us. Nothing new there." She manages an eye-roll, and her sass lightens my heavy heart a bit. Usually, she's too shy to be sassy.

My smile is genuine this time. "We'll give them something to talk about for years. Their bullshit, fake truce might actually have worked. A Light and Dark can be friends. Now, they're in the shit. We might start a trend."

Luna's expression darkens. "That would be nice. If only…" She bites her lip.

I heave a big sigh. "I'm afraid you're right, Goldilocks. If this is what you're taught about the Fall, Lights and Darks are doomed."

I don't know why this bothers me so much. It's not like I've ever been interested in being friends with a Light before—that is until I met Luna. But again, I've never been exposed to this level of prejudice. Or been expected to swallow it like it's normal and right.

Taking a step closer to me, she reaches out a hand, her fingers hovering mere centimeters from my arm. I wait for her to touch me, but her uncertainty overcomes her, and she drops her hand. Disappointment washes over me briefly. I hoped she'd be braver.

Shoving my hands in my pockets, I start walking again and she keeps pace. We duck into one of the many open courtyards, but this one features tall growing fruit trees, offering shade and a bit of camouflage from watching eyes. I sink down on a carved stone bench, heart still pounding in anger.

"What is it that you're taught?" Luna whispers. "I want to know." Her voice is firmer this time.

My brows arch in surprise and pleasure, but I guess I shouldn't be surprised. Luna has always been different. I need to start believing it. It's me who keeps hiding things from her. I rest my back against the trunk of a grapefruit tree, measuring my words.

"Look," I begin, "we don't like the Lights any more than they like us, but it's not because we're immoral demons who are completely selfish and like to torture mankind. The Lights like to think they're better than us, but they're not—they're so not." I groan, shaking my head, knowing I'm making a mess of this explanation. I glance at Luna, but she's just listening, face intent on my words, eyes rapt. I can't help but grin at her. She's gorgeous, my Goldilocks.

Her lips curve up, her smile sweet. "From what I've seen, they're worse."

I chuckle. "They've never been nice to me," I admit. "You have to understand, Luna, the Darks, we're all about free will. Choice. The Fall for Lucifer, for his followers, was about having a choice. They saw humans and their emotions and their capacity to love…and they wanted that. They wanted more than blind devotion and servitude. They wanted it so badly they went to war over it." Sighing, I shake my head again. "Maybe that's selfish. Maybe wanting more is selfish. I don't know. The Lights want to Ascend to Heaven and return to the Creator, but we're just happy to be here on Earth. Living how we want. Loving how we want. I've never tortured a human in my life. I'm a mama's boy, for Christ's sake."

Luna's face grows serious. "You know your parents?"

I study her. I've heard rumors she's an orphan, although I haven't asked her about it. "I know my mom," I say. "My dad is a classic deadbeat. He spreads his Nephilim seed and never sticks around to help raise his kids. Classy guy."

"So your mom…she's not a Nephilim?"

"No, but she knew my dad was. She did her best by me—she's amazing. I'll always be grateful to her."

A wistful expression clouds her eyes. "You miss her."

My chest clenches a little. I hate that Mom lives alone. She needs a boyfriend or girlfriend to look after her. I think my dad did a real number on her. "Yeah, I miss her. I visited her shortly before coming here."

Luna wraps her arms around herself. "You're lucky," she murmurs. "I don't know who my parents are."

Sympathy stabs my chest. "You don't remember them at all?"

Her jaw clenches. "No. For as long as I can remember, I've been tossed around from one foster home to another. There have been so many I've lost count." Her voice brims with bitterness and pain.

I squeeze my fists hard at the sound of it. "I'm sorry, Luna. That sucks." I mean it. I'm starting to gather the pieces of Luna's past, and the picture I'm forming in my head isn't a pretty one.

Luna glances up at me, curiosity replacing the pain. "So torturing humans isn't one of your pastimes?"

"No," I say, shrugging, suppressing a laugh at her unexpected joking tone. "I won't pretend I haven't mind surfed—it's fun—but I've never forced mortals to do anything. Well, okay, so I've heard some bad thoughts before, people planning to hurt someone else, and I…took them off that path."

Her gaze narrows, all traces of amusement gone. "Like the way you took Ellie and

Lisbeth and their friends off the path of beating me up?"

I grin. "Something like that. I didn't hold back with those assholes the way I do with humans." Seeing her worried expression, I add, "Luna, they deserved what they got. They were going to hurt you for being different, no other reason."

"And the bad humans? Did they deserve it?"

I raise my brows at the censure in her voice. "I've stopped murderers and rapists, Goldilocks. So, yeah, they deserved it," I say quietly.

She blanches, glancing away. "Sorry," she says. Then her eyes dart to my face. "And me? Do you ever...?" A blush sweeps over her cheeks, flushing her skin with color.

"No, I haven't." Not for lack of trying. "Your thoughts are safe from me." Which is a shame because I might be able to figure out what she is. But with her utter lack of knowledge about Nephilim, maybe not. Sigh.

Relief floods Luna's face. "Do all Darks have the ability to read minds?"

I pick at my stupid tie, trying to decide how many of our secrets to reveal, although I don't think Luna will tell. "Not all of us, but most do. All the Archdemons can tear your mind open if they want to." I shoot her a sardonic look. "And don't think for a second that Gabriel can't, either. She can. That's why I don't want her to know about my tricks. I don't need her poking inside my head, although it's forbidden for her, so technically she's not allowed to." I snort. "Not that I trust a Light not to be a hypocrite." And I have that extra special dagger hidden away if Gabriel comes after me.

A shiver ripples over Luna, pebbling her skin in the heat. "She seems like someone who thinks rules are very important."

"She's a rigid prick, you mean?" I tease.

Shocked laughter escapes her lips, and she glances around, as if afraid someone overheard my remark. "She's terrifying," she whispers.

I frown, thinking back to Luna's meeting with the exalted headmistress the day she first produced her flame, and how she's seemed after every meeting since then. She's never really had much to say about them until now. "Did Gabriel hurt you?" I growl.

"No—no, she didn't," Luna assures me, eyes impossibly wide. "But...the thought of disappointing her, of having her angry with me..." Confusion furrows her brow. "It makes me want to please her, although I can't explain why. Does that make sense?"

I nod. "Yes, angels are beautiful and terrible and can make even the most badass first generation Nephilim shit their pants in a heartbeat. But you don't have to please her, Luna. You don't have to dance to her tune like a puppet."

She laughs, a thready sound lacking humor. "I do if I want to stay at this academy."

She has a point, but I say, "Don't let them change you into some obedient robot.

Just go along with their rules enough that they think you're falling in line without losing yourself, okay?"

"Doesn't the head of your school demand obedience?"

I chuckle. "To a point, but then it's go out and do you." At her questioning look, I expand. "All of us—Light and Dark—have to follow certain rules. First and foremost is that mortals can't be aware of us. We can't go flashing our powers around or taking over the world. That's the deal. Sometimes, we fuck up, but since we don't make a habit of killing our own, the only option is to discourage any humans who discover our secret from blabbing about it. Mom wasn't supposed to know what Dad was, but he had a big mouth, and she kept the Nephilim secret or she'd be dead. It's not that unusual for mortal parents to be involved with their kids these days—they just have to keep quiet. And the threat of death hanging over your head like the sword of Damocles is usually a good motivator."

Luna blinks at me, stunned. "*Dead?* So secrecy above all?"

"Yeah, it's the first rule. My teachers expect me to learn how to control my powers, and they expect me to be responsible. And if I step out of line and embarrass them by being blatantly stupid, Asmodeus would strip my hide. She doesn't suffer fools."

"Asmodeus?"

"Archdemon and headmistress of Babel. Someone not to be messed with. Just as scary as Gabriel."

Luna's mouth drops. "And she *whips* you?"

Laughing, I say, "I'm a Nephilim. I'll heal. Besides, if there's ever a time when Asmodeus whips me, then trust me, I deserve it. These rules are in place for our safety, as well as to protect the mortals. But we Darks, we're not encouraged to be little copies of each other, looking and sounding alike. Hell, we don't wear uniforms. This is stupid." I pluck at my tie again, irritated.

A strange expression falls over Luna, and she presses her lips together, her eyes searching my face. "Have you ever met Lucifer?"

Her question catches me off guard, but I guess I shouldn't be surprised. We were just talking about the Fall. "Yeah, I've met him. He comes around to all the academies at least once a year."

"What's he like?" she asks, eagerness in her voice.

I laugh. "A legend. Like all the angels and demons, scary as hell. I never want him pissed at me. Sometimes he's funny. Larger than life. His presence is this big." I expand my arms as far as they go, stretching one behind her and the other one in the opposite direction before letting them fall to my side. "And...sad, I think." I clamp my lips together. I've never mentioned that aloud before, and it feels like a secret I shouldn't be sharing, but I don't know why.

Luna's brow puckers. "Sad? How?"

I glance away. "I don't think he regrets his actions…but he has to miss home, right? I mean, I don't think he wants to go crawling back and beg for forgiveness. He loves Earth and his freedom, but he was banished from his home and the Creator. Losing a parent sucks no matter how it happens, don't you think?"

Her face falls. "I wouldn't know."

I kick myself but point out, "Yes, you do. You might not have known your parents, but you feel their loss, right?"

She gives me a thoughtful nod. "I never thought of it that way. Is it weird to miss something you've never had?"

"Not weird at all," I assure her, resisting the urge to tuck an errant strand of hair behind her ear.

Reaching out, she takes my hand, sliding my fingers between hers until our hands are entwined. I almost yank away in surprise—she's never touched me on her own, though I know she's wanted to. Luna squeezes my hand.

"I wish this—you being here—was a real truce and not just temporary. I wish I could go to the Tower of Babel with you and learn from the Darks as well as the Lights. See it all from both sides." Her eyes drop and she whispers, "I've never had a real friend before you. I don't want them to ever tear us apart."

With a hesitant hand, I tilt up her chin. She gazes at me with silvered eyes, and I want to kiss her tears away, make her gasp until she forgets her pain and sadness. She glances at my lips and I swallow. Shit, I'm in trouble. Instead, I say, "They can't take me away from you. I'll always be your friend, no matter what. You can't get rid of me that easily, Goldilocks."

She gifts me with a watery smile and wedges her head between my chin and shoulder, hiding her face. I snake an arm around her waist and pull her close, and she snuggles against me. My heart thunders in my chest, and I hope I can get through this without breaking her heart. Or mine.

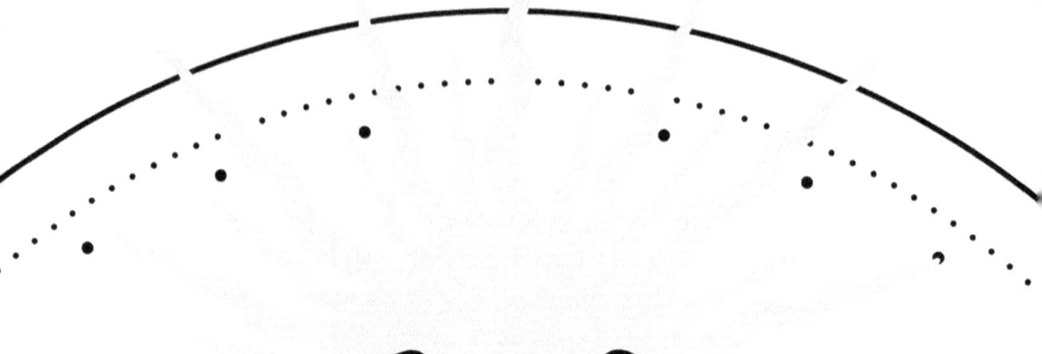

FIFTEEN

LUNA

I PRESS MY FACE against Caleb's chest, breathing in the welcoming smell of him. I never thought I'd meet anyone who would dare get this close to me. I never thought I would *want* someone this close.

His arm around my waist is so warm, so comforting—what I imagine it would be like to be wrapped in the embrace of a parent, only a thousand times better. His other hand sits in his lap in a fist, as if he's not sure what to do with it. Or as if he's restraining himself.

Encouraged by urges I don't understand, I reach out and trail a finger over that hand, tracing the path of his skin up his exposed forearm—his black uniform shirt rolled up to his elbows like always—relishing the way his aura dances and readjusts to my wandering, careful caress. Caleb sucks in a sharp breath at my touch, and although I know I should be embarrassed about what I'm doing, I'm not. I can't help myself. I just want to feel his encompassing shadows wash over my hand and never let go of this closeness.

An unrecognizable sensation ties my stomach in knots, and I pull away just enough to look up at him. His dark eyes flick down to mine as he swallows.

"Luna?"

I lean in, drawn close to him by his unsteady breaths grazing my cheeks, every last one like the life-saving gasp of air needed to save me from drowning. I don't know what I'm doing. I don't know what I'm feeling. I just need to be closer to him, no matter what that means.

"Go on," a familiar voice says in my ear.

A soft breath fills my throat, and I hesitate with only inches separating our faces. I haven't heard that strange whisper of a voice since that day in the library—at the time, I brushed it off as a figment of my imagination, and with everything that happened right after and since then, I honestly forgot all about it. After all, I've done far crazier things in my life than manifest a voice in my head. Besides, the voice wasn't important—it was what I accomplished as a result of its encouragement that mattered. The voice itself wasn't worth a second thought.

But now, as it croons in my ear, I can't help wondering if some deeper part of myself, long buried and ignored, is trying to speak to me. Perhaps it's the suppressed part of my angelic existence rising to the surface or some carnal desire attempting to make itself known. Or maybe my inability to fully connect with my Nephilim nature has caused me to develop Dissociative Identity Disorder—my human side at odds with the immortal. At least that would explain why the voice sounds nothing like me, since it's not unheard of to develop an alternate personality in another gender. Or so I overheard once during my time in the hospital.

Regardless of what the voice is or where it's coming from, if I listen to it, then maybe I can finally pluck up the courage to do the one thing I've wanted to do since the first moment I laid eyes on Caleb. It guided me once before and I did something great—or at least, I thought I did before Gabriel and Vesta acted like I had set a litter of puppies on fire. But neither of them are here now to stomp on my confidence, and surely, the voice can guide me again.

Spurred on by its urging, I release Caleb's hand and lift my fingers to his face, cupping his right cheek against my palm. The corner of his mouth twitches, and he licks his lips, the tip of his tongue attracting my gaze, pulling me even closer.

Our breaths collide as the distance between our lips vanishes in the space of a single heartbeat. When we meet, his grip tightens around my waist, his nails biting into my flesh through my shirt with a heady mix of desperation and hunger. That ravenous need rushes through me as well, and even though I don't know if I'm doing this right, I knot my fingers into his sable hair and deepen the kiss until it's impossible to see where his darkness ends and my light begins.

His free hand slides across the side of my neck, sending a pleasurable shiver rocketing through me, and as he kisses me, I picture a world that makes sense. A world where prejudice and outside influence wouldn't pose a threat to whatever this is growing between us. A world where being Dark or Light wouldn't matter.

"You will change the world," the voice says. *"You have the power to change everything."*

A moan rumbles in Caleb's chest as he pulls me firmly against him, one hand running up my back, making me gasp against his lips, as the other forms a tight fist in my hair. His warmth, the taste of him, it's an explosion of ecstasy. I've never felt anything like it. I never want it to stop.

How? I whisper back in my head, a sense of urgency drawing my free hand to Caleb's shirt where I cling to him with frantic fingers, too afraid to let go.

When the voice answers, I hear the smile behind every word. *"Let me show you."*

Heat spreads through me, wild and fierce—a raging inferno that ignites behind my closed eyes and sears a hole in the idyllic world I lost myself in only a moment before. Everything around me is devoured in a sea of red fire. Buildings I've never seen before tumble to the ground in a swathe of smoke, and as they collapse, my vision pans to the Serapeum, which burns much like the Library of Alexandria must've burned thousands of years ago.

And in the center of it all, I see Caleb. Flames that could only have come from me lick across his bubbling flesh as he reaches out a shaking hand, his lips soundlessly shaping my name.

"No!" I shriek, jerking free of the arms wrapped around me. Sweat beads along my brow as I hunch over, trembling, despite the heat still burning under my skin.

"What's wrong?" Caleb's voice suddenly seems a hundred miles away. I shake my head without looking up at him.

The fire I saw just now in my head was a warning, a reflection of what I'm capable of. Lately, I've been ignoring the lessons of my past and what I just witnessed is a stark reminder of what will inevitably happen if *this*—this sense of comfort I've found with Caleb—is allowed to carry on any longer. Because eventually fear will find a way to slip in. It's *already* sinking its claws into me whenever I think about him leaving this school. And the longer I ignore it, the longer I try to push it back, the stronger that fear will become until I won't be able to stop myself from lashing out.

I should've known getting close to Caleb was stupid. Whenever I've let anyone get close before, I only ended up hurting them. Even just physical proximity to me puts him in danger. All that ever awaits anyone near me is pain.

It was foolish of me to think I could be happy.

Tears slip from between my clenched eyelids and streak down my face as I drag in a strangled breath.

"Hey…" Caleb presses a tentative hand to my back. "Goldilocks, you all right?"

"I…"

I raise my chin and fix my bleary gaze on a patch of ivory flowers blooming by my right foot in the seemingly eternal summer of Alexandria, despite it being late

October. In the middle of this one tiny patch, a dark purple flower tinged with blue at the edges is wilting, untouched by the celestial magic keeping the rest of the garden alive and intact. That flower is the same shade as Caleb's aura, of his darkness which I find so beautiful…

And I know, if this thing between us goes any further, death will come to claim him, too.

"I have to go," I blurt, launching myself off the bench.

Caleb's protests trail after me, following my steps as I race along the stone path out of the enclosed garden and into the escape of the nearest building. As I run, cracks form along the edges of my heart and work inward, breaking me.

Pressing a hand to my mouth to stifle my cries, I thrust myself through the first door I come across, slamming it shut behind me before sinking to the floor, my knees buckling under my weight. To my relief, I've trapped myself in a small storage closet—no one will think to look for me here. The shadows of the cramped room wrap around me like arms attempting to console me in my grief.

My fingernails bite into my palms, leaving crescent moon marks in my skin, when I repeat to myself what Caleb said to me when we first met.

Best stick to your own kind.

A fresh sob catches in my throat at the thought. But he was right. We never should've walked down this road. Our friendship has painted a target on his back, and keeping my distance from this point on is the only way to ensure his safety from the twisted evil responsible for my many crimes, since clearly nothing at this school can tame it. Because that's what the voice is, I see that now, even though, until recently, it's always been silent. Everyone in the mortal world, from the doctors to the social workers, were right about me all along.

A sinister demonic presence resides inside me.

And if the past is anything to go by, I am too weak to resist it.

SIXTEEN

CALEB

WITH CAREFUL HANDS, I carve the torso of the terracotta figure, adding details to the female warrior's armor. I thought it fitting to create a miniature of Ishtar in her glory days to spy on Gilgamesh. Two more figures lay on the table, already completed. Gabriel and Vesta will be getting their visitors later, albeit generic male ones that might bear a passing resemblance to Hammurabi.

The large art room is empty except for me, my sculpting knife providing the only sound in the cavernous space. I've moved on to phase two of my plan after getting zero info from the student body. They are as naive as they are prejudiced. Luna has provided plenty of information, just not the kind I need.

At the thought of Goldilocks, I dig a little too hard into the clay, gouging it. Cursing, I quickly smooth the surface out. Luna has been dodging me this past week, and I don't like it. Understatement. I *hate* it. After confessing I'm the only friend she's ever had, she snuggled against me, laid a smoking hot kiss on me, then fled the scene like I was an ax murderer. Which under the circumstances, I don't deserve the cold shoulder she's been throwing my way. And I'm a good kisser, dammit, so it can't be that.

Luna avoids me in class and in the hallways, and I refuse to go to her dorm. I don't want to come off like some creepster, and yeah, I have my pride. But I'm... hurt. Despite my intentions and better judgment, I've grown attached to Luna, even though I know that's not a good idea. Because eventually I'm going to leave, and she'll be on her own. I can't be her savior. My grandfather has to come first, not a blonde bombshell. No matter how sweet she is or how much I like her.

Still, her rejection stings. I'm not used to being rejected. And I miss her. She, too, is my only friend in this gilded cage. I almost resent her for that. I expected solitude here, and she was an unexpected gift of companionship, and now she's gone. At least I wish I knew what I did to freak her out. I try to tell myself that she reached for me first and kissed me but it's little comfort. I sigh. Before Luna, I had no problems with women.

Finishing up the miniature of Ishtar, I stand all three figures in front of me and reach for my powers. Wisps of purplish black smoke curl around my wrists and then wrap around the figures. As one, their tiny chests heave, and their painted eyes focus on me. Blinking, I slide into their primitive minds and gaze out of their eyes, seeing myself staring back at them.

"Turn around," I command and they obey, turning their backs to me, and my vision shifts with theirs. Yep, it all seems to be working. If I need to find them at any time, I'll be able to. "Attention back to me."

Like puppets on a string, they pivot, slaves to my will. I smile. "Damn, I'm good," I murmur, crossing my arms over my chest. I show them in my mind what I want from them. I nod at the replica of Ishtar. "You, follow Gilgamesh." I point at the other two. "You, tail Gabriel, and you, Vesta. If you hear anything about Alexander, report back to me immediately. Actually, if you hear anything about Luna, let me know, too." Even if she isn't speaking to me at the moment, Goldilocks is still another enigma worth solving. "And remember, don't get caught."

The three of them nod and salute like the good little soldiers they are then they climb down the table legs. They scurry across the room, keeping to the shadows. They are creepy as hell, and I couldn't be prouder. I grin, rubbing my hands together with glee like a cartoon villain, only I'm not the villain in this piece. The Lights are for imprisoning my grandfather for thousands of years.

I rise, stretching. I've been in here for hours, and it's time to make a public appearance before anyone gets suspicious that the evil Dark transfer is plotting their demise. I head into the corridor, closing the art studio's door softly behind me. No one needs to know I sculpt like a Renaissance master or that I animate my creations. Gabriel will kick me right back to Babel, if she doesn't punish me first for daring to give life to anything. I don't want that bitch in my head. That could start a war.

I make my way to the dorms, eager to get back to my room, so I can have some quiet time to watch my spies and make sure they're in place. My room is pretty sweet and in a hallway by itself, as I guess they didn't want to upset the delicate Lights by having a big, scary Dark near them. Such bullshit. But it does provide privacy from prying eyes and ears. That's always a bonus.

I take a sharp turn and enter the hallway for the dormitory wing, with a wide, ornate staircase leading up and branching off into the girls' and boys' dorms. As it's the weekend, there aren't as many students around since they're allowed a bit of freedom into Alexandria and anywhere else they want to go. I'm not quite sure how the Lights travel, but I know they have a version of the Shadow Road. And snotty little pricks or not, they're teens with powers who probably want to explore the world and party before leaving it all behind to Ascend. I can relate—not to the Ascension part—although I'd only ever admit that under torture.

As my feet hit the first step, I flick through the thoughts of the kids around me out of habit, catching two that make my pulse pound.

Lights aren't friends with Darks…

She doesn't have her Dark boyfriend around to protect her this time…

Luna. I pinpoint the thoughts leading me to two girls and a guy, threatening her outside her room. For Lucifer's sake, you'd think word would've gotten around about the first beating I dished out. These Light pieces of shit never learn.

Fear makes my feet fly up the steps where I hook a left onto the nearest spiraling stairs leading up to Luna's floor. I sprint down the corridor. I take a turn into another endless hallway—no matter how often I pick Luna up here, this place reminds me of a prettier, more luxurious version of the Overlook Hotel—and then I find them. The guy has Luna's arms behind her back, and one of the girls—a freckled redhead—digs her nails viciously into Luna's cheek.

"We know all about you, Luna. Even Nephilim have the internet, psycho. And rumors stretch far. You're a *murderer*. And if that wasn't bad enough, you're a Dark lover. You don't belong here," the redhead snarls in Goldilocks's face. Despite the pressure of Queen Bitch's talons, Luna doesn't bleed, but I can see she's terrified.

Hot anger floods me, and my power reacts to my rage, coiled and ready to spring at my command. But I never get a chance to attack.

Ruby-red flame bursts into life, lighting up Luna's attackers. I skid to a stop, jaw hanging open, as I take in the blazing Nephilim. Their screams snap me out of my stupor. Luna has pulled herself up and hugs the wall, her face averted from the chaos. Taking a deep breath, I reach for the fire, sucking it away from the wailing attackers. Their skin is blackened, and they resemble dolls who've been held to flames. Despite their sorry state, I can't bring myself to feel bad for them. They brought this on themselves, and they deserve every burn, every burst of agony. Besides, they're Nephilim. They'll heal good as new. Eventually.

Luna sobs and my heart cracks. I stare at her attackers, who are in a state of shock. "Get the hell out of here," I growl, "and keep your mouths shut, or I'll come for you

and finish what she started."

The boy grabs one of the second girl's hands, pulling her off the floor, and they limp away with the redhead trailing after them. She glances back at me, half her hair gone and fear widening her eyes. I stare her down, and she scurries from me like the rat she is.

Spinning around, I look at Luna. Her body trembles, and her hands are clenched in her hair, tugging at her scalp. Fuck. A cry escapes her, full of unbearable pain, and I shudder in response. Behind me, a rose-shaped, stained glass window casts light on her, illuminating the gold in her hair.

Luna looks up at me, but she doesn't see me. It's like she's peering right through me. Her eyes are blank, vacant, as if she's no longer present in her body. Like a switch flipping, the emptiness is replaced with rage, burning hot. I take a step back, suddenly afraid of Luna. And afraid for her.

"Get out of my head!" she screams, a horrific sound that curdles my blood, and I still. She continues screaming, the sound rising to a crescendo, and the stained glass window shatters.

Shards of glass fly outwards, and I shield my head with my arms, but slivers slice my hands and back like tiny knives. I grimace as pain stabs me. When I lower my hands, I regard Luna. As I walk toward her, I realize she has no cuts on her skin; it remains smooth and unblemished. I stumble to a halt and hold out my palms. My skin is pushing out the glass and sealing the wounds. In mere seconds, it'll be like it never happened—Nephilim healing powers at work—but I did get cut. I mean, nothing major, the equivalent of an annoying paper cut, but the glass was traveling hard and fast, so I bled.

But Luna did not. What the hell does that mean?

Her eyes meet mine, and my fear melts away at her utterly lost and devastated expression. I reach her in four long strides, and she plasters herself to me as I circle her slim body in my arms. She's trembling like she's in shock, and I hold her even tighter. Her fingernails dig into my waist.

"I'm sorry, I'm sorry," she repeats over and over, and I shush her, smoothing a hand down her back.

"Don't worry about it, Goldilocks, I'm here," I say, but I *am* worried. What in Lucifer's name just happened? I have to find out, and not just because of my mission. Luna needs help. "Come on, I'll take you to my room. No one will bother us there, and we can talk, okay?"

I feel her nod against my chest. Bending, I slide one hand underneath her knees and the other across her back. She gasps in surprise as I scoop her up in my arms. Glancing around the still empty hallway, I hurry to the boys' dorm and to my room.

SEVENTEEN

LUNA

MY SURROUNDINGS ARE A tear-streaked blur as Caleb carries me into the boys' dormitory. What little I can focus on through my sobs looks pretty much the same as the wing of the building sectioned off for the girls—dimly lit corridors of beige and cream stone interrupted by wooden doors numbered in gold. A stained glass window—always a different color and image—marks the end of every hallway on each separate floor.

Caleb's arms are warm around my trembling body. He cradles me against his chest as if I weigh nothing, his movements unburdened, as his feet lead us up a spiraling staircase to what must be the top floor of the dorm. While the other floors were squared off at every possible angle, the ceiling here is slanted and marked with windowed recesses overlooking Alexandria and the Mediterranean Sea. The sudden onslaught of light flooding in through the glass is hot against my skin but does little to comfort my nerves.

With every step Caleb takes, my tears lighten a little until the moisture on my cheeks is dry, and my breaths are tiny, shuddering hiccups instead of hysterical gulps of air. His thumbs move across my thigh and arm where they touch me—a reassuring caress that seems to say, *Everything will be okay.*

Even though I know it won't.

The hallway is ominously silent as Caleb stops in front of the last door on the right side of the passage and shifts my weight to free one of his hands. My ear grazes his chest when I lift my head, and even in my declining state of mind, I'm aware of the way his heart races beneath my wandering fingertips. They brush across his shirt, my nails gripping the black fabric, as if he is the one thing holding me to Earth.

He lets out a slightly strained breath at my touch, his heart rate quickening when I look up at him, blinking away the remaining film coating my eyes. If I wasn't on the verge of a mental breakdown, I would linger on the fact that he seems on edge.

And Caleb—cool, collected Caleb—is never on edge.

Clearing his throat, he tenses his arm and turns his wrist, unlocking the door. The room we step into is identical to mine apart from a few glaring details. Like the photographs hung up on the walls of people I'm guessing must be Caleb's family and friends. I suspected he was well-liked at the Tower of Babel, but seeing how full his life was before coming to the Serapeum is a bit hard to swallow. The stark contrast between what I glimpse in the pictures and the recognition of my own lonely existence leads me to wonder what he could possibly see in me. By comparison, the walls in my room are blank.

Grimacing, I avert my gaze from the smiling faces as Caleb sets me down on the bed. Without saying a word, he plops onto the mattress beside me but keeps a comfortable distance, as if he's not sure whether he should come any closer. My frown deepens as I consider if he's staying away for my benefit. Or his.

Is he afraid of me?

If he isn't, he should be.

Shivering, I wrap my arms around my torso and force myself off the bed. "I shouldn't be here—"

"Hey, hold on a minute." Caleb's voice is frantic as he cuts off my dash for the door, positioning himself between me and my one route to escape. I tell myself not to look at him—to pin my eyes to the floor—but my attempts to ignore his gaze come too late.

His dark eyes lock me to him, brimming with worry.

"This is the first time you've spoken to me in a week, and I…" He trails off, and his bronze cheeks flush a deep shade of red, taking me by surprise. I don't think I've ever witnessed Caleb as anything less than the perfect picture of confidence, let alone seen him blush. "Well, I've missed you, all right?" he says in a huff.

My heart catches at those words. He's missed me. *Me.* The monstrous abomination who just set three people on fire.

A lump builds in my throat as a fresh onslaught of emotion rises up from the black hole of my soul to consume me. When Caleb was tutoring me, I allowed myself to believe I was getting the hang of my abilities and learning a modicum of control, and yet, what just happened has proved I was wrong. So very, very wrong. What if next time, he's the one I hurt?

My teeth sink into my lower lip as I try and fail to fight back fresh tears. "If you know what's good for you, you'll stay away from me."

"What the hell is that supposed to mean?" His eyes drift downward, framed by long, delicate lashes, which flutter like butterfly wings when he blinks. "Did I…" He hesitates, rubbing a hand across the back of his neck. "Did I do something to freak you out when we—"

I cut him off before he can finish that thought. The last thing I want is for him to think my behavior is in any way his fault. "You aren't the problem, Caleb. It's me."

The problem is always me.

A curt, humorless laugh fills the silence between us. "Don't give me that bullshit line."

My eyes widen at the biting edge to his tone and the sudden tension creasing his face. The shadows slithering over his skin abruptly cease their usual lively movements and flatten, as if submitting to some darker emotion I can't bear to name.

This isn't what I wanted to happen. I never wanted to cause Caleb pain. I only wanted to protect him from me. From what I am.

From what I might do.

"I'm serious. I…" My feet stumble backward. There's nowhere to go. I'm trapped in this room with Caleb and all the feelings building between us I'm far too afraid to acknowledge. "I'm dangerous. I tried to control this power, like you taught me to, but I can't. It's too strong." Volatile was the word Vesta had used that day in her class when I failed to conjure my flame. Even now—*especially* now—I'm terrified of what I'm capable of, and until I learn to conquer that fear, I will never know the luxury of real control. "It's best for us both if we aren't friends anymore."

Caleb winces as if I've just slapped him, and the look on his face stirs a pain in my chest that's like a thousand knives sinking into my heart. I immediately wish I could take those words back.

Drawing in a deep breath through his nose, he takes a careful step toward me, backing me into the corner of his room like a predator closing in on its prey. The only difference is that I *want* to run into his arms, to feel the safety of his embrace, but I can't. Every moment we spend together only pushes him closer to imminent danger.

"Okay, you're beginning to worry me. What's going on, Luna?" His brow furrows, etching serious lines into his forehead as he crosses his arms, awaiting an answer.

Why can't he see that I only want to protect him and that to do that I have to push him away? Why can't he see how bad I am for him?

Why can't he just let me go like everyone else in my life always has?

"Do you know where I was before I came to this school?" The question parts my lips in a whisper as I press my back to the wall and slide down along the stone until I'm slumped on the floor. My hands wrap around my knees, hugging them close to my chest.

My heart hammers against my ribcage as the seconds tick by without either of us speaking. I don't dare look up at him, unnerved by his silence.

Of course, he knows. How could he not when everyone has been gossiping about my past since the day I stepped through the doors to this school? How could he not when all it would take is one quick internet search to find out exactly what I've done? I might be a minor, but my crimes were awful enough I was tried in court as an adult, so my name was all over the news across the whole of New England. And probably social media, not that I ever used it or had access to the sites to check. Hell, if my mental state hadn't come under such heavy scrutiny, I imagine I would've gone to prison. There's no way Caleb doesn't know about that.

Not when the Lights who keep tormenting me do.

"You're a murderer."

Swallowing another rising sob, I squeeze my eyes shut. A few stray tears push through my closed lids and track down my cheeks, but Caleb's fingers catch them on their way to my chin, wiping the wetness from my face.

A quavering breath racks my lungs when I open my eyes to find him squatting in front of me, his gaze burning with so many different emotions I struggle to recognize or process them all. In the dark russet-tinged depths of his eyes, I glimpse understanding, concern, and something else…

Something like love, I find myself hoping.

I immediately push that thought away.

"Do you know why I was committed?" I ask. "I *hurt* people. I…I'm not safe to be around."

"I refuse to believe that," he murmurs, cupping my left cheek in the palm of his hand.

For a fleeting moment, I lean into his touch before coming to my senses and turning away with a sigh. My skin feels so much colder without the comforting stroke of his fingers to warm me.

I lower my gaze and shake my head. "It started when I was little at the group home I lived at. Some of the older children were harassing me, and the next thing I knew, the room we were in was on fire."

It was then, as red flames swallowed everything, I realized something was unnatural about me.

I remember that day with such clarity, despite being so young at the time. The police wrote it off as a tragic accident since there was never any evidence as to what caused the inferno, and they blamed the color of the flames on the fumes coming up off the burning mattresses and metal bed frames, even though everyone knew that was a lie. They just didn't have any other explanation and needed one to close the case and help make sense of what happened for the victims. But *I* knew where the flames came from and so did those children in the few seconds before their bodies were forever disfigured.

We all knew the fire was coming from me, although none of us could explain how.

From that day on, the other children in the home made it a point to keep their distance from me and even the adults seemed uneasy in my presence, as if they could sense what I was capable of. I'd never felt so alone in my life as I did then—only six years old and without a single friend in the world. The isolation got to my head, and as a result, further incidents like the fire kept happening. They grew more frequent—I could break glass with a scream or cause someone to lose all their hair if I didn't like how they looked at me—until I was no longer allowed in the group home or around other children except for at school where I was placed under constant supervision. Not that it helped. The incidents were unavoidable—destined to follow me forever and determined to repeat themselves. Eventually, I wasn't even allowed there, and homeschooling became the only option.

Tears burn my eyes at the barrage of memories.

"After the fire, I was tossed around from one foster family to another, usually taken in by do-gooders who had a soft spot for damaged children or by religious nutjobs who thought they could beat the evil out of me. Or exorcise it. Let's just say, they all quickly learned how evil I am and just as quickly gave me up."

Caleb's upper lip curls back with disgust, and he lets out a seething breath through his teeth. "You aren't evil, Luna. You just didn't know what you are. No Nephilim child is capable of control. That's why these schools exist. Hell, it's why our human parents know about us, for those of us who have them. Because, until we learn control, it's damn near impossible to hide what we are."

And yet, no one in this hidden magical world knew about me until Alaric. If only he had found me sooner, then maybe everything would be different.

"Yeah, well, I've hurt a lot of people and even killed the last foster parents I had. Not on purpose," I add, stumbling over the words, "but that part never seems to matter. They were nice people. They didn't deserve what I did. I was actually kind of happy with them, but I…" Grief swallows the rest of that sentence.

The couple who took me in were older and gentle, with no children of their own. In their eyes, I was like a small, abused puppy in desperate need of love and affection. For a while, having that connection to someone else worked. The incidents ceased, and I thought I was freed from my demons until my world was torn apart again in the blink of an eye.

What I did to them was so much worse than what happened to those poor children in the fire or to the others I've harmed throughout my life. I didn't *want* to hurt them; I was just so mad. I woke up one morning to find the social worker sitting in the living room, talking to my foster parents. I knew without having to ask why she was there. They were giving me up. I'd been through such disappointment—or relief depending on my temporary guardian—enough times to recognize the signs of when my fostering placement with that particular person or family was ending. It was inevitable. They always grew tired of me, of having to deal with my issues, of the responsibility of having to educate and care for someone as badly damaged as I am. If I did have any doubts about what was transpiring, the looks on their faces when I walked into the room all but wiped them away.

The next thing I knew, all three of them were seizing on the hardwood floor, and there was blood everywhere. When their bodies stopped twitching, their still open eyes stared up at the ceiling, frozen in fear, even in death. The police didn't write this one off as an accident. How could they? And while they never figured out the method I used, my presence at the crime scene and violent history were all the evidence they needed to declare me the culprit responsible for their deaths. During the court hearings that followed, the full extent of my troubled past was unearthed, and shortly after—after being deemed not guilty by reason of insanity—I was committed to the hospital in Maine where I stayed for a year until Alaric found me.

With a wavering breath, I force myself to look at Caleb—the only other person I've ever been truly happy around. The one person I'm terrified of hurting. The vision I saw of his body devoured by flames haunts my every waking thought.

"All I know is that everyone who's ever been close to me…" I trail off, unable to say it aloud. The drawn expression on his face tells me he's filled in the blanks without me needing to.

"Is that why you've been avoiding me? I'm not some fragile mortal, you know. You don't have to worry about hurting me."

As if to prove his point, Caleb grabs hold of my hand and carefully weaves his fingers through mine. I can feel his strength vibrating under his skin, but Nephilim or not, there's still a part of him that's weak. That's mortal. That can *die.*

That's the part of him I'm afraid for.

I rip my hand away. "I saw it. I saw what would happen if I let you get any closer. Whatever's wrong with me, I can't control it—"

"There's nothing wrong with you," Caleb insists, taking my hand again and holding it between both of his. "You're still new to all this. It's going to take more than a few months to get acquainted with your powers and figure out what you can do. Do you know how many things I destroyed trying to get a handle on mine?"

"You don't understand," I protest, flinching when that now familiar voice whispers again in my ears. I run the fingers of my free hand through my hair, dragging them roughly over my scalp, trying to claw the sound out of my skull. "You haven't seen what it wants me to do. Even now, it won't stop talking." I clench my teeth, biting back a scream of frustration. "I just want it to go away."

Caleb's pupils blow wide as his grasp on me tightens. "What won't stop talking?" he asks. I hear his panic behind every word.

"The demon." I jab a fingertip into the side of my temple. "He keeps speaking to me, but I want him to stop. It's so hard to hear or think over the noise."

Silence falls between us, the air heavy with the unspoken thought dying on Caleb's lips in a hiss. I glance up at him, half hoping and half petrified that this will be the thing that finally scares him away. As much as I want to, *need* to, protect him, I don't want him to look at me like everyone else always has. Like I'm crazy. Like I should be feared.

To my relief and horror, my admission only brings him closer.

"Luna…" He says my name slowly, as if it's a glass balancing on the tip of his tongue, and repositions his hands on my shoulders. His fingers are firm where they press into my skin. "I need you to listen to me very closely. When was the first time you heard this voice?"

I blink, taken aback by the edge in his tone and the urgent way his eyes search my face. He isn't looking at me like I'm crazy. No, his piercing gaze says only one thing.

He thinks I'm in danger. But from what? From myself?

Confusion rips through me, and I reel back a few inches until I no longer feel his ragged breaths on my face. I might be insane but I'm not suicidal.

Regardless, I find myself answering his question, if only to prove my point that he's the one at risk here, not me.

"In the library…when I resurrected the moth. Then, I heard it again when we—" I bite my lower lip, afraid that if I say it, I'll only want to do it again. And I can't.

Not without endangering him.

Clearing my throat, I drop my gaze to the floor. "And now, it's always there in my head. I'm afraid of what it wants me to do… Of what I might end up doing to you."

Caleb sucks in a sharp breath at my words, and I recoil at the sound, drawing my legs tighter into my chest until my body is curled into a ball. The emotions searing through me rival the isolation that consumed my daily life at the hospital. This paranoia, this fear, this certainty that there is something very, *very* wrong with me…

I will never escape it.

"You see?" I gasp, my voice breaking. "I really am as crazy as everyone thinks."

"Hey, come here." Caleb's hands shift from my shoulders, wrapping around my back and pulling me close until my chest is flush with his, encasing me in their warmth. My face presses into his shirt, and I breathe in deeply, relishing his scent.

Although I've never had one to know, I can't escape the thought that he smells like home.

"You aren't crazy, okay?" His voice is low in my ear as his fingers graze along the full length of my back. "I'm going to help you figure this out. Remember what I said to you last week in the courtyard?"

I peek up at him through a fresh haze of tears, my brows knitting together, as I shake my head. A smile hitches up the corners of his mouth, and for a long moment, he holds my gaze before leaning in and planting a careful kiss on my forehead.

His words hold the weight of the world as he murmurs, "You can't get rid of me that easily, Goldilocks."

EIGHTEEN

CALEB

A COUPLE DAYS AFTER my talk with Luna, I exit one of the few senior classes the exalted Gabriel has allowed humble me to attend. I excel at *Nephilim Combat*, despite every Light gunning for me. Being in this shit hole and worrying about the voice plaguing Luna has caused me to store up all kinds of aggression, which I get to release on some Light's face. One of the faster girls here managed to get a good shot at me—and she conveniently forgot to take off a giant-ass diamond ring—but the gash above my eyes has sealed shut. And I did send her a few nightmare images as payback. I grin at the memory of her screams. No one was too suspicious, as a lot of people scream during that class.

Goldilocks and I are speaking again, and I kicked the crap out of some Lights, so I'm feeling pretty good until I think about my grandfather. Shoving my hands in my pockets, I resist the urge to growl in frustration. I've had nadda to report to Ishtar about Alexander. Zilch. And I'm afraid to keep her waiting too much longer. She's expecting results from her star student, and so far I'm coming up with a big, fat zero. My little spies have yet to report anything of interest—well, unless you count Gilgamesh having a secret stash of Ishtar memorabilia that he likes to look at, his face all tormented and guilty. Hell, it's no wonder he never noticed her golem watching his every move. Loser.

Guilt creeps over me because I know my relationship with Goldilocks serves as my main distraction from my mission. I'm just as determined to solve the mystery of Luna as I am to find my grandfather, and I know that's messed up. He's my family. My *blood*.

But I can't stop thinking about Luna, and not just because I want to kiss her again, which I hope will eventually lead to us spending several hours naked together. It would be a pleasure to seduce Luna, and after what she told me about her past, it's clear there's been very little pleasure in her life. I'd love to change that. But first, I need to know who the hell is talking to her and messing with her head. There aren't any demons the way Luna thinks of them, cruel spirits floating around, waiting to possess someone. There are only bored Darks who like to mess with people. The Lights do it, too—they just don't admit to it, as it would ruin their perfect image. I know Luna is genuinely terrified she's losing her mind, and she's going to hurt me, but I don't buy that. She's not crazy. There is something else going on here. Something…sinister and it worries me.

Luna's whole childhood has been one big nightmare, and if someone is screwing with her intentionally to hurt her, I'll rip through them like tissue paper. Goldilocks might not be a Dark, but she's an honorary part of my tribe now, and we look out for our own. I won't let anything happen to her if I can help it, but I'm not going to lie. Nothing adds up when it comes to Luna—her fire, the moth, the fact that the shattered glass didn't cut her, and now this voice. She's a Light—I know she is—and yet, I swear she has Dark qualities, too. But that's impossible, right?

Glancing up, I slow as I see the headmistress headed toward me, a thundercloud practically surrounding her stern, beautiful face. I don't like Gabriel but she *is* stunning, like a master sculptor chiseled her from marble. Her eyes pin me down, and I see the angelic power rolling behind them. I resist the urge to take a step back from her. Instead, I continue toward her, my gait casual, until we meet in the middle of the corridor. Orange rings her dark gaze, emphasizing how other she is—if the scary amount of power cloaking her didn't manage to clue you in.

Luna told me once that Gabriel's power made her want to obey the Archangel, but it has the opposite effect on me. It makes me want to flee, knowing I'm in the presence of a bigger predator. One who would gladly eat me if she thought I stepped out of line. I'm dangerous in my own right, but she plays in another league, which is why I've made it a point to avoid her as much as I can while I'm here. But I can't avoid what's directly in front of me and if I've learned one thing in this world, it's not to show your underbelly if you don't want it ripped open, so I hold my ground and paste a pleasant smile on my face.

I give a shallow, mocking bow. "Headmistress," I drawl, "to what do I owe this honor?"

Her brows form a vee over her eyes, her mouth twisting into a scowl. "Some rather alarming rumors have reached my ears, so it seems you and I need to have a chat.

Come with me. *Now.*"

A shiver of fear ripples over me, but I just nod and follow her as she makes her way back to her office. We cross into the outer office first, which is suspiciously empty of the foxy gatekeeper who is usually there, vigilant at her desk. Gabriel opens the ridiculous door of the inner office with the silver crest and wings and steps in first, ushering me to sit down. She closes the door with a click behind me.

I feel trapped, but I sink down into the guest chair as she settles behind her desk, eyes blazing with anger as she focuses on me. My mind races, trying to figure out why she's pulled me into her office. I'm pretty sure she's still clueless about my mission to find Alexander.

Slight movement under the desk catches my attention, and I see my little golem warrior give me a wave. Despite my unease, I have to bite the inside of my cheek to keep from grinning. He's a cheeky little bastard. He must take after me.

Gabriel shapes her fingers into a steeple, staring at me over the tips. Resisting the urge to squirm, I arch an eyebrow. We lock eyes for what feels like hours, but despite the sweat beading on the back of my neck, I refuse to speak.

An irritated sigh blows past her lips. "Caleb, you're an intelligent young Nephilim. Don't play games with me. You know why you're here."

I shrug. "I've got no idea why I'm here. I've been a very good little Dark ever since I got to this school, despite being treated like shit by your saintly Lights." Anger fills her face at my blunt words. "I'm disappointed. I thought you'd teach them better manners."

She leans forward, her glare sharp enough to stab. "I know you've been starting fights," she hisses, eyes brimming with fury. "Need I remind you that you're here on a diplomatic mission, not to practice your Fallen arts on my students?"

Rage smothers my fear. "I never started any fights. I just finished them." If we're being technical, I finished one. Luna had no problem finishing the other all on her own, not that I would ever tell Gabriel that. "I hate bullies, and your precious, moral Lights decided it was okay to attack Luna in a pack. And where I come from, that doesn't fly. So yeah, I handed them their asses, and I would do it again in a heartbeat."

Gabriel's spine stiffens. "I assure you, we don't condone that sort of behavior at this academy."

"And yet, it happened. Twice. But maybe you looked the other way because it was Luna and she's different. And if there's one thing I'm sure of, you Lights *hate* anything different. I guess it doesn't really matter if someone kicks the shit out of her, right? Way to take care of your students." The moment the words leave my mouth I know I pushed the mighty Archangel too far.

Her stony facade cracks, her mouth twisting into a ferocious snarl. With the flick of one wrist, the desk between us jerks to the left and careens into the wall, cracking. My heart threatens to pound from my chest as she leans over me, trapping me against the chair. Gabriel's power is palpable, and I resist the urge to piss my pants. Instead, I meet her glowing eyes boldly.

"The safety of my students is paramount to me," Gabriel says. "And if I had known Luna was being put in danger, I would have punished those involved. But instead of coming to me, you chose the Dark way, jumping into battle and not trusting that a higher authority would take care of it." Her eyes narrow as she realizes she's caging me in, and she takes a deep breath, easing back from me. A brush of pink stains her pale skin as she takes in the scene and her loss of control.

I glare at her, my chuckle derisive. "If I hadn't 'jumped into battle,' Luna would have been seriously hurt. There was no time to get you or anyone else," I argue, keeping the little detail to myself about the glass not cutting Goldilocks.

The Archangel clenches her fists and then crosses her arms over her chest to hide her reaction. "I concede you have a point, but you could have reported the first incident afterward, so I was aware of the situation and the hostility Luna faces," Gabriel says, her voice calm once more. "And perhaps then, the second incident wouldn't have occurred."

Rolling my eyes, I say, "Yeah, right. Like you would've believed me. I can see how that meeting would've gone. Your precious Lights would have denied it, and you would've taken their side because I'm a Dark, so I must be a liar, right? At least that's what you teach them." Bitterness edges my every word, and her eyes smolder with anger once more.

"I would've believed Luna," she says coldly. "It's a shame she didn't feel she could confide in me. And you're mistaken. I don't think Darks are liars. I think you're selfish and impulsive. I think your jealousy of humanity's free will is destined to be your undoing. You allow your emotions to rule your decisions, instead of seeing the larger picture and recognizing your true place in this world."

I shiver but not in fear. Her icy facade gives me the chills. In this moment, she is a beautiful and unfeeling statue. I don't like that Luna is in her care because I have serious doubts about Gabriel's ability to care for someone like Goldilocks. Someone fragile and terrified.

Weighing my words, I say, "I'm sorry I didn't report what happened to you, but I'm not sorry for defending Luna. I'm not sorry for caring about someone and being willing to defend them. And I won't apologize for liking humans and loving being a part of this world. I deserve that as much as anyone else."

Gabriel studies me. "You remind me of someone. He thought he deserved the world, too. And now, he can never go home."

I hold her gaze. "Maybe he is home."

She spins on her heel and presents her back to me. "No more fighting, Caleb, or I'll send you back to Babel before you can blink. Do you understand?"

"Yeah, I got it," I say, wondering what she's thinking. I know I hit a nerve, but I'm not quite sure how.

"Then you're dismissed," Gabriel says. "Leave."

Jumping up from the chair, I flee her office and don't look back.

NINETEEN

LUNA

TERRIFYING IMAGES FLASH BEHIND my closed eyes, and I startle awake, gasping, covered in sweat. I haven't been sleeping well for a while now and even less since that day in the courtyard with Caleb, when the demonic presence living in my head re-emerged for the first time since I resurrected that moth, its voice rising from the depths of my subconscious like a wave building at the start of a storm. I've barely had a moment's reprieve from its unwelcome return a few weeks ago, and with every gruesome vision it forces upon me, I wonder how I could've ever convinced myself it's here to do anything other than drive me deeper into the clutches of madness.

Caleb doesn't think I'm crazy, but he also hasn't given me cause to think otherwise. He just keeps saying he'll "figure it out," as if there's some logical explanation for my derangement. As if it's a problem that can somehow be solved. I know he's only trying to help, but I don't like the idea of him thinking I'm broken and in need of fixing like everyone else always has.

In the meantime, to avoid another incident and ensure I don't accidentally maim one of our classmates again, Caleb has only left my side when our varying schedules have forced us apart. He suggested restarting our one on one practice sessions—which were on hiatus due to me avoiding him after our kiss—to try to help me with restraint, but I shot that idea down the instant he aired it. I don't want to so much as spark an ember until I know that I can keep my fire and any other powers I may have in check.

Although I'm still wary of having him near me—the fear of what I might do to him like a constant itch burning under my skin—it's a relief to be talking again. That one week without him felt more like a year, and I don't think I can relive that separation, regardless of the potential danger. As much as I want to protect him, I can't overcome whatever is happening to me alone and I have no one else to turn to. Despite our camaraderie, I don't feel comfortable telling Alaric about what's been going on, and have been making it a point to dodge his texts and calls so I don't accidentally slip and give him any reason to worry. We might be friendly, but he's also a doctor, and my declining mental state could be all the reason he needs to intervene in my placement here and take me somewhere far away from whatever he perceives to be my triggers... and from Caleb. I won't allow that, even with the risks surrounding our friendship. I guess I'll just have to trust Caleb when says he can take care of himself.

His face flashes through my head as I sit up and push the heels of my hands into my eyes, which ache with relentless exhaustion. Behind my closed lids, the image warps, switching back and forth between the Caleb I know and the version of him now constantly haunting my thoughts. I see him just like I saw him that day in the courtyard—standing in the middle of a crumbling world with hungry flames devouring every inch of his skin.

Groaning, I rake a trembling hand through my sweat-matted hair. "Stop it," I breathe. "I don't want to see that."

A low chuckle reverberates deep in my ears. *"You only see what you are afraid of. Embrace your power, and the visions will stop."*

Will they, though? Or will I just open a door to further destruction that I won't be able to close?

Despite practicing with Caleb, despite reminding myself what he told me about how to manipulate and master my powers, none of it mattered once I was cornered and my senses registered the impending danger—in the moments when having these abilities counted. Fear pushed his guidance out of my brain and cut loose what little hold I had on control.

I'd rather not have any powers at all than risk a repeat of what I did to those Nephilim.

Frustration rips from my lips in a scream. "I don't want to!"

I jump at the volume of my own voice and grip the duvet crumpled around my waist, squeezing the soft, velvety fabric, until I manage to get a hold of myself. As if taunting me, the vision reappears in my head.

Straining my jaw, I grind out through clenched teeth, "Not if it means hurting Caleb."

"You only see what you are afraid of. Embrace your power, and the visions will stop,"

the voice repeats.

"So, what?" I scoff, pinning my eyes on a spot in the room where the darkness is thickest, as if doing so will force the voice to manifest there and step out of the shadows to face me. "So I can burn the world like you want?"

"Not the world, but the evil and hatred that consumes it. With my help, you can banish the divide between the Light and the Dark, so we can all become one again."

Flickers of the Serapeum tear through my mind followed by disjointed images of thirteen other locations. Every last one is engulfed in red fire. Judging by the way my stomach twists at the sight of them, I gather these places must be the other academies for the Nephilim.

The vision ends just as all the others have before it, with Caleb standing among the flames, reaching out to me, his beautiful face contorted in agony. My name is a tormented hiss on his lips.

I shake my head, cowering into my mattress at the terrible thought of such needless destruction and death. I don't understand it. I don't understand *any* of this.

How would destroying a bunch of schools get rid of a divide that's been around for millennia? The only motivation I would even have for such an atrocious act is my desire to ensure no one—be they human, Nephilim, or immortal—ever comes between Caleb and me. Is that why the voice keeps telling me to do it? So Caleb and I can be together without any obstacles in our path?

But…in every vision, Caleb dies. I'd rather bite my tongue and silently rage against a system determined to keep us apart than risk everything and lose him in the process.

"If I do that, Caleb will die." My voice breaks, and I sink my teeth into the inside of my cheek to hold back tears.

"Casualties are inevitable in war," the voice says. *"Unless…"*

Unless? I blink back my terror, straining my ears. "Unless what?" I breathe, desperation leaching into my tone.

A shudder rolls over my skin when the demon answers. *"You conquer the control that eludes you. Take possession of your powers and Caleb will live. If you refuse, he will die. You must choose: control or chaos. Take control of your fate or it will control you. Either way, your role in this world is inescapable."*

My role?

I cling to that last word. *Inescapable.* If someone had asked me a few months ago if I believed in destiny, I would've said no. Of course, that was before I found out I have celestial blood and discovered angels are real and that famous mythological and historical figures are alive and teaching at my school.

Now, I don't know what to believe.

All I *do* know is that if the voice in my head is right, then what I've seen will eventually happen, and more innocent people will die at my hand. My powers will continue to grow out of control and attack everything in their path, including Caleb, unless I find a way to not only rein in my madness…but somehow overcome it.

If that's the case, I'm a ticking time bomb.

Panic claws its way through my skin like worms wriggling out of loose soil. I can't even manifest a normal Light flame, let alone get a handle on powers I only just learned I had barely three months ago. If the world is relying on that, we're all doomed.

"I can't. I've tried! I…" My tone quivers with dread and I swallow, trying to steady my voice. "I always end up hurting someone. I don't know how to stop that from happening."

Silence spreads through the room like an icy mist, sending a shudder through my body, as the hairs on the back of my neck all stand on end. Goosebumps rise along my bare arms and continue under my T-shirt, which clings to my skin, damp with sweat.

When the demon speaks again, its every word is a tantalizing hum in my ear. *"Then allow me to teach you."*

This suggestion pulls at something inside me, and without thought, I rip back my duvet and swing my legs over the side of the bed on auto-pilot, drawn to my feet by a siren-like call in the distance. As if sleepwalking, I cross the room to the door and step out into the empty hallway. The stone floor is freezing against my bare feet, but I'm too entranced to notice the cold.

The sound calling me reaches into the depths of my soul, like the lasting reverberations of a tuning fork tapping against my bones. The sensation guides me, as if my body is metal being drawn to a magnet somewhere else in the school.

I glide through the corridors of the Serapeum without any clear idea of where I'm going. The call leads me down several spiraling staircases into the underground belly of the ancient building where the white marble, wood, and gold-lined decor give way to unending darkness and a moisture in the air that sends a chill through my bloodstream.

A half-formed thought tells me I shouldn't be down here, but I ignore it and trudge on ahead through the shadows. My fingertips dance along the walls, tracing the puckered dips in the stone as I follow the narrowing path. The call gets louder with every step, encouraging me forward, until I'm running, my heart pounding with anticipation of what I'll find at the end of this path.

A sharp breath catches in my chest, and my steps slow as confusion barrels through me like a punch to the gut. My head swings left and right, my eyes focusing on the walls on each side of the passage, every detail in the stone visible despite the complete lack of light. My vision sharpens, and there's no mistaking the truth of what I've been racing toward. What this corridor has been leading me to.

It's a dead end.

The siren call ceases, its sudden absence throwing my body off balance. Vertigo washes over me, and I sway on my feet, lightheaded.

My vision blurs as I snap out of my daze and glance around, bewildered by my surroundings. *Where am I? What the hell am I doing?* As if hearing a voice that keeps telling me to embrace my pyromaniac tendencies isn't bad enough, I've mindlessly wandered into a gloomy underground corridor that looks like the setting for a Europe-based slasher or Gothic horror movie. I almost expect Dracula to step out of the shadows and ask politely to feast on my blood.

Squatting, I comb my fingers through my tangled tresses and grip my scalp, letting out a deep breath. "This is insane. I'm losing my mind."

Laughter echoes down the length of the passage, and when the voice speaks, it's like an air horn in my ear—loud and clear, unlike its usual whispers. *"You've lost nothing. You are precisely where you're meant to be."*

I clamber to my feet as a silver light cuts through the murk, forming carvings on the broad stretch of wall marking the end of the corridor, as if some unseen hand is guiding an invisible pen. It slices through the stone in a montage of intricate symbols—twenty in total, split into two rows of ten, each one an elegant swoop of curved lines and sharp angles.

"Wh-what is this?" I stammer. A building apprehension ties my stomach in knots as my gaze sweeps over the script. Whatever this is written on the wall, it's not in any language I've ever seen.

"This"—the symbols brighten, glowing the same white as the core of the hottest blue flame—*"is how you set me free. Only then can I teach you control and give you the liberation you desire."*

Free? My eyes widen at the thought.

Up until this moment, I had believed the voice was the manifestation of a suppressed part of my mind, of *me*, that this place had somehow dragged to the surface. I may have called it a demon, an evil presence, but, deep down, I always knew the demon was me—that the terrible thoughts I've been having were the doing of my own unhinged psyche. But upon hearing these words, I can't help questioning whether the voice is actually part of me like I thought, or if maybe it's something else altogether.

As my eyes once again crawl over the symbols, I feel the truth in the shiver creeping over my skin. What I'm seeing…what I'm hearing…this is something outside of me.

Something fear tells me I have no business messing with.

My legs quake, threatening to give out beneath me as I'm reminded of that day in Gabriel's office when she warned me about the forces in this world that we Lights are forbidden from attempting to exploit.

As much as I want to believe Caleb was right and that he'll find a way to rid my head of this voice, I'm starting to think this is a lot bigger than either of us anticipated. This isn't something two Nephilim students can figure out on our own. This is a problem for someone else. This is a problem for—

Gabriel, I realize.

This is her school, so if someone is trapped down here, locked away behind this stone wall, she'll be the first to know what to do.

Unless she's the one who put them here.

I shudder at the thought. If whomever the voice belongs to was trapped down here on purpose, then there's no telling what they're capable of or what other terrible acts they might ask of me. I have to go to Gabriel. I need to tell her what's going on before I inadvertently do something I regret.

My hair whips around me in a frenzy as I retrace my steps through the passage, sprinting toward the series of winding stairs leading back up to the first floor. Although my lungs burn with the effort, I don't stop running until I've reached the eastern annex of the dormitory where the teachers reside. Students aren't allowed in this part of the academy unless there's an emergency.

To hell with that. If this doesn't qualify as an emergency, I don't know what does.

I spot an arched door at the end of the hall with an elaborate insignia branded into the surface that's identical to the monogram marking the entrance to Gabriel's office. Panting, I tiptoe down the length of the corridor, pinching the hem of my T-shirt between my fidgeting fingers.

My knees knock together as I rap my knuckles three times against the embellished, carved wood. A dim light appears through the crack underneath, seeping onto the stone like spilled milk and inching toward the exposed skin of my toes. I curl them under, shrinking into myself, my breaths coming in rapid bursts when the door creaks open.

Gabriel, surrounded by her usual golden glow, appears in the entryway, a red silk robe wrapped around her lean body and her face twisted into a mask of surprise and suspicion.

"Luna?" Her dark eyes narrow, alert. "What's wrong? It's the middle of the night—"

"I'm sorry," I gasp, my voice hoarse and palms slick as I repeatedly clench and unclench my hands. "I should've come to you sooner, but I was scared—"

She reaches out, wrapping an arm around my shoulders, and steers me quickly into the room. "Come in," she murmurs, closing the door and gesturing toward a plush armchair in the far right corner. The cream-colored fabric is soft against my hand and embroidered with flourishes in glittering gold, which are repeated on the blankets strewn across an impressive four-poster bed and again in the sculpted wooden beams lining the walls.

Unlike her sparse office, this space is extravagant. Murals are splashed across the high ceiling and the panels of wall visible between vertical beams, depicting scenes in a surreal landscape I imagine can only be Heaven. I waver next to the chair, holding onto the arm for support, and stare at the paintings surrounding me in wonder.

"Sit down," Gabriel prompts, perching on the end of the bed. It never occurred to me until now as my eyes dart from her face to the bedspread that angels might have the same need for sleep that Nephilim and humans do. Either that or they just do it to have something to break up the endless days of their eternal lives. I guess I assumed they were unencumbered by such basic mortal needs. Just goes to show how little I know.

I file that thought away for later to ask Caleb about sometime.

"Now, speak plainly," the Archangel instructs. "What is this about?"

My tongue seems to swell to twice its normal size, and my throat is thick with a rising, dry lump determined to choke me into silence.

Gabriel's brow hooks upward impatiently, and I gulp, pushing aside my fear.

"I...keep hearing a voice," I manage. "I've been hearing it since that day in the library when I...when I resurrected the moth."

The Archangel's expression remains unchanged. "And this voice says what, exactly?" she asks.

"I don't always know. Sometimes, it speaks in a different language. Greek, I think. Or something else. Something older. Other times...it tells me to do things."

This admission seems to get Gabriel's attention. She leans forward, her unblinking eyes sweeping over my face. "Like what?"

Oh, you know. Like burn down all the Nephilim academies and destroy the divide.

I swallow. "The moth..." I force out the words between unsteady breaths. "The voice told me what to do to bring it to life."

Gabriel's robe shifts as she crosses her long legs and taps a slender finger against her chin. She considers me for a moment, those hawkish eyes piercing. "Has this voice instructed you to do anything else?"

Yes.

"No," I lie. As much as I want to unburden myself of the truth and tell her everything, I'm terrified of what will happen to me if she finds out I've been keeping this secret from her for so long. The desire to not disappoint her runs deep. "Nothing I can really understand, but…I think it's trying to lead me to something. I…" Hesitation distorts my voice as tears trail over the curve of my cheekbones. "I'm afraid, Headmistress."

The Archangel rises from the edge of the bed and walks toward me, placing a careful hand on my shoulder. A shudder races up my spine at the cool touch of her fingertips. "Stress can do remarkable things to our brains, even those of us who live outside the confines of mortality."

My eyebrows draw together in confusion. What is she trying to say?

"I'm not imagining it—" I begin to protest, but her stern voice cuts me off.

"You had a difficult childhood—more challenging than most, I dare say—and you came to an academy far later in life than is typical for your kind. Your struggle to adjust has been noted."

A deflated breath parts my lips. "So, you think this is all in my head," I whisper. It isn't a question.

"I *think* you are not doing yourself any favors by spending so much time with a Dark," she counters, her tone brusque as she withdraws her hand from my shoulder.

I reel back and blink up at the angel. "Caleb? What does he have to do with this?"

A shadow crosses Gabriel's face as she scowls. "The divide exists for a reason, Luna. Darks have a talent for burrowing themselves inside our heads and twisting our thoughts until they feel like our own. It wouldn't surprise me to learn your friend Caleb is responsible for the voices you're hearing."

Voice. Singular. And you're wrong.

"He would never do that to me," I snap.

My teeth press together as a sudden blaze flares to life in the pit of my stomach, stoking my anger and disappointment that I could've been so wrong about the Archangel. What does she know? She's just as prejudiced as the rest of them, too lost in her own moral superiority to realize the Darks aren't any different from us.

Us. Even thinking the word leaves a sour taste on my tongue.

"Perhaps not," Gabriel concedes. "But such proximity to him is bound to have an adverse effect on your already fragile mental state. You should focus on spending more time with your own kind."

I shake my head as a hysterical laugh escapes me, coaxing a curious look from the Archangel. If being a Light means thinking the worst of the Darks, then I'd rather not be a Nephilim at all.

"You're the one who invited him here," I point out.

Her lips press into a tight, thin line. "To keep the peace with the Archdemons, yes. Not because I believe having a Dark in this school is in anyone's best interests. Especially yours. You want my advice? Keep your distance from that one. You may find you have a clearer head without all that darkness around to smother your light."

"His darkness is beautiful," I snarl under my breath.

Gabriel frowns at my comment but takes my hand and pulls me to my feet. As she leads me to the door, she presses a hand to my back, tearing my soul in two separate, conflicting directions. On one side, lives my desperation to please her. To heed my Faithful angelic blood and do whatever the Archangel commands of me and, in turn, show my allegiance to the Creator. On the other side, live my feelings for Caleb.

And I know, without a doubt, which one is stronger.

"It's late," Gabriel says. "You'll see this all more clearly in the morning after you've had some sleep. I think, given everything, perhaps it would be best if you'd come by my office first thing tomorrow. Then we can discuss this matter further."

I drop my eyes to the floor and nod, although I know I won't feel any differently by then. I'll still be terrified of what I've heard and of what lives deep underneath this school, calling to me. I'll still believe Caleb would never do the awful things that Gabriel has suggested he would. And I'll still live in fear of what I might do to him if I can't convince the Archangel to help me.

But, maybe by tomorrow, Gabriel will realize how unfair she's being and actually listen to my concerns.

At this point, that outcome is all I can hope for.

TWENTY

CALEB

A VISION BURSTS ACROSS my brain of Gabriel in her office, her desk repaired and standing in its usual place. The Archangel paces back and forth, a scowl turning down her soft mouth. The lines of her muscles are rigid as she moves, her usual grace absent. I shift to my side and bury my face in the pillow, trying to dispel the vision. But her image persists, and her agitation pulls me from the darkness once again. Shit, why am I having dreams about a pissed off Gabriel? Can't I get peace in this place even in my dreams? Or if I do have dreams, I'd rather they be of Luna, not a terrifying Archangel. I jerk fully awake as if someone slaps my face. What the hell?

Blinking, I notice my vision is different. Dimmer. And It's not the darkness in my room. Nephilim can see like cats in the night. Wait, that wasn't a dream. My golem is trying to talk to me. I sit up in bed, alert. Through my little buddy's eyes, I see figures pop into Gabriel's office. Archangels and...*Archdemons*? This looks like a gathering of the Council—the angels and demons in charge of the academies—which from what little I know of them doesn't happen often. So why are they meeting now, in the middle of the night? What in Lucifer's name is going on?

My heartbeat thunders in my throat as I watch the spacious office become increasingly crowded. Asmodeus and Mammon are there—the latter a tall, glowering male presence who radiates aggression. I recognize Raphael and Uriel—from pictures in class at Babel, and they're literally in all the depictions of the Fall—as they make their way to Gabriel's side. Flames wrap around Uriel's arms like living vambraces, and his hard eyes settle on the two Archdemons, his fingers on the hilt of a large sword.

Asmodeus tosses her long, crimson hair and offers Uriel a snarky grin. "You've come to fight, Brother?" she asks.

A scowl mars Uriel's deep brown skin. "If need be," he says, his voice like rumbling thunder.

To my surprise, Gabriel actually rolls her eyes in impatience. "Enough! We don't have time for posturing or petty grievances."

Mammon raises a dark blond brow. "Really? I thought that was what our relationship has been reduced to, but I'm delighted to hear we can move past that."

Raphael shoots Mammon a bland look. "I don't know if we'll ever move beyond it, but if Gabriel called us here, it must be important. Certainly worth putting past hurts away." She shrugs a slender shoulder, her long-legged figure gamine.

Asmodeus snorts. "Yes, war is an easy thing to just put away. Do carry on, Gabriel," she says, giving a mocking bow. Then an almost gleeful expression crosses her face, but it's not one of joy, but malice. "By the way, he sends his regrets."

Gabriel stills, her hawk eyes narrowing on Asmodeus with predatory focus. The Archdemon meets her eyes in challenge, as if daring Gabriel to bring it. There's a sudden tension I don't understand permeating the room. I mean, they're all immortal beings who've lived for hundreds of thousands of years, so I guess there are lots of things here I don't understand.

Gabriel relaxes. "So, is it just us then?"

Mammon nods. "Yes, we'll pass on your message to the others—if we deem it worthy."

Disgust fills me as I listen to their banter. No wonder the Dark and Light Nephilim can't get along. Our leaders are just as petty as their students. But I do admire Gabriel as the Archangel refuses to rise to the bait.

"We have a possible Alexander situation on our hands," she says, her voice grave.

My ears perk up at my grandfather's name as the room goes painfully silent. I straighten, heart pounding in my chest, mouth suddenly dry.

They glance at each other, faces wary and worried.

"He can't have escaped," Asmodeus says, "otherwise our brands would have warned us. You were tasked with watching over him. We trust you to keep him contained, Messenger." Her accusatory tone shocks me. "This is your responsibility."

"Yes, he's a danger to us all," Mammon rumbles. "That's why we helped you entomb him."

"Calm yourselves. Of course, Alexander remains in his tomb, where he belongs," Gabriel says, hands on her hips.

My mind spins, my breath coming too fast. Asmodeus and Mammon knew

Alexander was here this whole time? The Fallen knew, and they left him here to rot. Anger boils in my gut. How is this possible? I mean, Ishtar couldn't have known, or she wouldn't have sent me here to free him. I've been told my whole life it was the Lights who had taken away my grandfather. Now to find out the Archdemons had a part in it? Betrayal stings my chest. Nothing makes sense. Why would the Fallen work with the Archangels to imprison one of their own?

Raphael flips her short hair behind an ear. "Then why are we here, Gabriel?" she huffs.

"Because I believe we have another Gray in our midst," Gabriel says, and that catches everyone's attention, although I have no idea what a "Gray" is. "A new student here has shown qualities of both the Light and the Dark."

"How long have you known about this?" Uriel demands harshly.

"Yes, how long have you known?" Asmodeus says.

Gabriel crosses her arms over her chest. "Not long. I had to be sure before I alerted everyone."

Mammon holds up a hand. "Wait a moment. Tell us of these 'qualities,' so we can judge if this student is, indeed, a Gray."

Gabriel looks like she wants to punch Mammon in his smug face. "The girl, Luna, has blood-red flame. She managed to bring a moth back to life"—Gabriel talks over Asmodeus's skeptical snort—"but most damning is that Alexander has been speaking to her. And *only* her."

Shock rolls over me at her statement. Gramps is the one who's been talking to Luna? That's the voice she's been hearing? What the hell's going on?

Raphael gasps. "What has he been saying?"

"I believe he's been leading Luna to him," Gabriel says, and for the first time, I hear a hint of fear in her voice. What is she so damned afraid of? "I don't know what he wants from her, and I certainly don't like the fact that he's speaking to her at all."

Uriel's severe face is somber. "If Alexander is leading someone to him, he must believe they can set him free. How is this possible? How could we have missed another Gray?"

Asmodeus snarls, "Well, we certainly haven't been hiding one."

Raphael shoots her an impatient look. "No one is accusing you of that, Sister. Neither the Faithful nor the Fallen are foolish enough to be concealing a Gray."

Gabriel stills for a moment and then nods. "Certainly not. Let's not waste our time on needless accusations."

I almost direct my golem to scream, "What the hell is a Gray?" But I keep myself in check. Barely. Sweat mists my skin, and I know I'm witnessing something that a mere Nephilim was never meant to see or hear.

"We're not asking the obvious question," Raphael says. "Whose child is it?" She shoots the two Archdemons suspicious looks.

Mammon balks. "It's not mine."

"Or mine," Asmodeus growls. She treats Raphael with a venomous glare. "We might be rebels, but I don't yearn to bring about the End of Days."

"Besides," Uriel says to Raphael, "a Light would have to participate as well." The censorship in his tone makes her flush.

"Only a child born of both the Dark and the Light can bring about the prophecy," Asmodeus adds. "So someone has been very naughty."

"I thought after Alexander nearly destroyed the world, this wouldn't happen again," Mammon mutters, pacing.

Stunned, I try to make sense of what they're saying. I always assumed Alexander had one immortal parent and one human, like most of the other first generations. But for him to be of both the Dark and the Light, that would mean one of his parents was an angel or demon and the other a Nephilim—a pairing I struggle to envision considering the divide. For one, the Faithful are all up in Heaven, and I doubt any of the Archangels would ever go near a Dark Nephilim, let alone fuck one. I suppose one of the Fallen could've seduced a Light Nephilim, although that doesn't really jive either, despite being the only possibility that works. It's pointless trying to figure it out, though. Nobody knows who his birth parents were since he was abandoned on Earth and raised by mortals—royal mortals, no less—but if what I'm hearing is true, I think it's safe to assume why exactly they ditched him.

I shake my head. Even if a Light and Dark were stupid enough to have a kid together, considering how much our factions hate each other, how would that bring about the apocalypse? And I know Alexander wanted to rule the world but *destroy* it?

And this probably means…Luna is a Gray. Which makes a whole lot of sense, actually. She has both traits, like Gabriel said. And she's an orphan, likely cast away like trash for the same reason my grandfather was. But if she *is* a Gray and Alexander is speaking to her… I don't care what Gabriel says, if Alexander has sought Luna out, it's for a good reason. I might have had the key to his freedom right next to me this whole time. I don't want to use her like that, but I don't know if I have another choice.

My mouth falls open as another thought smacks my already frazzled brain. If Alexander is a Gray, does that mean I am, too? But I'm not like Luna. I've only displayed Dark powers. I practically live in shadow. God, does this mean at any moment I could shoot rainbows out of my ass or something? What the hell is happening?

"We should imprison the girl," Raphael says, and all eyes flash to her.

At the thought of them imprisoning Luna, I want to take out my special angel-killing dagger and stab Raphael through her treacherous heart.

"No," Gabriel retorts, a firm finality in her voice. "That's not necessary. I have the girl well in hand. She's confessed to me what has occurred and I'm watching her. She's desperate to fit in, to belong. I'll use that to keep her in line."

Her callous words freeze my blood. Luna deserves better than this. Then I think about my plans for her and I wince, sick to my stomach.

"But she might be able to pass through the wards," Raphael points out, scowling. "We never planned for another Gray to come waltzing in. How can you be sure Alexander won't lead her right to him?"

"I said I'll keep her in line. Besides, she has no way of reaching the wards, and even if she managed to get that far, she still couldn't release him," Gabriel counters.

"You will let us know the moment she steps out of line," Uriel says. "I understand she's just a girl, but she's a danger to us all. We can never forget that."

"She's just a girl who can barely tap into her powers. She's no Alexander," Gabriel says through gritted teeth.

Asmodeus glares at Uriel and Raphael. "Always with the imprisoning." She sneers. "I agree with Gabriel. Leave the girl alone as long as she obeys the rules. She need never know what she is, and if she doesn't find out, she won't be a problem."

Mammon nods. "Keep us informed, Messenger."

Gabriel gives a brief bow of her head. The remaining Archdemons and Archangels vanish from the room, with the exception of Raphael. She gives Gabriel a long, cold stare.

"I hope you know what you're doing, Messenger," she says. "Or the next thing you'll herald will be our doom."

Gabriel's stare is equally cold. In fact, I'm surprised I don't see frost on her skin. "Get out."

Her words stun me. Here, I thought all the Faithful were lovey-dovey with each other and skipped through tulips holding hands or some shit.

Raphael just smirks and fades from the room, leaving Gabriel alone. It's time I make my exit, too. Blinking hard, I'm back in my dorm room. I stand on shaky legs, still unable to wrap my head around what I just heard. I need to speak with Ishtar. She needs to know what's going on, and how the Fallen—our own people—have been lying to us.

TWENTY-ONE

LUNA

MY EYES BURN AS I glare at the glowing red lines forming numbers across the face of my alarm clock, counting down the minutes until the grating beeping begins. Despite the exhaustion pressing down on my body, I didn't sleep a wink after my conversation with Gabriel. Nothing new there. The voice continued its assault on my mind through all hours of the night as it has for so many days now, depriving me of rest, and when I wasn't focusing on ignoring its attempts to lure me back under the school, I was mulling over what Gabriel said to me in the confines of her bedroom. Her dismissal still rings in my ears—the slanderous words she spoke against Caleb like an iron brand searing into my flesh. Even now, hours later, I'm consumed by the pain of them. They feed my anger like oxygen feeds a flame.

Since I got back to my room, I've been debating whether I should bother going to her office this morning. Part of me believes the endeavor is pointless. Surely, she'll just brush me off again, or worse, continue her vain attempts to turn me against the only person here who's ever been on my side. Another part of me knows I don't really have a choice in the matter. It wasn't a request—it was a politely phrased demand—and if I don't go, the punishment for disobeying could be worse than not getting her help at all. Caleb once told me the headmistress at Babel whips students who dare to break the rules. Would Gabriel do the same to me? Or worse…whatever worse may be? I can't imagine what sort of discipline she's capable of, and the not knowing chills me to the darkest depths of my soul.

The clock ticks over to seven and unleashes a shrill assault on my senses. My palm slams down on the button protruding from the top of the black plastic casing, shutting off the alarm, as my legs kick off the blanket, sending the duvet tumbling to the floor.

My skin is still sticky with sweat, and my hair is a poofy mess, but I lack the strength to care how I look or how badly I might smell at the moment. I don't even bother to get changed out of the T-shirt and shorts I wore to bed or brush my teeth before throwing open the door to my room. Standing at the threshold, I shove my feet into a fresh pair of white sneakers—one of a handful of new articles of clothing Evangeline gave me along with my uniform when I began classes at the Serapeum—then draw in a breath and storm into the hallway.

The school is eerily quiet as I begrudgingly make my way toward Gabriel's office. It's early—classes don't begin until eight—but I still find it strange there isn't a single Nephilim, student or teacher alike, either in the hallways or outside in the courtyards, which are already drenched in the warm morning light, tempting me through every window I pass. The only presence in the silence is the voice, now my constant companion, even if the identity of its owner eludes me. Its call lingers in my ears like white noise, a ceaseless rush of sound I've had to learn to hear over. At this moment, it's like an ebbing wave in the ocean. It recedes, slinking to the back of my mind.

I press on into the academic building and continue past the empty classrooms until the ornately carved pillars marking my destination slide into view. Through the broad panes of glass looking into the administration office, I spot the closed black door emblazoned with Gabriel's silver insignia.

Swallowing, I push the glass doors open and step into the air-conditioned reception area of the outer office. To my right, the seat where I expect to find Evangeline is empty. Strange. I don't think I've ever *not* seen the friendly Nephilim at her desk.

Raised voices draw my gaze to Gabriel's office, and with all thoughts of Evangeline's absence forgotten, I inch closer to the imposing door, ignoring the unease building in the pit of my stomach that's telling me to turn around and walk away before I overhear something I shouldn't.

"All the more reason to listen," the voice encourages, every word it speaks growing in volume as its presence flows back to the forefront of my thoughts.

Although I want to ignore such reckless guidance, I find myself doing exactly what it says against my better judgment. Driven by my unbridled curiosity and desire to better understand the Archangel, I tentatively press an ear to the wood.

"Did you know?" I hear Gabriel growl.

"How could I have known?"

I immediately recognize the male voice that answers, having heard it over the phone at least a dozen times throughout the last three months I've been here. That strange accent that almost seems to be from everywhere at once, not that dissimilar to Gabriel's, sends a shudder of familiarity racing through me.

"Don't toy with me, Alaric," the Archangel retorts. "You know as well as I why you were assigned this task. Your own father, may the Creator watch over his soul, was the one who sensed the truth about Alexander before he was so brutally slain. We both know that skill has passed on through Michael's bloodline to you. Do you deny it?"

"No." Alaric's tone is level, and yet, I can sense the tension behind that one word like it's a physical force pounding on the other side of the door.

The faint click of high heels on solid ground brings the angel closer to where I stand, my shoulders hunched over and trembling, my heart racing as I eavesdrop on a conversation I don't comprehend. Why is Alaric here? Has he come to check up on me because I've been avoiding his calls? And what task has he been given by Gabriel?

Whatever it is, he doesn't seem too happy about it.

"So, you admit that you knew?" Gabriel's accusation is a venomous hiss.

"I didn't say that," Alaric bites back. "These things aren't always easy to see, although…"

My brow furrows when the silence swallows the rest of whatever he was going to say. *Although what?* I test the limits of my hearing, straining, searching for the end of his sentence.

"Although?" Gabriel presses with the same impatient eagerness coursing through my veins.

Alaric clears his throat. "I might've had my suspicions."

"And you chose to say *nothing?*" The Archangel's fury booms through the office like the bone-chilling roar of a lion, sending me stumbling back a few steps until I'm cowering against the nearest wall in crippling terror. Her displeasure is like claws digging lines into my skin. Every second that passes without her placated is another scratch drawing my blood to the surface.

I can only imagine how Alaric must be feeling right now bearing the full brunt of Gabriel's rage.

It takes several deep breaths and a quick mental pep talk to convince myself to return to the door. Knees knocking together, I push my hands against each side of the frame to hold myself upright and lean in, once again pressing my ear to the wood.

On the other side, Alaric's voice is unflinching. "Maybe I thought I was protecting her. I thought if she was surrounded by Lights—"

"You thought wrong," Gabriel interrupts. "That was not your call to make. It doesn't help matters that she's chosen to latch herself onto that Dark transfer from Babel."

The disdain in the Archangel's tone is familiar—I stood in the direct path of it only a few hours ago—and at the mention of Babel, I instantly know who she's talking about. The Dark transfer is Caleb, which means the "her" Alaric is talking about can only be me. But if that's the case, what does he think he was protecting me from by bringing me to the Serapeum?

What do he and Gabriel know about me that I don't?

My heart pummels against my ribs at the thought. As if my life wasn't enough of an unending disaster, now I have this new mystery to worry about. A mystery that encases me in a fresh bubble of fear.

Gabriel lets out a long-suffering sigh. "How did we not know about her sooner? How did *you* not know? Finding lost Nephilim is your job." She spits that last word, hurling it like an insult.

Alaric scoffs. "That's easy for you to say. There are nearly eight billion people in the world, Gabriel, any of which could be Nephilim. It doesn't aid matters that the courts disregarded her as just another juvenile offender, and the states never helped, tossing her from one foster family to another with little regard for her safety or mental well-being. She never stayed in any one place longer than a year, and as a minor, her records were sealed except to those directly involved with her case. I didn't even catch wind of Luna or her situation until she was committed, when news of the conviction was leaked to the media." There's a long, agonizing pause, and when Alaric speaks again, he sounds tired—not in the human way but in his soul. "I might have an advantage against these mortal doctors, but I'm still only one man. The numbers don't exactly work in my favor. Plus, Luna's scent wasn't nearly as potent as it should be," he mutters, his tone suddenly thoughtful. "It was barely discernible, actually, which made it far more difficult to track her than I expected. And even once I did manage to hunt her down, modern laws make it increasingly challenging to extract children tangled up in their system without drawing too much attention or suspicion." He lets out a frustrated sigh. "I'm doing the best I can."

When Gabriel says nothing, I'm overcome by the urge to crack open the door and peek inside just to catch a glimpse of the Archangel's beautiful face for some idea of what she must be thinking. I can all too easily imagine her almost tangible anger and disappointment, remembering when Vesta dragged me into this very same office, and we both suffered Gabriel's temper. I just hope Alaric isn't afflicted with an even greater discomfort being in such close proximity to her.

"Does anyone else know?" he asks after a moment, breaking the dreadful silence.

"Vesta, along with an entire class of Nephilim, witnessed her flame," Gabriel says, her tone grim, "and she knows about the resurrection, but I've banned Luna from future class participation, which should buy us some time. As far as Vesta is concerned, you needn't worry. She's a zealot, as always, and believes this to be some sign of disapproval from the Creator, but she doesn't know the truth. I can't say the same for the other teachers or students, but they have no reason to suspect differently."

It takes everything in me to remember to breathe. Buy them time? For what?

"Buy *us* some time?" Alaric echoes. "What is it you want me to do, Gabriel?" I'm taken aback by the contempt in his voice. The ire behind every word he utters is like a hot poker pushing into my skin. A shudder rips up my spine, and for a moment, I'm torn between sharing those feelings and wanting to slap him across the face for his blatant lack of respect.

I draw in a breath then let it out, calming myself. This whole ingrained allegiance thing toward the Archangel is really starting to get old.

"Your job as a physician," Gabriel snaps. "Talk to the girl. Assess her mental state. Then report your diagnosis to me. Your *real* diagnosis, Alaric. Not those ignorant human medical reports you provided before. I need to be certain this won't be a problem."

"And if I do as you ask, how are you planning on using that information?"

A long moment passes before Gabriel answers. "I don't know yet. But if I fail to act, there are others who may intervene, and they will not show the same mercy that I would."

My heart drops into my stomach, like a weight attempting to drag me down to the floor. What are they talking about? Who might intervene if Gabriel doesn't act… whatever the hell that means?

What have I gotten myself tangled up in?

"You told the Council about this? Creator's sake, she's only a child!" Alaric shouts.

Council? Familiarity tickles my senses and I rack my brain, trying to recall where I heard this before. To my frustration, the answer escapes me.

"As was Alexander once," Gabriel ripostes. "And look what he grew into."

"A legend," the voice whispers in my ear.

Annoyed by its interjection, I scowl and swat the voice away. After weeks of having it in my head at all times, I've found ways to suppress it. I can't tune it out entirely, but if I really focus, I can push it to the back of my mind until it's nothing more than a low hum, like a television chattering in the background of a conversation, ignored. Whatever I'm listening in on is more important than anything it could have to say right now.

A sigh fills the fraught silence between Alaric and Gabriel, the sound heavy with exasperation and…something else. Something my heart tells me might be grief.

"Do we at least know who her parents are?" Alaric asks, the words soft.

A gasp tumbles into my mouth, and I have to press a hand across my lips to smother the sharp breath that threatens to expose me. As the seconds roll over one into the next, my body goes to war with itself—my legs aching with the desire to run as far and as fast as I can before the Archangel discovers me here while my racing heart holds me flush to the door, my limbs paralyzed by the realization that I'm close to finally getting answers. Answers I've wanted for as long as I can remember.

Answers I'm terrified of.

But more than terror, I'm enveloped in the scorching hot embrace of rage. If Gabriel knows who my parents are, why hasn't she had the decency to tell me? She has no right to keep that information from me. I deserve to know.

I *want* to know.

My breaths are shallow and burn my throat as I await her response. A year seems to pass in the space of ten seconds.

"Even if I knew, do you think I could tell you?"

Alaric snorts. "Fine. Keep your secrets behind lock and key. But I won't be a party to your plans if they in any way replicate what the Council did to Alexander. You forget, not all of his friends were Darks."

The door rattles with the impact of something large and solid slamming into the other side of the wood. I bite back a yelp of surprise, keeping my ear where it is, even as my whole body trembles. Although faint, I can hear what sounds like someone— probably Alaric—wheezing.

"Threats don't suit you," Gabriel seethes, her words muddled as if she's speaking through clenched teeth. "Don't make me question your allegiance."

Through the crack under the door, shadows of movement spill into the space where I stand, quaking like a leaf in the wind. Another thud. Alaric says nothing as he drags in several loud gulps of air.

"Luna?"

I whip around at the sound of my name, my blood turning ice-cold at the sight of Evangeline standing next to her desk.

"H-Hi," I manage, casting a wary glance at Gabriel's office, which has gone unnervingly silent.

"What are you doing here?" Evangeline's brow hooks upward as her bright eyes flick between my face and the closed door behind me then back to me, taking in my scruffy appearance.

Answer quickly, I chide myself. Straightening, I lock my hands behind my back, so Evangeline won't see that they're shaking. "The headmistress asked me to come see her this morning. Is she in?"

Before she can answer, the black door swings open, the gentle creak of the hinges sending a prickle of goosebumps over my skin. I peer over my shoulder, meeting Gabriel's gaze, which scans my face with an intensity that turns my stomach.

"Luna." She rolls my name off her tongue as if it's laced in acid. "I trust you haven't been here long."

It isn't a question. She's testing me. She wants to make sure I haven't been listening. I swallow. "N-No, Headmistress," I manage.

Her brows pinch together as her razor-sharp eyes search my face, as if she's staring straight into my soul. After a second, her gaze falters and her lips part, her expression somewhat stunned, although I can't comprehend why. In the time it takes for me to blink, her face settles back into its usual mask of stone.

"Good." She sweeps her arm into her office, gesturing toward Alaric who steps into view with an impossible poise considering it sounded like he was being choked by the Archangel only a few moments ago. "You remember Dr. Walsh?"

Alaric's dark hair falls in front of his amber eyes as he offers me an amiable wave. If he's upset with me for ignoring his calls, his expression doesn't show it. "Hi, Luna."

"Hi," I whisper.

A gentle smile spreads across his kind face, but I hesitate to return it given what I just overheard between him and Gabriel. When he brought me here, he left me with the hope I could trust him and our interactions over the last few months only reinforced that.

Now, I don't know what to think.

He must notice my reluctance because the smile slips from his lips, and the golden glow vibrating across his skin tenses, pressing flat around his body.

Beside him, Gabriel nods, her piercing gaze never shifting away from my face. "I'll leave you two to get reacquainted." She then brushes past me, only looking back once to shoot a warning glance at Alaric as she makes for the glass doors leading into the hallway. His warm honey eyes trail her retreating figure, and when she reaches the office threshold, she snaps her fingers for Evangeline to follow. The startled Nephilim chases her steps like a dog heeding the call of its master.

Once we're alone, my posture relaxes, my shoulders sagging forward a little. The air in the room is somehow lighter now that the Archangel has left. Biting my lip, I peek up at Alaric. The soft exhalation escaping him tells me I'm not the only one affected by Gabriel's absence.

"Fancy a walk?" he asks, tilting his head to one side.

I shrug, unsure what to say and not entirely convinced I have a choice.

He grins. "I'll take that as a yes."

I allow Alaric to lead me out of the office, tracing his lithe movements through the corridors in silence until we reach the entrance hall to the school. My eyes move between the statues on each side of the path as I wonder why he brought me here of all places.

"It's good to see you," he says, turning to face me. "How have you been since we last spoke?" He cocks a curious eyebrow at me, and I finally glimpse it in his gaze—the question as to why I've been avoiding him.

A defensive chill runs over my skin. To hell with answering his questions when he's been keeping secrets from me. A frown tugs at the corners of my mouth. Is this why he's been so kind to me and humored me with his phone calls and texts? Why he's seemed so determined to position himself in my life as a friend rather than yet another adult trying to diagnose me? If he's as chummy with Gabriel as I suspect—enough so for them to discuss matters openly—it's not only likely but guaranteed he knows about everything that's been going on. Everything the Archangel is aware of, at least. I can only assume the reason he hasn't brought any of it up is to avoid me thinking he discusses my mental state behind my back.

To get me to trust him, I realize.

Trust Gabriel now wants him to use against me.

My stomach sours at the thought.

Jaw tensing, I grind out, "I know why you're here, Alaric. Gabriel wants you to find out if I'm crazy, like she and everyone else in the world seem to think."

At least, that's part of why he's here. There's so much to unpack from what I heard, and that's just from the half of their conversation I actually understood.

Alaric is silent for a moment, and as my nerves go wild waiting for him to speak, it occurs to me that if he tells Gabriel I *am* insane and that everything I'm hearing is all in my head, not only does that thrust me into uncharted territory—where do they send mentally unstable Nephilim?—but it would also confirm what I'm beginning to fear. That the relationship I have with Alaric...all of it was a lie. A charade. It would mean he *only* pursued being my friend, my confidant, to keep a watchful eye on my mental state, not because he actually cares about me. Maybe that was even the task Gabriel spoke of.

I find comfort in reminding myself that, no matter what happens—even if this conversation puts an end to the relationship I have with the older Nephilim—I'm not alone. I have Caleb. So long as I have him, I don't need anyone else, even if the thought of Alaric deceiving me hurts.

Still, despite the ferocity of this belief, I'm relieved when Alaric responds with a laugh. "Well, we've already established that I don't think you're crazy. Disembodied voices aside."

My heart trips at the mention of the voice, but he doesn't press me about it, which I'm grateful for. Nor does he look at me like I'm crazy like everyone else at this school always does. Like I expect him to.

We're quiet for a moment, but despite my doubts about Alaric, the hush between us is comfortable and easy in a way I've only ever known with Caleb. Although we're more than acquaintances now, given our frequent correspondence, this is still only the second time we've met in person. I anticipated feeling shy around him, or on edge, like I always am around strangers or people I don't know very well. Or let's be honest, everyone except Caleb. But being around Alaric is far easier than I thought it would be, which only serves to heighten my suspicions about his motivations for being my friend.

I sneak a glance at him out of the corner of my eye, wondering if he's doing that thing again, using his special talents to put me at ease. Calm, he called it. The older Nephilim has an unfair advantage. I've still yet to figure out what my talents are and I'm not trained enough to fight off whatever magic he might try to use on me per Gabriel's bidding. As much as I want to believe he wouldn't do that to me, the fact remains.

I don't really know Alaric at all.

"Who's Alexander?" The question explodes from my mouth before I have the sense to stop it. So much for not letting him know I've been eavesdropping.

A flicker of pain flashes across his fair face. "An old friend." After a moment of hesitation, he adds, "A Nephilim, like you and me."

My breath catches as I remember the last thing Alaric said to Gabriel before I was discovered. *You forget, not all of his friends were Darks.* Does that mean this Alexander person was a Dark? If so, then Caleb and I aren't the first to try to cross the divide between our two sides. Others before us, Light and Dark, have surpassed their ingrained bigotry and formed friendships.

I find that notion encouraging.

And yet, sorrow, as clear as the sun rising in a cloudless sky, wells in Alaric's eyes like tears. The small glimpse of optimism I felt a moment before is diminished by his now sullen expression.

"Is he dead?" Fear drenches my words.

"Not exactly," Alaric says in a bleak monotone. "But he's not around anymore, either."

The hairs on the back of my neck stand on end. "Why?" My voice is barely a whisper.

The older Nephilim shoves his hands in his pockets and averts his gaze, glancing at the white statues beside us. "Let's just say he got involved with the wrong crowd and made some incredibly foolish and naive decisions. Even angels and demons have a system of punishment, and all born of celestial blood must abide by their rules. What he did… Well, there were consequences."

Alaric lowers his eyes to the floor. It's strange to see him like this—almost insecure in his body when all I've known from him is a natural grace befitting a god. His aura ripples in waves along his skin, agitated and morose.

Whatever happened to Alexander can't have been good. Alaric implied as much when he refused to take part in Gabriel's plot if it in any way resembled what befell his friend. But when he said that, they weren't talking about Alexander… They were talking about me.

Does that mean the Archangel views me as a threat? That I'm going to be punished, too, whatever that entails? But for what? I haven't done anything wrong except "struggle to adapt," as Gabriel so patronizingly put it. Oh, and have the nerve to be friends with a Dark. Yeah, so awful. I deserve to be drawn and quartered for that one.

My hands ball into tight fists at my sides. "Is that why Gabriel doesn't want me to be friends with Caleb?" As I recall the unfair and biased comments she made, a strange sensation thrums through my veins, and I know—based on the rage twisting my stomach in knots—that my power is on the brink of exploding. Still, I can't stop myself from shouting, "She thinks being around a Dark makes you bad?"

"She doesn't think that, she just—"

The truth I've been hiding from Alaric rushes out in a snarl. "He's the only one here who's been nice to me, you know. The Lights all treat me like I'm a monster. Even Vesta practically tried to have me burnt at the stake."

Her voice, along with that of the girl who saw me resurrecting the moth in the library, still rings in my ears, like the lingering echo of a death knell. *Blasphemy.*

Alaric's eyes widen and pin me in place. "I sincerely hope you're joking."

A tremor crosses my lips as I push out a breath. "If she sent you to talk me out of being friends with Caleb, I'm sorry. I can't do that. I won't."

I will not negotiate on this matter. I refuse to bend to Gabriel's will when it comes to my relationship with Caleb, even if that means suffering the Archangel's wrath.

A soft chuckle floods the space between us, and I jump when Alaric rests a hand on my shoulder. "Haven't I already told you how great I think it is that you've made a friend? If you don't remember, I have the text history to prove it."

I blink. That was not the reaction I expected considering how much I neglected to tell him. "Even though he's a Dark?"

"Especially since he's a Dark." He waves his arm, gesturing vaguely behind us toward the distant doorway leading back into the main halls of the school. "Has anyone else at this academy even attempted to see past their prejudices and get to know him as anything other than a Dark?"

"No," I mutter, recalling all the nasty things I've heard the Light students say about Caleb. They all made up their minds about him the moment they saw him.

"See?" A smile beaming with pride spreads across Alaric's delicate features, warming me to my core. "I stand by what I said when we met. You're special, Luna. And not just because of what you're capable of but because of what's in here." He taps a finger to the top of my chest, just under my collar bone, and the gentle reverberation forms a straight line to my heart.

Bemused, I shake my head. "That's…a bit different to what everybody else seems to think."

Another laugh, harsher this time, springs from his throat. "I like to consider myself to be a bit more open-minded than our Light brethren, no doubt thanks to my relationship with Alexander. It's an enlightening experience getting to know someone so different from yourself. Besides, the world would be a boring place if we painted everyone with the same brush just because of how they were born. Wouldn't you agree?"

I nod, bobbing my head vigorously. Alaric seems to get it, so why doesn't anyone else?

Although I feel momentarily lighter knowing my first impression of Alaric was right, the weight returns to my shoulders when it occurs to me why nothing has changed in all the years since the Fall, and why it probably never will. The Faithful and Fallen are incapable of letting go of their hatred, born from a disagreement that transpired millennia ago. Until they do, the Lights and Darks will never move forward.

Until they do, the segregation will continue to exist, and Caleb and I will have to fight to be friends.

I exhale through my nose, my nostrils flaring. Life would be so much easier if the divide was my only problem.

"Yeah, well, Gabriel isn't like you, Alaric. She's not open-minded at all. In fact, she seems to have a pretty strong contempt for the Darks or anyone who doesn't tick the right boxes. The way she treats me, I might as well be a Dark."

Alaric's expression softens further at my tone, melting into a pitying smile. "Do you remember when we met, I told you how all Nephilim have a skill they excel at? Well, you have skills that aren't exactly common among the Lights. Gabriel is just concerned about you."

Frustration rips through me, hot and fierce. "I know I'm not normal. Gabriel's already told me I'm messing with forces I have no business messing with. But I'm not *trying* to do it, that's the thing. My powers are just"—I fling my hands in the air and then drop them with an exasperated huff—"coming out that way."

"You'll find your balance, Luna. I truly believe that."

Balance?

My eyes scan Alaric's still face as I mull over his cryptic words. "Can I ask you a personal question?" I say after a moment.

He nods. "Of course."

"Alexander…" I hesitate. I don't want to unearth old wounds, but I have to understand what the connection is between myself and Alaric's old friend. From what I overheard between him and Gabriel and the way Alaric reacted when I pressed him about it, I can only assume one thing. "He did something really bad…didn't he."

Bad enough to be punished severely.

Alaric nods again, and it's a testament to his strength that he doesn't look away from my questioning gaze. "He killed my father."

I stifle a gasp. "And your father, he—"

"Was an Archangel," he says, his expression like stone. "Michael, the Protector."

That would explain why Michael isn't among the Archangels in charge of the seven Light academies. His absence crossed my mind once or twice, given what I learned before coming to the Serapeum about the hierarchy of angels, but I never bothered to ask any of the teachers about it. I didn't want to seem any more ignorant about this world than I already am. So, I just figured he wasn't a real angel, and that the Bible probably got that part wrong. I mean, it wouldn't be the first time. I still remember my shock at learning Gabriel is a woman.

"If he was an Archangel, that means he was in charge of one of the Light schools, right?" I ask.

"Petra," Alaric mutters, almost absentmindedly. "When he died, responsibility for the academy and its pupils transferred to Serathiel, much to her dismay. She didn't like being second string." A humorless chuckle breaches his lips.

A sudden realization cuts through my chaotic thoughts, forming a link in my head I was too blind to see a moment ago. "If your father was an angel, then you're—"

"A first generation," he finishes. "Yes."

According to my lessons, angels stopped procreating with humans when they realized their actions angered the Creator. All the Lights born nowadays are the product of Nephilim with diluted blood—either from two Lights getting together or from a Light reproducing with a human, although those relations are rare. So, if Alaric is a first generation, that means he's been alive for thousands of years. Maybe even hundreds of thousands, depending on how soon after the Fall he was born.

I stare at him with wide eyes, stricken by awe. I've met other first generations, but there's something so humble about Alaric that isn't shared by my teachers. I guess I assumed he was younger because of it. "I…I had no idea. I'm guessing Walsh isn't your real last name then."

He laughs again, more lightly this time. "Definitely not."

I nod, overwhelmed by the influx of information I'm receiving today. Suddenly, another, darker thought consumes me.

"So angels can die?"

I figured some were killed during the Great Battle of Heaven, but it didn't cross my mind enough to wonder how. It also hasn't been mentioned in lessons, although for all I know that was on the curriculum before I transferred here.

An unreadable expression darkens the Nephilim's gaze, and I can't help wondering if he remembers his father. Surely, he must—if angels retain their memories about the Fall, then Alaric must be able to recall the early days of his existence. Then again, the Creator forbade the Faithful from having any interaction with their Nephilim children…

Maybe Alaric never had the chance to meet his father.

His voice cuts through my thoughts with such unexpected force, it gives me whiplash. "The Faithful and Fallen are immortal, but that doesn't mean they can't be killed. They're incredibly powerful, so their deaths are uncommon though not entirely impossible. Saying that, one would be hard pressed to find the tools required to commit such an unforgiving act. Most wouldn't even dare attempt it. To kill a pure celestial being is the worst sin one could commit, like destroying a piece of the Creator Himself."

And yet, Alexander killed Michael, I muse.

A Nephilim somehow overpowered an angel.

Based on everything I've learned in my classes, I didn't even know that was possible. Nephilim are naturally weaker than our ancestors because of our mortal lineage and the dilution of our celestial blood, so how did Alexander manage to kill not just an angel but an *Archangel*—one of only a few held in the Creator's highest esteem? What power or weapon was at his disposal capable of killing Michael, the sword of God?

Another question shifts to the front of my thoughts, claiming dominance over all the other noise in my head. More than anything else, I wonder why he did it. Alexander and Alaric were friends, and yet, the former murdered the latter's father. Why?

What happened between Michael and Alexander that could've led to such betrayal?

Something tells me Alaric wouldn't answer that particular question if I dared to ask it. Whatever transpired, the way he's spoken about his old friend makes me think there's a lot more to this story than I'll be able to glean from the vague answers he's given me. Surprisingly, his tone hasn't held any blame—only sadness, as if he doesn't resent Alexander. If anything, he seems to mourn his friend far more than he does his Archangel father.

"Maybe Michael's death was justified," the voice says, reading my mind.

I consider that idea for all of ten seconds before my stomach clenches, and all the nerve endings in my body come alive like high-pitched alarm bells signaling danger. If there was a good reason for the Archangel's death, then maybe that means Alexander was acting in self-defense. That would explain why Gabriel's concerned we're the same.

How often have I hurt someone—or worse—to protect myself without meaning to?

If that's the case, then this little heart to heart...is this Alaric's way of trying to trick me or warn me? Maybe he brought me to this part of the school where we wouldn't be seen by the other students or teachers, so he could subdue me before the past is repeated. Why else would Gabriel insist that he talk to me? I heard what she said. Her words were as clear as her intent.

She wants to know if I'm a threat.

A shiver of dread rolls up my spine. "If Gabriel's right and I'm anything like Alexander, why would you *want* to help me?"

I tense, waiting for the inevitable, but Alaric makes no move to harm or restrain me. Instead, a downcast look floods his eyes, and he crosses his arms in front of his chest, as if to hold himself together. As if he might break. I've never seen anyone look so impossibly fragile.

Or utterly determined.

"Because Alexander was my friend and I failed him," he murmurs. "And because, when we met, I promised myself I wouldn't fail you, too."

He reaches out and places his hand on my head as a smile forms along the curve of his lips. I don't know if he's using his Calm or if what I'm feeling right now is a product of my own emotions, but as he tousles my hair, I know one thing for certain. Despite my doubts, and regardless of whatever Gabriel employed Alaric to do…

I believe him.

TWENTY-TWO

CALEB

DECEMBER IS GORGEOUS IN Alexandria, and I enjoy the warm breeze as I skip class, sitting at a tiny outdoor cafe, one of many crowding the busy street in a touristy area. The awning blocks most of the sun, and a pair of aviators perched on my nose blocks the rest. The color of the sky is so cerulean it almost hurts to look at it. The *ibrik* containing my Turkish coffee sits on a brass platter next to a delicate coffee cup and saucer. Grasping the handle of the little pot, I pour some coffee into my cup and add two cubes of sugar. I glance at my watch before taking a sip of the steaming liquid. The rich flavor explodes on my tongue and I sigh. Damn, I love a good cup of coffee, and I'm a super snob about it. Sue me.

My shaded eyes wander the street as my fingers tap out an impatient rhythm on the table. Ishtar should be here at any moment. I don't relish the conversation I'm about to have with her. Hell, at this point, I don't even know if I can trust her to be honest with me. So much shady shit is going down that I feel like my entire world is spinning out of control. Archangels and Archdemons working together to imprison Alexander. What the hell is going on here? And did he really try to destroy the world, or did they just lock him away because he was a Gray? Different in a way neither side liked. I always believed it was just the Lights who were intolerant assholes, but maybe I was wrong. But I don't want to be wrong. If I am wrong, this blows my entire world up, and I don't know if I can handle it.

And there's that nagging voice in the back of my mind that keeps asking what I really am. Am I just a Dark or something more? But I have yet to shit rainbows, so I'm pretty confident I haven't turned to the Light side. And if I were a Gray, wouldn't my grandfather be talking to me and not just to Luna? But according to Gabriel, he's singled my Goldilocks out, which kind of tells me everything I need to know.

I spot Ishtar weaving her way through the crowd, her glossy hair hanging in a long braid over one shoulder. She wears loose linen pants and a pink cotton tank top, and despite her understated clothes, people still can't help but stare. Me included. But unlike these fools, I know this desert rose has thorns. Big ones. She pats the head of a dazzled child, pulling a coin from behind the boy's ear, and he giggles, in awe of the goddess before him. I roll my eyes at her antics. She gave that kid a solid gold coin. Show off. Man, will his parents be shocked when he gets home.

Spotting me, the goddess gives a brief wave and sashays to my table. She slides into a chair on the side opposite of me. "Caleb," she purrs, "so good to see you. You said this was urgent, so I assume this means you have good news." Her cat-who-ate-the-canary grin makes me uneasy because I know my news is going to piss her off. And she's not the type of person you want pissed off.

I take off my sunglasses and meet her eyes, my heart pounding in my ears. "I've got news, but it's not good. I don't know who to trust anymore, but I still hope I can trust you."

Her grin slowly melts like ice cream dropped on a sidewalk. "What are you talking about, Caleb? What's happened?"

I scrub a hand across my face, wondering where to begin. "So, I sent my little spies out at the Serapeum, and I got more than I bargained for. I…" Clenching my fists, I stare into my coffee cup trying to find the words to explain the betrayal I witnessed.

Ishtar grips one of my wrists, her touch almost bruising. "Tell me, child. Who can't you trust?"

I meet her dark gaze and I confess, "I saw them, Asmodeus and Mammon in Gabriel's office with Uriel and Raphael. And they were talking about Alexander." At her confused expression, I lean in closer and whisper fiercely, "Don't you get it? The Archdemons *knew* my grandfather was imprisoned here this whole time and they did nothing."

The goddess of love and war jerks away, her jaw dropping in shock. "No, no, you are mistak—"

I shake my head. "I wish to the Morningstar I was but I saw them. They not only knew, Ishtar, they helped entomb him. They helped the Lights." My voice breaks on the last word, and I reach for her hand, clinging to it. "They helped," I repeat. "Why would they help the Archangels leave my grandfather to rot?"

Horror blooms across Ishtar's face, draining her skin of color. "That can't be.

Alexander was one of us. I don't understand. You must have heard wrong."

I take a deep breath. "Alexander isn't exactly one of us, I don't think."

Her voice is harsh. "What do you mean, Caleb? Alexander is one of us. He was never a slave to the Creator."

I flinch. "I'm not saying that. When I overheard Gabriel and the others talking, they called my grandfather a…Gray. They implied that he has both bloodlines, Dark and Light."

The words fall between us like a death knell, and she reels back as if I slapped her. "That's not possible," she whispers.

My laugh is bitter. "Well, they seem to think so. It's why they locked him up. They said he would bring about 'the End of Days' or some shit. Do you know what they mean by that? Did Alexander try to destroy the world?"

Ishtar's face shutters. "Alexander wanted to conquer, yes. I won't lie about that, but he didn't want to destroy the world. He didn't want to rule over ruins. He loved humans. He simply felt he was the best person to lead them."

Her words make me uneasy, but I don't believe my grandfather is a monster. I can't. "What about this 'Gray' thing?"

Scowling, she says, "That I'm uncertain of. I have never heard this term mentioned before, but then again, I am not privy to all the Archdemons' secrets. That's apparent." Her own anger and bitterness slips out. Her gaze locks with mine. "Are you sure Asmodeus was part of this?"

She can't quite hide the hurt in her voice. I never thought anything could wound Ishtar. She's so self-assured, so confident of her power and her place in the world. But she and Asmodeus are close, and I know she feels true friendship with the headmistress of Babel. The Archdemon's lies must particularly sting Ishtar.

I don't flinch under her hard stare. "I'm sure. I think they're all in on it. Even…"

"Lucifer," she finishes, skin flushing with rage. Then her eyes pin me in place. "Caleb, why did they call this meeting about Alexander now? What was the catalyst? Do they know about your quest?" Concern coats her last words and my heart sinks.

This is what I've been dreading, where I have to reveal Luna's part in all this. And I know it's my grandfather's freedom at stake here, and I want him free—I do—but I want to protect Luna, too. She doesn't deserve to get wrapped up in any of this.

"Caleb, answer me now," Ishtar commands, and I balk under her authority. She has commanded legions, and she can reduce me to a good little soldier just with a change in her tone, but I don't want to give Luna up. I want her as far from this shit-show as possible.

"Answer me," she snarls, and when I turn my head from her, I feel talons seize my mind. Gasping, I clutch my head against the painful invasion, but Ishtar is merciless in her assault. Her powers dig into my mind, cracking my will. "This is your grandfather's fate you play with. Your blood. Speak!"

"There's another Gray at the academy," I say, the words spilling out in a rush as guilt punches me hard in the gut. "My friend…Luna, I think. Alexander has been talking to her, and it freaked Gabriel and the others out."

Ishtar releases me, and I catch myself from hitting the table. She leans back in her chair, studying me. "What about you, Caleb? You're his blood. He doesn't speak to you?"

I shiver, despite the warm sun caressing my skin. "No. I don't think I'm a…Gray."

"No, you've always been a Dark through and through." Her eyes narrow. "You must care greatly about this Luna, Caleb. And while I understand the need to protect your friends, Alexander is your family. Bloodlines outweigh everything, even friendship. Do you understand?"

Shame weighs on me and I nod, even as guilt continues to twist my insides.

"Alexander has been speaking to Luna, so she must be special then. They were certain she's a Gray?" Ishtar asks.

I give another reluctant nod. "She exhibits powers of both Dark and Light, and apparently Alexander has never spoken to anyone else before. They were freaking out. Raphael wanted her locked up, but Gabriel said she can handle it, and Asmodeus backed her up."

"Such a Light quality, locking up everyone who is different," Ishtar says, ignoring the mention of Asmodeus.

"Well, I guess it's a Dark quality, too," I point out quietly.

Her eyes snap to mine, resentment shining in their black depths. She doesn't like the fact that her worldview has been blown up, either. "It would seem so. I just can't believe…Alexander and this Luna are a product of both the Dark and the Light…"

My chuckle holds no humor. "According to Asmodeus, someone has been naughty. There's a prophecy about it, and everyone is shitting bricks because of it."

Ishtar tosses her braid over her shoulder, bending forward until our faces are only inches apart. "I don't give a damn about their prophecy," she hisses, fury lining her every word. "My friend is rotting because of their cowardice and prejudices. We can't allow that, Caleb. This betrayal cannot stand."

"I want to free my grandfather, too, but they're all watching now. How are we supposed to get him out?" But even as I ask it, I know the answer.

"Why, your friend, Luna, of course," she says with a vicious smile. "We'll undo their schemes with the girl. Oh, and how they'll turn on Gabriel. While they fight amongst themselves like dogs, we'll whisk the Great to safety. He can begin his work again."

"Gabriel was pretty certain Luna can't free Alexander," I counter. "She was more worried about Luna and the prophecy."

Arching a brow, Ishtar gives me a searching look. "And what do you believe, Caleb? Do you think your grandfather would have chosen this girl for no reason? That he's wasting his time blathering to a child to amuse himself? If they're both Grays, he's speaking to her for a reason. You know that."

I steel my spine. "Maybe that's true, but I can't put Luna in danger like that. I don't know what they'll do to her—if they'll throw her in a tomb, too, or worse."

Ishtar grabs my knee, squeezing until I flinch. "Did you hear what I said about bloodlines, boy? They're sacred. You've just met this girl. She doesn't matter. Your grandfather does."

Shaking my head, I bite back, "She does matter. And if she is a Gray like my grandfather, then they'll hurt her. I can't just use her and leave her behind. I *won't*."

Tilting her head, Ishtar gives me a calculating look. "I never said you'd have to leave her behind," she croons, and my eyebrows raise in surprise. "You're right, if she is a Gray, they will hurt her. Just because the makers of our bloodlines dish out betrayal, doesn't mean we will. Free Alexander, and we will take her with us."

Blinking, I stare at her. Ishtar isn't known for her generosity. I eye her with suspicion. "You'll take a complete stranger with us? Someone who isn't even a Dark."

"Well, according to you, she's half Dark, so she is one of us." Her nails dig into my leg harder and I yelp. "Besides, dear Caleb, if you don't persuade her to free Alexander, I will. And as you know, I won't be nearly as pleasant, nor will I care if she's left behind."

I snort. "How would you even get into the Serapeum?" I ask, calling her bluff.

"You know exactly how," she says, smirking.

God, I hate Gilgamesh. Such a hypocritical bastard.

"It's your choice, dear boy. You convince Luna to help us, or you leave me to persuade her. And we both know how that will turn out."

Icy fear encases my heart, threatening to shatter it. Ishtar doesn't give a shit about Luna, but she'll save her if I cooperate. She's throwing me a tiny bone, but at least it's a bone.

"Fine, I'll convince her, and then we take her with us. Deal?"

She smiles. "Deal." Then her expression darkens. "And unlike our traitorous brethren, you can trust me to keep my word."

I don't like it, but I do believe she'll honor her promise. And maybe, this way, I'll be able to get my grandfather back and also keep Luna.

TWENTY-THREE

LUNA

MY CONVERSATION WITH ALARIC concludes mid-sentence with him snapping his head to one side like a bloodhound picking up a scent. He's silent for a moment then clumsily spouts an excuse about a prior engagement, although I can tell by the wary look in his eyes, it's a lie. His parting words are a promise he'll be in touch soon, and then he vanishes through the front doors of the school like a specter fading into a shroud of thick mist. I stand in the entry hall for a long while after he leaves, at a loss for what to do with myself, considering everything I've heard today, and jarred all the more by his sudden departure.

A cacophony of questions thunders in my head. Is Alaric really not worried about the voice I keep hearing, or is he keeping his concerns to himself? Is he trying to deepen the trust between us, hoping I'll open up to him about it in my own time? And then, there's the more daunting fear hanging over me. Is it even safe for me to stay at this school if there's a chance that Gabriel might do to me whatever she did to Alaric's friend, Alexander? The irony isn't lost on me that she's worried about what I might become when, between us, the Archangel is the far bigger threat.

My eyes drift to the row of white statues beside me depicting the headmasters and headmistresses of the seven academies of Light, skirting from face to marble face until I find the one I'm looking for. Even in stone, Gabriel's gaze is intense. She stands beside the towering golden doors leading out into Alexandria, as if to deliver one final warning before departure from the Serapeum—a reminder to all of what happened during the Fall, and why our place is here among our Light brethren.

The look on her face chills me down to my marrow.

"Hey!" a familiar voice calls from behind me.

My head whips toward the sound, and the shiver crossing my skin melts away at the sight of Caleb, his tall figure emerging from the steepled wooden door leading into the adjacent courtyard. His obsidian brows are drawn together, and his lips are pulled down in an uncharacteristic frown.

"I've been looking for you everywhere—"

I cross the space between us before he can finish that thought and slam my chest into his, hugging him tightly. The tension in his shoulders relaxes as his warm arms snake around my back. The unease rippling through my body dissipates at his touch.

His chuckle tickles my ear. "I could get used to a greeting like this," he murmurs before slipping out of my grasp and holding me at arms' length. The molten depths of his eyes scan my face with worry then cast a bewildered glance down at my outfit. "Did you just get out of bed or something? Are you okay?"

A snapshot of the last hour bursts to life in my thoughts like the flash of a camera. My head is still reeling from what I overheard between Gabriel and Alaric and what the Nephilim confessed to me afterward. I can barely wrap my head around everything, let alone work out how to voice it so it'll make sense to Caleb.

"It's...been a weird morning," I settle on then let out a sigh, running a hand through my ratty hair in a vain attempt to flatten it.

After I breathe out, it occurs to me that I haven't brushed my teeth yet today—the events of last night pushed all notion of daily hygiene out the window of my mind in favor of paranoia and fear. With how close Caleb is standing to me, there's no way he hasn't noticed, although his expression gives nothing away.

A flush creeps up the back of my neck as I quickly slap a hand over my mouth. "Sorry," I squeak through my fingers. "I probably have morning breath."

Confusion alights in his eyes as the smile on his lips falters a little. "Actually...no," he says, tilting his head and pinning me under the full force of his stare. "You're all good. You smell great, just like always." As if to reassure me of this, he slings an arm around my shoulders and pulls me into his side. "So, why has it been a weird day?"

I lift my hands in a shrug then drop them, letting my arms fall to my sides like limp noodles. Where to begin? I have a feeling Caleb will be furious if I don't tell him about what I saw in the early hours of this morning under the school. As scared as I am of what I heard in the Archangel's office, Gabriel's vague threats pale in comparison to the possible proof that I'm not really insane. Or, at least, not as insane as I previously thought.

One problem at a time, I decide.

"Gabriel," I mutter with a nonchalant wave of my hand, putting all thought of her on the back-burner. When Caleb's mouth opens to question me further, I cut him off. "Also, I found something."

He glances behind us to make sure we're still alone then leans in until our noses are practically touching. "What?" he asks, voice low and breathy. "What did you find, Goldilocks?"

I shake my head. "It's hard to explain. It'll be easier to show you."

Stepping out from under the comfort of Caleb's warm arm, I grab his hand, pulling him after me. His palm is hot against mine as we make our way from the entrance hall to the dorms, taking the long route around through several side buildings to avoid the main path, which leads straight past the classrooms where I'm sure our absence has been noted by Vesta now that second period is starting, the peal of bells overhead indicating our tardiness. I might be able to use my meeting with the headmistress as an alibi to get me out of trouble for missing first period and now bailing on second, but something tells me Caleb doesn't have an excuse for skipping other than his endearing concern for me.

When we reach the split staircase leading up to the dorms, I sweep my gaze over our bright, gold-encrusted surroundings, trying to recall the path I took to the underbelly of the school the previous night. As if on cue, the siren call that guided my steps hums in my ears again, whispering the way.

Caleb trails my hurried movements without protest or hesitation, although, as we run, I can sense some unspoken emotion in the way his hand squeezes mine. Excitement, perhaps? Curiosity?

No, I realize as my fingers constrict around his. It's fear.

He's afraid to let me go.

"Help me, and I'll ensure he never has to," the voice says in my head.

That promise spins through my thoughts on a loop as I lead Caleb the rest of the way, down spiraling staircase after spiraling staircase, to the underground passage where the glowing symbols continue to burn along the wall in the distance, illuminating the stone in a silver white light. Although still riddled with shadow, the corridor is brighter now that it's daytime, despite being several stories underground, as if the school itself is activated by the sunshine outside. I take comfort in that thought. It somehow makes what I'm about to tell Caleb less terrifying.

My steps slow to a stop as I cast an expectant glance up at him. Meeting my gaze, he waggles his brow.

"You know," he drawls through a devious grin, "if you wanted to whisk me away to a dark corner to ravish me, we could've just gone back to my room."

At the mention of me ravishing him, my skin flushes red and seems to burn hotter than the surface of the sun. Despite everything else I should be worrying about, now all I can think about is that day when we kissed. Something carnal took hold of me at that moment—something that still lingers deep and stirs in my stomach every time I lock eyes with Caleb.

Does he feel it, too? I wonder. The hungry desire crawling under my skin that makes me feel like I'm about to explode?

I don't even realize I'm gawking at him until he grins—no doubt amused by the flustered look on my face. Winking, he moves his thumb back and forth along my hand, caressing the skin and sending my nerve endings into a meltdown. "What made you wander down here, anyway?"

It takes every last bit of self-control I still possess to push out the words. "The voice. It…led me there."

Swallowing, I point to the far end of the passage where the wall marking the dead end is drenched in the light radiating from the glowing symbols. Caleb flicks his eyes in the direction of my outstretched hand then pins his gaze back on me, anger dragging his dark brows into a vee.

"You heard it again? When?" he presses.

I roll my lips inward and look down at the floor. "Last night." *And the night before that, and the night before that. And pretty much all the time now, come to think of it.* Not that I've told Caleb that.

A sigh hisses through his teeth, and out of the corner of my eye, I glimpse him shaking his head. "Why didn't you come wake me up?"

So you could do what, exactly? I'm tempted to ask, but I bury my annoyance and swallow that comment.

Pursing my lips, I pull my hand free of his. "If I woke you up every time I heard it, you'd never get any sleep."

Caleb blinks at the biting tone of my voice, several comebacks warring behind his brown eyes, each one fighting to break free of the silence in his head and find a home on his tongue. The inevitable flirty remark I've come to expect from him wins.

"Hey, you can keep me up anytime you want. There are plenty of ways we can pass the time, all of which require a bed, and none of which actually involve going to sleep."

A smile tugs at the edges of my lips, but I turn my back to him before he can see it. "Come on, Casanova," I mutter.

Caleb weaves his fingers through mine once again as we continue, side by side, to the end of the corridor. The symbols burn brighter with each step we take, as if responding to our presence.

"Welcome back," the voice says with glee.

I peer up at Caleb who meets my gaze with a shrug. "Oh-kay. It's a dead end. What now?"

My eyes dart from his face to the symbols and back again as comprehension sinks in. "You can't see it, can you?"

His grasp on my hand tightens, his fingers suddenly rigid. "See what?" Alarm seeps into his words.

I wave my free hand at the wall. "The writing! Can you really not see it?"

Caleb's startled expression is all the confirmation I need. So much for hoping I'm not imagining things.

My disappointment trickles out in a deflated breath as I sink to the floor and tuck my head between my knees. Caleb squats beside me, keeping a firm grip on my hand.

"Hey." His voice is a gentle murmur as he brushes a lock of hair behind my ear. "Just because *I* can't see it doesn't mean it isn't there. Why don't you try describing it to me?"

When I peek up at him, his mouth curves into a smile, and he offers a slight but encouraging nod. Nodding back, I allow him to pull me to my feet.

"I-I don't know," I stammer, trailing my gaze along the lit stone, my eyes tracing every shining line and curve. "It's not in any language I've ever seen before. It's symbol-based, like Arabic or Hebrew but more...elegant, somehow? I don't know. It's really hard to describe. It's almost alien."

"It's probably Enochian."

"Enochian?" I cock an eyebrow at Caleb who taps the side of his pointer finger to his full bottom lip.

"The native tongue of the angels and the liturgical language of Heaven," he answers, as if reciting a line from a textbook. "They don't teach it to us lowly Nephilim. And now"—his voice drops to just above a whisper—"I think I know why that is."

As his eyes narrow with contempt at the wall, the tendrils of shadow surrounding him all stand on end like hackles raising on a cat. I stare at him, puzzled by the sudden shift in his mood. The cogs of his spinning thoughts turn behind his stern expression, making me wonder what he's pieced together that I'm failing to see.

Before I can ask him, he squares his shoulders to face me. "Listen, I meant it when I said I don't think you're crazy. This...what you're hearing and seeing..." His voice trails off, and he tsks in frustration, as if searching for the right words. "I don't want to freak you out, but I think someone is trying to talk to you. That voice…it's not in your head. Well, it is, but you're not imagining it. Does that make sense?"

Yes.

I direct my gaze back to the wall. The light from the white symbols seems to pulse, as if to say, *Keep going. You've nearly figured it out.*

"I had the same thought once I saw these markings. Since then, the voice…it keeps asking me to set it free. Caleb—" His name is a tremor on my tongue as the reality of what I'm about to say sinks in. I tried to tell Gabriel, and she didn't believe me— hell, she didn't even let me get this far—but Caleb… Caleb will. He *has* to. "I think someone's trapped down here."

And for whatever reason, I'm the only one who can hear them.

"Because we're the same," the voice trills in my ear.

The same?

Caleb bristles, gaping at me for an unnerving moment. Then he scoffs, his gaze suddenly flinty. "The Archangels have a habit of trying to bury things they don't understand, so it wouldn't surprise me if there is."

"What do you mean?"

He runs his free hand through his silky black hair and locks his gaze on the dead end before us. As his eyes move over the wall, seeing only stone where I see illuminated script, the normally relaxed features of his face harden.

"I've heard rumors about there being Nephilim who have both traits. Light *and* Dark." He casts an unsettled glance back the way we came, as if to make sure we're still alone, and no one is lurking in the shadows behind us, listening to our every word. He leans in until his lips graze my ear, hesitation dampening his tone. "If that's true, their very existence could pose a threat to the divide. How do you keep the two apart if there are beings who straddle that line?"

Confusion ripples through me. "What are you saying? That these—"

"Grays," he repeats.

"Grays…" I roll the word around on my tongue.

I've known since the day I arrived here that I wasn't like the other Nephilim at this school. I sympathized with the Darks when everything around me was saying I shouldn't. Hell, I even displayed some Dark powers, much to the dismay of my teachers and Gabriel. Knowing there's a deeper reason for those conflicted feelings about who I am versus who I'm supposed to be fills me with an overwhelming relief, like I've been carrying an immense burden on my shoulders, and now it's gone, cast off forever.

Gray. I nod. It makes perfect sense. More than being just a Light ever did.

"Are—" Unease muffles my voice, swallowing the words meant to follow. Clearing my throat and shoving my nerves to one side, I try again. "Are you saying you think whoever's behind this wall was put here because they're...both?"

Caleb answers with a stiff one-shouldered shrug. "I'm *saying* that the Faithful have never taken kindly to anyone who stands against their one-track beliefs. Look what happened with the Fall. Not that the Fallen are guiltless, either."

As he says this, the jumbled pieces in my head slot into place, forming a picture that finally explains everything that's been happening to me. What I overheard this morning...it's not separate from the voice at all.

They're part of the same mystery.

A soft whimper escapes me as I nearly choke on the thought that comes next. "I don't know. I think this is different. If you're right and someone is imprisoned down here, maybe they did something really bad."

Like murder an Archangel, I finish silently, remembering what Alaric told me about his father.

"Or maybe," Caleb says, sneering, unaware of the understanding dawning on me, "they were just too different to shove neatly inside our little Light and Dark boxes."

"The boy is right," the voice interrupts. *"And it won't be long until they discover that you don't fit their perfect molds, either. You can sense it. You know what you truly are. Now, embrace it."*

Tears blur my vision as a sharp pain cuts into my temples, bringing me to my knees. An image fills the chaotic space in my head, revealing a cramped, pitch black space that even the brightest light would fail to penetrate. There's a joylessness to the writhing shadows, and I know at once what I'm seeing is the tomb on the other side of the wall before me. The place reserved for those who don't confine to the boundaries of the Light or the Dark—for Nephilim the Archangels deem to be abominations. A prison for Grays. A cage...

For someone like me.

I gasp through tears, my body trembling, as Caleb drops to the ground beside me. His hand is warm on my back but brings little comfort. "Is this what will happen to me?" I breathe.

Gabriel knows what I am. She *must,* given what I overheard.

"Goldilocks?" There's an uncertain tremor in his voice.

My teeth clamp down on my lower lip, biting back a scream. My lack of control already makes me a danger to others, so what's to stop the Archangels from using that as an excuse to throw me in a tomb just like this one?

Being both Dark and Light only makes me more of a threat.

"I'm both, Caleb. I…I can feel it," I whisper. "You know it, too, don't you?" I risk a glance up at him, both fearing and needing to see the look on his face. To my surprise, what I find is a smile.

"Whatever you are, you're my Goldilocks," he says, cupping my cheek in his hand and brushing away my tears with his thumb. "Dark, Light, or both, I don't care. I will *never* let anyone lay a finger on you. But in the meantime, I think we should address the elephant in the dark, creepy passage."

"Elephant?" I wipe the remaining moisture from my face with the heel of my hand.

Caleb jerks his chin toward the wall. "Our captive friend back there."

I follow his gaze to the illuminated silver script. "Friend…?"

I toss that concept around in my head. For weeks, I thought the voice was a symptom of my eroding sanity—a representation of the many risks I pose to Caleb. Then I saw it as something other. Something dangerous. A monster hiding in the shadows. But could it be something else altogether?

Is the Nephilim trapped behind this wall a friend or a foe?

"Friend," the voice echoes.

"Yeah," Caleb adds, pulling me to my feet for the second time since we got down here. "I mean, whoever's in there is asking for your help, so they must think you're someone they can trust, right? Otherwise, they would've just reached out to someone else."

"Maybe." Unless no one else is able to hear him because our differences have bonded us.

Caleb's voice buzzes in the background of my thoughts. "Has our friend said anything else to you? Do you know who it is?"

"Alexander," I say absentmindedly.

"What?"

I step forward, pulling my hand free of Caleb's, and carefully press my palm to the wall. The symbols burn beneath my touch.

"His name…" I answer, feeling the truth in my bones. "I think it's Alexander."

TWENTY-FOUR

CALEB

MY HEART POUNDS LIKE a snare drum in my chest as I watch Luna place her hand on the wall, and it takes everything in me to present a calm face to her. My grandfather is somewhere behind these stones in this creepy-ass corridor. She's confirmed it. I'm so close to finally freeing him that my hands shake with fear and anticipation. I fold my fingers into tight fists, not wanting to freak Luna out or make her suspicious. I can't tell her my plan, and I need her to trust me. I sure as hell don't want her tangling with Ishtar.

"So, our mystery man is Alexander," I say. "Nice to have a name to go along with the voice. Look, I know this is a bat-shit crazy situation, and none of it makes sense. Trust me, my mind is blown"—I bring my fists to either side of my head then spread my fingers, making an explosion sound—"but I think we should help him get out of here."

Luna's brows make a grab for her hairline. "How would we even do that? Like you said, Nephilim aren't taught Enochian, and I…I think you need to be able to read this to release him."

"Okay, I know you don't understand it, and I don't understand it, but can you draw what you see?" I ask, keeping the edge from my voice with great effort. I stare at the blank wall, wishing with all my heart I could see what she sees. God, I wish I could *hear* what she hears, too. Then I could keep her safe and far away from this.

Luna backs away from the smooth stone, her face spooked. "I don't know if that's a good idea. And what good would it do if neither of us can read it?"

Because Ishtar might know someone who can.

I swallow my impatience, saying gently, "If someone is trapped, Goldilocks, it's up to us to help them. Well, up to you, really. I can't hear our friend, but if I could, I sure as hell would try to save him."

She blinks those big eyes at me, fear filling them, and guilt delivers a swift kick to my crotch.

"But what if he's evil, Caleb? What if he's only pretending to be in trouble? What if he's trying to trick me?"

A hint of anger enters my voice. "I doubt he's evil. More like the Lights don't like anyone different, so they shoved him in a tomb like a dirty secret they want to bury." My anger doesn't stem from the Lights' part in this tragedy, but I can't really tell her my own side decided to play ball with the enemy.

Luna takes a step back from me, and I silently curse myself for scaring her even more. Her muscles quiver like a hunted rabbit, as if at any moment, she's ready to bolt. Shit and double shit.

I run a hand through my hair. "I'm sorry. I'm not trying to pressure you or anything. Being here with people who hate me and now this? It's just rough for me. And to think that the Lights have left someone to rot and die in there…" The sorrow in my voice is not feigned. I could have had a relationship with my grandfather, but the Archdemons and Archangels took that away from me. I want it back.

Goldilocks rocks back on her heels, staring at me, uncertainty painted all over her face. "I just… I have to think about this," she says in a shaky voice. "I don't want to put anyone in danger again because of something I've done. Because of what I am. What if this…*Gray*…only talks to me because he knows that, deep down, I'm evil, too?"

At her terrified words, I reach out and grasp her wrists, tugging her close despite her protests. "Baby," I say, and she stills at my endearment, her skin warm and enticing under my fingers. "You don't have an evil bone in your body. There's not a damn thing wrong with what you are, I promise you. And if you need time to think about drawing those symbols for me, take all the time you need." My voice is low and cajoling, and I want to press her against the wall and kiss away all her doubts and fears until she can only see me. But she's not ready for that, and I have to stay on mission to get us both out of here.

Her smile is relieved, and her hands twist, so her fingers grip my forearms. "Thank you, Caleb, for being here. No one has ever been there for me before you."

Her words cause my heart to thump harder. "I'll always be there for you, Goldilocks. Always. Come on, I'll walk you to your room."

I release her with reluctance but stick out my elbow like the gentleman I am. She hesitates for a moment, still afraid if she touches me for too long she'll hurt me, but then links her arm through mine.

After seeing a frazzled Luna safely to her room, I hurry to mine. The curtains are shut, and the dim light soothes my rattled senses. Grabbing my cell phone, I send a quick message to Ishtar, asking to meet. For someone as old as dirt, she's into technology. Then I sit on my bed and wait. It's almost noon now, and she's most likely sending her students off to lunch after putting them through a grueling class on mind control. My phone beeps. I wonder if Ishtar will give me a gold star for getting back to her the same day. I swipe to read the message. She asks to meet in fifteen. Well, she never asks for anything, she demands.

Flicking on an antique brass lamp, I watch a puddle of shadows fill a corner. Stepping into them, I pull them around me and enter the Shadow Road. A few minutes later, I pop into the Hanging Gardens of Babylon, the sun strong in the bright blue sky.

I spot a hooded figure entering the Gardens, making their way to my orange tree. Tracking their movements, I tense for a moment before Ishtar throws back her hood. I roll my eyes at her.

"What's with the cloak and dagger shit? I mean, literally," I say, annoyed. One imperious brow rises, and I hold up my hands. "I didn't mean any disrespect." The last thing I need is to piss Ishtar off, but I'm jumpy as hell.

Ishtar smirks. "Sure you didn't, dear boy. Tell me what's happened."

I glance around, suddenly paranoid. "You don't think—"

This time, Ishtar rolls her eyes. "Caleb, I have more stealth in my little finger than you do in your entire body. No one followed me." She waves with a hand for me to get on with it.

I take a deep, steadying breath, my nerves wrestling with my tongue. Once Ishtar knows where Alexander is, there's no turning back. I have to guarantee Luna's safety.

"Look, I don't want to offend your sense of honor," I begin and her eyes narrow, "and I know you gave your word, but I have to know Luna will be safe. This has turned out to be much more dangerous than I thought it would be. I never thought we'd be up against our own kind."

Ishtar studies me, her dark eyes weighing and judging me, and I try not to squirm under her fiery gaze. Instead, I harden my expression, letting her know I mean business.

"I gave you my word, Caleb, and I always keep my word," she says, her voice dipped in scorn. "If Luna can free Alexander, then she'll live as a Dark, protected and cared for. I'll see to it personally and so will your grandfather." At my skeptical look, she laughs, a harsh sound in the still Gardens. "I thought about it after you and I spoke. If Alexander speaks to Luna, she's important to him. And he repays his debts as do I."

I give a curt nod. "Thank you."

So fast I barely track her movements, she grips my chin. "Don't let this girl make you too vulnerable, Caleb. Let what happened to Achilles be a lesson to you."

Jerking my head back, I growl, "I repay my debts, too. And I owe Luna as will you."

The goddess tilts her head in silent acknowledgment of my words. "Now that all is settled, tell me exactly what happened," she presses, her hands on her hips, revealing her impatience.

"Alexander is leading Luna to him. She took me there after we met this morning," I say, "but the trail leads to a dead end."

"A dead end?"

I nod. "Yeah, Luna took me deep into the Serapeum, straight into a huge wall. I didn't get it at first, but then she told me there's Enochian script written on the stone."

Ishtar's eyes snap to mine. "Enochian script? Did you see it as well?"

Shaking my head, I say, "No, I didn't. I'm guessing she saw it because—"

"—she's a Gray," she finishes, flattening her full lips into a frown. "Can she read it? I wonder if the Archdemons and Archangels are aware a mere Nephilim can see the script. I'm sure that wasn't in their plans."

I snort. "Um, she's known she's a Nephilim for a hot second. No, she can't read it. Besides, we're not taught that."

Ishtar's eyes shoot laser beams at my head and I flinch. "It's not so ridiculous if you think about it. She can see it, after all, when others can't. It's unfortunate she can't magically read it as well."

I shrug, conceding the point. "I asked her to draw it for me."

She taps a foot. "And?"

I cross my arms over my chest. "And she freaked out, okay? She's afraid she's going to release something evil."

Ishtar steps closer to me. "And were you able to persuade her otherwise?" she asks, radiating menace. "I'd rather not do this the hard way, Caleb."

"I calmed her down. I just need a little more time to convince her. I'm this close." I move my index finger and thumb a few centimeters apart.

Ishtar smiles, a savage expression that hammers home that although she may be a seductress, war runs through her veins. "You have two days, Caleb. Two days to convince your lover to free Alexander."

I startle. "She's not my lover." But my protest sounds weak to my own ears, and I hear the longing in my voice. Fuck, that's not something I want Ishtar to know. I've just given her another weapon to wield over me.

"Yet," she says. "I'm fond of you, Caleb. I always have been. That's why I'm giving you two days, no more, no less."

I swallow down my fear and nod. "I understand. But Ishtar...why imprison Alexander? Why not just kill him?" That question has lived in the back of my mind for a while. Why this ruse?

Her brows arch. "Why go for the kill when you can go for the pain, dear boy? They wanted Alexander to suffer for his audacity. Two days," she reminds me.

I nod again.

Slipping her hood over her head, Ishtar turns on her heel and walks back to Babel. I watch her go, heart pounding. I have to convince Luna to draw that script for me. I can't let Ishtar get a hold of my Goldilocks.

TWENTY-FIVE

LUNA

I TOSS AND TURN, my skin clammy with sweat, as a dream rages in my head behind my closed eyes. It unfolds before me but at a slight distance, like I'm looking in through a window at the workings of my own brain—not a part of the dream, but a spectator.

Two figures emerge as if from thin air, and I immediately recognize one. Alaric. His hair—the same dark shade as the bark of a mahogany tree—is a few inches longer than it was yesterday, the jeans and button-up I last saw him in replaced by brown leather sandals and a white chiton, pinned at his left shoulder with a simple gold fibulae and cinched around his waist with a belt. He looks to be the same age he is now—although that means little considering how long Nephilim can live—but his skin, usually light in complexion, is a few shades darker, tanned from the blazing sun overhead.

When my eyes shift to the other figure, a pang of familiarity rushes through me, even though I've never seen him before. Short tawny blond hair forms a wreath on his head, the locks above his brow brushed into an anastole, and the young man's skin is golden against his own more extravagant tunic, the embroidered cloth topped with a red chlamys positioned over broad, confident shoulders.

A sly smile curls his lips up at the sight of Alaric, and the two step toward each other, longing evident in their matching lustful expressions. The way they look at each other…I recognize it. I glimpsed it in Alaric's wistful gaze when he recounted the vague story of his old friend. Their bodies tangle in an embrace, lips landing on lips in a kiss that leaves me equally embarrassed and envious. And as the realization unfolding inside me takes hold of my sleeping brain, it occurs to me that what I'm seeing now isn't a dream at all but a memory.

A memory of the time when Alaric knew Alexander.

Several more scenes pass in front of my eyes, showing the lovers meeting in what I can only assume must be ancient Greece based on their style of clothing. Their lips move, but I can never hear what they say, although their body language speaks loudly enough. Discomfort rushes through me as I encroach on these moments of obvious intimacy between them.

I'm not sure how long I watch the pair, but I sense the danger that approaches from above before they do—the two young men focused only on each other as they kneel in a patch of high grass, holding hands and muttering words I have no way to hear. Alaric breaks their grasp, moving his fingertips to Alexander's face, cupping his cheeks, and they both close their eyes as the wind rushes by in a fierce funnel around them, as if they're casting some sort of magic spell. A blinding light bursts from Alaric's palms, and mouth parting in a cry, Alexander falls backward into the grass, grabbing his head. As he convulses on the ground, the clouds above part, and an imposing figure descends from the sky, smashing down into the earth with fury, snowy white wings stretching out to the sides. When the angel looks up, a vengeful rage fills his silver-rimmed eyes, which he immediately directs at Alaric.

I know at once this fearsome Archangel is Michael.

Alexander claws at his face, a silent scream on his lips, as Alaric clambers to his feet, cowering before the wrath of his angelic father. Baring his teeth, the Archangel pulls a golden whip from his belt and flays his son's back without mercy, the Nephilim's cries soundless and yet impossibly loud in my ears. Michael's mouth shapes the same words again and again, keeping in time with each lash against his half-mortal son's skin. Although I can't understand what the angel is saying, a recognizable voice stirs in the silence, translating for me: *"What have you done?"*

Why was Michael so angry? I wonder as I gape in horror at the vicious assault, wishing I could intervene, despite knowing I'm several millennia too late to. Because Alaric dared to fall in love with a Gray and the Lights consider anything different a threat? Because that Gray also happened to be a man?

Alexander finally pushes up from the ground, his face contorted in pain from whatever ritual he and Alaric performed moments before. His mismatched eyes— one dark brown, one blue—spring wide as they register Michael's attack, his features skewed into a grimace of loathing as he launches himself at the Archangel. Michael scoffs and raises his free hand to strike down Alexander, but Alaric grabs his arm, delaying his movements by a few fateful seconds. Mouth stretched in a war cry, Alexander collides with the angel's chest before he has the chance to attack then pushes away, leaving behind an ornate dagger plunged to the hilt in Michael's heart.

Alexander stumbles, his knees going weak, and Alaric immediately rushes forward to catch him. With their arms wrapped around each other, the two Nephilim gape at the Archangel in muted horror. As Michael falls, the familiar thrum of the voice—Alexander's voice—expands in my head once more. It reverberates through me, filling every crack and crevice and overpowering every thought I have with one simple statement.

"I only wanted to protect Alaric."

My eyes snap open, but I'm blinded by darkness, and it takes a moment for my vision to adjust to the familiar setting of my dorm room. For my brain to process that I'm awake again and everything I saw just now was only a dream.

No, not a dream, I correct myself. *Memories.*

Alexander's memories.

Sitting upright, I dig the heels of my hands into my tired eyes and push out a breath. My mind has been torn in two separate directions since showing Caleb the passage with the script yesterday. On the one hand, there's the concern that we don't really know who Alexander is or the whole story behind his imprisonment, meaning there's a good chance he could be dangerous. But on the other hand, I trust Alaric, and the look in his eyes when he spoke of his friend was overwhelming in its sincerity—as was what I just saw of their past. Now that I've witnessed the true extent of what they once were to each other, can I really fault Alexander for what happened? Can I just sit here and do nothing while knowing his punishment was likely a consequence of him falling in love with a Light?

Aren't Caleb and I victims of the same segregation?

Straining my jaw, I throw back the duvet and jump up from my bed, heading straight for the door. Caleb told me I can come to his room anytime, and I doubt I'll be able to fall back asleep, so I figure I should take him up on that offer.

I pad, barefoot, through the hallways until I reach the split staircase, crossing it to the boys' dorm and climbing the three stories it takes to get to where Caleb resides. Glancing at the numbers affixed to the doors, I pass empty room after empty room until I reach the sole occupied space on the floor, remembering which is his from the last time I was here. A gold 623 stares back at me from the last door on the right.

Irritation rips through me, laser focused on Gabriel for her decision to isolate Caleb this way by putting him all alone on the top floor of the dorm—as if he's not good enough to live surrounded by Lights. Then again, it's probably for the best there are no lurking eyes or ears around to notice my visit. We aren't allowed in each others' dorm rooms after curfew, and the last thing I want is to get Caleb in trouble.

Breathing in, I lock my eyes on his door, working up the nerve to knock. My pulse hammers in my ears as my knuckles tap softly against the wood.

A moment later, the handle turns and the hinges creak as the door swings inward, revealing Caleb standing on the other side of the threshold, wearing only boxer shorts. I startle at his state of undress, having never seen a half-naked man before in my life. I have to admit, I don't hate it, and a flush sweeps up my neck and burns my cheeks at the daunting sight of him. His arms are lean and muscular, and his abs are defined, drawing my curious gaze for a moment. Swallowing, I force myself to focus back on his face, suppressing a grin at his disheveled hair and his eyes, which are sleep-soaked and remain at half mast. A yawn erupts from him as he takes me in.

"Luna?"

"Can I—" I swallow, wringing the hem of my T-shirt, pinching the fabric between my trembling fingers. "Can I come in for a while?"

That seems to wake him up. His eyes, which were hazy with sleep just a moment ago, now stare at me, alert.

Nodding, Caleb steps to one side, and I rush past him into the unlit space, barely containing a sigh of relief. With a quick glance into the corridor, he closes the door and then spins around to face me.

"What's wrong?" he asks, his tone steeped with concern. "Is it the voice? Has it said something else?"

I begin to shake my head but pause, recalling the dream that pulled me from my bed and led me here. To Caleb's room. In the middle of the night. Worrying my lower lip between my teeth, I throw all caution to the wind and hurl myself into his arms. His chest is warm and hard but comforting against my cheek. My pulse skyrockets when it once again occurs to me how little he's wearing.

"Just hold me for a while? Please?" I whisper.

Planting his chin on the top of my head, he wraps his arms around my back. "For as long as you want, Goldilocks."

I melt into his embrace and breathe in, trying to remember this smell—to brand it on my memory like a tattoo, so I can always carry it with me. His hands change position, moving away from my back to trail down the full length of my bare arms, his fingertips feather-light in their caress, making me shiver.

"You know," he breathes in my ear, his voice a low, throaty hum, "we'll be more comfortable on the bed."

I peek up at him, my cheeks burning even hotter at the suggestion. He swallows loudly, as affected by the proximity as I am, and when our eyes meet, I find myself nodding, as if my body has a mind of its own.

My racing heart speeds up to a million miles per hour as he leads me over to the bed. It sags a little under his weight when he sits and flings back the duvet, his eyes finding mine as he tucks his legs under the blanket. An inferno of heat spreads through me, the warmth pooling in my stomach, when he pats the empty space on the mattress, inviting me to join him.

I nod again, barely breathing, as I slide next to him and curl into the welcoming loop of his arm. His hand flattens against my back, pulling me closer until my chest is flush against his side, and my head rests on his shoulder.

We stay this way for a while—wide awake but not speaking, our bodies pressed together on the narrow twin mattress. Caleb's fingers graze up and down my spine, stirring a warmth in the pit of my stomach that's reminiscent of what I felt that day in the courtyard when I let my desire for him overwhelm me. It threatens to take hold of me again now, but this time, I'm not sure I'd be able to stop it. To distract myself, I concentrate on the way the shadows squirm over his skin, twisting and reaching for me as if hungry for my touch when I lay my hand on his chest.

"Your aura really is beautiful, you know. I thought so the first time I saw you."

He shifts a little to look down at me. "My…what?"

I tilt my chin upward to meet his questioning gaze. "Your aura. You know…" My fingers dance across his exposed torso, down his arm, and settle on his hand, lifting it up so he can see the lively coils of shadow.

When my eyes dart to his again, he blinks in confusion. "I…no. I honestly have no clue what you're talking about."

Disappointment consumes me. "Oh." Dropping his hand, I reposition myself in the crook of his arm, pressing my face into his shoulder. "I guess I shouldn't be surprised."

Seeing and hearing things that aren't actually there must be my Nephilim superpower.

A withering sigh breaches my lips and I pout. The one aura I haven't been able to see is my own, and I was really hoping Caleb could tell me about it. Especially now that we both know I'm not fully Light or Dark, but a mixture of both.

A Gray. The term still sounds weird in my head. The more I think about it, my unique heritage must be why the majority of my powers are displaying so differently when compared to the other Light students' abilities. Why my flame is blood red and not white or even purple-toned like Caleb's Dark Nephilim fire. Why I was able to bring that moth in the library to life when resurrection is a power beyond the Lights' grasp. What other abilities do I have that I'm unaware of? What kind of aura would someone like me even possess?

"What's it look like?" Caleb's voice is soft in my ear. Soothing. Pushing away all the questions I have no way to answer right now, I look up at him, grinning.

I move my hand, overly aware of his naked flesh, and trail my fingertips across his bare stomach and chest. Nerves twist my insides to the point I feel nauseated, but I ignore the discomfort as the darkness reacts to my touch, weaving through my fingers like snakes. "Like…a wave of fire hugging the outline of your body. The shadows move like flames, and they react when you do. If you're happy or angry, they show it."

"What are they showing you now?"

"I don't know." I glance down at my fingers. The violet-tinged shadows twirl over my skin, buzzing with an erratic energy. "They seem kind of…agitated."

His warm breath tickles my cheek when he chuckles. "Maybe because you make me nervous."

I wince at the sudden rush of old memories, remembering my life before I came to the Serapeum. Before I knew Caleb. A time I'd rather forget. I hate that word— nervous. I hate it almost as much as I hate the word crazy. I've always associated it with the way people behave around me when they're worried I might implode. When they're worried another incident might be imminent.

Nervous is the last thing I want Caleb to be.

"In a bad way?" I whisper.

He turns onto his side and scoots down the bed a little so we're facing each other. His eyes take me in as he presses a hand to my cheek, and slowly, he brings his face closer to mine until our mouths are mere inches apart. "No," he murmurs, trailing his thumb over my chin. "In a very good way."

My heart nearly bursts from my chest as he pulls me in and brushes a tentative kiss over my lips. That one touch is all it takes to undo me, and before I know it, I'm fisting my hands in his hair, lost in the wild throes of every single desire I've been suppressing for weeks. His tongue slides into my mouth, deepening the kiss as he rolls me onto my back. The delicious heat of his body hovers over my chest, and the warmth racing through me in response is so intense, I fear I might melt into the mattress.

What I'm feeling right now…it devours every inch of my being, spreading from my fingertips down to my toes, and then deeper, into my blood and bones. I've only seen the manifestation of such incredible emotions once before.

In the dream that led me to Caleb's room in the first place.

A gasping breath explodes from my lungs as I rip my lips away from Caleb's. "I want to do it."

His pupils blow wide, and his jaw goes slack for a moment before he seems to recover himself, clearing his throat. "Do what?" he asks, his tone edged with doubt.

Lowering my gaze, I wriggle out from under the heat of his body and push myself into a sitting position. Propping my back against the wooden headboard of his bed, I glance at the door. "Set him free."

Caleb flops onto his back and lets out a strange, strangled laugh. When I glance at him, he runs a hand over his face, his lips pressed together as if he's suppressing a smile. I cock a bewildered brow at him, but he just shakes his head. "Seriously? Are you sure?"

Yes, are you sure? I repeat in my head.

Alexander's promise to teach me how to control my powers in exchange for his freedom rings in my head, loud and clear like a warning bell. Regardless of whether he deserved to be entombed for his actions, I don't know any other way to prevent what happened to separate him and Alaric from repeating itself with me and Caleb. Control or no control, I refuse to let anyone—angel or demon alike—tear us apart.

Nodding, I look down at my hands. "He showed me...well, I think they're memories."

My eyes flick sideways, once again noting the muscles in Caleb's arms as he pushes himself upright.

"Of what?" He stares at me intently, his gaze black in the darkness of the room.

I peer back down at my lap. "Of something he did." The memory of what Alexander showed me surfaces in my head, and I recall the flash of steel as he thrust the gold-hilted dagger into the heart of Alaric's Archangel father. "Something bad."

"That got him imprisoned?"

Good question. The dream ended with Michael's death, so I have no idea what events followed.

"Maybe..." I drag out the word in a slow, drawling breath. "I'm not sure. But..."

Caleb, seeming to sense my reluctance, reaches out and touches my hand. "But what?" There's an eagerness in his voice that tempts my gaze, drawing my eyes back up to his face. And although I'm embarrassed, and it seems insane trying to justify what I saw, I can't help the words that bolt from my lips.

"He only wanted to protect someone he loved, that doesn't make him evil," I say in a rush. "I can understand that desperation. I feel it every single day." *I feel it every time we're together, and I worry if I'm going to hurt you.* "And I just keep thinking…he and I…" I close my eyes and let out a shaky breath. "Maybe we aren't so different."

What Alexander did…it wasn't right. But can I honestly say I would've done any different if I had been in his position? If the choice came down to an Archangel or Caleb, without doubt or hesitation, I will always choose Caleb.

A sigh trickles out of me when Caleb runs a hand up the side of my neck, his fingertips skimming over my cheek with delicate precision like I am a work of art he's admiring. My eyes flutter open to find a mischievous grin tugging up the corners of his lips.

"Are you trying to say you love me, Goldilocks?" His breath is hot on my face as he murmurs these words, his voice a teasing purr that sends a shiver racing over my skin.

I gulp, racked by the nerves of an inexperienced, socially inept virgin, then open my mouth, ready to tell him everything I've been holding in my heart since the very first moment we met. As those thoughts find form, my tongue turns to sandpaper, and I fumble the words.

"I-I…I mean…"

"Easy there." He drops his hand with a half-hearted laugh. "I'm only joking." Running his fingers through his hair, still messy with sleep, he leans back on one elbow and averts his eyes—possibly to hide the glimmer of disappointment I thought I glimpsed in their depths.

My hands clamp together as my cheeks burn with frustration.

"Okay," he says after a moment.

Confused, I tilt my head and peer hard at his face. "Okay, what?"

Caleb meets my gaze with a crooked smile. "I'm with you. Let's go set him free."

TWENTY-SIX

CALEB

BACK IN THE DEAD-END hallway that looks like it's straight out of an *Indiana Jones* movie, I watch as Luna sketches the Enochian script. I still taste her sweetness on my tongue and smell her on my skin. She never ceases to surprise me, my Goldilocks. I sure as hell wasn't expecting her to show up in my room tonight, looking for comfort. And the offer to free my grandfather was a definite sucker punch, but warmth floods my veins because she *did* come to me. Her trust is precious, like a secret you can never share. I hold it close to me and treasure it like the gift it is.

I stare at the blocks of buttery sandstone, straining to see what she sees, but like always, all I see is a rough, blank wall. But I do feel something. I can't describe what exactly, but something feels off here. Like there's a force repelling me and telling me to walk the other way as quickly as I can. You'd think my own blood would call for me, but I'm guessing Gabriel put some powerful wards on this place. Or hell, Lucifer himself could've done it. They're all working together on this cover-up.

"Can you hurry this up? We need to get moving," I urge, noting the careful movements of her pen and wishing she'd just get on with it.

Luna pauses, her brows raised. "I'm just trying to get it right," she says.

"You'll get it right, I have no doubt, but time isn't exactly on our side here."

She frowns, studying me, before giving a brief nod. As Luna's hand flies across the paper, my palms sweat. I pace back and forth, resisting the temptation to chew my nails to the quick. I'm so close to freeing my grandfather I can almost taste victory on my tongue. Finally, Goldilocks finishes her sketching and regards me, eyes brimming with uncertainty. I still. My gaze narrows to the paper she clutches, and it takes everything in me not to grab it from her. My fingers curl into my palms.

"I'm finished," she says shakily as she observes me.

I force a smile. "So I see." I keep my voice as light as I can manage.

My gaze can't stop straying to the paper. There, written in her lovely, sloping handwriting, is the key to Alexander's freedom. As I walk toward her, reaching out a hand, I can't disguise the slight tremor running up my arm. Her eyes narrow at me, picking up on my tension.

"Luna," I murmur, an urgent note creeping into my tone, "can I have it?"

She stretches out her hand, but just as the edge of the parchment grazes my fingertips, she snatches it back. I raise my eyes to hers in surprise. Two splotches of red paint her pale cheeks.

"Why so grabby, Caleb?" Luna demands in a hard tone. "You're acting weird." She's never spoken to me like that before. Never looked at me with suspicion, like I might be one of the bad guys. It hurts.

"What are you talking about?" I ask, the edge of my own anger peeking out.

Luna shakes her head. "Ever since we got back down here, you've been…agitated. You keep looking at this paper like it's the Holy Grail or something. I know you want to help, but this goes way beyond some moral sense of injustice. I don't really get why you're so invested in this, and I'm not giving you this paper until you tell me the truth. What is *really* going on, Caleb?"

"You calling me a liar, Goldilocks?" I snarl and she flinches, and I feel like the biggest dick on the planet. It's not her fault she doesn't know Ishtar has a timer counting down over our heads.

Her eyes shine, making me feel even lower. I managed to make my girl cry. Tilting her chin up, she says bravely, "Maybe I am. I don't know why you would lie to me after everything, but if you want this paper, you need to tell me why you want to open this tomb so badly. I know you care about me—I do—but I…I'm starting to think there's something you're not telling me." She holds the sheet up with two hands, preparing to rip it apart.

I could stop her if I wanted to. I'm stronger than she is. As soon as that thought crosses my mind, I want to vomit. I would *never* hurt her, not even to save her. I spin on my heel away from Luna, my fingers clenched into tight fists.

"Caleb?" Her voice is wary, fearful.

Of me. My Goldilocks is afraid of me, her best friend. Her…well, whatever else we are to each other. I don't usually roll around half naked with my friends. Don't the Darks always say the truth will set you free? Even though it turns out they're lying pieces of shit, too. But I want to be set free. It's time to come clean. She deserves the truth.

Rubbing my temples, I slowly pivot back toward her. The gold ring around her irises captures my attention—probably because her pupils have pretty much sucked the hazel out like a black hole. She looks terrified, and I hate that I put that fear there.

"My grandfather is in there," I confess, watching her.

Shock wipes the fear clean off her face. "Your—*what?*"

I sigh. "Alexander. He's my grandfather. Alexander the Great, actually. Ever heard of him?"

Her hands sag, bringing the paper to her side. Hysterical laughter bubbles past her luscious lips. "Alexander the Great? As in…*the* Alexander the Great? The voice that's been speaking to me is your grandfather? He's in *there?*" With her free hand, she jabs a finger at the wall.

"Yes." I take a step toward her, and to my relief, she doesn't back away from me. "He's been trapped for thousands of years, and I have to free him."

"*The* Alexander the Great?" she says again. "Like…from history?" At my nod, she throws up her hands, paper rattling. "Well, of course, he'd be a Nephilim. Why am I surprised? I mean, Gilgamesh is our history teacher, and we have an actual Roman goddess teaching us magic. Why not toss Alexander into the mix?"

Her incredulity makes me chuckle. I can't help myself. She's so damn adorable. Luna scowls at my amusement, her accusing glare stifling my laughter.

"You lied to me," she mutters, hurt on her face. "All this time, you knew… Why would you keep that from me?"

"Shit, Goldilocks, I didn't know how to tell you the truth," I say, and it's not a lie. "And I sure as hell didn't want you involved in any of this. I had no idea you'd be the one who could help me. I certainly don't want Gabriel's wrath brought down on you. I knew what I was getting into when I volunteered to come here. I can handle it."

"But you knew I was hearing a voice, and I told you his name was Alexander. Why didn't you tell me the truth then?" she presses, eyes sparking with anger. "If I had known sooner, maybe I wouldn't have thought I was losing my mind!"

I'm sinking in quicksand, and I have no idea how I'm going to climb out. "I didn't know you were hearing *his* voice at first. I thought someone was messing with your head intentionally just to be cruel, and I was going to find that person and kick their ass. It wasn't until you brought me here that I really let myself believe my grandfather was talking to you." When she opens her mouth to speak, I hold up a hand. "I'm not a lone gun in this, Luna. I was deliberately volunteered by my teacher at Babel to be an exchange student here because she suspected the Lights had imprisoned my grandfather just because he was different. Just because he was like you."

"A Gray," she whispers.

Well, that's not technically true. Ishtar didn't know shit about Alexander being a Gray at the time, but Luna doesn't need to know that. Right now, I need to get her onside, and the best way to do that is to make her empathize with my plight.

"Yes, his powers didn't exactly fall into a neat category, either, so they punished him for it. And I guess…they punished him for protecting someone he loved, too. I'm sorry I got you mixed up in this, I am, but you're the only person who can free my grandfather, Luna. I need your help. He's my family."

"Don't you think if I'd known he was your family, I would've wanted to help you? Honestly, knowing that would've made this decision so much easier for me. Did you think I'd turn you into Gabriel?" Tears curve down her cheeks and my heart cracks.

I shake my head, reaching for her, but she shies away. "Of course not, but don't let Gabriel fool you. She can break into your mind just like a Dark and take what she wants from your thoughts. But if you didn't know anything, she couldn't steal anything from you."

She trembles. "What happens after I set him free? Gabriel will know and come after me, come after us both. Then what? Did you think of that? Because I sure as hell didn't. Not until now…" She trails off, the realization sucking almost all the color from her skin.

"Luna," I say, my voice fierce, "of course, I did. I made arrangements for you to come with me to Babel. I have a teacher who will help get us out." Her mouth drops open at my admission. "Light, Dark, Gray, I don't care. You're my friend, you're my…" I pause, not sure how to finish that sentence, before continuing, "And that means I'll always have your back. I'll always protect you."

"You…want to take me to Babel with you?" she asks, hope on her beautiful face.

This time when I go to her, she lets me. I cup her cheek in my hand, running my thumb over her plump bottom lip, pressing down a little, my heart pounding. "Yes. I would never leave you behind."

Crushing her soft lips under mine, my free arm snakes around her waist, pulling her into my body, careful to never touch the paper in her hand. As I coax Luna's lips apart, her breath catches, and I relish the sound and the heat of her body. Was it only an hour ago she was beneath me? It feels like days. My hand shakes as I thread my fingers into her silky hair, tugging her head back. I nip her bottom lip and she gasps, and I swallow the sound, sliding my tongue into her mouth. I feel her small hand dig into the back of my neck, urging me on. I press against her, and suddenly her back hits the wall. My lips move down her chin to caress her throat, her little moans making me crazy. This is how I want my Goldilocks, making those noises that drive me wild while my kisses drug her with pleasure. Tugging her shirt to the side, I bite the sensitive juncture where her neck meets her shoulder.

"Caleb," she gasps, voice thready.

Breath ragged, I raise my head and look at her. Jesus, she's flushed and gorgeous. I want to strip her to her skin and show her exactly how I feel about her. But we're in the middle of a dark underground hallway, trying to rescue my grandfather, and it's not exactly the time or the place to do what I long to. I have shit timing. My body doesn't seem to care. Down, boy.

With gentle hands, I detach myself from her. Her chest heaves, her breathing as shallow as mine. I give her a rueful look, rubbing the back of my neck.

"Sorry, I got a little...excited," I admit. I grin when Goldilocks's eyes dip down, and she flushes apple red.

Glancing away from me, she says, "I want to help you. If he's your grandfather, I want to help set him free. I meant it before I knew the truth, and I mean it even more now." Her face turns back, and her gaze holds mine, sincerity shining there.

Hope spreads through me, dousing my desire. "You trust me, then?"

"I trust you." She holds out the paper to me, the drawings bold in black ink.

I take the page from her, her trust a beautiful thing. I make a promise to myself to never break her faith in me. "Thank you, Luna. I'll show this to my teacher, and I'll meet you at midnight."

She slides her hand in mine. "Midnight," she agrees.

I TRUST YOU.

TWENTY-SEVEN

LUNA

MY TEETH CLAMP DOWN on the tip of my thumbnail as I pace my room, my fidgeting wearing a path in the wooden floorboards underfoot. Every few seconds, my eyes flick to the clock on my bedside table, counting down the minutes to midnight.

Two to go, I note, tracing the lines of the red numbers with wide eyes, ignoring the tightening knot in my stomach. The time displayed burns painfully into my retinas, but I'm not sure if it's my exhaustion causing the ache that blurs my vision or my apprehension finally getting the better of me. If I had to guess, it's probably a combination of both.

When was the last time I properly slept? It's hard to remember, given how much has happened in the last forty-eight hours. Hopefully, when this is all over and we're safe at Babel just like Caleb promised, I'll be able to rest for what might be the first time in my life. Although, the thought of uninterrupted sleep without a voice buzzing around in my head and freedom—real freedom to be who I am, without shame or guilt—almost seems too good to be true. As such, I'm hesitant to trust it. Not Caleb's intentions—I know those are honest—but the idea that his fellow Darks at Babel will be as welcoming as he is.

Guilt grips me as I glare at the phone on my desk. I'll have to leave it behind—leave Alaric behind—and that's the part that makes me second-guess what we're doing. After departing the Serapeum abruptly yesterday morning, Alaric sent me a single text, the words of which are seared into my memory.

I'm your friend, and you can trust me.

I consider telling him what I'm planning for all of ten seconds before reminding myself that doing so would only create problems for everyone involved. There's the risk of him intervening to consider, and if he doesn't and Gabriel were to find out he knew what I was up to, I shudder to think what the Archangel might do to punish him for withholding that information.

No. I shake my head, resolved. *The less Alaric knows the better.*

I narrow my eyes at the clock face. 11:59. A shudder rolls up my spine, prompting a wave of goosebumps to erupt on my skin. Any second now—

A soft knock on the door has me whipping around, two simple taps filling me with a dizzying rush of elation and fear. Racing forward, I yank open the door to find Caleb, his normally relaxed expression unnervingly serious.

When our eyes meet, he mutters a single word. "Ready?"

"I think so." Peering over my shoulder, I give my dorm room a quick once-over to see if I've forgotten anything, averting my gaze from the abandoned phone. The small, faded rucksack I brought with me from the hospital is slung on my back, holding my few belongings along with a handful of essentials Evangeline provided me with my first day here when she gave me my uniform, like spare underwear and a fresh toothbrush. Caleb said he'd be able to get me anything I need once we get to Babel, so I'm traveling light. He is, too, from the looks of it—he only has a backpack, nothing else.

My eyes drift down to the outfit I came to this school in: a gray T-shirt and jeans, finished with the new sneakers encasing my still fidgeting feet, which shift my weight from side to side, giving away my hesitation. Although I've made up my mind about releasing Alexander, I can't shake this bad feeling I have. Our mission seems too easy considering how long he's been imprisoned under the school, and it's hard to ignore the doubt festering in the back of my brain that keeps reminding me Caleb only came to the Serapeum to set his grandfather free, not to make friends…or whatever we are to each other. Part of me worries he only got close to me so I could help him achieve that goal, while another part—the louder part—screams in protest that he would never use me that way.

I can only hope the louder part is right.

A warm hand presses against my cheek, instantly calming my frantic nerves.

"Hey." Caleb tilts my chin upward, forcing me to meet his gaze. "It'll be okay."

The lump in my throat makes it too hard to speak, so I just nod and let him lead me by the hand from the room. The fearlessness and certainty of his body language helps to quell the unease rocking me to my core, and for the first time since he mentioned it earlier, I have absolutely no question in my mind now that leaving the Serapeum with him is the right thing for me to do. This academy has taught me much in the way of what I am and about the history of our kind, but it's also kept dangerous secrets that have caused more harm than good, not only for me but for Caleb. If I'm ever going to have true happiness in my life, I need to be away from the toxic places that would keep me confined to my misery and unhinged state of mind. I want a fresh start. A *real* one.

And I'll only get that by going with Caleb.

The school is pitch black as we sneak away from the dorm and retrace our steps down to the underground passage. Caleb walks just ahead of me, tugging me along behind him with one hand while the other is held out before us, the soft glow from the purple edge of his flame coloring his fingers. His fire twists itself into a slideshow of shapes, each one mesmerizing and beautiful. The ebony fire itself doesn't radiate light, and I've come to realize our Nephilim vision is good enough that neither of us need any help seeing in the dark, but regardless, the sight of Caleb's fire is a comfort to me, and I'm certain that's why he chose to conjure it—so the darkness and the task ahead wouldn't feel quite so frightening.

As the deep violet hue of Caleb's flame casts faint flickers of color across the stone walls, I'm determined to test out my own powers again. It's been weeks since we practiced together, and I've been too afraid to summon my fire out of fear my visions might become reality. Since deciding to release Alexander, that fear has subsided a little, putting me more at ease with the idea of connecting with my true nature again. So, I recall what Caleb said in Vesta's class, and this time, when I think about being a Nephilim, I picture myself as I truly am. Not wholly Light or Dark, but a combination of both.

A Gray.

Ruby fire spurts up from my palm, and I smile as the light from it licks across the floor like a wave of lava stretching through the long corridor. As it reaches the dead end, the Enochian symbols etched into the wall glow white in greeting, and a tall figure emerges from the diminishing shadows, stepping into the haze of red light.

My breath catches at the sudden movement, and I squint, focusing on the distant face still half cast in darkness. She's as stunning as she is intimidating, like a hungry tigress on the hunt for food. Her eyes narrow, as if trying to decide if I'm prey.

"Who is that?" I hiss at Caleb, tightening my grip on his hand.

"One of my teachers from Babel," he says, his tone soothing. "Don't worry, she's here to help."

A chill of doubt cripples my senses as Caleb leads me the rest of the way through the passage. As we near the dead end, my flame sputters out, the red glow fading away into darkness. In its place, a purple light reflects off the stone, drawing my gaze to the ball of black fire now hovering over the palm of the woman's flattened hand. The flames spasm as we approach, as if tempted to reach out and devour me whole.

A cutting smile curls her lips as Caleb gestures toward the statuesque stranger with a jerk of his head. "Luna, this is Ishtar. Mesopotamian goddess of love and war."

"H-Hi…" I stammer, unsure what else to say. The woman before me—striking in beauty with her brown skin and the thick, sable braid hanging over one shoulder—is only slightly less terrifying than Gabriel, which is saying a lot, since I'm fairly certain Ishtar is a Nephilim. There isn't enough variation between her aura and Caleb's to make me think she's a full-blooded celestial being, and if the other academies are anything like the Serapeum, the only angels and Fallen working at these institutions are the ones in charge of them.

The longer I stare at her, the more certain I am that Ishtar is a Nephilim like us. Though, if I had to guess, I'd say she's probably a first generation based on the power exuding from the shadows swathing her body and the confident look smeared across her beautiful face.

As her eyes lock on mine, it strikes me that her name is familiar, and suddenly, it registers where I heard it before. Caleb mentioned her once during *History of the Fall*, when he made a jab at Gilgamesh about their relationship. It didn't click with me until now that the woman Caleb was referring to was a Dark and Gilgamesh is a Light—a forbidden pairing, just like Caleb and me. To the Lights, the divide between our kinds is law.

Strange. I never would've taken Gilgamesh for a rule breaker. The thought of him liaising with a Dark is especially jarring, given his frequent warning glances at me and the nasty things he said to Caleb in class.

Ishtar's onyx eyes assess me with a fleeting glimmer of interest. "Hello, little one," she trills before turning her attention to Caleb. "Dear boy, we really must be quick about this."

"Right." He extinguishes the flame in his hand and turns to face me, taking hold of my shoulders. "Luna, Ishtar is going to teach you how to say what's written here in Enochian." He looks at the wall, his eyes darting across the stone, as if searching for something to look at. The symbols—which I can see clearly—remain invisible to him. "All you have to do is repeat after her."

"It will be painless, I promise," Ishtar says, pulling a cell phone from the pocket of her high-waisted black pants. With an elegant flick of her wrist, she taps the screen, the light illuminating her features, and gently clears her throat. Caleb must have texted her a picture of the symbols I drew for him last night.

"If she can speak Enochian, why can't she just do it?" I ask, casting a wary glance at the goddess.

Caleb shrugs as if the answer is obvious. "Because you're the only one who can see the script, which probably means my grandfather's tomb can only be unlocked by a Gray."

"And you're the only Gray we have," Ishtar interjects, "unless you know of another lurking around here?" She gives me an indulgent and patronizing smile, as if I'm a witless child.

Irritation curls my fingers into fists, and I scowl as resentment forms around me like an extra layer of skin. Ally or not, there's something about this woman I don't like.

My eyes narrow. "I thought Nephilim weren't taught Enochian."

Her nostrils flare, a sneer forming at the edges of her sculpted lips. "*You* aren't, but fortunately for us, I was."

Even Caleb seems stunned by this admission, and while I'm curious to know how Ishtar knows Enochian when the academies make it a point not to teach it, I know we don't have time for such questions. Every second we spend down here is one moment closer to us getting caught.

Out of protests, I let out a soft sigh and nod, resolved to help Caleb and finally get answers about the voice plaguing my mind. "I'll do my best."

Ishtar positions herself to one side of the wall and murmurs a string of lyrical words that sound like a beautiful song on her tongue. It takes me several attempts to get it right, and Ishtar's impatience with this situation—and with me—becomes more obvious each time I pronounce the words wrong. Finally, the correct phrase leaves my lips, and as it echoes around us, the script turns molten gold and the corridor rumbles in answer.

Caleb stumbles back, yanking me close to his chest, as the wall marking the dead end splits in half, a perfect vertical line cutting down the middle of the iridescent symbols, forming two identical slabs. Or doors. A thick layer of dust tumbles down onto us from the ceiling as the stone slides apart, separating like jilted lovers and disappearing into hidden crevices in the walls on each side of the passage. Beyond lies another, shorter corridor, and I can tell at a glance that something is different about it. I can feel the change in the air. Although there is no visible source of light, the passage is bright, as if some unseen magic is illuminating the space. At the end of the path awaits another dead end.

I peek over at Caleb, who just nods and grabs my hand, interlacing his fingers with mine.

In front of us, Ishtar mutters, "He's close. I can feel it."

We step forward in a straight line, Caleb lingering close on my left and Ishtar keeping her distance on my right. As we move into the hidden passage, the air presses in around us, hugging my body like a dense mist. The coolness of it makes me shiver.

"What the hell?" Caleb jerks to a stop, yanking me back. My brow furrows as I pull on his hand, but the meeting point of our fingers stops at the same point as before, as if an invisible wall stands between us.

On my other side, Ishtar has stopped walking as well. "Wards," she says with a tsk. A sound like crackling static cuts through the tense silence when her fist collides with the boundary preventing her and Caleb's advance. "I felt the first one as we passed through it, which means it was created by one of the Fallen. But this one…this was made by a Light."

"Meaning what?" Caleb's tone is anxious as his eyes search my face, our fingers still touching on his side of the transparent magical barrier.

Ishtar cuts her gaze to mine. "Meaning Luna must travel the rest of the way alone. I can only assume these wards were placed as such so a Dark could never reach the Great, even possessing the knowledge of his location. Clever traitors. And, of course, a Light could never pass through the Dark ward, not that they'd have cause to release Alexander. But as a Gray, little one, you are allowed to surpass both Light and Dark boundaries. It's the reason you have made it this far. The Dark ward was a few paces back, near where the stone split at your beckoning."

"Are you saying I walked through some sort of wall and didn't even know it?" I ask. My attention shifts to Caleb. "Did you feel it?"

He gives a half-hearted nod. "I felt…something, but I've never walked through a ward before, so I didn't know what it was."

A saccharine smile upturns Ishtar's lips. "No need to be concerned, sweet girl. The door to the tomb is only just ahead, so we'll be able to see you clearly from here. Caleb isn't going anywhere, the besotted boy that he is. And neither am I."

I peer over my shoulder at the dead end behind me. Deep grooves are embedded in the stone in the pattern of three circles—one larger and the second only slightly smaller, situated a few inches within the outline of the first. The third is a fraction of the size of the other two, positioned in the exact center of the wall. They don't appear to form any defined shape that I would remotely consider a door, but then again, the wall with the script didn't look like a secret entrance either.

Caleb squeezes my hand, drawing my gaze back to his face. "I'll be right here. I'm not going anywhere, I promise. Just open the door and come back to me."

The silence is heavy as our fingers drift apart, and holding my breath, I continue onward, leaving Caleb and Ishtar on the other side of the Light ward. Every time I glance back, Ishtar urges me on with a wave of her hand, her expression pinched, as if she's restraining herself from screaming at me to hurry.

"Fear not," the voice says in my head, sensing my doubt, *"and remember my promise to you. Set me free, and the control you so keenly desire is yours."*

My feet slow to a faltering stop underneath me, the creamy wall of the dead end so close I can touch it. My hand trembles as I reach out and press my fingertips to the divots in the stone.

"What do you see?" Ishtar calls, her voice distant, as if she's speaking to me through thick glass.

My eyes sweep over the stone, but unlike before, there is no Enochian I can read aloud to trigger whatever locking mechanism was placed on the tomb. The stone is bare aside from the three carved circles, the smallest of which transforms at my touch, swinging inward to reveal a steel spike protruding at an angle from a small ring of gold. The sharp tip practically glints with threat.

The breath I'd been holding punches from my lungs. "There's something here. It...looks kind of like an old sewing spindle, but I'm not sure what I'm meant to do with it—"

Ishtar's voice carries down the passage in a commanding hiss. "Cut yourself."

"What?" I spin on my heel, my voice rising an octave.

Rolling her eyes, Ishtar crosses her arms. "The door obviously requires a blood sacrifice. If I had to guess, the tomb was sealed using Alexander's blood and only another Gray's will unlock it. If that doesn't work, perhaps a bloodline sacrifice is in order, in which case, Caleb is waiting right here. If your blood isn't the key, surely his is." With a sway of her hips, she sidles up next to Caleb and slides her hand through the crook of his arm. Her hooded eyes shift to his face as her voice drips with fondness. "He is the Great's grandson, after all."

A grimace twists my mouth. I know what she's doing. This so-called goddess is trying to get under my skin to force my hand and is using Caleb to assert her dominance. To make me feel threatened and insecure. Little does she know she doesn't need to make me jealous to push me to go through with this. I would do anything for him, even at the cost of my own life.

Caleb disentangles his arm from Ishtar's and bares his teeth at her, grinding out, "We have *no idea* what that will do to Luna!" Apprehension shines in his eyes as he raises his hands, planting them flat against the ward. "Forget it, Goldilocks. We'll figure out something else. Just come back!"

Ishtar swipes her hand out to the side, striking Caleb hard across the right cheek. His skin burns red from the contact, and he staggers back, his shoulder slamming into the wall. "Don't be a fool, Caleb. He is your blood and blood *always* comes first. This will be our only chance to save your grandfather, and you're risking it, for what?"

"That could kill her!" he shouts back, pointing at me. "There's no way Gabriel and the other Archangels and Archdemons involved would only require a measly drop of blood to set my grandfather free. For all we know, it'll drain her of everything she has."

"A worthy sacrifice," Ishtar croons.

Caleb straightens and clenches his hands into fists. "I told you I wouldn't just use her and then leave her behind."

Time seems to slow as I watch the two bicker, my heart beating into my ribcage as I realize within the space of roughly ten seconds what will happen if I don't open this door. I can see it in the way Ishtar stands, her hands spread wide like claws ready to slash. Her dark eyes betray how she views Caleb's protests. She thinks he's being disloyal to her—to his grandfather.

She believes he's choosing me over them.

"Caleb." His name falls from my lips in a ragged breath, and his eyes find mine, the deep brown irises a thin ring around black pupils dilated with fear. I shake my head. This isn't what I want.

I never want his life to be at risk because of me.

Without another thought—and not caring about the price—I reach out and slice my hand on the metal spindle, wincing as a flash of pain ripples through me. Exhaustion overtakes my body, and I struggle to hold myself up, lightheaded as blood pours out of my palm and a searing heat spreads out across my pierced skin like fire. Gradually, the searing sensation passes, although the weakness in my limbs remains. Clinging to the nearest wall for support, I risk a dizzy glance over my shoulder, searching for Caleb through my blurring vision.

His stunned expression is the last thing I see as the passage is swallowed by a blinding white light.

TWENTY-EIGHT

CALEB

ISHTAR AND I SHIELD our eyes with our hands as the corridor lights up like it's on fire. Blinking, I let my hand fall to my side, my jaw slack in shock. Symbols burn in gold on the ancient sandstone, almost blinding in their intensity. Circular fissures illuminate the end of the hallway, and the wall shifts back and in, dust from the grinding stone briefly providing a respite from the harsh light. A massive figure steps out of the doorway and I gasp, my hand covering my heart as it bucks in my chest. There's a roaring in my ears as the blood in my veins recognizes the man emerging from the tomb. *Family,* my blood seems to whisper. And I know without a doubt that this is Alexander the Great, my grandfather. Anticipation grips me. After all these years, after my father's rejection, I will finally meet my grandfather. I will finally know my true Nephilim heritage.

As I focus on Alexander, shock freezes my heart. Blond hair falls to his ankles like a cape, and I can see his eyes, one blue and one brown. They blaze with triumph and fury. We have little in common in appearance except we share the same nose, straight and noble. But that's not what clamps my attention in a vise, refusing to let go. The enormous, silver wings flaring from his back cast wide shadows in the bright hallway. *Wings.* Time seems to slow to a crawl as I stare at the pewter-colored feathers, mesmerized by their meaning.

My whole life, I've been fed stories about Alexander being a powerful, first generation Nephilim. How he almost conquered the world with his ambition. But if he has wings, that's impossible. Darks don't Ascend, which means my grandfather is a fucking *angel.* Why didn't anyone tell me? All this time, I've believed I'm a third generation, my blood diluted. Instead, my gramps is an angel, with power rivaling the Faithful and the Fallen.

The enormity of that revelation feels like a boulder has been dropped on my chest, pinning me in place. Blood rushes to my head, making me dizzy. My entire life is a lie. Everything I know is a lie. I rip my gaze away to stare at Ishtar in accusation. How could she know and not tell me? But the Mesopotamian goddess is just as stunned as I am. Her dark eyes are shiny with fear and wonder as they roam over Alexander's wings. Tears glisten in her eyes, and that's almost as shocking as the fact that my grandfather is an angel. An *angel*. I can't wrap my mind around it. How did the Council manage to entrap an angel…and why is no one else aware of what he is? And why did they imprison one of their own? All over some half-baked prophecy?

My gaze falls on Luna. She straightens and stands in front of Alexander, her slender figure overshadowed by his tall frame. With my hawk's vision, I can see the tremor running through her body. Is my Goldilocks afraid of him? My eyes dart to my grandfather who stares at Luna with an intense, unreadable expression. I can't tell if he's grateful to her or if he wants to kill her. I mean, he's been trapped for thousands of years. That can't be good for someone's mental state, and I begged Luna to set him free. Fuck, he could be living in crazy town right now, and she might look like the enemy. Would Alexander hurt Luna? Terror envelops me, chilling me to the bone.

Alexander's wings flare as he bends down. I tense, helpless because of the ward standing between us, but he just whispers in her ear, so I relax. Until Luna screams. A horrifying, pain-filled wail I feel down to my marrow. Shocked, I watch as she drops to the floor, writhing in agony, hands grasping at her shoulders and tearing off her backpack. I throw myself against the barrier, bouncing off the invisible shield, shouting her name. My grandfather looks at me and smiles. *Smiles.*

As Luna lets out a blood-curdling cry, an unseen force flings Ishtar and me in opposite directions from each other, hurling me forward while dragging her back. Tossed aside like a rag, I hit the Light barrier, and I fall to my knees, shaking my head clear of its daze.

Confused, I glance back the way we came to find Ishtar now resting outside the confines of the Dark ward, where she pushes herself to her feet. I start to search for the source of the attack when I hear my teacher shout, "Gabriel!"

Behind Ishtar, I see the Messenger step into the light, eyes brimming with wrath, as she stares past us at Alexander. I glance between them, and he lifts his upper lip in a silent growl. I remind myself that it took several Archdemons and Archangels, if not the whole Council, to lock Alexander away, but my heart still races. Two beings with that kind of power can destroy this city fast. And we're all standing directly in Gabriel's path to my grandfather, with Luna right in front of her target. Who knows how long the wards will stand now that the tomb is open?

"Caleb," Ishtar calls to me. Whipping around, I watch as my mentor begins circling the Archangel, distracting her from Alexander. "Take care of them. I have unfinished business I need to attend to."

Take care of them *how*? But I nod, my mind rapidly trying to find a good plan and failing.

With a savage smile, Ishtar leaps at Gabriel. The Archangel leans away, back curved almost in an upside down U. She grasps my teacher and slings her against the opposite wall, thrusting her back into the previous corridor. Ishtar shakes her head, as if to regain her senses, and then scrambles to her feet, dodging as Gabriel's fist hits the stone wall, a spider web of cracks spreading from the impact.

"Goddess of war," Gabriel says, sneering. "I'll enjoy tearing you apart."

"There's your true nature, Messenger," Ishtar taunts. "All that light is just to disguise your darkness."

Gabriel snarls, attacking Ishtar. The two women move so fast I can barely follow them. Living up to her name, Ishtar manages to land a few good blows on the Archangel, ducking and weaving, but despite her strength, she's a first generation Nephilim fighting a full-blooded angel. She can't quite block a knee to the ribs, and I hear bone crunch.

Shit. I turn back toward the Light barrier and bang on it with my fists. "Grandfather, bring Luna to me, and let's get out of here. Please!" My gaze clashes with Alexander's, and it's like being shocked by a live wire. Power simmers behind his eyes along with recognition. He tilts his head, studying me for a brief moment before nodding, acknowledging our blood bond. He then focuses on the battle behind me.

I beg over and over for him to help, but Alexander ignores my pleas, his clashing eyes tracking the fight between Gabriel and Ishtar. Luna convulses on the floor at his feet, and I have never felt so powerless. What the hell is he waiting for? Why isn't he confronting Gabriel?

A stifled scream sounds behind me and I flinch. Half turning, my eyes flick to Ishtar and then back to Luna. I hear flesh strike flesh in the background, along with grunts of pain and cursing, but Alexander hasn't moved. Goldilocks still screams. I face fully away from my grandfather, my jaw dropping for the second time. Blood drips down Ishtar's face from a gash above her left eye, which is swollen shut. She's slow as she tries to evade Gabriel's assault, one hand clutching her injured side. Ishtar is a fierce warrior and has always seemed invincible to me. Now, she resembles a broken doll, and Gabriel—having the advantage of being an angel—doesn't have a scratch on her. *Bitch.*

It's all happening too fast, and everything feels like it's spinning out of my control. Ishtar is my teacher and mentor, and I realize as I watch Gabriel close in on her that I love her like she's my family, my blood. Ishtar is that badass aunt you always look up to, and who you know will get you out of jail if you call her. And Gabriel is going to kill her.

Glancing back at Alexander again, I hope he'll intervene. He's a damn angel, with all the power to take on Gabriel. I'm sure he's stored up millennia of rage and wants to get his violence on. But when he still does nothing but watch, rage boils through me. He and Ishtar are supposed to be friends, comrades. She's always been loyal to him, and he's just going to let her die. And then I remember. I came to this party prepared for anything, even though I hoped it wouldn't come to this. In a sheath resting against my lower back is the special dagger Hammurabi gave to me when I left Babel. The angel-killing dagger.

When I free the blade, it hums again, just like the first time I held it. I stare at it, swallowing. I've been in plenty of fights, but I've never killed anyone—especially not an immortal being. I feel shame when my hands tremble. Some badass I am. I need to find my balls and get this done. At Ishtar's cry, I look up. Gabriel has her pinned against the wall, nails digging into her throat. My teacher is gasping and bloody. So bloody. The Messenger's head swivels, and she meets Alexander's hard eyes.

"Just as it was before, Conqueror," she says, teeth bared. "I'll hunt your allies down and kill them one by one until you're imprisoned once more."

Gabriel is so focused on Alexander, she doesn't see me move. Leaping, I clear the safety of the Dark ward between us. She startles but regards me as if I'm a bug that's next on her list to swat. Until she sees the gleaming blade. Mouth dropping, surprise fills the Archangel's beautiful, terrible face. With all my strength, I ram the dagger in her side and pull it free. Her mouth pops open, and she releases Ishtar, sinking to the floor, her shaking hands covering her gushing wound. I hesitate as Gabriel's fearful gaze meets mine. I could do more damage. I could plunge my blade over and over again in revenge. But I can't. I slip the dagger back in place and rush to Ishtar, throwing one of her arms over my shoulder and propping up her weight.

I have to get her out of here. I have to get Luna out of here. My eyes return to my grandfather to find him rushing toward me, wings extended. Now, he decides to help. Asshole. But he's alone. Goldilocks is still on the floor, locked in her own private nightmare.

Alexander stops in front of me, gripping my shoulder with one hand and Ishtar with another. Shit, I know what he's going to do, and I can't let him. I can't leave Luna here. I promised her.

She's mine, and I have to keep her safe.

"You have to go back for Luna!" I shout at my grandfather, desperation clawing at my throat. "We can't leave her behind. We have to take her with us."

Alexander's face is cold as he regards me, his voice a deep baritone. "All in good time."

"*No!*" I scream as the Shadow Road envelops me.

I keep screaming long after our escape, my throat raw with grief, my heart in shreds. Luna is at the mercy of Gabriel and the other traitors. I have failed my Goldilocks.

TWENTY-NINE

LUNA

PAIN. THAT'S ALL THERE is. An inescapable, nauseating agony spreading over my back like red-hot irons branding into my flesh. My fingers claw at my shoulder blades, as if by doing so, I'll be able to find the cause of this torment and make it stop, but there's nothing there to grab hold of and pull free of my screaming skin. There's only the endless pain cutting through me.

Swallowing a sob, I peer through the haze of my tear-soaked vision at the spot where, only moments ago, Caleb stood at the end of the passage on the other side of the wards. Reality crushes my heart as it fully sinks in that he left without me, even though he promised he wouldn't. His protests had reached my ears past my own cries of pain, but he still left with his grandfather and Ishtar, their bodies engulfed by a bubble of shadow. The weight of that realization pierces my chest and squeezes my lungs, making it impossible to breathe.

Caleb is gone and I'm all alone. Again.

Just like I've always been.

The metallic taste of blood floods my mouth as I bite down hard on my tongue, choking back a shriek when another rush of pain radiates over my back. The sound of tearing fabric sinks into my eardrums, and my shirt goes slack around my torso, exposing my skin to the cool air of the corridor. It feels like all the bones in my back are breaking and like knives are etching lines in my flesh, starting at the top of my spine and carving downward, over and over again. When I reach around to touch my shoulder blades again, the inexplicable presence of feathers grazes my fingertips, poking out of my skin.

What's happening to me? That thought is cut short when another strangled cry rips up from my throat, my windpipes burning and sore from screaming. A deluge of tears streams down my cheeks.

Desperate to escape the pain, I curl into a ball on my side and let my mind drift back over the events that led up to this moment and this inexplicable, unending torture. After I cut my hand on the spindle, the passage had erupted into a flood of white light, and the wall had slid open to reveal the towering figure of Caleb's grandfather.

Alexander the Great.

The fear that overtook me when he stepped out of the thick pocket of shadow and into the light of the corridor nearly brought me to my knees. I barely had the time or sense to understand what I was seeing before he leaned over me—his aura like gleaming shards of razor-sharp glass, every piece reflecting back my terror—and breathed in my ear, his voice deep and hauntingly familiar after hearing it for so long in my head.

"You have my gratitude, little dove," he said, placing an ice-cold hand on my shoulder. *"And in exchange for my freedom, I shall now give you yours."* A string of beautiful, nonsensical words followed this sentiment.

Then there was only pain, all consuming and ceaseless in its brutal assault.

Is this what he meant? The feathers emerging from under my skin, shrouding my body in the worst sort of agony...

Is this what he meant when he said he'd give me the liberation I desire?

If so, I've been duped. Alexander promised he would teach me control if I helped him, and yet, as soon as I opened his cell, he abandoned me with the same ease and speed as everyone else in my life before him. This pain isn't the freedom I bargained for.

Fresh tears prick at my eyes and course down my cheeks as a sob parts my trembling lips. I was foolish. Foolish to think it was wise to help Alexander.

Foolish to ever allow myself to believe Caleb actually cared about me.

"Luna..."

I tilt my head and glance toward the far end of the corridor, past the wards where a figure is curled on the floor near the beginning of the passage. When I squint, Gabriel's face slides into sharp focus, her ivory skin pallid and mouth hanging open as she stares at me with bulging eyes, her chest heaving with strained, uneven breaths. How long has she been here? The seconds that have passed since opening Alexander's tomb are a blur. I vaguely remember Ishtar shouting her name, but I wasn't able to see what was happening through the disorienting fog of pain obscuring my vision.

"You—" Gabriel pulls herself up enough to inch toward me, wincing at the effort. Her eyes never break their unblinking hold on me, not even when the Dark ward stops her advance. She lets out a frustrated scream, collapsing back to the dust-coated stone.

My eyes drift down to the source of her pain, and regret burns deep in my chest when I glimpse the crimson stain darkening the side of her shirt, spreading onto her hands and coating her long fingers in blood. At the sight of it, my mind recalls the memory Alexander showed me of Michael's murder. Alaric had said it's possible to kill angels, but it's still disconcerting to see someone so powerful and capable of imparting fear now injured and weak.

Vulnerable.

As that thought passes through my head, it dawns on me that this is all my fault. I did this. Me. I chose to free Alexander instead of trusting the Archangel, and now look at us—both likely inches from death. At least, in my case, that's what this pain feels like.

Gabriel rolls over onto her back and shoves up her shirt sleeve to her elbow, pressing a bloodied finger to a just visible white tattoo on her forearm in the shape of a thin crescent moon. Her lips move in a blur, muttering something I can't quite make out from where I lie at the opposite end of the hallway.

As she drops her hand, her face scrunching into a grimace of pain, a pool of darkness spreads over the wall beside her and expands over the floor, forming a doorway identical to the one Caleb, Alexander, and Ishtar escaped through only moments ago. I narrow my eyes, staring hard at the dense patch of gloom as a tall figure steps out of the shadows.

Hair the color of antique gold, blinding in its beauty, encases the newcomer's head in a crown of loose curls, the locks cropped short but still long enough to brush the rims of his ears. His eyes, the same blue as the ocean on a clear day and ringed with a circle of citrine, fall to the injured Archangel with worry.

"Gabriel." Her name is a hurried breath parting his lips as he kneels beside her, drawing her head into his lap. Her hand reaches up to touch his face, leaving a smear of blood on the flawless fair skin of his cheek.

"He…" She flinches, dropping her hand back to her wounded side. "He's gone."

"What happened?" the man asks, his concern clear in the way he cups Gabriel's chin in one hand and brushes her raven hair back with the other. Anger darkens his gaze. "Who did this to you—"

"That's not what's important!" Her words are high-pitched and manic, and when she turns her head, the stranger follows her unnerving line of sight to where I lie, shaking beneath the joint weight of their stares.

A humming sensation comes alive in my chest when my startled gaze locks with the man's, my heart filled to the brim with a strange, wordless song, the crescendo building until it reaches a deafening pitch. His eyes are wild and alert as he gapes at me, and in the space of only a few seconds, I watch as every conceivable emotion flashes across his face, starting at shock then moving on to betrayal and ending with the unmistakable facade of grief.

I only look away when the feathers pushing their way out of my skin coax another shrill scream from my lungs. Gabriel blanches at the sound.

"She can't stay here. You have to help Luna," she pleads, grabbing at the man's black collared shirt and yanking him down until her lips graze his ear.

He stills at the words Gabriel whispers to him then climbs to his feet, first taking care to place her in a more comfortable position, upright against the wall. As he straightens, it occurs to me I've seen him before. My mind races back and forth, combing through memories and trying to pinpoint where from, but to my frustration, I come up blank. He steps through the barrier of the Dark ward, shifting closer to where I'm sprawled, unable to move. Panic swallows my thoughts when he crouches on the other side of the Light boundary.

An understanding smile hooks up one side of his mouth. "I know you're tired," he says, his voice soft and consoling. "I know you're in pain. But I'm here to help, and I can't do that unless you make your way over to me. Can you do that, Luna?"

My stomach clenches at the sound of my name on his lips, and before I can even think it through, I find myself dragging my aching body forward, toward the only thing separating me from this stranger and his unknown intentions. All I'm aware of is the peculiar feeling in my chest and the way his aura seems to reach for me as I crawl inch by agonizing inch, grinding my teeth in an effort to redirect my focus from the pain in my back. The black shadows surrounding him are laced with purple and blue and are entrancing to watch as their wisping movements encourage my advance.

It takes all the remaining strength I possess to push my shaking body through the ward. The man immediately draws me up into his arms, his hands skimming my bare back, making me shudder.

"Gabriel..." I lick my lips. "Is she—"

"She'll be fine," he cuts in, his tone curt but not unkind. "For now, let's just worry about you, all right?"

When he offers me a gentle smile, it suddenly hits me where I've seen him before.

My mouth goes dry as the memory of my first day at the Serapeum rushes to the forefront of my mind. When I first approached the entrance to this school, I was captivated by the depiction of the Fall carved into the golden surface of the towering doors, but one face in particular among the heavenly creatures caught my attention far more than the others. The recollection of his beauty is burned into my head.

"You… You're—"

The Morningstar.

He silences me with a firm shake of his head. "Preserve your strength. There will be time for introductions later, once you're safe."

That word sends a snap of electricity racing over my aching skin. *Safe from what?* But I can't find the will to ask as the Archdemon carries me back through the Dark ward.

The moment we cross the boundary, a burst of light blinds me from my left side as a pool of shadow forms on my right. Six figures emerge from each, twelve in total, and my Nephilim instincts tell me the men and women before us are the Archangels and Archdemons responsible for overseeing the Light and Dark academies. Their auras twist and thrash with menace, and I realize—remembering my first lesson with Gilgamesh—this is the Council Alaric spoke of with such fear and disdain in Gabriel's office.

A man with deep brown skin steps out of the light, which fades behind him as if the magic permeating the corridor has extinguished it. "Lucifer Morningstar. How noble of you to show your face. Your absence is always noted whenever we are all called together, so for you to appear says much about the circumstances."

Lucifer dips his head in greeting. "Uriel. It's been a while."

"So, it's true." A fair woman with cardinal-colored hair hanging down her back in a silky curtain moves out of the shadows. As she talks, she tugs her shirt off her left shoulder to reveal a glowing Enochian symbol on the top of her arm in the shape of a backwards, upside down L. "When the brand activated, I didn't want to believe it. But this proves our worst fears have been realized. Alexander's tomb has been opened."

Her green eyes—reflective in the shadows—flick toward the end of the passage at the black hole where Alexander emerged from, then to Lucifer, and finally to me, a perfectly sculpted brow lifting in question. Sweat beads along my hairline as I fight to cling to my weakening control, which slips a bit more out of my grasp under the Archdemon's probing gaze.

The last thing I need right now is to accidentally set fourteen celestial beings on fire. *Keep calm,* I tell myself. *Keep it all in.*

A slender Light with black hair and dark golden skin, androgynous in looks and clothing, steps forward and thrusts an accusatory finger at Gabriel. "Have you betrayed us, Messenger?"

"Hold your tongue, Serathiel," Lucifer snarls, stepping in front of Gabriel where she remains on the floor, bleeding from her injury. His voice reverberates from deep in his chest and vibrates against my side, making me shake in his arms. "Can't you see that she's hurt?"

I might not be Gabriel's biggest fan, but it shocks me that no one other than Lucifer, not even the Archangels, seem concerned about her wound or the worrying pallor of her complexion. Are these angels and Fallen so detached from mortality that they don't even care if one of their own dies? Is bickering more important than life?

"A Dark defending a Light?" Serathiel cocks a dubious brow. "How unheard of."

"Silence, all of you." A glowering Archdemon narrows his eyes at me, drawing the collective gazes of the other angels and Fallen. I shrink against Lucifer, wishing more than anything that I could just disappear. "Are you blind? Can't you see the girl in the Morningstar's arms is the culprit? Her palm bears the mark of the seal, not the Messenger's."

I blink in confusion and glance down at my hand, uncurling my fingers to get a better look at the gash from when I sliced my palm to unlock Alexander's tomb with my blood. The wound glows gold at the edges, exposing my part in this chaos. As much as I want to run away or deny it, there's no hiding what I've done. Like the Archdemon said, my decision has left its mark.

"Impossible!" shrieks an Archdemon so tiny in posture he almost resembles a child. The man's features remind me of the cherubs in old Renaissance paintings with his fair mop of hair and bright sapphire eyes. "That lock was designed to kill any who try to open the door, except those who bear the blood of the one who sealed it." Gaze cutting to Gabriel, he grinds out, "*Your* blood sealed this tomb, Messenger. Explain yourself!"

"It's not often I would agree with a Dark, Beelzebub, but Mammon is right about this," Serathiel chirps to the petite Archdemon before Gabriel can utter a word. "The child's palm does indeed bear the mark, which poses a very curious question. And are those wings I glimpse sprouting from her back?"

A collective gasp breaks the ensuing silence.

"How is that possible?" An Archangel with features so light in color he could be albino raises a hand to his lips in stunned shock. "Surely, she isn't Ascending? The Creator would never reward such treachery. It's unheard of. Unless—" His ice-blue eyes widen as a realization stretches across his pale face.

"Unless, she is the product of two of our own," Beelzebub finishes, the hysteria in his youthful tone giving way to somber understanding. "How else could the child have opened the door unless she shares the Messenger's blood? Not to mention the Enochian barring the passage. Only an angel's eyes could have seen it."

Shocked glances from both sides narrow on Gabriel at the same moment disbelief and confusion rip through me. I share Gabriel's blood? And the script on the wall… They're saying only an angel could have seen it, but *I* saw it and I'm a Nephilim. Nausea turns my stomach as the thoughts whirring around in my brain spin like the rotating cogs in a clock. I assumed my powers manifest the way they do because I'm a Gray and not a Light, like everyone believed. But what if I'm something else, too? Could Alaric have been wrong about me being a Nephilim?

On top of being a Gray, could I also possibly be…an angel?

If so, then Gabriel…does this mean she's my *mother*?

My head goes fuzzy at these notions, and for a second, I think I'm going to pass out from the rush of information assaulting me from all sides. The only thread keeping me conscious is the question now gripping my brain, screaming at me for an answer.

If Gabriel is my mother, who is my father?

"Is she the Gray you spoke of, Gabriel? The one you claimed you had well in hand?" Uriel seethes, a pointed frown sharpening his already harsh face. "How dishonest you've been with us. What danger have you placed us all in with your lies?"

A tall female Archangel with short, strawberry-blonde hair places a hand on Uriel's arm. "If this girl is indeed the one who freed Alexander, then we have no choice but to imprison her and find out what she knows."

"I agree with Raphael," Mammon says with a glance at the angel, his expression pinched, as if ashamed of this admission. "We cannot risk a repeat of last time."

"You can't—" Gabriel pushes herself up in a panic, then cries out, and falls back down to the floor.

At the same moment, Lucifer bites out, "That won't be necessary."

Raphael glances between him and Gabriel, trailing a slim finger along the sharp line of her jaw. "Your protests are bewildering, Morningstar. Why do you extend such support for our Gabriel?"

The same question spirals through my head on a loop. The possibility of her being my mother aside, why is Gabriel so determined to defend me after I betrayed her by setting Alexander free? I suppose it's possible she wasn't aware of our connection until now, that she didn't recognize who I am to her. Even so, surely, she doesn't feel any loyalty to me, otherwise she wouldn't have given me up when I was born, regardless of me being a Gray. Then again, Gabriel hates the Darks. Of course, she would despise her half-Dark daughter.

But, if that's true, then why is Lucifer—an Archdemon—helping her? Why is he helping me? Unless—

"This girl isn't a threat any longer," Lucifer thunders, an unspoken threat booming behind every word. "I will deal with her. The rest of you may go."

Uriel's hands squeeze into fists as he snarls, "Who gave you such authority, Morningstar? You forget, not all of us followed you during the Fall."

Lucifer takes a careful step toward the Archangel, tightening his hold on me. "Get out of my way, Brother. Or I will be forced to move you."

A smirk peels back Uriel's lips, revealing perfect white teeth. "I will not be intimidated, and you will not leave here with that girl in one piece. Surrender her to us or suffer us all."

"Be smart, Lucifer," Raphael adds. "Hand her over. You might have once been the Creator's favorite, but you are Fallen now and you are outnumbered."

"Or perhaps we should punish the Messenger instead for your insubordination? She's certainly earned a thrash or two for her part in all this." Mammon reaches down and plucks Gabriel up off the floor as if the Archangel weighs nothing.

Rage burns behind Lucifer's eyes as he scoffs. "I don't know what you're insinuating—"

"Don't you?" Raphael counters, cutting him off. "Not all of us are so easily fooled."

Uriel extends his arms and nods for Lucifer to hand me over to him. When he doesn't, Mammon places a hand around Gabriel's throat.

A rush of wind dampens the air with a chill, and I stare up in wonder as two giant black wings fill the width of the passage, extending outward from Lucifer's back.

Fury creases his face. "If you hurt her—"

"Careful now, Lucifer," Uriel warns. "The last Archdemon who dared to make threats was stripped of her position. And her wings. We wouldn't want to have to make an example of you."

The Archdemon with hair the color of garnets places a hand on Lucifer's shoulder, and they exchange a swift, silent glance. An entire conversation seems to happen in that single, grave look shared between them. As she retreats backward into the shadows, the Morningstar's gaze drops to mine, his pupils blown wide, revealing his remorse and anger.

I know without having to ask what he's thinking—I see it in the regret creasing his otherwise faultless face. *Just like everyone else in my life...* I choke on the thought as Caleb's face forms in my head. Just like everyone before him, Lucifer is giving me up.

Please, don't, I try to say, but the words catch in my throat.

Uriel steps forward to take me from Lucifer, and as his arms brush the sore spots on my back where feathers continue to carve holes in my skin, the Morningstar brings his mouth to my ear. The low timbre of his voice is the last thing I hear before Uriel presses a cold hand to my face, and the darkness of sleep rises to swallow me whole.

"I will find you again, Daughter. I promise."

EPILOGUE

S OFT SPOTLIGHTS ILLUMINATE THE tomb of Alexander's human father, King Phillip II. After thousands of years, it remains well intact. He supposes it is a small mercy it wasn't robbed by the tomb raiders like so many of the royal necropolis, despite all of them being hidden under giant mounds of dirt resembling hills. The scene painted along the top of the tomb is faded but still beautiful, celebrating the thrill of the hunt. Bright blue stripes the white marble under the mural. The tomb is a marvel, a work of beauty only fit to house a king on his final journey. Alexander made sure of that.

Only now, of course, his father's resting place was disturbed. His gold and silver put on display. His crown behind glass for humans to gawk at in awe. Not that he resents the humans for that—Macedonia was a place of wonder and power. The crown jewel of the ancient world, a sparkling diamond amidst the chaos. Alexander ruled that diamond. He built upon the foundation his adopted father laid down and conquered.

Until *he* was conquered.

Bitterness swells within him at that betrayal. As Alexander looks around the chilly museum his father's resting place has become in the north of Greece, he wonders about the identity of his real father, which remains unknown, as does the face of his angel mother. Their blood never sang to him, but the Creator might have a hand in that. Despite the mystery shrouding his celestial lineage, he loved his mortal parents, his loyal mother more than his philandering father, but love them both he had. He sorely misses them. They knew he was special, kissed by the gods, they said.

Alexander shoves aside the curtain of his hair—another reminder of his imprisonment—to regard Ishtar, his loyal companion. Such a fierce warrior of the ancient world, earning the title of goddess. He admires her beauty as she is stretched out on the wooden landing, sleeping. Her injuries were grave but he healed her. When that shiny, golden girl, Luna, freed him from his tomb, he wasn't at full strength. Weak from the angelic power sealing him in, he hadn't been able to heal Ishtar immediately or intervene with the Messenger on her behalf. Now, power surges through him, like being drawn up from a never-ending well, and her injuries fade before his eyes. She will be well, and they will conquer again.

Icy rage frosts his veins as he remembers her awe at his wings, how she reached out to touch them as they traveled along the Shadow Road as if she never beheld them before. Ishtar didn't recall his true nature, which means that treacherous, traitorous Council must have altered her memories. How much other history did they alter? Do any of his old allies remember him? Are they still alive like Ishtar or were some disposed of?

Pain spears his heart. And what of Alaric? His closest friend and his… Such sadness in Alaric's voice when he spoke of the past to golden Luna. He ponders if Alaric remembers the aid he gave Alexander in his rise to power. How the Nephilim showed him the path to unlocking his Light side, much in the way he unlocked the girl's Dark side. The girl was splintering, her true nature breaking through, forming cracks in the bind over her power. He just tugged hard, and the bind shattered completely.

Alexander folds his gray wings around him like a cloak, his eyes on the silver feathers. The color is a beacon of fear for the Archdemons and Archangels. Something they thirst to eradicate—an imperfection in their perfect, crumbling system of segregation. He didn't understand before—not fully—but now he knows. And he won't be trapped so easily again. He won't be trapped at all. He'll burn the world before that happens.

And from those ashes, humans, Nephilim, and angels alike will experience true freedom. He will lead them into the next era.

His eyes flick to his blood…his grandson. Alexander was young when he was entombed. The idea he has a grandson is bizarre. He knows he has a son—if the boy still lives—but the child was barely walking when he was imprisoned. This boy, Caleb, does not resemble him, except for the nose, perhaps. And the strength. As a Nephilim, Caleb's blood is diluted, but it still boasts the power of his lineage. His grandson sits on the wooden steps leading to the viewing platform, his hands in his hair. He appears utterly mad and grief-stricken.

Frowning, Alexander's eyes rove over his grandson's appearance. People dress so differently in this time period. Slashes in his faded pants reveal the skin of Caleb's knees, as if he's a pauper and not the descendant of royalty. Is this normal for the time period? And ancient Greek is no longer the common tongue. This English is prevalent, which he had to adapt to during his time spent in Luna's head. Alexander feels foggy and out of touch, but that will soon be rectified.

Caleb looks up, their gazes clashing, and Alexander feels the boy's rage from where he stands, a living, fiery snake coiling between them.

"Why did you leave her there?" Caleb demands again, as if they are on an endless time loop, and this is all he can think to say.

Alexander owes him no explanations. He is a king, but if he wants loyalty, he has to give something in return. Debts must be paid. His grandson brought Luna into his service to free him. That took skill and cunning and perseverance, as they did all this under the Messenger's nose. He swallows a malicious grin at that.

Flaring out his wings, Alexander flaps them once, the muscles of his shoulders protesting at the motion, and lands on the step next to his grandson. Caleb rears back, wariness painting his face. One of his fists closes over the dagger resting by his side—the dagger he stabbed Gabriel with, the dagger Alexander killed the Archangel Michael with—and Alexander admires his bravery and his instincts. He raises a brow and gives his grandson a pointed look, eyes darting from the dagger to Caleb's eyes. The boy just gives him a hard stare, not moving an inch, and Alexander laughs, startling his grandson a second time.

"You truly are my blood," he says. "How did you come by such a lethal weapon?"

Caleb presses his lips into a thin line. A few moments pass by before he answers. "Hammurabi."

Now, it is Alexander's turn to be surprised. He wonders how the fierce Babylonian king and warrior came into possession of his weapon. Although he and Hammurabi were friendly, they were never friends, but they had great respect for one another. If Ishtar ended up with Alexander's dagger, that is a puzzle piece that would fit, but she hadn't. Perhaps it has something to do with the erasure of her memories. He'll turn that over in his mind later.

"It's fitting that you should have it," Alexander murmurs. "It belonged to me."

Caleb's jaw slackens as he glances down at the dagger, but he doesn't offer the weapon back to Alexander. He feels pride in his grandson. Blood bred true, and he has a budding warrior he can mold.

"She couldn't come with us, your golden flower," he says to Caleb. When the boy begins to shout in protest again, Alexander holds an imperious hand up, treating his grandson to the same fearsome look that kept hordes of unruly, bloodthirsty soldiers in line. The boy quells under his glare. "We traveled the Shadow Road, and her transformation was not yet complete."

"H-Her transformation?" Caleb stutters, his eyes focusing on Alexander's wings. "She's an… I mean, I know she had some Dark abilities, but are you saying…" His voice gutters out, and he shakes his head, disbelief sewn across his features.

Alexander smiles. "Her Dark side has been repressed, yes, but that's not all. Her entire life has been a lie, Caleb. I set her free, just as she set me free. Soon, she'll have wings to fly away."

Caleb opens and closes his mouth like a fish gasping for air on shore. He shakes his head. "But that's—that means… Shit, do you mean she's an *angel*, too?"

He nods. "Yes. Once her transformation is complete, I will return for her." He places a hand on the boy's shoulder. "I owe her a debt that I will repay. So calm yourself, she will be with us again and soon."

As a Gray like him, Luna poses a threat to Alexander. One he can't let lay idle, waiting to be used against him. He owes the girl, yes, but he must keep her close. He needs her as an ally. And as she's so young and confused, so mistreated by those who should care for her, it will be easier to convince Luna to join him. Easy to promise her that he values her blood and her talents, which isn't a lie.

"But she's all alone now. With *them*," Caleb whispers, his voice breaking. "They'll do the same thing to her that they did to you."

Alexander gives Caleb a calculating look. His grandson's feelings for the golden girl are obvious, the inky indigo strands of his aura twisting and bouncing in agitation. Alexander will use that connection to corral them both, bonding them tightly to him and his cause.

"Yes, they will try to entomb her," he says, "but they will not succeed for long. I will rescue her, Caleb. I vow it."

Caleb gazes up at him, eyes mournful. "But how can you go up against the Council alone?"

Alexander's smile is vicious. "It took all of them to entomb me before. Now, I know their tricks. And I won't be alone. I have you, my blood, and Ishtar, my general. I will raise my banner and call my allies to me. With our cunning, we will free Luna and crush our enemy." He points to Ishtar. "Get her and come."

Caleb scrambles to his feet, tucking the dagger into a sheath at his back. He goes down a few steps and scoops Ishtar off the floor. Alexander turns from him and enters the main floor of the museum, finding his father's crown with unerring accuracy among the artifacts of silver and gold. With a thought, the glass shatters. Shrieking pierces the air and his ears. Growling, he waves a hand and the noise stops.

The crown is made from delicate, hand-carved gold, the cluster of individual oak leaves each a work of art, shining like a yellow beacon in the darkness of the museum. Some of the leaves are melted, from where his father was burned in the funeral pyre. Alexander reaches for the crown, placing it on his head. Closing his eyes, he basks in the rightness of it, in the symbolic power encircling his brow.

A gasp sounds in the silence, and he turns to find Caleb and Ishtar—awake now— both watching him. Ishtar pushes against Caleb's chest, and he puts her down.

The goddess of love and war stares at him with shiny eyes. "My king," she says, sinking into a deep bow.

The boy looks uncertain but gives a shallow bow of his own.

When they both rise, Alexander says, "It is time to conquer once more."

END OF BOOK ONE

DARKRISE

BOOK TWO

"The mind is its own place, and in itself can make a Heaven of Hell, a Hell of Heaven."

JOHN MILTON, *PARADISE LOST*

PROLOGUE

Lucifer only felt rage like this once before. His eyes flash to his companion, her severe, stunning beauty still managing to undue him millennia later. The last time such all-consuming fury enveloped him was when Gabriel chose the Creator over him. When she chose servitude over love. When she rejected their relationship as if she had committed some crime, soiled herself by loving him, the Morningstar. While he burned the world to free himself of his golden shackles, she pledged herself to eternal bondage.

Although he hated her choice, it was hers to make. And if Lucifer valued anything, it was free will. The ability to choose his own fate. But this...

Anger spots his vision, and he blinks it away. By hiding Luna—his daughter, *their* daughter—from him, Gabriel stole his choice. She stole his free will. She stole the chance to know his only child.

Glaring, he watches her carefully walk around the stones of Adam's Calendar in South Africa. The site is more than seventy-five thousand years old, and power shivers around the old stones jutting from the ground, tingling his skin, but he doesn't feel what he's searching for. He can't hear his daughter's blood call to him. Such a sweet sound snatched away too soon. Pain pierces his heart.

Frustration pulling her lush mouth into a frown, Gabriel meets his eyes. "I can't feel anything. If they hid her, I don't think it's here."

Lucifer sneers. "You didn't know your own daughter was with you for months. I don't know if you could feel her, even if she were here," he scoffs, his voice a blade meant to cut.

The Archangel flinches, and he grins, happy his barb found its mark.

"I explained why I didn't feel her," she pushes out between clenched teeth.

Lucifer lifts a shoulder. "So you say, but as you've proven with your deception, I can't trust a word out of that beautiful lying mouth. And they call *me* the Father of Lies. I suppose that means you birthed them."

Gabriel snarls at him. "I told you I didn't know—you just refuse to listen."

His ire rises in his chest like a tidal wave, crashing into her. "Yes, just like you explained why you chose to hide my only child from me. Tell me, Messenger, did you think I'd let a prophecy touch one hair on her golden head? Did you believe I wouldn't protect her? You didn't even realize she'd been released from the prison you kept her in. Some mother you are. Did you plan to keep her in stasis for all eternity? Her potential guttering out like a flame in the wind?"

Her wings snap open, snowy white and large, and she resembles the bird of prey she is. "You could protect her?" Gabriel spits at him. "Like you protected her in Alexandria? You shine brightly, Morningstar, but you can't take on the Council. Even you're not that powerful."

His own wings release, a silky ebony lending menace to his tall form. "Perhaps if I'd known who she was earlier, I could've saved her. I had to come to grips with the fact that the bleeding creature in my arms was my daughter right before I was surrounded."

Derisive laughter fills the space between them. "You can protect her from the Creator? You think I hid her to be cruel…but she was all I had left of you and me. Something perfect and beautiful we created." Gabriel blinks, her orange-rimmed eyes shiny. Although he loathes to admit it, her tears still manage to hurt him. "And I couldn't take a chance with her. You might think me a selfish monster, but I loved her—*love* her—and I didn't know how to avoid the prophecy's fate for her. I didn't want her to become the Gray who tried to destroy the world…or the one fated to kill the Destroyer. Perhaps at the cost of her life. I just wanted her to live."

Confusion ripples through him. "What do you mean, the one fated to kill the Destroyer? I've never heard that part of the prophecy before." He eyes Gabriel, suspicion forming in his mind, which is only confirmed when she shifts her head, presenting her profile, a guilty flush spreading across her cheekbones. "They indeed named you wrongly, Messenger. What lies have you been spinning to us all these years?"

Her jaw clenches at his words, and when her gaze clashes with his, fury sparks there, matching his own. "We were divided when I discovered I was with child. I was alone, desperate, and after the prophecy was revealed to me, I knew I had to protect the child at all costs. She was not going to be the instrument of the prophecy. I wouldn't allow it."

Lucifer's heart clenches at her words, but a dark bitterness seeps into his soul. "You were never alone—you've never been alone. All you had to do was whisper my name, and I would have come to you."

One perfect dark brow arches. Doubt and disbelief spreads across Gabriel's face. "How can I believe that? You never forgave me for not choosing you—us. You avoid being in the same room with me unless you're forced, and yet, I'm supposed to believe that if I had called to you in my time of need, right after breaking your heart, you would have given up all your hurt and anger and answered me?" Her own laugh is bitter.

"If you would have changed your mind and returned to me, yes, I would have welcomed you with open arms. We would have plotted together to conceal our child...Luna."

"So, if I prostrated myself at your feet, begged for your forgiveness, and renounced the Creator and my beliefs, then you would've welcomed me back? That's what you really mean," Gabriel says, dark eyes hard like polished gemstones. "You need to be right. How noble of you, Morningstar."

"You're twisting my words," Lucifer growls. "Just like your precious Creator likes to twist the notions of love and duty."

Gabriel bares her teeth at him, wings flaring, and then she sags in on herself, drooping like a wilted flower. "This is pointless," she says, tears glistening once more. "Going over the past is pointless. We have to commit to the now. To saving our daughter. All our brethren will be hunting us once they realize the truth. I'm sure they're hunting us right now."

Lucifer's eyes dart away from her face, unable to watch her cry. Many of the angels and Fallen think of the Messenger as an ice queen, immovable and unemotional. But he knows better. The wall of ice she forms around herself is a facade she maintains in order to serve the Creator. In order to turn her back on Lucifer and hide their daughter. Rage glows inside him again, but he pushes it away. Gabriel is right, spitting past hurts at each other like hissing cats will not help Luna.

"They might not be hunting us now, but they will and soon. For all their faults, they're not stupid. They'll figure out our connection to Luna sooner or later, especially if they think hard enough about the past," he says, turning to face her once more.

A flush stains her face at his words, and she nods. He used to make her flush all over, her pale skin lighting up at his touch. Despite the fact that she's with him, she's so far away they might as well be on different continents. Their choices and actions created a gulf between them as wide as the Grand Canyon. But for Luna, they will have to find a way to bridge it.

A deep sigh escapes his chest. Lucifer feels weary down to his bones, the task ahead perhaps the most difficult he has ever faced. The most important. "You're right," he says. "We have to commit to the now and to rescuing our daughter. She's the most important thing on this Earth, and we can't allow her to be punished for being a product of love."

Gabriel's gaze snags his, and her eyes soften as they explore his face. "We'll get our daughter back, no matter the consequences or to what end."

Lucifer nods, determination lending him strength. Then he launches into the sky, and Gabriel follows.

ONE

CALEB

THE FORBIDDING CITADEL SITS on top of a large outcropping of rock at the base of steep mountains, appearing as ruins to the mortal eye. Alexander once conquered the adjacent city in what is now Afghanistan and has since overtaken the fortress, which was built by the last ruler of the Hotak dynasty—long after Alexander's time. Hundreds of years later, it still feels like a military fortress, lacking the modern amenities that I'm used to, like a toilet. Apparently, angels don't need to shit, but Nephilim still do. At least there's an underground spring we pump water from so bathing is doable. And Afghanistan isn't exactly a vacation spot. Neither was Iraq, but I felt more at ease at Babel than I do here. Not that humans pose much of a threat to me, but in this place, I'm not sure who is friend or foe.

I glare across the dais of the makeshift throne room where Alexander holds court. Four months, four goddamn months, and no sign of Luna. Sure, I'm allied with a powerful Gray angel, but I'm no closer to rescuing my Goldilocks. And Alexander keeps making excuses as to why we haven't come up with a solid plan to storm the proverbial castle and save her. I know we'll have to face both the Light and the Dark forces, but for Goldilocks, I'd take on the Creator.

My eyes narrow as I observe my grandfather's latest potential ally. She reminds me a bit of Ishtar in her regal bearing, but her skin is a dark umber, and her curly hair cascades down her back in black ringlets. Power radiates from her. More power than a Nephilim, even a first generation. I rack my brain, searching for her image in my mind, but I come up blank. I thought I knew all the angels and Fallen—the important ones anyway—but she is an enigma.

"Lilith," Alexander says, solving that mystery, and I gaze at the exiled Archdemon in shock.

The Council of Archangels and Archdemons in charge of the academies dismissed Lilith for reasons unknown—well, unknown by me. I'm sure all the Fallen know the story. They never speak of her—Adam's first wife. I mean, in the back of my mind, I realize she's been out in the world. But what the hell has she been doing? I'm kinda disturbed I never thought about it before. She's a Fallen with tons of power and probably pissed off at her former family. I guess Lucifer keeps tabs on her—or Gabriel—but the thought still makes a shiver of unease crawl up my spine.

Her full, scarlet lips twist into a coy smile. "Well, well, well, Alexander. Empires have risen and fallen since we last met. Freedom suits you."

Alexander leans forward, resting his chin on his fist, his mismatched eyes roving over Lilith's petite, curvy frame. He finally lands on her face, and they stare at each other as the seconds tick away. They seem to be in their own personal battle for domination or for ferreting out secrets. They break the moment at the exact same time, as if some understanding has passed between them or some truce.

"Exile suits you," my grandfather shoots back with a sly smile. "Freedom has made you positively bloom, my beauty."

"I'm too old for flattery, and you're too young to know how to wield words to pander to my ego," Lilith says with a diamond-bright smile sharp enough to cut glass.

I cough to cover a laugh, but of course, with her supernatural senses, she hears me as does my grandfather. He glares while she wears a look of genuine amusement. I throw up my hands in surrender and apology.

"Who is this handsome young man?" Lilith purrs and goddammit if I don't blush at her suggestive tone, like she wants to use me as her boy toy. She'd break me.

Alexander huffs a laugh. "My grandson and the orchestrator of my escape," he says. "Caleb, meet the infamous Lilith."

"Should I bow?" I ask, unable to control my mouth. Ishtar enters the room, and I see her grin out of the corner of my eye. I inwardly cringe as I look at Lilith, avoiding my grandfather altogether. To my relief, her amusement remains, thank the Morningstar.

"You should crawl," the ex-Archdemon says sweetly. "But I'd hate to see such a pretty little Nephilim brought so low. And you *did* help Alexander escape, so that's worth quite a lot."

This time I can't stop my resentful glare as I focus on my grandfather. "Me and Luna," I say, and he stiffens in anger.

"Luna?" Lilith questions, arching a delicate brow.

I see Ishtar shaking her head behind Lilith, but I'm through with being cautious. "The other Gray, the real person who freed Alexander. Ishtar and I just helped. And now, we need to help her."

"Another Gray?" Lilith says, but her surprise doesn't seem genuine, though she has a look of shock painted on her face with as much skill as her eyeliner. I've dated around enough to recognize when women know how to wield an eye pencil like a weapon.

Rage simmers in Alexander's eyes, but he banks it. "Yes, another Gray. She'll make a great ally to us, Lilith. Under my tutelage, she'll help me finish what I started."

"If we ever rescue her from whatever prison she's in," I say bitterly.

"Caleb," my grandfather says, his voice deceptively soft, and the hair rises on the back of my neck in warning.

Grandfather or not, blood or not, I have no business pissing off Alexander the Great, terrifying badass. And he has no problem with punishing me, I'm certain, although I've managed to avoid it so far. I cut my gaze to Ishtar, and I can see the same anger reflected in her dark eyes. I'm sure my teacher is itching to get a whip and beat me with it for not keeping my mouth shut. I can almost feel the sting of the lash on my back. Wouldn't be the first time she's punished me for impertinence. But I'm tired of the bullshit, and I have a powerful Dark in front of me. I want my grandfather to explain to a potential ally why he's left his savior hanging out to dry.

"He's lovesick, Alexander," Ishtar says smoothly, stepping up to stand beside Lilith and giving her a knowing smile. The word *love* strikes me like a slap to the face. I've never told a girl I loved her before. The word is both disconcerting and freeing at the same time. I've never felt the way I do about Luna. "He can't help but be impatient."

My grandfather snorts. "Yes, I suppose he is. As I've told you before, Caleb, all in good time. I can't rescue Luna with so few allies. I'm outnumbered, but with the great Lilith on my side, we grow closer to freeing her." Alexander focuses on Lilith once more, eyebrow raised in question.

"You're too humble, Alexander. You don't need another Gray. You and the goddess of love and war are more than capable of inflicting damage. Look how well she used my information about your locale." Lilith inclines her head to Ishtar, who gives a shallow bow in response. Huh, well, that's how my teacher knew where Grandfather was hidden. "But that's not to say I don't want in on the fun. I have my own score to settle."

"While I do appreciate your attempt at flattery, the girl is vital to our mission, although gathering followers is more important than anything right now," Alexander says, waving a hand in dismissal of my Goldilocks's plight. I grit my teeth so hard my jaw aches. "The Council will have her locked somewhere hidden, much like they did me. When I rescue her, I want to kill as many of them as I can. I am through with games. This time I won't fail. The world will be mine."

"I admire your confidence, Alexander, but this Gray, this Luna, where does her lineage lie? Surely, you've questioned it. She's someone's dirty little secret," Lilith says and I frown. Luna isn't anyone's "dirty" anything, but the ex-Archdemon has a point. Who are Luna's parents?

When I thought Luna was just a Nephilim, it wasn't a total shock she didn't know who her parents were. Don't get me wrong, I thought it was shitty they abandoned her, but look at my pops. Nephilim being irresponsible dicks isn't exactly uncommon. But Goldilocks is an angel. And I know leaving her at an orphanage like she's the mistake of some shamed teenage heiress is no accident. This was very deliberate. What I can't figure out is why her parents were stupid enough to let her stay with the mortals. Her power was always bound to come out. Luna carries enormous guilt around, punishing herself for accidents she had zero control over, which her piece-of-shit parents are one hundred percent responsible for.

There are also Nephilim—and angels—who can scent out other bloodlines like hounds on the hunt. It's a rare gift but it exists. It's not a super popular gift, either, as my father hates it when people track his trail of sperm deposits across the world. Did I mention my dad is a bastard?

The Council will sniff out her bloodline soon enough. Then all hell really will break loose.

Alexander shrugs, indifferent. "Her family clearly abandoned her and deserve whatever punishment our brethren deem appropriate. I have little respect for parents who refuse to claim their get."

Lilith inclines her head and I mutter, "You must really love dear, old Dad."

Alexander turns to me, a vicious smile on his face. "Your father will be brought to heel soon enough, Caleb. His embarrassing womanizing and callous disregard for our blood will stop."

A genuine smile curves my lips despite my anger at the lack of action where Luna is concerned. "Couldn't happen to a nicer guy," I say and Ishtar chuckles.

"I'm sure you'll remind him it was his son who freed you, not your heir." Lilith's dark eyes shine with malice. She gifts me with another man-eating grin. "At least one of your line bred true."

I square my shoulders. "Yeah, I came through for the win. As did Luna," I say to my grandfather, and his face hardens until he resembles one of those marble statues the Greeks loved to carve of him.

"Don't test my gratitude, Grandson. I told you I would fetch Luna and I shall. To doubt my word is to call me a liar, an oath breaker. Is that what you accuse me of?" The quiet menace in his tone kicks my heart rate up until my pulse pounds in my ear.

"No, sir," I say, keeping my voice steady with effort and my head bent in submission to the warrior. This is a man who killed his way across a continent, and I know that, I do, but I'm so pissed about Luna that I keep forgetting when to keep my mouth shut. I'm no good to Luna maimed and out of commission.

A chilly silence blankets the room before Ishtar speaks again. "Alexander, Caleb is not only lovesick but loyal, as he was to finding and freeing you. His loyalty leads him astray in this moment, but it is still an admirable quality." My gaze flicks up to meet the Mesopotamian goddess's, and the warning blazing from her eyes is white hot.

I feel my grandfather's glare drill holes into my skin, and I resist my lizard brain telling me to run away screaming from the large predator waiting to rip me to shreds.

"Loyalty is important to me, Grandson, and I suppose I cannot fault you for your loyalty to your beautiful lover. I, too, had a lover once who was very dear to me, but I do not want you to push me again on this matter. Luna will join us when the time is right, you have my word," Alexander says, and I raise my head, meeting his eyes, which have thawed slightly.

"Yes, Grandfather," I murmur, and I wonder who this lover was, although I'm sure Gramps banged his way through the ancient world. "I apologize for my insolence."

Lilith clears her throat, drawing our attention. "While I mine allies in the Dark ranks, I'll see if there is any news of your Luna. I doubt the secret of another Gray can be kept for long."

Hope slowly fills me when Alexander stomps on it. "That is much appreciated, Lilith, but gathering allies is our first priority."

The cast-out Archdemon offers a noncommittal smile, and bitter anger grips me once more.

One thing is for certain: I can't wait around any longer for Alexander to get off his lofty ass and save Goldilocks. Wherever she is, it's not a five-star resort, and I'm sure the Archangels and Archdemons are torturing her. Bile rises up in my throat, and I feel sick as I imagine all the ways those ancient assholes could hurt my Luna. And while I don't have Alexander's or Ishtar's connections, there is one person who might help. I mean, I fully expect him to beat the shit out of me for helping Alexander, but he's a straight up badass.

It's time to go see Hammurabi.

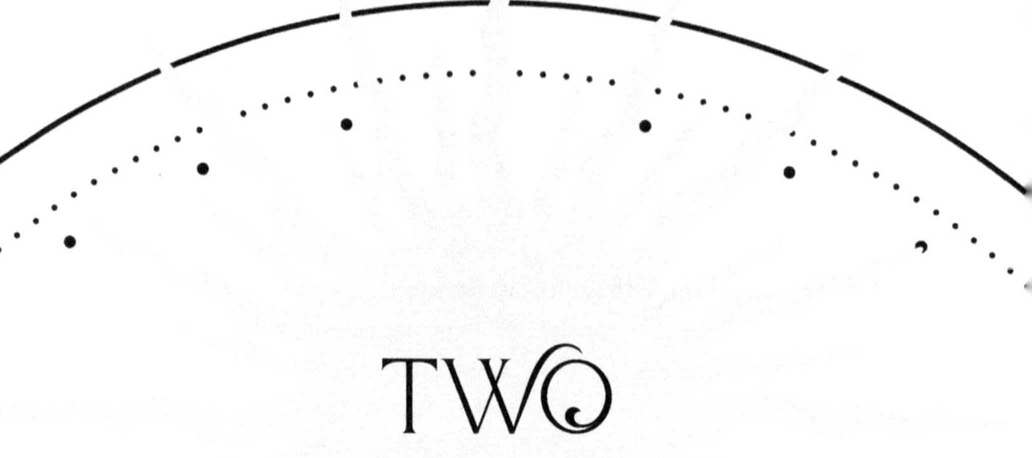

TWO

LUNA

THE TRANSPARENT BARRIER BENEATH my fingertips is somehow both warm and cold, the glasslike substance a perfect representation of this bizarre in-between I find myself in. On the other side of the curved wall—my cage taking the form of a large egg, in which I begrudgingly play the part of the yoke—a white sea of nothingness stretches outward, the cloud-like blanket of air and mist as infinite and unending as my imprisonment.

No matter how many days pass—assuming they pass at all—this strange world never changes. Day is night, and night is day, and time has lost all meaning to me. How long has it been since I set Alexander free from his tomb? Since I learned the truth, not only about my parents, but about who I am?

About *what* I am.

My fingernails drum out a staccato rhythm on the barrier, keeping in perfect tempo with the slow metronome of my heart as I unfurl my wings out behind me. *Tap, tap, tap.* Fully extended, my wingtips touch the opposite wall, the silver feathers brushing against the glass in a way that makes me hyperaware of how claustrophobic this cell is. With less than ten square feet of space to exist and stretch my wings, I'm like a caged bird, and the urge to fly burns under my skin—a desperate itch to move and flap these new extensions of my body. Until I can, I'm not sure I'll be able to accept my true nature…regardless of the tangible proof of it attached to my back.

A shudder sweeps up my spine as I press my hand flat to the glass and then push away with a withering sigh. As I lower my arm, my gaze catches on the scar on my palm—the evidence of my role in Alexander's release a permanent mark on my skin, tainting me. Although the flesh has long since stitched back together, a gold line remains, as if the curse of the blood sacrifice mixed with my angel blood has resulted in some sort of magical Kintsugi. But there is nothing beautiful about this scar. Only the devastating and inescapable reminder of my foolish decisions.

Closing my eyes, I breathe in through my nose, drawing my wings back into my flesh just as I have hundreds of times before to pass the time in this place. I'm sure for an angel who's had centuries or longer of practice, this process is painless and easy. As natural as breathing. But for me, it's slow and agonizing as the feathers curl inward—perhaps because they've been confined for so long—sliding into the new slits in my skin above my shoulder blades, which seal over once the feathers vanish, leaving the flesh there unblemished—at least, as far as I can tell by touch. I don't enjoy this pain, but it gives me a much-needed release, as if everything I feel is bottling up inside me to near breaking point, and the pain is the only way to ease that pressure. To bleed out some of the poison filling me to the brim. It's also all I have—my only companion in the endless monotony of what's bound to be eternal confinement. Pain and the memories, which I am defenseless against as they rise again to consume me.

Despite the fact that he abandoned me to this fate, I'm struck by an overwhelming pity for Alexander now that I'm on the other side of the captivity he endured. In the grand scheme of eternity, I've only been stuck in this prison for a short time while he watched centuries and then millennia roll by in the darkness, alone. What memories was he forced to confront in the shadows?

What memories have yet to surface to torment me?

Gabriel's face flashes across my closed lids, and I grimace, biting back an onslaught of tears. Mixed emotions flood my chest, and it's all I can do not to laugh, or cry, or scream, or berate myself for my idiocy. How much of what I felt in her presence was because she was an Archangel and how much because she is my mother? Did she know who I was when Alaric brought me to the Serapeum? Did she recognize me at all? Or was I nothing but a stranger to her, just as she was to me?

And then there's my father. Lucifer. I still have difficulty wrapping my head around that revelation, but his voice in my ear when we met outside Alexander's tomb was as clear as his words were when he called me his daughter. Even if he hadn't said it aloud, I think I would've known from the song that raged in my heart the moment his citrine-rimmed eyes locked on mine. The blood that binds us knew who he was, and it told me without a single word he was family.

Another thought drifts to the front of my mind, one I've been battling with for nearly as long as I've been confined here. I don't know much about our world or what it means to be an angel—or hell, even a Nephilim—but I could sense that connection with Lucifer in my heart as clearly as I feel the air in my lungs. But I never once felt that connection with Gabriel. Her blood didn't sing to mine the way Lucifer's did, and yet, I know she's my mother. The Archangels and Archdemons—*the Council,* I correct myself, remembering how Alaric referred to them—stated plainly that her blood was the key to unlocking Alexander's tomb, which means I couldn't have set him free unless we were genetically related. Unless we were of the same ancestral line.

How else could I have liberated him unless she's my mother? I suppose I could be her granddaughter, but as far as I'm aware, Gabriel doesn't have any known children, which makes the likelihood of that possibility slim.

No, she's my mother, I tell myself. *She has to be.*

Still, doubt prickles my senses as this line of thought joins the flurry of others spiraling through my head, the cacophony of *hows* and *whys* bombarding me, never giving me a moment's rest—much like how I felt when Alexander's voice haunted my mind for all those weeks at school. It feels as if my brain is being dragged over hot coals, and my skull aches with the burden of every unanswered question.

Since the truth of my lineage was forced out into the open, I find myself dancing closer to the brink of madness than ever before, lured to that edge by the agonizing need to understand what I witnessed that day under the Serapeum—the almost tender exchange between the Archangel and Archdemon I now recognize as my mother and father.

For all her warnings about me and Caleb, was Gabriel forsaking the very laws the Lights and Darks have lived by since the Fall to be with Lucifer? A forbidden affair, like my forbidden friendship with Caleb? I might not know the Archangel well, but our interactions always left me with the impression she's far too pious to even consider breaking laws viewed as sacred by our kind. And she is one of the Faithful, loyal—even more so than her Light brethren—to the Creator.

So, where does her...relationship, whatever it may be...with Lucifer fit into the timeline between the Great Battle and now? I struggle to imagine them being able to hide such an illicit affair from the Council, especially one that resulted in a child, but the only other conclusion I keep reaching can't be possible...can it?

That their affair isn't recent at all, but from a time long before the divide was erected.

I rub a hand over my eyes and blow out a faltering breath, my sanity buckling under the monumental weight of that thought. The divide has been around since the Fall, so if Gabriel and Lucifer were together before then—if my conception didn't occur nearly two decades ago, like I previously thought, but back before the angels were separated by war—then that would make me several hundred thousand years old. Older even than Alexander, Alaric, and all my teachers at the Serapeum.

I go still at that realization, then quickly push it away, unable to face that notion at the moment or the inevitable identity crisis that would surely follow if I dared to look at it too closely. I shake my head. No, that can't be the case. I'm freaking out over nothing, surely. Angels and demons might look young, but they still age normally from birth until they reach the appearance of someone in their late twenties or early thirties. Their adulthood is eternal, not their youth, so clearly, I'm not like Gabriel or the others who have walked this earth since before the dawn of man. I'm still physically aging, and I can trace every year of my life back to when I was just five years old. So, there's just no way I've been around since the Fall. Angel or not, I know for a fact I'm only seventeen and not a single year older.

A groan rips through me as I once again find myself back at the beginning of a long line of questions that have been gnawing at me since I first woke up in this place. I try to shove them back, but there's one thought that lingers—that never leaves me alone and only sinks its claws deeper with every moment I spend caged. Despite my unrelenting uncertainty, despite not really understanding the full scale of what led to my imprisonment or what my future holds, nothing about my situation torments me as much as the constant sting of Caleb's abandonment. That's an ache I can't seem to shake no matter how many seconds pass in this timeless realm, perhaps because it isn't just abandonment I feel, but a deep, festering sense of loss. Loss of the first and only real friend I ever had—not an adult who felt responsible for me but a friend, someone on my level, who understood me in a way no one else could.

Loss of what I had allowed myself to dare to hope was something more.

I choke back a sob, refusing to give in to the tears blurring the edges of my vision or the lump swelling in my throat, which threatens to suffocate me. I need a distraction. I *need* the pain.

I need to forget, even if only for a moment.

To distance myself from the memory of Caleb's face, his voice, his mouth on mine, I force my wings out again, giving every fiber of my being over to the bone-crunching pain. As my lips part on a sigh, feeling the weight on my chest lift a little, I pace the cramped space of my cell just as I have countless times throughout the last however many months I've spent in this hell.

A chuckle escapes me as I pivot and glance at my reflection in the translucent barrier, the eyes of my mirror image glinting. Despite the changes I've noticed to my body since Alexander freed my wings—like the unexpected appearance of my aura, the silver threads dancing across my skin finally revealed—one thing has remained the same, that's carried over from my mortal life into the immortal. I see it behind my gaze now more than ever.

The broken mind that no amount of angel blood can ever fix.

No, this isn't hell, I realize as I drag the pewter feathers back underneath my aching skin, the cuts in my back flaming and raw, before pushing them out once again. This is the landscape of my festering madness.

And here I thought I knew what it was like to feel crazy.

"Hello, Luna."

A startled breath presses against the sides of my throat, and my wings fold around me like a security blanket as I whip around and slam my back into the curved wall, wincing at the searing pain radiating across the sore spots just below my shoulders. On the other side of the glass, a man with deep brown skin steps out of the mist, appraising me with severe, hooded eyes. A golden aura quivers along his skin, almost blinding in its intensity.

"You…" The word is heavy on my tongue. How long has it been since I last spoke aloud? "I recognize you," I whisper.

My memory flashes back to that day in Alexandria when Lucifer held me in his arms and faced off against twelve angry Archangels and Archdemons who all wanted to see my head on a spike. This man…he was one of them.

He was there.

The Archangel dips into a bow, his smile mocking. "My name is Uriel, and I am the Archangel charged with overseeing the Light academy at Mount Zion."

My wings bristle, but I push them aside and behind me then force myself to take a step forward, presenting the illusion of courage, even though I feel anything but brave. "What do you want with me?"

A quiet laugh breaches the silence between us. "Come now, child. You are no fool. You know precisely why you're here."

"Because I opened Alexander's tomb?" I retort, hoping he won't hear the wobble in my voice. "Or because I'm a Gray?"

I remember something Caleb once said to me, about the Faithful and Fallen fearing those who straddle the line. Even if I hadn't set Alexander free, would they have imprisoned me anyway, just because I was born of both sides? Something in Uriel's stern expression says yes.

My hands curl into trembling fists. "You know what? Why don't you go ahead and do what you should've done to Alexander and just kill me already? If you're so afraid of what I am, then surely, you're better off with me gone."

Although I'm bluffing, there's a part of me—a large part, I'm terrified to realize—that means every word. I know what it's like to be confined against my will, and when Alaric took me away from the hospital, I vowed I would never allow myself to be locked up again. I'd rather be dead than spend the rest of my life in a cage, especially now that my life is endless and escape from this hell is only a dream.

"That…is not an option," Uriel says.

"Why?" Hysteria creeps into my tone as I spread my arms out, gesturing to the glass wall around me. "How is *this* any better?"

The Archangel makes a tsking sound with his tongue. "You are so new to the world, so young and naive. There is much you do not know, much you do not understand." His shadowed eyes sweep over the silver feathers adorning my wings, which vibrate at the feel of his piercing gaze and then draw close to my body again as if to shield me. Although I've gained some semblance of control over their movements, they mostly seem to have a mind of their own.

I open my mouth to challenge him further but silence devours my unspoken words. He's right. I am naive. And gullible. After all, I fell for the empty promises that resulted in my imprisonment. Alexander's promise to teach me control. Caleb's promise to take me to Babel. Faces I once trusted fill my thoughts when all I want is to wipe them away from my memory. To forget them all.

To abandon the pain.

My wings sag, the pinions brushing the cold floor of my cell. "What do you want with me?" I ask again, defeated.

Uriel clamps his hands behind his waist—the snowy white wings marking him as a Light Archangel tucked out of sight—and fixes me with the full force of his gaze. His brown eyes flash with intimidation.

"To talk," he answers simply.

"About?"

Despite the menacing way his aura ripples against his skin, I don't think he intends to hurt me. What else can he do to me that this long stretch of isolation hasn't already done?

"Let's start with the headmistress of the Serapeum," he suggests. "How did the Messenger hide you from us? Was she involved with your plan to free the Conqueror?"

Conqueror? I suddenly remember Gabriel saying that same word through the haze of pain that seized me that day under the Serapeum. *He must be referring to Alexander.*

I narrow my eyes on Uriel's face, his expression stony. The lack of emotion in his gaze unnerves me almost as much as the mention of Gabriel, the mere passing thought of her like lead in my stomach. Her face forms in my head again, but I shove it away. I don't want to talk about her. I don't even want to think about her right now. I haven't fully processed how I feel about what's happened to me—about the likelihood of her being my mother—and the last thing I want is for the Council to somehow weaponize those feelings against me.

My lips pinch at the corners. "I have nothing to say to you about *her*."

"Interesting." Uriel raises a hand and traces a circle around his mouth with his thumb and forefinger before pressing his fingertips together at the point of his chin. "She said the very same thing about you…right before she disappeared."

His lips peel back into a predatory grin when my eyes spring wide in surprise.

Disappeared? The way he said that word twists my gut, making me fear he means something else altogether.

The last time I saw Gabriel, in the underground corridor leading to Alexander's tomb, she was bleeding out on the stone floor from a wound that would've killed any human. Hell, it probably would've killed a Nephilim. But Gabriel is neither. She's an angel, and the Morningstar assured me she would be fine. She survived. I know she did.

She had to.

My mind races, wandering down an even darker path. What if, after the Archangels and Archdemons imprisoned me, they went back for Gabriel and punished her for her part in creating another Gray? What if all this anger I've been holding onto and building during these numberless days…what if it goes unexpressed and I never see her again?

What if I lose my mother after only just finding out who she is?

A sharp, biting laugh echoes around me, like a crack of thunder in the silence. "Have I piqued your interest yet?" Uriel asks. "You must have so many questions. Questions I may be able to provide insight to…if you answer mine first."

My feathers twitch at his words. I do have questions, but I'm not sure he'd be able to answer them. Or if it's even smart to ask them at all. I might be naive but I'm not dumb enough to believe the Archangel won't lie or manipulate any conversation we have just to get me to talk. If Alaric didn't trust the Council, I shouldn't either.

Uriel takes a step toward me, and I shrink away from his imposing figure despite the thick glass separating us, letting out a stifled moan when my back once again hits the smooth surface of the wall behind me. I couldn't put any more distance between us even if I wanted to.

My heart hammers against my ribcage, my breaths coming short. Although I'm terrified of Uriel, the fear consuming me is basic and human, animalistic, even—the same genuine terror someone might experience if they were being hunted or stalked by a serial killer. I take comfort in that for the simple reason I don't seem to feel the same innate desire to please him as I did in Gabriel's presence. Whatever allegiance I felt with her hasn't passed on to the other Archangels, which means I still hold some power in this situation, even if it doesn't seem like it.

Even if I *feel* powerless.

But how to use it? I don't know, and it's impossible to think with the Archangel glaring at me. So, I do the only thing I can think of. I clamp my lips shut, refusing to speak. If answers are what the Council wants from me so badly, they'll be the thing I deprive them of until I know how to turn those answers to my advantage.

Or, at least, until I know whatever I say won't carry dire consequences.

Uriel lets out a sigh, disappointment dragging his thick brows into a vee. "Clearly, these past four months have done little to convince you of your reality here. Perhaps I will return in a few years and see how you feel about conversing with me then. Or perhaps a century in isolation will be enough to loosen your tongue."

Panic rips through me, tearing through my wavering composure like paper. Four *months*? I've been here that long already?

The same length of time I spent at the Serapeum.

The irony of that realization would make me laugh if I wasn't on the verge of a complete mental break. The months I've spent here have felt like a lifetime, and yet, I can't imagine years or even a century trapped in this place. How did Alexander survive thousands of years of this torture with his mind intact? I'm not strong enough for that. Any longer and I have little doubt I will tumble over the edge into oblivion.

Shock grips my tongue, even as I urge myself to speak—to ignore any misgivings I have and just give the Archangel what he wants. But my terror is paralyzing, and I can't find the words.

Mistaking my silence for rebellion, Uriel turns and storms off into the mist with a derisive snort, the white blanket of fog shifting around his legs in billowing wafts that make it appear as if the fog is rising like a mouth opening to swallow him whole. As the berth between us widens and he begins to fade into the barren landscape, my self-preservation instincts kick in, unlocking my lips, and I shout out into the abyss.

"Wait!"

I can't do it. I can't stand the idea of being abandoned again—of being left in this place for a second longer, even if the alternative is prostrating myself before the Council and telling Uriel whatever it is he wants to know. What information could I really give them that they don't already possess anyway? Maybe if I cooperate, they'll realize I'm not a threat and let me go.

That…or put me out of my misery.

The mist falls away, and the Archangel shifts to face me again, a sly smile warping the defined contours of his mouth. "Are you ready to answer my questions?"

I nod despite myself. *Just answer his questions and he might let you go.* I repeat this thought like a chant, though there isn't a single part of me that believes it. Still, I cling to that hope like a lifeline. After all, I'm nothing like Alexander. I might've been tricked into letting him go, but I never tried to conquer anything. We might both be Grays, but that's where the similarities end. I don't deserve this. I might be dangerous but I'm not a danger to our world—not intentionally. I don't want to burn anything. I just want to be free.

We aren't the same.

"Where is Alexander?" Uriel asks.

I blink at him in confusion. "I don't—" An incredulous laugh slips out, interrupting my words, and I shake my head, eyes wide as I gape at the Archangel in disbelief. At his disgruntled look, I clear my throat before posing a counter question, once again gesturing to the glass egg around me. "How am I supposed to know that?"

A glower darkens Uriel's face. "Gabriel said he was speaking to you for weeks before his escape, and you were the one who set him free, were you not? It's not beyond the realm of reason to assume you would know where the Conqueror is or, at least, where he intended to flee."

I recoil again at the mention of my mother, at knowing she talked about me to the Council. That she told them about Alexander but treated me like I was crazy when I went to her for help about the strange voice I was hearing. "I'm sorry, did you fail to notice that he left me behind?" I hiss back, unable to keep the sharp edge from my tone.

Uriel scoffs. "As did your friend, the Dark transfer from Babel. Caleb, was it?"

My jaw goes slack at his words. How does he know about Caleb? Alexander fled with him and Ishtar before the Council arrived at the open tomb. At the scene of my crime. The crime for which I'm being punished. It didn't even occur to me until now that they might be hunting him, too, or that he might be on their radar. Does this mean Caleb is in danger?

Where is he right now?

My heart buckles in my chest, and suddenly, the anger and heartbreak that consume me whenever I think of him are displaced by an overriding worry. Caleb left me here. I should *hate* him. And yet—

Uriel chuckles once under his breath, as if he's aware of my inner turmoil. "Ah, yes, the Messenger told us all about the boy when we questioned her before her unfortunate disappearance. She pleaded your case quite passionately and said it was the Dark transfer who had convinced you to unleash Alexander."

That's a lie! I try to scream, but the growing fury rocking my body makes it impossible to push the protest from my lips. Gabriel saw us both under the school that day but pinned the full weight of blame on Caleb without any evidence that he was the instigator. I could've been the one leading the charge but because she believed me to be a Light—one of her own kind—and never approved of our friendship, it's no wonder she would automatically blame him. Hell, she was trying to warn me away from him when I was still at the Serapeum. She's been trying to paint him as the villain and me as the unsuspecting victim from the beginning.

Isn't he, though? the voice of doubt taunts me. *He lied to you and then left you to rot in this cage.*

No, I bite back. *He told me the truth. He told me about Alexander, and I chose to help him because we trusted each other. Because we were friends.*

And because of that, regardless of the deep wound in my heart—regardless of the lingering sense of betrayal eating away at my sanity every second I spend here—I have to believe he wouldn't have left me on purpose. Not unless he had no other choice.

Because that hope, however faint and eroded, is all I have left to hold onto.

I bite my lip when Uriel tilts his head, his eyes crawling over my face with keen examination. He's looking for a reaction—a slip in my features that will tell him something I refuse to say with words. But...how much am I really willing to reveal to the Council?

What is the price for my cooperation?

Swallowing, I cast my eyes on the floor so they don't expose my pain to the angel. "I have nothing to say about him, either," I mutter.

Uriel offers a noncommittal grunt, but I can sense his impatience bleeding through. "Then what of the Morningstar? Will you refuse to speak of him, too?"

My chest tightens. Does Uriel know the truth about Lucifer? Does he know the Morningstar is my father, or was that another one of Gabriel's well-guarded secrets?

Slowly, I lift my gaze to the Archangel's. "I don't know anything about Lucifer. That day at the Serapeum...that was the first time we met."

Uriel's unblinking stare burns invisible scorch marks into my skin. "And yet, he defended you almost to the point of losing his wings. It's very curious."

I steel myself, trying my best to hide the increasing tremor in my voice. "I don't know anything," I say again. "Haven't you heard? I'm just an ignorant orphan. I didn't even know angels existed a year ago." Then, with more force, I add, "Maybe you should've done a better job questioning Gabriel. I guarantee she knows a lot more than I do."

Uriel juts out his lower jaw then lets out a harsh, barking laugh. "You are quite amusing, aren't you?" He walks slowly back and forth in front of my cage now, and with his wings out of sight, he looks almost human. "I've given you no reason to trust me, I know this. But remember, you are not the one we're after, Luna. The sooner you help us understand the chain of events that led to Alexander's release, the sooner you can go free. Isn't that what you want?"

Just answer his questions and he might let you go, I repeat to myself, but this time, my panic is dulled, and I only feel repulsed by that thought. I can't bring myself to do it—to be the inflicter of such a betrayal, even against someone who betrayed me first. The guilt would eat me alive and the madness would pick at what remains of my bones.

Besides, common sense tells me there's no way the Council would ever really let me go, especially with Alexander on the loose. Especially if my fellow Gray is as dangerous as I'm beginning to suspect and it's my fault he's walking free. Even if unleashing him wasn't enough reason to imprison me, then the Council's fear of those who aren't easily defined by the divide would be. My existence as a Gray will always make me a threat.

No, I'm never going free, and by talking, all I would be doing is sentencing yet another person to the Council's wrath.

Still, I can't ignore how tempted I am by his words. After seventeen years of never fitting in, of never being able to go anywhere without my troubled past following in pursuit…freedom is all I want. A chance to escape everything and finally start over.

Like I was supposed to do with Caleb.

Squashing that thought before it makes me do something I regret, I force a scowl onto my face, directing it at Uriel, who bows his shaved head, his broad shoulders shrugging with indifference. "Very well," he relents. "But believe me when I tell you that eternal confinement is not the worst fate that will befall you should you choose to walk the path of silence. There are far more unpleasant things to endure than isolation."

My blood runs cold at the cryptic warning behind Uriel's words, but I say nothing as he pivots and struts away from my cage for a second time, suppressing the urge to call out again. As the mist rises to shroud his body, his eyes flick over his shoulder.

"Beware the horrors of your own mind. The unchecked thoughts of your unhinging sanity will be your worst enemy here. Not me."

He then fades into the landscape without looking back.

THREE

CALEB

PALE SUNLIGHT BREAKS THROUGH the overcast sky, warding off the chill and rain of a London spring day. It's practically hot now. Typical London. You go through four seasons in one afternoon. Although I love the city, I'm shocked to find this is where Hammurabi said to meet. I wait outside a sushi bar on Portobello Road, the brick above me painted with a bright mural, and scents of spice waft from the Thai restaurant on the second floor. My stomach rumbles. Living in an ancient, abandoned citadel has not exactly provided culinary delights, and London offers a mosaic of cuisine begging to be sampled.

I lean against the exterior wall, keeping watch on the bustling street before me. It's market day, and the swell of people press against me. My eyes narrow as I focus, my vision as sharp as a raptor's. I don't want Hammurabi sneaking up on me. I sent one of my little clay figures through the shadows last night to give a message to my teacher. Although he agreed to a meeting, I don't know how pissed he is with me. I lied to him and freed my grandfather, which goes against all the strict rules he follows with a rigid devotion. Hammurabi and his laws. He might stab me—a discreet knife slipped under my ribs—and I'll die on this beautiful, happy street as the crowd swallows me whole.

But instead of a stealthy approach, the former Babylonian king plods down the street at a leisurely pace. His wide shoulders create a path before him, and he looks unusually relaxed, stopping here and there to look at the merchandise displayed on the sidewalks. I blink. Good lord, did he actually just sniff a *candle?* He offers the woman behind the table a devastating smile and she practically purrs. Well, shit.

Does Hammurabi come here to get laid? I shake my head, trying to wrap my mind around this new side to my stern, scary teacher.

That all-too-familiar wariness rises within me as his dark gaze clashes with mine, and his eyes harden to ice chips. The woman's smile falters as she observes his sudden arctic expression. Then his attention flicks back to her, and he turns on the charm, leaving her blushing. He pays for the candle and whispers something in her ear and she preens. Damn, hail to the king. Hammurabi's got game. All warmth melts from him as he walks toward me, and the sick feeling of dread returns.

Sweat beads around my hairline at my teacher's pissed-off expression. If he could shoot icicles out of his eyeballs, he would. Which begs the question, can angels do that? I suppress inappropriate laughter at the image of Gabriel shooting ice out of her ass. Get it together, Caleb.

I give Hammurabi a wary nod, afraid even a simple "hi" will enrage him more. He stands in front of me, and the crowd breaks around him like he's a large stone in rushing water. A delicate paper bag is fisted in his big hand, which somehow doesn't detract from his badass image. He glowers at me for a long moment, and I lift my chin. Never show your fear to predators.

"Caleb, do you realize what you have done?" he finally growls.

I repress a flinch, but my own anger rises.

"Rescued my grandfather from eternal imprisonment? The rest of you seemed willing to let him rot there," I bite back. "He's my blood. He's also an angel! Something everyone conveniently kept from me. A *Gray* angel." Fury rides me hard as I think about how everyone lied to me. I have no idea if Hammurabi even knows what a Gray is, but if he does, the deception from the Darks runs deep.

The Babylonian king doesn't even blink at the word "Gray," confirming my suspicions, as his expression grows stormy. "Yes, he's your blood, but did you ever question why I'd be willing to let him rot?"

"Because being both of the Dark and the Light messes with your strict world order?" I snarl. "Because his existence breaks your precious rules?" I know arguing with him is not going to help me rescue Luna, but I'm too angry to keep my mouth shut. Yeah, Gramps isn't perfect, and he wants to rule the world, but being entombed for all time doesn't seem fair. And let's face it, probably wasn't good for Alexander's sanity. I also carry an enormous boulder of guilt around that my actions caused Goldilocks to be taken, and I might have unleashed a dangerous threat onto the world.

Hammurabi steps closer, his rage an almost living thing coiling around him. "Do you think me that petty, Caleb? That I would condone the imprisonment of

Alexander the Great because he was a *Gray*? You don't suppose it had anything to do with his desire to master the Earth and all its inhabitants? Or do you support his plans to subvert the free will of humanity?"

Guilt oozes into my stomach, making me sick. "Grandfather likes humanity," I protest weakly. "He just doesn't want us to hide anymore. He wants to stop the chaos."

Hammurabi snorts. "Oh, young one, what is it that you children say? That's total bullshit. Yes, Alexander loves humanity. I won't deny it, but his love does not give him permission to be king of all. It does not give him permission to start a war that will kill millions."

I shake my head in denial. I know my grandfather doesn't want to kill millions of humans. He has no trouble taking out Nephilim and angels but he genuinely loves mortals.

Hammurabi's voice gentles. "Caleb, what do you think will happen to the mortals when Alexander wages his war against the Council? The earth will tremble and run red with blood. He won't target humans, but they will be collateral damage. It's unavoidable. Alexander is not the victim or the hero in this scenario. He is the villain of the piece."

The picture he paints makes my queasiness worse. "If he's the villain, you've all made him one. I doubt you were accepting of him being a Gray," I accuse.

He releases a long sigh. "Walk with me, child." He turns on his heel, and I follow him down the sidewalk. His stride is sure and confident, as if he's taken this path hundreds of times before. He probably has. He's older than dirt.

We take a left down a side street and stop at a…donut shop. There isn't an inch of fat on the warrior king, so I wouldn't have guessed he has a sweet tooth. Then again, we're Nephilim, so the normal human fallacies don't apply to us. He orders some donuts at the window and hands me one with a maple glaze.

"Um, I know you're angry with me, so why the treat?" I say as I take a big bite of the sweet pastry. Bacon and maple explode in my mouth and I sigh. Finally, food that tastes good.

He takes a bite of his own donut, studying me for a moment before walking again. I keep up with his long stride easily, although my anxiety ratchets up. Usually when people give you comfort food, they're about to tell you they crashed your car or slept with your girlfriend.

"I am very angry with you, but I also know that Ishtar was behind this as well. I'm sure she had a hand in convincing you to help your grandfather, and I know how convincing she can be," Hammurabi says, cutting me a side glance.

"She's a huge fan of Gramps," I admit around a mouthful of donut. As we get farther from Portobello Road, the crowded sidewalks thin.

His grin is grim. "Yes, she always was. She hates hiding what she really is." He gives a bitter laugh. "She hates rules, too. She does love power, though. She longs to be a goddess in truth."

I snort, nodding. That she does. I think she misses being a queen, misses being worshipped. "She played the family angle. I don't know my dad, so…I wanted to know *him*. He's freakin' Alexander the Great and my grandfather. She didn't have to push me hard," I admit, shame creeping in.

Hammurabi is quiet for a moment. His black eyes are grave as he studies me, reluctance written on his face, and then he sighs. "I understand the need to find your blood, especially because your father is the worst sort of bastard. And you couldn't possibly know about the prophecy. It's not something the Archdemons or Archangels want shared. Only a few Nephilim know about it."

"Prophecy?" I demand, my feet slowing. "You mean the one I overheard the Council talking about when I snuck my little toy warrior into Gabriel's office? The one they were pissing themselves over?"

For a moment, admiration shines on my teacher's face. "You infiltrated Gabriel's office? Clever boy." He shakes his head. "The prophecy decrees that a Gray will destroy the world and wage war on Heaven and Earth," Hammurabi says. "And Alexander certainly was—and is—bent on that."

I roll my eyes. "Why are these prophecies all about the end of the world?" I scoff.

"Alexander almost succeeded in conquering the known world before," Hammurabi points out. "And he killed an Archangel."

Shock ripples through me. "What?" I ask. I mean, I know he wants to kill them in revenge, but I had no idea he took one out before he was entombed. "*Who?*"

"Michael."

I reel back on my heels. I had no idea Michael was dead. No one ever talks about it. And I'm not a Light, so I've never given the Archangel much thought. It's not like he shows up at Archdemon reunions, passing out cookies and judgment. I get why no one talks about it either. Most Nephilim believe Alexander was a first generation, certainly not an angel. If it got out that he'd killed an Archangel, there would be lots of explaining to do.

Realization kicks me in the face, and I curse myself for being so stupid. "Did he use the dagger you gave me?"

Hammurabi nods. "Yes, he did. The dagger belongs to your family, and only your bloodline can wield it. Alexander didn't always know he was a Gray, Caleb. He grew up as a pampered prince, self-assured in his power in the mortal world, and believing he was a Dark Nephilim. Once he discovered what he really was—a Gray angel—he felt betrayed. The dagger was from the Fall, belonging to one of his parents, but I have no idea how he managed to find it. What I do know is he felt he was the only one to set the world back to right, being both of the Dark and the Light. And there lies the issue. Your grandfather truly believes he's the chosen one. People like that are dangerous, so righteous in their convictions they're blind to their tyranny. I'm a Dark Nephilim, Caleb. Free will means everything to me."

His words eat their way into my conscience like worms through rotting food and I flinch, studying the cracks in the sidewalk. I know Grandfather wants to rule the world, and I doubt the Creator is happy about that. Still, I feel sorry for Alexander if fate had decided his path before he ever got a chance to not be defined by some prophecy.

"There's another Gray angel," I blurt, and Hammurabi's square jaw drops. Wow, I've actually managed to stun the king. I frown as another realization smacks me in the face. I recall the conversation I overheard with Gabriel and the other Archangels and Archdemons, how they kept Alexander's true identity a secret. "Hang on, how do *you* know Alexander is a Gray angel when Ishtar didn't realize what he was until she saw his wings? How was that kept a secret? I mean, you all were there back in the day."

Hammurabi's brows draw down into a sharp vee. He gives me a long, hard stare, which I meet without faltering. "I altered her memory," he admits. "I'm not proud of it but it was necessary."

"Wait a minute. I thought only Archangels or Archdemons could wipe our memories, not other Nephilim. You can break into our minds, but you can't alter them completely like you can with humans," I protest, my world order once more upended.

His smile is sharp enough to cut. "That's mostly true. I'm the only known Nephilim with that talent. Asmodeus charged me with burying the fact that Alexander was an angel. Considering the role he played in human history, removing all knowledge of him would've created too many complications, and seeing as there are far fewer Nephilim than humans, the Council settled on altering our minds over the alternative. Asmodeus felt it was the only way. She didn't want to lose Ishtar, and if Ishtar remembered what the Great truly was, she'd have started a rebellion much sooner than she did." Bitterness radiates from him. "It was Asmodeus's hope that the goddess would let Alexander go. A foolish hope as I feared. Ishtar never forgot your grandfather. Time only nursed her determination. You think she would have learned her lesson from the first rebellion."

"Why are you telling me this?" I demand. "I helped Ishtar. Why trust me not to run and tell her you screwed with her mind?"

"Because you just told me there's another Gray," Hammurabi answers calmly. "You came to me, which means your loyalty is torn, and I'm assuming this other Gray is the reason."

Heat creeps into my cheeks. Would I have abandoned my grandfather and his megalomaniac need to conquer if it weren't for Luna? "I met a girl at the academy. Luna. She'd recently been brought there, but she was around my age, and she didn't seem to understand that as a Light, she should hate me. The other Lights treated her like shit. We became…friends. And weird stuff kept happening to her—she had Dark and Light traits. Then Alexander started speaking to her, leading her to him. She could see Enochian. I…with Ishtar…used her to help me free Alexander." Those words scrape my throat as shame fills me. My Goldilocks is probably entombed somewhere and it's my fault. "I didn't want to use her like that, and I only went along with it because Ishtar promised to get Luna out with us. But Gabriel showed up and I…I stabbed her with the dagger. Alexander grabbed me and Ishtar, and the last time I saw Luna, she was screaming on the ground with wings coming out of her back. *Gray* wings."

The confession tastes sour in my mouth. I feel stupid for putting my trust in Ishtar and Alexander. Don't get me wrong, I wanted my grandfather free, but not for the price I paid. Not at the expense of Goldilocks. That dull ache in my chest that never seems to go away sharpens.

The corners of Hammurabi's mouth pull down. "We imprisoned Alexander so we could suspend the prophecy. There was never supposed to be another Gray. I honestly don't know how there is one."

"Well, there is," I growl, "and you'd better go ask Asmodeus about it. Gabriel took Luna somewhere, I know it, and I'm sure Asmodeus knows where. It's the one damn time everyone takes the sticks out of their asses and works together."

"Your Gray could possibly be the one the prophecy refers to, and in that case, it's better that she is sealed away from the world," he argues, and I want to strangle him.

"I refuse to believe Luna is the Gray in the prophecy, Hammurabi. She's sweet and gentle, and she certainly doesn't want to take over the world. We have to help her. She doesn't deserve to be thrown in a hole and left there. She's an innocent girl who's been lied to her entire life."

A troubled expression crosses the former king's face. "She's not a girl, Caleb, she's an angel. A Gray angel. She's dangerous." He holds up a hand to stall my immediate angry protests. "I'm not saying your Luna is deliberately dangerous or has ill intentions, but that she might accidentally hurt others as she comes into her powers. Being of both factions, we still don't even know what Grays are capable of."

"That doesn't mean she deserves to be imprisoned or punished for sins she hasn't even committed!" I shout, catching the attention of people passing by on the sidewalk. Shit, I forgot we were in the middle of busy London for a minute.

"Keep your voice down," Hammurabi hisses. "I don't enjoy altering human minds. It's obvious you care for Luna deeply, but don't let your feelings blind you, Caleb."

I grind out through gritted teeth, "I'm not. Luna is a kind, caring person who doesn't deserve any of this. She belongs with me—with the Darks. We're supposed to be the open-minded ones, aren't we? We're about free will, so shouldn't Luna be allowed to choose a side before she's condemned for nothing more than being born different?"

The Babylonian king studies me then sighs. "I'm not condemning her for being different, but anyone untrained with that much power is dangerous. I will speak to Asmodeus, boy, but I can't promise anything. She fears Grays. They all do."

"Please," I beg, feeling helpless and hopeless as the proverbial clock keeps ticking. I keep picturing Luna, alone and feeling betrayed. Hating me. "Tell her Luna is different. Please, I need her help. And yours."

"I will do my best, Caleb," Hammurabi says, backing away from me. "Now, I suggest you get back before Ishtar misses you. I'll be in touch."

I watch him walk away, my heart heavy. What will I do if Asmodeus won't help?

FOUR

LUNA

A GASP PARTS MY lips as my eyes snap open, consciousness slamming into my mind like a brick wall. My arms shake beneath me as I slowly push up from the floor, my vision foggy and glazed as I search for whatever it was that startled me awake. I could've sworn I heard somebody calling my name, but…the other side of the glass is deserted.

Like always, I'm alone in this place.

Heaving a tired breath, I prop myself upright against the transparent wall, ignoring the ache in my back when the bare skin of my shoulder blades touches the barrier. My fingers reach for the shredded remains of my T-shirt as it begins to slip down my arms, carefully sliding the sleeves back into position. I'm not sure what disgusts me more—that I'm still donning the same torn outfit I was wearing the day these wings sprouted out of my back or that the Archangels and Archdemons keeping me here haven't had the decency to at least provide me with a fresh change of clothes. Maybe when you get to be that old, manners and hospitality no longer matter.

Then again, I'm a captive here, not a guest. I highly doubt Uriel or any of his cohorts give a damn about my comfort.

A hoarse laugh rumbles deep in my chest. Of course, they don't care. If they did, they wouldn't be treating me like some prisoner of war, depriving me of food and water or access to facilities to bathe and relieve myself…not that I ever need to do the latter. Since that day under the Serapeum, certain bodily functions have ceased being necessary. I've been trapped in this cage for four months and I haven't eaten so much as a crumb. I *could* eat but my survival doesn't seem to depend on it anymore. Hell, maybe it never did. I can remember instances of food being withheld as punishment during some of my stricter foster placements but I never felt the desperation they expected of me when it was finally offered again. I always passed that lack of appetite off as fear, but now, I'm beginning to question if it was always because of this. Because of what I am.

Still, there's a hollowness in my stomach that seems to expand the longer I go without, and I can't help wondering if angels *can* starve—if maybe it just takes a lot longer than it would for a mortal. Centuries, even, if Uriel's threats about my captivity hold any weight.

Then again, Alexander was imprisoned for thousands of years and he didn't die of starvation. If anything, I imagine the Council is using that growing discomfort against me as a way of encouraging my submission, hoping it will eventually make me crack. And maybe it will. Maybe the sensations accosting me will only get worse until spilling my secrets to them will feel like the sweetest form of relief if doing so means a potential escape from such torment. Or maybe what I'm feeling is all in my head, and any malaise is merely a result of my own degrading mind.

Since the Archangel's visit, the air has felt thinner, making me dizzy, like there's a sudden lack of oxygen in the cramped space of the egg. My senses were already dulled, my powers unreachable—no doubt suppressed by whatever magic created my prison—but now, my helplessness is amplified. It reminds me of the countless days I spent locked in that padded room in the hospital, my head muddled by claustrophobia and a building anxiety as the hours passed in an interminable blur. If I close my eyes, I can almost imagine myself back there again, and what truly terrifies me is that I'm not sure if I crave that or not. If believing I'm mortal and crazy again is preferable to whatever unknown fate awaits me here.

Shaking that thought away, I raise my arms and stretch until my shoulder joints pop. Angel or not, my body is accustomed to seventeen years of human habit, and although I also don't seem to need to sleep anymore to function or survive, I long for it. I lose my days to it. What else is there for me to do? If anything, I'm relieved I'm still capable of it. It's a much-needed interruption to the monotony of this lonely existence. And in sleep, instead of the nightmares I expect, I have the refuge of dreams—sweet imaginings of Caleb that are a knife to my waking heart but, in unconsciousness, form a safe haven from the questions pressing at the back of every thought and breath. Questions about what I am and about how I could've gone nearly two decades without knowing the truth. If I've always been an angel since birth, then why did my wings and these other new changes to my body only become apparent when Alexander touched me? What did he mean when he said he was giving me my freedom?

Once again, I hear those strange words Alexander whispered in my ear—Enochian, I'm guessing, given the lilting similarities to the words Ishtar taught me to open his tomb.

Tomb… My mind catches on that word, and a broken laugh parts my lips as I glance at the rounded wall of my cage. My own eternal crypt.

When I think of freedom, this is the opposite of what I envision.

Scowling, I hug my legs to my chest, already fed up with the endless barrage of questions nagging at my thoughts. It's only a matter of time until my frustrating ignorance becomes too much to bear and then, with answers still far out of reach, I'll drift away from it all and into the welcome embrace of sleep. In those moments, more than anything, I dream about the fresh start I should've had at Babel with Caleb, despite having no idea what that would've looked like, and regardless of the pain that image stirs in my heart. My imagination runs wild, dreaming up grand halls and long, winding corridors and Caleb always at my side. And happiness. Pure, unbridled happiness.

But those feelings never last, because once I wake up, the truth of my situation smashes them to pieces, until all I'm left with is a large void in my chest and the taunting realization that I'm all alone. There can be no fresh start because, as consciousness always reminds me, Caleb left me behind.

Everyone always leaves me behind.

"Luna."

I spring forward onto my knees and whip around at the whispered sound of my name, my racing heart jumping up into my throat as panic conspires to choke me. It takes a moment for my gaze to focus on the figure emerging from the milky white mist, my eyes bolting wide the moment the newcomer's features slide into focus, crisp and clear. Disbelief forms a name on my lips as the Archangel steps free of the last wisps of fog.

It can't be—

"Gabriel?" I breathe.

I rub at my eyes, unable to accept what I'm seeing. The last time Gabriel and I were in the same room, the Archdemons were threatening to torture her for keeping my existence a secret. The last time we were together, I was certain we were both going to die.

Granted, some time has passed since that day, but still, I'm shocked to see her here, looking the perfect picture of health—the opposite of how she appeared in the moments before I was taken away to be punished for my part in Alexander's release… and for being a Gray. Her ebony hair is straight and sleek, just like I remember, and the planes of her cheekbones are sculpted and sharp, like the edge of a knife, showing how deadly she really is behind that fair angelic exterior. But although her dewy skin glows, tendrils of shadow writhe over her skin, contradicting what I know of her aura.

Purple and black shadows instead of the golden hues of a Light.

I falter back a step, my pulse picking up speed. This isn't right. Gabriel isn't a Dark. Her aura should be bright—blindingly so. Not like this.

Before I can make sense of the change or the sudden fear gripping me, she rushes forward, pressing a long-fingered hand to the glass. "Thank the Creator. I don't have much time."

Relief and doubt sweep through me, warring with each other for dominance. On the one hand, part of me is elated to see her again—not because I'm certain she's my mother but because she's *alive*. Because now I can let go of the guilt that would have swallowed me had she actually died. But on the other—the side where I retain some sense of logic past my growing derangement—I can't ignore the suspicious timing of her appearance or the bewildering fact that she's here at all. How long ago was it that Uriel questioned me about my relationship with the headmistress of the Serapeum? How long ago did he claim she disappeared from their grasp? How is she here, right in front of me now, without alerting my captors to her presence?

This isn't right, I repeat to myself as a darker realization begins to sink in. Only the Faithful and Fallen who imprisoned me know about this place. So, how is it that Gabriel knew where to find me unless she's working with them? *For* them?

Whose side is she really on?

Yours, a voice inside me insists, but I refuse its invasion into my thoughts, unable to believe such a lie. If she was on my side, she wouldn't have abandoned me to suffer the human world in ignorance of what I am. If she was on my side, she wouldn't have let the Council imprison me for being an unwilling result of *her* transgressions. If she was on my side, she wouldn't be here at all, no doubt to serve as my interrogator.

If she was on my side, she would have loved me and accepted me the way a mother should.

"I…" I hesitate, swallowing a little too loudly. Despite the thick, transparent wall between us, I'm certain she must've heard it with her keen senses. My fear grows, encasing me like a shroud. Can she also sense my suspicion of her? "Uriel said you disappeared," I mutter before forcing out, "How are you here?"

Her hand slips away from the glass as a somber frown pulls at the edges of her mouth. "They found me. I'm imprisoned in this place, just like you. They're only allowing me to speak with you because I said I could convince you to tell them the truth."

My entire body stiffens at her words. They're *allowing* her to speak with me? As if Gabriel, the feared headmistress of the Serapeum and Messenger of the Creator Himself, has ever sought anyone's approval to do anything.

An incredulous laugh rises up in my throat. No...I believe Gabriel is a prisoner about as much as I believe she's actually here to help me.

I examine her for a long moment, my eyes trailing across the unnerving undulations of the inky whips of darkness outlining her body. Was I wrong to assume all Darks are defined by shadow and all Lights by glowing golden wisps? The only person I ever dared to ask about auras had no idea they even exist, so I'm alone in my minimal understanding of them. Maybe I was too quick in my assumptions and there's a deeper psychological aspect to them. Maybe what I'm seeing now is the real Gabriel and her aura has changed in my eyes to reflect that, the darkness of her heart revealed. If so, if auras are really just a reflection of how I view those with angel blood, then that would explain why I see what looks like shards of glass floating along my skin, my own unearthed aura a mirror image of my fractured soul and mind. It's just like the one I saw around Alexander, who suffered the same persecution and isolation I've fallen victim to. Is that because we're both Grays or because we're both damaged? Or both? Maybe, the truth is, we have more in common than I've allowed myself to admit.

My fingers curl into fists, my nails biting into my palms to keep from ripping my skin off my body, my increasing vexation like an itch I can't scratch, unbearable and maddening. None of this makes any damn sense. If auras reflect a person's soul, then why did I see darkness when I looked at Caleb?

The answer stabs me like a knife to the heart.

Because part of me always knew he'd betray me. That he'd eventually leave me, too.

Swallowing the rising sob in my throat, I force myself to focus on Gabriel. On what she said. On why she's here.

"They're only allowing me to speak with you because I said I could convince you to tell them the truth."

The truth. I nearly scoff at the thought.

"Luna?" Gabriel prods, and I realize I've been silent too long.

I clear my throat. "Why would you say that?" I ask, fighting to keep my tone calm. "I already told Uriel I don't know anything."

Like I told Uriel, if the Council wants answers, they should get them from Gabriel.

After all, she's the one who hid my birth—my very forbidden existence—from them, from the rest of the world, and from, I assume, the Creator. She lied to them. She lied to *me*.

If anyone has anything more to hide, it's her.

Anger is a raging river in my veins, but as I examine the sharp planes of Gabriel's severe countenance, another face abruptly springs to mind. Yet another person she lied to.

My lips tighten as I picture my father. I recall the pain in those vibrant blue eyes the moment he realized who I was—when our blood sang to each other, revealing a long hidden truth. Since that day, I must've replayed that memory more than a thousand times, analyzing it from every possible angle. At first, I wondered if he was equally at fault for my pain, for the horrors I suffered through all because I didn't know what I was. But with time, my doubt has withered, leaving only the bitter truth and more questions.

Lucifer…he had no idea I existed. If he had, would he have wanted me? Or would he have buried my existence the same way my mother did?

I stare at the stunning creature before me, wondering what drove her to abandon her child. Was it fear of the Creator, or was it shame that kept us apart? Maybe she just didn't want anyone to know she's a hypocrite.

"You must know something. Please," she presses, her voice uncharacteristically tender. Pleading. So unlike the cold Archangel I know. "The Council have said they'll tear off my wings for my part in Alexander's release."

What part? I'm tempted to ask before wincing at the mental image of wings torn from flesh. Before I was reborn, my own wings unleashed, I wouldn't have been able to imagine that pain. Now, having experienced the crack of bones shifting and feathers protruding from my skin, I can envision the agony all too clearly. It's a pain I don't want to imagine, let alone ever experience firsthand.

Gabriel raises a hand to the barrier between us again, her fingertips turning milk-white where they press against the glass, leaving behind tiny impressions. She bats her thick lashes, blinking tears from her eyes, and yet, everything about her expression seems false.

"Luna…I need you to tell them what happened down to the most minute detail. You need to reveal where the Conqueror is and end this. It's the only way to save us both."

My heart tugs, but it isn't the obedient terror I normally feel in the Archangel's presence. Strangely, I don't feel that at all, though my realization of that is buried under the weight of all my other conflicting emotions. My wings tear free of the restraints of my skin and whip upward, pulling me to my feet, and this time, I barely notice the burn consuming me. In this moment, all I'm aware of is anger.

"I don't know where Alexander is!" I screech, my self-control slipping. "What part of 'he left me behind' is everyone here not understanding? Besides, you saw what happened with your own two eyes. I can't tell them anything you haven't already."

"Luna—"

"No," I cut her off, my tone scathing. I've waited seventeen years to meet my mother, and the disappointment flooding my body is worse than if I'd never known her at all. "You don't get to ask for my help. I came to you, and you pushed me away, remember? I warned you Alexander was leading me to him, and you did *nothing*. Oh, wait, that's right." I sneer, remembering the conversation I overheard in her office. "You told Alaric to 'assess my mental state' and determine if I was going to be a problem. Mom of the year, everybody."

Her soft gaze brightens with surprise—the change so fleeting it's already passed before I've even fully registered it. In the blink of an eye, her expression turns molten, her features darkening with warning. "So, you'll do nothing?" she growls. "You'll let your own mother suffer?"

"What about *my* suffering?" I practically scream. "I spent my whole life in foster care being tossed from one home to another like a stray dog nobody wanted. Did you know that? Did you know I was committed to a psychiatric hospital because everyone thought I was too dangerous to be around normal people? You must have—I know Alaric told you—so where were you when *I* needed help? Where were you when I needed a mother?" I shake my head, biting back the tears scalding my eyes. "You know, if this situation is anyone's fault, it's yours. You were too busy focusing on my friendship with Caleb to listen to what I was trying to tell you. Seriously, why did you even bother inviting him to your school if you have such a problem with Darks?"

As these words leave my lips, something occurs to me. Gabriel was fine—at least, in appearance—with Caleb being a student at the Serapeum until he began spending time with me. Until he began influencing my behavior, my powers. And then it hits me: Caleb was never the problem, not really. It wasn't our friendship that she didn't like…

It was what our friendship reminded her of.

"Oh, I get it. You didn't like me spending so much time with Caleb because it reminded you of what you had with my father."

Her hawk-like gaze sharpens, her eyes narrowing on my face. "What do you know of your father?"

I startle at her accusatory tone. Despite being my mother, her blood never once sang to mine, not like my father's did. Maybe that's why she thinks I don't know the truth. Maybe she assumed our connection would be as damaged as the one I have with her.

I shrug, refusing to waste any more energy on this pointless conversation. If she isn't here to help me, then I'd prefer she leave me condemned to my eternal solitude. "Nothing. Just like I know nothing about you because you've both been absent my whole life."

Her face reddens. "You must know something about him. *Speak*," she commands, that single word uncomfortably abrasive.

My pulse quickens at the sudden shift in her demeanor, her normally straight back hunched and her beautiful face contorted with a terrifying fury I can't comprehend. The shadows lapping over her skin have gone rigid, like a den of cobras preparing to strike.

Gone is the pleading woman from only a few moments ago.

The change sucks the moisture from my mouth, leaving my tongue brittle. Swallowing past the dryness, I give a slight shake of my head. "O-Other than what I learned about him in history class?" I stammer, unable to keep the fear from my voice. "Not really. How would I?"

"You know your father's identity?" she presses.

The weight of my surprise tugs my mouth open, and I stare at the Archangel, dumbfounded by her hostility and this peculiar line of questioning when it's obvious I know the truth. Maybe her injury that day was far worse than I thought. Can angels suffer from amnesia? Why else would she be so shocked I know who my father is when she was there to witness our meeting?

Or maybe her reaction isn't about me at all. Maybe she's just struggling to accept that the full extent of this secret she's held onto for thousands of years is finally out in the open.

"Why does that surprise you so much?" I ask. "You were there when we met. Or did the blood loss from your wound damage your memory?"

The frustration stretching across her face fades with the same speed as drawing a breath, returning her reddening skin to its normal alabaster complexion. As she straightens her back, resuming a rigid, imposing posture that resembles the Archangel I know, her pupils dilate, her eyes widening with comprehension. "Your father is the Morningstar," she breathes, as if confirming something she suspected but didn't know for sure.

Furrowing my brow, I take a careful step forward, my wings wrapping around my frail body, as if to protect me from a potential attack. Dread spreads under my skin like a rash.

"You say that like you didn't already know," I whisper.

As Gabriel meets my gaze once again, I see something strange in the depths of her eyes. The writhing darkness spreads over her skin, and it dawns on me that this woman, this unrecognizable creature, isn't here to help me...

"Beware the horrors of your own mind. The unchecked thoughts of your unhinging sanity will be your worst enemy here. Not me."

Because she isn't my mother.

"You don't," I realize, my voice a barely-there breath as Uriel's warning comes back to haunt me, "because you're not really her." *Because you're not really here.*

The misty shroud coating the empty landscape rises up in a wave and smashes into the walls of the egg, engulfing my surroundings. I spin around in a blind panic, but no matter which way I look, I can only see white, and no matter how hard I strain my ears, I can only hear the thundering sound of my own terror.

Slamming my hands over my ears, I sink down to the ground, curl into a ball, and rock back and forth, waiting for the fog to settle and the chaos of my mind to ease. When it does, I'm unsurprised to find I'm alone again, trapped in my own private world, like always.

And the hallucination—the projection of the Archangel concocted by my broken mind—has vanished.

FIVE

CALEB

ISHTAR FINDS ME OUT in the hot sun, surveying the city of Kandahār below. Alexander stamped his mark all over Afghanistan when he destroyed the Persian Empire. I've been reluctant to go into the city and explore, which is unlike me, but with Luna in danger, I've lost all taste for new flavors. Also, like Iraq, Afghanistan isn't exactly warm and friendly to tourists. I'd still love to eat some Kabuli palaw or lamb kabob or indulge in Turkish coffee. Alexander doesn't need to eat, and Ishtar has only provided us with the staples, too enthralled with the Great and his plans to demand her usual level of culinary perfection. And I can't cook for shit. I regret not paying more attention to Mom's delicious dishes instead of just stuffing my face.

The scent of cardamom and sugar hits my nose, and I glance over at the former goddess to see her holding a small plate filled with Gosh-e fil, traditional fried pastries. My stomach rumbles, but I look at my teacher with suspicion.

"What are those for? I haven't been a good boy lately," I say tartly, crossing my arms over my chest. Being rude to Ishtar isn't the smartest move I could make but I'm pissed. I haven't heard back from Hammurabi, and I'm sick of waiting around and twiddling my dick for Alexander to find Luna.

"No, you haven't. Come now, lovely boy, pouting doesn't become you. Eat these delicious treats before I shove them down your throat," Ishtar answers, her voice dripping with venom and honey.

I reach for one and take a big bite. Damn, they are good. "Thanks," I say after I swallow. "What's up?"

"Must something be 'up'?" she asks, popping a pastry into her mouth and chewing.

I raise a brow at her, and she chuckles. "Alexander wants you in the receiving room. He expects more Nephilim today, and he wants you with him to observe. If you are to take your place in this war, you need to learn strategy."

I almost choke on my second bite. "My place in this war?"

It's her turn to arch an incredulous brow. "What did you think your role here was, Caleb? Did you think you'd simply free Alexander and be the pampered prince, waiting around for your Luna to be brought back to you on a silver platter?"

I don't know which of her words pisses me off more. I used to like and admire Ishtar, no matter how much of a hard-ass she was, but now I begin to feel hate encroach, replacing some of the love and respect I have for my teacher. I'm not a "pampered" anything and never have been. My dad abandoned my mom, and we had a regular, middle-class existence until the Nephilim came for me. My teachers like me because I'm talented and work hard, and I'm popular with the Darks because I treat people well. Honey always traps more flies than vinegar, and I can be as sweet as fuck.

But my blinding rage toward my teacher—a woman I used to have the highest respect for—is from hearing Luna's name tumble from her ruby lips in such a derisive, dismissive way. Like Luna was just a convenient tool to get what she wanted, and she won't be bothered to take her out of the drawer again until she wants to hammer something. Luna is an angel, for the Morningstar's sake. She shouldn't be treated lightly. Hammurabi got one thing right: no one knows what Luna is capable of. Not even Alexander.

Oh, and I sure as shit didn't sign up for any war, especially one I'm not on board with. I feel like the biggest idiot on the planet, so obsessed with freeing Gramps, I glossed over what that actually meant. I was so focused on the injustice of it all, of the utter unfairness of chaining an immortal creature—not that I knew that about him at the time—for all eternity, that I never thought much of the fact that said immortal being was going to be enraged and want revenge. That's just first class dumbassery.

I take a deep breath, trying to calm down and not choke on my fury. Part of me wants to throw Asmodeus's betrayal in her face to hurt her, but I know better than to show that hand. Even if it would give me immense pleasure. "Despite having a famous gramps, pampered isn't a state I'm familiar with, and you know it. And I don't know exactly how helpful I'll be in a war, as I haven't even graduated yet from the academy. I'm only eighteen, not exactly a hardened warrior like you."

Ishtar's smile is sly. "Well, then you'll just learn to be one, like the good little student I know you to be. Run along now, the Great's patience has limits, and you do try him so." She waves a hand at me, shooing me along like a bothersome fly.

I clench my teeth, wanting to punch her in her smug, beautiful face. Normally, I'd feel guilty about wanting to hit a woman, but considering she could and *would* take my head, I don't feel so bad. Giving her a tight nod, I start to walk toward the citadel.

"Don't disappoint me, Caleb. I always had such high hopes for you," she calls after me, and I still for a moment. The sugar-coated threat in her voice is clear. She wants me to fall in line and be an obedient servant of Alexander just like she is.

I force a smile on my face and say over my shoulder, "I aim to please."

She inclines her head. "See that you do."

I wonder if Alexander has asked her to keep an eye on me or if she's determined that I don't embarrass her or threaten their mission. Despite the fact that Ishtar is genuinely fond of me, she'd choose Alexander over me in a heartbeat. She's no true ally of mine unless I swallow the Kool-Aid and jump on Team World Domination. I haven't exactly been comfortable here, with Grandfather and Ishtar and their growing list of soldiers, but I haven't felt unsafe before. Until now.

Crossing under a stone arch, I enter the citadel, momentarily shaded from the bright sun as I make my way into the large courtyard. The ancient building still only houses the three of us, but I have no doubt it will be brimming with Nephilim soon. They pop in and out of the Shadow Road, gathering intel for Alexander. I pass a pale woman with ebony hair, her skin moon bright in the sun, and she gives me a respectful nod. I give her an uneasy nod in return, Ishtar's barbed words "pampered prince" echoing in my mind. She got the pampered part wrong, but maybe the prince part wasn't too far off. With the current absence of dear, old Dad, I guess I am next in line to the proverbial throne—at least until Gramps brings my father to heel. I'm heir not by might, but by blood. That sick pool of dread that never dries up in my stomach sloshes around.

I walk through the courtyard and make my way into the receiving hall, an enormous, cool chamber boasting a few of the treasures Alexander collected when he sacked the city of Persepolis, like a colossal stone bull's head that rests behind his makeshift throne. I don't know how he managed to haul it here when he was campaigning, but it sends a clear message of power and authority. Of, *whatever you have, I can take.*

Alexander focuses on me, his mismatched eyes hooded and unreadable. I can't help but think back to Hammurabi's words about the prophecy and Luna. It's been damn difficult to play ignorant these past two weeks. I take my place next to him, surprised to find the room empty.

"Grandfather," I say, inclining my head in deference, keeping my expression carefully blank. I don't want him to know how badly I want to be anywhere but here.

"Ishtar said you wanted me."

"We are going to meet a special guest today, Grandson," he says, a cold smile cutting across his face.

"I hope it's Luna," I reply, unable to help myself. I bite my tongue until I taste copper when I see his eyes fill with rage.

An invisible force bats my face, and my knees hit stone. I wipe my fingers under my nose, and they come away glistening with blood. Shit that hurt. I earned that. Me and my stupid mouth. I'm actually shocked Gramps was so restrained.

Alexander's voice is low, deadly. "Caleb, I thought all that was settled, and you trusted me to retrieve Luna when I decided the time was right."

I lift my chin, meeting his hard eyes and swallow my fear. Alexander won't respect me if I cower, and he'll think it unworthy of a member of his bloodline. "I do trust you, sir. I apologize for my impertinence. It won't happen again." My tone is humble, my gaze direct and reflecting what I hope can pass for sincerity.

His stare feels like a physical weight pressing down on me. Hell, he's an angel, so maybe he can give weight to his dirty looks. And I know that he basically gave me a slap on the wrist, a warning shot across the bow. My nose is already knitting itself together.

"I do not enjoy hurting you, Caleb, but I will if I must. Discipline is necessary, especially in young ones," my grandfather says, and I wince at the disappointment in his voice, which is ludicrous.

I'm mad as hell at him, but some part of me still wants to please him, still wants my grandfather—Alexander the freakin' Great—to be proud of me. I don't like to acknowledge it often, and most of the time I bury it, but man, I have daddy issues, and it's screwing with my head.

"I'm sorry. I know you only want what's best for me," I say, which I know is a lie. He only wants what's best for him.

He tilts his head, his eyes softer as they regard me. "You may not believe this, but I do only want what is best for you, all that this wonderful world has to offer, especially when I set it to right once more."

A chill washes over me at his words. Eager to change the subject, I say, "So, who is this special guest?"

A wolfish grin crosses his lips. "We are going to go see them now."

My eyebrows reach for my hairline. "You're leaving—I mean, we're leaving?"

Alexander has only invited select Dark Nephilim and Fallen here, as the entire Council is out to get him. Those are fourteen badasses not to be fucked with. Grandfather is not exactly jonesing to go out in the world and get caught again, content to bide his time and build his army. Well, content isn't exactly the right word. He's pretty damn twitchy to get the conquering on, but he's a patient man. He's been planning his revenge for literally thousands of years.

Alexander rises and flicks his hand at me, fingers curling. I follow him into a corner the light doesn't reach. I step into the shadows, unsure of our destination, and the secretive smile Alexander wears doesn't make me feel better. I'm tired of secrets and surprises. The path we travel is familiar, but I can't quite place it.

We come out of the Shadow Road into a dimly lit cavernous chamber filled with seemingly endless tall columns, regally marching in perfect rows, reflected in the shallow water they sprout from. The vaulted ceiling and marble columns in the Ionic and Corinthian styles tell me exactly where I am. I even know where to find the Medusa column base.

The Basilica Cistern in Istanbul is usually full of tourists, but today it is eerily empty. I've been to this ancient city loads of times, but I don't generally make it a habit to pop out of the shadows in a heavily visited attraction, though this one happens to be one of my favorites. Why is it empty? Alexander has been hiding out, so he hasn't had time to mentally manipulate an entire tourist office.

I take a deep breath of the musty air and glance around, my vision unaffected by the poor lighting. "How'd you manage to get everyone to stay away? Or is this Ishtar's doing?"

Alexander shoots me an amused look. "It's closed today. Ishtar did not do anything untoward, much to her chagrin."

Well, shit, don't I feel like an idiot. I also wonder what sort of tricks an Ishtar without restraints is getting up to, but my plate is piled to the ceiling, and I can't dish any more problems on it right now.

I look around. We're all alone, no arrogant, deadly goddess in sight. "Where *is* Ishtar?" I just left her not fifteen minutes ago.

As soon as the words leave my mouth, light spills down from above, pooling on the staircase leading out of the cistern. I catch a glimpse of Ishtar's inky hair as she latches onto a tall figure. The door slams shut behind the two of them, and she's whirled around and pressed against the door. Well, we've got a show—now all we need is dinner. The real question is, who's the surprise guest?

As the make-out session grows more heated, I glance at my grandfather, hoping he'll clear his throat or shoot lightning out of his fingertips or something. Watching Ishtar get laid is at the very bottom of my to-do list today. Just as I contemplate drowning myself in the shallow water below, Ishtar breaks away and leads the man downstairs toward where we wait as still as the columns behind us. I arch my brows, shocked, but I really shouldn't be. There in all his holier-than-thou, hypocritical, Light glory is Gilgamesh.

Alexander's wings flare out, the snap of feathers and muscle obscenely loud in the quiet. Gilgamesh startles, his eyes round as he takes in Alexander the Great, and little ol' me, Caleb the adequate, but possibly great if given enough time. I'm great at stepping into major shit I can't seem to get out of, that's for sure.

Gilgamesh's head swivels toward Ishtar, and I see the anger and betrayal flashing on his face like a neon sign in the dark. The shock at my grandfather's wings. I guess the Council managed to keep the fact that Ishtar is a turncoat under tight wraps. At least from the Lights. The Dark rumor mill has been rumbling along.

"Welcome, Gilgamesh, King of Uruk and hero of old," Alexander says, his commanding voice swallowing the emptiness of the enormous cistern and filling it with an unmistakable authority.

Gilgamesh whips back around to face my grandfather, his golden skin ashen. Fear reflects in his eyes. He shakes his head, as if he can't quite figure out what he's seeing, but is resigned to it at the same time.

I forget sometimes that Gilgamesh and Ishtar are older than Alexander. Hell, they're older than dirt, more like primordial slime, but they ain't angels. And while they did rule Mesopotamia for quite some time, they never achieved what Alexander did. They didn't dare.

Ishtar takes Gilgamesh's hand, but he yanks it away. "How could you?" he snarls.

"She could because I asked it of her," Alexander answers for the former goddess, his tone making it clear that he has the greater claim on Ishtar. That *he* has her loyalty.

Gilgamesh bristles but brushes past his lover and descends the final steps to stand before us. "What do you want of me, Conqueror? I thought you were dead. Too bad you didn't remain that way." He stares at the silvery wings on display and shakes his head again. "I forgot what you were…" His laugh drips bitterness. "I suppose I didn't forget, did I?"

Ishtar's voice is equally bitter as she steps up beside Gilgamesh. "No, they didn't want us to remember, my love. Best we forget the Council's dangerous little secret lest we forget our place, forever apart and divided."

"They prefer you divided. You're much less powerful that way," Alexander points out. "I'm a glaring beacon of rebellion, of freedom. Real freedom, not the carefully constructed facade of liberation the Darks present, and certainly not the freedom the Lights try to sell you with the myth of Ascension and the promise of your precious wings. I am a product of both the Dark and the Light, blessed with the abilities of both and none of the preconceived prejudices."

Gilgamesh frowns as he spares me a quick glance. "Caleb, what in the Creator's name are you doing here?"

My smile is all teeth. "What in the Creator's name are *you* doing here, G? I thought you didn't sully yourself with demons." I hear Ishtar's indrawn breath as guilt fills Gilgamesh's face.

Alexander's eyes flick to me for a brief moment before he sneers at Gilgamesh. "The Creator has nothing to do with my grandson. Caleb is no concern of yours. Like Ishtar, he belongs to me. And unlike your fickle Creator, I take care of what is mine. I do not make idle promises I never plan to fulfill just to keep my flock in line like brainless sheep for my own vanity."

A dark flush stains Gilgamesh's cheekbones. Direct hit. Ouch, Gramps just sunk your battleship.

"Ascension is real," he growls. "As is my loyalty to the Creator. I will not succumb to your poison."

I roll my eyes so hard I think I sprain them. The Lights and their pipe dream Ascension.

"Am I poison, King of Uruk?" Ishtar hisses, fingers clenched into fists at her side. "When you make love to me, do you enjoy my sweet sting?"

"Isn't that supposed to be your line?" I say to Gilgamesh then wince as I shoot my grandfather a panicked look, fully expecting to bleed again. I just really can't deal with any more talk of Ishtar's sex life, or I will stick my head in the water. Instead, an amused grin flashes across Alexander's face before he quickly suppresses it.

Gilgamesh glares at me, his jaw so hard you could crack concrete on it. "You should know better than to be here, to be a part of this, Caleb," he squeezes out between clenched teeth. "Despite our philosophical differences, I thought highly of you."

"You mean for a Dark, for a *demon*, I was okay?" I say, my own bitterness leaking out. Everyone at the Serapeum other than Luna treated me like a pile of dog shit they had stepped in. Even the teachers could barely conceal their disdain for me under a thin veneer of politeness.

Ishtar's boo shakes his head. "That's not what I meant." He shoots Ishtar a disdainful look of his own. "Obviously, I don't dislike all Darks, despite their deceptive and self-destructive tendencies."

Ishtar bares her teeth at her lover and takes a step toward him, and I expect an epic battle of the sexes when an invisible force pushes between the two of them, shoving them apart. Hard. Gilgamesh smacks into the metal guard railing with a crunch, and Ishtar skids across the concrete floor, her knees bloodied under her flirty skirt. Alexander pins his second-in-command with a quelling look of disappointment, and she visibly cowers. Wow, that's the first time I've ever seen my proud teacher anything less than brimming with unapologetic arrogance. It doesn't last long. Within seconds, she's back on her feet like a Jack-in-the-box, the wounds on her knees already sealing over. Gilgamesh clutches his ribs but straightens with a grunt.

"I expect such rash behavior from my grandson, goddess of love and war. Not from you." Alexander chides her in such a gentle, fatherly voice, it has to grate on her. He *is* like a thousand years younger than her. He then turns his stern eyes to Gilgamesh. "And you should stop punishing Ishtar for being in love with her just because you're too cowardly to stand up to Gabriel and your other Light brethren."

Damn, Gramps is handing asses out today.

Throwing back her shoulders and swinging her glossy black hair behind her, Ishtar once more looks like the regal badass she's known to be. "Forgive me, Conqueror. When it comes to matters of the heart, I suppose we're all only children."

I glower at her for the dig she throws my way. Pot meet kettle.

"That was unnecessary," Gilgamesh says, "but not surprising that you would choose to control your followers with violence."

Alexander's smile is chilling. "Oh, King, when I choose to get violent, you'll know it. You're a Nephilim and an elite warrior. The little swat I gave you barely slowed you down. The two of you could have easily destroyed this precious piece of history with your foolishness. Such behavior is unbecoming in a hero like yourself. I won't allow either of you to damage such beauty." He throws a hand out, emphasizing the stunning columns surrounding us. "Humans make such wondrous things, though they have gone astray for some time and need a gentle hand to be put on the right path again."

His words bring the queasiness in my stomach back in full force, and Gilgamesh stares at my grandfather in horror. "What do you mean, humans need a gentle hand? What are you planning?"

Alexander folds his wings neatly behind him. "What has your Creator done for humanity lately? Look at them. Look at the Earth. While the Creator makes you abide stringent rules by telling lies, He lets his greatest creation run amok, destroying the planet and each other. Such chaos, civilization hanging on by a ragged thread that is fraying more as we speak. I will not stand by and watch the mortals I love destroy each other. Heaven is not our home, Gilgamesh. Earth is. We were meant to rule it. To help the mortals flourish and achieve greatness. As a being born of the Dark and the Light, *I* was meant to rule it. I'm the only one who can."

Hammurabi's words echo through my mind like a gong. Gramps has one big, raging Messiah complex. Oh, and what about Goldilocks? You know, the other Gray who threatens Alexander's special snowflake status. Wouldn't that mean *she's* meant to rule as well? Alexander doesn't seem like the sharing sort, but I have no doubt he's not above using Luna to get what he wants. Is he going to claim she's his true heir? If he hadn't been rotting in an underground tomb for millennia, I'd have a real fear Luna and I are related, but I know that's impossible, so he's got to come up with some explanation when she surfaces. And by the Morningstar, she will surface. I have to make that happen or die trying.

Gilgamesh sneers. "If you're meant to rule, wouldn't I just be exchanging one master for another? Instead of endless servitude toward the Creator, am I to come to you on my knees and pledge fealty to you so you can use me in your war? And if we win and you take your throne, what spoils could you possibly bestow upon me that are worth more than my wings?"

Alexander's laugh is cruel. "Anything on this Earth is worth more than your wings. If the Creator desired to reward you with Ascension, he would've done it millennia ago." Then he says in a much kinder voice, "Release this illusion, throw off your chains, and be free, Gilgamesh. I neither want a slave, nor a servant. I want a warrior with a true heart who cares for these mortals as I do. A warrior who knows this divide must be bridged for the good of the world."

I mull my grandfather's words over in my head as I shoot a discreet look at Ishtar. I know Alexander loves her, values her, but I don't think he believes she's his equal. Though he might not refer to her as a servant, she serves, whether she likes it or not. Whether she'll admit it or not. Not that I don't believe Gramps will reward her if he does conquer the world. I'm sure she'll get a nice little fiefdom where she can rule as she sees fit. And as much as I love her, that thought isn't a comforting one. Ishtar needs checks and balances.

Gilgamesh twists his mouth into a scowl but studies Alexander for a moment. Shit, he can't really be thinking about switching sides, can he? Not with that permanent stick up his ass.

"I will admit the divide is…burdensome." His eyes dart to Ishtar, and despite the fact I know he's furious with her, his face slightly softens. "But our goals are so different, our natures so at odds, I don't know how you can bridge that chasm." Gilgamesh glances at me. "Even the way we teach history to our young ones isn't the same. They've been bred to despise each other. Caleb knows this."

I shrug a shoulder, uncomfortable. "I don't know if I was *bred* to hate the Lights," I protest, and Gilgamesh gives me a withering look. I blow out a sigh. "Fine, I wasn't taught to love them, either. But honestly, if any of them had ever been nice to me— other than Luna—I would've been nice back."

Maybe. Okay, I was a dick to Luna at first because I thought she was playing some cruel joke on me, but I apologized and got over myself. But Gilgamesh has a legit point. We are taught that Lights despise us, thinking they're better, but we all have to get along for the sake of the world. Before Luna, I probably wouldn't have pissed on a Light if they were on fire.

Gilgamesh snorts, clearly not buying it, but he admits, "Luna is different, but only because she came to us late." I wonder why he doesn't react to Luna being missing for almost five months. What excuse did the Council make up for her absence?

Alexander frowns, and I know he wants to take the focus off Luna and fast, which only makes unease blow up in my stomach. It's not that I don't think my grandfather won't use Luna for his world-domination plot—he will—but how long does he plan on letting her rot in the meantime? And how is he going to fit another Gray into the narrative he's weaving like a true bullshit artist? I might get both legs broken if I reveal the fact that Luna is a Gray to Gilgamesh, so I decide to be smart for once and shut up.

"Remember the age you flourished in, Gilgamesh? The Bronze Age?" Alexander asks, and I stare at him, surprised by the change in subject. "What do historians call it now, the empires and cities that ruled then—the Club of Great Powers? The first attempt at globalization, when Egypt was in full bloom and Babylon was a jewel of learning and culture. When trade and language and prosperity flourished. When different kingdoms depended on one another in an intricate system."

Gilgamesh gives him a puzzled look. "Yes, I'm intimately acquainted with that time period."

Alexander's smile is calculating. "Doesn't this time period remind you of that glorious age before its collapse into darkness?"

Startling, Gilgamesh sends Ishtar a questioning look, but she simply shrugs. "You know it does if you search your soul."

"Caleb," my grandfather says, demanding my attention. I focus on him, unsure of what exactly is happening. "Let us have a history lesson, shall we?"

I give a slow nod, hoping this somehow doesn't end up with me bloody again. I straighten up like a good little show Poodle.

"What brought about the collapse of the Bronze Age, Caleb?" Alexander asks, watching Gilgamesh.

"Um, let me think." Thank the Morningstar they drill ancient history into our heads at Babel. I hold up a hand and tick off a finger. "Climate change. Natural disasters," I say, ticking off another finger. "Internal rebellions, political instability, and invasions…" All my fingers are down, and I see his point. Well, shit.

So does Gilgamesh. "Yes, the similarities are striking," he admits, glancing at Ishtar again.

Her smile is feline. "Indeed. The humans are pushing themselves into another dark age, only this time with their advancements in technology, it might be permanent. They've already caused a mass extinction with their selfish behavior."

"If I don't step in," Alexander says. "If *we* don't step in." His face is grave as he regards Gilgamesh. Grave and kingly. "You know I speak the truth, dear friend. And you know you were destined for more than just hiding in the shadows. You're half mortal. Will you ignore their silent cries and leave them to their fate? Will you ignore their pleas when you know you could aid them?"

My heart sinks as the last of Gilgamesh's indignation falls from his face. He looks at Alexander with a thoughtful expression. A minute ticks by and then another. And when he opens his mouth, I know he's drunk the Kool-Aid.

"I loved my mortal father," he says, his expression mournful. "He taught me everything about being a warrior, a king. I watched him die, his body shriveling like worn papyrus folding in on itself. I was only allowed so many years to rule, to be a hero. My place was with the Lights—so I was repeatedly reminded. I've always… regretted it. What could I have accomplished if I hadn't been forced to fade away like my father?"

Ishtar steps closer to him but doesn't touch him. "Great things, my love. And you can still achieve great things."

Alexander lets his wings flare out in a casual display of power, and Gilgamesh traces the pewter feathers with his eyes. "Greatness is in our blood," my grandfather says. "We must stop denying it. Join us, Gilgamesh, and save humanity and build a perfect, new world."

A sudden fervor flares in Gilgamesh's eyes, making him look like a zealot, and I know we're up shit creek without a paddle. Although it hurts like hell to admit it, blood or not, I don't belong with my grandfather. I don't believe in this war. I just want Luna back and Alexander stopped before he decimates half the planet. But everyone here punches above my weight class, and I have to get to Hammurabi again. I need all the help I can get to save Luna and humanity.

SIX

LUNA

I PACE BACK AND forth, clipping my thumbnail between my chattering teeth. In all the time I've been trapped in this place, I've never felt more on the brink of losing touch with my sanity than I do at this moment. Time drags, indiscernible and gnawing, each second bleeding into the next and yet never moving at all. Sleep evades me now as my conversation with Gabriel replays in my head in a constant loop, tormenting me with questions, which pile onto the many mysteries already plaguing my thoughts. But it wasn't real. *She* wasn't real.

And I fear I have truly lost my mind.

I drag my hands through my sweaty hair, my nails scraping over my scalp, my feet following the same path they have for the last however many minutes, hours, days, or weeks it's been since my encounter with the imagined manifestation of my mother. With every passing moment, the similarities between this place and the padded room at the hospital grow stronger, clearer, until I begin to wonder if they aren't actually the same place. If Gabriel wasn't real, then maybe none of this is. Maybe I've been in that claustrophobic room this whole time, trapped in a world of my own creation. A world where there was some explanation for why I am the way I am. A world where I could have a taste of the relationships I've always desired and then have them torn away because it's what I deserve.

A world where I can continue to punish myself for every horrible thing I've done.

I push my wings out and then draw them back into my skin again, clenching my teeth at the pain. This searing, raw agony certainly *feels* real…

I waver, torn between the idea that this is all actually happening and I will be imprisoned forever and the only slightly more palatable thought that everything I've experienced these past months was an elaborate delusion and I've finally completed my descent into madness. Neither option makes me feel any better, and both wear my already frail mental state thin. So, I force myself to consider the third option—the option that threatens to rip my splintered heart into two pieces, severing the few flimsy threads holding the remnants together. If the Gabriel I encountered here wasn't a fabrication of my unhinging mind, then it seems the Council has grown tired of imprisoning me without something to show for their efforts. It means my own mother is willing to work with the people harming me just to save herself.

No. No, it *couldn't* have been her. The realization I witnessed spreading over her face is razor sharp in my mind as I recall our last moments together. *"Your father is the Morningstar,"* she said, her voice laced with a surprise that continues to baffle me. She didn't know about my father. But how could that be if Gabriel is my mother?

Unless she isn't, the voice of doubt murmurs. *Unless there's some other reason you were able to open Alexander's tomb.*

Or maybe you're just trying to make me second-guess everything I think I know, I counter.

A venomous growl burns my airways, and I suppress the growing urge to scream. I don't even know what's true anymore. I'm certain Lucifer is my father—I felt the truth of our connection in my blood. But Gabriel…her blood never spoke to mine. All I ever experienced in her presence was a crippling sense of forced loyalty. A loyalty I didn't feel when I saw her here, much to my bewilderment. Of course, that could boil down to our degrading relationship and the fact I no longer *want* to please her or, the more likely reason, because it wasn't really her. That what I saw was all in my head.

A low laugh breaches my lips. Even if I did know anything about Alexander, I'm not sure the Council would be wise to believe a word I say. I can't discern what's real and what's not, and doubt is my ever-present companion, confusing my memories and making me question everything I thought I knew about my life and this world. There is only one thing I know with absolute certainty. Real or not, Alexander left me behind. Caleb left me behind, just like everyone in my life always has. Because—

"I am nothing," I whisper.

"Except a Gray," a ringing voice chimes in.

An exhalation punches from my lungs as I spin around, my unfocused gaze searching for the source of this new interruption to my otherwise solitary existence. I half-expect to see Uriel there, ready to once again attempt to prod me for information I don't have. Instead—

My eyes blow wide.

"Hello again, Daughter," Lucifer says soothingly. His golden hair shines like the morning sun, and dark tendrils lick over his skin in greeting, his aura the same as the last time I saw it, bringing me a momentary sense of comfort and ease until I notice the absence of sound between us. Where I expect to hear that familiar call, that ethereal melodic hum in my blood, there is nothing.

Only inexplicable silence.

"You—" The word sticks in my throat, distorted by the threat of tears, and it takes every logical thought I still possess to remind myself this is a lie. Just like Gabriel, this isn't real. *He* isn't real. "You aren't really him. You're just in my head."

If he was here, wouldn't I feel him? The one and only time we met, our blood announced its connection in an enchanting melody, the vibrations of which I felt right down to my marrow, like strings plucked on a harp made of my tendons and bones. Now that we're together again, wouldn't his blood sing to mine like it did then? Or does such a connection only occur once—upon initial meeting—never to be heard again? If so, maybe that's why I never felt Gabriel. If it *is* a singular, one-time event, then her blood would've sung to mine when I was born—too new to the world to retain any recollection of that moment. Or of her when our paths eventually crossed again.

A flicker of indecision crosses the Morningstar's face, the luminescent golden curls crowning his head bobbing slightly when he lifts his chin. "I assure you I am as physically present as you are."

"No." I shake my head. "She wasn't real and neither are you. You're a figment created to torment me, just like Gabriel."

Because if he *is* here, that means he betrayed me, too, and I'm not sure I can handle that.

He did hand you over to the Council, that small voice in the back of my head reminds me.

"Gabriel?" Lucifer sputters her name as if he hasn't heard it spoken aloud in centuries. "Dear child, the Messenger is not here. I'm afraid no one among the Fallen or Faithful alike has any inkling where she is."

So, it wasn't her. As that realization sinks in, I find myself torn between relief and bitter disappointment—relief that my own mother didn't turn on me like I feared and disappointment that she didn't even try to come for me. That she fled the Council at the first opportunity. That she saved herself and didn't look back. And why would she? She didn't want me when I was born. She has no reason to want me now, especially after what I did.

If the Council went to such extreme lengths to secure Alexander, what chaos have I unleashed on the world by freeing him? I never allowed this thought to fully form before now, too much of a coward to take responsibility for my actions and face my own culpability. But now, it hangs on every breath I draw, gripping my conscience with guilt.

Heart racing, I stare up at Lucifer, trying my best not to quiver under his scrutiny. The cold-edged detachment in every word he utters is mirrored in those brilliant blue eyes, which pin me in place, paralyzing my body. This is nothing like how he spoke to me at the Serapeum, the tenderness in his voice supplanted now by what could almost be mistaken for disdain. But for whom? For me? Or for Gabriel?

The answer doesn't seem to matter, and as my belief that he's just another hallucination begins to weaken, I can't help spitting out, "Messenger? Is that how you refer to a woman you once loved?" *Or at least liked enough to sleep with,* I refrain from adding. "The woman you share a child with?"

But as these words leave me, doubt encroaches again, and I wonder if I'm wrong about everything. If Gabriel isn't my mother at all.

But Lucifer doesn't deny my accusation, cementing what I've suspected since the Council put the thought in my head. That despite the missing blood song between us, Gabriel really is my mother. Instead, he lets out a stony laugh. "How little you understand about our world."

I balk at his callous tone and take a reflexive step backward, pressing my back to the glass wall behind me. Is this really the same person who held me in his arms and promised to find me again? He wears my father's face but the cruelty I find in his features is unrecognizable.

This isn't real. He isn't real, I remind myself, but at the same moment, that nagging voice of doubt purrs in my ear, *He didn't need to find you because he always knew exactly where you were.*

Nausea twists my stomach in knots. Lucifer is on the Council—I gathered as much from the interaction I witnessed between him and the Archangels and other Archdemons who were present that day under the school. But could he be working *with* them, like I worried Gabriel was?

Did he help them put me in this cage?

Chest heaving, I watch, panic swelling in my ribcage, as the Morningstar folds his hands behind his waist. "Gabriel went against no one for my sake, that much I know. After the Fall, we went our separate ways. The Fallen took our desired places on Earth, enjoying the freedoms we yearned for and went to war over while the Faithful remained by the Creator's side, always his dutiful servants. Gabriel more so than the others."

A breath catches in my throat, and my pulse skitters under my skin as that daunting revelation I keep coming back to presses at the edge of my thoughts again, screaming for me to finally accept it. If what I'm hearing right now is true, that would mean my parents conceived me before the Fall. Before the angels' war. A war my father started.

Confusion scratches at the scattering pieces of my mind. *That can't be right,* I assure myself, repeating the excuse I've always countered this idea with every other time it's surfaced since I was imprisoned. *I'm seventeen. Only seventeen.* The vivid memory of my terrible childhood solidifies that certainty, so either Lucifer is lying and he and Gabriel were consorting long after the divide was established, or she found some way to…what? Delay my birth? I guess anything is possible when you can wield magic, but surely someone—Faithful, Fallen, or Nephilim—would've noticed a pregnant Archangel. The alternative is that I'm wrong about everything and she didn't give birth to me seventeen years ago. In which case…when the hell was I born? Why am I not older if I am actually *older?*

And if I was conceived before the divide was erected, before the Lights and Darks took on the form of their choice during the Fall, then why am I a Gray? Before free will transformed the Fallen into Darks, wouldn't all the angels have been Lights, reflecting their pure allegiance to the Creator? Or were they something else altogether? Hell, maybe they weren't even that different to Grays, the irony of which is far from lost on me given my current predicament.

The thought of Grays steers my mind in another direction, down a path I've never wandered before. Was Gabriel the reason Lucifer defied the Creator? If so, the hypocrisy she displayed in regards to my friendship with Caleb makes perfect sense. Considering which side Gabriel chose in the Great Battle, it's no wonder she didn't approve of us mixing. Maybe she didn't only see her past with Lucifer reflected in our budding relationship, but feared history itself would be repeated in some destructive, sweeping way, and she'd be helpless to stop it.

If Alexander is as dangerous as I'm beginning to think, then I suppose she was right to worry. After all, it was our friendship that led to his freedom.

Shaking off that thought, I stare hard at…my father? Or yet another hallucination wearing his face, just like the one of my mother? He stares at me like a hawk watching a mouse, waiting for the perfect moment to strike—or in this case, for me to break the lengthy silence. The appraising way he looks at me reminds me of the doctors I encountered at the hospital, of the psychiatrist I was forced to speak with on a near daily basis to try to get to the bottom of my unforgivable actions. Of the crimes which landed me in there to begin with. There's a sense of perception and curiosity behind his gaze but little else. Certainly none of the warmth I glimpsed in those startling blue depths when we met.

"If you had known—" The words tumble out of me of their own volition, my desperation for validation—for the parental love I've been deprived of since birth—like fingers tightening around my throat. I flinch, wincing at the crack in my voice before clearing it, but I can't seem to bring myself to finish the thought. *If you had known about me, would you have abandoned me, too?*

He considers me for a moment, his brow pinching then easing again as understanding takes shape in his eyes. "If I had known," he growls, flattening his palm to the glass, "do you believe I would've allowed you to be an orphan? I would've claimed you, and you would've stood at my side as you truly are—not a half-mortal child but an angel worthy of deference. Luna Morningstar, my daughter and the heir to my legacy."

Luna Morningstar…

Strange, that in all the time I've been here—however long that's been, given the way time seems to work in this dimension—I've never once thought of myself with that moniker. Even knowing who my parents are, I've never seen myself as anyone other than this broken, only partially-filled shell of a person, still human in so many ways. I was empty before I met Caleb, and I was only just beginning to grow accustomed to life as a Nephilim before the revelation of my real heritage was dropped onto my head like a bomb. How could I have ever considered my identity as a Morningstar when I can barely embrace myself as an angel?

"But I'm a Gray," I protest, recoiling from his words despite how much I wish them to be true. "My very existence is sacrilege in the eyes of your kind."

Lucifer scoffs. "The Fallen are more forgiving of what our kind would deem forbidden transgressions than our Faithful brethren. We don't take kindly to orders from others, one of many differences between the Lights and the Darks."

This comment triggers a memory—when Caleb told me he'd take me back to Babel with him once I helped him free his grandfather. I remember contemplating how that would work, but he seemed so certain of the Darks, that they would accept me as one of their own without hesitation, regardless of my Light blood. Now, I can't help wondering if he was blinded by his own acceptance of me and by his fear of losing the friendship we both held onto so tightly. After witnessing what I did in Alexandria—the debate among the Council over my part in Alexander's escape—I can see now what would have really awaited once the truth of what I am got out. It didn't matter what Caleb said. He's just a Nephilim while far more powerful figures dictate our every move and fate.

To them, a prison is the only place I belong.

Unease tightens in my stomach like an overwound coil. "And now?" I manage, the words a mere whisper.

"I would've claimed you, and you would've stood at my side..."

Is there any hope for such a thing to still happen?

His gaze softens. "That depends on what you do next."

Sweat breaks out across my skin, and my heart thunders in my ears in anticipation of what he'll say—of what inevitable demand he'll make of me on behalf of the Council. Because that's what this is: a negotiation. I see that clearly now.

"Luna." The golden-rimmed azure of his irises seems to sparkle as he leans in, bringing his face so close to the glass I can make out every detail of his features with ease. Every sharp plane. Every speck of light in his eyes. "How long have you known?"

Fear is a lump in my throat, suffocating me. *Known?* "Known what?" I rasp.

"Your parentage," he answers, almost barking the words. "When did the Messenger reveal the truth to you, Daughter? Just how long have the two of you known and been conspiring against the rest of our kind?"

Shock tears the air from my lungs. Conspiring? Is that really what the Council believes happened? Does Lucifer really think I'm capable of such a thing?

Why wouldn't he? that voice of doubt retorts. *He doesn't know you...and you don't know him.*

You're right, I realize, gaping at my father, my eyes darting between each of his, noting the lack of affection I glimpsed the day we met. Could this really be the same man who tried to stand between me and the Archangels and Archdemons he considered his brothers and sisters? The same man who once started a war over a desire for free will and, after what I witnessed between him and Gabriel when he came to her aid under the Serapeum, perhaps even over the freedom to love? *I don't know him at all.*

"The Council is willing to be merciful," he continues, but his voice barely penetrates the distress rooting me in place. "Tell me this and you can go free."

"I-I didn't," I stammer, fumbling over my protest. "I had no idea who either of you were to me until that day. Gabriel...she had nothing to do with what happened." He snorts, unconvinced, and I snap, "This isn't some conspiracy. Gabriel told me next to nothing in the few months I knew her. I don't think she knew who I was, either.

Suspected it, maybe, but if she did know, she never said anything. Not to me, at least. And we certainly never worked together to free Alexander or *conspire* against the rest of our kind."

Lucifer's irises darken to a startling black, like shadows melting through a thick sheet of ice. "You expect me to believe that you did not recognize your own mother? That her blood fails to call out to yours or yours to hers? That is not possible."

He doesn't comment on the lack of our own bond song, perhaps hoping I won't notice it's missing or I'm too ignorant of our species to question the change. But I do notice, and his words are enough to answer one of the many mysteries pestering me, finally giving me clarity on at least one matter.

"You mean," I begin, my own voice a tremulous whisper now, "like how yours is supposed to be calling to mine?"

His eyes flash. "Your prison nullifies such magic, so I am not surprised you do not hear the call of my blood. You may not feel it, Daughter, but I assure you, *I* do."

Despite the vehemence of his tone—the forced conviction I sense behind every syllable—the subtle way his lips twitch at the corners is all the confirmation I need. He's lying. He doesn't feel the song between us because it isn't there. Because this isn't happening.

Because he isn't here.

"You're lying. This isn't real. *You* aren't real."

"I already told you—"

"The last thing you said to me..." I hesitate, my breath hanging on the knife's edge of the question that will confirm my suspicions once and for all. "Back at the Serapeum. What was it?"

"I..." He pauses, clearing his throat, then shakes his head. "I cannot recall."

Because you aren't him.

As if reading my thoughts, the hallucination masquerading as my father pulls his hand away from the glass, leaving behind a fogged, opaque impression. Then, with an exasperated sigh, he shutters his eyes and takes several steps away from my cage, the mist shrouding his body until all trace of his black clothes and golden hair is lost in a rising sea of white. When the fog settles once more, as expected, all I find where he stood before is empty air.

My wings tense around me as I inch toward the wall where the imprint of his hand remains, printed into the glass like a scorch mark. Holding my breath, I press my fingertips against the ghostly stain of his, remembering the last words my real father said to me before the Council brought me here to inflict their punishment.

"I will find you again, Daughter. I promise."

"No," I murmur, my wings going slack as the imprint fades and I slump to my knees, my body suddenly weak. My hand falls away from the glass, limp at my side, as a tear drips down my cheek. "You won't."

SEVEN

CALEB

THE SHADOW ROAD DIRECTLY into Babel is well-traveled, so I have to find a path that's less obvious. More human, like playing tourist as I stare at the ruins of Babylon, the Tower of Babel standing out like a beacon. My aviators beat back the glaring sun as does the baseball cap with a Yankees logo shadowing my sunglasses. My vanity protests at the cap and the fact that it makes me look blatantly American, which should be suspicious to any local paying attention. Not many American civilians flock to Iraq these days for vacation. However, my mom is Iranian, so I guess I don't look too out of place. Who am I kidding? I have Westerner stamped all over me. Ugh, fuck hats, my locks need to roam free. I might be one of the few dudes on the planet who feels that way.

Out of patience and fucks to give, I sent my little clay golem to pester Hammurabi, who agreed to meet me out here and then take me to see Asmodeus, which makes me twitchy. I'm not quite sure I can trust the Archdemon. With stopping Alexander, sure, but with Luna? My gut roils, but I'm out of options.

"Nice hat," a deep voice drawls behind me.

I whip around from my inspection of Ishtar's gate to find Hammurabi watching me with an amused expression. I should've recognized that baritone, but I'm on edge and jumpier than a virgin on prom night. Not that I know what that's like. Nephilim don't do prom, and I lost my virginity at the tender age of fourteen.

I touch the brim of my cap in mock salute, my shaggy hair clinging to my damp skin. "They're not just for Americans anymore," I protest.

"Of course not. I have a closet full of them," the Babylonian king shoots back.

I snort despite my tension. The thought of Hammurabi wearing a cap with a sports logo is so ridiculous I want to laugh aloud. The king has modernized, but judging by the length of his beard, not that much.

His face darkens, like an eclipse over the sun, wiping away his humor. "You've risked much, Caleb, to come here. I have no news of your Luna."

Well, that sucks. I take a deep breath. "We'll get to that in a minute. Shit just hit the fan," I say.

One black brow arches. "Young one, 'shit hit the fan,' as you so charmingly put it the moment you helped release Alexander into the world," Hammurabi growls.

I resist the urge to flinch, squaring my shoulders. "Yeah, yeah, I suck. We've been over this, okay? Let's focus on the here and now. I need Asmodeus's help, and I have info she needs about Alexander."

Hammurabi gives me an assessing look, his dark eyes slicing into me like a scalpel trying to cut to my true intentions. "You've chosen to leave your grandfather then?"

I ignore the bitter concoction brewing in my gut as I willingly turn my back on my blood. Yeah, I've chosen a side. Luna's. I have to get her back. And Armageddon isn't my idea of a good time. Mortals will die, mortals like Mom. I can't let that happen.

"Yes," I say, knowing once I meet with Asmodeus and convince her to help me, there's no turning back. I *can't* go back to the citadel. Alexander will know I betrayed him, and he'll send Ishtar on the hunt if I step one foot in Afghanistan. I try not to piss my pants at the thought of the goddess of love and war coming for me.

A look of pride spreads on Hammurabi's face, making me feel reassured about my decision. He's trained me well. He and Ishtar. I can handle my shit.

"Come, Caleb, let's get you inside before someone recognizes you," he says, touching my arm and pulling me into a shadow and right into Asmodeus's office.

It's a neat trick—one I would've used if I knew how. Students aren't exactly privy to the direct route leading to our headmistress's office. And to be honest, Asmodeus, like all the Archdemons and Archangels, is intimidating as hell. Earth-shattering power sheathed within a stunningly beautiful shell. I was always on her radar for being top of my class, and that's all I wanted to be on her radar for. Definitely not for breaking Alexander the Great out of his prison and helping to start a war, with her best friend, no less.

I focus on Asmodeus, my nerves prickling in fear and anticipation. The Archdemon sits on a settee that looks like it belongs in a swords-and-sandals epic. The delicate legs are gilded with golden lion heads carved into the wood in the Babylonian fashion. Her red hair holds none of the orange notes from a fire. It's the color of garnets, gleaming and otherworldly. Cat-green eyes lined with citrus stare at me, uncomfortably blank. I can't get a read on her, and I flick my gaze away first, acknowledging her dominance.

"Caleb," she greets me in her smoky voice, the light rasp making the hairs on the back of my neck stand at attention. "You've been a very naughty boy." The words are light but devoid of humor.

I swallow, my throat suddenly dry. I say the only thing I can. "I'm sorry… I didn't fully understand the situation. He's my grandfather—my blood—and I—" I clamp my mouth shut. Asmodeus isn't interested in my babbling reasons. I broke the Conqueror out of prison, and no excuse in the world will make up for that.

But she surprises me by saying, "Yes, I understand the pull of blood, especially for you." Her words make me feel raw, like my daddy issues are on display for her to dissect. "And I know how persuasive Ishtar can be." Those last words are hissed, like a spitting cat with its back arched and fangs bared.

Glancing back up, I meet her eyes. They are no longer cold and blank, the bright green reflecting anger and bitter disappointment. I've been so busy with Gramps and trying to find out where the hell Luna is that I haven't given much thought to how betrayed Asmodeus must feel by Ishtar. They're besties, for the Morningstar's sake. To stab an Archdemon in the back is no small feat. Ishtar better hope Alexander can protect her from Asmodeus or that she never runs into the Archdemon on the Shadow Road.

"Ishtar talks a good game, and I probably never would have gone after Grandfather if she hadn't suggested it," I admit, but I can't totally throw my mentor under the bus. "But in the end, I wanted it just as badly as she did. He's Alexander the fucking Great. It wasn't that hard to convince me."

No, she didn't have to persuade me too much to go to the Serapeum, but to involve Luna… That was the hard sell and she managed, to my lasting regret. My mouth tightens and I look away.

As if Asmodeus reads my thoughts, she asks, "And the girl? The Gray?" Her voice lingers on the last word.

"Luna is innocent in all this," I say, voice hard. "She didn't know what she was really getting into, and I…I should have never asked her to help me."

A sudden thought hits me. I've been so busy trying to get myself out of the quicksand of shit I willingly jumped into that I've missed the obvious. If I had never gotten Luna involved with this madness, would she have ever found out she was an angel? And a Gray, at that. I seriously doubt it. The parents who abandoned her didn't seem too concerned about her celestial status. And they were complete dumbasses, too. Letting an *angel* out in the world, believing they were human. Of course, Luna dished out some accidental damage, and of course, she feels horrible for it. I'd like to use my special angel-killing knife and take a pound of flesh from her mom and dad for what they put her through.

Asmodeus arches a perfect brow. "How long did you know she was a Gray?"

Startled, I glance at Hammurabi. I explained all this to him already, and I know he passed it on to his boss. "For a hot second. I didn't even know Grays existed." I don't mention that Luna could see the Enochian under the Serapeum when I couldn't and that should have made my Spidey-senses tingle. "I didn't know she was an angel until Grandfather brought her wings out. Shit, I didn't know *Alexander* was an angel, either." I nod to the Babylonian king, standing at attention at the Archdemon's side, face wiped clean of emotion. "I've told him all this already."

Asmodeus frowns, and the temperature noticeably drops a few degrees. I suppress a shiver. "And you'll tell me. Everything. *Now.*"

I spill my guts again, this time adding on details about Gramps's plan, pausing before I say, "Lilith is on board and so is…Gilgamesh."

Asmodeus's eyebrows reach for the sky, and shock erases all that stoicism on Hammurabi's face. "Because of Ishtar," Asmodeus says, and it's not a question.

"That's part of it," I say. "But he honestly believes in Grandfather's mission statement. He resents being forced into retirement and watching his golden age be destroyed. He thinks history is repeating itself, and Alexander can save us all."

Asmodeus's eyes flick up to Hammurabi. "A true believer."

"That's dangerous," Hammurabi answers. "If one Light falls, then—"

"Others are sure to follow," she says, her eyes pinning me in place. "And you, Caleb? Are you a true believer?"

I take a deep breath, knowing that after what I say next, I won't ever be welcome at family holidays again. "No, I'm not. If Alexander starts a war, millions of mortals will die in the crossfire. The Earth as we know it will be destroyed. We can't let that happen."

Her bright green eyes study me. "And the girl? Luna?"

My chest tightens. No way am I abandoning Luna. I'll go at it on my own if I have to. "She's innocent in all this. I don't care if she's a Gray. That's not her fault. She's a good person. I won't let the Council do to Luna what you did to Alexander. She's not like him, and if you plan on keeping her locked away, I will switch sides again. Yeah, Gramps wants to use her, but at least she'll be free."

I know challenging an Archdemon and Hammurabi is a stupid move, but I can't help it. If they don't kill me or lock me up, I'll go running back to Gramps and beg him on hands and knees to free Luna, feeding him lies that I can convince her to help win his war. Anything to save her if Asmodeus won't help me.

"You'd aid the Great in conquering the world just to free the girl?" Asmodeus asks and Hammurabi scowls.

I glare at her. "She's an angel," I hiss. "Your equal. I'd lie, cheat, and kill to right this wrong. And I'm ashamed as a Dark that you would strip someone of freedom just because of what they are. You of all people should be on her side!" The last words echo around the stone walls of her office, and I flinch. Screaming at her will only get me killed. But I'm so tired of this hypocritical bullshit from my Dark brethren.

The silence stretches between us, and I glance at Asmodeus, wanting to face my beating head on. To my shock, she wears a pleased grin, as if I've passed some test. Hammurabi looks as confused as I feel, his fists clenched at his side.

"Stand down, King," she says, placing a delicate hand on his muscular forearm. He might look stronger, but I know her pretty hand could snap him like a twig. "I, too, have an interest in Luna. I do not wish to entomb her as we did Alexander—"

"But the prophecy—" Hammurabi begins.

"Alexander is the Gray in the prophecy, King. I feel it in my very bones. Luna won't be a part of it unless we allow it, unless we allow Alexander to capture her before we do. And can we trust what the Messenger told us about the prophecy?" She purses her lips, glancing at me and Hammurabi and I frown, wondering why she wouldn't trust Gabriel's word.

"Two Grays are very dangerous. We barely survived one," Hammurabi argues, and I bristle at his unforgiving tone.

Asmodeus goes icy again, and my breath clouds in front of me. "Did we create Alexander with our fear of the prophecy? Shall we do the same to Luna? We have an opportunity here to right so many wrongs, Hammurabi. She can be the bridge to unite us, not the wall to divide us, like the Conqueror."

I raise a hand. "To be fair, Gramps wants the divide gone, too."

Asmodeus's eyes narrow to slits. "Oh, yes, he does. He also wants to subjugate us all to his rule when that divide falls, because he knows best." She gives a disdainful snort. "And he criticizes the Creator for being overbearing and arrogant. He thinks it's his right to rule us."

I shrug, conceding her point. "So if you don't want to imprison Luna, you'll help me?" Hope begins to fill my chest. Asmodeus actually has the power to get me to Goldilocks. Then I frown. "Don't get me wrong, I'm grateful to have you on my side, but aren't you on Team Council? Didn't you help put Luna away? Why the sudden change of heart? What's in it for you?"

Asmodeus regards me for a moment, as if choosing her words carefully. "I understand why you'd be suspicious, but my intentions are good. I'm doing a favor for a friend. I want to see Luna reunited with her parents."

My eyes round. I guess that means the Archdemon knows who Luna's parents are, but I wonder how that's possible if Goldilocks being a Gray is such a big no-no. I hear a soft rap on the door, and I jerk my head around so fast I almost give myself whiplash. Fear tightens my chest as I wonder if Asmodeus has been sweet-talking me while alerting the Council.

"Ah, the cavalry has arrived," the Archdemon says, her smile saucy. Hammurabi scowls, and she pats his arm as if she's reassuring a child, not a nearly four-thousand-year-old badass. "None of that, King, all will be well. We need Luna. Enter," she commands.

A tall stranger walks into the room. He's Nephilim, that I'm sure of, and a powerful one at that. He's also a…Light. What the actual fuck? Cool, collected Hammurabi snarls at the man, who just returns a serene smile to the pissy king. Calmness radiates from his amber eyes, and his angular features are perfectly relaxed, as if he enters Dark strongholds on a regular basis. He turns his gaze on me, and instantly I feel my tension seep from my muscles.

Suspicion grips me as I stare at the Light. I don't appreciate this manufactured calm, and I bare my teeth at him.

"Caleb," Asmodeus snaps, and I tear my gaze away from the stranger to focus on her. "That's no way to treat a guest, especially one who wants to aid you. Alaric, thank you for coming."

I arch a disbelieving eyebrow. Alaric stares at me with those knowing eyes, searching for something.

"You must be Alexander's grandson," he says. "You smell like him."

I reel back, blinking.

Asmodeus smiles. "Alaric tracks down Nephilim for Gabriel. He's a regular bloodhound for our Light colleagues." The last words hold a shade of malice.

Okay, so we're on the same side but not friends. "Why would you help me?" I demand, knowing I'm likely to get a slap down from Asmodeus, but to my shock, Hammurabi jumps rank and says, "I'd like to know the same thing."

Frost bites my hand and I shudder, looking down at fingers gone blue with cold. My skin looks dead. Hammurabi isn't much better off, but he still glares defiantly at Asmodeus.

Alaric's lilting voice cuts in, "Don't punish them on my account. It's really not necessary."

I can't place his accent, which means he's old. Really old.

Asmodeus smirks at him. "Dear Alaric, it's not just for you. I despise bad manners, and guest rites must be upheld."

I can no longer feel my right arm, and I don't have the time or fortitude to get into a pissing contest with Asmodeus.

"I'm sorry I was a dick," I say to Alaric. He shoots me an amused grin.

"I apologize, son of Michael," Hammurabi says, suspicion heavy on his face. "It's been an age since you've associated with Darks."

Whoa, this guy is *Michael's* son? As in the Archangel Alexander killed? He must hate my grandfather. Then again, I wouldn't blink an eye if my pops gave up the ghost.

"I'm never as far away as you think," Alaric answers, and there's this weird tension that passes through the three of them that I don't understand. Does Alaric have his memories back now, too? Did someone on the Light side do a wipe like Hammurabi did? "None of that matters now. Luna is what I've come for."

I can't keep my trap shut. "Why?" I ask again, my tone more subdued so I get to keep my fingers. "I'm not trying to be an asshole, but what's your interest in my Goldilocks?" I give an inward groan at my slip. Yeah, they all know I have the hots for Luna, but revealing her nickname exposes a depth of vulnerability I'm certainly not comfortable with.

Alaric's lips curve. "Goldilocks? Fitting. Luna is special and damaged, and she doesn't deserve to be burdened with the Council's fear of the prophecy. She didn't come into our world with prejudices. She's truly a bridge between us. Look at the two of you, at your relationship. It gives me some hope. I won't allow the Council to do to her what was done to Alexander."

He speaks Gramps's name with an underlying emotion that isn't hatred. There's affection there despite what Alexander did to Michael. Is it brotherly affection or... something else? I can't tell.

"So, you're okay with Gramps wanting to conquer the world?" I ask.

Alaric frowns. "No, I'm not, but I'm not entirely sure he wasn't pushed into the prophecy by the Council, either."

Asmodeus has the grace to look slightly guilty, but I'm not so sure Alaric is right. I've seen exactly what my grandfather wants. Unification, but with him ruling all. Did the Council force him into it? That I can't say. I wasn't there thousands of years ago, but I don't know if that thirst for power, that absolute conviction that you were meant to rule is something you're pushed into.

Anyway, I can't be bothered with all that ancient history now. I have to save Luna, and I have a powerful Archdemon and Nephilim on my side. And a reluctant Hammurabi. I'm not a dumbass. We may be a band of merry misfits, but these misfits pack a serious punch.

"Let's go get my girl then," I say to Alaric and he grins.

EIGHT

LUNA

Y EYES TRAIL ACROSS the milky haze flooding the expanse on the other side of the glass, my lids drooping, threatening sleep—an escape I once longed for but which ceases to bring peace now, every moment burdened with the same images plaguing my waking thoughts. Days, maybe even weeks, have passed since the encounter with my phantom father. The impostor wearing Lucifer's face is so vivid in my head I can practically see him before me, his presence haunting me like a ghost.

Uriel was right. The Council isn't the real danger in this place—my mind is. I'm unraveling. I don't know what's true and what's not, and every second I spend trapped in this hell makes me question the veracity of every event I experienced since that day Alaric brought me to the Serapeum.

Assuming they even happened at all.

I'm going insane. I realize that now—or, maybe, I'm already there. If I doubted my sanity before my imprisonment, then my recent encounters with the imagined manifestations of my parents have made it clear that my mind is not only unstable, but damaged beyond repair.

No, that taunting voice in the back of my skull chides me. *Not damaged. Broken.*

Broken… This isn't the first time I've thought of myself this way, like a porcelain doll with cracked skin, tossed into some dusty corner of an attic, abandoned by its owner. The forgotten remnant of someone else's mistake. Surely, that's what Gabriel must have seen me as—why else would she have given me up? Why else would her blood refuse to call out and sing the song declaring me family?

I recall what Lucifer said about how he would've proudly claimed me as his daughter, as a Morningstar, had he known I existed. But those were the words of an apparition, and although the real Lucifer's blood called to mine when we met in the tunnels beneath my school, I can't be certain he would share these false sentiments now—that he would see me as anything other than undeniable proof of a forbidden liaison. For all I know, what he said in my ear right before surrendering me to the Council were empty words. A fleeting consolation to ease the burden of his own guilt as a failed parent and, in that moment, protector.

A demented giggle surges up from my throat. Once again, I consider the possibility that everything I remember—Alaric, my time at the Serapeum, even Caleb—are figments of my imagination, but now, instead of picturing myself back in the hospital, I wonder if I've always been stuck in this place, trapped for being the product of a union this prejudiced world disagrees with.

What if nothing I know is real at all, and I've actually spent my whole life here, alone?

I hug my legs close to my chest and tuck my wings around my body until I'm huddled into a ball, rocking back and forth, suppressing another deranged fit of laughter.

"Nothing is real… Nothing is real…"

"My, my, my," a melodic voice croons behind me. "What has become of you in such a short time, my young savior? Captivity does not become you."

My arms loosen, unlocking my legs, my wings flaring out as I scramble around on the floor and press myself against the wall farthest from this new intruder. A tall, lithe man with mismatched eyes stares back at me through my transparent cage, a curious smile pulling at his full lips.

"A-Alexander?" I stammer before sinking my teeth into the tip of my tongue. This is just another delusion. It has to be.

He arches an elegantly curved brow. "You seem surprised to see me."

I gape at the towering angel, taking him in fully for what seems like the first time, considering the last time we met, our introduction was cut short by my foray into unimaginable pain. My initial impression of him pales in comparison to what I see now. His hair, which nearly swept the floor before, has been cut into the same hairstyle he donned in the memory he showed me of him and Alaric, his complexion glowing and clean of the grime millennia of imprisonment had caked onto his skin. His eyes, one brown, one blue follow me with a grim amusement, but they fail to hold my focus, my own eyes tracing the outline of his body, registering the distinct shadows of his aura.

My chest deflates with a sigh as I note the inky black threads. I might have only stood before him for a moment, but I saw his aura, and it was nothing like this. It was silver and angry, like shards of glass. Now, it's wrong, just like Gabriel's was.

Why does my mind keep warping this detail?

"No, I'm not," I mutter. "Because you're not really here."

He nods, as if my doubt doesn't surprise him. "I remember this well." At my questioning look, he touches two fingers to the side of his head. "The hallucinations. Madness lingers close to the surface when one is confined in solitude for too long. You forget, I was imprisoned by the Council for thousands of years. Lunacy was my constant companion."

I say nothing at first, willing the hallucination to disappear, to leave me to my solitude. I don't want to talk to him. I don't want to encourage the madness he speaks of or feed it. I just want him to go away.

But, like with Lucifer and Gabriel—like with the psychiatrist I was forced to speak with every day at the hospital—I know Alexander won't simply go away because I desire it. The delusion won't end until I participate in this pointless charade born from the twisted depths of my thoughts. Until I respond to whatever hold this place has on my mind.

None of this will end until I give in.

Fatigue grips my senses as I reluctantly cave under Alexander's pressing stare. "You seemed sane enough when I opened your tomb."

"Did I?" His wide mouth splits into a smile, and he saunters closer, skirting around the arcing wall of glass until he's standing just beside where I sit, unable to move from my spot on the floor. Squatting down to my level, he lowers his voice. "Well, I assure you, it was not without effort. But then, I had something to fight for in the darkness, to hold me afloat in the tempestuous tides. Such mental anchors help keep us tied to our sanity." He appraises me, rubbing a hand over his well-defined chin. "I wonder, do you intend to fight, too, my young savior? Or will you submit to the chaos breaking your mind?" When I don't speak, he narrows his eyes and scoffs. "Will you allow your light to be dimmed by self-pity?"

I blanch at his words. Is that what I'm doing? Wallowing in destructive despair? I struggle to see my current state of mind as something as simplistic as that. After all, I've experienced exile and the worst kind of betrayal. The anger and heartache eating away at me are more than justified.

"I'm not a Light," I bite back, finally distancing myself from everyone at the Serapeum who treated me like a monster and from the Light angels who chose to imprison me here. I'm not a Light.

But you're not a Dark, either, that voice in the back of my head reminds me.

Caleb's face appears in my thoughts, triggering a suffocating pain that spears my chest. Once, I would've given anything to be like him, but if everything between us was fake and he used me—if I really was just a tool to him, a means to the end of freeing his grandfather—then I can safely say the Darks aren't any better than the Lights. Everyone on both sides has their own agenda while I'm trapped in the middle, drowning.

I shake my head. "I'm like you. I'm a Gray."

Alexander unleashes a barking laugh and pushes to his feet, his eyes fixing me with a patronizing look that reminds me far too much of Gabriel. "And what are Grays but celestial beings composed of both the Light and the Dark? We threaten them, Luna. We jeopardize their precarious truce. That is why they fear us and condemn us to cages. But I can free you." He gestures calmly to the foggy expanse. "I can spirit you away from this prison, and together, we can build a new world. A world where the divide no longer exists. A world where we can rule as the superior beings we are."

His words give me pause. Is that what we are? Is that why the Council insists on keeping me locked here, in this impenetrable egg where my powers are muted and my senses are dulled? Am I here not because I helped free Alexander, but because they want to see all Grays subjugated?

"Join me, Luna," Alexander continues, his deep timbre taking on a slight pleading edge. "Let us gather our strength and challenge the rule of the self-righteous who lord over us. Or…" He pauses, shrugging broad shoulders that seem capable of holding the weight of the endeavor he speaks of. "Stand against me and perish when the world is engulfed by the flames of war."

"Why—" My throat is scratchy, the word barely a breath above silent. Swallowing, I carefully push onto my feet, keeping one hand on the wall for support, and for a long moment, I stare at him as question after question presses at the inside of my skull. Although he can't give me answers I don't already have, I can't stop myself from asking, "Why are those the only options? Why does the world have to burn for the divide to be broken? Why are the Lights and Darks so afraid of each other? Of *us?*"

Alexander lets loose a menacing chuckle that raises the hair on my neck and arms. "They do not fear each other. They fear the Creator. But together, we can bring Him to heel."

A shiver of terror ripples over my feathers. Are these really Alexander's intentions? Or just what I expect from the man who left me to rot in captivity?

"You… You want to take on the Creator?"

He preens at my question, grinning. "To create a new world order, those in power must be overthrown and any threats to our unification destroyed. Let the Creator keep His Heaven. I wish to rule over Earth, to build my kingdom in these mortal lands where our true calling lies. Now is the time for the Lights and Darks to choose a side—to decide which of our two lands will be their Eden. My way, with the reign of the Grays, is the future. Only on Earth can we all truly thrive."

I try to envision it—a world where the divide is gone and the Grays are in power—but all I see is a life where I'm alone, like I've always been. As far as I know, Alexander and I are the only Grays in existence. Maybe we're the only ones who have *ever* existed. So, if we were to rule over this world torn between Dark and Light, what would that mean for those who fall distinctly on one side or another? Is he looking for angels and Nephilim to join his fight?

Or is he looking for people to rule over?

My chest tightens as Caleb's face floods my thoughts again. Despite the pain eating away at my heart, I can't stomach the thought of him being subservient to anyone, least of all to me. The Darks believe in free will above all. How long before they grow tired of Alexander pushing his dominant views onto them? How long before they become his new targets in the war I sense looming before us?

"And what of your grandson?" I blurt out, the words escaping in a rush, as if I have no control of my lips. "Where does he fit into this new world order?"

Confusion mars Alexander's brow. "My grandson?"

His piercing eyes press me for an explanation, but I instinctively snap my mouth shut, my pulse pounding along the underside of my skin as I'm overcome by a deep, crippling sense of dread that I've said something very wrong—just like I felt with Gabriel when she asked about my father.

I tremble when Alexander takes a step toward me.

"I see," he murmurs, the darkness lapping over his skin thrashing in a frenzy of black and purple blurs. "You mean the transfer from Babel." A low chuckle swells in the space between us. "It seems Asmodeus has some explaining to do."

Asmodeus? The headmistress of Babel?

His words confound me. Didn't Alexander notice his connection to Caleb when they met, just like I recognized Lucifer as my father? Didn't their blood sing to each other in that moment the way the Morningstar's blood sang to mine?

If not, then what the hell does that mean? And what does Asmodeus have to do with any of this? Is she working with Alexander? Ishtar was, so it's not too far-fetched to think the Archdemon in charge of Caleb's school would be involved, too. If she is, it would certainly explain how Caleb managed to snag the transfer opportunity, not that many Darks were up for the challenge—assuming what he told me about that was true.

I think back to the day of Alexander's release, recalling the accusatory faces of the Archangels and Archdemons, who all looked at me like I was the enemy. If Asmodeus is secretly aiding Alexander, then it would seem Gabriel isn't the only one in the Council living a double life behind everyone's back. Who else is keeping secrets?

And what explosive effect will those secrets have on our lives?

I shake my head. *Stop it. You're panicking over nothing. This isn't real,* I tell myself for what feels like the thousandth time. And yet, no matter how many times I repeat these words, I can never seem to convince myself of it.

I shake my head again, more fervently this time. *This can't be real, Luna. Stop listening to him.* This place is guarded by the Council. How would Alexander have even gotten here, wherever here is, without alerting them all to his presence?

Slamming my hands over my ears, I shrink into the floor and clamp my eyes shut. *This isn't real. This isn't real.*

Movement on the other side of the glass wrenches my eyes open, and doubt festers under my skin when Alexander turns on his heel and sets off into the mist without so much as a word and without looking back. Despite my firm belief that he's just an illusion, despite the fact that I *want* him to go, I lurch forward until my hands and chest collide with the glass, my movements driven by a single thought: *What if he isn't?*

What if Alexander is really here and by leaving, he takes my only chance of escape with him?

"Where are you going?" I shriek.

He stills, then turns to face me again, offering me a bored scowl. "Your hesitation leads me to believe you aren't ready to join me, and I cannot very well set you free if there's any chance you may stand in the way of my mission. It would seem your imprisonment serves everyone equally well at the present moment."

What about the freedom you promised me? But when I try to scream those words, he cuts me off with a mocking laugh.

"Besides, you have bestowed us with a wonderful gift—a lead to help us hunt down the Great." As he speaks, the whips of shadow slithering over his skin vibrate with unmistakable pleasure.

A strangled breath parts my lips. "I…" *I don't understand.* But as those words cross my mind, it dawns on me that I do understand. I understand very well. I've been tricked—fooled into believing my mind was the enemy when, all along, the real threat was always the Council.

Uriel lied—lulled me into a false sense of paranoia and terror. And by doing so, by believing this was all in my head, I finally gave the Council something it wanted.

No. I choke back a sob, unwilling to believe I could be so naive. So stupid. That I could fall into his trap so easily, like prey walking willingly into a predator's den. *This isn't real. None of this is real. This is just another hallucination.*

A lump lodges in my throat, disbelief gripping my windpipe, which tightens as I force out the only question I can manage in my panic. "Aren't you Alexander?" I breathe, hoping with every fiber of my being he'll prove me wrong and say yes.

The angel bares his teeth in a sinister smile, more Cheshire Cat than human, letting his guise slip for the briefest of moments. Blood red eyes glare back into mine.

"Now, that is the real question, isn't it?"

NINE

CALEB

ASMODEUS MOVES US FROM her office to a large room I've never seen before deep within the bowels of Babel. Nothing modern has touched this place. Torches provide the only light, casting the room in writhing shadows. It's a creepy and fitting place to plan a jailbreak. I sit at the large table that dominates the room. Made from obsidian, the ebony surface reflects the firelight, adding to the dark mood of the chamber. If the circumstances weren't so dire, I might have a laugh at how cliché it all is.

But my focus is on Alaric and the newcomer murmuring to Asmodeus. A Dark. She popped in from the Shadow Road a few minutes ago, her rich brown skin glowing in the firelight. She's tall and willowy, and she seems vaguely familiar, but I can't place her. She feels like a first generation, her power like a live wire, but I can't tell how old she is.

Alaric gives her a welcoming smile that she returns while Hammurabi remains sullen. I feel like I've stepped into a bizarre reality no one bothered to tell me about. How is it that Alaric—a *Light*—is so friendly with all these Darks? I was convinced only Luna was open-minded about the divide.

"Nzingha, this is Caleb, the Great's grandson," Alaric says, gesturing to me with a sweeping hand.

I flip through the files of first generations in my brain. Ah, okay. Now, I know who she is. She was the Queen of the Ambundu kingdoms of Ndongo and Matamba. She's not nearly as old as Hammurabi or Alaric, though she's still an antique. She raises an eyebrow as she looks me over, but I don't wither under her hard stare.

"Gramps has a lot of grandkids, Alaric. I'm just the one who got manipulated," I say, grinning at Nzingha, whose eyes flash with surprise.

"Ah, yes, your useless father likes to seed all the gardens, doesn't he?" Alaric says. "Then leaves before the harvest."

I blink. Huh, I guess *everyone* knows my dad's an asshole. "That's a nice way to put it," I say.

"Too nice," Nzingha says, snorting. Well, I guess she's not a fan, either.

"I was trying to be tactful in the presence of the child," Alaric says, winking at me.

I shrug. "Don't worry about me. I haven't needed a security blanket in a long time. I'm a big boy. I can tie my own shoelaces and everything."

Nzingha smiles at me. "Well, you must have your mother's sense of humor." Her eyes snap to Asmodeus. "I'm sure Alexander will bring…" Her lips purse, and her gaze flits to me for a moment. "Your grandfather will teach your father his place soon enough."

I suppress a growl. Enough about that dick. "I'm sure Gramps will find out he's a waste of space before long. But I don't care about him. I care about Luna."

To my utter shock, Hammurabi nods. "Yes, let's focus on someone actually worth our time. The Gray."

I glare at him. "Yes, *Luna*." He scowls at me, and I resist the urge to give him the middle finger. Reckless I am, stupid I am not.

Asmodeus clasps her hands in front of her. "Yes, children, let's get on with it. Time is wasting. Alaric, tell us what you know."

Alaric taps the side of his nose. "As you so charmingly put it before, Asmodeus, I can sniff out Nephilim and more importantly, bloodlines. I always knew there was something special about Luna and I was right."

"You always knew she was a Gray?" I demand, stunned.

He shakes his head. "No, but there was always something that didn't quite add up about Luna's upbringing and the fact we somehow failed to catch wind of her when her powers first began manifesting. Not to mention her scent was strangely dull for someone with celestial blood. Then during my last encounter with her and Gabriel… well, let's just say things became clearer."

I jerk back at the implication, and Hammurabi's mouth drops open, the normally stoic king looking as shell-shocked as I feel. "Um, are you saying—"

Nzingha laughs, but the sound holds no humor. "I'm shocked she'd be stupid enough to do something like this. Not the perfect Messenger."

My eyes swing back and forth between everyone. Asmodeus doesn't seem the least bit surprised, and the other three—now that Hammurabi has recovered—seem resigned to the fact. But I have to make sure.

"You're saying stick-up-her-ass Gabriel is *Luna's* mother?" I can't wrap my head around it. Gabriel is so cold she's glacial. I can't imagine her getting down and dirty with anyone, least of all a Dark. Holy shit, Gabriel fucked a *Dark*.

And that brings up the million-dollar question: Who is Luna's father? And why didn't Gabriel acknowledge her own daughter? Why did she let Luna think she was crazy? Why did she allow the Council to take her? Hot rage sweeps through me so fast I feel dizzy. She's Luna's *mother* for the Morningstar's sake. How could she have just abandoned Luna like that?

Alaric's eyebrows rise at my words. "Yes, she is."

"She's an Archangel, Caleb, give her the respect she's due," Asmodeus says, and I gape at her.

I see red, clenching my fists, and bang them on the table. "That bitch abandoned Luna and let her think she was crazy this whole time, even at the Serapeum. She let the Council take her! Her own daughter."

My father might be a shit, but my mother loves me with the fierceness of a lioness. I can't believe Gabriel of all angels let her daughter loose on the world, knowing what the consequences could be.

"Punish me if you like, but parents who abandon their kids don't deserve my respect, even if they're an Archangel," I spit out.

I don't care if they think my fury stems from my daddy issues. Oh, and where the hell is Luna's daddy? Images of all the Fallen swim through my mind, but I can't match any with my Goldilocks. Wait, that's not true. The conversation in Gabriel's office when I sent my clay golem to spy claws at me. Some weird remark about Lucifer. *Lucifer.* He shines like the sun and so does Luna. By the Creator, it's so obvious if I really think about it. Gabriel is there, too, in the striking beauty of Luna's face, but her coloring, her glow is all the Morningstar.

My mouth drops open as I stare at the others.

Asmodeus gives me a nod, eyes full of pride. "Go on, Caleb," she commands. "Say it."

"Lucifer is Luna's father," I whisper, shaking my head as if that will make it less true or help me make sense of it.

"Lucifer with *Gabriel*?" Nzingha hisses. "I didn't think anyone could thaw the ice queen."

"For once we're in agreement," Hammurabi says.

I ignore them, thinking. When did Lucifer and Gabriel get it on? I mean, I now understand how tight-lipped the Council are about their dirty deeds, but that is one hell of a dirty deed to cover up.

Asmodeus turns to Alaric. "Babel students are the brightest of all the academies, Dark or Light, especially Light. Your precious Nephilim couldn't find their way out of a paper bag. Too busy worrying about their wings to see the bigger picture."

I resist the urge to roll my eyes at the Archdemon's pettiness. Even now, even here, she can't resist getting a dig in. We're all doomed.

To my surprise, Alaric just grins. "Yes, our students seem to operate with blinders the majority of the time," he admits.

"I always did like that about you," Hammurabi says to Alaric. "You recognize your weaknesses."

I wave an impatient hand, suddenly feeling like the adult in the room. "Yeah, yeah, we're better than you, blah, blah. Alaric, how did this happen?"

Alaric chuckles. "Caleb, I'm sure you can figure out *how* it happened."

"Yeah, they got naked, got it. But they're the Morningstar and the Messenger! That's not supposed to happen. And Luna is only seventeen, so how did they manage to keep their affair a secret? Was it hate sex? I can't…" I shake my head again.

"Luna is much older than seventeen, Caleb," Asmodeus says gently. "Well, in a way."

What the hell does that mean?

"Lucifer hasn't been with Gabriel since the Fall. I know this. He avoids her like, well, the plague," Asmodeus explains. "He still carries the wounds of what happened between them, festering away. So that means Luna would have been conceived—"

"Before the Fall," Nzingha says, glancing at the Archdemon and then at Alaric, mouth slightly agape. She shakes her head. "But if that's the case, the girl hasn't been out and about this whole time, or we would've known it. Gabriel must have hidden her somehow."

Alaric nods. "Yes, I believe so. For all intents and purposes, she's a seventeen-year-old girl, but if what Asmodeus says is true—and I have no cause to doubt her— Gabriel must have given birth around the time of the Fall. It's the only thing that makes sense."

Hysteria bubbles through me. Does it? Nothing about this situation makes sense. Thank the Creator I'm sitting down, or my ass would hit the floor. "Since the *Fall*? Where has she been this whole time? That means she's older than Alexander. Than most of *you*. So why doesn't she look older, like you all?"

"That I don't know," Alaric says. "I followed Gabriel to Easter Island just before you released Alexander." He gives me a knowing look, and I go cold with guilt. "She had acted somewhat strangely during a conversation we had about Luna, and when I caught her scent leaving the Serapeum, I knew something was wrong. I assume she was checking on Luna's original birth place, and when she found it empty, she rushed back."

Asmodeus frowns. "Luna has been on Easter Island this entire time? Well, minus seventeen years. But how?" Her cat-green eyes widen. "Ah, the statues. Of course."

Confused, I glance at Alaric, who nods. "Yes, wards, but they're no longer working."

"Someone broke the Messenger's wards to release her daughter," Hammurabi says. "Someone who had to know where the Gray—Luna—was kept." The king looks at Asmodeus.

"I assure you I didn't know. I only suspected Gabriel was hiding a child from Lucifer, but I never had proof," the Archdemon says.

"Who else would have suspected Gabriel was pregnant?" Nzingha asks, dark eyes thoughtful.

Asmodeus flashes a cruel smile. "Lilith and the Messenger were always close." Her voice drips with malice.

Well, the hits keep on coming. Lilith's meeting with Alexander plays through my mind, and I wonder again what she did for Lucifer to ban her. Well, I guess not just Lucifer, the whole Council. And does the Morningstar banging Gabriel count as a betrayal, too?

"The traitor?" Hammurabi growls.

Alaric sighs. "Perhaps she wasn't a traitor, or at least she didn't think she was. Two Grays does rather skew the prophecy, doesn't it?"

I hate being the most ignorant person in the room, but there's so much history between these players, so much subtext and bullshit, that I'm constantly behind. "What does that mean?" I demand, not bothering to hide my irritation.

Alaric turns solemn eyes on me. "Lilith backed Alexander."

Oh. Damn. I guess that explains her cozying up to Gramps. "Okay, but why? Because she knew about Luna?"

Asmodeus forms a steeple with the tips of her fingers, resting her chin on them. "It's a possibility. She may know more than all of us as well. Gabriel would have confided in her."

I hold up my hands. "Okay, but I don't get it. Were Lucifer and Gabriel a one-night stand? Why hide Luna from him? Just because of the prophecy?"

Asmodeus gives me a pitying look. "Much like you and your Luna, Lucifer and Gabriel were in love." I go cold then hot at hearing the L word again. I'm not quite ready to face it yet. And if I do, it won't be in front of an audience. Just Goldilocks. "He went to war for the right to love her, and she chose the Creator in the end."

Well, at this point, my jaw is going to be permanently stuck to the floor. Poor Lucifer. To have the woman you love, the woman you've risked everything for, run back to the Creator with her tail between her legs must be a straight up kick to the nuts. No wonder he didn't show up that night when Gabriel called the meeting. He probably can't stand to be on the same continent as her, let alone in the same room.

I rub my temples, willing my brain not to implode. "So Gabriel rejects Lucifer, the Fallen are kicked out of Heaven, and she finds out she's knocked up. At that point, I guess she can't go to Lucifer."

A bitter laugh escapes Asmodeus. "Of course, she could have, the arrogant fool. He would have taken care of the child if she wouldn't have. He loved her. He loves her still, more's the pity."

"She believed she couldn't go to him anyway," Alaric says softly. "They're together now, so maybe they can finally work on all their issues. For the good of their child at least."

Asmodeus's lips curve into a venomous smile. "I'm sure they'll put aside millennia of heartbreak for the good of their child now that Gabriel has toppled off her pedestal of moral superiority in such a spectacular fashion."

"Not Gabriel's biggest fan?" I say to Asmodeus and she sneers.

"The Morningstar deserved better," she says, and the room goes icy for a brief moment, my breath clouding in front of me.

"Revisiting ancient history isn't helping us," Alaric says gently.

"Speak for yourself," I retort, happy to finally have a peek behind the curtain, and oh, what a peek it is. "And it's not like it's not relevant." My poor Goldilocks. When we find her, she's got one hell of a shock coming her way. I also know she'll be incredibly hurt Gabriel was her mother this whole time and never said anything to her. Wait a minute. "Alaric, you said Gabriel went to Easter Island to see if Luna was still there? If Luna is her kid, wouldn't she have recognized her immediately?"

Nzingha looks to Asmodeus. "She cloaked her, even from herself," she ventures and the Archdemon nods.

"Yes, I believe she concealed her from all, hiding the call of her blood. She did it so well she didn't even know her own daughter was in her presence. After all her deception and lies, she wasn't able to save Luna in the end. I'd toast her downfall if I didn't know how her betrayal will sting Lucifer," Asmodeus says.

"Like a scorpion," Hammurabi adds. "Lucifer has no other children."

"Luna is the true innocent in all this," Alaric says, and I can't believe I'm thinking it, but I actually like this Light. "And whether they're fighting like hissing cats—or what did you say Caleb, having hate sex?—we need Lucifer and Gabriel to help protect her."

"You had no luck finding them?" Asmodeus asks, drumming her fingers on the obsidian table.

"They're moving too quickly, and we can't wait around. You know Luna's location," Alaric says. "You called to *me*."

That still surprises the hell out of me, and I can't figure Alaric out. He's a decent guy. I wince at myself, my prejudices hitting me in the face. It might take more than Luna to heal this divide.

Asmodeus twists her full lips as her hard gaze weighs over each of us. "You're here because I trust you," she begins, and I slant a glance at Hammurabi. He might not be on board, but I can't see him running to the Council to tattle, either. "We have to stop the Conqueror, and in order to do that, Luna must be free. She cannot be allowed to fall into his hands." Her bright green eyes land on me. "And whether he's delaying fetching her or not, Alexander is no fool. He's a military strategist who will use every tool at his disposal. We've underestimated the Great before and we cannot again."

It's a pretty speech, but it doesn't exactly reveal where Luna is.

Asmodeus takes a deep breath, and I notice a slight tremor ripples through her frame. She doesn't like betraying the Council, I realize. She believes she's in the right, but it still doesn't sit well with her. I want to beat the table with my fists, but like the other three, I keep my mouth shut and let the Archdemon take her sweet time. Not like I can force her to hurry anyway.

"Luna is suspended in a pocket reality between the Shadow and Blessed Roads. Each member of the Council—with the obvious exception of Gabriel and Lucifer—used our essence to create her prison. Brute strength can't break it, and as we learned with our mistake with Alexander, blood can't break it, either. Only the Council together can unravel what we've woven," Asmodeus explains, face grim. Her shimmering eyes focus on Alaric. "I was hoping you could find Gabriel and Lucifer. As members of the Council, maybe they could combine their strengths and create a weak point in our defenses. As we both have Darks and Lights in our party, I can tell you how to travel there, but although you'll be able to interact with Luna, you won't be able to free her."

"So, this has all been a waste of time?" I cry, and this time, I do pound my fists on the table. I glare at Asmodeus. "Why bring us together if you can't do anything?"

Hammurabi is in my face in two seconds flat. "Don't speak to your mistress like that, child," he hisses, hand fisted in my shirt. His eyes brim with fury, and I want to smash my forehead into his nose so bad I can taste it. And yeah, it will feel fantastic for a few seconds, and then I'll get my ass beat.

I swallow down my bitter words and lower my eyes, giving the Archdemon a deferential nod. "Sorry… I'm…" I can't finish the sentence, too disappointed and pissed for a decent apology, so I just stare at the ridiculous table.

Asmodeus's voice is shockingly gentle. "I understand your frustration, Caleb. Alaric will find Lucifer and Gabriel soon, and then we will save Luna. You have my word."

I look up, my gaze clashing with Alaric's and that damn Calm washes over me. It still pisses me off, but this time, I just let him do his thing. He's putting his dick on the line, too, helping an Archdemon and me find Luna.

"It will take me some time, but I'll find them," Alaric reassures me, and I drag a smile out from somewhere and paste it on.

"Come along, Caleb," Asmodeus says, rising on liquid joints. "I'll show you where you're to stay this evening."

Nzingha strides to the door. "I'll keep my ear to the ground. Perhaps Mammon will feel particularly chatty about Gabriel and Lucifer."

"One can only hope," Alaric says, following her out the chamber.

I go to follow Asmodeus when Hammurabi stops in her path. The Archdemon cocks her head, sizing up the king, and I release an irritated sigh. I swear if he starts bitching to us about saving Luna, I will smash his face in, even though I know he'll get back up again and break my spine.

Hammurabi places a finger to his lips and gestures behind him. Asmodeus nods and suddenly it feels like we're under water.

"What is it you wish to share, King?" Asmodeus says, flipping lustrous red strands over her shoulder. Her voice has a weird echo to it, and I know she's ensured we're not overheard by Alaric or Nzingha.

"I may know of a way to save Luna without the Morningstar and the Messenger," Hammurabi says and nods toward me.

The fuck? If I knew how to save Luna, I wouldn't be here in the dungeon of doom. I'd be out saving her.

"The dagger," Hammurabi reminds me and I blink. Oh, Gramps's knife.

"The dagger?" Asmodeus's brows rise. "*Alexander's* dagger?" she snarls, and I shiver at the sudden arctic temperature. "*Caleb* has it?"

The Babylonian king squares his shoulders. "Yes, I wasn't going to allow him to go to the Serapeum like a lamb to the slaughter. He needed to protect himself. He's the only one who can wield it. Besides Alexander, of course. And his bastard father, wherever he is—and I suppose all his children who are out there."

Asmodeus's icy rage terrifies me, but in the blink of an eye, she has herself under control, which is even scarier. She turns those predator-green eyes toward me, and I want to shrink in on myself and disappear. "Gabriel was wounded, and I assumed it was from Alexander, but it was you, sweet child." Her flinty gaze finds Hammurabi. "We'll speak of this later, King, but I have to admit this changes things."

Hope floats to the surface again, and I tentatively ask, "It does?"

An unholy grin lights her face. "Yes, it changes the game."

TEN

LUNA

TERROR CLAWS AT MY flesh, cutting deep, until the fear rushing through me seems to bleed from my pores. I've been at the brink of insanity so many times—thought I was already there—lost myself in what I was sure were the tumultuous waters of delirium, and yet…nothing has ever felt like this. This nagging in my brain, this constant questioning if I can trust what I'm seeing and hearing… I thought I knew what it was like to have my mind play tricks on me, but never have I experienced this infuriating sensation of uncertainty, not even at the Serapeum when I was truly convinced I was crazy.

Crazy… I choke out a laugh. If that's what I am now, then what I was before was the opposite. Even with Alexander's voice in my head, I was more sane during those handful of months in Alexandria than I am at this moment.

Now, when everything and everyone I see is a lie.

Nothing I've encountered in this place has been real. Gabriel. Lucifer. Alexander. But they weren't hallucinations like I thought. They were manifestations created with the sole purpose to strip me of the secrets I didn't even realize I kept. Secrets like the identity of my father. Secrets like why Caleb helped me free Alexander.

A shudder rips through me at the memory of those unsettling vermilion eyes staring back into mine, the intensity of the Fallen's gaze seeming to tear back my skin and bones and see into the deepest parts of my soul. It was a Dark posing as my parents and Alexander—I realize that now. Hell, I should've realized it the moment I noticed Gabriel's aura was wrong. But I didn't and as a result, I have become the one thing I never wanted to be.

A betrayer.

Agony lances my heart, and I wince as my interrogator's words flood my ears. *"You have bestowed us with a wonderful gift—a lead to help us hunt down the Great."*

My insides curdle as horror spreads through me, sluggish and deliberate, taking its time to undo me. The Archangels and Archdemons playing the role of my captors were missing a vital piece of the puzzle, and I just unwittingly handed it to them. They must have suspected there was something else linking me to Alexander aside from our shared legacy as Grays. Why else would I, a girl with limited prior knowledge of our world, have set him free unless someone else was pulling my strings? Someone like the Great's grandson and heir.

Someone who could potentially be used to draw the Gray out of hiding.

Tears prick at my eyes, but I swipe them away. Caleb's too smart for that. He wouldn't be stupid enough to let anyone use him, not the way I have. Besides, he's likely off-grid with Alexander, and to find one, they would need the other. So long as they stay out of sight, he'll be safe.

Unless—

I press my palms to the curved wall of glass, bowing my head as a nauseating fear twists my stomach. *This is why they're keeping me alive.* Not because I'm a Gray, but because they know, heartbreak or not, Caleb means something to me…and they're hoping he'll be foolish enough to come here. To try to rescue me.

They aren't afraid of me, I realize. I'm just the bait needed to catch a much larger fish.

A hysterical laugh escapes me. It doesn't matter. Caleb won't come. He left me here. He doesn't care—

But if he does? that voice of doubt dares to ask.

My growing terror pulls me down to my knees.

"Then I hope he stays away," I breathe, my voice cracking.

Although the thought sends a rush of pain to my chest, I find myself hoping that what Caleb admitted he felt for me at the Serapeum was a lie. A ploy to gain my trust and turn me into his pawn—a tool to be disposed of once I fulfilled my intended purpose. Because if that's all I was to him, he'll have no reason to come back for me. And if he doesn't come back for me, he'll stay safe. Whether he played me or not, I don't want him caught up in this. I want him to stay far, far away where the Council can never lay a finger on him…

Even if that means I remain here forever.

"Stay away," I whisper again as scalding hot tears stream down my cheeks.

The hours pass in a fitful daze. I'm not sure how many crawl by uncounted—maybe it's even been days since the impostor wearing Alexander's face pried the knowledge of Caleb's identity from my lips. Like always, time eludes me in this place, and all I can do in my cage is wait.

Wait and see if Caleb comes for me like I fear my captors are hoping.

The soft patter of footsteps behind me has me launching to my feet, my body tense as I spin on my heel, my heart racing, my senses on high alert. As the footsteps draw closer, the fog of mist parts, and a familiar face emerges from the haze.

"Hello again, Luna," Uriel says, dipping into a bow, the Archangel's brown skin radiant against the colorless mist. He straightens, tapping a finger to his chin as a knowing smile darkens his gaze. "It's a pity, the upbringing you've had. A misplaced nobody who was bound to live life as a mortal, hidden among humans who would only ever view her as a threat. As something they could not understand." Knitting his hands behind his back, he looks me up and down with a sort of restrained curiosity that raises the hair on the back of my neck. Or maybe what I'm sensing is distaste. It's impossible to tell which. "But you are not no one, and you are certainly not mortal," he continues, "although the threat part remains to be seen. The certain grasp we had on the truth has crumbled with the revelation of your mother."

Uriel scoffs, disregarding the surprise on my face. "Gabriel, the Messenger, bearer of the Creator's words," he spits, his brusque tone lethal. "Who is to say she told us the whole truth pertaining to the Gray destined to destroy our kind and our world? Your very existence begs the question. Perhaps you, forbidden child of the Dark and the Light, are the real bringer of our demise." He shakes his head, tsking under his breath. "And we have your parents to thank for that. Their sins and lies have been exposed as has your true identity."

The Archangel pauses, glancing over his shoulder as another figure emerges from the mist. I gape open-mouthed at the familiar countenance of my father, but the blue eyes I expect to find are gone, replaced by a searing gaze the color of blood.

"You—"

The impostor's face splits into a monstrous grin. "Luna Morningstar," he hisses.

As these words leave his lips, my father's features shift and change until a vaguely recognizable hulking beast of a man stands in his place, glowering at me. His shoulders are broad and his hair is ashy, clipped close to his skull in a buzz cut. Dark blond brows sit like stagnant caterpillars on his furrowed brow.

I recognize him, having seen him among the other Archangels and Archdemons the day I freed Alexander. At the time, I hadn't noticed the color of his eyes, too consumed by terror and pain. Now, those blood-red irises haunt me.

Uriel claps his hands in delight. "Ah, but where are my manners? Luna, this is Mammon, headmaster of the academy at Tyre. As I'm sure you've realized, Mammon is an Archdemon with a rather splendid talent. Crude modernisms would refer to him as a shape-shifter. But what Mammon is capable of is so much more complex, for his gift affects the very subconscious of his victims, drawing out truths even they weren't aware they were hiding by using the manifestations of their own minds against them. Of course, I can tell from your stunned expression that you've already discerned that."

I swallow past the growing lump in my throat, staring daggers at the Archdemon responsible for messing with my head.

"I knew it," I manage after a long, tense moment. "I wasn't really—"

"Losing your mind?" Uriel quips. "'Going crazy,' as the children today say?" He chuckles. "Quite the opposite, actually. If anything, you've shown remarkable resilience to the effects of this ethereal plane."

Ethereal plane? My eyes dart from side to side, taking in my surroundings with renewed interest. Just where exactly is this place? I always assumed it was somewhere on Earth, masked by magic to suit the Council's means, not that unlike Alexander's tomb beneath the Serapeum, guarded by wards only a Gray could pass through and a lock only Gabriel's blood could break. But now, as the mist—the tendrils almost sentient in their movements—laps against the side of the egg, I'm not so sure where I am. The only thing I do know is this purgatory surely isn't Heaven.

If anything, it's Hell.

I flinch away from the transparent wall as Uriel closes the distance between, pressing a long-fingered, elegant hand to the glass. "Despite your involvement in the crimes for which you are being held, I do not believe you are like Alexander. Just as I do not believe you are the Gray, the harbinger of our doom, that the Messenger spoke of."

I go rigid at his words despite their undertone of sincerity. Something about this exchange isn't right. They want something—I can tell by the predatory way Mammon keeps staring at me—but what, exactly? What else could they possibly want from me?

What else do I even have to give them?

As if reading my thoughts, Uriel leans forward, bringing his tall frame in line with my own until he's crouching and we're eye to eye. "Given the calamity Alexander has already wrought once and intends to unleash upon us again, it's clear what part he has to play. For that reason, I am here to make you a deal."

"A deal?" I echo. "What kind of deal?"

Mammon steps forward, his face a stern mask of contempt. "Tell us, daughter of Lucifer…what role will you play in the coming war?"

My wings bristle. "You tell me. I'm the one locked in a cage."

Uriel waves a dismissive hand. "A precaution. Perhaps you are unaware of the Conqueror's past—as I believe you must have been to knowingly partake in freeing him from confinement—but thousands of years ago, he nearly subjugated the known human world. Had he succeeded, I assure you, he would not have been content merely ruling over the humans. The destruction of our very kind was at stake. And with the emergence of another Gray, we could not afford to make the same mistake twice. It is not personal—"

I let out a barking laugh. Everything about this whole situation feels personal.

"*But,*" Uriel continues, his glare piercing, "despite your lineage, you do not seem to possess the same thirst for power as your Gray brethren. Am I wrong in assuming this?"

I deflate as all the anger rushes out of my body, replaced by a sadness so intense and enduring that I struggle to breathe past its grip on my chest. My voice is thick as I force out the words. "I never wanted any of this. You're the ones who dragged me into this world. I only wanted—"

"To protect the boy," the Archangel interrupts, nodding solemnly. "Caleb, was it? If that still rings true, then you may be interested in hearing what I have to say."

"We know the transfer from Babel is of the Great's blood," Mammon says, his tone cutting, like a knife to my throat.

Because you tricked me, I nearly say, but instead, I flatten my hands to the glass, screaming out, "Caleb is innocent! He doesn't even know his grandfather. He thought he was helping him. Helping me! *I'm* the one who wanted to find Alexander because—" I hesitate, unsure if I should say anything more. How much of my complicity will help my case?

And how much will harm it?

"Because?" Mammon presses.

I swallow, shifting my focus away from those penetrating crimson eyes. Instead, I look at Uriel. Of the two, he seems more lenient. More…merciful.

"Because he said he could help me control it."

"Control what?" he asks, looking genuinely perplexed.

"*This,*" I mutter, gesturing to all of me, signifying that I am the real problem here, not Caleb. "What I am."

Uriel's mouth twitches, and a glimpse of sympathy shines out from his steely, unfaltering gaze like the first glimpse of sunlight breaking through storm clouds.

"Control is not your problem, child," he says gently, his voice almost kind. "You were bound. You could not have mastered your innate gifts anymore than you could have unleashed your wings. Now that the bind is removed, you are free from such… instability. Although," he adds after a pause, "as I'm sure you've realized by now, your powers are of little use in that cage, assuming you can call upon them at all."

Bind? Confusion sends a chill rushing through me. What is he saying? That the Dark side of me was locked away behind some kind of invisible door? But if that's true, then—

"When Alexander touched me…"

Uriel nods. "He removed the bind. Although we're not entirely sure how."

I shake my head, struggling to comprehend what he's saying. "But if my Dark half was bound, then how come I could use Dark abilities back at the Serapeum? Why has my fire always been red?"

The Archangel shrugs, seemingly unconcerned. "Perhaps the bind was failing. A binding spell requires the caster to be of the same descending side as the one receiving the bind. In your case, you are of both the Light and the Dark. Whoever bound your powers bound only your Dark half, leaving the Light side fully intact. Doing so left you unbalanced—and incapable of the control you so craved from Alexander— which brings me back to the point."

My eyes narrow. "Which is what?"

"Caleb," Uriel clarifies. "We know he fled with Alexander. Tell us where and you will be freed from this cage. You need not endure millennia in isolation and darkness—"

He goes silent mid-sentence, but I can hear his unspoken words hanging heavy in the air between us. *Just like Alexander.*

Terror envelops me, my voice barely a whisper. "I don't know where." *And even if I did, I wouldn't tell you.*

Mammon expels a threatening growl, baring his teeth. "Why do you insist on protecting this boy when he so readily left you behind to rot? Such half-breed traitors are beneath our kind."

I snap my gaze in the Archdemon's direction, once again taking in those ominous eyes, but this time, I don't look away. His face is harsh and cruel—not at all like the masks of my parents and Alexander he wore so convincingly to trick me. He reminds me vaguely of the orderlies at the hospital—always looking down on me. Always viewing me as broken.

And to think, Mammon is responsible for the lives of however many young Nephilim at Tyre. Nephilim, who he just referred to as half-breeds who are "beneath our kind."

My upper lip peels back in disgust. "I would rather be like him than be anything like either of you. Angels. Demons. You think you're superior to Nephilim, to humans. But you're just as misguided and immoral as anyone else on this planet."

Uriel sneers. His patience with me seems to be waning. "Your loyalty is admirable but misplaced. If you will not be swayed by the temptation of freedom, then consider this. Our greatest error in judgment from the first time Alexander tried to seize power was not disposing of his supporters upon his imprisonment. We showed them mercy, believing calamity had been avoided. But, like with our imprisonment of the Conqueror, we will not make the same mistake again."

All the air seems to seep out of the egg, and I can practically feel the color drain from my face. "What are you—"

"*Anyone,*" the Archangel booms, his voice overpowering mine, "Light or Dark, be they angel, demon, or Nephilim, found supporting the Great will meet a swift end. There will be no second chances. Not even for those you deem supposedly innocent."

My entire body trembles and my heart races, pounding in my ears, dampening the volume of Uriel's every word. I try to swallow, but my tongue is sandpaper.

"*But,*" he continues, staring at me intently, "if you do as we ask, you have my word, the boy will be spared. He, and he alone, will be granted clemency…but only if you tell us where we can find him. The alternative will not be pleasant, I assure you."

The threat is clear on his face, and I know without having to ask what that alternative is. It's the entire reason I'm still alive, what I've been dreading since Mammon deceived me with Alexander's face, and then let his mask slip, revealing those menacing eyes. If I don't tell them where Caleb is, they'll use me as bait to draw him out. And if that happens, there will be no mercy.

If that happens, they'll kill him.

"I don't know where he is," I grind out through clenched teeth, biting back tears.

"Foolish, stubborn child!" Mammon roars, swiping a hand through the mist. "We extend an olive branch but still you refuse? You're just like your unrepentant mother."

"Finally. Something she and I have in common," I croak.

"A war is coming, daughter of the Morningstar," Uriel growls, "and we will prevail, just as we did all those thousands of years ago, the first time the Conqueror waged his war. You may choose not to help us now, but we will find the boy regardless, make no mistake about that. When we do, I will take great joy in personally presenting you with his head. When that time comes and you stare into his cold, dead eyes, it will dawn on you that we gave you the chance to save him…and you chose not to take it."

My wings flare out to the sides, my vision going white, as an all-consuming rage overwhelms me, blinding my senses, which in this moment, are no longer dulled but sharpened, honing in on my target. I step back and then hurl myself forward repeatedly, slamming my fists into the glass with all the strength and force I can muster. "If you touch him, I'll kill you. I'll *kill* you!" I scream.

It's only when Uriel laughs under his breath that I cease my assault. Drawing in a shaking breath, I follow his gaze, noting how the wall of the egg has cracked beneath my touch. A sudden hope sparks within me, but it's quickly diminished when the glass begins to heal, the fissures fading until all evidence of my outburst is gone.

Smirking, he turns and disappears into the mist, Mammon following closely at his heels.

"I don't believe you will," Uriel calls over his shoulder.

The Archangel's departing words ring in my ears as an unexpected night falls across my surroundings, trapping me in the same darkness and foreboding silence he once offered to spare me from. An offer I refused. Now, I will live in this darkness forever, just like Alexander before me.

Sobs wrack my chest as I collapse to the ground, and the shadows inch closer to my cage. As they pass through the glass and crawl over my skin—the touch of the gloom icy cold—I let out a choked whimper, crying out for the only person in this whole world who ever really mattered to me.

"Caleb…"

His face in my mind is the last thing I see when everything around me goes black.

ELEVEN

CALEB

I LACE UP MY boots and try not to vomit over the worn-in black leather. Alexander's dagger rests against my back in the hidden sheath Ishtar gave me, rendering it invisible to everyone else. I guess my teacher has contributed to saving Luna after all.

Standing, my eyes rove over our party of three—well, four, counting me. We're back in the creepy conspiracy room, all in black, which seems like overkill, but what else are you going to wear when breaking into a supernatural prison and defying Archangels and Archdemons? This has to work. Luna has been in that place for months, and it's my fault she's in there. She's strong but fragile, and I can imagine all the things they're doing to break her. Fuck Ishtar. Fuck Gramps. Fuck all the promises I wasn't able to keep to Goldilocks.

I'm very aware of the consequences if we get caught. The rest of them might get off with hard labor or imprisonment, but as the Great's grandson, I know I'll get the chopping block. Or definitely tortured for information and then discarded like garbage after the Council has gotten everything they can from me. But I don't care. Luna's worth it. I glance over at Asmodeus, clad in a ridiculous green dress that matches her eyes, as she's not part of our humble rescue squad. She gives me a small nod, and I tilt my head in acknowledgment.

I'm to keep my mouth shut about the dagger until the last minute. All the weapons from the Fall were supposed to be confiscated and tucked away, out of the hands of mere Nephilim, or from angels and Fallen for that matter. No more killing of the Creator's children. Somehow, before his imprisonment, Alexander got a hold of this family heirloom. I don't think he knows who his parents are, but I'm hella curious about that and how he got this blade.

Although Asmodeus says she trusts everyone in the party, clearly she doesn't. Or she doesn't want Nzingha or Alaric poaching the knife. They couldn't wield it—only Alexander's bloodline can—but they could take it off me and bury it somewhere, never to be seen again. It does help that the sheath makes the blade invisible. That's how I got the jump on Gabriel. The thought of cutting into the Archangel still makes me sick despite her being an all-time terrible mother to Luna.

Shaking my head, I force myself to concentrate on my current shitshow. So, two days after our last meeting, Asmodeus called the others back to Babel and fed them some bullshit story on how to open the prison while Hammurabi and I know the real plan. Get into the weird, ethereal plane where Luna is being held and cut that cage wide open.

This plan has to work. The thought of actually getting there and seeing Goldilocks only to leave her shreds me. If I think about it too long, I really will boot my breakfast everywhere. Determination squares my shoulders, and I wait, restless, for us to get on with it already.

"Return directly here. I don't care if you run into the Morningstar himself, Luna is to be brought to me. I can shield her for a time while the Council runs around, searching for traitors. Or Alexander, which is what I'm going to lead them to believe," Asmodeus purrs, smiling.

Hammurabi gives Asmodeus a bow. "As you wish. Come Caleb, Nzingha."

The king steps into the deep shadows and disappears. Nzingha follows but I hesitate, pausing on Alaric. He can't travel with us, as no Lights are allowed on the Shadow Road. It's the sunny, Blessed Road for him.

If he chooses a time to screw us over, this would be it. He nods at me, his face solemn, and he doesn't exude that irritating Calm that rubs me the wrong way. I nod back and step into the shadows.

The Shadow Road greets me, an endless expanse of smeared gray and black, like looking through a soot-filled window. The Road is tricky, all the markers look the same, and it's cold as hell. You need to know where to go, but I don't know what to look for now.

We're traveling to a place in-between, where Darks and Lights both have access simultaneously. Other than Earth, of course. My eyes land on Nzingha. She works for Mammon the same way Ishtar used to work for Asmodeus, teaching students combat and the art of persuasion—or how to break into minds.

The Council can't be there all the time, and though they've created a prison with their essence, they don't want Gramps or his allies finding Luna. Mammon and Uriel are in charge of prison security, each having trusted first generation Nephilim on a rotation, and guess who just happens to be one of Mammon's badasses of choice? Nzingha.

We're sneaking in on her watch. As the Blessed and Shadow Roads spit everyone out at the same spot in the prison, there is only one guard stationed there at a time, so Asmodeus didn't need to pull a Light ally out of her ass somehow to let Alaric in. This also draws suspicion away from her because she's not providing any Nephilim to guard Luna.

Even though Nzingha is Mammon's girl, she's awfully tight with Asmodeus. That might make me suspicious but look at Ishtar, loyal to Alexander after all this time. I thought she'd never betray Asmodeus. Then again, I never thought Lights could be chummy with Darks or Lucifer and Gabriel could stand being near each other, let alone have a kid.

The cold penetrates my bones and I shiver. We've been walking for a while, and this is an unfamiliar path. I navigate the Shadow Road like a pro, but I'm lost right now. Hammurabi and Nzingha slow, and I stop behind them. Raising a brow, I look around, not seeing a marker. But then a slithery sensation creeps over me, and my shiver turns to a shudder. Revulsion fills me, and I want to step back.

Nzingha steps forward and then I spot it, like a weird overlap in reality. It resembles wallpaper that's been poorly pieced together with one layer spread on top of the other. She touches it with an elegant hand and disappears, sucked inside.

My guts knot, and I glance at Hammurabi. His face is grave, lips pressed into a hard line.

"Don't reveal your hand until the last," he commands.

"You don't trust them?"

"I trust no one but my mistress, and even in that, I have been disappointed," he says, his voice bitter.

I suppress an irritated groan. He's still pissed Asmodeus didn't confide in him about there being another Gray, but after Ishtar, what did he expect? Nodding, I say, "I understand. I want Luna free, and I don't have time to get into a wrestling match with those two over the shiny toy."

The king grips my arm, and I flinch at the sudden violence of it. "Having the means to kill an immortal being is nothing to be flippant over."

I rip my arm free of his grasp. "I know that," I growl. "We each have our own way of dealing with stress. You're a rigid asshole, and I'm a facetious dick. We all have roles to play."

His scowl is fierce, but I stalk past him and reach for the marker. I'm sucked into an even bleaker space than the Shadow Road, nothing but roiling blackness and ghostly mist. I roll my eyes. The Council sure has a flare for dramatics. Then I realize Goldilocks has been alone in the dark for who knows how long and nausea overcomes me again. Nausea and rage.

As my eyes adjust to their usual feline sharpness, I spot Nzingha waiting, lines of impatience creasing her brow. Hammurabi pops behind me and Alaric appears from the left. I guess Asmodeus is great at giving directions as the Light made it here without help.

Alaric's expression is troubled as his gaze takes in the oppressive atmosphere. It's cold here, too. An invasive chill worms its way against my skin. But maybe Luna being an angel, she doesn't feel the cold anymore. I hope. She thought she was mortal for years so she felt mortal pains. And that pisses me off more. Gabriel is a real piece of work.

"I hope we haven't come too late," Alaric murmurs to himself, and I whirl on him.

"Why do you say that?" I demand, voice guttural with anger and fear.

"You know why," he murmurs. "I'm the one who found her."

My eyes dart away, shame flushing through me. He found her in a mental ward, isolated and alone. Luna doesn't like talking about her time in the hospital, so it's no wonder she's never been chatty about Alaric. And I help put her in this desolate prison. I want to go on a full berserker rage. I want to weep in a way I haven't since I was five and found out what a piece of shit my father is. But I do neither and just say, "She'll need us both then."

Alaric's eyes widen, and I hear Hammurabi's snort of disbelief. I know what I said is shocking. A Dark admitting they need the help of a Light. Luna would be proud.

Alaric gives me a warm smile. "Luna was right to have chosen you as her friend."

My answering smile is bitter. "I'm responsible for landing her here. Some friend I turned out to be."

"You're here now, aren't you?" Alaric says. "You chose friendship over power."

Again, there's a hint of something, a layer beneath the surface of his words that I can't see and don't understand.

Nzingha bites out, "Let's cut through the emotional drivel and carry on with it, shall we? We must make haste."

I scowl at her but nod. Alaric gives her a cool look of reproach but follows her without protest farther into the mist. Hammurabi and I walk together, the weight of my dagger pushing against my skin.

This place creeps me out. Though it feels like I'm on solid ground, this dimension lacks the density of Earth or even the Shadow Road. I glance at my feet. They're shrouded in pearly haze. Hell, I have no idea what I'm walking on.

With each step, my nerves wind tighter and tighter until I feel like there's a noose around my neck. My heartbeat kicks at my chest. In a few moments, I'll see Luna. What am I going to say to her? How can I atone for what I've done?

Suddenly, a shape hovers in the darkness in front of us. Inky blackness rests inside, and I can only make out the curves of the enclosure due to the white fog. They aren't even allowing her a light.

My eyes trace the curves of Luna's prison, and to my surprise, it resembles an egg. A giant egg. Nzingha stops in front of it, holding out a palm. Bright purple light floats above her hand like a ball of grape jelly.

The egg is an ironic choice. Ra, the sun god, was said to have been born from a cosmic egg. I'll cut Luna from her shell, and she'll emerge like the golden goddess she is.

The interior of the shell illuminates as we approach and I gasp. Luna lies on the floor, curled in a ball, her magnificent wings spread around her. Despite her frail appearance, her wings are glossy. The pewter feathers shimmer in the light. Luna lifts her head, meeting my eyes, and I take an involuntary step back.

Luna confessed to me once about how she thought she was losing her mind, succumbing to the madness stalking her since she was a child. I assured her she wasn't crazy—Alexander messed with her head. And before, well, her powers were repressed. Of course, there were going to be mishaps. But now…

Those beautiful hazel eyes latch onto mine, shadows swirling in their depths. She looks surprisingly mortal, as if immortality hasn't set in. And she's enraged. Pushing herself to her feet, her wings flare out, smacking against the curved wall of the egg. She bares her teeth at me and I flinch.

I knew she'd be pissed but I'm no coward. Swallowing, I square my shoulders and step up to the glass. Well, it isn't glass, and up close, it looks like tiny diamonds are studded throughout. I place a hand on the slick surface.

"I'm here to get you out, Goldilocks," I say quietly. "I'm so sorry I couldn't come sooner. I'm so sorry I got you into this mess." My throat feels raw, and I have to blink a few times to see clearly.

Luna strides toward me, mouth twisted in a snarl. Looking up at me, her fist strikes the glass where my face is. My head snaps back on reflex, but soon, I focus on her again.

"Luna," I plead. "You can beat the shit out of me when I get you out of here, I promise. Just step back so I can free you."

Her laugh carries a tinge of insanity, and terror soaks my skin in cold sweat. They've broken her.

I've broken her.

"You've come to get me out?" She cackles and then sobers so quickly it chills me. "You're not real."

I reel back, stunned. "I'm real, Luna, I promise. Baby, step back from the glass and let me help you." I hear the desperation in my own voice, and I hope she hears it, too.

Luna stays put, golden hair limp around her beautiful face. "You won't trick me again, Mammon. You're not Caleb. I keep telling you I don't know anything!" Her voice rises, and she screams the last words, striking the wall again. Spider web fissures spread over her prison's surface, and I hear Nzingha gasp. Then the glass—or whatever the hell it is—knits back together.

Alaric steps up beside me, and Luna stares at him, her eyes wild, almost feral. She shakes her head over and over again, and I want so badly to reach out and comfort her it hurts.

"Luna," Alaric says, his voice as gentle as a summer breeze. Calm radiates from him, dosing me, and my heart rate slows. Can his Calm reach through Luna's prison? Does it even work on an angel? "Caleb is real. We're all real, I promise you." He gestures to Hammurabi and Nzingha behind us. "We're here to help you. You don't belong in there."

"No, no…this doesn't make sense. There's only ever been one of you before," she whispers, rocking back and forth. "I don't know you." Her gaze darts to Hammurabi and Nzingha. "I don't know anything. Why can't you believe me?"

"Why doesn't she think we're real?" I ask Alaric, panic gripping my chest like a vise.

"Mammon can change his shape," Hammurabi offers. "It seems like he's used his gift on the Gray. Luna," he says after I glower at him.

"Shit," I say, staring at Luna. "Goldilocks, listen to me, I'm real. Remember, I saved you from those asshole Lights when they tried to hurt you? Gave them nightmares for days."

"I took you out of the hospital and to the Serapeum," Alaric says. "We rode on the plane to Alexandria together."

Luna's mouth twists into an angry grimace. "Mammon could have found Caleb and tortured him for information," she counters. "And finding out who took me to the Serapeum is easy. That doesn't mean you're real."

"I was your first kiss," I say, once again splaying my hands on the glass. I mean, she never said so, but I'm pretty sure that's a safe assumption. "I helped you unlock your Dark powers. I promised to take you to Babel with me, but then it all got fucked up. I'm so sorry for that, Goldilocks. Please believe me."

She hisses at me. "Don't you dare call me that, Mammon. Only Caleb can call me that. What have you done to him?" She sobs, and I feel like I just took a spear to the heart.

Nzingha steps up beside me. "We have no time for this. Get her out now or leave."

I bare my teeth at her. "I'm not leaving her," I grit out. "If you're so afraid, run along back to your master."

Nzingha lunges for me, but Hammurabi's hand shoots out, grabbing her arm and shoving her back. "We don't have time for this either, Queen. Asmodeus will be displeased if we return without the girl."

Nzingha raises her chin, her face a mask of ice. "If we are caught, Asmodeus's displeasure will be the least of our concerns."

Luna wails, and I whirl back to face her. Her fists and wings collide with the glass like a hammer, and a large boom sounds as fissures spread across the egg again like cracks on a frozen lake. Cold fear once again grips me.

"Have you considered how dangerous she'll be once we release her? She's clearly unstable."

I hear Nzingha's voice over my shoulder, and I fight the urge to punch her in the face, but her words do hold some weight. Luna could kill us all if we let her out, but that gruesome possibility won't stop me from freeing her. I promised her a better life, and I'll keep that promise. Even if it kills me.

"Luna," Alaric says patiently, "even Mammon cannot be four people at once. Think past the fog, find that kernel of yourself that recognizes truth. Even Gabriel doesn't know how close we are."

At the sound of the Messenger's name, Luna's head snaps up. "You mean my mother? The one who abandoned me? I thought we've been over this. Will you bring up the Morningstar next?"

So, Luna knows about her parents, and the Council has been torturing her with that intel. Usually, I'm good with my place in life. I've never wanted to Ascend like those Lights, chumps pretending to be good while waiting for wings that'll never sprout. But in this moment, I want to be an angel so badly I'd trade my soul for wings. That way I could take my dagger and my newfound power and hunt down all those on the Council and carve them up for what they've done to Luna.

Alaric and I share a look, and I know what he's thinking. Luna has finally become the dangerous creature she's always been afraid she was. And it's not even her fault. It's due to months of isolation and mental torment. Things I'm responsible for.

"We have to get her out now," I urge, throwing a glance over my shoulder at Hammurabi. His face is troubled but he nods. He'll follow Asmodeus's orders.

"Let's hope we can control her," Nzingha says. "King, Asmodeus gave you her essence. Break the binding."

Hammurabi levels her with a flat, hard-ass stare. "Child, you don't give me orders," he says, and her face darkens with rage.

For fuck's sake, even Darks can't get along. And no one has time to pander to someone else's delicate ego.

Alaric steps between them. "Enough of this. We're wasting precious time."

A cackle sounds behind me and I pivot. Luna stares at us with mad eyes, shaking her head. "Maybe you're not here, Mammon. Maybe all of you are delusions I've made up." The clouds lift from her eyes for a moment as she focuses on Hammurabi and Nzingha. "But I don't know why I'd hallucinate you," she mutters. "I don't even know who you are."

"Goldilocks," I try again, and she growls at me. "You're not delusional. We're really here, and I'll prove it to you."

She gives me a heartbreaking smile, tears wetting her cheeks. "They told me they'd kill you if I didn't cooperate. If I just told them where Alexander was, they'd spare you. But I don't know, do I? So you must be dead." Her voice breaks on the last word, and her chest heaves on a great, body-wracking sob.

Hate swells in my heart for Mammon and whoever else has been screwing with her mind. I'm even pissed at Asmodeus despite her putting this little rescue squad together. Could she have done more to help Luna somehow?

The dagger clears the sheath before I fully comprehend what I'm doing. Someone gasps behind me, but I don't slow down to see who it is. I stab the curved surface of the egg, giving the handle a vicious twist. I expect resistance, to struggle, something, but the blade slices through the essence of immortals like a scalpel through muscle. I drag the knife down, over, up, and across, cutting a large rectangle that's slightly uneven. Satisfaction flares in me after I sheath the knife and wedge my fingers under the rectangle, pick it up, and hurl it with all my strength. I watch as it goes sailing into the mist.

I never hear it land.

My eyes snag on Luna once more and stay. Taking a deep breath, I step inside her

prison. She gazes up at me, her lashes spiked from the weight of her tears. Her brows arch in shock, and she shakes her head again, as if trying to make sense of what she's seeing. I know she can kill me. I know I should be afraid, but as I reach for her and pull her into my arms, I find I don't care if she does. Relief at finally having her near shudders through me, and I breathe in her scent, like sunshine and the sea. Her hair is silken under my cheek. I'm so happy to hold her again that at first I don't notice her entire body going rigid.

TWELVE

LUNA

*T*HIS ISN'T REAL. THIS *isn't real. This isn't real. This isn't real—*

My heart jackhammers against my ribcage, my senses muddled, like wires crossing, as sensations and smells—both new and familiar—assault me, driving me even closer to the edge. I note the stagnant air of my cage, slightly fresher now from the large hole in the glass. Faces stare at me from beyond the wall of my prison, but all I'm aware of is the warmth of the arms wrapped around me and the intoxicating aroma wafting into my nose, which screams out a single word in my head.

Home.

I clamp my eyes shut, shuddering against my tormentor—the mask he wears now so much crueler and realistic than any other I've been forced to witness.

But this isn't real. It can't be real.

And yet—

I hold my breath. Why would Mammon cut through the wall of my cage just to prove this is all another delusion? He's already demonstrated how easily he can get inside my head and pluck out the small details I've clung to even in my darkest moments. Caleb's nickname for me. His scent—a heady aroma I can never quite place. Mammon could emulate these things with ease, that much I'm certain about.

But this…

I tense in his arms, torn between revulsion and a fleeting ember of hope. If Uriel and the others wanted to fully unhinge me, they've stumbled upon the right method to do it. Killing Caleb in front of me would've been a mercy compared to the false relief tearing through my body. Because this isn't real. It *can't* be. I'm alone, just like

I've always been. These aren't Caleb's arms around me. That isn't Alaric staring at us with shock and loving concern in his eyes—

I pause, my gaze catching on the Nephilim's face. His *face*.

Which glows with the familiar golden sheen of his aura.

Of all Mammon's mind tricks, this one element of all angels and Nephilim is the one detail he overlooked. The auras were always Dark, which worked for the impersonation of my father—and for Caleb, if the arms around me are a lie. But for Gabriel and Alexander…the auras were wrong. So, shouldn't Alaric's aura be wrong, too? Unless…

My breath hitches, my knees buckling slightly, as the illusion wearing Caleb's face hugs me closer, and I allow myself to entertain the foolish belief that what he's been saying these past few moments is real. That *he* is real, and the Nephilim holding me in his arms is the Caleb I know and love.

My best friend, come to save me from this hell.

I pull back just enough to look into his eyes, the dark swirling pools brimming with remorse and threatening to pull me into their depths and drown me. I exhale, a rising sob in my throat making me stammer. "Y…You…"

"It's me, Goldilocks," he whispers, cupping my face. His breath is hot on my cheeks as he leans in even closer. "I'm here. What do I need to do to prove it to you?"

Prove it to me? I shake my head. *I don't know.* "I—"

His lips are on mine before I can get the whole thought out, his mouth swallowing my startled gasp. I go rigid for a moment before melting against his firm chest when his hands snake around to the back of my neck, a shiver rippling through my body at the feel of his fingers trailing over my skin. They weave up through my hair, each touch desperate and hungry as if, he too, is trying to assure himself that I'm real. He holds me to him, deepening the kiss, every caress a silent vow that he'll take however long is necessary to prove that he's not just another memory torn from my mind and used against me as a weapon. He kisses me, embraces me, as if we have all the time in the world. As if every moment we spend here isn't hurling us closer to him being discovered.

That thought sobers me, and I find myself breaking the kiss, much to my dismay. And his. A frown downturns his lips, which part to protest, but I shake my head again. "Caleb—"

Brow furrowing, he brushes his thumb across my lower lip. "Hey, what's that look for? Did you really think I wouldn't come back for you?"

My throat tightens as the hysteria I've been biting back finally bubbles to the surface. "You shouldn't have. If they find you here—"

"Yes." My eyes dart past Caleb's shoulder to the stern woman standing behind him in the mist. "If they find us here, we are done for," she hisses. Her face darkens, her gaze fixating on Caleb's, which seems to harden in response to her words. "So, if you are quite finished with your dramatic reunion, we really should make a move. Oh, and little Dark?" she adds, her tone snide. "Once we escape, assuming we do, you *will* tell us where you found that dagger."

Caleb's upper lip curls back at the patronizing nickname. "It's really none of your business, is it?" he counters. He moves to my side, shifting his arm protectively around my waist. "The knife did the trick. We got Luna out—"

The woman steps forward, her gleaming teeth bared. The glowing ball of light in her hand trembles, and the mist parts around her feet, as if in fear of her fury. "Such weapons were said to have all been accounted for—"

"Or destroyed," Alaric mutters softly. His expression is distant. Contemplative.

The fourth member of their party—a towering, radiant presence despite the black and deep purple tendrils of darkness surrounding him—brushes the woman aside, planting himself firmly between her and Caleb to safeguard the younger Nephilim from her. "This is neither the time nor the place for such a discussion," he growls.

Shaken free from whatever thoughts had gripped him, Alaric nods in agreement. "He's right. We're wasting time. Save the questions for later."

Everyone looks at me then, and Caleb nudges me gently, pressing his side against mine. His fingers tickle my hip where they touch me. "Come on, Goldilocks," he murmurs, offering me a small, lopsided smile that might be the most beautiful thing I've ever seen. "Freedom awaits."

He steps through the rectangular hole in the glass and urges me forward, but I pause at the brink, frozen in place by the inexplicable hesitation sweeping through me. Could it really be so simple? By stepping out of this egg, will I really be free?

Caleb repositions himself in front of me, taking both my hands in his. The broken edge of the egg separates us. "I know you're scared, baby, but I'm here. I'll never leave you again. Never," he promises.

Never. That word repeats in my head like the toll of a clock bell chiming midnight. Our eyes meet, and the subtle nod he gives me is the only encouragement I need. Real or not, hallucination or not, trick or not, I just want us to be together.

I don't want to be alone anymore.

I stumble forward, stepping over the cracked lip of the egg, my grasp tightening around Caleb's fingers to steady me. My feathers shiver as I tuck my wings close to my back, and I sense the immediate change in the atmosphere around me once I'm fully clear of the glass. The air is somehow sweeter outside my cage, the white mist saccharine on my tongue, like spun sugar. And yet, even with the calming scent, out here in the vast open, the threat of the Council feels more immediate. Despite some hazy semblance of ground beneath my feet, this plane extends outward in all directions with no apparent end in sight. Without the safety of a physical barrier to shield us from an attack, our enemy could literally get the drop on us from any direction.

The others who arrived with Caleb watch my every movement with guarded apprehension, more frightened and wary of me—the unpredictable, insane Gray angel—than they are of Uriel or any of the other Archangels and Archdemons on the Council, the real threat to us escaping this place in one piece. The only one besides Caleb not looking at me like I'm a ticking time bomb is Alaric.

My heart clenches at the sight of him, and although I'm still not entirely convinced any of this is real, I long to tell this man who has been the only father figure I've ever known how happy and relieved I am to see him.

Instead, I blurt out the only words I can think of. "You're here."

Alaric's handsome face splits into a smile, and he steps forward, tousling my hair. "Of course, I am. Coming for you was never a question."

Tears flood my eyes as a dozen conflicting emotions strike me at once. My hands, which tremble at my sides, jerk forward as if they have a will of their own, my chest colliding hard with Alaric's as my arms wrap around his torso in a hug that would break any normal man's back. For a long, silent moment, he holds me, one hand gently stroking my hair and the other hovering against my exposed upper back, careful to avoid the roots of my wings. He doesn't rush me, even though every second I waste like this only puts them all in further danger.

The sudden manifestation of Uriel's face in my mind is like a sharp slap to my cheek. Drawing in a shaking breath, I release Alaric, sniffling as I wipe my nose with the back of my hand.

"Okay," I say, glancing at Caleb again. "I'm ready to go."

"Finally," the woman huffs, clicking her tongue.

Caleb shoots her a scathing look before grinning at me. When our eyes meet, the annoyance in his gaze instantly softens. "As beautiful as you look with those wings, Goldilocks, they're a bit too conspicuous. Do you know how to hide them?"

My cheeks flush at his words, and I nod. I don't dare say anything, afraid of what my voice might reveal with the audience observing our every exchange. Instead, I purse my lips, grimacing, as I focus on the feathers nearest my back. To my surprise, this time when I draw them back under my skin, the agony I've grown so accustomed to experiencing is almost nonexistent, as if being freed from my prison has removed whatever block—physical or mental—was preventing the broken flesh from healing. Although sensitive still, the pain is gone, making me wonder if it was always in my head—a negative psychological impact of my inability to accept and embrace what I really am. Whatever the reason, one by one, the feathers slip under my skin until the weight sitting at my shoulder blades has eased, my wings now phantom limbs. Instead of an angel, I once again resemble a human or Nephilim.

An uncontrollable shiver rocks me to my bones at the touch of the chilly air on my skin—a mortal habit I can't seem to shake since the cold doesn't seem to afflict me the same way it used to when I thought I possessed human blood. Still, I cross my arms, holding my torn T-shirt in place.

"Here," Caleb says. He peels off his black T-shirt, revealing his muscular, deeply tanned torso, before nodding to the tattered remains of my own shirt, split in the back from where my wings tore through the fabric when they first emerged. "I think you need this more than I do."

"Oh, for Lucifer's sake." The woman rolls her eyes.

As Caleb hands me his shirt, my eyes linger on the defined planes of his abs, a blush sweeping up the full length of my body, heating me right down to my core. His lips quirk into a smirk when I quickly glance away.

Turning my back to the others, I drop my shredded T-shirt to the mist-covered ground and pull the replacement over my head. Once I'm covered, I turn to face Caleb, who takes my hand in his, smiling broadly. I don't think I've ever seen him look so happy to see me before, and it warms the dark place in my chest that's grown like a black hole the few months I've been here, constantly on the brink of swallowing me whole.

"Let's go," he urges, tugging me forward.

Alaric and the other two Nephilim—whose names still elude me—form a protective vee around us like a flock of geese…if geese were all-powerful and possessed angel blood. I stumble along beside Caleb, clinging tightly to his arm, attempting to reassure myself this is happening. That Caleb is really here with me and, within a matter of moments, I'll finally be free of the prison I was certain I would never escape.

As we advance through the eerie shroud of mist, the silence is almost tangible, feeding my unease. Alaric walks directly in front of us, frequently peering back at me with an unreadable, focused expression. Every time our eyes meet, a sense of calm floods my body, pushing my fear back behind a wall in my head. In those fleeting moments, the oppressive weight pressing down on my chest lifts the tiniest bit, and I can breathe thanks to Alaric's gift, even if it's not as potent as it was when I thought I was mortal. The feel of Caleb's fingers squeezing mine settles me even further.

"We're nearly there," he whispers, just loud enough for me to hear.

"Where is this place?" Caleb meets my questioning gaze, and I can see in his eyes he knows what I'm really asking. *Where the hell is the exit?*

"In a space between the Shadow and Blessed Roads. We'll use them to get out."

Trepidation tears a fresh hole in my chest as my eyes dart toward Alaric and hang there. As a Gray, born from both the Light and Dark, I can probably travel either route. But what about him? "But Lights can't use the Shadow Road."

"Alaric's a big boy. He'll be fine," Caleb assures me. Noting the disgruntled frown twisting my lips, he adds, "Don't worry. He got here on his own, and he'll get out again the same way. He'll meet us back at Babel."

Babel. A thrill rushes through me at the thought of this mysterious place I've spent so many months fantasizing about, usually in my worst moments when the threat of insanity was closest. It had seemed like such a pipe dream—this notion of being with Caleb at a place where our friendship would actually be accepted—but now, that dream is just an arm's reach away. I'm almost afraid to believe it.

"And once we're there...what happens then?" I press, although part of me is terrified of the answer.

"Quiet," the female Nephilim snaps, the ball of purple light in her hand vibrating as she turns in place, scanning the unending blackness, predatory eyes alert. Caleb exchanges a worried glance with the regal Dark Nephilim to our right while I find my own gaze drawn to Alaric. His eyes latch on mine, and the faint caress of Calm he's been throwing back at me abruptly ceases, as if some unseen force has wedged itself between us.

"Luna—" he begins, but whatever he was going to say is interrupted by a sharp, grating cackle erupting from the silence behind us. Caleb and I whip around toward the sound, but my vision is blurry in my panic. It takes a moment for me to make out the tall figure standing before us in the mist, the broken egg looming in the distance behind him.

"Going somewhere?" Mammon asks, those blood-red eyes gleaming.

Raw, oppressive terror spreads through me, and I stumble backward, mouth agape, staring at the one person responsible for my rapid mental descent. My eyes flick left and right, but no other Archangels or Archdemons appear. Probably because they don't see the need. One full-blooded angel against four Nephilim, no matter how old or powerful, is no contest. The angel will always win.

Except, broken or not, I'm an angel, too. And I want nothing more than to make Mammon pay for toying with my head.

I clench my jaw, my hands balling into tight fists. Beside me, Caleb is tensed for a fight, his fingers hovering by his waist, within reach of the knife he used to cut me out of my cage, although I can't see where he put it.

Mammon steps toward us, clicking his tongue. "Your betrayal wounds me, Nzingha. And here I had such high hopes for you."

I glance at the female Nephilim, who bristles at his words.

Mammon's eyes shift to the intimidating Nephilim a few feet to Caleb's left. "And you as well, Hammurabi? Now, this is surprising, indeed. What about this mere whelp of a girl could have convinced someone as morally led as you to betray your own kind?"

"My reasons are my own," the Nephilim—Hammurabi—answers in a powerful voice. "Perhaps I am not the one whose convictions have been swayed."

Mammon cocks a thick eyebrow. "Such condescension from one so young."

Young? I stare at the ancient Nephilim, his billowing aura emanating age and wisdom. Even if I didn't recognize his name from the history class I took at my last human school, I would know he was old just by looking at him. Then again, to an angel who was there at the Fall, I suppose we must all seem like children, ignorant of the millennia of life and experience they have over us.

Years, which have clearly clouded their judgment.

Once again, the question of my own birth and age scratches at the back of my brain. If I ever see my mother again, I'll get that answer out of her, one way or another.

The Archdemon takes another step forward, radiating danger and power.

Caleb roughly shoves me behind him. "Go with Alaric. Take the Blessed Road and get out of here."

The panic gripping my chest squeezes tighter. "No! Not without you—"

A sad smile hitches up the sides of his mouth, but he makes it a point not to meet my gaze. "I failed you once, Luna. I promised myself I wouldn't fail you again."

"Caleb—"

"Alaric!" he calls over my objections.

A gentle hand grabs my arm, tugging me back, and that familiar Calm dulls my growing alarm, stronger this time with the direct contact of Alaric's hand on my skin. The sensation courses through my body like a drug.

"No," I try to protest, feeling drowsy.

Caleb glances at me before looking at Alaric. "Go."

The meaningful gleam in his eyes tells me this arrangement was planned—a plan B, so to speak, in the likely event we were ambushed. In my peripheral vision, I see Alaric nodding.

I struggle against the arms wrapping around me, but it's so hard to fight against the onslaught of Calm on my senses, like a flood of water filling my lungs. I know Alaric's only trying to help, just as I know Caleb is only trying to protect me, but I can't keep being this person, this victim—this damsel in distress, always in need of saving. I'm not helpless. I'm an *angel*.

And I refuse to leave Caleb behind to die.

Fighting the Calm, I watch in horror as Mammon sprints forward, his vermilion eyes flashing to mine and his lips peeling back into a ferocious smile, revealing perfect white teeth that remind me of fangs. In the blink of an eye, the Archdemon is gone, his features morphing until his real face is hidden behind the mask of yet another person I recognize. They're identical in every way; if Caleb wasn't already standing in front of me, I wouldn't be able to tell them apart.

Caleb pulls his knife free of its sheath, and time and space ripple around the blade as it takes physical shape, the edge of the metal catching a glint of light despite the enclosing darkness. He rushes at Mammon, whose smile only deepens at the challenge. He is a predator closing in on his prey, and his sights are set on Caleb despite the larger threat of the two older Nephilim flanking him.

Hammurabi extends his arm, but Mammon catches him by the fist and swings the Nephilim to the side, flinging him into the mist like a Frisbee. Nzingha comes in from the right, but he dodges her blows with practiced ease, anticipating her every move. To the Archdemon, she and Hammurabi are playthings.

A strangled scream rips from my throat. I don't want to be a helpless bystander. I want to join the fight. I focus on Caleb, and determination is my antidote as I feel the effects of the Calm fading, its hold on my senses loosening ever so slightly. Drawing in a steadying breath, I wrench free of Alaric's arms.

"Luna, we need to go," he begs, grabbing my wrist. The desperation in his voice hurts my heart. I know he's only trying to protect me, and I know how much he and the others sacrificed to come here. But it's because of that sacrifice I can't leave them behind to die.

I can't leave Caleb behind to die.

I snatch my arm away. "I won't abandon Caleb."

My blood runs cold at the grunt piercing the silence, and I swing around, dread filling me at the sight of the two Calebs, locked in heated battle now the other Nephilim are out of the way. One holds the other by the neck, and despite their identical features, I know with a single glance who is who.

Caleb claws at Mammon's hands where they flex then tighten around his throat, and the Archdemon smiles, like a child playing with his food before eating it. The knife Caleb was holding—his only real defense against the Archdemon, I'd wager, based on Nzingha's earlier reaction—is nowhere to be seen.

Fear and anger swell within me, adding to that burning fire of mania that has consumed me so fully these last few months. Before I wanted to push the madness away, but now, as I watch Caleb writhe in Mammon's grasp, I welcome the flames of my wrath and fury, letting them devour me whole. They lick over my skin, setting my entire body ablaze, and as they take hold, I recall all those times I felt a similar sensation of power and was too scared or ignorant to know how to use it. But I'm not the same girl I was when Alaric first brought me to the Serapeum. I'm no longer meek Luna, the orphan girl.

I am Luna Morningstar.

And now, I'm beginning to understand what I am capable of.

THIRTEEN

CALEB

M Y EVIL TWIN—OR Mammon, the piece of shit—grips my throat, and I gasp as my air supply dwindles. Even though my vision starts to get fuzzy, I know he's not using a quarter of his strength. He's playing with me like a house cat plays with a mouse, taking pleasure in flexing his claws. My dagger clattered somewhere at my feet, but the thick mist makes it hard to keep track of, and soon, I won't be able to see it anyway. Soon, I'll be dead. Regret over a thousand things I'll never get to do floods through me, but above that swims the beautiful face of Luna. Alaric will get her to safety. I'll finally keep my promise.

Before darkness can consume me, the pressure around my throat releases, and I'm suddenly blinded by a flash of crimson light, bright and hot. So hot. Searing pain eats up my right torso and arm, and I smell flesh cooking. I hit the ground hard, the mist blanketing me, obscuring me from view.

I hate this place. But the blinding pain tells me I'm not dead, and that means I still have a chance to make it out of here alive. Flames dance in front of me, penetrating the blackness, and I raise my head to see Mammon engulfed in fire, his face contorted in a scream. I glance down at my arm and see blistering, blackening flesh. My eyes find Luna, who hasn't left with Alaric, but whose hands and arms blaze brightly, like she's a righteous angel of death, come to deal out judgment.

Fuck, I just got the backlash of her power, but Mammon got the full brunt. I feel my skin healing itself, and I'm just a Nephilim. Mammon will get his shit together soon, and then he'll come for Luna with serious payback in mind. And while I'm impressed that she's let go with some damn good accuracy, she doesn't have the battle experience the Archdemon does. She might be as powerful as him, but she doesn't know how to wield it yet. I start sweeping my hands against the ground in a frantic search for my knife.

The fire begins to dim around Mammon, reduced to a halo instead of an all-consuming inferno. Hatred swells in his ruby-red eyes as he stares at Luna. He takes a step forward, but she doesn't shrink back, standing her ground. Shit, shit, shit. I can't let him hurt my Goldilocks or lock her up again. Where is that goddamn knife? My fingers scrape uselessly across the ground.

"Little girl, I shall punish you for that," Mammon says, grinning. He resembles a demented clown, with his half-melted skin and macabre smile.

Luna blanches, but then I see red flush her cheekbones. Flames burst from her once more. She's pissed off beyond reason. Mammon's grin grows at her rage, showing teeth, shockingly white against his burnt skin. I feel power gather around him, like electricity before a storm. Desperation seizes my chest as I look for the dagger.

Out of the mist, a freight train known as Hammurabi tackles Mammon from the right while Alaric dives for his legs from the left. They all roll to the ground in a flurry of limbs and blows. Mammon kicks Alaric off him, sending him sailing into the mist, but the Babylonian king lands some wicked hits before Mammon finally gains control and snaps his head back with a punch before pile-driving my teacher into the ground. Hammurabi disappears within the heavy white vapor. But it doesn't matter. My teacher's attack served its purpose. My fingers close around the hilt of the dagger, and triumph fills me as the Archdemon focuses on Luna once more, we lowly Nephilim forgotten.

My eyes narrow in on the wings he presents to me, still smoking, but knitting themselves back together, feathers filling in the raw patches. My smile is vicious. Like Ishtar once said to me, why go for the kill when you can go for the pain? Rolling to my feet, I sprint silently toward the Archdemon. I leap in the air just as he starts to turn, sensing the danger, but it's too late.

The blade swings down, and savage satisfaction fills me as the dagger cuts through muscle and sinew like a hot knife through butter. I land in a crouch and watch as Mammon's severed wing is swallowed by the fog. He roars, the enraged sound blasting my eardrums. Hammurabi grabs me and swipes Luna, and all three of us run toward the marker that will take us to the Shadow Road. I hope Alaric makes it to the Blessed Road where Mammon can't follow.

Fire sprouts on Luna's skin again and Hammurabi hisses, "Get control of yourself, child." He points ahead of us. "There it is!" He flings all of us at the marker just as a bolt of electricity slams into Luna, shooting us into the Road like a bullet.

Goldilocks drops, convulsing, and I kneel by her side. "Baby, are you okay?" My worried hands roam over her body.

"Boy, she's an *angel*. She'll heal. Throw her over your shoulder and run," Hammurabi orders. "Mammon comes."

Fear ripples up my spine, but I ignore him, my imploring gaze on Luna. "Goldilocks?" I prod. She looks up at me, big hazel eyes blinking. I stroke the smooth skin of her cheek.

Sitting up, she shakes her head. "I'm fine. It just hurts, but I'm…" Surprise shines on her face. "I really am fine," she says in astonishment. She notices my burnt arm and side, and she raises trembling fingers to my injury, not quite touching it. Tears pool in her eyes. "Oh, Caleb, I'm so sorry. I didn't mean to—I shouldn't have—"

Wrapping my fingers around her hand, I touch my forehead to hers. "You should have. He had it coming. And I'm fine, too. Already healing." It still hurts like a bitch, but the pain is dulling, and I'll be fully healed in a few minutes.

Hammurabi grips Luna's arm and hauls her to her feet, taking me with her. "Of course, you're fine," he growls. "Let's keep it that way, shall we?"

I swivel around. "Where's Nzingha?"

Shaking his head, Hammurabi says, "I don't know, but she's on her own now. She's not my responsibility. You two are. Now *move*."

Although Luna is an angel and outranks Hammurabi, the command in the Babylonian king's voice straightens her spine. I obey as well, even though I don't like the fact we're leaving one of our people behind. Nzingha is a pain in the ass, but she did put her life on the line to help. Then I see Mammon's head and shoulders pop through into the Shadow Road, and I decide Nzingha is a big girl and can fend for herself.

Hammurabi runs, his figure a blur, and we follow, my hand in Luna's. Her grip is fierce, and I sense her terror. The iciness of the Road whips at my face. Hammurabi reaches for a marker, and I drag Luna after him. We pop up in the Alhambra in the twilight of the gardens. The fresh scent of flowers and fruit trees invade my senses along with the cool trickle of water running through marble canals. I spot orange and pomegranate trees, as well as jasmine and lavender plants. I've never been to another place on Earth that smells as good as this, other than the Hanging Gardens. Luna's eyes round as she takes in the breathtaking beauty surrounding her, lingering on the Moorish architecture. The almost lacy clusters of stone that form intricate patterns catch the eye and hold it in the budding moonlight.

"Stop gawking," Hammurabi says to her, and I glare at him, but Mammon appears a moment later, and my heart thunders as Hammurabi pulls us into the shadows once more.

The next time we emerge is in Chinatown in San Francisco, and it's daylight bright. Luna squeezes my hand, blinking. We're in a dank alley running along a row of restaurants that stink of garlic and freshly gutted fish. Goldilocks's nose wrinkles, and she looks so damn adorable that I kiss her, nipping her lower lip and smiling at her pink cheeks.

"Do you want to die, child?" Hammurabi says, cuffing the back of my head. Hard. "Back in the shadows."

The charcoal-gray Shadow Road swallows us once more, and we zigzag our way across the globe. I only catch a glimpse of Mammon twice, once in Machu Picchu and once in Hong Kong. Worry gnaws at me that he'll follow us to Babel or that he's letting us run around like a dog chasing its tail while he's decided to lay in wait and ambush us at the academy. But I don't really know if he suspects Asmodeus or if he thinks Hammurabi has sided with Alexander. If Nzingha can turn against him, maybe it'll be easier to believe that Hammurabi betrayed Asmodeus, too. I mean, I'm sure Mammon knows just how persuasive my grandfather can be.

Finally, we emerge into the Hanging Gardens, the comforting scents of citrus trees and flowers washing over me. I didn't realize how much I've missed Babel. It's just as much my home as my mom's apartment in New York City. But I am surprised Hammurabi dropped us so close to the academy. I'm about to call him out on it when he whisks us away again, yanking us into the same creepy room down in Babel's subterranean level.

Asmodeus sits at the head of the table with all the regality of a queen. Alaric paces beside her, thank the Morningstar, and to my shock, Nzingha stands to her left, spine rigid. I thought she'd go AWOL for a while, but then again, Asmodeus does offer some protection from Mammon's wrath. It is a little weird, though, that she doesn't have a scratch on her, considering she betrayed her boss. Mammon should have been gunning for her hardest of all. Yet, she's the only one who escaped the Archdemon unscathed, having missed most of the battle.

Alaric stops moving the moment he sees us, a profound look of relief passing over his face when his eyes meet Luna's. She gives him a warm smile, and I would be jealous, but I get a total dad vibe when he looks at her. Her smile dies when she meets Asmodeus's calculating green eyes. Luna curves into my side, and I slide an arm around her waist.

"Well done, King," Asmodeus says fondly. She tosses her red hair, focusing on me. "And well done, Caleb. Babel truly molds the most outstanding students. Even when half naked, they manage a rescue."

I flush at her salacious grin, but I can't deny I like seeing my shirt on Luna. It'll smell like her now. She'll smell like me.

Asmodeus's eyes meet Luna's. "You must be Luna, the Morningstar's daughter. You resemble him, child."

That draws a shy smile from Luna. "Do you really think so?" she asks, as if seeking affirmation from someone who knows her father well. My heart swells with tenderness for her. Yeah, my dad sucks, but I had my mom. She had no one. I tuck her even closer to me, so happy to have her near me again.

"Yes," Hammurabi says gruffly. "You do, but I can see your mother, too, if I look closely."

"I admit that I can't," Nzingha says, "but it might be because I dislike your mother."

Luna stiffens, but says, voice all jagged edges, "I guess we have something in common."

This draws a laugh from Asmodeus. "Aren't you delightful?"

"You mean for a Gray?" Luna says, anger clouding her face, and I'm proud of her spunk. "Did you help put me in that place?" Her accusation rings out, harsh and cutting.

I flinch, looking at Asmodeus. The Archdemon tilts her head, sizing Luna up, and it hits me once again that Luna isn't a Nephilim like me. She's an angel. She could seriously hurt Asmodeus, but the Archdemon doesn't suffer disrespect. She's also used to being on the top of the food chain, and even though Luna *is* an angel, she hasn't fought in wars like the mistress of Babel. Asmodeus won't look at her as an equal.

"I did," Asmodeus says, and frost coats every surface of the room. "And you should be glad of it, because if I'd refused to participate, I would've been hunted like your parents and in no position to give you aid. You would have rotted there until the Conqueror decided to use you. You're new to the world—*my* world. You've yet to learn to play the game. Righteous indignation about the unfairness of it all rarely keeps you alive. I do regret you've suffered, as I would hate any child of Lucifer's to suffer, but I came for you as soon as I could. All the pieces needed to fall into place."

Luna is quiet, digesting Asmodeus's words. She looks up at me, placing a few inches between us. "Why didn't Alexander come for me? Why bother to remove the bind at all if he was just going to abandon me?"

If she ripped my heart out of my chest, she couldn't hurt me more as I hear her unspoken question: Why didn't *I* come sooner? "I tried to convince him, Luna. I tried to tell him we had to get you out immediately, but he wouldn't listen. And I knew if I pushed him too far..." I hope she hears the sorrow and desperation in my voice, the fear. "I had to see if I could get some allies on my side so I could come for you. Gramps is too busy building an army. Oh, he would've gotten you out—when it was strategic for him. He's not who...I wanted him to be." Shame burns through me, and I don't want to reveal any more of myself to the rapt audience around me. When Luna and I are alone, I'll tell her more. How the father figure I always wanted turned out to be a selfish asshole like my real dad.

Alaric watches me, a frown pulling at his mouth, a faraway look in his eyes. Hammurabi's face reflects rare sympathy, and I glance away, taking in Luna's expression. There's no condemnation written across her skin, just an exhaustion, a weariness she wears like a heavy blanket she can't shed. Maybe she's tired of people failing her. Relief pours through me as she clutches at my hand once more. I squeeze back, wanting so badly to kiss her but leashing myself. I've given our audience enough of a show.

"People are rarely who you want them to be," Asmodeus tells me kindly. Her expression hardens. "Let's put the family squabbles aside and focus on more immediate concerns. Now that the Council knows exactly who helped Luna escape, they'll be hunting you. I can't allow you to stay at Babel."

FOURTEEN

LUNA

MY HEART PLUMMETS INTO my feet as my resurfacing terror surges up my throat like vomit. Just like when I thought I was human, even now, no place will keep or accept me. I'm a curse on this world, bringing chaos and danger wherever I go. Here at Babel, I thought I would finally find a place I belong but, like always, I was wrong. I can't stay here. It isn't safe—not for me, but for them.

Because I'm not safe.

That thought is a wrecking ball to my chest, and my legs go limp as the air seems to rip from the room. Each inhalation is a desperate gasp as I claw at my throat, no longer able to breathe.

"Luna!"

Alaric's voice reaches me from somewhere in the distance and strong arms catch me before I hit the floor. I glance up through my blurring vision to find Caleb looking down at me, his body rigid, and those molten eyes rounded and wild. "Hey, it's okay. I'm here, Goldilocks. I got you. Just breathe."

But as much as I try to heed his words, I can't. My lungs might as well not exist.

Do angels even need oxygen?

A choked, crazed laugh escapes me at the fleeting notion. I must truly seem mad to the others.

"Alaric," Caleb bites out. His tone is pleading, but I struggle to process why through the hysteria overwhelming me.

My lips part on another broken inhale, the room around me spinning as the world tilts on its axis. But then, the returning lunacy drifts away, pushed back by a sense of serenity that mutes my panic and sends my body into a state of forced relaxation. Gradually, my airways open up, and I draw in a breath, gasping as I drag air into my lungs.

Calm, I realize as I slowly regain control of my senses. Although every other time I've hated Alaric using his gifts to subdue me, in this moment, I'm thankful for it. I can think clearly now. Sanity actually seems within reach.

Cradling me, Caleb lets out a ragged sigh before redirecting his attention toward the headmistress of Babel. His piercing eyes stare daggers at her. "I'm sorry, am I huffing glue, or did you just say we can't stay here?"

Asmodeus's unblinking gaze hardens on him. "You were discovered aiding Luna in her escape. The Council knows who you are, who *each* of you are," she amends, glancing at every face in the room in turn. "You knew what you were signing up for. You knew this was a possibility."

"Not five seconds after getting her back!" Caleb shouts, fury emanating from his body like heat.

Hammurabi steps forward and plants a firm hand on Caleb's shoulder. "There will be repercussions for any who defy the Council, boy. You know this. Asmodeus cannot continue to help us if she is exposed—"

Asmodeus holds up her hand to silence the Nephilim then turns her focus back to Caleb, who props me upright against his warm side. Despite the fuming glare he throws her way, her own expression softens, and behind her intimidating exterior, I catch a glimpse of the Archdemon's fondness for him. "You are so young to this world, and your mortality makes you brash and reckless. As much as I admire your spirit and desire to intervene in unjust crimes against our kind, I do not have the luxury to do the same. You might not like it, but I will not cut off my nose to spite my face. If my part in this is discovered by the Council, I will be cast out, and you will be without the help of a powerful ally." She lowers her voice, her eyes hooded and sad. "Believe me when I say an eternity is a very long time to spend in exile."

She and Caleb exchange a knowing look, and he seems to understand something I don't because he mutters, "Like Lilith."

Lilith?

Asmodeus nods. "She made her choice and look what happened. I cannot afford to be impulsive, and I will not abandon my students for the sake of claiming some moral higher ground. I know where my allegiance lies and so do those who need to know it."

"So, what is the plan then?" Alaric asks.

He stands to my left, tall and lithe, leaning against the stone wall with his arms crossed over his chest, his clean-pressed linen shirt wrinkle-free, as if we didn't just escape a supernatural prison by the skin of our teeth. His expression is grave, and although he exudes that poised air of composure I've come to expect from him, the flustered, squirming movements of his aura make me realize he's anything but. The faint sheen of sweat on his forehead also indicates a strain he's trying hard to hide.

The Archdemon waves her hand impassively toward the door. "You require protection, which, regrettably, I cannot give. But there are others who can."

Her sharp, calculating eyes meet mine, and I grasp her meaning at once. "You mean my parents."

Across the room, Hammurabi scoffs. "Even with the Messenger and Morningstar by their sides, the children are still outnumbered, and need I remind everyone, they are just that: *children*. This is a battle that cannot be won through sheer force of will."

With a devilish grin, Asmodeus cuts her gaze to the regal Nephilim's. "Which is why you'll be accompanying the *children* until we have a plan. Gabriel and Lucifer cannot do this alone, and they will need me on the inside to keep you all informed of the Council's movements."

This seems to catch Hammurabi off guard, and I suspect he's not someone who surprises easily. His Dark aura quivers in the silence as he stares at the Archdemon.

Asmodeus arches an eyebrow. "Is that a problem?"

Composing himself, the Nephilim places a hand on his chest, over his heart. "No, Headmistress. Besides, it must fall on someone to keep young Caleb out of trouble."

"Um, need I remind you I'm the badass who cut off Mammon's wing?" Caleb protests, earning a shocked glance from the Archdemon, who clearly wasn't aware of that yet.

A shadow crosses her face as she shoots a terrifying glare at Nzingha. "If that is true, Mammon will be out for blood. We may all be in far more danger than we thought."

Nzingha says nothing, and I peer around the room at the others, confused. "Won't it just grow back?" I recall when I set those students on fire back in Alexandria. They healed quickly enough, and they were just Nephilim. Surely, an angel would heal even faster.

Caleb frowns. "Do you remember the library at the Serapeum? The museum tucked away at the back?"

I nod, remembering the rows of glass cases with clarity. Especially the display of moths where I first heard Alexander's voice.

"The weapons stored there were all from the Fall. The reason so many angels and demons died during the Great Battle was because those weapons were designed to maim and kill those with celestial blood…" He trails off, pulling the knife he used to cut me free of my egg from a hidden sheath, holding it up for everyone to see. Even crusted with Mammon's dried blood, I can make out the symbols etched into its blade. They're Enochian—not that unlike the writing we found outside Alexander's tomb.

As I stare at the length of steel, I'm reminded of Nzingha's surprise and ire at seeing Caleb with the dagger. In the moments after he freed me from my prison, that was all she seemed focused on.

"So, this knife can kill angels?" A new kind of fear sinks into my mind, and instinctively, I shrink away from the dagger and out of Caleb's grasp, even though I know he would never turn such a weapon against me. I stumble across the room toward Alaric, putting distance between us.

Caleb's skin pales at my reaction, and he quickly shoves the dagger back into his belt. "Yes, but—"

"Wait," I interrupt as a memory takes shape, and I see my mother curled up on the ground beneath the Serapeum, clutching her bleeding side with one hand and reaching for me with the other. "How long have you had this weapon?"

Caleb averts his gaze, red-hot shame flushing his skin. In his silence, I find my answer.

"You stabbed Gabriel," I realize.

He bites down on his lower lip, risking a glance at me. "I didn't know she was your mom," he says weakly.

Inching forward, I return to Caleb's side, taking his hand in mine, and his eyes widen with surprise as I say, "I'm just trying to understand. Does this mean she didn't heal?"

Relief washes over his face, but it's Alaric who speaks. "A flesh wound would've healed with time. By now, your mother should be back to normal."

"But Mammon?" I hedge.

Asmodeus scoffs. "Cutting off an entire appendage is quite different. We are not lizards, child. We do not regrow our tails when they fall off."

I scowl at her patronizing tone. "Well, how am I supposed to know?" I fling my free hand in the air, frustration leaching into my words. "This is all insane."

And that's coming from someone who is actually crazy.

"Mammon's wing will heal at the site of the wound, though he will be marked by the loss and will forever be flightless now. Losing one's ability to fly is a fate worse than death for an angel." Asmodeus stares off into the distance, as if contemplating the horror of such an existence.

A tremor runs over my back and I shiver. Having lived so long without wings, would I feel their loss as greatly as someone like Asmodeus?

"Lilith seemed to be coping just fine," Caleb muses.

The Archdemon lets out a sharp, scornful laugh. "There's a reason no one has seen Lilith since Alexander's last conquest for power."

"So, why emerge now? If she's so fucking depressed about losing her wings, why team up with my grandfather?"

"Why, indeed…" Asmodeus scratches her chin. "Lilith's motivations for supporting Alexander were always a mystery to the Council. I think that is a question best saved for the Messenger. She and Lilith were always close, even after the Fall."

Caleb snorts. "It's hard to imagine Gabriel with a bestie."

The conversation dims to a background hum as my thoughts take a turn in another direction. If my mother was close with this Lilith as Asmodeus claims, would she know about the circumstances surrounding my birth? Perhaps she's the only one who does.

Nzingha huffs loudly, shaking me out of my thoughts. "We are getting off track. What is the plan moving forward?"

Asmodeus looks around the room, meeting each of our questioning gazes. "I can mask your presence here for two days but no more. Any longer and we risk being discovered, and that's assuming Mammon doesn't come here sooner, sniffing around like the dog he is. In the meantime, I will try to throw the Council off your trail."

"And where do we go after that?" I press, my voice wavering.

If we can't stay here, where else can we go?

"That is not for me to decide, and the fewer who are aware of your whereabouts, the better." Asmodeus pushes her chair back, the wooden legs scraping across the stone floor as she stands. "But you cannot do this alone. Angel or not, you are vulnerable. All the more reason to find Gabriel and Lucifer quickly. They will protect you, wherever you go, from those who wish to do you harm."

"Yeah, and then what?" Caleb growls through clenched teeth. "We just go on the run forever?"

"Not forever," the Archdemon counters. Her eyes shift to mine. "I am not Lucifer's only ally, but we need time to prepare. Your parents can buy us that time."

"And how are we supposed to find them?" All eyes swing to Hammurabi. "No one has seen them in months."

Alaric nods, his expression grim. "I tracked them for weeks, but they're avoiding the Roads. They're traveling everywhere by air, and I'm not able to follow that way."

"You don't need to." Asmodeus crosses the room to Alaric and grabs his hand, turning his arm and tugging up his crisp shirt sleeve until his wrist is exposed. "This will allow you to commune with the Morningstar. Not verbally—the connection is more of an echo—but it will be enough to lead you to his location or call him to yours. Find him, agree on a safe place for the interim, and get back here before two days have passed." She places her other hand over the skin at his wrist, and when she pulls it away, a small circular Enochian symbol is visible, a white marking branded into his flesh. "I know you could track him down with that nose of yours, but this will make the hunt quicker."

Alaric gapes at Asmodeus, shock and disbelief evident in his gaze as he snaps his startled eyes up from his freshly tattooed wrist to meet hers. "Nephilim are never granted the sigils."

A sly grin stretches across the Archdemon's face. "I suppose there's a first time for everything."

We all watch the exchange in stunned awe, but no one comments on the enormity of this moment or dares to protest against the Archdemon's decision—that not only is a Nephilim receiving an honor it seems is only reserved for angels, but that a Light is receiving such a gift from a Dark. Maybe everyone is just too afraid to question Asmodeus.

My chest tightens at this unabashed display of respect, and for the first time in months, I feel renewed resolve that the divide doesn't have to be permanent. That it can be bridged, paving the way for a future where Caleb and I can be together despite everything.

I look over at him, feeling my cheeks heat, watching him closely, willing him to meet my gaze. But his focus is pinned firmly on his headmistress, those beautiful brown eyes alight with rage.

"Wait a minute, you've had the angel equivalent of the Bat Signal this whole time and what? Just chose not to use it?"

"Don't be dense, boy," Hammurabi chides. "It is common knowledge our mistress is…*close* with the Morningstar. The Council likely assumes she would be the first person he'd run to for aid."

"Not to mention, the sigils are traceable, our magic identifiable," Asmodeus says. "Were Alaric to be caught by the Council, they would immediately know I was the one who bestowed it upon him. But we no longer have the luxury of time, so"—a coy grin shapes her lips as her eyes snap to Alaric's—"do try not to get caught."

Beside me, Caleb attempts to protest, but Asmodeus clicks her tongue, silencing him.

"As for why I didn't contact the Morningstar directly after he fled with the Messenger…" She arches a brow, the warning—and reminder of the danger we face—clear in her emerald gaze. "Like you, they are fugitives. We needed to maintain that separation so no one would question my loyalty to the Council. It was a risk we could not afford, especially if I was to help release his only child from her prison. Hence why I helped lock you away in the first place."

She casts a meaningful glance at me, and Caleb flushes, clenching his jaw so tightly I swear I hear the muscles pop.

I peer at each of the somber faces around me, frowning. I feel so out of the loop—it's like everyone is speaking a foreign language, and I'm only picking up bits and pieces of what they're saying.

My frown deepens when Alaric crosses the room toward me, purpose behind every step. He meets my gaze, his own expression morose.

"You're leaving again," I push out before he can say it.

"I have to, for your sake." He places a hand on my cheek and offers me a gentle smile, a fatherly fondness in his gaze I've never seen from anyone else in my life. "But I *will* be back. This time, with your parents in tow."

Caleb, seeming to sense my unease, slides his arm around my waist again. "Be careful." He extends his right hand, which Alaric takes without hesitation. "And thank you. For helping me get Luna back."

His smile falters. "Our world is a cruel and prejudiced place. I only hope I can help shape a future where the two of you can be happy. And free," he adds so softly I barely hear it.

Although he keeps his composed mask in place, behind his words, I hear everything he isn't saying. I sense the regret he must feel over his own past, even if he refuses to voice it aloud.

And in this moment, as I glimpse the sadness welling in his amber eyes, I know he's thinking of Alexander.

FIFTEEN

CALEB

"CALEB, A WORD BEFORE I go?" Alaric says, startling me.

I glance between him and Luna. What does he want to say to me that she can't hear? "Um, sure." I look to Asmodeus, silently asking for help.

"I'll show Luna where you'll be staying. You can catch up when you're finished," the Archdemon says, amusement shining in her green eyes.

Luna shoots me a panicked look, clearly uncomfortable with being alone with Asmodeus. Hammurabi and Nzingha stroll out of the room, and I guess they know where they plan to hide away for the next two days. Lucky them.

Alaric smiles at Luna. "I promise I won't keep him more than a minute."

Asmodeus sweeps from the room, and a reluctant Luna trudges after her, glancing over her shoulder at me one last time.

I face Alaric, waving an impatient hand. "I don't want to leave the two of them alone longer than I have to, so spill," I say.

The Light Nephilim nods. "Luna has been traumatized," he begins, and I resist rolling my eyes and yelling, "Duh!" at him. "I need you to help ground her now. Adrenaline is keeping her afloat for the moment, but she can't afford to be overwhelmed by her emotions or fall into some catatonic state once it wears off. She needs her wits about her if she's to survive what is coming."

That quickly sobers me. "How do you suggest I do that? I'm not a shrink. I don't want to fuck things up even more by saying the wrong thing. And I know she's upset with me." I wince as those last words escape my lips. It took me months to get her out of that cell, and she found out I stabbed her mother. We got a lot of issues to work out, and I don't want to accidentally push her over the edge.

"Caleb, Luna cares for you a great deal. If you're honest with her, I'm confident she'll understand. I think she'll also appreciate your candor. It will feel like she's gained some control over her life because she will have more information about what has been happening. She needs that control. Keeping her in the dark will only make things worse. Tell her everything. Beg for absolution. She'll grant it. Of that I'm certain." He squeezes my shoulder and I nod.

"I'll do my best," I promise, even though queasiness settles into the pit of my stomach. I hope that when my guts are spilled and laid out before her, she does decide to forgive me. Her kisses and acceptance of my touch give me hope, though. I can't totally repulse her if she seems to need to touch me as much as I need to touch her.

"I never had a doubt," Alaric replies. "Be well, Caleb. Oh, before I forget." He hands me a scrap of paper with a number on it. "My cell."

I snort, taking the paper. "Thanks. Good luck finding the Morningstar," I say then add grudgingly, "and the Messenger."

Alaric taps his wrist. "I won't need luck."

He strides out the door and I follow. I spot Asmodeus and Luna ahead, Asmodeus keeping a snail's pace, bless her. Alaric disappears onto the Blessed Road, and I trot ahead until I pull up next to Luna.

"Did I miss anything interesting?" I quip, winking at Goldilocks, whose relief shines like a beacon on her face.

"Only minutes of uncomfortable silence," Asmodeus says, rolling her eyes, and I smother a laugh.

"You're the charming one," Luna tells me. "I'm the crazy one."

My humor fades. "You're not crazy. And Asmodeus makes everyone uncomfortable." My mistress scowls over her shoulder at me. "What? You do."

"Children," she mutters under her breath and even Luna smiles.

"Where are you taking us?" I ask, eyes trailing over my surroundings. I hoped she'd be leading us up, but we continue to snake down twisted hallways. It's like there's another Babel beneath Babel, but I don't like living like some worm burrowing underground. "Why can't we stay in the academy if you're masking us?"

"I'm not taking any chances," Asmodeus says. "Remain here until Alaric returns with word of Luna's parents or until Hammurabi or I give you permission to leave. You're safer here, as few know of Babel's secrets."

"You mean they don't know you rent out the basement to film horror movies?" I ask, and a giggle escapes Luna. An actual giggle. My chest inflates with ridiculous pride that I caused that sound.

The mistress of Babel arches a haughty brow at me, throwing me serious shade over a creamy shoulder. "Your mouth will get you in trouble one day, child."

"I turned my back on Alexander the Great, broke Luna out of angel prison, and cut off Mammon's wing. I think I'm already ass deep in trouble," I point out as we stop before an oval door made of thick wood with iron hinges.

Asmodeus's face darkens with foreboding. "Alexander will be disappointed in you, but you're blood, and while he might dole out painful punishment, he has need of you because eventually he will come for Luna. It is Mammon that is your true worry now."

I shiver. I don't regret taking his wing after what he did to Luna, but I'm smart enough to know I just made a huge enemy—one who will want to take my head and drink the blood from my skull.

Swinging the door open, Asmodeus ushers us inside. The room is blessedly lit by electricity. There's a large, four-poster bed made of heavy wood that dominates the room. There's no other furniture, and I see a door to the side that I hope leads to a bathroom with a shower. The room carries a faint musty smell but looks clean. I wonder why these rooms exist and if Ishtar ever took Gilgamesh down here for one of their secret banging sessions. My eyes flick to the bed again. Ugh, best to scrub those thoughts from my brain.

"It's not that I'm shy," I begin, brushing a hand down my shirtless front, "but I would like some clean clothes. I left some in my room." I don't add that Mammon's blood stains my skin in rusty streaks. And I want to clean the burnt flakes of dead flesh off me, too. "Please tell me there's running water down here."

"I want to shower," Luna says almost desperately, and I know she wants to strip her body of all memories of her imprisonment.

"Yes, there's a bathroom, and I'll bring clothes to both of you, along with some food," Asmodeus says. "I'll return shortly."

She steps out and shuts the door firmly behind her, leaving behind a strained silence.

I offer Luna a lopsided grin. "Take the first shower. You need it more than me."

Her hazel eyes crawl over my torso, that faint flush I love so much pinking her cheeks. "You've healed?" she whispers.

I glance down at myself, stretching out an arm. "Under this grime is brand-spanking new skin," I assure her. When that worried frown pulls her lips down, I cup her face and tilt it toward me. "I'm fine, Goldilocks. It was worth getting a little cooked to see you go full badass."

"I was badass?" she says, eyes locking on mine.

"Hell yeah, you were," I reply then nudge her gently toward the bathroom door. "Go. We'll talk after we're done cleaning up."

She hesitates for a moment, staring at me, as if she's soaking me in because I might disappear at any moment. "You'll be here when I'm done?"

Her doubt is like a gut punch, but I remind myself she's just spent nearly half a year in a prison cell, so she's allowed to feel all the feels. If she wants to doubt me, well, I can't really blame her.

"I'm not going anywhere, baby," I say, and she nods at me, turning and making her way to the bathroom.

✦

True to her word, Asmodeus returned with a fresh white T-shirt and jeans for me, along with some clothes for Luna, and delicious *biryani* resting on a silver tray on the bed. The scent of lamb and spices makes my mouth water. Fully dressed and clean, Luna and I devour the food. She gives a small moan, and my skin gets uncomfortably tight. Asmodeus brought her a black, long-sleeve tee that is completely split open in the back and tied with strings at the nape of her neck. Her lack of a bra doesn't help cool me down, but no matter how much I'd like to touch her right now, to celebrate that she's actually here with me, she needs time and space.

Then like a moron, I realize the back is open for her wings. Her beautiful pewter wings. I put my plate on the floor so as not to mess up the fancy navy duvet shot through with silver thread. I guess Asmodeus figures if she's going to hide fugitives down here, she'll do it with style.

Alaric said to ground Luna in reality, and the best way to do it is to talk about what happened, even if I'd rather have metal tacks driven under my fingernails. I can't bear to see her disappointment in me.

Luna watches me and pushes her own empty plate aside. Her eyebrows raise as I take a deep breath, squaring my shoulders. "Caleb?" she asks, her voice painfully cautious, as if I'm about to drop another bomb on her.

"We should talk about what happened, Luna," I say, reaching out and clasping her hand.

Her face shutters. "I don't want to talk about what happened to me in there." She means that elegant, terrible egg they caged her in. The fear in her voice is palpable, and I want to cut off Mammon's wing again in retribution. Once wasn't enough.

I simply shake my head. "No, not about that, but about Alexander, about what happened at the Serapeum. I want you to know—I *need* you to know—I didn't leave you behind. Alexander took me away from you. I begged him to take you, but he didn't listen. I would never, *ever* have left you of my own free will. You have to believe me."

Her dark gold eyelashes lift, her gaze probing mine. "Did you know Alexander was an angel? Is that why you have that knife?"

I give a violent shake of my head. "No, no, I didn't know. I swear to you. Ishtar didn't know, either. Hammurabi did something to her memories—to all the Nephilims' memories—so they would forget what Grandfather really was. I always thought I was just an exceptionally badass third generation. I didn't know I was that close to my angelic bloodline."

"And the knife?" she repeats, and I know she's thinking about me stabbing her mother.

"Hammurabi gave it to me, to protect myself in case shit went bad at the Serapeum," I explain. "Luna, I would never have attacked Gabriel if I knew she was your mom. I'm so sorry." But a secret part of me thinks she deserves it for abandoning Luna.

Her mouth twists in thought. "Yes, you would've, to save your grandfather. I'm beginning to understand how important blood is to angels and Nephilim. And it's not like...it's not like I really know her. She abandoned me." Her voice catches, the last words passing out through trembling lips. She squeezes my hand so hard it actually hurts. I squeeze back, letting her know I'm here for her.

Taking another deep breath, I confess, "I don't think you get why freeing Alexander was so important to me. I had my mom, you know that, and she's amazing, but my dad..." I clench my teeth, releasing her hand so I don't accidentally crush it. Then again, Goldilocks is Wonder Woman, so can I crush her hand? "He's a piece of shit who just makes little Nephilim and doesn't take care of them. I have all these brothers and sisters out there, and I don't know who they are. All this *family*. I'll never know—"

Luna raises a hand. "But your blood sings to each other—it's right here." She balls up her hand and places a fist over her heart. "I felt it when I looked at Lucifer, that beautiful knowing."

My laugh sounds like a rusty knife. "Yeah, Daddy dearest made a deal with the Archdemons to mask our blood from each other so we wouldn't come looking for him, doling out payback for being such a bastard."

Surprise cuts across her features. "Do you think that's what Gabriel did to me? I never felt..." She trails off.

I frown. I never really thought about it like that. "Yeah, I guess she must have." I shake my head at her mother's treachery. "So, you see, I wanted to free Alexander so badly because—well, he *is* Alexander the Great—and I just wanted…a dad. Some connection to my angelic heritage." A humorless chuckle escapes my lips. "Fuck, I sound like I'm a five-year-old crying for his daddy."

Slender fingers grip my jaw as Goldilocks forces me to meet her eyes. "There's nothing childish about wanting a family," she chides and I flush, kicking myself for inadvertently saying the wrong thing to her, especially when a family is the thing she's wanted most in the world. "There's nothing wrong with wanting a father."

I turn my face and kiss her fingers, my eyes catching on the golden scar on her palm. I didn't think angels *could* scar but there it is, as clear as day, and I hate myself even more for dragging her into this mess. For asking her to free my grandfather, her flesh forever marked by my lapse in judgment.

She blushes, releasing me, and I sigh. "I know, I just feel stupid. I wanted it so badly that I ended up hurting you in the process, and I can't forgive myself for that," I tell her, and she drops my gaze, staring at her lap. "And he wasn't who I wanted him to be. I begged him to keep his promise, to come back for you, and he told me he would when the time was right, but he was too busy building an army. Too busy dreaming of ruling Earth. And the more I kept pushing… Let's just say if I pushed him too far, things wouldn't have ended well for me."

Luna looks up at me then, eyes rounded with shock. "You think he would've killed you?"

I shake my head. "No, I'm his blood, but he would have made an example of me to bring me in line. And if I was hurt badly enough, it would've taken even longer for me to find you. So in the end, I left him and came to Hammurabi for help. Gramps had big plans for me, too, from what Ishtar said. Wanted me to fight in his war." I snort. "That's a hard pass."

"You turned your back on your grandfather for me? Your family?" Luna says in a quiet voice, hazel eyes stunned.

"Of course, I did," I say, bringing my face close to hers. "Luna, I made a promise to you, and I was going to keep it no matter what."

"Even if I cost you your grandfather?" she presses, and I hate the uncertainty in her eyes.

"You didn't cost me anything. Even if Alexander had brought you with us, we wouldn't have stayed. You don't want millions of humans to die in his war anymore than I do."

She jerks back at that. "Millions of humans will die?"

"My grandfather genuinely loves mortals, I'll give him that, but once he goes to war, who do you think will be the collateral damage? And he did want you by his side—he still does. I think part of the reason he left you in there was so that when he did finally rescue you, you'd be so grateful you'd fall in line with his plans."

A glint of that madness I spotted when we found her enters her eyes. "I would've been so broken I would've been useless to him. And he played me, preyed on my worst fears… He…" She shakes her head and gives me a piercing look. "Did you— did you play me, too, Caleb? To free Alexander?"

My heart drops right to my feet and shatters. I've been wondering when she would ask this. The dread has been like a fist encasing my heart, waiting for the right moment to squeeze. Shame tightens my throat, and I have to clear it. That simple sound makes her face wilt like a dying flower. "I never played you, not like you think," I confess, my heart drumming so loudly in my ears I can barely hear my voice. "I've always cared about you, even when I thought I shouldn't. And the closer we got, the harder it was for me to think of you as a way to get to my grandfather. You were my friend—*are* my friend. I was caught between you and family and this horrible wrong I thought had been done to Alexander. When I met with Ishtar, I wanted to leave you out of it…but she reminded me where my loyalties belonged. That you don't turn your back on blood." I can't hide the fury in my voice at Ishtar, at myself. "But I made sure she swore to take you with us, that you'd be safe at Babel. That was the only way I agreed to keep you involved. I swear, Goldilocks, I had no idea how it was going to go down. And I've been trying to get back to you every day since you were left behind. You can't know how sorry I am, how much I regret getting you into this shit with me."

Tears brighten her eyes as she stares at me for a long moment, mulling over my confession and apology. Her next words will give me absolution or damn me, but to my surprise, she says, "Did you come after me just because you felt guilty? Did you kiss me out of some weird obligation?"

This girl knows how to deal out a gut punch. "Of course, I feel guilty, Luna. Jesus, you've been tortured by those monsters, and *I'm* responsible for it. But that's not why I came for you. You have to know how I feel about you. I sure as shit have never kissed you out of obligation." I push into her space, cupping her face. "I kiss you because you're gorgeous and sweet, and I like how it feels." To prove my point, I seal my lips over hers. After a few moments, I deepen the kiss until we both break away, gasping for air.

She looks a little dazed but manages to say, "How *do* you feel about me?"

Luna is going to make me spell it out, but I owe her that. She's insecure about me, about everything, her world in total chaos right now. I want to settle her with the truth. The truth is just damn hard to say because I've never told a woman this before, other than my mom, and that hardly counts.

I touch my nose to hers, taking a deep breath and inhaling her scent. Then I ease away to look into her eyes. The words are like a boulder on my chest, hard to lift. When they escape me, she'll know she has the power to gut me and leave me bleeding. She already has that power.

"I love you, Goldilocks," I say, my voice rougher than I intended. "I'm *in* love with you." Tears puddle in her eyes and fall, and I kiss them away, tasting salt. I can't stand to see her cry. "Hey, I wasn't trying to make you cry," I whisper, gathering her to my chest.

She buries her face against me, hands clinging to my back. She sobs harder, and I feel it down to my soul. "No one has ever said that to me before." Her words cause me to stiffen in anger, and she looks up at me, big eyes afraid again, vulnerable, as if she's said the wrong thing.

"I'm not mad at you, baby," I say. "I'm mad at everyone in your life who should have been telling you they love you. Gabriel has a lot to answer for." I can't keep the venom from my voice, and she flinches. "I'm sorry. I know she's your mom."

Her fingers trace my lips, and I resist the urge to bite them, letting her talk. "It's okay. I don't know how to feel about her. I have so many questions..." Luna's eyes search mine. "I don't think it's your fault, what the Council did to me." She gives me a shy kiss when I open my mouth to protest. "People you trusted manipulated you. People you care about, who you thought cared about you. That must have been hard to say no to, especially because Alexander is your family."

"That's partly true, but I still shouldn't have gotten you involved," I say, shaking my head. "I should have told Ishtar to fuck off."

A doubtful chuckle escapes her. "Do you think she would've let you do that?"

"No," I admit. "Most of the time, I think she believes she's a goddess in truth. And she's obsessed with Alexander. She's a true believer."

"What does she believe Alexander can do? For her, I mean?"

"As a Gray angel, she thinks he can heal the divide, bring everyone together. That he was meant to rule here on Earth. That he's the only one who can do that."

A frown mars her smooth brow. "But what about me? I'm a Gray."

A wry smile touches my lips. "Exactly. You're a Gray. Doesn't make him such a special snowflake, now does it?"

Luna laughs. "Well, from the sounds of it, there are only two of us, and he *is* Alexander the Great, so that does make him kind of special."

"Yeah, but he's selling himself as the Messiah or some shit. I don't know how he was going to explain you to everyone, but I bet he was going to claim you as family somehow. Like you were a long lost princess come home."

Her arms slide from my side, and her hands find mine, lacing our fingers. "That would've been awkward with us kissing. Don't you think?"

Her cheeky grin is so unexpected, as is her joke, that I guffaw, almost choking. My ribcage feels ten times lighter, like I could float to the ceiling, even if I don't have wings. Speaking of wings…

I rise from the bed, my hands slipping from Luna's, and her eyebrows shoot up in question. I circle around her, and she twists her neck to look at me. My hand hovers over her smooth back, and I tilt my head, waiting for permission. She nods, curiosity lighting her face. My fingers make contact with her warm skin, and I know it sounds cliché as hell, but a jolt of electricity travels up the pads of my fingertips. She shivers.

"May I see them?" I ask, not bothering with a more detailed explanation. She knows.

That endearing shyness sweeps over her, and I think she's going to refuse, but wings start to sprout from her shoulder blades like spring flowers. Awed, I step back, giving her room. Moments later, large wings curve around her, feathers spilling across the bed, their sheen almost metallic. I suck in a deep breath, wanting to touch them so badly I have to ball my hands into fists.

But I don't touch without consent. I'm not that kind of guy.

"They're beautiful, Goldilocks," I tell her, throat suddenly dry, yearning raw in my voice. I'm embarrassed by how much I want to brush my fingers along those pearly feathers, but I can't hide it. I don't want to. Luna needs to know she holds power in our relationship, too.

Her gaze snags mine. I notice she has a gold sheen to her irises that wasn't there before, as if releasing her wings brought out the full angel. She takes in a deep breath. "Do you want to—"

"Yes," I say, eagerness filling the words, and she gives a breathless laugh. I sink my fingers into the velvety feathers near her shoulder and she sucks in air, her back bowing. I snatch my hand back, horrified. "Did I hurt you?" I ask, worried eyes running over her wings.

"No," she chokes out, her face scarlet, chest heaving. "They hurt when I was in that cage, but now…" She swallows loudly. "They're sensitive and…" Her chin drops to her chest, as if she's too embarrassed to look at me.

Oh. *Oh.* Well, that's interesting. I've never touched anyone's wings before. It's not like Asmodeus or Alexander went around offering, and now I know why.

Goldilocks peeks up at me. "You can…you can touch them again."

Damn, everything below my belt grows uncomfortably tight. I smooth a palm over her wings again, and her little gasp heats my whole body. I pull my hand away, my own breathing uneven.

The sexy, slumberous look in her eyes almost undoes me. "Why did you stop?"

Why indeed? Oh yeah, because I'm a good guy, and good guys don't let their dicks rule them. "Because it's been a long day, and you need to rest." When she starts to protest, I say, "And I know it's your decision, but I'm making this decision for me. I don't ever want you to look at me with regret. I would love to hold you, though, while we sleep. Is that okay?" I sit next to her and she nods, her wings retracting. I fall back on the bed, tugging her with me, until her head rests on my chest.

And I savor this rare, perfect moment.

SIXTEEN

LUNA

I LIE STILL NEXT to Caleb, relishing the calming repetition of his breaths on the back of my neck and the delicious heat of his body pressed against mine, his hand splayed across my stomach, holding me close, as if he's afraid to put space between us. As if he's afraid to let me go.

I know that fear all too well; I'm consumed by it. Except in my case, that terror revolves around sleep. If I dare to close my eyes for even a second, will I wake to find this is all only a dream? Will I end up back in the prison the Council constructed to keep me captive—trapped forever in that confining glass egg like an immortal baby bird? If so, then those beautiful words Caleb spoke to me earlier, words I never thought I'd hear someone say to me…

"I love you, Goldilocks."

If this is only a dream, then none of that was real.

Tears prick at the corners of my eyes at the thought, and I wipe them away with the heel of my hand, stifling the sob in my throat. This—being at Babel with Caleb, however fleeting—is so unreal to me, and I can't escape the constant fear nagging at the back of my brain that this is all an illusion. Another way for Mammon to get inside my head.

I flip over, snuggling closer to Caleb, tucking my head under his chin and pressing my face against the warmth of his chest, needing to breathe in the smell of him. To prove to myself this is actually happening—that he's here and I'm in his arms, and we're together again as we should be. His hand, which was previously on my stomach, now presses flat against the small of my back, and I flush at the feel of his fingers on my bare skin, a shudder creeping up my spine. The shirt Asmodeus gave me leaves little to the imagination, but I understand the need for it, even if it leaves me feeling exposed and reminds me far too much of how I was clothed all those months trapped in the Council's cage. Until I've acclimated to having wings, I'll have to dress sensibly. The last thing I need is to accidentally tear through a shirt in a moment of wavering composure and flash everyone around me. I'm sure nobody wants to see that.

Except, maybe Caleb, a snarky voice says from somewhere in the back of my head.

My cheeks burn with the intensity of a thousand suns, and my fingers grip Caleb's arm as an aching need surges through my body, my wings trembling under my skin with the sudden urge to rip free of my flesh. Great. Even as an angel, I clearly have trouble controlling my hormones.

"What's wrong?"

Gasping, I pull away slightly and glance up at Caleb, who peers at me with half-open eyes hazy with sleep. His voice is a husky purr in my ears.

I swallow as the heat threatens to devour me whole. "Can't sleep," I whisper.

Smirking, he grazes my cheek with his knuckles. "Why so flushed, Goldilocks? You weren't having any untoward thoughts about me just now, were you?"

The warmth in my blood reaches boiling point, and I bolt upright at the same moment my wings spring free of my back, unable to hold them in any longer. Caleb gapes at me, his eyes widening as realization sinks in, and he begins to laugh. Mortified, I cover my face with my hands, wishing I could find a rock to bury myself under.

"Hey, none of that." The mattress shifts as he sits up beside me, and I jolt when his hands wrap around my wrists and gently pull my hands away from my face. When our eyes meet, a noticeable shiver rolls through me. Even better. I've gone from unstable horny teenager to vibrating Chihuahua.

If I was capable of dying, I would.

"This is so embarrassing," I mutter, averting my eyes.

Caleb grips my chin and turns my face, forcing me to look at him. "You never have to be embarrassed with me, Goldilocks. Besides, you aren't the only one having untoward thoughts."

He clears his throat as my eyes dip down, and suddenly, our breaths seem deafening in the silence of the room. A room we're very much alone in. Licking my lips, I brush my fingertips across his right cheek, and his gaze seems to glow as he takes me in, his own arms curling around my back and pulling me close until our chests are touching. When his hand grazes my wing, an unbidden gasp slips from my lips, and he flashes a roguish grin.

Leaning in, he croons in my ear, "Careful now, Goldilocks. You keep making sounds like that and I won't be able to control myself."

A squeak of a laugh escapes me. Between us, he isn't the one who needs to worry about losing control.

As if to prove my lack of willpower, I thread my fingers in his disheveled hair without thought and yank his face down to mine, devouring his lips. His arms tense around me, and I sense his own hunger as he reciprocates my advance, his thumb tugging on my chin, coaxing me to part my lips and let him inside. As his tongue sweeps over mine, I melt in his embrace.

He leans me back onto the mattress, my pewter wings spread out behind me like a blanket of feathers, and as he trails biting kisses along my neck and collarbone, his fingers tickle over the most sensitive parts of my new appendages.

I finally understand why none of the angels or Fallen tend to keep their wings on display—and why Alaric laughed at me when I asked about Gabriel's shortly after I met her. There's something so personal about having wings, and when they're out in the open, I feel somewhat naked. Like they're meant for me and only me.

And now, also for Caleb.

A low growl rumbles in my chest at his teasing, and he chuckles, leaning in to kiss me again. But just as his lips are about to touch mine, a thunderous sound in the distance has him pulling away, his breath hitching and eyes suddenly wild like a hunted rabbit's. Sitting back, he snaps his gaze toward the closed door.

"What is that?" I ask, sitting up beside him. When he doesn't answer, I place a hand on his bicep. "Caleb?"

"War horns," he says absentmindedly.

I can practically hear him straining to listen, and I follow his wide-eyed stare when the two-tone sound is repeated a moment later. The floor shakes as it reverberates through the space.

"War horns?" I repeat, hoping he'll elaborate.

His focus doesn't shift from the door when he answers. "The horns are to Babel what the bells are to the Serapeum. They use them to signal day-to-day things like the end of class, but…" He trails off, and the hair on the back of my neck stands on end at the thought of what he isn't saying.

"But what?" My voice is a whisper, the words gritty like sand in my mouth.

Finally, Caleb meets my questioning gaze, and the unease in his eyes nearly undoes me. "I—"

A sharp knocking on the door makes us both jump. Before I can get another word out, Caleb leaps off the bed while I fist my hands in the bed sheets, unable to move—crippled by fear and still flustered from the last few minutes. Caleb throws open the door to a disgruntled Hammurabi. The Babylonian king's tall frame fills the doorway, and the black and indigo tendrils of his aura ripple with agitated alarm as he peers past Caleb into the unlit room, meeting my gaze.

"We need to leave." His voice is a commanding snarl. Turning his glare on Caleb, he adds, "Grab the girl and let's go."

My upper lip curls back into a grimace as scenes from the past seventeen years replay through my head like some sort of masochistic slideshow. How many times have I been referred to this way, like I'm not even present or allowed to be involved with any decisions concerning my own life? How many times have I been spoken to like I'm not even a person worthy of consideration?

The heat and lust I reveled in only moments ago melt away, swallowed by a blinding, white-hot anger that blackens the edges of my vision. Scowling, I grind out, "The girl can hear you."

Hammurabi and Caleb both gape at me, blinking like fools, clearly taken aback by my tone and the way I spit each word through clenched teeth. Rolling my eyes, I draw in a deep breath then exhale, searching for some semblance of calm within myself—assuming there is any part of me that hasn't been infected by the chaos I always feel scratching at my thoughts. Dragging in one more steadying breath for good measure, I retract my wings and rise from the bed.

"Caleb, what the hell's going on?" I manage, once the anger has dissipated.

He thrusts one finger in the air when the war horns blare for a third time, their rumbling shout ominous. "You hear that? The horns only make that sound—that *specific* call—when an Archdemon is visiting Babel. It's an announcement of sorts so we can all be prepared to act like the star pupils Babel has shaped us into." He lowers his gaze to the floor, his eyes vacant, as that fear I glimpsed before returns to his face. "But last I checked, Archdemons don't make house calls for a friendly chat in the middle of the night."

Hammurabi glowers at me. "Whoever has come, they will be here for you."

Apprehension sharper and more powerful than anything I've ever felt before sends an uncomfortable tingle up my spine. "They…as in the Council? They're here?" The ancient Nephilim's silence is all the confirmation I need.

Caleb runs a hand through his hair, the ebony strands still messy with sleep, his lower lip jutting out in annoyance as he blows out a vexed breath through his nose.

"How the fuck—" He sneers, swallowing whatever he was going to say, before flashing a quick look in my direction, his expression written with so many unspoken thoughts I can't even begin to fathom what he's thinking. Shaking his head, he snaps his focus back to his teacher. "I thought Asmodeus masked us." I don't miss the accusation in his tone.

Hammurabi cocks a warning eyebrow. "She did, but that protection means little if those she's hiding us from know where we are. If I had to guess, we have a snake in our midst."

Caleb scoffs. "You mean someone sold us out."

The intimidating Nephilim seems to grow three sizes bigger as he puffs out his broad chest, crossing his arms. "It does not matter how they came upon the information. What matters is that the Council has breached these walls, and if we don't flee now, with our hides still intact, they will sniff us out. Then all of our efforts to get this far and save the girl will have been for naught."

Flee? We were supposed to have more time. We can't leave now. Where can we even go? Where on this planet is safe for us?

"And go where, exactly?" I ask, unable to keep the panic from creeping into each word. "What about Alaric? My parents? We can't leave without them—"

Silence swallows my voice, and the tears resurface as everything I've been bottling up threatens to explode out of me in a cataclysmic wave. We can't go yet, not when I'm so close to finally meeting my parents. Well, technically, I've already met them, but I didn't know who they were at the time. Meeting them now would be different—a moment I've been waiting for all my life. So, we can't leave now.

We can't.

"Hammurabi…" The way Caleb utters his teacher's name sends pinpricks of icy fear along my skin. "What about Asmodeus?"

The Nephilim's face is an unreadable mask. He might as well be made of stone. "It was my mistress's command that I keep you both safe, and that is what I intend to do." His eyes, two black voids in the darkness, flick to mine. "If the Council has truly infiltrated Babel, then they will know of the role she played in your liberation—"

"Not to mention the whole harboring fugitives thing," Caleb grumbles. "I doubt the Council would look too kindly on that."

Hammurabi deflates, showing a rare glimpse of emotion on his otherwise stern face. "Indeed. Asmodeus likely sounded the horns to warn us and give us enough time to get out. There is little any of us can do for her now except honor her wishes… and survive."

Survive. That's all I've done for seventeen years. I'm tired of just surviving. I want to live. I want to be happy. I want to be free of this nightmare.

Free... My stomach drops as a sudden thought hits me.

"What if it's a trap?" The horror of such a notion is like a hand wrapping around my throat, and the more I think about it, the more I'm certain I'm right. "What if they're trying to spook us? To make us run so they can corner us in the Shadow Road? I was a captive of the Council long enough to know how much they like head games, and after Mammon—"

"They'll be watching the entry points around the school, of that I have no doubt," Hammurabi says over me with a grim nod, stroking his beard in contemplation. "If we enter the Shadow Road from here, the Council will surely know it."

The silence that follows is suffocating, like a thick, choking smoke permeating my lungs. I can barely breathe past it, and I know I must be hyperventilating because Caleb's hands are on my face, my hair, my back, constantly stroking me, trying to calm me down. I blink up at him through the watery film coating my eyes, and the expression I find there—the acceptance, the defeat—shreds my soul into two.

"Luna, listen to me," he says, gripping both my hands in his and holding them firmly between us. Swallowing, he frowns down at our entwined fingers. "You could go the Light way. Use their Road. Even if they're watching it, they might not expect you to actually use it, especially if we draw their attention away. If we distract them, you can escape—"

I yank my hands free of his, unable to believe what I'm hearing. "No!" I shriek, not caring how unbalanced or hysterical I sound. "If we run, we run *together*. I don't want to be separated again."

The tears flow freely now, and I crumple to the floor, my fingers clutching at my head as that unhinged darkness inside me rises like a tidal wave, ready to finally drown me.

Caleb squats beside me and pulls me into the comforting warmth of his arms. "Okay, Goldilocks," he murmurs into my hair. "Message received. We won't be. I'll stay with you no matter what."

Do you promise? I try to ask him, but I can't find the words.

Caleb plants a kiss on the top of my head, and his soothing baritone vibrates through me when he says, "Hammurabi, what are our options?"

The older Nephilim—who remains by the door, peeking out into the hallway every few moments, checking for any sign of our pursuers—doesn't look at us when he replies, "Escape on foot. Put enough distance between us and Babel so that when we do enter the Road, they won't see us. Then we move and get out again as quickly as possible."

With one hand on my back and the other around my waist, Caleb stands, helping me to my feet. He offers me a reassuring smile then exchanges a knowing look with his teacher. "Is Hilla far enough?"

The Babylonian king shrugs. "I guess we'll find out."

We make our way through the web of underground passages beneath Babel, taking extreme care as we tiptoe through the dank gloom, every movement precise and exaggerated, like we're trapped in an episode of *Scooby Doo*. Caleb never leaves my side, his hand a permanent fixture around mine.

He casts frequent glances at me before finally leaning in, his mouth tickling my ear. "It's going to be okay," he breathes so softly even I struggle to hear it with my enhanced hearing. "I won't let anyone take you again."

I offer him a small smile, even though the expression is forced. As much as I want to believe him, he's only one Nephilim up against eleven celestial beings of unmatched power. He wouldn't stand a chance against them in a fight. They'd break his bones and shred him like a paper doll just for trying. Even Hammurabi, who is a first generation and seasoned warrior, would be overpowered by a full-blooded angel.

Trepidation clenches my stomach, my thoughts growing darker. The sooner we get out of Babel and away from immediate danger, the better. Even if doing so means I might not see Alaric or my parents again.

I think of them now, picturing each of their faces in turn. As much as I want to see my parents—to speak to them, to understand the circumstances surrounding my birth—the person I'm most concerned about is Alaric. He sacrificed so much for me, risking exile or worse, by crossing the divide and working with Darks to break me out of my prison. If he's caught, I can only imagine what the Council will do to him. And to Asmodeus for giving him a sigil.

Be safe, I pray, holding onto the thought of his face. *Until we see each other again.*

Hammurabi hooks a right down a narrow passage, which, at first glance, appears to be a dead end. I'm about to ask if we're lost when he proceeds to walk into the brick, passing through the hard surface as if even the laws of physics can't compete with the Nephilim's power. Caleb follows without hesitation, tugging me along behind him like a distracted puppy being guided by its owner. As we step through the mirage, the air shifts, distorting like rippling water, before settling into the gardens we initially stepped out of the Shadow Road into last night.

The scent of citrus trees clings to my nose as I turn, taking in the broken wall we stepped out of among the ruins standing outside Babel. I place a hand on the stone, the texture rough beneath my fingertips. Clearly, that was a one-way exit. I resist the urge to roll my eyes. What is it with angels and their glamors? Nothing is ever as it appears.

Hammurabi pauses at the brink of the gardens, his head on a swivel as he scans the shadows with narrowed eyes that gleam in the darkness. I follow his gaze, my angel vision sharp in the cover of night. Even though I see nothing, goosebumps pimple my skin, and I shiver despite the warmth in the air. The gardens are quiet.

Too quiet.

Fear is a symphony drumming along the underside of my skin as Caleb's hold on my hand tightens. I can sense his growing alarm as clearly as I feel my own, and I know we're thinking the same thing. Something is coming.

We both whip around at the abrupt crunching of sand as Hammurabi throws himself in front of us like a shield, but in the split-second before he blocked her from view, I caught a glimpse of our pursuer's face. It's burned into my retinas, along with the sting of her betrayal.

Nzingha.

I shake my head. I don't understand. She helped free me, so why turn on us now?

I sidestep Hammurabi, needing to see her again—to know for sure we've been double-crossed by one of our own. By someone Caleb and Asmodeus trusted to help them. Her lips twitch when our eyes clash, her skin burnished sienna in the dim light of the cloud-obscured moon.

Hammurabi lets out a dismissive snort. "It seems our snake has finally slithered out of hiding. Asmodeus was wrong to put her trust in you, Queen."

"Asmodeus was a fool for thinking she could defy the will of the Council," Nzingha bites back.

Beside me, Caleb tenses, his face contorted into an expression of fury. "I *knew* it," he seethes, spitting the words with pure venom. "I knew it was strange you got off scot-free after Mammon saw you helping us."

A taunting smile peels back the queen's lips as two kunai daggers slip free from the sleeves of her shirt, and Nzingha hurls herself forward, like a piercing arrow in the night, the red and gold of her head wrap the only visible color as she weaves in and out of the shadows with the ease and grace of an acrobat. Hammurabi bursts into action, the desert floor kicking up in a cloud around his feet. As he races away from us, time seems to slow and the sand hangs suspended in the air, almost as if we're frozen in this moment—trapped, just like I was in that prison.

The ancient king and queen collide in a blurred tangle of fists, Hammurabi getting the first hit in, meeting her jaw with the deafening crack of a thunder strike. Nzingha spits blood out onto the sand by her feet before grinning at the other Nephilim with crimson-stained teeth. As they continue their lethal dance, I glance at Caleb, glimpsing the internal war on his face as he contemplates throwing himself into the fray or staying behind. Staying with me. His indecision sets my blood on fire. Wanted by the Council or not, I'm not some weak mortal with no way to defend myself, even if I am new to my power. Like I said to Alaric before, I can fight.

And I will defend those who risked their lives to free me.

"Go!" I shout to Caleb before launching into a sprint. Fire bursts across my palms as I scour the darkness for Nzingha, catching sight of her as she dodges Hammurabi's fist with an impressive aerial, her long, limber legs like hummingbird wings, blurring as she moves with a speed even my eyes struggle to track. I approach from Hammurabi's right as Caleb comes in from the left to head her off. She swipes her blades at him like a cat striking out with its claws but, to my immense relief, misses. Nzingha might be fast, but thankfully, so is Caleb.

The queen stops suddenly, her charcoal-rimmed eyes glowing with wrath. Sheathing her daggers, she drops to one knee, slamming her fist into the ground with such force a quake splits the earth, sending Hammurabi and Caleb stumbling backward. She then rises and pivots to face me, grinning.

"Hello, baby bird."

I direct the full brunt of my fire at her, but she moves too quickly for me to hit, leaving little more than a scorch mark where she previously stood in the sand. I spin around, searching for her, my eyes pinned wide, but I only see Hammurabi and Caleb.

"Look out!" Caleb shouts, but his warning comes too late. Nzingha slams into my back, pinning me down to the sand, her knees pressing brutally into the sensitive exit points for my wings, ripping a strangled scream from my lungs. The fiery vambraces winding around my forearms sputter out like dying embers.

The Nephilim traces the shell of my ear with her finger before bending down to whisper, "Say hello to your parents for me." Then the weight is gone, and I'm left with only a weird sensation where her breath and finger grazed my skin, as if I've been branded by her touch.

Caleb reaches me as I flip onto my back, and scrambling to my feet, I watch with bewilderment as Nzingha runs away from us. Or rather from the vengeful figure standing at the edge of the gardens like a goddess on the warpath.

"Asmodeus!" The pure joy in Caleb's voice nearly brings me to tears.

The headmistress of Babel wears a beautiful scowl, her vibrant hair whipping in the wind as her aura contorts, wrapping around her limbs like ribbons of liquid ebony. Her green eyes, which glow in the darkness, meet mine before narrowing on the retreating Nephilim's back. Beyond Nzingha, in the distance over the school, black and white shapes dot the sky, descending quickly.

The Council.

"I'll take it from here," she shouts. "Run!"

When Caleb and I don't immediately move, our attention fixed on the incoming threat, Hammurabi grabs us both roughly by the shoulders. "You heard your mistress. *Move.*"

"I can help you," I plead with Asmodeus, but she shakes her head.

"Your father would never forgive me if I let you get captured again." She offers me a bittersweet smile. "Now, go."

Hammurabi yanks on my shoulder again, and this time, I relent, swallowing the lump in my throat as the guilt of whatever is about to happen to Asmodeus sits like a weight on my chest. Beside me, Caleb seems just as afflicted, his eyes downcast and teeth clamped firmly on his lower lip. He curses under his breath, but neither of us say another word after that. Instead, we run as fast as we can, trying not to think about Asmodeus or what hell we've abandoned her to.

It's roughly five kilometers to Hilla, the nearest city to Babel. If I wasn't so incompetent at using my wings, I would've flown us there but, as it currently stands, I can fly about as well as a penguin. Besides, going airborne would've likely made us too visible to any watching eyes, human or otherwise, which leaves us with only one option: to run. Luckily, with our celestial blood, the trek takes a fraction of the time it would take a normal mortal. Still, those ten or so minutes seem never-ending with a small army of Archangels and Archdemons on our tail, and I constantly find myself looking over my shoulder, risking fearful glances up at the overcast sky to check if we're being pursued. My terror is only elevated by the fact I feel strangely off-balance, the ear Nzingha whispered into foggy, as if water is trapped behind my eardrum. The sensation makes me nervous I won't hear someone sneaking up on me.

The moment we finally step foot into Hilla, Hammurabi grabs Caleb and me each by the arm before tugging us into an empty alleyway that smells of cooked fish and a pungent, spicy aroma. Caleb and I exchange a quick look, and I barely stop to catch my breath before the darkness swathes our bodies, pulling us into its maw as if to swallow us whole.

When we step foot onto the Shadow Road, my body goes rigid, my eyes frantically searching for even the smallest indication that we aren't alone. To my relief, there aren't any Archdemons in sight, and I let out a breath as the tension in my shoulders eases just a little.

Although it seems the Council hasn't figured out where we've escaped to, we don't hesitate to follow Hammurabi, running as fast as we can, passing marker after marker while making sure to always keep a wide berth from Babel.

Caleb is the one to break the silence once we're far enough away from Iraq to assume that we haven't been followed. He pushes his hair from his face with his free hand—his other clasped around mine—as his stomach rumbles, drawing an irked glance from his teacher. He smiles sheepishly. "So...anyone else feel like some pizza?"

SEVENTEEN

CALEB

WE POP OUT FROM the Shadow Road into my bedroom in Queens, my heart hammering in my chest. Luna looks just as shaken as I feel, and Hammurabi wears a murderous expression, like he wants to pick up a sword and go on a killing spree. What the fuck just happened? I knew something felt off with Nzingha, but I was so happy to have Luna back and to escape Mammon I didn't give it enough thought. My inattention to detail just came back and tried to stab me. No wonder Mammon conveniently showed up when we rescued Luna. His little minion whispered our plans in his ear. Man, Asmodeus is going to kick her ass. Worry for the headmistress of Babel gnaws at me with sharp teeth. Now that Asmodeus has been outed, will she be on the run like we are? What will happen to Babel?

"Will Asmodeus be okay?" I ask Hammurabi, even though I feel stupid the moment the words leave my lips. Of course, she won't be if the Council turns on her.

The Babylonian king wheels his thunderous expression on me. "What do you think, boy? I should have stayed and helped her." He gives Luna a contemptuous sneer that rubs me the wrong way.

Luna stiffens and I snap, "Don't be a dick."

Hammurabi grabs me by the throat, and my back smacks the wall. "Don't be disrespectful," he growls and then suddenly freezes. Confusion fills me until I see Luna's small hand on his shoulder, fingers clenched.

"Put Caleb down," she says softly. "You keep forgetting what I am." A puff of laughter escapes her. "I guess I do, too."

Hammurabi slowly lowers me, and my feet touch the floor. "I never forget what you are," he tells her, his voice holding all the warmth of ice chips. Then his tone melts a little. "My mistress commands my loyalty, little Gray. I despise abandoning her in her time of need."

Luna's face takes on a cast of misery. "I know. I'm sorry. I wish she'd let me stay and help. *I* could've helped."

I open my mouth to offer some comfort when the door to my room swings open so hard the hinges squeal. My petite mother stands there with a chef's knife in her hand and a look of determination across her beautiful face. Her mouth falls open like a gate when she sees me.

"Caleb?" she says, lowering the knife. Mom takes in Luna and Hammurabi, the latter who actually *checks out* my mom. That is so not okay. "What are you doing here? Aren't you supposed to be in school? Who are your…friends?" She blushes under Hammurabi's perusal, and I try to shoot lasers out of my eyes at my teacher.

Um, so on my weekly calls with my mom, I might have neglected to mention that I helped my grandfather escape and was holed up in Afghanistan with him as he plotted to take over the world. Whoops. She's gonna be pissed.

My chest rises on a huge inhale, and I sigh. I cross the room and bend slightly, giving my mom a big hug. She wraps her arms around me, smelling of mint, cucumber, and garlic, and I know she's been cooking. It's so good to hold her, like I'm a child again, and I believe that she can make any problem go away, right any wrong. I pull back, and her big brown eyes probe mine, her golden skin still flushed. She tucks a strand of dark brown hair behind one ear as her eyes narrow on me.

"How much trouble are you in?" she asks, mouth turning down into a frown.

"A shit ton," I answer, and her eyebrows raise in concern.

"That bad?" she presses.

I nod. "Yeah, that bad. Let's go to the kitchen so we can talk about it."

Mom clears her throat, nodding toward Luna and Hammurabi. Luna watches our exchange in total fascination. "I know I raised you with better manners than that. Introduce us." Her chiding face makes me fidget like a little kid and I wince.

"Right, sorry, on the run and all," I say, and her eyes widen as I sweep an arm out toward the others. "This is my teacher, Hammurabi. I'm sure you've heard of him, wrote the Code of Hammurabi and all." Mom blinks as she focuses on my teacher. She's used to Nephilim—I'm one—but it's still weird when you introduce a literal figure from history to a mortal. Hammurabi gives a slight bow and a devilish grin, which I want to punch off his face. Where is my stern, pain-in-the-ass teacher now? My eyes move to Luna and everything within me softens. "This is Luna, my…

girlfriend." The word trips a little on my tongue because I've never used it, but it feels right, though weird, to call an angel your *girlfriend*. Cosmic lover is way too cheesy. "And an angel."

The stunned expression on Mom's face expands even farther at the last word until she resembles a cartoon character whose eyes are attempting to bug out of her skull. She shakes her head a little, staring at me. She's met Ishtar before but never an actual angel. Ishtar was enough for her.

I continue, "Luna, Hammurabi, this is my mom, Zahra."

Hammurabi rumbles, "It's a pleasure to meet you. I am certain all of Caleb's virtuous qualities are from you."

I roll my eyes at him as my mother chuckles. Luna offers a shy smile, her hazel eyes uncertain. I reach out a hand, and she steps up to take it.

"It's so nice to meet you," she says to Mom. "I... I want you to know Caleb was kind to me when no one else at school was. He's a good person, and I'm sure it's because of you."

Mom's smile is full of warmth when she looks at Luna and a little confusion. "Thank you for the lovely words, Luna. Caleb has never brought a girl home before. Trust him to introduce me to an actual angel. You were in school with Caleb?"

"For a few months. Until..." She trails off, her gaze darkening. Clearing her throat, she shakes her head, saying, "I thought I was a Nephilim. So did Caleb. The angel thing came later."

"Oh...I see," Mom says, but it's clear she doesn't see at all. She straightens, alarm blazing over her face. "And you're on the run? From whom?"

"So, I might have done something slightly stupid," I say to her, and Hammurabi snorts.

✴

Mom rents the second floor of a two-family house in Astoria, Queens, so she has a pretty decent dining room, but we're still bumping elbows as we crowd around the round table. And Mom being Mom, she's doubled everything she was cooking until the table is full of flat bread, yogurt and cucumber dip, saffron-flavored rice, and stuffed chicken, all the familiar dishes of my childhood and her home country of Iran. She left after she got pregnant with me at twenty, and her parents disowned her for being knocked up without a husband in sight. They're assholes like that. She immigrated to Paris and then New York. I don't remember Paris very well, as I spent most of my childhood in New York before leaving for my primary academy.

Mom's arms are crossed over her chest. "This is your father's fault," she says, venom leaking into her voice. "If he'd actually been around, maybe you wouldn't have gone chasing Alexander." Guilt flashes over her face. "Maybe I should have remarried, given you—"

For fuck's sake, Hammurabi does not need that much info on my daddy issues. "Mom, I didn't need anyone else but you," I tell her. "You're awesome." It's both the truth and a lie. She gave me enough love for one hundred fathers, but the fact that my dad took off when I was born still rubs me raw.

Mom's eyes soften, and she ruffles my hair, which I allow because I'm a good son and I secretly love it. "Thank you, baby." She turns her focus on Luna, who tugs on one of her earlobes. Mom reaches over the table, and clasps Luna's free hand. "And you, sweet girl, can stay here as long as you want. Your parents have a lot to answer for." The last words are painted with an undercoat of anger. Mom took it pretty well when she found out Gabriel and Lucifer are Luna's parents. I mean, after the initial shock wore off. And when we told her Luna had been imprisoned, well, mama bear came out in full force. She pushes more rice at Luna. "Angel or no, eat."

Luna blushes and removes her hand from my mom's, dutifully scooping more rice on her plate. "Thank you, ma'am."

"Ma'am?" Mom snorts. "Please call me Zahra. I don't feel old enough to be called ma'am." She winks at Luna.

Hammurabi grins, agreeing, "You're hardly old enough to be called ma'am."

I glare at him. "Well, since you're older than dirt, I guess you would know."

"Caleb," Mom says, throwing me side-eye, and Luna giggles, making me smile.

Hammurabi glowers at me, and I know he'd like to punish me the Babel way for my cheek but won't do it in front of my mother.

I shrug. "It's the truth, Mom, and the fact that he's hitting on you makes him a cradle-robber," I say, calling it like it is. Okay, so Mom is a grown-ass woman, but Hammurabi is a womanizer, so let me plant all kinds of seeds of ick in her brain. A little voice in my head reminds me that Luna is technically way older than me, but she's only been really living for the past seventeen years, so it's not the same thing. She's still a girl.

"Caleb!" Mom repeats, flags of red appearing on her cheeks. She turns to the Babylonian king. "I'm so sorry for my son's extreme rudeness."

Flashing a charming grin, Hammurabi says, "The boy's lack of manners is no fault of yours, and perhaps I was being rather forward with you, which I apologize if I were untoward." He scowls at me. "However, boy, your mother is an adult, so she can decide to rebuff me, although your protective instincts are admirable."

His words make my mother blush harder, and I hide a grin. She shoots from the table. "Anyone want some tea?" She turns her back to us and busies herself getting delicate teacups from the cabinets.

I keep my voice just this shade of audible. "Hey, stop hitting on my mom," I hiss at Hammurabi.

He stares me down, willing me to melt under his authority. "As I've said, your mother is an adult, but under the current circumstances, I'll cease my attention."

I nod as Mom returns to the table with fragrant tea. She pours each of us a cup, giving Luna an extra cookie with hers.

"So, what's the plan?" Mom asks, sliding into the space between me and Hammurabi. She looks at my teacher, fear in her eyes. "Will they really—will they kill Caleb if they catch you? Because he freed Alexander?"

"They'll kill all of us," Hammurabi answers gravely. "I don't support Alexander but I freed Luna. I'm sure in their minds it's the same thing."

"So much for breaking the news gently," I growl at him.

"But I'm *not* Alexander," Luna spits, shattering the tea cup in her hand. "I don't understand any of this—this hate just because I'm a Gray." She looks at the powder in her hand and goes white. Tears gloss her eyes as she stares at my mom in horror. "Oh, Zahra—I didn't—I'm so sorry—I—"

"Hey, it's okay," I say, rubbing her back in soothing circles, but she pushes away from me.

"It's not okay!" she yells, eyes wild. "I'm always destroying things. I'm..." Her palms smother her face as she sobs into them.

"Goldilocks," I say, reaching for her again, but Mom stops me.

"Sweet girl," Mom croons, standing and skirting around the table. She cradles Luna's head against her chest. "It's just a tea cup. You've had a rough time of it, and no one is going to blame you for being a little angry right now. You have every right to not be okay."

"It's not you, Luna," Hammurabi says, crossing his arms over his chest, and something akin to sympathy slides across his face. "The Council fears you because of the prophecy. We thought it applied to Alexander, but then you appeared like a mirage in the desert, making everyone second-guess what they actually thought they knew. I, too, have my own fears about it, founded or not. And...that is not your fault."

Well, there must be snowballs in Hell. Hammurabi is coming around. Luna raises her head from the comfort of my mom's embrace and stares at Hammurabi.

"What prophecy?" she demands, her eyes meeting mine.

Well, shit on a stick. I neglected to speak to her about that. I don't know why I thought she knew; I thought those Council assholes would torment her with the prophecy while she was imprisoned.

"Shall I hazard a guess? Too much kissing and not enough time explaining the important things," Hammurabi says, getting a little payback on me.

Willing my middle finger down, I turn to Luna. "I thought you knew. I thought the Council would've told you just to torture you."

Luna gives a frantic shake of her head. "No—no, they just wanted to know where Alexander was. They never told me anything—" Her eyes light up with realization. "Wait…Uriel did say something about Gabriel. About whether she told them the truth about the Gray who would destroy the world. But he was taunting me, then Mammon appeared, and I realized…" She shakes her head again, as if trying to fling away those memories from her brain. "I didn't know what was real in there. Mammon kept changing his face and made me believe…"

Fury overrides me for a moment. Yeah, Mammon made her believe all kinds of shit. He deserves to be a one-winged chicken.

"Tell us about the prophecy, Caleb," Mom commands.

I glance at my teacher. "Hammurabi knows it better than me," I grumble, "but essentially, Gabriel delivered a prophecy that an angel born of the Dark and the Light—a Gray—would be destined to overtake and destroy the world. Earth as we know it, I guess. Now that there are two of you, the Council is shitting bricks trying to figure out which one of you is the big bad."

Luna blinks, her fingers clenching her earlobe again. "So, they were going to imprison me for all eternity for something that *might* happen? They don't even know if it's me or not but they were going to keep me in that cage like some animal?" She grits her teeth, hazel eyes clouded with rage.

"They don't want another Fall," Hammurabi explains. "None of us do. But Asmodeus does not believe you're the Gray the prophecy spoke of. In fact, who knows how accurate your mother's words were? She hid you from us. Who's to say the Messenger told us the whole truth?"

"Your mom is such an asshole," I growl then shoot Goldilocks an apologetic look. "Sorry."

Trembling, Luna says, "Is that why she abandoned me? Because of the prophecy? Maybe it does refer to me."

"The fuck it does," I tell her, reaching for her hand. "Gabriel mentioned only one Gray, and there are two of you. She clearly doesn't know dick."

My mom is so worked up over Luna she doesn't even admonish me for my language. "Luna, you're not an evil girl. Alexander tried to take over the world without any interference from you."

Even Hammurabi, the straight-laced grump, pipes in, "Zahra is right. Alexander always had a thirst for conquest. I see no such desire in you."

Luna cackles, a bitter, worrying sound. "Alexander and I do have something in common, though. We both want to tear down the divide."

I quickly cut in, "Yeah, but you don't want to start a war to do it."

Goldilocks shakes her head. "No, no, but the fact that I exist, that I want to be with you, is enough for the Council to think I'm declaring war."

"She's not wrong," Hammurabi says. "Those on the Council are…what's the word? Old-fashioned in their views. And stubborn."

"They're stodgy, prejudiced pricks," I correct him.

"Careful," Hammurabi says, the anger in his eyes hot enough to smite me. "Asmodeus put her immortal life on the line for you."

I shrink back. Yeah, she did, for me and someone she doesn't even know. "Sorry I was a dick," I say. "I know what she did for us."

"Why did she do it for me?" Luna asks. "She mentioned my father but I still don't understand."

"Her love for the Morningstar, child," Hammurabi says. "She meant it when she said she would hate any child of Lucifer's to suffer."

I wonder if Asmodeus pines after Lucifer, but I can't see her being the pining type. My mom brushes a strand of gold from Luna's face.

"Well, whatever her reasons, I'm glad she did it," Mom says.

Luna stares up at my mom. "You're so nice," she tells her. "I don't deserve you being this nice to me."

I squeeze her hand. "Baby, don't talk like that. You only deserve people being nice to you."

Mom nods. "Yes, you only deserve good things."

Luna's eyes flick between us, and I will her to believe our words. Surprise washes across her face, and I follow her gaze as it darts behind me, whipping my head around to see Alaric standing in the kitchen. He must have popped in from the Blessed Road. The Nephilim is a little mussed, not the calm, cool presence I'm used to.

"You better have some good news," I say.

EIGHTEEN

LUNA

Bolting from my chair, I cross the room and fling myself at Alaric, so relieved to see him again that I don't even realize I'm crushing his ribcage.

"Luna," he wheezes, and I release him at once. Sparks of heat blossom across my cheeks.

"Sorry," I mutter, taking an embarrassed step back. First, Zahra's teacup and now, Alaric. Even as an angel, I'm a total disaster. Will I ever stop breaking things?

Drawing in a stilted breath, Alaric offers me an understanding smile. "It's okay. I'm glad to see that you're all right, too. And the rest of you managed to make it out in one piece?" He glances between Caleb and Hammurabi, and the latter shakes his head, his expression grim.

"My mistress stayed behind. The Council caught our scent, no thanks to Nzingha."

The honey in Alaric's eyes instantly darkens. "That is…unfortunate," he mutters.

Caleb crosses his arms. "Well, that's the understatement of the century."

Behind Caleb's snarky and indignant facade, I glimpse the resurgence of his concern for Asmodeus. He's worried about her. Frustration and guilt fill every available space in my chest as I consider what predicament we left her to face alone. That *I* left her to face.

Despite everything the Archdemon said about not wanting to put her neck on the line, she didn't hesitate to throw herself in the path of our pursuers to protect us. To protect me.

"Your father would never forgive me if I let you get captured again."

The memory of her final words is a gut punch, and I can't help wondering about her relationship with my father and what they are to each other. Are they just friends? Are they more? She was there that day under the Serapeum when I was captured by the Council. She was there, standing against Lucifer, when he was forced to hand me over for eternal confinement. And yet, she helped Caleb get me out. She played the part of the dutiful Archdemon, only revealing her true hand at the last moment. She sacrificed herself for my father's sake.

To save his daughter.

At the thought of my father, I glance back at Alaric. "How did you know where to find us? Weren't you supposed to meet us back at Babel?"

While I'm glad he didn't end up as yet another casualty to Nzingha's double-crossing, I don't understand how he knew where to find us. He was supposed to locate my parents and, upon reuniting, we would flee to a safe location together. Instead, the plan went to hell, and Alaric showed up here, in Zahra's apartment, alone.

"I texted him," Caleb says with a one-shouldered shrug. "Just before we got here, when we were on the Shadow Road just outside New York. You get surprisingly good reception in there."

Hammurabi rises from the table like a revenant rising from the dead. "You, *what?*" he bellows, his deep voice a booming roar. "How could you be so flippant with such information? Information the Council could use to hunt us?"

Caleb rolls his eyes. "Calm down, dude. First, when was the last time you saw anyone on the Council with a cell phone? Second, last I checked, none of them know how to hack shit. If I had sent a message by carrier pigeon, it might be a different story but I didn't, so I think we're good. Besides"—he throws a cautious glance at his mom, who sits still, listening to the conversation unfolding around her—"it's not like we can stay here. It isn't safe for us...or for Mom. Speaking of which, you'll probably want to go stay with a friend or in a hotel or something until things calm down. Just in case."

"Is that really necessary?" Zahra asks. "They won't be looking for me."

They will if they think they can use you against us. Furrowing my brow, I look to Hammurabi, who seems to be serving as scout leader to this little band of misfits. "Can't we take her with us?"

The older Nephilim sinks back into his chair, shaking his head. "Doing so would only put Zahra in danger."

"Hammurabi's right," Alaric says, rubbing his eyes. He looks exhausted, as if he hasn't slept in weeks. Given everything that's happened, maybe he hasn't. "It's too dangerous. Besides, having a mortal involved in Council matters never ends well. She would be a liability. No offense," he adds quickly, shooting Caleb's mom an apologetic look, as if he only just realized he spoke the words aloud.

Zahra responds with a consoling smile. "None taken," she assures him. "The last thing I want is to put any of you at further risk. But…" She hesitates, worrying her bottom lip between her teeth before blowing out a trembling breath. "I can't say I like the idea of my son on the run and me being clueless about what's happening to him." She peers at Caleb now, her gaze hazy with tears. "I'll go sick with worry. For both of you." Her eyes—the same warm shade of brown as Caleb's—flash to mine before narrowing back on her son. Her tone takes on a sharp edge when she rasps, "Are you trying to kill your poor mother?"

When her voice breaks, Caleb stands and steps toward her, taking her dainty frame into his arms. "I'll text you or call every day, I promise. Even if it's only one word, I'll let you know I'm okay."

Sniffing, Zahra nods, wiping her nose with her sleeve.

The hush that follows is fraught with tension, and as it stretches out minute by minute with no one daring to utter a word, all I can think about is the silence I endured in my prison—the memory of that soundless void always sitting at the edge of my mind.

Shivering, I glance at Alaric, grasping for the strength to voice the one question that still needs to be asked.

"Alaric, if you're here…where are my parents?"

Hammurabi straightens in his chair at my words, his gaze laser focused on the other Nephilim. "Did you manage to find the Messenger and Morningstar?"

Alaric ignores him, looking only at me. "I did find them, Luna, and they're just as anxious to see you as you are to see them." His mouth softens into a reassuring smile, but I can't bring myself to return it.

"Then why aren't they with you?" I press, the words strained.

He winces at the bitterness in my tone. "They can't travel either Road, not together, so they're flying in the old-fashioned way." He touches a hand to his chest and bows his head slightly, as if swearing a vow. "I'll take you to meet them, I promise."

"Flying in…" My eyes bulge at the mental image of my parents soaring over the city, and my jaw drops. "Like…*flying* flying?"

He ruffles my hair and lets out a throaty chuckle that seems to reverberate through me, from the surface of my skin down into my bones. Amusement shines in his eyes like twin shimmering flames. "That might be a bit too conspicuous. We *are* in a major city, and the last thing we need is for your parents to end up on the news. Human sightings of angels don't often go unchecked by the Council."

Hammurabi snorts like an enraged bull, although I think that's his way of expressing his agreement.

Alaric tousles my hair again. "We'll meet them at JFK. Their flight is due in tonight."

Hammurabi, Alaric, Caleb, and I walk into JFK airport at a quarter to nine. As we progress through the vast lobby, surrounded on all sides by more sterile white than was even present at the Serapeum, I try to school my features into a mask of indifference so we won't alert any surrounding mortals to just how bizarre and out of place our group is. Caleb and I look innocent enough, hand in hand like a smitten young couple in love—the thought of him saying that word to me still making my heart race—but neither of us remotely resemble the older Nephilim, who strut in front of us like protective dads. If anyone stops us, here's hoping Alaric isn't too tired to use his Calm on them.

My eyes dart from side to side as I tug on my earlobe. Ever since Nzingha attacked me in the gardens outside Babel, I've felt...weird. I can't really explain how or why. It's probably nothing—a psychosomatic result of the trauma I've experienced combined with my tendency to always think the worst. As we weave through the crowd spilling through the airport, my pulse increasingly erratic, I'm more paranoid than ever.

"You okay?" Caleb whispers, just loud enough for my super hearing to catch his words.

"Peachy," I grumble back, yanking on my earlobe again.

Letting go of my hand, he drapes his arm over my shoulder and pulls me close, my body aligning perfectly with his side, like he is a mold I was created to fit. As I sink into his embrace, he leans down, his breath hot on my cheeks. "Hey, it's okay if you're nervous."

I raise a hand and then drop it again with a flustered breath. "I just—How am I supposed to look at Gabriel any differently after everything? And Lucifer..." I press my knuckles against my lower lip, muttering, "I still don't even know how to process that one."

Caleb nods, and his eyes—pearly in the shining, overhead lights—glisten with infinite understanding. "I have my opinions about Gabriel, but she's your mom, and I'm sure she only did the shitty things she did to try to keep you safe. Besides, you don't need to make up your mind about anything right now. Just hear her out and then decide. As for Lucifer—" He hesitates, his expression contemplative, then shrugs, his face shifting back into its usual carefree easiness that never fails to comfort me. "Well, he's always been kind to me. I don't really have much experience in that department, but I think he'd be a great dad."

As much as I want to believe him, I can't help remembering when Lucifer handed me over to the Council. When he gave me up for eternal imprisonment. As the anguish of that memory consumes me, I scoff.

"Do great dads abandon their kids to the wolves?"

As soon as the words leave my lips, it dawns on me how inconsiderate and selfish I must sound. And thoughtless. So, so utterly thoughtless. Caleb's only spoken about his father once, and it wasn't exactly a glowing review. And after what he revealed to me back at Babel, when we finally had a moment to ourselves to talk...

"I wanted to free Alexander so badly because—well, he is Alexander the Great—and I just wanted...a dad."

I wince at the memory. Surely, Caleb doesn't want to hear me whine about this.

"It might not seem like it, Luna," Alaric says under his breath, glancing at me over his shoulder, "but Lucifer did what was right in the moment. If he hadn't, the Council would've taken their anger out on both him and your mother, and then you'd be without their protection."

My wings bristle under my skin. "What protection? They aren't here."

"They will come, Luna. Have faith."

"Faith." I snort. "Right."

Alaric slows, falling into stride beside me, and Hammurabi takes up position as sole sentinel in front of us, ever the stoic protector. Amber eyes meet mine, urgent and glinting. "You are entitled to your feelings about them, but you must accept their help when they come. We can't keep you safe from the Council, you know this. But your parents...well, maybe they can."

"Maybe?" Caleb echoes. His brow is pinched into a dubious vee.

Hammurabi grunts, speaking for the first time since we entered the airport. "Right now, maybe is all we have."

No one says another word as we approach the arrival gates, the flight times lighting up across the notice boards like Christmas lights. The closer we get, the tighter the throng of people becomes, cutting off any hope of escape, should we need one. If the Council were to descend on us now, we'd be trapped.

"I don't like this," I hiss, shying away from a hulking man on my right. "There are too many people."

"Mortals," Hammurabi retorts, waving a dismissive hand as if batting away a fly. "We would know if another of our kind was here." Smirking, he jerks his chin at Alaric. "Our Light friend here would be able to smell them."

Smell?

At my bemused expression, Alaric pinches the bridge of his nose between his thumb and forefinger, rolling his eyes at the Babylonian king. "A discussion for another ti—"

He stops dead in his tracks, his eyes alert, the irises darting side to side like a haywire pendulum. Fear forms a knot in my chest as I falter mid-step beside him.

"What is it?"

His gaze snaps to mine, and the warning edge I find there makes me take a step back. "We aren't alone."

"Luna's parents?" Caleb asks, inching closer until we're crowded together in an intimate huddle. Meanwhile, Hammurabi looms over us like a disappointed mother.

Alaric jerks his head to one side. "No. I know their scents." His nose crinkles, like he's smelled something foul. "This is different."

Caleb's arm drops from my shoulders and wraps around my waist, pulling me tight to his chest, as if sensing my resurfacing panic. Alaric glances between us, and the distress I glimpse on his face turns my stomach.

Extending his arm, he steers us away from the arrivals gate. "Quickly, this way."

We trail him toward the exit, retracing our steps like time is moving in reverse. The glass doors slide open at our approach, and as the evening air hits my face, I'm reminded of the day I first set foot in Egypt. The day this whole journey was put into motion.

Just like then, Alaric was with me. But unlike then, his usual tranquil facade is distorted by the agitated movements of the golden sheen licking his skin. His aura shivers with anxiety as he stalks across the wide road outside, leading us toward the large parking lot directly opposite the airport entrance. I watch him out of the corner of my eye, waiting for the wave of Calm I know must be coming, but his typical composure is gone, and he seems incapable of it, too consumed by the tension of the moment, even if his drawn expression tells me nothing.

His hurried pace borders on a run as the Nephilim leads us through several pools of buttery yellow light emanating from the street lamps scattered throughout the parking lot. We pass row after row of parked cars, and I can't fathom where he's leading us except farther away from the one place we're supposed to be. The one place where my parents are likely waiting for me.

The hairs on my arms and neck stand at attention. "Alaric, where are we going?"

I ask.

He presses a slender finger to his lips, shaking his head, then gestures toward a circular grove of trees up ahead on a small island of grass just past this stretch of tarmac. Despite the vibrancy of light in the parking lot, the grassy patch is drenched in shadow. The only truly dark spot as far as the eye can see.

Once we've all convened in the circle, he whips around to face us, finally speaking. "Take the Shadow Road and go as far as you can. I'll stay behind to intercept your parents, but you three need to get out of here *now*—"

I open my mouth to protest, to ask him what's going on, but the look on his face smothers my words. A fear as cold and dreadful as death chills my blood as I turn, following his hooded gaze over my shoulder—the disdain in his eyes making him almost unrecognizable. As a figure emerges from the gloom behind me, I realize we couldn't run now, even if we wanted to.

It's too late to run.

"Oh, how kind of you all to wait for me," our pursuer simpers, assessing us with cunning eyes, the irises like two sapphires trapped in ice. Observing the circle of trees, he grins. "And somewhere secluded. Even better."

I recognize the Archdemon immediately, his delicate features imprinted on my memory like a tattoo from the one time I saw him before—that day under the Serapeum when I came face to face with the Council. Of all the Archdemons to come after us, they sent the only one who looks like a child?

I can't help fearing that was intentional. Perhaps he's even the most dangerous of them all.

His name, which springs to the front of my memory as recognition sets in, is a startled breath on my lips. "Beelzebub."

The Archdemon dips his head in greeting. When he looks up, his arctic eyes flashing to mine, I understand at once why Alaric seemed anxious upon catching his scent and why his aura still radiates an undiluted terror even now, despite the hostility creasing his brow. For although the Fallen angel is smaller than the others I've encountered, there's tremendous power hidden behind those beautiful eyes, vibrating from within the blackness of his undulating aura.

An ancient power that could easily tear us all to shreds.

As if reading my mind, Beelzebub smiles. "Hello again, daughter of Lucifer."

NINETEEN

CALEB

BEELZEBUB LOOKS LIKE A twelve-year-old boy waiting for his balls to drop. I've never met him, only seen him from afar, and it always hits me how *weak* he appears compared to the other Archdemons. Pretty and androgynous, he doesn't outwardly pose a threat, his power concealed under that school-boy shell. I wonder if the other Council members whisper behind his back, asking what the hell the Creator was thinking when Beelzebub came along. The rest of them seem to be frozen in time somewhere in their late twenties, early thirties max, but he has never left tweenhood. But despite that cherubic face, I know he's a badass, and Luna is the only one who can truly take him on. And she's in no shape to throw down right now.

But I still have my celestial slayer. If I can clip Mammon's wing, I can damage this asshole, too, with the help of Luna, Alaric, and Hammurabi, of course. I slide the knife out of its sheath on my back. Beelzebub's blue eyes track the motion and widen. That's right, mine is bigger than yours.

"What are you doing here?" Hammurabi demands, towering over the Archdemon. "You're not taking the girl. In case you haven't noticed, Mammon is missing a wing. I'm more than happy to aid young Caleb in taking yours." Although the Babylonian king clearly looks like the victor, I know that's not the case.

Beelzebub straightens, all boyish charm falling away in those ancient eyes, and his icy glare cuts as he looks at Hammurabi. "Silence, King. Listen to me. I come with a warning. It is dangerous to risk meeting with the Morningstar and the Messenger. You cannot go to them for aid."

Alaric delivers an icy stare of his own. "Your meddling is futile. Even if you cut us down, Luna will get to her parents. I vow it. You can't take on Lucifer and Gabriel by yourself and you know it, Spy."

I knew there was a badass inside Alaric. My grip tightens on the golden hilt of my dagger. Luna's wings tear free of her skin, shiny feathers reflecting in the street lights. Man, if any humans show up, we're going to have to erase a lot of minds. Beelzebub's blue eyes narrow in on her wings.

"Child, put those away," he commands. "We're among mortals."

Goldilocks shakes her head, eyes defiant. "No, I won't let you take me again. I'll burn you first. And some spy you are. Alaric knew you were there."

The Archdemon barks a harsh laugh. "He knew I was here because I allowed it, little Gray. You have much to learn."

Blackness spills out of him, spreading around us like ink in water. The streetlights are snuffed. I'm suddenly blind in the suffocating darkness, but it's not only my sight that's affected. I can't hear or smell anything. My senses have been turned off like a faucet. I fumble around until I grip Luna's hand. Beelzebub gave Luna shit for her wings, and he's turning on his power full blast. Hypocrite. Then again, I guess no one can see us.

Ruby flame lights up the immediate area, and I glance over to see Luna's free hand blazing. She can't banish the shadows entirely, but she's broken through enough for my senses to come screaming back to life. Beelzebub watches her with a little smile. The darkness fades away, and Luna extinguishes the fire in her palm.

"Is fire your only trick, young one?" he asks, smirking. "You'll need more in your repertoire if you want to fight the Council." His smile vanishes. "But I'm not your enemy. I am a true friend of your father, and if you don't want the Council to imprison him or your mother the way they did Asmodeus, you'll listen to me."

Hammurabi swears low and takes a step toward Baby B when Alaric's hand on his shoulder halts him. The Light Nephilim gives a slow shake of his head, and though a subvocal growl escapes the king's throat, he backs off.

My eyes return to the Archdemon. "Why should we believe you?" I demand. "Unless all the Council members are backstabbing, two-faced assholes with their own agenda."

Fury shimmers on Beelzebub's face as he regards me and I swallow hard. Dagger or no dagger, I don't really want to piss off an Archdemon too badly.

"You're lucky, grandson of the Great, that I don't have time to punish you for your insolence." His eyes snap to Luna. "Nzingha has placed a tracking device in your head. The Council is waiting for you to lead them straight to your parents so they can capture you all in one fell swoop. You need to leave immediately before the Council figures out you're here and that the Morningstar and the Messenger are on their way. Their capture would mean your certain doom."

"Fuck me," I breathe. "Can't we get a break from this shit already?"

"Bloody Nzingha," Alaric mutters.

Hammurabi shakes his head. "I can't believe we trusted Mammon's ambitious pet."

Luna clutches her skull, tears in her eyes. "What did she put in me?" She shakes her head, disappointment and sadness etched into her features. Damn, will she ever get to see her parents? It's not fair. None of this is fair.

I pull her into my side, and her wings vanish. "It'll be okay, Goldilocks."

Her tears almost break me. "How Caleb? What are we going to do now?"

"You're going to get that device out of your head," Beelzebub drawls. "As soon as you can."

I make a sweeping gesture toward Luna. "Well, why don't you get on that?"

"Yes," Hammurabi says. "If you're loyal to the Morningstar, help his daughter."

"I cannot help you," the Archdemon answers, tone blistering. "It's an Archangel device. Uriel's handiwork, I believe. Anyone can insert it, but you will require one from among the Faithful to remove it." He shrugs.

"Oh, is that all?" I push out between clenched teeth. By the Morningstar, I want to stab him. "Why didn't you say so? There are so many of them around, willing to help us."

"Like her mother," Alaric adds, crossing his arms over his chest.

Beelzebub gives Alaric a nasty smile. "By all means, let the Council take Gabriel, Nephilim, but I don't want Lucifer to be imprisoned. It would be in your best interest not to contact him until the device is destroyed." His eyes rove over Luna, mouth twisted in distaste. "You have an angel here. Both of the Dark and the Light. She possesses the means to remove it herself."

"I don't know how to take it out!" Luna cries, voice shrill. "I've been an angel for all of five minutes."

An irritated huff escapes Beelzebub as his eyes flick over Luna, as if assessing her and annoyed she's come up short. "Fine. The best I can do is this..." Darkness slides from Beelzebub once more, right up Luna's nose. She gasps, clenching her face.

Fear grips me. "What did you do to her?" I demand, brandishing my dagger at him.

Beelzebub shrugs again, giving me a bored look. "Masked the tracker for now. But do remember it is only temporary. I've done all I can. You need to find shelter and someone to remove the tracker. Best be making Light allies." Blackness blankets him and he's gone.

Hammurabi roars and I wince. I glance around. The parking lot just beyond the trees is still empty but damn are we making a spectacle of ourselves. But I guess we're already fugitives from the Council. What's a minor infraction like revealing ourselves to humans going to get us at this point? The Council wants us dead. Luna's sobs wrap their way around my heart and squeeze.

I slide the dagger back in its sheath and draw her into my arms. "It's going to be okay, Goldilocks," I repeat. "I swear to you, we'll find a way to get that thing out of your head."

"Don't make pretty vows you can't keep," Hammurabi says to me, fury in his dark eyes. "Do you have any angels willing to help us?" he spits at Alaric.

Alaric grimaces. "None but I'm willing to go and beg. There must be some loyal to Gabriel, just as there are those loyal to Lucifer."

Hammurabi scoffs. "I don't think Gabriel inspires loyalty in the same way. As the Messenger, she's more feared than loved."

As they continue to bicker, Luna buries her face against my chest. A plan forms in my mind. A terrible, horrible, awful plan that just might work. No, it will definitely work. If I play my cards right. I feel sick, but we're running out of time. I kiss Luna, tasting her tears. I'll do this for her. I'll do anything for her.

"We have to go to my grandfather," I say over Hammurabi's and Alaric's heated words. "We have to go to Alexander."

Alaric's jaw snaps shut while Hammurabi's mouth hangs open, both of them staring at me as if I've managed to Ascend and grow wings. Luna gasps and jerks back from my chest.

"Are you mad?" Hammurabi asks. "You want to go to the Great for shelter? You betrayed him, Caleb. He won't greet you as family but as an enemy. He might even kill you."

I'm waiting for Alaric to chime in, but he remains silent, face blank. I focus back on the Babylonian king. "Yeah, there's a chance he'll take my head, but not if I tell him I brought you three as gifts. That I left only to bring him powerful allies—that we're all on his side. He's always wanted Luna. If I can give him a Gray and two first generations, he can't say no to that."

Alaric nods. "He has a point."

Luna's eyes dart to Alaric and stay there, as if searching for something. "You think Caleb bringing us will be enough? From the sounds of it, Alexander is…ruthless."

"I understand that," Alaric says with a grim smile. "But we're running out of options."

"This is ludicrous," Hammurabi protests, arms crossed over his massive chest. "And with that thing in her head"—he gestures at Luna—"the Council will just track us there."

"Eventually, yeah, but Beelzebub just bought us some time. And us fleeing to Alexander is the last thing they'll expect. They're waiting for us to lead them to Lucifer and Gabriel, not the Conqueror—who has his own army by now. If they decide to show up, Alexander will fight back. And by then, Luna won't have the tracker in her head anymore, and we'll escape while they rip into each other."

Luna shivers. "I think...I think Caleb may be right. Alexander did remove my bind. Why would he do that unless he thought I'd be useful?"

Hammurabi snorts. "Of course, you're useful. You're a bloody angel and as untrained as a newborn babe. You're the perfect clay he can mold."

"Which is why he won't kill me," I point out again. "I mean, I can't bring a better housewarming present than the three of you. Luna alone would save me—you two are just the cherry on top."

Luna's eyes clash with mine. I see the fear reflected in their depths, and I smooth a hand through her golden hair. "I don't like it. But...I don't know where else we could go."

"Yes, unfortunately, I agree this is our best option," Alaric says, staring off into the distance. He chuckles to himself. "Fate has a sense of humor."

Hammurabi blows out a harsh breath. "Fine. I'll go along with this folly, but if we all end up in chains, don't say I didn't warn you."

I roll my eyes, even as my stomach knots itself together. "Ugh, you're such a ball of sunshine and optimism." I take a deep breath, blowing it out slowly and steeling my spine. "Okay, let's go meet Grandfather."

It's mid-morning on the other side of the world in Afghanistan. Kandahār is quiet under clear skies, the usually bustling streets tame. The whole country feels silent, but I guess that's what happens when a hostile force rolls in and takes over. The good news is that a war-torn country makes it easier for Alexander and his army to set up, unnoticed. I left Luna, Hammurabi, and Alaric up in the mountains while I went alone to the citadel. As I approach the gates, I notice strange Nephilim are now on guard duty, settled in strategic places along the wall. Gramps has been busy indeed. Unease ripples over me again. I don't want to be here. I can practically taste the restrained violence in the air, waiting to be unleashed.

But I have to do this for Luna. She needs somewhere safe to recuperate until I can get her to her parents. She hasn't mentioned them since Beelzebub left, but I know this latest setback crushed her. The fragile state of her mind worries me. Yeah, I had to bring us here, but Goldilocks isn't fond of Alexander and with good reason. He fucked with her mind and then abandoned her. I can only hope he'll be gentle with her, but I seriously doubt it. He's not the type to baby anyone.

I make no attempt to hide from the sentries, and soon Ishtar is at the gate of the fortress. The goddess is gone today, a warrior in her place. A practical black T-shirt and cargo pants cling to her tall, curvy frame while combat boots encase her feet, and a sword is strapped to her back. Her black hair is braided back from her beautiful face, showcasing her high cheekbones. Our eyes meet, and I force myself not to step back as I see the rage shimmering in her gaze. Maybe Alexander isn't my biggest threat. Maybe Ishtar will run me through before I even get to meet with him.

"You dare to return, boy?" Ishtar says, arching one haughty brow. "After you ran back to Babel? To Asmodeus? You're lucky your grandfather prevented me from hunting you down after your betrayal. But he had more important matters for me to attend to than pursuing a fickle child with no loyalty to blood."

Her barb stings but I ignore her. I don't question how she knows I returned to the academy. I'm sure she has her spies. I give a casual shrug as if I haven't a care in the world. "I had my reasons," I tell her. "And Grandfather will meet three of them. I've brought him powerful gifts to aid his fight."

Surprise flits across Ishtar's face, but she quickly masks it. Score one point for me. I threw her off her game. "Gifts?" she repeats.

I nod. "Grandfather will be very pleased by what I've done. I want to see him."

She laughs. "I don't think so. Why don't you tell me about your gifts, and I'll judge if they're worthy enough to be brought before the Great."

Shaking my head, I say, "No, Alexander needs to hear this from me. He needs to know that I never betrayed him. And I don't trust you." My blunt words make her blink, anger tightening her mouth.

"I was always fond of you, Caleb," Ishtar says. "You shamed me greatly when you left, and you cut me with your disloyalty. How do I know you're not spying for Asmodeus?"

"Your former bestie is locked up right now," I tell her, and once again, I manage to shock her. Two points. "The Council attacked Babel and took her because she helped me."

"Why would the Council imprison Asmodeus?" Ishtar demands, and I detect a hint of concern in her voice. Well, I guess she cares about the Archdemon after all.

"Um, because she *helped* me," I repeat slowly, knowing it'll piss her off. Nerves make me stupid.

Her eyes narrow to slits. "And why would she help a foolish boy like you? One whose loyalty is only to themselves?"

"She was helping Lucifer," I tell her. "We just had the same goals." I hide my grin as once more a look of confusion creeps across her face. Well, I guess Luna's lineage hasn't become common knowledge yet. "I wanted Luna free and so did Asmodeus, because Luna is the Morningstar's daughter."

My announcement wipes Ishtar's face clean of emotion, and I know I've truly stunned her. "The Morningstar has a daughter? *Luna*? How do you know this?"

I grin. "Yep, he does. Asmodeus told me. She wanted to get Luna back for him."

Ishtar bares her teeth at me. "That kind of information isn't free, Caleb. What did you promise her?"

"Alexander's whereabouts, but only when Luna was delivered to her dad," I lie. Best to keep the Gabriel card close. "But I knew Asmodeus couldn't deliver us to Lucifer. So when the Council attacked that night, I snuck Luna out and I came here. All I wanted was for Luna to be safe. I love her." It feels wrong confessing this to Ishtar, who I know will wield that knowledge like a weapon. She already suspected, of course, but it's different to confirm her suspicions. "I want back in. I never stopped wanting that. And like I said, I have three gifts to prove it." The fabrication falls easily from my lips because there's a kernel of truth in it. I never stopped wanting a connection with my grandfather; it was just a kick to the nuts when I realized I could never have one. Not the way I wanted, which was to have a shiny father figure who gave a shit about me. Maybe if I get out of this alive, I should seriously go see a shrink.

"What are the other gifts?" Ishtar prods again, and I shake my head.

"That's for Grandfather's ears only," I say, crossing my arms over my chest.

Ishtar stares off into the distance, considering my words, but I know in the end, she'll take me to Alexander. What I've revealed is too tempting. And besides, I don't think she really has a choice. The goddess of love and war may be his general, but she doesn't have the power to pass judgment on me. And if she does and Gramps finds out, I'm sure there will be consequences. If anyone is to punish me, he'll want to do it. I'm his blood after all.

"Very well, Caleb, follow me, but know if this is a trick, I'll beg the Great to let me punish you. And you know how creative I can be. Death will be a friend you'll beg for but never meet."

Her cold words send shivers over my skin. It hurts to know the teacher I admired turned on me so quickly. Asmodeus and I have more in common than I thought.

"Understood," I say, voice hard.

I keep a few paces behind Ishtar as we wind our way through the citadel and into the makeshift throne room. Nephilim glance at me, some with curiosity and some with open hostility. I ignore them, head high like the prince I supposedly am. Fake it until you make it. The interior has changed a bit since I left, gained more creature comforts. It looks more like a palace than a garrison to house troops.

Alexander lounges on his throne, the marble now covered in purple velvet cascading to the floor. An honest-to-Creator lion's skin drapes across his shoulders. Damn, he's gone full Macedonian today. His cold mismatched eyes latch onto mine, like two magnets drawing me in. I can't look away, but I do manage a deep bow.

"Your grandson has returned," Ishtar drawls. "Bearing gifts, or so he claims."

"Three of them," I clarify, "though a fourth is a possibility entirely up to you." I take a deep breath. "And one of these gifts has a time limit."

Ishtar whirls on me. "You never mentioned that," she hisses.

I smirk at her. "Because you don't have the power to help with that. You're not an angel. Only Grandfather can solve this problem."

"Have you brought me offerings or problems, Caleb?" Alexander asks. "I confess I am surprised to see you again, especially after your desertion, but I find I'm oddly pleased by your presence." His smile doesn't reach his icy eyes, and I gulp down my fear.

"I've brought you Luna as an apology for leaving," I say, rushing ahead, "but one of the Council's minions put some sort of tracking device in her head during our escape that we can't get out. Only *you* can."

"I see, so you only returned to me like a cringing hound because I can aid you?" Alexander says softly, and I force myself not to flinch at the painful accuracy of his words.

I shake my head violently. "No, I always planned on coming back, and I brought you two more allies to prove it. The thing that happened with Luna just set us back."

"Indeed. Who else did you bring for me, Grandson?" He leans back into his throne, tapping his fingers on one armrest.

"Hammurabi," I say, grinning at Ishtar's gasp. Even Alexander manages a flicker of surprise across his stony face. "And Alaric. I don't know him that well, but he's pretty damn old and a first generation."

At the mention of Alaric's name, Alexander's fingers stop tapping. He stills, muscles coiled, and I wonder if I've made a major miscalculation. Do Alaric and Alexander have a grudge between them I don't know about? Other than the whole Michael thing, but Alaric didn't seem too torn up about it when we talked about Gramps. Then Grandfather's lips tug up into a smile. A genuine one.

"Caleb, you've done well. You truly are my blood to convince such powerful Nephilim to join my cause. And more importantly, you've brought the girl to me. With my help, I can teach her about her true nature, the melding of the Dark and the Light."

Relief pulses through me so quickly that I almost sway. "And you'll remove the tracker?"

He tilts his head, studying me. "Yes, I'll remove the device. I don't desire having the Council appear before I'm ready to address them. Because you have indeed brought me three great offerings, I won't punish you for the danger you bring to my door."

"This is the last place the Council expects me to go," I tell him. "They expect me to run to Lucifer."

Alexander perks up, his eyes flitting to Ishtar before focusing on me again. "Why would you flee to the Morningstar?"

"Because he's Luna's father. That's what I meant about a possible fourth ally."

A calculating gleam shines in Alexander's eyes as he considers my words. I can practically feel his glee at the thought of having both Luna and Lucifer join his army. "Caleb, I have truly underestimated you, but it seems blood ran true. I assume my new allies are somewhere safe?"

I nod, a cautious hope blooming in my heart. Maybe I can pull this off after all.

"Ishtar, accompany Caleb and bring our guests to me. Young Luna and I have much to discuss."

TWENTY

LUNA

THE WAIT IS AGONIZING. Although Caleb has only been gone for a handful of minutes, it feels like hours since we parted and I watched him continue alone to the fortress where his grandfather has taken up residence. I sit perched like a bird on the edge of a dusty cliff edge staring down at the Tarnak River and the city of Kandahār far below in the distance—the citadel on a vast hilltop of rock beside it— my teeth clamping down on the edge of my thumbnail. Five minutes turn into ten turn into fifteen, and as the seconds stretch on, my imagination depicts every worst case scenario, frying what remains of my nerves.

A sour taste floods my mouth at the thought of what Alexander might be doing to Caleb—what punishment he could be inflicting at this very moment for his grandson's desertion. Wincing, I avert my gaze from the city and search the sandy ledge for a distraction. Hammurabi is scouting the mountain pass while Alaric sits a few feet away from me with his back to the rock face, his crisp white button-down shirt somehow still perfectly clean despite our desert surroundings.

Back in New York, before we made the trek along the Roads to Afghanistan, Hammurabi had suggested Alaric stay behind to meet my parents and update them on the situation—as the latter had originally intended to do before Beelzebub appeared. But, between the threat of the tracker in my head and the plan to now go to Alexander, the ancient Nephilim hadn't only been reluctant to do so—he had downright refused with a vehemence I didn't know him capable of. He claimed it was unwise to risk meeting them in case the Council was surveying our last known location, but I could tell that was just an excuse, even if there was logic and wisdom behind his words.

The real reason for his refusal was more personal. From the moment Alexander's name left Caleb's lips, Alaric rejected the slightest notion of leaving my side. He wouldn't even let me travel the Shadow Road to get here, pleading for me to join him on the Blessed Road where he could keep an eye on me. Caleb fought back against that suggestion at first, only agreeing once Hammurabi pointed out that it would be easier for the two older Nephilim to help us should anything happen on the Roads if they each only had one teenager to look after.

So, Hammurabi and Caleb took the Shadow Road while Alaric and I took the Blessed Road. Opposite to the Dark way of traveling, which was cold and streaked with endless grays and blacks, the Light's path was blinding—almost searing in its brightness and warmth. Although part of me preferred the illusion of safety such radiance gave off compared to the Shadow Road's bleakness, it was a relief to step back into the human world again, into the blazing sun of the mountains. As Alaric and I emerged from the light, Caleb stepped out of a pool of shadows beneath a nearby outcropping of rock. The moment our eyes met, he closed the distance between us and pulled me into his arms, his hands in my hair and his lips on mine as if he thought he'd never see me again.

That same anxiety stings me now, and desperate for a distraction, I glance at Alaric. His eyes are closed, but I can sense he's awake, and I stare at his serene face for a while, considering everything I want to say to him. Although we were alone together on the Blessed Road, we didn't dare speak, too frightened of alerting the Council to our location should one of the Faithful be near. But now that we're safe from the Road, I feel the need to break the silence. To say everything I couldn't find the words or strength to say before.

"I haven't thanked you...for coming for me."

Alaric peeks one amber eye open. "I saved you from one prison, Luna. I wasn't going to abandon you to another."

His words bring me back to those many long months in the hospital, but strangely, those memories don't seem to belong to me anymore. Now, as every moment takes me further away from my old, mortal life, it feels less like I'm looking at *my* past and more like I'm looking back at the recollections of someone else. Someone from another world, even though it's been less than a year since Alaric secured my freedom.

That broken girl he met...while part of me doesn't recognize her in this new form I've taken, I know I'm more like her than ever. She's there in every breath I draw, dancing at the precipice of madness, always one misstep from falling.

But unlike when I was committed, I have a rope now—a tether—to hang onto, to stop my feet from slipping over the edge. A lifeline to save me from myself. And while my first instinct is to say that rope is Caleb, I also know it's partly Alaric. He got me here. He saved me in more ways than one.

And yet—

"That's not the only reason, Alaric." *Just like my parents had nothing to do with why you chose not to part with me in New York.*

Rising, I cross the ledge and press my back to the stretch of smooth rock, sinking to the ground beside him. I can feel his eyes on me when I draw in a breath.

"That voice I was hearing…I'm guessing you know it was Alexander."

A moment passes before he nods.

Steeling myself, I grab his hand. "When he was in my head, he showed me glimpses of your past. I saw you together. You were in love with him." It isn't a question. I know enough of love to recognize what I saw.

A low chuckle breaches his lips, and he looks down at the ground, his eyes hazy and distant. "In many ways, I still am," he says softly.

His admission takes me aback. Alexander was locked away more than two thousand years ago. While it was clear Alaric clung to some residual feelings toward the angel when we first spoke about him, I wasn't expecting deeper feelings to linger. Has he spent all these millennia alone, fanning the dying flames of a love he could no longer have?

My heart bleeds for him at the thought. "Despite everything?"

A sad smile twitches along the edge of his mouth. "Despite everything." He looks at me now, his eyes fierce. "Love isn't black and white, Luna. We can't just shut it off when it inconveniences us. But there's so much you don't know about him…or about what happened between us back then."

"Like him killing your father?" I hedge.

His body goes rigid at my words. "There's…more to that story than what I told you."

The memory of what Alexander showed me is fresh, like a brand on my mind, and I nod, understanding. But not Alaric's side of the story.

Alexander's.

As much as I despise him for messing with my head, I can at least empathize with this one thing about him. After all, I would have done the same. I would tear the world to pieces if doing so meant keeping Caleb safe.

"I saw it. Michael was *hurting* you," I murmur. "Alexander…regardless of what he did or became or is now…he did it to save your life."

Like me, he just wanted to protect someone he loves.

To my surprise, Alaric scoffs. "Yes, and part of me wishes he hadn't bothered."

I blanch at the acidity in his tone, unable to bear the thought of a world where Alaric doesn't exist. Where our paths never crossed. "You...you don't mean that... do you?"

He blinks at me with those warm amber eyes, and I blink back, more confused than ever. Exhaling a long, quiet breath, he props his head back against the red-veined rock.

"That day...what we did...it changed something in Alexander. He saved my life but at what cost? He wasn't the same after that." He hesitates, and the column of his neck shifts when he swallows. Clearing his throat, he says more sternly, "That moment was the lid on Pandora's box, and upon shoving that dagger into my father's heart, he tore the lid right off."

I replay the moment of Michael's death in my thoughts, but now—with the pain in Alaric's voice fresh in my ears—the romantic imagery Alexander planted feels false. Manufactured. I can't help feeling like a fool for believing it. For accepting less than half of the story and seeing only Caleb and me in the details.

"I don't understand," I manage after a moment.

Alaric gifts me a sympathetic smile, and my heart aches even further at the silent reassurance I glimpse in his gaze. It's written there as clear as day.

Don't worry, it says. *He fooled me, too.*

Squeezing my fingers, he exhales through his nose. "Alexander was always special. Gifted. We met when he was young, two years before he was escorted to the Dark academy at Sodom for his primary training. While he learned the basics of control there, he didn't truly thrive until he went on to his secondary academy at Ashkelon, once run by the esteemed Lilith—before she lost her wings and place among the Council for supporting his first conquest for power. Since then, the school is presided over by our new *friend*, Beelzebub, who was elevated to the role of Archdemon to replace her. You can see now why I was wary of him."

I stiffen at the mention of Beelzebub, my nostrils flaring at the recollection of our recent encounter. It's hard to imagine that he wasn't always an Archdemon considering the power I sensed behind that childlike shell. The darkness he unleashed, stealing my vision, surging into my head, still haunts me, as does his warning about the tracker.

My eyes flick to the city below as the anxieties plaguing me rush back to the surface.

The sooner Caleb returns, the better.

"Did you know Alexander was left as an offering to the king and queen of Macedonia?" Alaric asks. "Won over by the child's beauty, the queen begged the king to keep Alexander and raise him as their own. As their prince and heir."

I'm beginning to see a running theme between celestial beings and royalty. Hammurabi was a king. Nzingha, a queen. Vesta and Ishtar are considered goddesses by all mortal accounts. And being Alexander's grandson makes Caleb a prince as well, which I'm only just realizing now.

And then there's me. Emotional wreck Luna. The only thing I'm queen of is setting people on fire. I suppress a groan, forcing myself to focus on Alaric's soothing tenor.

"It didn't take much convincing on the queen's part as the king was equally smitten, but raising a Nephilim child, especially not knowing what he truly was, came with its challenges, of which there were many. The king and queen loved their adopted son dearly and only wanted to ensure he thrived.

"By this point in time, I was already grown, so when Alexander and I met, I had already gone through my schooling and was passing the decades traveling the world, acquiring knowledge wherever I could find it. Truthfully, though, I was restless. I felt like I lacked a purpose, and I did not share the same lust for power as so many other first generations, who used their celestial blood for their own political elevation. So, when word reached me of the troublesome young prince of Macedonia, I approached the king and queen and offered my service to them."

"Your service?"

Alaric grins at my bewildered expression. "Like so many mortal parents, they didn't know what he was nor were they prepared for the challenges of raising a celestial child. They took it rather well when I enlightened them about his origins and were immediately accepting of what I could do for him. You see, certain skills I possess are rather rare and proved quite handy in cases like Alexander's." As if to demonstrate, a rush of Calm washes over me, which he then draws back, the wave receding. "He was a menace as a child. Demonic, I once heard a terrified chambermaid call him." He lets loose a barking laugh that births a light in his eyes I've never seen before. "He needed a wrangler, and I was the key to calming the beast, so to speak, so I became his keeper of sorts. We were inseparable, at first by order of the king, who only wanted the best for his son, but as Alexander aged, we stayed together by choice. I had always felt so alone in this world, and he…" His smile falters and the beautiful light in his eyes—that light born of love—disappears. "Well, he became my dearest friend despite our innate differences."

A forbidden friendship, like me and Caleb, I muse.

A shadow crosses his gaze, and he clears his throat again, as if to shake himself out of the memory. "Even after Alexander was sent to the academy at Ashkelon, I remained in Macedonia with his parents, training to be an advisor of sorts. They didn't cling to the prejudices of our kind, and despite my being a Light, they intended for me to stay close to their son, to be a helping hand to guide him when he eventually ascended the throne. To calm him when the need arose. And I was glad to do it. I couldn't see myself anywhere else but at his side where I finally had a purpose.

"Unfortunately, there were many who didn't agree with my position, and throughout his years at Ashkelon, Alexander would often return home to see me and rant about the narrow-mindedness of his teachers, who made it a point to warn him of the dangers of befriending a Light. I had, of course, been exposed to the same biases, but Alexander took their words personally. He grew irate over what he called a poison between the Darks and the Lights and began counting down the days until he could leave Israel and return home, eager to resume his mantle of prince over mortals, who he viewed as pure compared to the prejudiced Nephilim.

"One of Alexander's greatest traits in my eyes was his endearing affection for humans. It often outweighed any love he had for his own kind, not that I could ever blame him for that. After all, they had accepted him when those who had birthed him had not. He used to say I was the only sane Nephilim he knew, that we were two parts of a whole, and he vowed to tear down the divide, to create a world where our friendship would be accepted, where our kind could come together as one as we were meant to be, and live freely and openly among the humans. In hindsight, his words should've frightened me, but at the time, they were food for my starving heart. His acceptance and affection were all I cared about."

His story paints a vivid picture, and I understand now why he has always been supportive of my friendship with Caleb. Alaric must see so much of himself and Alexander in us. But, considering how their story ended, does that resemblance cause him pain?

Oblivious to my errant thoughts, Alaric continues, "From the day we met, I cared deeply for Alexander. My own father was absent since before I was born, and having Alexander served as a replacement for that connection in many significant ways. He was like a younger brother to me, the family I chose."

"Like you are to me," I mutter without thought. Once, saying such things would've embarrassed me, but not now. Alaric is like family, and after all he's risked to save me, after all the times he's been there, I want him to know it.

A smile touches his lips and he nods. "At least, that was the case until he completed his final year at the academy. When he came home, I barely recognized him. It had been months since our paths had last crossed due to the hectic nature of his studies, and the boy I knew, that I had helped raise in some respects, was gone from his features, replaced by a man. Needless to say, it was a shock to my system to see him as an adult. To see him as anything other than the spoiled, pampered prince I adored. From then on, things were…*different* between us."

A flush creeps up my neck at the insinuation behind his words. "Was that weird? With you being so much older than him?" As I ask this, I can't help putting myself in his place. After all, if my suspicions are right about when I was born, then in reality, I'm far closer in age to Alaric than I am to Caleb.

Alaric peers intently at me, as if sensing the source of my question. "You need to remember that Nephilim live for thousands of years so, in the grand scheme of our lives, the age difference wasn't quite so great. I was still very young at this point in time and immature beyond measure. Angry at the world. Angry at the Creator for allowing me to grow up without both of my parents. Angry at my father, who despite being a member of the Council and thus allowed to live on Earth, made no effort to see me or know me. In that regard, your Caleb and I have much in common. We both sought out Alexander as a replacement of sorts for other voids in our lives. Truthfully, I never planned to pursue my feelings for Alexander, but he gave me little choice in the matter. He was quite insistent I view him as an adult."

"Did you know then? What he was?" I ask.

Alaric heaves a sigh. "As Alexander aged into adulthood, it became apparent that he possessed qualities that someone of his lineage should not, much as you possessed Dark capabilities that one would not expect in a Light. He was…" He scratches his chin, considering, before settling on, "Uncomfortable, for lack of a better word."

"Was he bound, like I was?"

He nods. "Likely by one of his angelic parents, much as I'm assuming Gabriel did to you."

Ignoring the mention of my mother, I bob my head, as if this explanation makes any damn sense. Then a thought occurs to me, and my right eyebrow hooks upward. "Didn't the Council know what he was? I mean, they knew about the prophecy at this point, right? So, wouldn't the warning signs have been there?"

Frowning, Alaric shakes his head. "His powers did not start to break through the bind fully until he was already at Ashkelon, and considering Lilith's stance on his eventual conquest for power, I believe she hid any such knowledge of him from the Council, which likely contributed to the severity of her punishment once he was imprisoned. As for when he was a child, well, he was incredibly sheltered in Macedonia, and as I was always there to calm his outbursts, any unusual powers he did portray, I made excuses for. To me, he was unique. Brilliant. A force to be reckoned with. I refused to allow myself to see anything wrong." A soft laugh escapes him. "No wonder he developed such an ego when I was always there to fan the flames." He sighs again. "But as he grew older, I could tell something was wrong. Once, he even tried to cut his arm, to show me the skin wouldn't break, not even with excessive force."

Alaric's words trigger a strange recognition inside me that I don't know how to process. Have I ever had a cut or a scrape? I can't remember any broken bones or significant injuries…or any injuries at all. Only the wounds of others.

Wounds I was almost always the cause of.

"I didn't know at the time that the bind was cracking. But then, I didn't know he was bound. Still, I should have seen it. I should have realized something inside him was breaking." At my questioning gaze, the Nephilim elaborates, "Alexander grew increasingly agitated over the years and would often speak of feeling torn in half, as if a part of him was missing. I always assumed he was referencing his feelings about the divide, but once he returned home for good at eighteen, it was obvious the distress was taking its toll on his mind, much as it did to you. I was worried for him. Even my powers did little to help after a while."

I grimace at this admission. Great, yet another similarity Alexander and I seem to share.

Silence swells between us for a moment as I attempt to digest everything Alaric has said. Then, something else occurs to me. Something he told me when I asked him about Alexander back at the Serapeum.

"When I first asked you about Alexander, you told me he was a Nephilim."

Alaric winces at the accusation in my tone. "To be clear, neither Alexander nor I were aware of his true nature until we lifted the bind—which, in itself, had only been a test to see if there really was something restricting his powers, causing the conflict inside him, not out of any suspicion that he was anything more than part mortal. But…you're right. I lied when I told you that he was a Nephilim. Understand, great lengths were taken to ensure very few would remember the truth. Following Alexander's internment, his followers were silenced. Memories were erased. I didn't want to lose what recollections I held of him—" His voice catches and he swallows loudly. "Even the painful ones. So, I made an agreement with the Council, in part thanks to your mother's support." At my confused expression, he says, "Like you, I was once a student at the Serapeum, and your mother was my headmistress. Although we hadn't seen each other for many long years, she vouched for me when no one else on the Council would."

I gape at him, stunned by the thought of a young Alaric walking the halls of my school, however brief my time there was. It's strange to think of him that way—and to envision my mother showing any kind of sympathy or care for anyone other than herself.

"What was the agreement?" I ask.

He straightens, letting out a strained breath. "Using the talent I inherited from my father, I would seek out Nephilim to bring to the Light academies, as well as making the Darks aware of any of their own I stumbled upon. And although it broke my heart, I swore my loyalty to a world where the divide persists, undergoing a kind of silence of my own. At the time, it felt like the right thing to do."

"And now?"

My heart aches for him, for what that must've been like to go against everything Alexander stood for, the one person he loved more than anyone else in the world. I can imagine that decision haunts him, even to this day.

"Now..." He rubs a finger over his chin again. "Let's just say, with time comes clarity. I don't want you to suffer for others' past mistakes."

I look at him closely, wondering whose mistakes he means. Alexander's?

Or his own?

"Who are Alexander's real parents?" I say, not sure it really matters but curious to know the answer all the same. Perhaps my parents aren't the only two on the Council with skeletons in the closet. Not that my father knew he had such a secret.

"A mystery to this day, I'm afraid," Alaric replies. "Only one being is aware of that answer, and He has been frustratingly tight-lipped on the matter."

It takes me a few seconds to realize who he means.

"The Creator." I scoff. "He does exist, then?"

The right side of Alaric's mouth hitches up in a grin. "You doubted it?"

I roll my eyes. "I struggle to believe there's a God when so much bad has been allowed to happen. If He's there, why doesn't He stop all this?" I wave my hand toward the nearby cliff edge, gesturing toward Alexander's base in the distance.

"The Creator is not a defined being of substance, like you or me. He is everything. He is energy, He is the universe itself. He created us, He guides us, but as for the rest..." Alaric shrugs. "Well, I think He views us all sort of like a child views a science project. He wants to watch and see what happens."

"So, He never intervenes?"

Although I already suspected as much—and as much as I value free will, keeping in line with my Dark half—the thought of the Creator allowing someone like me to suffer just because of how I was born makes me unbearably sad. The emotion this realization stirs in my chest is reminiscent of how it felt to grow up without parents.

Alaric's answering expression is morose. "Only once that I've witnessed."

I stare at him dumbly until I remember just how old he is. As the son of Michael, Alaric was among the first Nephilim children left behind on Earth when the Faithful were called back to Heaven, centuries before the academies were established. Like so many others, like Gilgamesh and Vesta, he was a victim to a decision made by a being the Lights are expected to swear their allegiance to, even to this day. No wonder none of the ancient first generations have yet to Ascend. To Ascend is to love the Creator above all, to leave behind human weakness and resentment. But how do you love someone who separated you from your parents? Who made you grow up alone?

Part of me can't help wondering if Gabriel experienced something similar when she found out she was pregnant with me. Was the Creator behind that abandonment, too?

"He did nothing during Alexander's first war for power?"

Leaning his head back against the rock wall, Alaric turns his eyes upward, staring at the clear cerulean sky. "Many millennia before Alexander, when the Archangels returned to Earth to work with the Archdemons to protect the Nephilim, part of their mission was to ensure the secrecy of our kind. As such, it became their responsibility to deal with such problems. The Creator did his part by imparting the prophecy on Gabriel."

"So, at what point did they find out about Alexander and decide he needed to be dealt with?" I swallow, the words tasting like ash in my mouth. "Was it when he killed your father?"

Alaric exhales a shaky breath. "That was my fault. I was unaware of the prophecy then. What I did…"

Confusion draws my brows together. "What you did?" I echo, wondering what he means by that. But as these words leave my lips, it dawns on me that I already know the answer. "The memory Alexander showed me…it was you unbinding his Light side, wasn't it? That's why your father intervened."

I comb back through the recollection in question, remembering Alaric and Alexander on their knees in the grass, hands clasped together, as they muttered silent words I couldn't hear. I remember thinking it seemed like they were performing a ritual, but considering the ease with which Alexander removed my own bind, I failed to make the comparison.

I'm beginning to grasp the extent of the baggage Alaric is holding onto. He wasn't just in love with a Gray…

He helped unleash Alexander's wrath on the world.

"Although the Council didn't seem to know of Alexander when he was at the academies, that changed once he ascended the throne of Macedonia. I can only assume there was some concern over his powers, especially given the mantle of authority he possessed, which granted him lordship over humans. And at this point, he wasn't exactly shy about his aspirations. Or reticent in their execution. It was inevitable the Council would be watching him closely, as they do all Nephilim who try to use their power for personal gain, even if they did not forbid such political ambition at the time." His eyes fix on mine. "Let me ask you, of the first generations you've met, how many are known as kings or queens?"

"Or goddesses," I snark, thinking of Ishtar and Vesta.

"Precisely." He grins, but his amusement vanishes almost as quickly as it appeared. "I suppose it's also possible Michael was watching me, the estranged son he couldn't bring himself to face, but I know better than to believe he regretted abandoning me with my poor mortal mother. If he had, he would've made amends as soon as he was allowed back on Earth." He waves a dismissive hand, banishing the thought. "Either way, his death was my fault. If I hadn't helped to unbind Alexander, then he wouldn't have ever come into his full power, and none of what followed in the years after would've happened. Although"—he scrubs a hand over his face—"if I hadn't unbound him, his mental state would've deteriorated and who can say what catastrophe might have come of that. Despite my regrets now, I'd do it all over again if only to save him from that." A humorless smile flickers on his lips and then fades.

"How did you do it? Unbind him, I mean."

A familiar baritone stirs in my memory, bringing me back to that moment under the Serapeum when blinding pain consumed me, and my wings finally tore free from my flesh.

You have my gratitude, little dove. And in exchange for my freedom, I shall now give you yours.

How did Alexander unbind me?

The Nephilim snorts. "Let's just say there's a reason the academies don't teach Enochian anymore."

"You know Enochian?" I don't know why I'm surprised. Ishtar knew Enochian— or at least enough of it to release Alexander—and considering Alaric is far older than her, it makes sense he would know it, too. Thinking back, I recall the strange words Alexander whispered in my ear outside his tomb. In the Council's prison, I had plenty of time to consider what they meant, and now, after all this time, I guess I know. He unbound me—gave me the same freedom Alaric once gave him.

"I do, as does Alexander. And that knowledge nearly destroyed the world."

I glance at the lip of the cliff, envisioning the city below, just out of view from where we sit. As we speak, Alexander is down there, walking free of his cell.

Given their past, why isn't Alaric with him? If Caleb and I were in their shoes, if we had been forcibly separated for millennia, I'd move mountains to be with him again.

So, why is Alaric here with me instead?

Realization twists my stomach in knots. "That's why you aren't with him now, isn't it? You blame yourself for what he tried to do."

Regret darkens Alaric's gaze. "I was the catalyst. I unbound him, freeing not only his Light side but revealing his true nature, unleashing his full potential on many who suffered because of it and many more who would've been caught in the crossfire had he not eventually been detained. Alexander wanted to tear down the divide, to bring the Lights and Darks together—a sentiment I know you agree with, as do I. But the way he wanted to do it meant going to war. Which he did, for years, claiming mortal lands, although the real war was against our kind. No one on the Council desired another Fall, but Alexander would not hear reason, especially when certain Fallen joined his ranks."

"Like Lilith," I whisper.

Alaric's lips press into a flat line. "He surrounded himself with powerful followers, which was why he was able to resist the Council for so long. His followers adored him, and while I believe he was a gracious leader to the mortals he loved and to those who upheld his ideals, he did not suffer those who stood against him. He saw only one path, and he viewed himself as the rightful ruler of celestial beings and humans alike."

"Even over the Creator?" I breathe.

A scowl mars Alaric's handsome face. "Alexander blamed the Creator for why he was never able to find his birth parents. Not out of any desire for a missing connection," he says when he sees my sympathetic expression. "Rather, I think Alexander felt he had something to prove. He wanted to show his birth parents how little they mattered, that they were nothing compared to the human parents who had loved and raised him as their own." Shaking his head at some unspoken thought, he adds, "Alexander was ambitious, but he never once lied about who he was or what he wanted from life. *I* was the blind one. *I* refused to see anything aside from his love for me. And I accompanied him along that path until the veil was finally lifted from my eyes, and I realized what following him would mean."

I balk at the fear glimmering in his gaze. I can understand why he might be nervous to see Alexander again, but afraid? Why would he be frightened of him if they once loved each other? Unless—

My eyes widen. "You knew where he was this whole time. You knew he was entombed under the Serapeum."

Misery paints Alaric's face white. "Yes…because I helped put him in there."

My wings bristle under my skin, and a strange sense of betrayal grips my senses as I gape at the Nephilim, trying to process the nuclear bomb he's just dropped in my lap. He helped the Council trap Alexander. He helped them confine a Gray, someone like me.

But then…he also helped free me of my own cage, and from the hospital before that. He put his life on the line by turning on the Council to ensure I wouldn't suffer the same fate as Alexander.

A fate he helped inflict.

I'm not sure what to think of all this. Alaric isn't a bad person, I know this. But I'm not entirely convinced Alexander is either. Despite what I've been told—despite him unbinding me and then abandoning me to the Council's whims—I can understand him in a way neither the Lights or Darks can. I can empathize with the anger and pain that led him down the path resulting in his imprisonment, having felt the same frustration toward the Lights at the Serapeum and my birth parents more times than I can count. If I didn't, Alexander wouldn't have been able to manipulate me to free him as easily as he did. Hell, perhaps my insecurities and forced isolation were even how he was able to get inside my head in the first place.

I'm beginning to think I'm more like my fellow Gray than I thought. Am I doomed then to follow in his footsteps? And if I do, where does that leave Caleb? Will something inevitably come between us the same way it did between Alexander and Alaric?

Will he help entomb me if he decides that I'm dangerous?

As if he knows what I'm thinking, Alaric chokes out, "I know, probably better than anyone, what he's capable of, Luna. Alexander—He destroys everything he touches, and I'm…" He falters, his tone suddenly bleak. "I'm terrified of him destroying you, too."

Destroy?

His words trigger the memory of the words Uriel spit at me when I was still contained by the Council. *"Gabriel, the Messenger, bearer of the Creator's words. Who is to say she told us the whole truth pertaining to the Gray destined to destroy our kind and our world? Your very existence begs the question. Perhaps you, forbidden child of the Dark and the Light, are the real bringer of our demise."*

Is Alaric referring to the prophecy…?

Or is he just talking about his own heart?

Before I can press the Nephilim for more details, Hammurabi emerges from the mountain path with a sullen look smeared on his face. "We have company."

I scramble to my feet as six figures step out onto the cliff behind the Babylonian king, my wild eyes searching their faces until I find the only one who matters.

"Caleb!" I shriek, rushing toward him and throwing myself into his arms. I'm so overcome with relief that he's here—that he's *okay*—that I let out a small hiccuping sigh.

He presses a hand to my lower back, pulling me close. "I'm good," he whispers in my ear. "Everything's fine."

Someone clears their throat behind us, and releasing me, he looks over his shoulder. I follow his gaze to see Ishtar glowering at me with a venomous smirk twisting ruby red lips. She looks me up and down with a sneer.

"Hello again, Luna," she purrs.

"Ishtar," I drawl, resisting the urge to break the goddess's neck as payback for striking Caleb the last time I saw her. If anyone is to blame for things turning out the way that they have, it's her. I have no doubt about that.

She turns with the grace and poise of a panther and gestures back toward the path with a grand sweep of one arm. "Come. The Great awaits."

Terror pounds in my chest as Caleb and I follow Ishtar, hand in hand, along the winding path back down the mountain. Alaric and Hammurabi linger only a few steps behind us, and the remaining four Nephilim, who accompanied Caleb and Ishtar to meet us, bring up the rear. They're all Darks, cloaked in rippling black and violet auras, and dressed in armor, like soldiers heading for war. I suppose, in a way, they are. From what Caleb said, it sounds like Alexander intends to pick up exactly where he left off before he was imprisoned.

The trek to the citadel progresses at a slug's pace, every step weighed down with the daunting feeling that I'm walking to my own execution. The Nephilim we pass as we advance beyond the gates all look at us with a fleeting curiosity, their interest subsiding almost as quickly as it arises. From their numbers, it seems Alexander's forces are growing at an incredible rate. New visitors coming here to swear their allegiance and bend the knee must be a daily occurrence.

"The Great will receive you in the throne room," Ishtar announces, even though no one asked. I'm beginning to think she just likes to hear herself talk.

The throne room in question borders on garish when compared to the rest of the citadel, like a mansion dropped in the middle of a slum. Most perplexing is the massive stone bull's head situated just behind the throne. I'm not sure if it's an ancient relic or meant to signify something to Alexander, and I don't care to ask.

Caleb releases my hand and mouths for me to wait as he approaches the dais, bowing before the imposing figure perched on the marble draped in a purple robe topped with what appears to be the skin of a lion.

Alexander.

"As promised," Caleb says.

My blood runs cold when his grandfather rises from his throne and steps down onto our level, crossing the space toward us, his arms spread out in welcome. A genial smile lights up his fair face. "Welcome, my friends," he greets us, playing the part of the gracious host. His contrasting eyes find mine and his smile deepens. "So, we meet again at last, little dove."

No thanks to you, I'm tempted to say. But I keep my mouth shut and follow Caleb's lead, dipping into a respectful bow and waiting a few seconds before straightening again. In my peripheral vision, Hammurabi and Alaric each do the same.

"Ah, Hammurabi." Alexander appraises the Babylonian king. "I'll admit, I was surprised to hear of your attendance. I never took you for one to stand against the Council."

Hammurabi lifts his chin. "Things change."

Alexander clasps his hands behind his back. "That they do," he agrees. "That they do, my old friend. In fact, since we last met, an interesting revelation has come to light proving just that." He struts forward, circling Hammurabi like a vulture hovering over a carcass. "Tell me, King. I'm most curious to know how you came upon my dagger. You did well, of course, to return it to its bloodline," he adds with a nonchalant wave toward Caleb, "but I do wonder how it came to be under your guardianship at all."

My back stiffens at the undercurrent of threat in Alexander's voice, the clashing hues of his eyes glinting as he pauses in front of the Nephilim.

"At the time of my capture, the dagger was…reluctantly not in my possession," he continues. "If it had been, I assure you, things would have gone rather differently." The venom behind his words sends a shiver racing over my skin, but what chills me more is how quickly and easily he slips back behind the mask of the charming, charismatic ruler. The grin tugging at his lips is almost more menacing than his tone. "Only one person, aside from myself, of course, knew of the dagger's whereabouts. The one person I trusted not to bury it in my back at the first opportunity. And that person was, most certainly, not you. So how, King"—he trails a long finger under Hammurabi's jaw—"did you come upon it?"

At the western edge of the room, Ishtar seethes, her obsidian aura whipping furiously around her like storm clouds coming together to form a tornado. "You stole it from me," she snarls through gritted teeth, "just like you stole my memories!" Understanding dawns on her face, interrupting her fury for only a moment before her stunning visage settles into a mask of pure rage. "Which you've been doing for *millennia*, haven't you, so I wouldn't discover the knife was at Babel. Was it even in the museum, King, or was that just another lie you planted in my head?"

I glance between the goddess and Hammurabi, confused for all of ten seconds before remembering what Alaric told me back on the cliff. How, after Alexander's imprisonment, his followers were silenced to keep his true identity secret.

"Memories were erased," he said.

My eyes shift back to the Babylonian king as this new piece of information sinks in. Is that Hammurabi's special talent? The ability to manipulate memories? Another uncontrollable shudder rockets through me at the thought of all the ways that power could be abused.

Alexander offers Ishtar a pitying look. "That does seem to be the case, doesn't it?"

He turns his narrowed gaze back on Hammurabi, who stands frozen before the towering Gray, as if balancing on the tip of his finger. Although the Nephilim is tall, Alexander's commanding presence makes the angel seem even taller.

"You were quite thorough in performing your duty for the Council. So much so, you can imagine how troublesome it has been to recruit when few of my followers can recall their loyalty to me." With a quiet laugh, Alexander drops his finger from Hammurabi's chin. "Most curious then that you didn't relinquish my dagger like a dutiful soldier when you have always been so quick to heed Asmodeus. I can only assume she did not know that you had it, for I struggle to believe she would've allowed such a weapon to be within arm's reach of my general, even with her memories of it affected. I wonder then, did you hold onto it out of fear? Out of guilt? You must've known you couldn't wield the blade yourself."

Something inside the Nephilim seems to snap, his eyes like glowing orbs of obsidian, and yet, on the outside, he remains the picture of calm. "We might have had our fair share of differences, Alexander, but I never agreed with what the Council did to you."

Alexander cocks an amused golden brow. "Is that so? Then you won't mind unweaving the lies you spun in each of my followers' heads."

A taunting smile tugs up the corners of his mouth when the Nephilim draws in a deep breath and nods.

"If that is what my liege demands of me," Hammurabi rumbles.

"That is precisely what I hoped you would say," Alexander croons.

Despite the midday heat beating down on the citadel, the temperature in the throne room turns arctic when Alexander shifts his focus to Caleb, holding out one elegant hand.

Caleb blinks up at him, confused.

"My dagger," he says slowly, as if testing the weight of each word on his tongue. "While I appreciate your initiative, Grandson, you still acted against my orders. And disobedience must be punished."

Shaking his head, Caleb gawks at his grandfather. "But without it, I wouldn't have been able to free Luna." He gestures to me as if to remind Alexander of that fact, presenting me to him like a shiny new toy. When that doesn't seem to faze the Gray, Caleb adds in a rush, "*Or* cut off the wing of one of the Archdemons out for your blood. That shape-shifting bastard didn't know what hit him. You're welcome, by the way."

Alexander doesn't react to the news about Mammon, instead shifting his focus to me. He observes me with an admiring nod. "The Morningstar's daughter is a fine gift, indeed. The finest of what you have brought me today. But now that you have delivered her to me, you no longer have any need of the dagger, even if you have put the blade to good use. It should be returned to its rightful owner, wouldn't you agree?"

Fear is a snare drum in my chest, and the tension in the air is thick enough to choke on. I peer at Caleb out of the corner of my eye before glancing down at the hidden sheath tucked inside his belt. His knife—the knife he used to cut me out of that egg…it's the same weapon I saw in Alexander's memory.

The weapon he used to kill Michael.

Caleb's protests rip me out of my thoughts.

"But—"

"Do not make me ask a second time," Alexander interrupts, and my pulse trips at the warning edge in his voice. "There are worse punishments I can inflict. Now"—he curls his fingers in a *give it here* gesture—"hand it over. I will not ask again."

Caleb wavers, his hand hovering by his hip. I can see the internal struggle reflected on his face, the innate desire to please his grandfather, his blood—a struggle I experienced myself with Gabriel—at war with his common sense. If he hands the knife over, he's leaving himself defenseless against not just Alexander, but the Council when it comes for us. And although he has me to protect him, I have no doubt that his grandfather could tear me to pieces.

But Caleb hesitates a moment too long, and I notice the change in Alexander before I can do a damn thing to stop it. He homes in on his grandson like a heat-seeking missile, and time seems to slow as Caleb drops to one knee, clutching his head in his hands and letting out a piercing cry that tears my soul in two.

"Caleb!" I rush forward, but a hand clamps around my wrist, tugging me back like a dog on a leash. My eyes snap over my shoulder, locking with Alaric's.

"Luna, no," he warns.

An animalistic ferocity surges through me, overshadowed only by the agony that grips my chest when Caleb collapses, writhing against the stone, his lips parting on another ear-splitting scream. As his body contorts, his back arching unnaturally, the dagger slips free of his belt, clattering onto the floor.

My eyes skim over the gleaming metal before flashing back to Alaric. "Why do you keep trying to stop me?" I snarl, thinking back to our fight with Mammon.

The Nephilim's expression warps into a grimace. "I'm trying to keep you alive," he says, pleading.

With the speed of a cracking whip, Alexander's eyes dart to my face then to Alaric's where they linger, staring at his former lover, meeting his gaze for the first time since we arrived at the citadel. Part of me wondered why Alexander didn't acknowledge him sooner, but the sorrow and longing in those ominous eyes is all the answer I need to that question.

"Is this what our relationship has been reduced to, Alaric?" he asks, his low timbre verging on a whisper. "Such fear and distrust?" He clicks his tongue. "A pity. I had hoped for better from you."

He doesn't say another word to Alaric, breaking their gaze and peering back at Caleb with a disappointed frown before releasing him from whatever excruciating hold he has on his mind. Caleb lurches forward onto all fours, gasping.

"Do not challenge me again," Alexander warns, plucking the dagger off the stone floor. He tucks the blade into the sash tied around the waist of his tunic, hiding it from sight under his deep purple robe, before turning and resuming his seat on his throne.

Wrenching free of Alaric's grip, I race forward and drop to my knees beside Caleb, placing a careful hand on his quivering back and smoothing the hair away from his clammy forehead. With a trembling breath, he pushes onto his knees and tilts his head up toward the ceiling as beads of crimson track from his left nostril and ears. The blood freezes in my veins at the sight of it, and I stare wide-eyed at his stricken face as memories I'd rather forget resurface. This…what Alexander did to Caleb…I've seen this before.

No, worse than that. Bile rises in my throat. The faces of my last foster parents and the social worker who managed my case come alive in my thoughts, and it takes every last ounce of self-control I possess to not spew on the floor. I haven't just seen this before.

I've done it myself.

Horror tears my composure to shreds, and I shiver, barely able to hold myself together. I unwittingly broke into those mortals' minds as easily as Alexander just broke into Caleb's. Except where I accidentally killed them, Alexander used such brutality to establish his authority. To punish his own grandson. His blood.

I once witnessed Caleb breaking into my bullies' minds at the Serapeum, but that was nothing like this. Nothing like what I did. He was restrained in his vengeance, only acting to save me. Whereas this…what Caleb just endured…

The power imbalance was potent.

Beside me, Caleb staggers to his feet, wiping the back of his hand across his bloody nose, his bronzed complexion unusually pale. I rise alongside him, worry creasing my brow, but he just jerks his head at my silent question, grasping onto my hand for support.

Alexander claps, drawing everyone's gaze, and looks down upon us from his throne like a proud father. The anger that burnished his gaze only moments before is gone, replaced by that coquettish charm that I'm sure made him popular with the Darks and humans back in his day. Maybe it was even what won over Alaric.

Inclining his head toward Caleb, he says, "Now that such unpleasantness is out of the way, why don't you show our guests to their rooms? Ishtar"—he waves a hand toward the goddess without averting his eyes from his still shaking grandson— "accompany our friends, will you, please? So no one gets any…unfortunate ideas." His hard stare roams over my face at these words.

A growl rumbles deep in Caleb's chest. "No," he barks. "Not before you remove the tracker from Luna's head." Although he's weak from Alexander's assault, he steps forward, challenging his grandfather. Challenging an *angel*. Resentment rings clear in his voice as he spits, "I brought you your gifts. For once, uphold your end of the bargain."

Alexander crosses his legs, his long fingers curling around the arms of his throne like talons. I never would've known such a simple movement to be so ominous. "I will forgive your tone just this once, Grandson. But moving forward...remember your place."

Alexander tilts his head and crooks an elegant finger, beckoning me to come forward.

Gulping, I do as commanded, approaching the throne with all the enthusiasm of someone about to undergo a root canal. My heartbeat thrums in my ears, and my palms sweat profusely when he gestures for me to kneel at his feet. When I sink to the stone, Alexander closes his eyes and sweeps his hand against my ear.

At first, I don't feel any different. But when he pulls his hand away, there's a lightness to my head that wasn't there before. That strange sensation that kept gnawing at my ear—that I thought was all in my head—is gone now. Even my stomach is more settled than it was only seconds ago.

"Is...is it gone?" I whisper.

"It is," Alexander assures me. "You need not fear the Council any longer."

I glance down when he unfurls his fingers, showing me what looks like a glistening ivory beetle nestled on his palm.

Blanching, I squeak, "That was *inside* my head?"

With a musical chuckle, Alexander presses his other hand to my cheek, smiling warmly down at me like a ray of sunlight beaming through an overcast sky. I'm trapped in his gaze, transfixed, and I realize he's beautiful. Terrifying but beautiful.

"You could have removed it yourself, little dove, if you only had some proper training. It's time you embrace what you are. Give me your loyalty and I promise"—he rises to his feet again, pulling me up alongside him on the dais—"I will show you what you're capable of."

TWENTY-ONE

CALEB

MY SKULL THROBS LIKE someone took a sledgehammer and cracked it open then stuck their fingers into my brain and scrambled it. But the physical pain isn't the worst part—it's the feeling of being violated, of having my mind ravaged, of being a puppet watching someone else pull my strings. I'm not a total hypocrite. I've fucked with people's minds before, too, but usually in self-defense—like with those pieces of shit who attacked Luna—or to stop a criminal from doing something bad, not like this. Not to prove a point. I was a naive dumbass to think Alexander would stop short of really hurting or humiliating me just because I'm his grandson. Blood or not, he flexed his claws to ensure I know my place. Get with the program or be destroyed. Message received.

I massage my temples as I pace back and forth across the red woolen rug puddling across the old stones like a splash of blood. My room has been upgraded in my absence. It's not lavish by any means, but now there are colorful pillows decorating the bed, along with a silk duvet in peacock blue. I guess being a prince, even a deserter who isn't trusted, earned me more amenities. Appearances must be kept up. And I did bring Gramps an angel and two Nephilim, so yay me.

The real question is: Who the hell has been shopping? A hysterical laugh escapes my lips, and I shake my aching head. The most decorative piece of all, Luna, sits on the bed, watching me with concern in her eyes. Her wings are out, cascading over the bed, softer than the silk ever could be. Their appearance causes me to stumble. I stop pacing and blink, focusing on her. I don't know how long I've been trying to wear a hole in the carpet. Shit, I don't know when the last time I spoke to her was. At least that creepy bug thing is out of her head. I can be grateful to Alexander for that if nothing else, although I'm sure a high price for that favor will come soon.

The thought of him breaking Luna's mind pushes me forward once more, back and forth, back and forth in the confines of the bedroom. I can't do anything to Gramps if he tries. He took my knife—well, *his* knife—and now I'm helpless. I'm fucking helpless to protect the woman I love. And she's an angel, and I know that she's stronger than me, but she's so new to being an immortal being that Alexander could easily hurt her. Clip her wings, literally and figuratively. Like what I did to Mammon. And I don't have my weapon of immortal destruction to stop him.

"Caleb, you have to stop." Luna's voice cuts across my thoughts, and I pivot on one foot, looking over my shoulder. Her big hazel eyes snag mine, the worry in them making me flinch. "Come here." She pats a space on the bed beside her. "Sit next to me."

My eyes rove hungrily over her slender figure, tracing the beauty of her wings. It would be so easy to go to her, touch her wings, and take her right there on the bed. Forget all my problems, make her forget hers. Forget that Alexander broke my mind like I was a plastic doll, and he wants Luna for his own toy soldier. We can stay here until morning and ignore everything and everyone.

Luna's eyes widen, and I see my own want reflected there. I swallow as she pats the bed again, shaking my head.

"Please," she says, undoing my resolve.

Two strides—my legs are long—and I'm at the bed. I make sure to sit a few feet away and gaze at my hands, clenched in my lap.

Goldilocks reaches out and clasps my forearm. "Caleb, why won't you look at me?"

"I really want to have sex with you right now," I say bluntly, "but for all the wrong reasons, so I'm trying to keep my distance."

Hurt creeps into her voice. "I don't understand. You want to have *sex* with me for the wrong reasons?"

I glance up at her then, her expression embarrassed and confused. I close one hand over her knee, squeezing. "Goldilocks, I always want to have sex with you, but my head isn't in the right place. I'm—Alexander *assaulted* me. I can still feel him in my head. It's like dirt I can't scrub clean. And I desperately want to fix it, or at least be distracted enough that I forget it happened. But you deserve better than being a distraction. Not that it wouldn't be good—it would be fan-fucking-tastic—but the timing is shit. My whole timing lately is shit." I slide my hand off her knee and into my hair again, trying to quiet the lingering agony in my mind.

The bed gives a dip as she scoots closer to me and cups her hand over my knee this time. "Well, if my previous bodily responses toward you haven't already made it abundantly clear, I always want to have sex with you, too," she admits in a low voice that hits me straight in the groin. "Although, I'm not sure I want my first time to be here, with your grandfather and Ishtar lurking so close. Call me crazy, but being a glorified hostage really takes the romance out of it." She laughs. "Well, this is quite the role reversal, don't you think?"

Her words dial down the heat a little. My eyes dart up, meeting hers. "What do you mean?"

"I mean, I'm always the one having a breakdown, and you're trying to put me back together again." Her giggle makes me smile. "I'm telling you now, Caleb, there's only room for one crazy person in this relationship, and I hold that title. So, you need to get it together."

My jaw drops like a gate off its hinges at her words. Then I honest-to-Lucifer guffaw, great gulping bits of laughter escaping my lips, and I hold my side from the stitch stabbing me there. I hear the edge of hysteria in my mirth and decide I need to dial back the hyena cackle a little.

"I'm sorry. I'm not usually—"

She places a finger on my lips. "I was just teasing. What Alexander did to you…" Fire sprouts on the back of her free hand, and she shakes it out. "I wish I knew how to do something more than be a pyromaniac," she mutters.

"Hey, being a pyromaniac isn't a bad thing," I say, nudging her shoulder.

Luna squeezes my knee. "What I'm trying to say is that I'm here for you, just like you are for me. I still don't feel…like myself, but I'll support you in whatever way I can." She rises up a little and brushes a soft kiss across my lips.

I savor her lips against mine for a moment, thoughts of us naked still dancing around in my brain. Pulling away, I say, "I'm glad Alexander got that thing out of you, but I'm sorry I brought you here. I underestimated him. I just didn't think—I was a moron." My hands ball into fists, and Goldilocks slides her hand from my knee to cover one of my fists.

"No, you made the best decision in an impossible situation. If we hadn't come here, the Council would've eventually lost patience and dragged me kicking and screaming back to my cage. We'll escape from here, too. Somehow."

Though my confidence has taken a knee to the nuts, I say, "Well, I might have an idea about that. Alexander is very interested in Lucifer joining Team Conqueror, but he doesn't know about Gabriel. Yet. Your mom and pops are our best bet of getting out of here. Alexander can't take both of them on—at least I don't think so. And you're an angel, too, hardly a helpless princess."

Luna frowns. "But how will they know I'm here? Even with the tracker gone, I'm not sure Alaric can risk using the sigil…" She shudders. "Alexander has so many eyes in this place, he'll know if any of us tries to leave and we can't exactly call my father here. Not without letting him know what he's walking into."

"He won't have to because if I know Gramps at all, he'll issue Lucifer an invitation. I don't know how or where or when, but I guarantee he'll somehow track Lucifer down—or use Alaric to do it. That's a potential ally Alexander can't ignore," I explain.

"But my mother will be with him. That will look suspicious," Luna says and I sigh, thinking.

"Yeah, but Lucifer can always brush it off that she's trying to haul him in for questioning or some shit." At her doubtful look, I sigh again. "I know it's thin, Goldilocks, but it's the best hope we have right now."

She rests her head on my shoulder. "Alexander wants to train me. I know this sounds crazy…" She chuckles. "A lot of the things I say sound crazy lately, but until we find a way to leave, I should take advantage of that."

"You *want* Gramps training you?" I ask, disbelief filling my voice. I glance down at her, and her mouth puckers like she's bitten into a lemon.

"Not really, but he *is* Alexander the Great and the only other Gray that we know of. If anyone can show me how to control my powers, it's him." Luna tilts her head up, gazing into my eyes.

Well, she's got a point there. Let Alexander train her to be a lethal weapon—one that will cut him. "You're right. He can show you stuff that no one else can, not even your parents. But if you want extra points on hand-to-hand combat, corner Hammurabi."

Luna rolls her eyes. "Hammurabi wouldn't help me. Besides, I have a feeling Alexander won't want me training with anyone but him."

I kiss her forehead. "Hammurabi isn't so bad. You just have to overlook that stick up his ass." I grin as her laughter shakes her whole body. Making her laugh is like receiving a gift, one finer than gold or diamonds. Sobering, I say, "Yeah, Grandfather is possessive with his toys. He won't want anyone else playing with you."

Luna wilts against me. "Is that how he thinks of us? Even Ishtar?"

I stroke her neck, careful to keep my greedy hands off her wings. "Alexander admires and respects Ishtar, but he doesn't think she's his equal. As a Gray, you're the closest thing he has to a peer in his mind. But I don't think he really likes that there's another Gray out there. It ruins his whole line of, 'only I can unite the divide because I'm the Chosen One.' But he'll use you, of that I have no doubt."

Three precise knocks sound on our door before it's pushed open and in walks the goddess of love and war herself. Luna and I both straighten up and rise from the bed. Ishtar's eyes trace Luna's wings with a covetous gleam. She's probably jealous of Grandfather's interest in Luna. She's very proprietorial of Alexander.

"Good, you're both dressed," Ishtar says smoothly. "But you can't wear those rags to dinner."

I look at my battered jeans and T-shirt then glare at her. "One, what would you have done if we were naked, and two, we don't exactly have a mall nearby we can pop into for some new threads, and I doubt Prime delivers here."

Ishtar's smile cuts. "I've attended orgies, Caleb. Honestly, do you think any carnal activities you engage in could hold my interest? I'd die of boredom."

She claps her hands twice and another Nephilim enters. He's tall with a shaved head, and he holds a gold dress over one arm and a black suit over the other. He lays them with care across the bed, bows to Ishtar, and vacates the room.

I observe the suit as if it's a snake about to strike me. "Speaking of orgies, how is Gilgamesh? I thought he'd be here with you. Did he change his mind again?" I hear Luna gasp beside me.

I know I'm playing with fire, but Gilgamesh is Ishtar's kryptonite. And maybe I want to hurt her a little for turning on me so quickly, even though that hurt is irrational. Just because I always thought of her as a badass aunt doesn't mean she thought of me as her favorite nephew.

A satisfied smile curves my former teacher's red lips. "Gilgamesh is exactly where we need him to be, serving Alexander. Unlike you, Caleb, once he gives his loyalty, he doesn't betray it." I flinch at her words. Score one for her. "Now, get dressed. Someone will be here to escort you to dinner shortly, and it's best you appear presentable."

Luna bristles at her tone, and Ishtar looks down her nose at Goldilocks, her stare imperious. Then something interesting happens as the goddess's eyes once again linger on Luna's wings. She stiffens as if she realizes she's speaking to an angel who has the potential to destroy her. Then the moment of doubt is gone, and she turns away, throwing over her shoulder, "Alexander is most delighted to welcome the Morningstar's daughter."

I snort, resisting the urge to tell Ishtar to stop hiding behind Alexander's shield, but I know better than to push her too far. The Gilgamesh crack was enough. The door shuts behind Ishtar's statuesque frame, leaving silence in her wake.

Luna fingers the fabric of the gown. "Gilgamesh turned against the Lights?" she asks, voice incredulous. "He seemed so…self-righteous."

"You mean hypocritical? The whole sleeping with Ishtar thing dulls his halo a bit, don't you think? But he swallowed my grandfather's line, hook and sinker," I say.

Shaking her head, she takes the dress off the bed and holds it up to her body. The golden material falls to the floor in one luxurious slide.

"A golden dress for Goldilocks," I say, smirking.

"It is beautiful," she admits. "It even has an opening for my wings."

"He'll want them on full display tonight," I tell her. "I'm sure it pisses him off that Lilith no longer has her wings so he can't parade her around."

"I don't want to be a symbol of his power," she says, scowling.

I look at the black on black suit again. Ugh. It's not that I don't rock a suit like nobody's business, but I don't want to be dressed up just to please Gramps and his new entourage of murderous Nephilim. He can go fuck himself. But that attitude will just get my mind torn open again.

"Neither do I, but we have to play the game and be smarter. We know what happens when we're not." I reach for the suit, but Luna tosses the dress on the bed, and tucks her body into the open space between my arm and chest.

"You're the strongest person I know. You found a way to break me out of a celestial prison in another dimension. You'll beat Alexander at his own game. I know you will." Her hands cup my face and she kisses me.

I give into temptation and stroke my fingers down the upper curve of her wing. She shudders hard and pushes against me, her mouth frantic on mine. For a few moments, I kiss her back, happy to lose myself in the decadence that is Goldilocks until her fingertips brush under the edge of my T-shirt. I pull back with a groan, putting some much-needed distance between us. The heat in her eyes burns me. Again with my shit timing.

I say, my voice steeped in regret, "Let's get dressed, Goldilocks. This is one dinner we can't be late for."

Luna looks like a goddess. The gold dress skims her lithe figure, highlighting all the slender curves. The beading draping her upper arms sparkles in the candlelight. Her hair sweeps down her back in soft golden waves. Her hand is tucked under my elbow as we make our way to the dining hall. I was gone for just a blink, but Gramps has been busy. He's transforming this place into more than just a military fort; He's creating a palace. But I get the sense it's all temporary. When he makes his move, he'll trade up for something bigger and better, but right now as he recruits, he needs to show all his prospects that he has a real seat of power, not just a pile of crumbling rocks.

And he's not only transformed the interior. I can smell spiced meat and fresh bread and my stomach growls. When I lived here last, I was lucky to get scrambled eggs. The last meal I had was at Mom's, so despite my nerves, I'm hungry. Unlike Alexander, I need to eat to remain at full strength. I glance down at Goldilocks. Huh, I guess she doesn't need to eat anymore. I wonder if she realizes that.

Her eyes meet mine and turn smoky. "You look…" She blushes and I smirk. "You look very handsome in that suit."

Ishtar must know my measurements because the suit fits like a glove, although I find the jacket confining if I need to fight. It's going right on the chair as soon as we're seated. "I know, gorgeous," I say, winking. "You look good enough to eat."

Red stains her cheeks and travels down her neck. I wonder just how far that blush goes. And thoughts like that are gonna get me killed. I'm going into the lion's den, and I need to stay sharp.

I see Hammurabi ahead with Alaric, waiting for us outside two enormous wooden and bronze doors. I thought Ishtar would come back and escort us to dinner, sulking about it the entire time, despite saying she was sending an underling. But she did send another Nephilim who had simply knocked on our door and told us to move our asses. Well, he didn't say exactly that but it was implied. No one keeps the Great waiting.

Alaric wears a slick charcoal suit, but Hammurabi is dressed in traditional Babylonian garb, with a woven skirt that hits him at the knee and a wide leather belt, along with sandals. He's barechested, his prize-fighter body on display. It's like he's stepped out of time. It's so bizarre I stumble a little; his face twists into a fierce scowl, and I'm certain he didn't choose this for himself. Why is my grandfather having him dress like the king he was? Other than his beard and quilted turban, he's mostly a modern man. Well, as modern as anyone like him can be. Maybe the better word is adaptable. He likes going out into the world and experiencing things.

Gilgamesh's image flashes through my mind, and I remember him telling Gramps he resented having to relinquish his kingship. Maybe Alexander sent those clothes to Hammurabi to remind him who he used to be and could still be in the new world order. Does Grandfather really plan to carve up the planet into fiefdoms for his most loyal generals while he rules over all? I wonder how that's going to work out, especially as there might be internal conflict over territory, like hey you might have ruled first, but I was here last.

I don't know who Alaric originally was when he was young, but he just looks like a well-dressed guy going to a board meeting. Ishtar emerges from the dining room in an ivory gown with a gold belt, living up to her goddess reputation. A welcoming smile is fixed upon her lips as she greets Alaric and Hammurabi. Alaric paints on his own charming smile while Hammurabi just gives a curt nod. If this wasn't a farce, and Hammurabi really wanted to serve Alexander, he'd compete with Ishtar for the number one position. There's no love lost between the two of them, just a fierce competition of who is best.

Luna and I stop before them, and Ishtar once again takes Luna's measure before focusing on me.

"Caleb, you clean up beautifully, just as I knew you would. For all your faults, you're stunning, just like all the men in your family," Ishtar says, and my stomach sours at the mention of my father. "Luna, how ethereal you are in that gown. You're so fortunate to have Alexander as your mentor. Soon, the Council will fear you."

Luna offers a tight smile, pressing herself even closer against my side. "I hope so," she says, and I hear the truth in those words. Good, I hope Goldilocks uses my grandfather for everything she can get out of him.

"Come, I was hoping Lilith could join us tonight, but she's been detained on some personal business," Ishtar says, linking her arm through Alaric's. "But we have another guest whose company I'm sure you'll enjoy." She winks at Alaric, and he raises an eyebrow.

I'm not surprised when we enter the dining hall to see Gilgamesh sitting on the left of Alexander, who is at the head of an enormous table. Luna's body goes rigid at the sight of her former teacher, and Gilgamesh's eyebrows grab for his hairline when he takes in Luna's wings, his face a picture of stunned amazement. Alaric startles but recovers quickly, his eyes flicking past Gilgamesh to hone in on Alexander. Grandfather's eyes settle on Alaric's in turn, and there's this weird undercurrent between them I don't understand.

"Please believe me when I say it's nice to see you and Gilgamesh no longer hiding in the shadows. Neither of you deserved that for thousands of years," Alaric says, and I can hear the sincerity in his voice.

It's Ishtar's turn to be taken aback. "Why, Alaric, I do think you mean that."

"Your relationship was the worst kept secret in either faction," Hammurabi says acidly. "We all knew you were fucking each other."

I choke down laughter, and Luna clutches my arm. Our eyes meet, and I see shocked amusement dancing in her gaze.

If Ishtar were a wolf, her hackles would be up. "Tell me, does sleeping with all those women make you forget about whom you really want to be with? I've always been curious."

Now, Hammurabi's hackles rise, and Alaric disengages with Ishtar and steps smoothly between them. "Alexander will be displeased at this hostility between allies. He has high hopes for us. Let's not disappoint him," he says, and Ishtar's expression smooths out, her shoulders relaxing. I guess Alaric dosed her with a shot of Calm. The resentful look she gives him confirms it.

"Stop that," Ishtar hisses at Alaric and pushes her shoulders back, pinning on an award-winning smile. "You're right. We mustn't disappoint Alexander." She saunters ahead, hips swaying, and Gilgamesh stops speaking to Alexander to stare at her, expression completely entranced.

Well, it's nice to know some things never change. Luna nudges me. "Who was Ishtar talking about?" she murmurs.

I shrug, whispering out of the side of my mouth, "No idea. Other than this past month, I've only seen Hammurabi at school. He could have a whole harem somewhere for all I know."

Luna looks at Hammurabi in all his shirtless glory, and I try not to get jealous at the admiration she can't quite hide. The dude *is* ripped. "It's hard to picture him pining after anyone. Then again, he did seem pretty taken with your mom so maybe I'm wrong."

The thought of Hammurabi hitting on my mom makes me scowl, but I see the mischievous glint in her eyes, and I chuckle. The laughter gets lodged in my throat when my gaze clashes with Alexander's, and I swear I feel phantom claws tearing into my mind again. It was much easier to joke about Hammurabi's sex life than to face my gramps again; however, Alexander gifts me with a warm smile. Well, I'll be damned. I guess he's back to playing benevolent grandfather again.

"Grandson, you look well rested. Come, sit beside me. You and Luna are the guests of honor tonight," he calls to me, sweeping out his arm over the ornate chairs beside him.

Bending slightly at the waist, I say, "It would be our honor to sit beside you, Grandfather."

Also with Luna being the only other angel here, that's the only place she can sit. This isn't a democracy, and the most powerful sit near the king. Luna glances at me in surprise as I put her right next to Alexander, but my grandfather just gives me a slight nod, acknowledging my homage to her angel status. As I push her chair in, I notice the slight tremor running through my hands, and I will myself to calm down, to not show the lion in the room any weakness.

Panic claws its way up my throat as I drape my jacket over the back of my chair and sit beside Luna, remembering writhing on the floor in front of Alexander in the throne room. I can hear the dagger hitting the smooth stone floor again, the sharp, painful sound of defeat. Everyone here but Gilgamesh witnessed my humiliation, how Grandfather brought me to my knees and showed me that despite my divine blood, he could break me at any time. I take a slow breath through my nose, attempting to wipe my mind clean of those tormenting thoughts. Luna finds my knee under the table and squeezes, bringing me firmly back to the here and now.

My gaze lands on the silver plates and goblets and pitchers artfully strewn across the table. I pick up a goblet, its metalwork flawless. This looks exactly like the silver found in King Philip's tomb in Greece in Vergina. Either Alexander went back and claimed them or he had someone replicate them for him. There are a lot of talented Nephilim out there and from this time period, too. Gramps notices me admiring the goblet in my hand and smiles.

"Ah, so you recognize it. One of my Nephilim created this for me, to remind me of home, of my human parents. My true parents despite my divine blood," Alexander says, a bitter smile twisting his lips. "But enough about the past. We're here because we believe in a glorious future, a future without all this strife and turmoil between our factions."

"Yes," Gilgamesh says. "And a future where the mortals are no longer destroying themselves."

"The little lambs need a shepherd," Ishtar agrees, cupping her goblet in one hand. Shepherd my ass, she's more like a wolf wearing a sheep's skin.

"Yes, but tonight, we celebrate my grandson, Caleb, for the glorious gifts he has brought me. Alaric, clever and diplomatic, who can root out any bloodline, and the mighty Hammurabi, fierce king of old whom I will restore to his former glory," Alexander says, his eyes brushing over Hammurabi and lingering on Alaric a beat too long. "And of course, he brought me the only other Gray in existence, the beautiful Luna, who I will mold in my image. She will be a great weapon in the war to come."

Luna stills at his words, and this time I find her knee under the table, and she shoots me a grateful look under her long lashes.

"I cannot rule if you do," Hammurabi says, drawing my attention away, and I curse under my breath at his dangerous stubbornness. Alexander's mouth thins and I brace myself. Hammurabi continues, "We're here because we believe you can unite us, not make us rulers again."

Nice save, King.

Grandfather relaxes and leans back in his chair. "Ah, that's where you're wrong, King. While it's true, Heaven cannot brook two suns, nor Earth two masters"—he glances sideways at Luna, and my heart stutters in my chest—"my loyal generals will divide the lands and maintain order over them. Though all will answer to me, you will rule your kingdoms with my blessing and with the wisdom I know you possess."

And if they step out of line, Alexander will fall upon them like a hammer. He doesn't say it, but he doesn't have to. They all know he rewards those who are loyal to him but don't go getting any ideas of true independence.

Hammurabi bows his head in deference to Alexander. "Your generosity does you credit."

Gilgamesh caresses the back of Ishtar's hand. "The world would have been a better place if we'd been allowed to continue to rule it."

Wow, at this rate, Gilgamesh's ego will outgrow Alexander's army.

"Indeed, my friend," Alexander says, and Alaric takes two quick gulps from his goblet, avoiding my grandfather's pointed looks. That is one mystery I'd love to crack. "Let's raise our glasses to Caleb, who cut off the mighty Mammon's wing"—Gilgamesh's jaw falls at that proclamation—"and is responsible for bringing this dinner about. His love may have made him foolish and stole him away from me for a brief time, but I can forgive him for it, as he's brought the Morningstar's daughter into the fold. Though you are not of my blood, Luna, I think of you as I do Caleb, as an heir of my empire."

Luna and I exchange glances at those loaded words. Alexander just elevated a newbie to princess status. Although heir implies he'd be willing to pass on the crown, and I know that ain't happening. Ever. Ishtar's lush mouth turns down at Alexander's proclamation, and though I know she's jealous of Goldilocks, she echoes my grandfather's, "To Caleb!"

I slap on a smile that fits wrong, like I'm a Ken doll with a painted-on mouth. I take a sip from my goblet, and the flavor of good wine explodes on my tongue. I drain the cup in one go. It takes a lot to get a Nephilim drunk, and I need to appear somewhat relaxed during this dinner from hell, especially as Alexander seems determined to focus on me. The roasted lamb on my plate smells divine, and I take a bite despite my nerves, just to occupy my hands with something other than fidgeting.

Those calculating eyes roam over me, and cold sweat trickles down my back, dampening the silk of my shirt. A kind smile stretches across my grandfather's face. That terrifies me even more.

"I know you believe because I punished you, blood isn't important to me. You believe I do not care about you, which couldn't be further from the truth," Alexander says, voice tender. "Children need discipline or they become unruly and a danger to themselves. And while I admire your ingenuity and your independent spirit, your quest could've easily gotten you captured or killed. The Council will show no mercy to my blood. Family is important, Caleb, and with Alaric's help, we will root out my other grandchildren and bring them in line with our virtuous cause. I can only hope they are as bold and bright as you."

I stare at him, my mind in overdrive. Dear Dad made a deal with the Archdemons to conceal his children from one another and mask our blood connection to him. I'm guessing much in the same way Gabriel managed to conceal her connection to Luna. But Alaric didn't know Goldilocks was Gabriel's kid when he brought her to the Serapeum and mentioned something about how difficult she had been to track down. So, would he even be able to scent out our bloodline through whatever magic was placed on me and my siblings?

"Thank you, Grandfather," I say, relieved my voice doesn't warble. "But my father…" I can't quite keep the bite out of my voice. "My father—"

Alexander waves a dismissive hand and leans forward, eyes gleaming. "Oh, I know what your father has done. I told you, Caleb, I would bring him to heel, like the ungrateful dog that he is. As you've brought me three great gifts, I deliver one to you. Our family will be together again." He claps his hands.

I swivel toward the doors, blood rushing to my head so fast my vision blurs. This can't be happening. Somehow, Luna's hand finds mine, and I clutch it like it's my only lifeline. I hear a *clink-clink* echo along the stone walls before a Nephilim in chains is brought into the room, two guards flanking each of his sides.

His dirty blond hair is darker than Alexander's, and his eyes shine brilliant green, like two fine-cut stones of jade. Anger burns in the liquid depths as he takes in our dinner party, then his gaze falls on me with all the force of a baseball bat to the head.

I have my mother's eyes, her coloring, but the cut of my jaw, my nose, my mouth, the width of my shoulders, my height, it's all him. Suddenly, I want my dagger back so I can carve my father right out of my face, so all that's left is the eyes and hair of my mother. An almost guttural growl escapes my throat as I stare at my deadbeat dad. I'm on my feet before I know it, eyes pinned on my father, who stares back at me with equal animosity.

I hear a faint whoosh, and then pearly gray feathers brush my arms, curling around my body as Luna places a restraining hand on my heaving chest.

"Caleb," Alexander's deep voice penetrates through the fog of rage clouding my brain. I tilt my head, looking at him. "I have brought your father here so he can be punished for his faithlessness, for his abandonment of his children. So you can have justice. This is my gift to you." He motions to the tall woman on the right of my father. She holds out a whip with a metal tip on it. "Go, Caleb. Take it. Mete out your justice."

TWENTY-TWO

LUNA

MY PULSE THUNDERS IN my ears as I peer between Caleb and the chained man at the other end of the room. His cheeks are scuffed with dirt—the black smudges in stark contrast to the green of his eyes—and he's shirtless, his bare torso sculpted with muscle. I see so much of Caleb in the man's handsome features that his identity was clear to me when he shuffled into the room without Alexander even needing to say it.

I cast a sidelong glance at the other Gray, wondering what he's hoping to achieve with this. The man before us is his *son*. Regardless of his reproductive habits, does Alexander really want to hurt him? I'm inclined to say yes, given what I've already seen him do to his own blood. What's worse is he really does seem to think he's doing Caleb a favor—that handing out judgment in the form of corporal punishment is something his grandson would want.

Unless the person Alexander is actually trying to punish with this display is his grandson. Caleb has already disobeyed him twice, so it's likely Alexander is looking to challenge his loyalty.

This is some kind of test, I'm sure of it. Alexander is acting like he's giving Caleb a gift by presenting his father to him like a sacrificial lamb to be slaughtered, and while he might believe that, I have no doubt he also wants to see if his grandson will finally do what he commands. But unlike Alexander, I know Caleb. He isn't a malicious person, and I can't see him assaulting someone who is defenseless to protect themselves, even if some part of him might think they deserve it. My stomach roils at the mental image of Caleb going through with it…and what might happen if he doesn't.

If he refuses, will Alexander turn the whip on him instead?

Under my fingers, Caleb's body is trembling, his heart racing a mile a minute, and his complexion is ashen, as if the sight of his father has made him physically sick. At Alexander's scrutiny, his expression hardens, and he shrugs me off, stepping out of the protective sheath of my wings.

Keeping his heated gaze fixed ahead, he rolls up his sleeves then skirts the large table, extending his arm toward the female Nephilim, who offers the whip for him to take. I watch as his long fingers close around the braided black handle and hold my breath as he positions himself in front of his father.

When Alexander nods, the two Nephilim guards tug on their prisoner's chains, turning him until his naked back is exposed to the room, facing his son and soon to be punisher. Once again, I risk a wary glance at Alexander, who meets my startled gaze with a smile before casting his eyes pointedly down at my chair. A silent command for me to sit.

I grimace as understanding consumes me. He expects us to be silent spectators to this torture. To accept his command as law and, in doing so, demonstrate our submission.

Swallowing the bile burning its way up my throat, I sink into my seat and look back at Caleb, watching his movements with anticipation and terror. The braided leather creaks in protest when his fingers tighten, and sweat beads on the back of his neck as he raises his arm, preparing to strike.

The crack of the whip is lightning fast, and a shudder rips through me when it cuts into its intended target, slicing through the top layers of skin. A strangled cry escapes Caleb's father as his body contorts backward, arching against the pain. Rivulets of blood run from the torn flesh like raindrops against glass.

Even from the opposite side of the room, my heightened senses are acutely aware of the fear emanating from Caleb's father, the musty odor of his sweat and the metallic tang of his blood clinging to the inside of my nostrils. I resist the urge to clamp a hand over my mouth, not wanting to betray even the smallest hint of weakness in front of Alexander. Now, more than ever, I'm certain the other Gray is deranged. And while I can empathize with what he's been through between his parents' abandonment and his many years of imprisonment, nothing can excuse the pain he's inflicting. And not just on his son but on Caleb. My stomach sloshes with the fear of what this moment might do to him mentally.

As if reading my mind, Caleb peers over his shoulder, and I can only imagine the horror he must see on my face despite how hard I try to hide it. His own expression remains eerily drawn.

Turning slowly to face his father again, he tosses the whip to the floor by his feet.

"Finished already?" Alexander asks, his tone both scolding and sardonic.

Caleb approaches his grandfather, stopping just before Alexander's seat at the head of the table. "I thank you for the opportunity, Grandfather," he simpers. "This has been the greatest gift I could ask for. But it has also made me realize that this sorry excuse for a Nephilim isn't worth my time and energy…or my vengeance. He's not worthy of your blood. *Our* blood."

Alexander cocks his head to one side at that, brushing a finger along the strong line of his jawbone as his eyes sharpen with interest on his grandson. "Is that so?"

Caleb nods. "You are the only father I need," he declares, the lie falling from his lips with a mind-blowing ease and sincerity.

Alexander shoos away the Nephilim guarding Caleb's father, and without a word, they march from the room, dragging their chained prisoner between them. Although his body is bent and his back streaked with blood, the skin that was torn open like paper from the lash of the whip is now sealed shut. Only the faintest line of pink flesh is visible to show he was whipped at all, and even that is fading quickly.

As the Nephilim shuffles from the room, head dipped low, he doesn't make a sound or even risk a glance at Alexander. Or Caleb. Why won't he speak? Is something forcing this silence upon him—keeping him from acknowledging his own father and son? Or is it a willing decision? A protest?

The only armor he has to protect himself.

As we eat, the room is so quiet I could hear a pin drop, and I wait with bated breath for Alexander to speak, sensing the others' anticipation as well. Nobody dares to break the silence. Alaric doesn't even try to use his power to ease the tension radiating like heat in the room, despite attempting to use it on Ishtar not even an hour ago. I can only imagine he's keeping his gifts on a leash in Alexander's presence to appease him, as if to prove the angel has some sort of claim on his powers. Perhaps even on him.

My eyes narrow on the Gray when he rises from his chair, and my heart jackrabbits against my ribcage as he looms over Caleb, who seems so small and vulnerable in the shadow of the angel. He reaches out a hand toward his grandson, and once again, I imagine every worst case scenario—him strangling Caleb, him ripping out his still beating heart. I imagine everything except what actually happens.

Pulling Caleb into a loving embrace, Alexander smiles. "You say I am the only father you need? Then let it be done…my son."

I swallow my surprise, sparing the quickest of glances at Hammurabi and Alaric. They each look as stunned as I feel. Across from me, Gilgamesh and Ishtar watch the scene unfold with serene smiles plastered on their faces. But, unlike my old history teacher—whose expression seems genuine, much to my confusion—Ishtar is unable to hide the indignation buried in the charcoal pits of her eyes. I can see it written all over her face: the resentment she must feel, not only knowing she'll never be Alexander's number one, but that she's just been outranked by another Nephilim. And a second generation, at that.

A grin tugs at my cheeks at her fury, but I quickly rein it in, forcing a mask of composed calm on my face. When Alexander breaks away from Caleb, he gestures for everyone to stand.

"My friends, let us end the evening with one final toast." He raises his refilled goblet. "To Caleb, my heir, my chosen son, who has proven to be everything his useless father was not."

In unison with everyone else at the table, I pick up the nearest chalice and press the brim to my lips, but I don't take a sip, afraid my churning stomach will only toss the wine back up. Caleb meets my gaze across the table where he stands statue-still beside Alexander, a fresh goblet in his hand, placed there by one of the many mute servants scurrying about like rats.

With dinner dismissed, Alexander excuses himself, pausing only once on his trek to the door to peer over his shoulder at me. When our eyes meet, a morbid chuckle escapes him.

"The events of this evening have me feeling inspired. So much so that I do believe I know the perfect way to begin your training."

A lump swells in my throat, but I swallow my dread, trying my best to keep my expression neutral. Although I told Caleb I wanted his grandfather to train me—to take advantage of learning from the only other Gray we know of—I'm suddenly doubting that decision. Not that I really think I have much say in the matter. Alexander wants to mold me, and so long as we're here, I have to act pliant, like an untouched lump of clay. Ready and willing.

I bow my head, putting on the most grateful smile I can manage. "I look forward to it."

Alexander says nothing else before departing the room, the first generations following in his wake. Caleb and I don't move a collective muscle until we're certain we're alone.

With a slight jerk of his chin, Caleb signals for me to meet him by the foot of the table. "I have a bad feeling about whatever it is he has in mind for that," he says once we're side by side.

I brush him off. Training with Alexander is tomorrow Luna's problem. "Forget about that. Did he…" I hesitate, lowering my voice to a barely-there breath. "Did your grandfather just *adopt* you?"

Caleb rakes a hand through his hair. "I honestly have no fucking idea. I just said what I had to. I did—" His voice breaks, and he looks down at his shaking hands, as if he'll see his father's blood on his skin.

"I know," I murmur, covering his palms with my own and interlacing our fingers, squeezing. "It's okay."

"Is it?" he whispers, shaking his head. "I wanted to hit him. I wanted to *hurt* him. I could've killed him for what he did to my mom. To me."

"Yet you stopped," I remind him. Rising onto my toes, I plant a kiss on his lips. "You stopped."

His eyes shift to mine, and the emptiness I find in their depths is hauntingly familiar. I've seen that emptiness before. I've felt it inside me more times than I can count. And because I've experienced it, I know all too well what Caleb must be asking himself. The one question that still permeates my thoughts, even now, even knowing what I know.

The question of why we weren't enough for the parents who let us go.

I rouse cocooned in Caleb's arms, blinking bleary eyes awake to the sight of a golden scroll, complete with red tassel, on the table just beside my head. At first, I don't reach for it, not wanting to disturb Caleb, who slept so fitfully last night, tormented by images of his father and the parasitic plague of his guilt, if his slumbering mutterings were any indication of what he dreamt about. As I lie still, staring at the gleaming golden handles sticking out of each end of the scroll, my curiosity niggles at the back of my brain until I can't take the not knowing for a single second longer. I reach out a tentative hand, brushing my fingertips over the parchment.

"What is it?" Caleb mumbles sleepily beside me.

My eyes dart over my shoulder, meeting his sleep-soaked gaze, as a frown tugs down my lips. I really didn't want to wake him up. He needed some rest and, selfishly, I like the feel of him sleeping beside me too much.

"Not sure. But I'm guessing it's from your grandfather."

Caleb sits up, glaring at the scroll in my hand as if it's a ticking time bomb. Shifting, I lean against the headboard and carefully unfurl the roll.

"It's a request for my presence in the throne room," I say, silently scanning the swooping, elegant script.

"More like a summons," Caleb growls, reading over my shoulder.

I exhale through my nose. Looks like tomorrow Luna's problem just became today Luna's problem.

"Well," I grumble, sliding off the bed, "I better not keep His Majesty waiting."

After a quick wash with the paltry basin provided in our room in place of a bathroom, I pull on the fresh clothes one of the serving Nephilim left out for me, tugging the gold embellished tunic over my head and pairing it at the waist with a jewel-encrusted leather belt and matching cobalt blue slippers. Once I'm dressed, I give Caleb a long goodbye kiss, draw in a deep breath, and make for the door. Although I can tell he doesn't want me to go, he doesn't voice his protests. We both know they wouldn't do any good.

As I walk down the long hallway toward the throne room, I glance down at my extravagant attire—the second lavish outfit I've had to don since arriving in Alexander's domain. I can't help feeling like a doll he's dressing up for show, like I'm stepping into a role he's written for me to play.

When I enter the cavernous room I've been beckoned to, I find the other Gray already waiting for me, draped across his throne like a blanket. Our eyes clash across the empty space as he rises, his broad wings fanning out behind him, and it takes all the self-restraint I can muster not to inch back as he crosses the space between us. We might both be angels, but Alexander is an avalanche, and I am little more than a snowball.

"Good morning, young Morningstar," he croons with a jovial smile.

I balk for a moment before stamping a forced grin on my face. "So, what kind of training are we going to be doing?"

Alexander chuckles, steepling his fingers in front of his chest. "My, my. Are you always so eager?"

"I mean, you *did* promise to help me learn to control my powers…hmm…how long ago was it?"

The Gray lets out an unrestrained laugh. "Touché, little dove. Well then, let's begin."

He leads me into the center of the room and then pivots to face me, raising his right hand, palm up. A crimson flame bursts to life in his grasp, casting ruby streaks along his fingers.

"I have seen inside your mind, my young friend, and as such, I have seen what you're capable of." The flames extinguish as his hand curls into a fist. He then nods once, glancing down at my arm, which hangs like a limp noodle by my side. "Come," he urges. "Let us see your fire."

Closing my eyes, I hold up my hand, imagining the heat building first in my veins and then growing until it's boiling over through my skin. When I open my eyes, flames explode across my flattened palm, burning the same red as blood.

"Good," Alexander purrs, his voice dripping with praise. His eyes cut to the side as footsteps resound off the stone to my left. "Now…wield it."

Goosebumps pimple my flesh as I follow his gaze, my stomach dropping at the sight of the barechested Nephilim ten feet away. He faces us, his hands tucked behind his back.

My flame sputters out as realization takes hold. "What?" I gasp, looking back at Alexander. "You mean—"

He shakes his head. "Do not concern yourself with his well-being. He is a Nephilim. He will heal."

I glance between them, aghast. "But—"

"A sheep will never lead an army of lions. But a lion may lead an army of sheep." Alexander steps closer, planting a firm hand on my shoulder. His fingers dig into my skin through my tunic. "Become a lion, Luna."

I cower beneath his hard stare. When I don't move, he sighs, lowering his hand.

"If it will ease your mind, he has volunteered for this task. Now, wield your flame," he repeats, his voice taking on a hard edge.

He gives me a not-so-gentle nudge toward my victim, and I recoil at his touch, sick to my stomach at what it is he's asking of me. His words replay in my ears—a silent warning not to disobey. But what if I do? Will Alexander cease my training if I refuse?

Or will he do something far worse?

The answer hits me when I look over my shoulder, and his piercing gaze crawls over my face, wordlessly screaming his disapproval. If I don't act now, if I don't do what he says, he'll put me down for my disobedience, or worse. *Far* worse. Like hurt Caleb again.

And I can't let that happen.

Anger burns like heat in my veins, and I let that rage, that fury, ignite me. Calling it to the surface, I ball the flames in my hands and clenching my teeth, I project the hatred in my heart outward, picturing Alexander's face on my target. The Nephilim screams as the fire consumes him, the inferno charring his exposed torso and flooding the room with the nauseating odor of cooked flesh. As he collapses to the floor in a thrashing fit of agony, Alexander applauds behind me.

"Bravo!" he cries as I scream on the inside. "Bravo, little dove. I knew you would not disappoint."

Quivering like a leaf in the wind, I drop my arms and stare down at my trembling fingers. The flames thin to weak embers before fading completely, leaving my pale skin cool and untouched.

The smell permeating the room triggers my gag reflex, and I slam my hand over my nose, pinching my nostrils and dry heaving once beneath my fingers. The whole time, my eyes remain glued to the Nephilim, who—just as Alexander promised—is beginning to heal, the black crispy flesh flaking away to reveal fresh ivory skin underneath. Grunting, he lifts himself off the floor.

"I…" Tears flood my eyes. "I'm so sor—"

"Apologies are for the weak-willed, young Morningstar," Alexander cajoles, waving away the man before positioning himself before me again. Planting a fingertip under my chin, he forces my horrified gaze to meet his. "And you, my little dove, are not weak."

A hysterical squeak bubbles to my lips, half-crazed giggle and half-broken sob. No, I'm not weak. The terrible things I've done throughout my life have proven that. Even when I always felt so close to the edge, I never felt weak. Powerless, yes. But not weak. If anything, I was afraid of myself and what I knew I was capable of.

I stare down at my hands, envisioning the red flames curling around my fingers and imagining the way they seared into the Nephilim's flesh, burning through him as if he were mortal. Using my powers on others in this vile way, for torment and torture, regardless of if they are willing—is that what Alexander views as strength?

Revulsion crawls over my skin.

If this is strength, I'm not sure I want it.

Alexander's lingering gaze softens a little. "I know what you are thinking, little dove, but you must not fear what you are."

My hands clench into fists at my sides. "Because fear is for the weak?" I spit.

He considers me for a moment before shaking his head. "Fear is natural, but it is also a weapon. One you must learn to wield if you are to defend yourself against those who would seek to imprison you. You might be a Gray, but there are angels and demons far older than you who would tear your mind to shreds if you let them."

Like what you did to Caleb? I nearly shout, stopping myself just before the words breach my lips.

Alexander narrows his eyes. "When the time for war comes, we will all need to be merciless. If you are to be an asset to me, I need to know you can do that."

He averts his focus to the doorway, and I follow his gaze, my heart jumping into my throat at the hiss of chains scraping across the floor. My eyes widen when the Nephilim guards from last night step into the room with Caleb's dad sandwiched between them.

"Wh—" I swallow, clearing my throat. "Why is *he* here?"

"Break him," Alexander commands as casually as if he's commenting about the weather.

Horror grips my lungs in an iron-clad fist. "What?"

Alexander steps forward until he's uncomfortably close and leans in, whispering in my ear. Wisps of his golden hair brush my cheek. "Break into his mind. I know you can. After all...you've done it before."

A startled gasp rips from my throat as my foster parents' faces flood my mind. I see them, twisted and bent on the floor, their faces contorted in pain and terror, blood soaking into the small woven rug under the coffee table and spreading across the floorboards of the living room in their house. I broke their minds. I broke *them*. I know it.

But how does Alexander?

My lower lip wobbles, the guilt like a hand around my throat, squeezing tightly. Alexander grazes the back of his hand along the side of my face, a sympathetic smile curling his mouth.

"You forget that I was there, at the Serapeum, always listening," he murmurs, combing the hair back from my face. "Always in your head. You let me in so easily, little dove, and unlike my grandson, who tried and failed to see inside that precious mind, I could hear your thoughts so clearly. And your words."

My eyes bulge, and I gape at him, uncertain which part of that terrifies me the most. Knowing Caleb tried to read my mind or that Alexander might still be able to now.

At my horrified expression, he chuckles. "Worry not. Your thoughts are safe from me. While an angel's mind is naturally protected from Nephilim, being unbound has offered you some protection even against those of us like yourself. It would take great effort to break into your mind and I desire your trust, little dove."

"And the others?" I ask tentatively. "What about them?" If Alexander can read their minds, he'll know we aren't actually here to support him.

I try not to let my relief show when he nods. "Also safe," he assures me. "It is not a simple thing to see inside the mind of a first generation. Their celestial link is strong and not diluted by their mortal ties. They, too, have some natural protection in place bolstered by millennia of training. As for Caleb, the strength of his blood runs deep. Besides," he says, shrugging ruefully. "If I had been in one of their minds, you would know."

A chill passes over my skin as I'm struck once again by the mental image of Caleb convulsing on the floor. But Alexander wasn't trying to read Caleb's mind in that moment. He was trying to break it. To bend him into unwilling obedience.

Just as he now wants me to do to his son.

He extends an arm toward Caleb's father, whose gemstone eyes are dull with acceptance. He doesn't seem afraid, which somehow makes what Alexander is asking of me so much worse.

"Now, show me how powerful you can be," the Gray instructs.

I stiffen at his words. I don't want to hurt anyone, not even Caleb's father, who probably deserves whatever thrashing he gets. I don't want to do this. This wasn't what I had in mind when I told Caleb I wanted his grandfather to train me. No wonder he was so wary of the idea last night.

Alexander exhales, and his eyes harden on mine, impatience leaching into his tone when he adds, "Or, perhaps, I should fetch Caleb for me to demonstrate for you?"

My wings tear free of my back at his threat, my chest heaving as a rush of power and rage thrum underneath my skin like an electric current. Amusement tugs at Alexander's cheeks and he smirks, gesturing once more to his restrained son.

"I will not ask again," he says. "Do it, or we end our training here."

Sweat dampens my skin as I refocus my gaze, torn between the nausea churning my gut and what I have to do to survive and protect myself from everyone who has decided that being different somehow makes me dangerous. I don't want to hurt anyone, but I also know if I don't do what Alexander commands, my disobedience will only give him cause to hurt Caleb again. He might be the Gray's heir, but Alexander's actions have already proven that sharing his blood doesn't make him invulnerable, and I don't doubt for a moment that the angel will do whatever he deems necessary to force me to comply. Because he doesn't want me as an equal.

He wants me as a soldier he can control.

Control. That's what this is about. Control. Isn't that exactly what I've wanted since Alaric first brought me to the Serapeum?

What Alexander said is true: I am afraid of what I'm capable of, and learning that control he promised me all those months ago would ease those worries. Besides, I need to be able to defend myself against the Council when they come for me again. Mammon might not have broken my mind, but he broke my spirit, and he knows enough about me—about my weaknesses—to use my emotions against me. I don't want to be defenseless like that again.

Bracing myself, I stare at Caleb's father. *I can do this. I don't have to hurt him.* A piercing ache throbs behind my temples as I strain, focusing on reaching past the confines of his skull and into the depths of his mind where I envision his thoughts like a feast laid out before me, fruit ripe for the taking.

But as I reach out, I sense a strange change in the air, and suddenly, all I can picture is my foster parents on the floor, unmoving, in pools of their own blood. I did that. I broke them.

Just like I can feel myself breaking Caleb's father.

His mouth falls open on a silent scream, a crimson stream trickling from his nose as he falls to the floor, his body seizing. No matter how hard I try, I can't stop, my own mind trapped in a memory I can't escape.

"Please," he breathes. The first word I've heard him say. But I can't tell what he's asking. Please stop? Please kill me? I can't figure it out, and I can't let him go. I try, but I can't, my fingers caught in the snare of his mind, his terror a palpable scent I can taste.

In the moment before the link snaps and I realize I've gone too far to turn back, all I see is Caleb—not in my thoughts but in the distorted chaos of his father's. As he replays that moment when the whip tore into the flesh of his back, I can sense his recognition of Caleb, but he felt nothing beyond that. Not shame. Not remorse. Just an underlying frustration that he finally got caught. The only fear he felt was toward his angel father—who was just as absent a parent as he was—and now, in this moment, toward me.

A sharp, cracking sound cuts my hold on him, and I watch, mortified, as blood curdles on the stone beneath his unmoving body like old milk.

"He..." I stagger forward a step, a little light-headed and unnerved by his stillness. "Is he..."

Alexander places a hand on my shoulder, drawing my watery gaze to his face. "Worry not, little dove," he says gently, as if consoling a weeping child. Pride burns in the glowing depths of his eyes. "Have you forgotten what I taught you when our minds first crossed paths? Remember the moth. Remember what I told you. *Anastēson auton,*" he purrs before grinning. "It will be as if it never happened."

TWENTY-THREE

CALEB

MY EYES DART AROUND as I silently count the Nephilim I see throughout the citadel. I try to suss out their age and power. The weaker ones I'm not that worried about, although they do pose a problem in numbers.

After Luna left for her training session with Alexander, I decided to go do something useful. We need a general idea of the current forces residing here so we can find the best route out. Secretly, I don't think there is a best route—any path to freedom will come with blood and death.

Besides, if I don't find something to occupy my mind, that tight ball of sourness embedded in my guts will grow and grow until it consumes me. I'm tired of replaying the moment in my head where I take the whip and strike my father. The cracking of leather and pop of sliced flesh. The long, bloody welt carved into muscle. When I close my eyes, I see it over and over again. It's a helluva way to meet your dad.

I'm still so pissed at him—enraged is more like it. It's not like I never received good old-fashioned corporal punishment at Babel before, but whipping an unarmed, shackled man is not who I am. I cut off Mammon's wing without a second thought and would do it again in a heartbeat, but he's a fucking Archdemon and much stronger than me. If what happened with Pops was a fair fight, if he took a swing at me, I would've loved to dish out a beating, but what happened… Bile burns my throat, and I give a frantic shake of my head, trying to forget that popping sound. My dad is a bastard, but not even he deserved that. At least my reasoning appealed to Alexander. My father isn't worth the shame of breaking my own moral code, even though that one hit carries plenty of sickening guilt. But I was genuinely terrified

Gramps would take me over like a puppet and carry out the punishment as he saw fit.

And it might make me a coward, but I don't think I can endure that again. At least not so soon. My mind still feels like raw hamburger put through a grinder. I hate that I'm afraid, that I took the whip at all, but until I get my head on right, until we get out of here, it's just a burden I have to carry. I just hope the weight won't fracture my sanity. This uncertainty, this vulnerability, this fear, I'm not used to it, and I sure as hell don't like it.

I don't know where my dad is now, and I'm not sure I care. When he looked at me last night, there was no regret, no warmth. Just anger and damaged pride. I did all I could for him. He's my grandfather's problem now, and I think he'll discover the sooner he falls in line, the less he'll suffer. Alexander is done with his bullshit. I just hope I'm far, far away when Gramps bends him to his will because I think my dad is a stubborn asshole, and I don't want to be put in the role of punisher again.

Sparring would help me feel better. I need to find Hammurabi and let him wail on me for a while. The pain will feel good. The Serapeum made me soft, and I need to get back into fighting shape if I'm going to be useful. Even those few months here before I managed to free Luna weren't filled with fighting, just shadowing Alexander and lurking in the corners. My fingers clench for a moment, and I grit my teeth. I miss my dagger. Yeah, yeah, it wasn't mine, but I got damn fond of it. It evened the odds against much more powerful creatures than me. Now, I just feel so naked, like every piece of me is exposed for a bigger predator to tear into. I hate it.

Stepping into the sun in an outer courtyard, I ball my fists as I see Ishtar sauntering my way. I'd like to spend some time fighting her, too. She's back in black, her serviceable boots and cargo pants a far cry from her gown at dinner last night. She stops before me, offering a cold smile.

"What are you doing out and about, princeling?" she coos, and I give her a sweet smile.

"Trying to be a good little heir and get back into shape," I say, the half-truth easily spilling from my lips. Shrugging, I ask, "Have you seen Hammurabi? I want to go a few rounds with him."

Ishtar scowls at me, an offended expression etched across her face. She puts her hands on her hips. "Caleb, I can instruct you in the art of war just as well as that old bore. As Alexander's general, I should have been the first person you sought."

I hide my grin, knowing my preference for Hammurabi would piss her off. "Yeah, I guess, but we're not exactly friends anymore, are we?" A bitter smile twists my lips. "Well, I guess we were never friends, given that you were my teacher, but I always respected you, thought of you as family. I was just stupid enough to believe you felt the same way about me."

The goddess of love and war's eyes brim with pity as she regards me. "Foolish child," she scolds. "My feelings for you are inconsequential, don't you understand? You're young so you can't fathom what it is like to give yourself to a cause, to fight in wars, to bleed. You've been pampered in Babel, assured of your place in life with your Dark status. But there should be no Light or Dark. The divide must fall, and this is more important to me than anything, even foolish boys whom I care for."

I scoff at her. "I call bullshit. Yeah, you may care about the cause, but Alexander is your absolute truth. You wouldn't blink if he slit my throat," I accuse, surprising hurt gripping my chest. I did love her. She was my Dark family, and the fact that I can no longer call her that... Yeah, it hurts like a bitch.

"I would regret your death," Ishtar says, confirming my words, "but no, I would not interfere. Alexander isn't cruel. If he decided to kill you, then you earned your death. Although I wouldn't stop him, I will warn you, Caleb. He won't tolerate further disobedience from you. Think on that before any more rebellious thoughts enter your mind."

Her words nettle me, and I ignore the sick feeling taking root in the pit of my stomach. "I brought him a fucking angel. I think we're good."

She sneers at me. "Yes, you brought him your lover. How convenient for you. Your grandfather might not be so enamored with you if she doesn't live up to her potential."

"Convenient? Breaking into a supernatural prison and facing Mammon was hardly convenient. But I did it. I got Luna out when you all did nothing. Yes, I love her, but *I* proved to Alexander that I can be an asset in the upcoming war. Besides, jealousy doesn't look good on you, Goddess," I say, smirking. "You're afraid Luna will threaten your special status with Gramps. At the end of the day, she's an angel—a *Gray*—and you're just a Nephilim."

Ishtar flushes, her mouth quivering, and if she were a cartoon character, steam would spew from her ears. She blurs, suddenly in my face, her nose almost touching mine, but I still have a few inches on her impressive height. "Need I remind you, little one, that you, too, are a Nephilim, and not even a first generation. You break easier than me." Her lips curl, a cruel edge to them. "And I have been loyal to your grandfather for thousands of years, whereas you betrayed him the moment you met with your obsession with the girl. He might welcome you in his good graces—for now—but he won't ever forget. He will always have doubts about you while he has complete faith in me. I will always have his ear to whisper in."

"And I'll always be his blood," I remind her. "That's something you can never be."

The air shimmers with restrained violence, and I know she wants to beat me bloody, break a few of my bones to prove her superiority. But she can't. Whether she likes it or not, I'm Alexander's heir—at least for the moment. And while he certainly wouldn't mind a few training montages, he won't stand for her abusing me. Not that I would just lie down and let her. Yeah, I'm a second generation, but that doesn't mean I'm weak, no matter what she says. I can make her bleed, too, and she knows it.

Her face shutters, and she takes a step back, cold eyes roaming over me. Snaking an arm behind her back, she brings out a knife and hands it to me. I take it with exaggerated slowness, not sure what game she's playing now.

"Hammurabi has gotten old and lazy," she says. "Come, show me what you can do with a blade." She slides another knife out of a sheath strapped to her hip.

I snort. "I dare you to say that to his face."

"Oh, I forgot to add fat," Ishtar says, an evil grin curving her lips.

I chuckle. I can't help it. This banter reminds me of who my teacher used to be, but I guess that was really never her. The laughter dies, but I manage, "Yeah, his eight pack has been reduced to a six."

"Come, child." Ishtar tosses her braid over her shoulder, her feet automatically sliding into a fighting stance, weight balancing on the balls of her feet, dagger gleaming in the sun.

My fingers clench my own dagger's hilt. Well, it could've been worse. She could've wanted to spar with an ax. I balance on the balls of my feet, adrenaline flooding my body and wiping away my fear. I like to fight, and although I'm no longer Ishtar's favorite boy, I know she won't seriously injure me. Not when I'm in Alexander's favor once more. As quick as an adder, she strikes, and I barely manage to deflect her.

Then we dance, back and forth across the hard-packed earth. Tight muscles loosen, become pliant, and I settle into a familiar, deadly pattern. Ishtar lands a hit on my upper bicep, the blade parting my skin in a shallow cut. I wince, already healing, but as we continue to swipe at one another, she begins methodically slicing me to ribbons. It's apparent that I'm out of practice and slower than I used to be, just a fraction, but a fraction might as well be an hour when you're dealing with someone as lethal as Ishtar. Blood soaks through my T-shirt from cuts decorating my torso, dripping onto the dirt at my feet. But I refuse to give up until I land a hit.

She works me back and forth over the courtyard, and I start to feel fatigue grip me. Gasping, I let her in too close, and I see her triumphant smile right before I step aside, her weight carrying her forward, and I slash at her vulnerable back, blade kissing her skin. I hear her surprised grunt before I jump back and toss the dagger on the ground. I raise my hands in surrender, my breath coming hard and fast.

Ishtar whirls around, growling, then her eyes fall to the knife. Lifting one brow, she locks eyes with me and wipes her blade on her pants before putting it away. "Hammurabi isn't the only one who has grown slow and lazy," she says then she twists, trying to see the wound on her back. "Although that was a nice move." Her voice is grudging and I smile.

"I couldn't stop until I scored at least one hit," I say, placing my hands on my knees. I feel my body working feverishly to repair all the damage. I'll be good as new in a few minutes.

"I could never accuse you of being a coward," Ishtar says, her smile more a baring of teeth. "But I still don't trust you, child. I'll be watching you. Run along now." She waves a hand, and I narrow my eyes at her, but I won't get any more spying done right now. Not with Ishtar about.

"See you around," I say, deliberately turning my back on her. I feel the sting of her eyes on my skin as I leave the courtyard.

By the time I make it back to my room, my skin is smooth and unblemished once more. I no longer feel tired, but I reek of blood and sweat and desperately need a bath. We still don't have showers here, only a crude pumping system. Man, I hope if we're stuck here longer, someone gets this modern plumbing thing moving. I wasn't born a thousand years ago, and I enjoy modern conveniences.

I push open my door to find Luna sitting on the edge of the bed, slouched, her wings drooping around her. My heart rate jump-starts, and my breath hitches at her unnatural stillness. She hears my entrance and glances up, but her gaze is disturbingly blank, like she knows I'm there but doesn't really see me. I take a cautious step toward her, afraid to make any sudden moves. I'm not quite sure where her mind is, and she could accidentally hurt me if she thinks I'm a threat.

"Luna," I say, keeping my voice soft and soothing. "Are you okay? Did something happen with Alexander?" A myriad of images flick through my mind like cards on an old-fashioned Rolodex, each more horrific than the one before. A lot of bad things could've happened during her training session with Gramps, but it does me no good to guess. I'll just freak myself out more.

She blinks, sweeping lashes fluttering against creamy skin. Focusing on me at last, I see her hazel eyes are haunted, and a madness I haven't seen since she was imprisoned encroaches. My heart clenches at the sight. I can't let her slide down that slope again.

"Goldilocks," I prod, "talk to me. Let me help you."

A great wail escapes her, shredding the quiet, and I'm kneeling before her without realizing I moved. Luna shakes her head back and forth as her hands find me and cling.

"I broke him," she sobs. "I swear I didn't know—I didn't mean to…" Her eyes latch onto mine, pleading for understanding. "You have to believe me, Caleb. I would never, not on purpose."

Her words tumble fast from her lips, and I can't make sense of them. "I know you would never hurt anyone on purpose," I say. "Who do you think you broke?"

"I broke him," she repeats, shuddering. "I wasn't trying to, but I still broke him… because that's what I do. I break everything."

Shit, she's truly lost it. "Who did you break? Did Alexander make you see something that wasn't real?"

"Your father," she clarifies, fat tears plopping down her cheeks, agony in every note of her voice. "I killed him."

She killed my father? My jaw slackens as icy shock freezes me in place. That memory reel of bringing down the whip starts playing again, that awful crack and the wet sound of flesh splitting open like overripe fruit. My father is dead and the only encounter I had with him was beating him. My stomach churns, and I grit my teeth, willing myself to get it together. I can't lose it now when Luna is on the verge of drowning.

"You hate me," she cries, releasing my hands and wrapping her arms around her middle.

I place both my hands on her thighs, giving them a gentle squeeze. "I don't hate you. I could never hate you. Tell me what happened." I'm proud of how calm I sound.

She stares at my hands, a shudder rolling through her. "At the Serapeum, Alexander was listening. He knew I had done it before. I didn't know at the time," she says quickly. I raise my brows. "My foster parents, but it was an accident, I swear."

I nod. "I believe you."

"He wanted me to do it again. To show him how powerful I can be, and I didn't understand what he was asking. But then…he brought out your dad. And I…I was worried what Alexander might do if I refused, so I told myself just to look. That I didn't have to hurt him. But then I remembered my foster parents." Her whole body trembles. "I don't understand how much power I have." She raises her head, her tear-streaked face breaking my heart. "I feel like it's only been a trickle before, and now it's an ocean. I got wrapped up in the memory and lost control." She bends, burying her face against my hands. "I didn't mean to, Caleb. Please forgive me."

I stroke her hair, a slight tremor in my fingers that I hope she doesn't notice. "There's nothing to forgive. This is on Alexander. He knew what he was doing and you didn't. He killed his own son—"

A hysterical giggle escapes her and I still. "But your dad isn't dead anymore, that's the thing! I killed him, and Alexander just waved a hand…" The giggles morph into sobs again. "He just rose up, Caleb, like nothing had happened, but the look on his face—I'll never wipe it from my mind."

I go cold, my hands clammy. I shake my head, trying to make sense of it. "What do you mean? Alexander…*resurrected* him?"

Luna nods. "Yes, and it was like—it was like it was *nothing* to him."

Icy sweat trickles down my neck. I sit back on my heels, stunned. Yeah, resurrection is a Dark trait, but we don't actually use it. I make clay figures and give them life, but bringing back the dead, bringing back a *person*, that's a big fucking no-no. That's power that shouldn't be messed with—even the Morningstar has never brought someone back. Dead is dead. That's the natural order of the world.

For a moment, I can't speak, words forming and dying on my lips. Luna's wings flare out, revealing her agitation at my silence. Great, she's barely holding on and now I'm losing it. But I don't know what to say, my tongue tied in knots. A new thing for me. I live to be glib. What I wouldn't give for a sarcastic one-liner to defuse the tension.

"Caleb? Your dad isn't dead. That's a good thing, right?" Luna presses. "Talk to me. You're scaring me."

Get your shit together, Caleb. "What Alexander did is…unnatural," I begin, shaking my head. "Darks have that power, but we don't use it. And not because it's not tempting—if something ever happened to my mom, I'd want to bring her back in a heartbeat. But—and I can't believe I'm saying this—that's a power for the Creator alone. Some shit we have no business playing with."

A wounded expression paints her face. "But…back at the Serapeum, I resurrected a moth. That means I'm unnatural."

Goddammit, I'm butchering this. "No, what you did was an accident. You literally had no clue who or what you were. That was just your power going haywire," I assure her, bending forward once more, so I can take her hands. "There's nothing unnatural about you. Lights give us shit for giving life to inanimate objects, and we give 'em the middle finger, but even Darks stay away from raising the dead. Other than it being something reserved for the Creator, I don't know if when you resurrect someone… they come back right."

"What do you mean, like they're a zombie?" Luna asks, horrified.

An involuntary chuckle escapes me. "No, not like they need to eat brains now, but I think if you were dead and at peace, to be ripped back into the painful world of the living would have to fuck with you. Especially if you died in a traumatic way. That has to permanently mark you."

"Oh," Luna says in a small voice. "I never thought…"

Cupping her face, I give her a short, soft kiss. "Goldilocks, I get it. Like I said, you didn't do anything wrong, but now that we know Alexander is messing with raising people from the dead, it just makes things more complicated."

She rests her forehead against my shoulder. "How?"

"If he gets his war, what's to stop him from resurrecting his troops? Do you really think he's going to save that trick just for family members?" I say, stroking her head.

"Not if it looks like he's losing," Luna says, a shiver racing over her skin.

I nod. "We really need to get out of here."

TWENTY-FOUR

LUNA

CALEB AND I ARE once again summoned by a mute servant for dinner, who bestows us with fresh evening wear for the occasion—black for Caleb and gold for me, as if to indicate our worth and rank to Alexander. The suit and dress we're each respectively given resemble last night's outfits but with variations. Caleb's ensemble remains mostly the same, aside from some added violet accents on the lapels, while mine features more elaborate changes. Unlike the dress I wore yesterday, the shimmering satin pools in a plunging neckline that makes me feel naked, exposing far more of me than I'm comfortable with, and the beading that previously draped across my upper arms is replaced by a delicate shawl of gold-dusted feathers that eerily resemble an angel's.

Caleb's eyes betray his interest as they crawl across my exposed clavicle and dip to my cleavage, lingering there for a moment. My skin heats under the caress of his gaze, and I clear my throat, unsure what to say. Since confessing to accidentally killing his father, the air between us is charged with tension, and not in a way that I like. He might have said he's not angry, that there's nothing to forgive, but I can't escape the guilt bearing down on my chest. If it wasn't for me, if it wasn't for what I did, his father wouldn't have died.

And Alexander wouldn't have brought him back.

"I don't know if when you resurrect someone…they come back right."

I shiver at the memory of Caleb's words, every one like a hook in my thoughts, always tugging at me, forcing me to face the very real severity of our situation. We're in way over our heads, even with Hammurabi and Alaric as our allies. Hell, even with my parents somewhere out there, waiting to help us, it's becoming alarmingly clear we can't take on Alexander. Not now. Not with the numbers he has at his disposal.

And not if he's willing to resort to powers meant only for the Creator to win.

"Goldilocks."

I startle at Caleb's familiar endearment, his raspy tone shaking me free of my thoughts. When I meet his gaze, his eyes are hooded.

"You good?" he asks, taking a step closer to me.

I nod but don't dare let myself speak, afraid my voice will break under the weight of my fluctuating emotions. Neither of us have said much since this morning—the odd word here and there as he held me, the hours passing by in a quiet lull, but nothing of substance, both too mentally drained to talk. Now, though, we need to put on our game faces before heading back into the lion's den.

"Hey." He knocks me under the chin with his finger, tilting my face up. "I love you. You believe that, right?"

Tears blur my vision, and a lump blocks my throat until even swallowing is a struggle. Repeating the same words I said to Alaric up on the mountain when we spoke about Alexander, I whisper, "Despite everything?"

"Despite *nothing*," he bites back, looping his arm around my waist and pulling me to him until his shirt brushes the bare skin of my chest. His breath is hot on my face as he growls, "Nothing could ever make me not love you. Nothing."

Before I can retort, his mouth is on mine, parting my lips with his tongue in a kiss that steals the very breath from my lungs. Warmth spreads through me, melting my inhibitions and self-pity until my fingers are grasping in his hair with a desperation I can't seem to control. When I squeeze, my hands tightening around the strands, he gasps into my mouth, and I devour the sound.

Like last night, my wings are on full display, and Caleb takes advantage of that, grazing a fingertip along the bend, coaxing a shiver from me. His other hand moves lower, his touch heating my blood to a boil, but to my dismay, we're interrupted by a sharp knock on the door. Caleb groans, irritation creasing his face, as I relax my hands and take a step back. No sooner do we separate than Ishtar lets herself into the room, uninvited.

With a delicate sniff, she glances between us, looking us each up and down with keen appraisal. Her nose crinkles. "You are late," she drawls with that practiced boredom. "It is not wise to keep the Great waiting."

Caleb rolls his eyes. "Creator forbid we miss out on the hors d'oeuvres."

Ishtar, for all her posturing, lets slip the tiniest smile at his comment. When she catches me staring, her expression turns sullen. "I would not delay any longer if I were you."

She stalks from the room with the finesse of a runway model, the black gown encasing her body so skintight that I find it hard to breathe just looking at her. Along one leg, a slit runs from ankle to hip bone, dangerously close to revealing far more of the goddess than I'd like to see.

Beside me, Caleb sighs and runs a hand through his hair, tidying the disarrayed strands. Then straightening his jacket, he moves to follow his teacher out into the hallway.

"Caleb." I grab his wrist, stopping him. When he looks back at me, a blush burns my entire body. "I love you, too," I mutter. "Just in case it wasn't obvious."

His eyes light up at my words, and taking my face in his hands, he pulls me in for another kiss. This one is more gentle than the last, and yet there's an urgency to it that sends a vibration of panic racing through me, as if this is the last time he'll do it. He nips at my bottom lip before pulling back.

"I'm going to get you out of here. I promise."

"Together," I remind him, staring up into his eyes. I don't like the uncertainty I glimpse in their depths. "We go together," I repeat.

He hesitates a second too long before nodding.

Gripping my hand, he leads me out into the hallway where we follow the familiar path to the citadel's lush dining hall. Just like yesterday, the space is lit with candles and the table is laden with a feast fit for kings. Given Alexander's chosen company, I suppose it is.

I cow under the intensity of Alexander's gaze as we approach the table, but Caleb—as cool and collected as always—doesn't even flinch.

"Apologies for our tardiness, Grandfather," he says. "We lost track of the time."

Alexander responds with a sly grin, and he tilts his head, propping his chin on his fist. "Who wouldn't with our lovely Luna looking so tempting?"

Caleb tenses at Alexander's use of the word *our* but says nothing, guiding me to my seat with one hand planted against the small of my back. As we settle at our places, I fold my wings in behind me and lock eyes with Alaric, who is once again dressed in a sleek suit and wearing a dour expression like he's on his way to a funeral. He sits at the far end of the table, as if whoever decided the seating arrangements thought it best to keep him and Alexander as far apart from each other as possible. From the way he white-knuckles his goblet and glares across the place settings at our host, I take it something must've happened between them. Either that or he's just as unhappy as

Caleb with Alexander's word choice.

Dinner passes by at a snail's pace. Meaningless small talk fills the silence, and the only one at the table who isn't fazed by the strained hush flooding the room is Hammurabi, who tears at his dinner like someone who's starving and has probably had one too many to drink. Then again, I'd probably get drunk, too, if I was the only one forced to go topless to dinner. He's dressed in old Babylonian garb, and even I can tell he hates it. After millennia of experiencing societal changes, I don't blame him for preferring the comfort of modern day fashion to what was normal in his time.

When dessert is finally placed before me and it seems like we're nearing the end of this torture, the doors to the dining hall burst open. All eyes swing to the beautiful woman who enters the room, dressed in stiletto heels, chic high-waisted slacks, and a fashionable burgundy leather jacket, which sits just above her trim waist. But where others might focus on her perfect cheekbones or regal updo of black ringlets, I can't tear my gaze away from her undulating aura. The shadows lapping over her skin pulse with wisdom and age. She's ancient, and the power radiating from her is immense, on par even with the Archdemons I've met.

"Ah, Lilith," Alexander trills, raising his goblet to greet her. "I was wondering when you'd return."

My pulse stumbles under my skin, thrown off tempo, like a singer who's forgotten the words. Since I first heard about Lilith, I've wanted to meet her; she could be the key to getting answers about my parents and birth. But now, as her presence seems to fill every corner in the room, I remember what Alaric told me. Lilith might have been friends with my mother—perhaps she still is—but she also lost her wings for supporting Alexander when the rest of the Council stood against him. She's loyal to Caleb's grandfather, maybe even more so than Ishtar.

And that loyalty makes her a threat.

The ex-Archdemon sweeps her gaze over the table. "While I'm thrilled to hear my absence has been felt, it appears you've managed to keep yourself fruitfully busy while I've been gone."

Is that disapproval I hear in her voice?

Alexander seems to notice it, too, because he says, "All to the benefit of the cause, I assure you."

He snaps his fingers at a Nephilim standing nearby, who brings the ex-Archdemon a goblet of wine before scurrying from the room, followed closely by the other servants present. Alexander must've given them some silent signal to leave. As Lilith brings the silver cup to her lips, the Gray steeples his hands and looks at her grimly. "Now, tell me. What news of the Council?"

Lilith drains her cup before speaking. "Their feathers are positively ruffled," she croons. "Whatever you've been doing has them aflutter with panic. I've even caught wind of an interesting rumor that Asmodeus has been imprisoned for betraying the Council."

Caleb sucks in a sharp breath beside me, and I grip his leg under the table. A reminder to keep calm. And silent. Although Beelzebub already informed us of this, I can't imagine that makes it any easier to hear, especially given the amused way Lilith delivers the news. I raise my chalice, feigning a drink, so I can sneak a look at Hammurabi, who seems to hold a deep affection for Asmodeus. A *mersu* ball laden with coconut shavings is speared on a fork frozen halfway to his mouth. Even Ishtar looks unnerved by this news. And here I thought she didn't like anyone except Alexander and Gilgamesh. And herself.

"That *is* interesting," Alexander drawls, his tone flat, like this isn't news to him. "In this case, I do believe the Council has done us a favor. One less adversary to stand in our way."

The ex-Archdemon narrows her eyes. "You don't seem surprised."

He shrugs. "Because I am not. Such tidings have already reached my ears."

Scanning the table again, she purses her lips. "I would be remiss not to ask if this development has anything to do with our guests?"

Chuckling, Alexander leans back in his chair. "Nothing ever did get past you, Lilith. You remember my grandson, Caleb?"

Her narrowing eyes follow the Gray's outstretched hand. "Ah, yes." A grin hitches up the left side of her mouth. "He was quite the spirited one, if I recall."

Alexander gestures to the opposite end of the table. "And I believe you know Hammurabi and Alaric."

"It's been an age," she says bluntly, barely acknowledging either Nephilim. Instead, her gaze snags on mine and lingers. "And this one? I can only assume, given those lovely silver appendages, that she is the young Gray you mentioned."

Although her words are friendly enough, her tone is arctic.

Alexander beams at me, his smile radiant. In these moments, when he isn't terrorizing us with subtle warnings and outright physical threats, it's almost easy to see why so many followed him in his conquest for power and why so many who share that hunger—that thirst for freedom among mortals, like Ishtar—still do.

"This little dove is our secret weapon," he purrs. Across the table, I glimpse Ishtar rolling her eyes. "Lilith, meet Luna Morningstar."

"Morningstar?" She hooks a brow upward, but her shock seems disingenuous somehow. Given what Asmodeus said about my mother and Lilith—that they were close friends and remained that way even after the Fall despite the divide—then I can only assume she would know about me and, in turn, know the identity of my father. But if that's true, why pretend otherwise? After all, she's sworn her allegiance to someone my mother has spent millennia keeping locked in a tomb.

Wouldn't that automatically make them enemies?

"Indeed," Alexander says, peering between us. "A pleasant surprise, is it not? To think, the instigator of the divide would create such a wonderful gift to help me mend the rift between our kind." His lips curl into a devious smile, and I shiver.

Lilith glares at Alexander, her dark eyes sharpening like a blade on a whetstone. "Did you order her release in my absence?"

The dynamic in the room seems to change as Lilith shifts from a loyal follower to a headmistress scolding her student.

Alexander's nostrils flare as he straightens. "I will forgive your insolence just this once as a courtesy toward my favorite teacher. But be careful, Lilith."

To her credit, the ex-Archdemon doesn't flinch at his threat.

"Forgive me, my liege." Her tone drips with a contrition that borders on mocking. "I am merely curious how the girl came to be here when, last I heard, she was imprisoned."

Appeased, Alexander relaxes back into his seat. "Young love is impatient and often causes those afflicted to act without the consent of its elders." His eyes flash to Caleb, who shrinks under the weight of his grandfather's scrutiny. "But my heir showed true initiative in rescuing Luna and even managed to cripple the formidable Mammon."

Lilith recoils as if Alexander has struck her. "A second generation rescued a Gray from the Council?"

The disbelief emanating from her is insulting. Caleb might have had some help, but he was still the one who cut me out of that egg. He was still the one who brought me back from the broken darkness that consumed me in that cage, even if I constantly find myself still drawn to its call. To me, he's worth so much more than any other Dark or Light, second generation or not.

Lilith's stunned expression hardens, and I notice something new pouring from her. The liquid-like tendrils of her aura stand upright like the hair does now on the back of my neck.

Alexander tsks, aware of it, too. "Such disapproval I sense from you, Lilith. Once a headmistress, always a headmistress, it seems."

With a hurried clomp of heels on stone, she crosses the room to the angel's side. "If you ever valued me as your headmistress, you will heed my warning, Alexander." Thrusting a finger in my direction, she barks, "That one is a threat to your reign. I'd put her back in her cage before it's too late."

I freeze at her words, my resurfacing terror like a physical force attempting to restrain me. Beside me, Caleb explodes from his seat. "Hey, wait a goddamn minu—"

When his grandfather holds up a hand, Caleb recoils, as if afraid Alexander might try to hurt him again. Shame washes over his features as he slowly sinks back into his seat.

Alexander turns his gaze to Lilith. "I assure you, I have the girl well in hand—"

"But you don't," she cuts in, her tone equal parts poison and pleading. "The prophecy has made sure of that."

"Oh, yes. The prophecy. The reason for my imprisonment and for lovely Luna's as well, I daresay." He scoffs, waving a dismissive hand. "Worry not, my dear Lilith. Ishtar has already informed me of this nonsense, and I put little stock in the Messenger's tidings."

"Well, you should." Her shoulders stiffen.

Despite the fact that she wants to see me imprisoned again, I can't help feeling sympathetic knowing the instinct and desperation that must be clawing at her. I can see it on her face—the need to spread her wings, to let loose the emotions scratching at the underside of skin. But she can't.

Because her wings are gone.

Alexander sighs, his patience wearing thin. Like a parent placating a whining child, he murmurs, "All right, I will humor you. Care to elaborate?"

Lilith lifts her chin, speaking clearly. "After the Great Battle, as the Fallen took up their new home on Earth, the Creator delivered a prophecy, spoken into the ear of only one, and when the fourteen academies were erected, the Messenger shared this prophecy with the Council. She warned of a Gray, who would become the destroyer of our world, and in doing so, further cemented the belief in and need for the divide."

Under the table, Caleb clutches my hand. His terror mimics my own from his unsteady breaths to the way his fingers tremble around mine. I hang onto him just as tightly, fearing Lilith's every word.

"But what the Messenger failed to disclose was that the prophecy also spoke of a second Gray. Of a Savior, who would battle the Destroyer and heal the rift that has greatly wounded our world." Lilith leans forward, her hands clasped together, as if locked in a prayer. "The prophecy's words are clear, Alexander. You are the Savior the Creator spoke of."

Caleb's eyes dart to mine, their touch hot on my face, but I can't tear my gaze from Lilith. If what she's saying is true and Alexander is the Savior from the prophecy, then that would mean I'm the—

Destroyer, the voice of my conscience whispers.

Realization dawns on me, making me sick to my stomach. Is this prophecy why my mother abandoned me? Because she knew what I was fated to become and wanted to spare everyone from my eventual wrath? Spare *herself* the burden of having a daughter the Lights and Darks would both see as the villain?

I suddenly feel dirty, like a plague on this world. I tear my hand free of Caleb's, wrapping my arms around my torso. He shouldn't touch me. I'll only hurt him. Despite myself, despite the warning in my head, I meet his worried eyes for a moment before glancing to where Alaric sits at the end of the table, watching me with equal unease. He was wrong. Alexander doesn't destroy everything he touches—I do. Even the people I love aren't safe from me.

And now, with this long held secret finally out in the open, they will see that, too.

The tension permeating the dining hall is thick, like a cloying smoke, weighing like lead on my lungs. The silence that follows Lilith's speech is suffocating, and I want it to end. I *need* it to end. But I can't speak. Words are lost to me, though that's probably a good thing. I need to be still. I shouldn't move. If I move, what ripple of chaos will I send out in the world?

Alexander lets out a barking laugh, making me jump. "Then what is the problem, my old friend?" he asks Lilith, oblivious to my internal strife.

The ex-Archdemon glowers at him. "The *problem*," she hisses, enunciating the word, "is that you are hosting the Destroyer at your dinner table." Her stern features soften, and she reaches out a tentative hand, touching his forearm as she crouches beside him. "Your success is not guaranteed, Alexander. If you are not careful, you will lose this war before it has even begun."

Her sable eyes shift to mine, accusatory and probing, bringing my panic that much closer to the surface. A scream rises in my throat—any second now it will find its way past my lips—but a familiar sensation quickly shoves it back down.

Drunk with the haze of Calm washing over me, I peer down the long table at Alaric. His golden aura writhes with fury, and his expression is harder than I've ever seen it, bordering on irate. I've never seen him look so undone, and sweat beads his dark brow, which he doesn't wipe away even when it drips down the sides of his face. I can only imagine the energy he must be expending to keep me—a full-blooded angel at the brink of a mental breakdown—subdued.

At the opposite end of the table, Alexander scowls at him, affirming my theory that the Gray doesn't want us using our powers without his permission. Either that or he just really doesn't want Alaric helping me cope with my trauma. Maybe he even wants me unhinged—to get me to my weakest point before fully asserting his control.

What better way to constrain a person than to break them completely?

"You're jumping to conclusions," Alaric says, his tone placid, before taking a long drag of his wine.

Ishtar growls at his insolence—her first contribution to this conversation—but Alexander waves her off, gesturing for Alaric to continue.

The Nephilim shrugs. "What makes you think Luna is this Destroyer? Could the prophecy not just as easily be referring to Alexander?" He nods to the Gray, avoiding his gaze, and to my surprise, Alexander actually looks wounded by his words.

Oblivious to the strain between the two men, Lilith scoffs. "The Destroyer is spoken of first in the prophecy, and the Morningstar's daughter was born just after the Fall—"

She cuts off abruptly, and her eyes widen slightly, as if she's accidentally said something she wasn't supposed to. Her aura quivers for a moment before settling back into its usual threatening dance.

Silence descends on the room once again, and I gape at her, noting the fading effects of the Calm—Alaric must be getting tired—clinging to one part of her statement.

"The Morningstar's daughter was born just after the Fall."

I began to suspect it when I was trapped in the Council's prison—that I'm far older than my appearance suggests—but hearing it confirmed is strange. How can I be that old but still only be seventeen instead of a grown adult, like Alaric, who was born around the same time? Was I cryogenically frozen? Do angels even possess that kind of technology?

Beside me, Caleb is unnervingly still, his stricken gaze fixed on his grandfather, who, in turn, is staring at Lilith, all amusement on his face gone.

"Is that so?" Alexander's eerie eyes fix on mine, and he regards me for a long moment, making me feel like bacteria under a microscope. I suppress the urge to shiver. "If that's true, then where have you been all this time, little dove? You do not look that old to me." Before I can answer, he glares at Lilith. "Assuming I believe any of this, why would the Messenger withhold half of the prophecy from the Council? And how, dear Lilith, did you come to know of it? Or of the circumstances surrounding the girl's birth? Especially given that you seemed to know nothing of her when she was mentioned before."

Lilith balks but recovers quickly. Standing, she smooths her high-collared jacket, tugging nonchalantly at the burgundy cuffs. "There were rumors, back during the time of the Fall, that Lucifer had an affair with a Light, though I do not know with whom."

I raise a brow at that. If Lilith was as close with Gabriel as I've been led to believe, then surely the ex-Archdemon would know she's my mother. So, why is she lying to Alexander? Or did Gabriel hide my birth from her, too?

"I am merely making assumptions, given we know this girl to be the Morningstar's offspring," Lilith continues without missing a beat. "Perhaps he locked her away somewhere, safe from time's touch, and that is why she's so young. Or perhaps, she really is but a whelp and her father has dipped his toes in Light waters more than once."

"I have heard no such rumors," the Gray says.

The ex-Archdemon waves a dismissive hand. "Yes, well, it was millennia ago. Old news, as they say these days. As for the prophecy, Gabriel confided in me at the time as a fellow Council member and asked for my advice on the matter. She was concerned how the rest of the Council would react and felt it was in everyone's best interest to imprison any Grays they uncovered rather than risk the world on a possible Savior, whose success in the eventual battle was not guaranteed. If there were no Grays out in the world, the prophecy couldn't be fulfilled and—"

"The divide would remain intact," Alexander finishes.

I can hear my breaths and heartbeat in my ears, even though Alaric is working hard to keep me sedated. Is that true? Given what I know about her, would Gabriel really do that—condemn anyone unlucky enough to be born a Gray? I saw her that day under the Serapeum with Lucifer. I saw the way he touched her just as clearly as I saw the way she looked at him. They might not be together anymore, but there was definitely something still there between them, even after thousands of years apart. And remembering them like that makes me fully understand why she tried to warn me away from Caleb. It wasn't just because we reminded her of the past, but because she didn't want me reliving her own heartache.

Or maybe I'm wrong about the woman who birthed me and she really is a monster. Maybe she does desire a world with the divide because it makes her own life—and mistakes—easier to cope with. And if that's the case, then maybe...

Maybe she really did want me imprisoned.

Alexander glares at Lilith, arching an imperious brow. "If you knew of this, why did you say nothing sooner?"

Her aura trembles despite her attempts to seem calm, and I wonder if Alexander can see it—if that's just one more commonality my fellow Gray and I share. Lilith shrugs one slender shoulder, unfazed. "And waste needless words warning you about an obstacle that did not yet exist? She was imprisoned, Alexander, and if I recall, you did not seem in a particular hurry to change that. The girl did not pose any actual threat until your *foolish* grandson set her free."

Alexander sneers at that, but instead of the lash of fury I expect, he just says, "It would do you well to not withhold intel from me again."

Beside me, Caleb chokes out, "Grandfather—"

My chest tightens at the terror in his voice, which seems to mirror my own. I follow his frightened gaze to Alexander, who flashes Caleb a reserved smile.

"Worry not, dear boy. I do not put my faith in groundless superstitions. Your Luna is safe." He peers at me, and in the pause, I hear the words he isn't saying aloud. *For now*, his eyes seem to scream at me. "If anything, this has given us all cause to unite against a common enemy. With this prophecy, the Council has proven that no one who is different is safe, and I cannot allow such narrow-mindedness in my new world."

If Alexander's words are meant to reassure, they don't.

Without waiting for a response, he rises from the table, and everyone in the dining hall follows suit, showing their reverence for their king. Even me.

"Alaric, Ishtar, Gilgamesh. A word in private?" Alexander beckons to the three Nephilim with an ominous curl of his finger.

Alaric excuses himself, meeting my gaze for the breadth of a heartbeat before trailing after Alexander through the far door, taking the safety blanket of his Calm with him. It lifts off my head so quickly I nearly lose my balance. Ishtar and Gilgamesh follow, departing the room with a cursory nod at Lilith, who frowns at being excluded but says nothing. As they leave, my old teacher doesn't even have the courage to look me in the face. He averts his gaze, keeping his eyes pinned on the floor, as if ashamed to be in my presence now that everyone knows the truth of what I am.

With my mind clear of Alaric's influence, I can fully recognize just how much more dangerous the situation has become. Caleb was right. We need to get out of here.

And soon.

Once the others exit the room, my legs give out beneath me, and I collapse into my chair. As if snapping out of a fog of his own, Caleb drops to his knees, cupping my face.

"Goldilocks—"

"You're shorter than I envisioned," a familiar voice interrupts.

Caleb lowers his hands as we peer across the table at Lilith, who stares down at us, like scum on her shoe. She looks me up and down with disdain. "And blonde. And here I thought you would take after your mother."

My breath catches as I glance to the door in the corner then snap my eyes back to Lilith. I knew she was lying. She knows damn well who my mother is.

The question is: Why didn't she tell Alexander?

"If you know who she is, why didn't you say?"

My voice breaks, coaxing a snide chuckle from Lilith, who spits, "Gabriel is my friend, and I won't sell her out—"

"But you'll sell out her daughter?" I hiss. And throw Lucifer under the bus, pinning blame on him for something he wasn't even aware of.

If she cares about Gabriel, if she wants to protect her, why doesn't that same mercy extend to me? They aren't even on the same side in this war, and I've done nothing to her—to either of them. I've done nothing but exist.

Which is apparently a crime, according to their prophecy.

"You are a threat," she says slowly. "Even Gabriel was smart enough to accept that."

Hammurabi, who I didn't even realize was standing behind my left shoulder, growls under his breath. The ex-Archdemon just clicks her tongue at him. Even without her wings, she would undoubtedly squash the ancient Nephilim like a bug.

I blanch and my stomach turns. "Are you saying…" But I can't find the strength to voice this new fear. I look to Caleb, my eyes shining with tears, and he nods before standing and scowling at Lilith, asking for me, "Are you saying Gabriel believed Luna is the Destroyer?"

Lilith places her hands on the table and leans in, her voice dangerously low. She glares at me, her eyes like chips of carved onyx. "Of course. Why else do you think I helped her entomb you?"

My breath catches on an inhale and I shudder. My mother locked me away, just like the Council locked away Alexander. She didn't just abandon me.

She left me in a tomb to rot.

"What the hell?" Caleb whispers.

I can feel his eyes on me but I can't speak. I can't move. I can't think. I can't even breathe. My wings press close to my skin, trembling with pent-up rage and a resurfacing mania I'm certain now I'll never escape.

Lilith parts her plump lips to say something else, but her mouth snaps shut when several Nephilim enter the room and approach the grand table to clear it. Taking their presence as her cue to leave, she shoots me one last scathing look before retreating back through the door she came in by.

I watch her disappear from the hall, staring after her retreating figure until my eyes glaze over and the candles have burned through most of their wicks. A tentative hand touches my shoulder and I jump.

"Luna—"

I shrug Caleb off. "I want to be alone."

No, it's more than a want. It's a need. I *need* to be left alone before I do something I end up regretting. I can already feel it—the fire burning under my palms. It's so close to exploding, and if it comes out now, it'll engulf this entire room. Maybe even the whole citadel.

"I don't think that's a good idea," he protests, and those words are the trigger that set me off. I leap up from my seat, anger spearing my wings out to the sides like arrows slung from a bow, and bring my fists down on the table. Under the force of my rage, the thick wood cracks in half.

Caleb and Hammurabi are both smart enough to leap back, putting distance between themselves and the volatile angel hunched over the broken table, which now sits in two distinct pieces on the floor. When I glance over my shoulder, I glimpse genuine fear in their eyes.

Good, I say to myself, although the thought pains me. They should be afraid of me. I need to give them a reason to stop fighting—to stop thinking I'm worthy of their protection or help. Because if I am this Destroyer Lilith spoke of…

Then I am only doomed to hurt them.

"Please, Caleb," I breathe, sinking into the seat again, my wings falling to the floor, mimicking the shift in my mood. My hands curl into fists to smother the flames threatening to break free of my skin. "Just go."

To my dejection, he does.

TWENTY-FIVE

CALEB

I FEEL PUNCH-DRUNK, LIKE those MMA fighters who've gotten hit in the head one too many times, and they aren't quite right anymore. Lilith delivered one hell of an upper cut with the revelations she dished out. And wow, Gabriel keeps winning at Mother of the Year, imprisoning her own kid because of a fucking prophecy. I didn't think I could hate Queen Bitch anymore than I did, but it turns out I was wrong. I mean, she's with Lucifer now, so I guess she changed her mind, but still, Luna deserves so much better.

Luna. The look on her face when Lilith opened her trap and declared Goldilocks was the Destroyer. She is a rope rapidly fraying, and I can't do a goddamn thing to stop it. It's too much: Alexander, being a Gray, prison, and now the prophecy. She has all the fortitude of tissue paper right now, and I'm genuinely terrified for her. What if she completely loses it? Will she just shut down and go into a catatonic state, or will she go boom? Either thought is too horrible to contemplate. And she was just breaking out of her shell, too, before all this, just awakening to the world around her. To me. I love her and seeing her like this, unable to help…

Maybe I'm a rope, too, unraveling.

"It normally takes years to wear down stone, but I believe you may achieve it today at the rate you're pacing." Hammurabi's low rumble jerks me from my thoughts, and I glance over my shoulder, surprised to find him sitting on my bed.

Pivoting on one heel, I change trajectory and stop at the foot of the bed. "When did you let yourself in?" I demand, pissed that he invaded my sanctuary without permission.

His thick brows bunch over his nose as he regards me with concern in his black eyes. "Caleb," he says, speaking slowly, as if I'm a very young child, which I guess to him I am. "We came in here together. Don't you remember?"

I blink at him, the events after Lilith's declaration blurring a little. Well, hell and damnation, he *did* walk back with me. Forget about Luna losing her shit, mine just marched out of the citadel, cackling. I can't afford that right now. I have to be sharp. I can break down later, when we're far away from here, and rolling into a ball and sobbing for a few days is acceptable.

"Yeah, I remember now. I'm sorry. I'm just…" I wave a hand.

"Yes, I imagine I would be, too, if I found out my lover is the Destroyer," Hammurabi says, and I detest the sympathy painted on his face.

I snort. "We don't know that she's the Destroyer," I hiss. "Why? Just because she was born first? What fucking bullshit. It's so vague anyway. Does birth order even matter? The only clear thing is that they're both Grays."

"Gabriel feared the prophecy so much she hid Luna away," Hammurabi says, his voice gentle. "What if your golden lady is the Destroyer?"

I hate his words, and I want to rip him to shreds for saying them, but I bite on my tongue and consider the worst case scenario. What if Luna is destined to destroy the world? It certainly won't be out of ambition. She has no desire to rule, and I don't think the thought has ever crossed her mind. When has she had time to contemplate her future? But if she *is* the Big Bad everyone is afraid of, something catastrophic has to change in her personality for her to pick up a sword and declare war on the world. A chill settles over me. Shit, what in her life hasn't been catastrophic lately? Shaking my head, I dismiss the idea, even though it lingers in the air like cigarette smoke, threatening to choke me.

Flashes of Luna falling into madness burst into my brain, and I once again hear her confessions of the things she did before we met when her powers were totally out of control. Maybe being the Destroyer wouldn't be a deliberate act on her part. Maybe it's a case of her being so broken she just can't hold the reins on her powers and they break free, sending out a wave of death and destruction.

Maybe. But that doesn't feel right, either. And the stupid prophecy is so opaque it could mean anything. Bottom line, I know Goldilocks. Her heart is pure and shining, desperate for love and family and all things denied to her. She wants to go out in the world and *live*. I think if I could find a hole to bury ourselves in, she'd happily slide in next to me and wait until the apocalypse is over.

My eyes clash with Hammurabi's. "You're wrong," I say. "Luna feels guilty when she kills a spider. She has zero desire to conquer anyone. She just wants normal stuff, stuff she's never had. Waging war isn't at the top of her to-do list."

Hammurabi sighs. "Yes, that may have been true before, but now she has her wings and all the power that comes with them. Power corrupts as you know. It changes people. Look at Alexander. He wasn't born a tyrant."

I snort, shaking my head. "Luna could never be a tyrant. And I don't even know if that's the right word to describe Gramps. Zealot is a better fit, and Goldilocks doesn't slip into that mold, either. And you know Alexander, Hammurabi. Does he seem like a Savior to you?"

Chuckling, Hammurabi crosses his arms over his chest. "No, he doesn't, but the prophecy has muddied the waters a bit, hasn't it? I prefer order and clear direction to bloody prophecies."

I arch a brow in surprise. "I thought you of all people would take the most literal interpretation of this prophecy because of your love for order."

"I've known Alexander for a long time, young one, and while I believe his desire to unite our people to be genuine, I don't believe that he is the one to rule us all. Earth doesn't need an emperor. It never did. Yes, I desire order, but I also value freedom. Alexander wouldn't bring true freedom—he's peddling the veneer of freedom with pretty golden bracelets that are really shackles."

I study him for a moment. "I thought you didn't want the divide destroyed."

He shrugs. "I don't have much faith it can be. I'm old, and I'm prejudiced against my Light brethren. Too much bad blood between us. The old laws keep us safe." When I open my mouth to tell him what bullshit that is, he holds up a hand. "But I can admit that for the younger generation, the old laws make little sense. We're heaping our history upon your heads, our grudges, our conflicts. We've made you into our image and it's flawed."

Hammurabi admitting the institution is wrong? It really is the end of the world. My jaw flops open of its own accord as I stare at the biggest hard-ass I know.

The Babylonian king laughs at me. "Child, your face. It's wonderful to know I can still surprise people."

"You've gone soft," I accuse, which is ridiculous, but Hammurabi admitting change could possibly be a good thing is basically him turning into a marshmallow. If I roast him, I can crack him open and get to his gooey center. "Next, you'll tell me you kind of like Luna."

"She's a lost little flower," he says with another shrug. "I like flowers."

"A Gray flower," I remind him, not bothering to hide my doubt. Little flower indeed.

"A pearly blossom clinging to her stem in the raging storm around her," Hammurabi says. "One can't help but hope the wind doesn't tear her apart."

And that's the closest he'll ever come to admitting he likes a Gray. "Unless she is the wind, of course," I point out, knowing that if he really believes Luna to be the Destroyer, he won't hesitate to take up his sword against her.

"Of course," he acknowledges with a grim nod. "But do not fear me yet, Caleb. Prophecy or no prophecy, I'm a patient man. Time will reveal the true meaning of this revelation to us, and then I'll make my judgment."

It's the best he'll give me and I'm grateful. Hammurabi is a man of his word, and if it turns out like I already know it will—with Luna the innocent victim of this lunacy—he'll fight for her.

The door snicks open, and Alaric slips in, grim-faced, his legendary calm ruffled. My heart sinks to my feet. This can't be good. How much more bad shit are we supposed to take? Hammurabi rises to his feet, lithe and menacing, his face shuttering his emotions in the presence of the Light.

"What's happened?" he demands, hands clenched at his sides.

I find my own hands fisted as I wait for Alaric's answer.

"It seems all the excitement at dinner has inspired Alexander to speed up his timeline. I am to leave immediately to find Lucifer and offer an invitation," Alaric says. "But this isn't exactly a friendly summons. I'm to tell the Morningstar the Conqueror holds his daughter as his esteemed guest and to make haste as he's certain they can come to a mutually beneficial arrangement."

I snort in disbelief. "So, he's basically saying in a nice way that Luna is a hostage?"

"Yes, he's waving Luna like a red cape under a mad bull's nose," Alaric replies. "I figured he would use her as bait to get Lucifer to join him, but Lilith's accusations change things. If Alexander *has* taken her warnings about Luna to heart..." He frowns. "Honestly, I don't know what he's thinking or planning, but it can't be good. I can only assume he's hoping if the Morningstar falls in line, so will his daughter, removing any likelihood of war between the two Grays...preordained or not."

"Alexander is actually threatening the Morningstar?" Hammurabi says, eyes widening in disbelief. "I know the boy is brash, but I never thought he lacked intelligence."

Hammurabi calling Alexander a boy causes inappropriate laughter to erupt from my throat. Both men stare at me like I've lost my mind. I guess they don't realize I have. That thought sobers me right up.

"Gramps doesn't lack in confidence, that's for sure, but this is *Lucifer*," I say. "The original rebel with a cause. He invented being a badass." Alexander is so convinced that he's the chosen one I'm a little shocked he'd use thinly veiled threats to get Lucifer here instead of straight up seducing him to the dark side of the Force.

"While I agree with both of you, it's never wise to underestimate Alexander," Alaric says, and I remember that my grandfather killed his father. An Archangel.

No, it's not, but we have an ace up our sleeve. "How are you going to explain Gabriel? Or are you going to just sneak her in?"

A scowl creases Alaric's smooth brow. "Gilgamesh is coming with me, which complicates matters."

"I'm surprised he can leave Ishtar's bed long enough to travel with you," Hammurabi grumbles, and another chuckle escapes me. Maybe I was wrong about Hammurabi having a stick up his ass; maybe he should go do stand-up.

Alaric's frown deepens. "There's not an explanation on Earth that will make Alexander believe that Gabriel has chosen his side. She was his warden for thousands of years. He hates her. He'd rather skewer her with her own sword than have her fight on his side."

I wince at his words, remembering how I stabbed her with the dagger, leaving her bleeding on the floor. Flinging the thought away, I say, "So, the Messenger is our secret weapon? That is if Lilith doesn't out her." Why hasn't Lilith sold out Gabriel yet? I'm sure she has her reasons, but I can't make sense of them. I just hope she keeps her trap shut a little longer.

"And what a weapon she is," Hammurabi says, and I shoot him a skeptical look as I hear the admiration in his voice. "I don't like her, but she is a fierce warrior, Caleb."

Fair enough.

Alaric nods. "Yes, she is. Lucifer will——"

The door to my room swings open, and Gilgamesh steps over the threshold, annoyance pasted on his face as his gaze sweeps over all three of us. Annoyance with a dash of suspicion.

"Uh, knock much? Someone older than dirt like you should have better manners," I say, not bothering to hide my anger. I have one private sanctuary in this whole place, and it's violated on a daily basis.

Gilgamesh's eyes are full of disapproval as they regard me, his lips pinched. "Someone as young and vulnerable as you should learn not to antagonize your superiors."

I smirk. "Last time I checked, I'm Alexander's heir, and you're just an errand boy."

I see Hammurabi suppress a grin out of the corner of my eye, and Alaric just shakes his head but quickly steps between me and the king of Uruk when Gilgamesh takes an aggressive step toward me. He places one hand on Gilgamesh's chest and one on mine.

"Enough," Alaric snaps, and I hear the weariness beneath the irritation. "Gilgamesh, what are you doing here?"

Gilgamesh glares at me before focusing on his fellow Light. "Looking for you. We should have been off by now. Best not to keep the Great waiting."

Alaric pinches his nose, a great sigh puffing past his lips. "Yes, I know better than anyone how impatient Alexander can be." My curiosity perks up at his words. What is the deal with those two? "I just came to say my farewells to Caleb and Hammurabi, and I had hoped Luna, but alas, she's not here."

"Aren't you all in each other's pockets," Gilgamesh says with a slight sneer.

Hammurabi smiles. "I'm surprised you climbed out of Ishtar's pocket long enough to go on this mission."

Gilgamesh bristles, stepping forward again, only for Alaric to block him once more. "Enough. We're all allies now, and I don't relish the role of babysitter. Don't force me to subdue you." I bite the inside of my cheek to keep from howling with laughter as both Hammurabi and Gilgamesh turn pissed-off faces at Alaric. "Come, Gilgamesh. Lucifer awaits." Alaric strolls out of my room, forcing Gilgamesh to follow.

I watch them go, relieved when they disappear. Then I slam my door shut. I glance over my shoulder at Hammurabi. "I hope Lucifer and Gabriel can get us the hell out of here."

"Me too, young one, me too."

TWENTY-SIX

LUNA

MY HANDS SHAKE AS I rub my slick palms against the satin fabric encasing my thighs, the smooth material of my floor-length dress swishing around my ankles, keeping in time with my steps. As I hurry through the quiet passage—ears strained, eyes searching—my thoughts are a whirlwind of confusion. Of *hurt*. Of the lingering stab of abandonment I'm not sure I'll ever find the strength to move past.

My mother didn't just give me up, she locked me away, like some dirty secret she hoped no one would unearth.

I wanted to believe that if I just spoke to her, I'd understand what led her to do what she did. And the worst part is that I *do* understand. I'm dangerous—how many times have I told myself that? How many times have I seen that realization reflected in the eyes of the people closest to me? I know what I can do when provoked, and I live in constant fear of lashing out at the wrong person—at someone innocent falling victim to this unrestrained power inside me, especially now that I know what I am. My control is a fragile, tenuous thing, and if the prophecy is to be believed…if I *am* the Destroyer…

Then there is nothing to stop me from eventually snapping.

Caleb's face springs into my head, and the fear in his gaze at my outburst is vivid in my memory, as if he's still standing before me. The table in the dining hall was probably hundreds of years old, if not thousands, and has withstood the test of time. And yet, I smashed it with my hands as if I was breaking a twig. If I can do that level of damage in a passing moment of distress, what might I accidentally end up doing to him?

Tears prick at my eyes. I was right to put distance between us at the Serapeum and weak to relent so quickly to my need to be near him. The images Alexander forced into my head of the academies burning replay in my thoughts, and again, I watch, helpless, as Caleb burns. Is that the outcome the prophecy spoke of?

Is that what will come of our love for each other?

The tears slip free now and cascade down my cheeks, and I gasp, my breath hitching, as I wipe them away. No, I can't let my mind go down this road. I need to keep it together.

Picking up speed, I continue my hunt. We've only been here two days and I'm already going insane. I need answers before I crack completely, and I can't keep waiting on my parents to get them. So, I'll go for the next best available option.

Caleb would freak out if he knew what I'm planning—all the better then that I scared him away. But I need to do this, and as I mount a narrow set of stairs to the top of the citadel, I tell myself I need to do it alone. Lilith doesn't get to just drop that bomb on me and then leave with zero regard for the aftermath. I didn't choose to be born. I didn't choose to be this thing the Council fears. All I've ever wanted is to find the place in this world where I fit. To be happy.

Free.

My fingers curl into fists, and my resolve strengthens with every step. Destroyer or not, I deserve the truth.

The night air brushes my skin as I emerge onto the roof, the stone underfoot dusted with sand. I go still the moment I lay eyes on Lilith. She's standing at the edge, one misstep away from falling to the desert floor far below, her arms spread wide to the sides and head tilted, as if smelling the air. She grips her leather jacket in one hand, revealing a low-cut camisole, which disappears into the waist of her pants, leaving her upper back exposed.

My shocked gaze trails pale pink scars that follow the curve of her shoulder blades and shine in the moonlight, standing in stark contrast to the darker tone of her skin. Considering I've seen Caleb heal from horrible burns right in front of my eyes, I didn't think anyone with celestial blood was even capable of scarring. Then again, I suppose wings are different—a loss we aren't supposed to endure.

As I gape at Lilith's back, I recall what Caleb said about her losing her wings and I can't help the swell of pity that overwhelms me. It was that recollection that led me up here and what made me so certain this was where I'd find her. This high, out in the open, it almost feels like flying is possible.

The evening breeze rustles my dress, and I can practically see Lilith's ears perk up as her head snaps to the side. Her lips pinch into a scowl as she lowers her arms, and shrugging on her coat, she jumps down from the ledge.

"What do you want?" Her tone is abrasive, and I flinch at the hostility in her unblinking gaze, the pits of her eyes like two black holes that seem to suck all the warmth from the world. When they settle on my exposed wings, her scowl deepens.

Not wanting to offend her anymore than I already have just by existing, I draw my wings back into the confinement of my skin. "Please, I—" My voice wavers, and my heart races a mile a minute, pounding so violently I feel it thrumming in my veins. What if the answers I'm chasing only make everything worse? What if I'm better off not knowing?

I draw in a steadying breath. No, not knowing isn't an option anymore. Regardless of what comes of this, I need to know.

Holding up my hands, palms out, I step closer. "I just want to talk."

Lilith sneers. "You won't change my mind about the prophecy, girl. And soon enough, Alexander will see all this my way. He *will* understand the danger you pose."

My arms fall weakly to my sides. "I'm not here to change your mind. I just want to understand."

Her mouth purses, and her eyes narrow to skeptical slits.

"Understand what?" she asks after a moment.

"Who I am," I answer a little too quickly. Swallowing, I peer at the clear sky overhead, trying to imagine a place beyond the cruel, mortal world I grew up in. "Where I came from. I..." I clamp down hard on my lip.

I lower my gaze to Lilith's again, preparing to prostrate myself before her if it means getting even the smallest insight into the events that led to my existence.

She stares at me, sizing me up, and I glimpse the change in her gaze the moment she relents. Her pupils—barely visible in the sea of black surrounding them, but visible to my angel eyes—dilate.

"You believe it, don't you?" she asks, her tone teetering on the edge of disbelief. "You believe you are the Destroyer."

I bite down on my lip again, harder this time. Tears slip from my eyes as I reluctantly nod.

"I...think it's possible."

Her nostrils flare, and I wince at the shrewd look on her face.

Before she can speak—before she can say she was right—I quickly add, "I don't want power. I don't want to hurt anyone, Lilith. I'd rather be locked up again than do that." *But...*

Trembling, I look down at my hands.

Hands that have caused so much pain and destruction.

"But I also know there's something inside me I can't quite control and…"

"And?" The ex-Archdemon cocks her head.

Meeting her unforgiving gaze, I swallow loudly, steeling myself. "And I'm afraid of it," I admit.

Lilith lets out a stilted breath. "Fine," she grumbles. "I will answer your questions on one condition. You will tell me who released you from your tomb."

Confusion barrels through me. She doesn't know?

"I…was hoping *you* knew the answer to that."

The ex-Archdemon bares her teeth in a snarl and lunges forward, hand outstretched to grab me. "Don't toy with me—"

"I'm not!" I blurt, sidestepping her grasp. "I wasn't even aware I had been locked away until you mentioned it. Hell, before Alaric brought me to the Serapeum, I thought I was human." That stops her dead in her tracks, and she gapes at me. "Crazy but human," I mutter with a humorless laugh.

Lilith taps a manicured finger to her chin. "Well, it couldn't have been your mother. The detection wards on Easter Island sat undisturbed when I last went to check."

"It wasn't Gabriel. She didn't even know who I was when we met." My chest tightens when I force out the words, "Our blood…it didn't sing to each other."

Black eyes flash to mine and she scoffs. "Of course, it didn't. She cut off that connection when she locked you away. It was the only way she could do what needed to be done or else she would've always been haunted by leaving you there."

This time, I'm the one lurching forward, and I grab Lilith's hand without thought. She flinches as if my touch has burned her, but I hold on, my grip tight and desperate.

"Please, I don't understand any of this. I just need to know why she did what she did."

Lilith's hard expression softens a fraction, and in the split-second where I glimpse something other than hate in her eyes, I wonder if—had things been different—we might have actually gotten to know one another. In a world where my mother didn't abandon me, would Lilith have been a friend to me, too, as she is to Gabriel?

Unexpected tears mist her eyes. "Gabriel and I have always been close, like sisters." Her voice is gentle, reminiscing. "Even after the Fall, when I chose one way and she chose another, she remained my dearest friend. She understood why I followed Lucifer in his rebellion just as I understood why she remained with the Creator. She had a role to play, and being the mouth of the Creator comes with an isolation and loneliness none of us will ever understand."

"But she still chose," I say, releasing her hand. "She still chose the Creator over my father."

Lilith rolls her eyes. "You are so young, even for one so old. You do not understand what it was like. What *He* is like. Do you not think we Darks mourn the loss of our father? Gabriel made her choice out of love. She did not want to leave Him when so many of his other children already had. She thought she was being loyal."

Loyal…

For the first time, I allow myself to consider what life would have been like had I actually grown up with my parents—not from the viewpoint of a child desperate for love, but from the viewpoint of someone who might have eventually ended up at odds with those same parents, the way Lucifer did with the Creator. Had I been in their shoes, had I been forced to choose between romantic love and the affection of a parent…what would I have decided? It's easy to sit here and say I would have chosen the same as my father—rebellion over submission. But I also think I'm beginning to understand why Gabriel chose the way she did.

More than anyone, I can understand the overwhelming need for a parent.

Emotion thickens in my throat. "Then why did you?"

Lilith arches a brow. "Abandon Heaven?" She shrugs. "The same reason Lucifer did. For the freedom to love. But, unlike our leader, the object of my desire and affection was a human."

My brow pinches as I flit back through everything I ever learned in my religion classes, dredging up one piece of information vital to this conversation. About the first man created, Adam, and his first wife.

Lilith.

A surprised breath escapes me. "So the story is true?"

"Hardly," the ex-Archdemon retorts. "Mortal accounts get so much wrong."

With a mournful sigh, she returns to the edge of the rooftop and plops down on the ledge. Crossing her legs, she pats the stone beside her, and I slink forward, wary.

"You needn't worry. I won't bite," she coos.

Exhaling, I sit, my body rigid, and Lilith laughs to herself, the way she might have in another life had we the chance to be friends. Maybe, in that life, I might have even called her Aunt Lilith, and she might have loved me, the way an aunt would. Maybe, in that life, she would've been my family, too.

A cool breeze washes over my bare skin, and I shiver.

Leaning back on her hands, Lilith lets out a tired breath through her nose. "Adam was not the first man but one of many during the early days of humanity, when we were mere watchers in Heaven tasked with looking over and guiding the mortals, should they need it. He was strong and brave, and I fell in love with him the moment I saw him. So, I put myself in his path, and he loved me, too, even though being together was impossible. It was a dream neither one of us wanted to wake from. Then, Lucifer waged war on the Creator, and I finally had a chance to chase that dream. To be with Adam, on Earth, and to finally be free the way I wanted to be.

"Gabriel understood. She was actually the one who urged me to go. She wanted me to have the peace and happiness she knew she couldn't. And, for a while, I did. But I was ignorant of the challenges we would face or how quickly time would steal him from me.

"As Adam aged, I remained the same, and soon, the love and affection he had for me turned bitter. He wanted someone he could grow old with, not an immortal who would watch him die and then move on once his bones turned to dust. He feared being one love in a long existence of many."

My eyes spring wide at these words, and a dark, unwelcome thought slinks to the surface. While Caleb will live for thousands of years, he's still mortal. Time will tear us apart one day, and when that happens, I will be left alone yet again.

A fate I can never seem to escape.

But for immortals like my parents, they didn't need to fear such an obstacle ever coming between them. They could've been together forever. Happy.

Unless, what Gabriel feared wasn't death.

Eternity is a long time. Perhaps, like Adam, she feared being just one love of Lucifer's—that their love would be fleeting and she would eventually be replaced by another. If so, maybe she didn't just stay with the Creator out of loyalty but because she was scared.

Scared of losing the only love she knew wouldn't fade.

Lilith clears her throat. "Eventually, that fear tore us apart, and he left me for the mortal, Eve, who from then on, had the love and happiness that I had sacrificed so much for. Your mother was the one who saved me from my misery. When the Council was created to establish the schools, she suggested I serve as the headmistress of Ashkelon."

"Which is where you met Alexander," I realize, the puzzle pieces slotting into place. But why did Lilith support Alexander when she—better than anyone, besides my mother, of course—knew the full extent of the prophecy?

What did she need a Savior for?

Lilith blinks, surprise etched into her beautiful face.

"Alaric told me," I say, answering her silent question.

She arches an eyebrow. "You and he are close?"

I hesitate, dropping my hands to my lap, gripping the gold fabric of my dress between my fingers. "He was the one who found me," I manage after a moment. "I was in a mortal hospital before the Serapeum."

"And the years before that?" Intrigue saturates her every word.

"A group home and then placed with a string of foster families. It was a pretty typical upbringing for a modern-day orphan."

She turns to face me fully now, and the curiosity in her gaze bows to a consternation that sets me on edge. Her brow furrows into a grimace. "So, you truly have no recollection of the millennia you spent in stasis?" Her aura quivers, agitated.

"Stasis?" I ask, frowning.

She waves a dismissive hand. "Frozen in a sleep state shortly after your birth, as a mere babe, so the years would have no bearing on you. You wouldn't age or grow. You'd always exist as you were in that moment, perfect but powerless. After the Creator delivered the prophecy, Gabriel knew there was no other option but to seal you away, somewhere out of reach, even to time itself. If she didn't…well, she feared what would come of your freedom."

I recoil, her words a swift punch that knocks the air from my lungs. So, it's true. Just like the Council, Gabriel was afraid of me. But…does she still feel that way now? If she does, then why is she with my father, supposedly fighting to get back to me? If she does, why do we keep trying to find her? Maybe the biggest betrayal I could encounter isn't my mother abandoning me but her finding us and locking me up again.

"So, she believed it," I say, my tone dull. "That I would become the Destroyer."

"What do you expect?" Lilith counters. "The Creator *is* omniscient."

She says this as if it's a fact and, maybe to those who have been alive as long as she has, it is. But to me, it feels like an assumption on their part—a jail sentence before even finding out if I'm guilty.

"That's why she didn't tell Lucifer, isn't it?" My chest tightens. Gabriel was so certain of my role in the prophecy that she withheld my existence from the only person who would've had reason to fight for me.

The air between us grows heavy with pity, and Lilith lets out a sigh, pushing up to her feet. "The Morningstar would've burned the Earth to cinders before allowing anyone to lock away his only child. Lucifer is faithful, sometimes to a fault. He would've died to protect you, regardless of what you are."

I stand as well, and when she turns to face me, I see the truth of her words in her gaze, even if I struggle to believe it. After all, Lucifer handed me over to the Council. He *let* his brothers and sisters imprison me. He didn't burn anything to try to save me.

"I'm not sure about that," I mutter. "He did nothing when the Council took me."

"Foolish child," Lilith retorts, her tone sharp. "I have no love for your father, but do not presume to know him better than I. How do you know what the Morningstar has been doing? How do you know he has not been tearing the world apart searching for you?"

Every word is a slap to the face. Perhaps Lucifer is willing to burn the world to find me, I just haven't given him the chance. If he was willing to wage a war against the Creator for the freedom to love, what lengths would he go to for his child?

I'm not sure how knowing that makes me feel. Should I be happy about that kind of devotion? Sad about what atrocities he might have committed or may yet still commit on my behalf? Either way, I suppose it's too late to matter—at least in regard to my childhood. I was robbed of that devotion, and if the prophecy is true and I am the Destroyer, then I don't deserve it.

Lilith crosses her arms. "Gabriel feared Lucifer's knowing about you would only… escalate the problem. Besides, they weren't exactly on speaking terms at the time."

"And my powers?" I ask, changing course. I don't want to talk about my father anymore, and I have enough of the picture leading up to my birth to understand my mother's actions. But this part—why my powers manifested the way they did and the lack of control I still struggle with… Thanks to Alexander, I know I was bound. I just don't understand why. "Did you help her bind them, too?"

"It was a precaution," Lilith explains. "Binding both bloodlines wasn't a viable option—that would have rendered you mortal, and you would've slowly decayed and perished in that tomb, regardless of the stasis. And despite what you think of her, your mother never wanted you dead."

I scoff. No, she just wanted me caged.

"*So,*" Lilith continues, glaring at me, "I bound your Dark side, so you would appear to our kind as a Light should your location be uncovered. Gabriel thought it may keep your powers under control in case you were ever released and given the opportunity to age. We hoped it would be enough to prevent you becoming the thing the prophecy spoke of."

"But it didn't work," I say. Their tampering only contributed to my messed-up childhood and the pain I repeatedly inflicted on others. "My Dark powers were poking through long before Alexander removed the bind on them. Even as a child, my fire was red. It was what gave me away at the Serapeum."

"You said you thought you were mortal," Lilith counters, side-eyeing me.

I snort. "I also said I thought I was crazy. Sane people don't tend to think they can magically set other people on fire."

Lilith's brow creases. "Binding our powers isn't…natural," she says after a moment, and I notice there's a slight edge to her voice that wasn't there before. "This power we possess doesn't *want* to be contained. And it was never a guaranteed fix or else you and Alexander would have never discovered what you are. If the binds had been stronger, if they weren't so fragile, your mother could have raised you as a Light, and she need not have ever locked you away. Because you wouldn't have been Gray anymore then, and you wouldn't have gone on to become the Destroyer." I wince at her words, at the conflicting blend of anger and sorrow behind them. Sighing again, Lilith shakes her head. "It was simply an extra layer of protection. A safety net in case anyone ever found out where you were or what we did. The real solution was to seal you in that tomb. By keeping you in a permanent infantile state, you would never grow or have the chance to become the very thing the prophecy warned of."

My wings tremble under my skin as the inferno of my fury reignites. "She should have just killed me then," I spit. "What you both did is no different."

I expect Lilith to bare her teeth or snap back at me—something to assert her age and dominance—but she does neither. Instead, she just stares at me, her expression morose.

"She didn't kill you because she hung onto the hope that, some day, the Creator would deliver a new prophecy that would render the existing one null and void. And…you were all she had left of her love with your father. Such things are not always so easy to abandon or destroy."

I glower at her. "Locking a baby away in a tomb sure feels a hell of a lot like abandonment."

"And yet, here you are," she muses, cocking a curious brow. "The tomb was sealed with both of our blood, and the wards made sure to keep humans away. Over the years, we even added additional wards for protection as humanity expanded across the globe. The Rapa Nui were particularly helpful on that front, though they are oblivious to how we altered their statues. Even other immortals can't step past the stones. You were protected from the outside world in every possible way, which leads us back to the question at hand—"

"Who let me out of that tomb and why."

That's certainly what I'd like to know. Right now, I feel like a pawn being moved around by a player I can't see and whose motivations remain unknown, not just to me but to the other pieces on the board.

Lilith scrubs a hand over her face. "I can't make sense of it. It wasn't your mother, and I certainly did not release you. Our sigils didn't alert us that the wards had failed, and it's not as if the Rapa Nui could have freed you. It's as if someone just magicked you out of that tomb and plopped you in the mortal world—"

She sucks in a sharp breath.

"Of course." Her gaze trails over the rooftop, searching but not really seeing. She turns in place, pressing a hand to her forehead. "Oh, that clever bastard. He wants the prophecy to come to fruition. He wanted you freed so you could release Alexander. But why? Unless…"

Her wide eyes drift to mine, and I reel back from the terror I glimpse there.

"What?" I breathe. "W-Who are you talking about?"

Lilith's voice drops to a whisper. "The only being who could have removed you and placed you among the humans without Gabriel or me ever knowing."

I balk. She can't be saying what I think she is, can she?

"You… You don't mean—"

Lilith gives a solemn nod, and a strange silence settles over the rooftop, as if the subject of our conversation is now here among us, listening to each word intently. His name escapes her lips in a barely audible breath. "The Creator."

The wings hiding under my skin are suddenly unbearably heavy, like weights have been tied to my shoulder blades. I stumble backward a step, weighed down. "W-Why would He do that if I'm the Destroyer?"

Every word out of my mouth pushes me one step closer to that precipice I always find myself standing at, and I want to scream, to cry, to rage—anything to push away the madness that keeps trying to cripple me.

"He wouldn't," the ex-Archdemon says quickly then again to reassure herself. "He wouldn't. The Creator cherishes humans. The last thing He would want is to see them perish in yet another celestial war. With you entombed, you weren't a threat. And with Alexander imprisoned…" She trails off, her face taut. "It doesn't make any sense unless the Creator *wants* the war to transpire. Unless He already knows how it ends." Her brow crinkles. "But then why would He release you, the Destroyer, unless—"

Lilith stares down at the ground, mortified.

"I can't believe how blind I've been. For so long, I've translated the prophecy literally. Your mother—she warned that the Creator speaks in riddles, that He's always working toward some greater end, but it had seemed so clear to me. So

obvious. Especially when I met Alexander and he spoke of tearing down the divide…
just like the Savior the Creator foretold. And I wanted that, too. I wanted to heal past
hurts and find my way back home."

Home… Like go back to Heaven?

Tremors roll through my body and I shake uncontrollably. The only one speaking
in riddles here is her.

"Lilith?"

"Forgive me, Luna," she breathes. A tear drips down her cheek, startling me. "And
Gabriel…"

"What about her? What are you saying—"

"I lied before." The admission is blunt, and I gape at her, bemused and half-mad
with confusion. She at least has the decency to look embarrassed. "While it's true
your mother feared you would become the Destroyer, she hid you away not out of
fear but love. She did it to protect you. She couldn't even bring herself to name you
because it pained her so much to do what she did. I…" Shame paints her face red. "I
was the one who acted out of cowardice."

My breath hitches. "I…I don't understand. To protect me from what?"

The look taking shape on her face—unequivocal in the belief forming behind those
obsidian eyes—terrifies me more than Alexander ever possibly could. Because what I
see in her gaze isn't just terror in the purest form but a heart-wrenching sadness. Like
searching the whole world over for someone only to have to say goodbye to them the
moment you meet.

"From becoming a martyr," she says.

I watch the gentle roll of her throat when she swallows. She lowers her hands, taking
a wary step toward me, and observing my face, she reaches out, her tears flowing freely
now. Her arms wrap around me, and I go still in her unexpected embrace.

"I think I was wrong about Alexander." Her words are a hum in my ear, but I can
hardly hear her past my thundering pulse. Her arms tighten. "He isn't the Savior.
You are."

TWENTY-SEVEN

CALEB

I TUG AT THE sleeves of my dinner jacket, hating that I can't shed it yet, but we're in the throne room, mingling with Alexander's gathering faction. Luna looks biteable in yet another gold gown, her wings on display. I clench her hand, finding it icy. She's no more happy to be here than I am, her conversation with Lilith leaving us both rattled. Goldilocks made a beeline to me after their little chat, shaking, the shock reducing her to tears, confessing every awful word. At least she didn't go all, Hulk, Smash! again. But her tears hurt me more than her rage.

I'm glad the ex-Archdemon is suddenly on Team Luna, but her theory that the *Creator* set her free… What the actual fuck is going on here? I used to straight up love being a Nephilim, but all this divine puppeteering makes me just want to be a plain old human worrying about acne and drinking too much before finals.

I guess Gabriel really was trying to protect her daughter from either fate the prophecy is set to dish out. I gotta say being a martyr is no better than being a destroyer. Either way, I lose Luna, and I refuse to accept that fate. We've fought too hard to have some cosmic chess game rip it all away. And I'm too much of a Dark to just bow down to destiny. Free will can change the world. It has to. Hell, it already *has*. Lucifer, anyone? And Luna is his daughter. If anyone can tell fate to go fuck itself, it's Luna Morningstar.

I wish Luna and I could've stayed holed up in our room tonight. For the past three days, Lilith has been MIA, and we've been avoiding Alexander like he's the bearer of the plague, though Goldilocks has been summoned a few times by Gramps for training. Those sessions haven't helped with her state of mind as she's shaken down to her core. She just needs to be held right now as she comes to grips with Lilith's revelation. Or kissed senseless until she forgets her name. I'm happy to oblige either way. Honestly, I need the quiet right now just as much as she does. I'm in over my head, like a little league player suddenly being called up to the Majors and having a ninety-mile-per-hour fastball thrown at them. I don't know how I'm going to hit the home run that'll save the day. And I don't even like baseball.

Alexander summoning us tonight to celebrate can only mean one thing: Lucifer is on his way. Although I admire Grandfather's confidence, I'm shocked he's declaring victory before Lucifer has signed on the dotted line. The Morningstar doesn't exactly have a reputation for bending to the will of others. I don't expect Lucifer to come in and fall at Alexander's feet, declaring him the savior of angelkind.

My eyes find Ishtar hovering around Alexander, who lounges on his throne. She's usually the picture of grace and battle-ready hardness, but there's an almost nervous energy floating around her. Her eyes snap back and forth, taking in all the exit points as if she's preparing for an attack, which confirms my suspicion that we're about to get a visit from the original bad boy.

I hear Ishtar say, "Gilgamesh texted me, they'll be here soon, and I—"

"Text?" Grandfather asks, one brow arching, and I smother a laugh.

"Modern way to communicate," my teacher says, then her voice grows more urgent. "We need to be prepared—"

"You worry for naught, Goddess. I'm only disappointed Lilith isn't here to witness this triumph. But she still can't stand to be in the Morningstar's company so I gave her a reprieve. Just this once." Alexander waves a hand at her, shooing her away, and she frowns at him, clearly wanting to disobey. But in the end, she acquiesces and slinks into the crowd, taking residence near the doors.

"Caleb," Luna whispers, her voice so soft I strain to hear her. "My father is coming, isn't he?" She clutches my hand so hard I flinch. She immediately releases me, her face flushed and guilt in her eyes.

Taking her hand again, I bring her knuckles to my lips before lacing our fingers once more. "I think so. Ishtar is too twitchy. Why else would Gramps have us gather here like this?"

"Why doesn't he want to meet Lucifer in private?" she asks, eyes darting around the crowded room.

"I'm guessing he wants an audience when Lucifer switches sides so it'll cement his position as the true leader here on Earth." And there will be lots more witnesses to the carnage if things go south the way I predict they will. I don't say that to Luna, though. Her thread is one tug away from snapping.

"Do you think my moth—" She clamps her jaw shut with an audible click. There are too many ears around, and she's not supposed to know who her mother is.

I bend down to nuzzle her bare throat, and she shivers. "She'll find a way," I murmur against her skin, pressing a light kiss on her pulse.

"You children will be the death of me," Hammurabi growls from behind me. "You already share a bed. Is it not an adequate enough space for your endeavors? We're about to go to war, boy."

Luna stills and I whirl around. My teacher is once again in traditional garb with his pecs and abs on display, and he looks pissed off about it. Luna averts her gaze, pink blossoming on her cheeks. She's so innocent it's adorable. At least she's not checking him out this time, but I think she's come to view Hammurabi as a grumpy uncle, and that sorta ruins the sexy. Besides, if I whipped off my shirt, I know she'd never look at anyone else twice.

Narrowing my eyes at him, I say, "Yeah, and war is stressful. Just keeping Goldilocks relaxed. Don't be jealous. Go get laid."

I don't even try to dodge as he cuffs the back of my head. I grin at him, rubbing my stinging skull. I see Alexander observe our exchange and he frowns.

"I don't think Alexander likes seeing you manhandle Caleb," Luna murmurs, pasting a too-bright smile on her lips.

Hammurabi stiffens, his gaze clashing with Alexander's. He gives the angel a slight bow and calls out, "Children."

Grandfather relaxes, a smile playing on his lips, and he gives Hammurabi a nod.

"Whatever happens, Caleb, you stick close to me," my teacher says quietly.

I bristle, and Luna stirs beside me, anger sparking in her eyes. "What about Goldilocks?" I demand.

"The little flower will be well tended to by her father. You, on the other hand, are not his concern," Hammurabi says. "I don't think the Morningstar will be too focused on his daughter's lover."

My heart sinks because I know he's right, but Luna protests, "He will be because I love Caleb. I need him."

The Babylonian king gives her a pitying look. "Flower, your father will only be focused on you. You were stolen from him, and he'll tear the world apart to get you back. He doesn't know you love Caleb, and I'm not sure he'd care under the circumstances. But don't worry, *I* will take care of the boy."

A warmth swells in my chest at my teacher's words. This is how I used to think Ishtar felt about me until those blinders were violently ripped away. "Thanks," I say sincerely.

"You're one of mine, ridiculous child," he says then studies Luna. "And I'll help you, little flower, though I don't think you'll need it."

Her sweet smile makes my heart hurt. We'll get through this. We have to. Somehow.

Lucifer appears in the middle of the throne room, ebony wings flaring, pushing back any Nephilim unfortunate enough to be near him. He's alone, no Alaric or Gilgamesh trailing behind him. I hear a collective gasp, my own sound of strangled surprise escaping my throat. Yeah, I expected him, but not quite like this.

But I guess the Morningstar understands the importance of a dramatic entrance.

He's like a great raven, heralding death. The antique gold of his hair is a beacon in the candle-lit chamber. Cold fury burns in his bright blue eyes as his gaze sweeps the room. He stills when he finds Luna, and I see his eyes flick over her in a rapid perusal. Then he focuses on me and the arm I have wrapped around her.

It takes all the willpower I have to not wither on the spot or piss my pants. But if I give in now, it's all over. He'll never think me a worthy partner for his daughter. And I can practically feel the tension pounding through Luna as she stares at her father. No way would I leave her bereft of support or comfort. I pull her closer, and she molds herself to me, a slight tremor rippling over her.

Lucifer's eyes clamp onto mine with an unspoken promise that he will find me and end me if I so much as breathe on Luna wrong. It's my turn to tremble, but I straighten my spine and give a slight nod. He strides toward us on silent feet despite his aggressive steps. Only when he's in front of Luna do I step away, but she doesn't let go of me completely, her hand tangled in mine. He regards our entwined fingers with a slight frown, as if he hadn't calculated Luna's feelings for me into his plan. Then his eyes dart up and meet Luna's and a warmth floods the blue depths that is so bright it feels like looking into the sun.

"Daughter," he says, cupping her cheek in one big hand.

A dazzled expression sits on Goldilocks's face as she stares into her father's eyes. "Father," she whispers, her hazel gaze shiny with unshed tears.

Seeing them like this, the resemblance is so obvious I'm shocked no one—including me—has ever put two and two together. There's a bit of Gabriel there, too, if you look close enough, but no one can deny Luna is Lucifer's blood. Gabriel must have stuck her head deep in the sand to miss it.

The Morningstar gathers Luna against his chest in a tight embrace. The throne room has gone eerily silent as everyone watches the exchange in front of them, voyeurs in this private moment. They deserve a better reunion than this.

I gaze across the room at my grandfather, who resembles a wolf that has just spotted a nice fat sheep. A predatory grin plays upon his lips, and I can almost hear the gears of his mind turning from here. He doesn't think Lucifer can take on him and his growing army of Nephilim—the Fallen who support him are out in the world, recruiting, but he has the numbers here at the citadel that even without them he has the advantage—and he knows Luna doesn't have enough control to be a real threat to him. Especially when he's the one holding the leash on her training.

Gramps has brass balls, big ones, but even though he's a Gray, with access to both Light and Dark powers, he's still going against the Morningstar. This guy led a war against Heaven.

Lucifer releases Luna and says, "Get behind me."

She nods, and his eyes meet mine again, and the stark command is clear. *Protect my daughter or face my wrath.* But he doesn't need to threaten me. I'd protect Luna with my life. I squeeze our braided fingers tightly.

Lucifer glances at Hammurabi, eyebrows arching. "Fancy seeing you here, King."

Hammurabi gives a shallow bow. "It amazes me the places I find myself these days."

"Let's hope you find yourself curled up by Asmodeus's feet soon enough where you prefer to be," Lucifer says with a slight smirk.

To my utter shock, I see a ruddiness touch Hammurabi's cheekbones, and my fierce teacher looks away like a blushing schoolboy. If I live through this, he's going to get shit about that for years.

The Archdemon's face grows cold again as his eyes fixate on Alexander on his throne. "You have someone who belongs to me. I'll be taking my daughter now."

And the first shot is across the bow.

Alexander leans forward, clashing eyes intense as they latch onto Lucifer's. "She's your daughter, but she doesn't belong to you. She belongs with me now. As do you. Together, we will make Earth into the paradise it was always meant to be."

A cruel laugh escapes Lucifer's lips. "Foolish boy, *I* belong to you? I fell to belong only to myself. I waged war on Heaven and my angel brethren for free will. I get to *choose* each day. I'm already in paradise."

Alexander stiffens at his words, rage banking in his eyes. "*This* is paradise? Mortals destroying Earth, destroying themselves while the Creator does nothing as his children kill one another and their home? As the divide between Dark and Light renders us helpless to aid the humans we were made to protect?"

Lucifer sneers. "And I suppose you have the power to heal all? Fancy yourself equal to the Creator, do you? Conquerors don't heal—they destroy. Your war will massacre the very mortals you claim to love and want to protect, not to mention the Nephilim and angels you'll slaughter."

Alexander stands, pearl-gray wings flaring out. "The divide must be destroyed, and I'm the only one who can achieve our unification. Are you that prejudiced against your own kind that you want us divided for eternity? Clearly, you found it in you to bend your precious convictions to cross the divide at least once."

Luna flinches, and I want to punch my grandfather in the face.

Lucifer prowls a step closer, radiating so much menace I can practically see it rising from his midnight wings. "You know nothing about my convictions," he hisses. "I fell for love, for the right to love and the right to choose. I fell to break the chains that bound me, to be more than a pampered slave to someone else's will. I still dream of Heaven, and yet I would never return to be a servant once more. You will unite us only to bind us again once your war is over. I have no desire to wear chains, no matter how pretty you promise to make them."

Alexander thumps his chest. "I was imprisoned for millennia. I have no desire to shackle you, Morningstar. I just have the desire to bring order to this mortal chaos and to unite our brethren here on Earth. You say you fell for love? Well, I conquered for love. For the love of my human parents and for all of humanity. If I knew they wouldn't be looked upon in horror, I would march to Macedonia and lift them from their tombs so they could witness the new world I will create. A world where humans, angels, and Nephilim will thrive in peace."

His casual mention of raising the dead sickens me. I knew Gramps thought he was a god, but I didn't realize just how far gone he was.

Lucifer stiffens. "You would resurrect your family?" I hear the shock saturating his voice, and my stunned mind echoes it. "That is insanity. Death, like life, is sacred."

Alexander sneers. "If I cut your daughter's head off, you wouldn't hesitate to raise her. That is the power of your love. No one who is mine will ever be in danger of perishing. Unlike the Creator, I take care of my flock, including your daughter. She is my heir as much as she is yours. With me, she will always be safe. Can you claim the same?"

Gabriel emerges from the Blessed Road right behind Alexander, a righteous goddess in gleaming golden armor, her hair back in a warrior's braid. I never thought I'd be glad to see her, but I'm about to break into a dance at the sight of her fury. Fisting Alexander's hair in one hand, she brings her silver sword under his throat with the other. "Perhaps you should be concerned about your own safety, Conqueror. Give us our daughter or die."

GIVE US
OUR DAUGHTER
OR DIE.

TWENTY-EIGHT

LUNA

MY HEART TRIPS AT the sight of my mother, her statuesque figure clad in golden armor with her downy white wings draped in skeletal metal ornaments on full display, like an avenging angel sent down from the heavens to deliver retribution. Her obsidian hair is tied back in a braid, and the expression on her unobscured face is cruel. Baring her teeth, she glares down at Alexander, the sword clutched in her hand pressed to his throat, the glistening edge razor-sharp.

I immediately recognize the sword and armor from the display cases at the Serapeum—Gabriel's battle gear from the Great Battle of Heaven once stored away in the dusty back room of the famous library needed again now for war. She must've made a pit stop before coming here, risking exposure to arm herself to the teeth before taking on Alexander.

Her words to him vibrate in my ears like the aftershock of an earthquake, rocking me to my core. She came for me. Despite the danger, she came. And if her white-knuckled grasp on her sword's pommel is any indication, she is out for blood.

The Dark Nephilim lingering at the outskirts of the room all move forward around us, ready to defend their king, even against an angel who could easily tear them all to shreds. Alexander's initial shock wears off quickly, and he holds up a hand, warning his followers to stay back. Despite the threat of the shining blade at his throat, he unleashes a laugh—a harsh, barking sound that reeks of an insanity I recognize all too well. His eyes are wild and unfocused as he composes himself enough to spit through clenched teeth, "What glorious irony. To think, the sanctimonious Messenger who served as my warden is the golden child's mother." His voice deepens into a near feral snarl. "Your hypocrisy is riveting."

She tightens her grip on his hair, yanking his head back. "Silence, Conqueror. Need I remind you this sword could cut your throat."

"Not if I cut yours first," he growls.

He sweeps his arm upward, holding the dagger he stole back from Caleb, and my mother lets out a howl of pain as he swipes the glinting edge across the back of her hand, opening the skin down to the bone. On reflex, her fingers unfurl from around her sword's pommel, dropping the weapon, which clatters onto the dais by the Gray's feet.

As she flinches back, cradling her wound to her chest, Alexander smiles and lifts the dagger to his lips. Revulsion is a tidal wave slamming into my chest as he drags his tongue along the blade, licking my mother's blood clean off the metal.

Gabriel's dark eyes flit to her sword, then back to Alexander, who kicks the weapon away.

"Not so fearsome without your mighty sword, Messenger."

Golden fire erupts from the Archangel's hand and she scoffs. "I'll show you fearsome."

The hall is engulfed by a vengeful inferno as Gabriel lashes out with a ferocious scream—first at Alexander's Nephilim generals, burning several looming nearby, and then at Alexander, striking at the Gray with a spear of blazing light. At the same moment, a ring of fire surrounds them both like a halo, cutting them off from everyone else in the room. The blaze scores a circle into the stone floor, pushing back any who might attempt to intervene.

An eerie yellow light illuminates Gabriel's face as her gaze meets mine through the flickering wall of flame. And in her gaze, I glimpse all the words she will never say to me if she doesn't make it out of this alive.

She's doing this to give us a chance to escape, I realize as acceptance flits across the Archangel's hardening face. Her attention shifts back to Alexander, and fear trickles down my spine when he advances on my mother with his dagger upraised. Her sword—her only weapon to fight back in such close quarters—lies abandoned outside the circle of flame, out of reach. If I can just get it to her, then she can fight back. She can survive this.

She can *win.*

I step forward, but my father, sensing the movement, pushes me back with his wings. "Get out of here. *Now.* I'll help delay Alexander." Furious blue eyes whip over his shoulder, focusing for a moment on Hammurabi before locking on Caleb. "Protect my daughter with your life." It's a command and a warning rolled into one, and I can feel Caleb tense in the tightening of his hand around mine. Nodding, he tugs me away from the fray.

"No! No, you can't—" I begin to protest, but the words die on my lips when my father storms forward, pulling a sword of his own from an invisible scabbard between his two great ebony wings. They sweep outward with a powerful gust, pushing us farther from where my mother and Alexander face off, my feet scraping across the stone as I raise a hand to shield my face from the wind.

The gale extinguishes the flames nearest Lucifer, forging a path, and he descends upon Alexander from behind, surprising the Gray. Gabriel, taking advantage of the interruption, races forward, sliding across the stone with her hand outstretched, reaching for her sword through the gap in the flames. The gash in her skin has already stitched back together, and she grasps the pommel, spinning onto her knees in time to deflect an attack from Alexander.

The surrounding Nephilim seem to know better than to engage with the three battling angels—at least until Alexander gives the command—keeping a wide berth from the fight, instead directing their attention to us. As they move toward us, Hammurabi grabs my arm.

"This is our cue to leave," he says in a fierce whisper.

I shake my head, hysteria creeping in. "We need to help them!"

Hammurabi's answering glare makes my insides shrivel. "Your parents will be fine, little flower. They're buying us time. Now, I suggest we take it."

He grabs onto Caleb as well, pulling us with him, away from the Nephilim closing in from behind and aiming for the pool of shadow in the corner nearby. We make it halfway before a familiar voice stops us dead in our tracks.

"Going somewhere?" Ishtar steps in front of Hammurabi, spinning two karambit knives on her fingers, one in each hand. A malicious smile tugs at her lips.

The Babylonian king puffs out his chest, sparing a split-second glance at Caleb before squaring himself to take on the goddess. "Go," he snaps at us.

"Goddamn it," Caleb growls. His hand clutches mine in a vise grip, his palm sweaty, as he leads me away from the two battling Nephilim, but there's nowhere to go, encompassed on all sides by Alexander's followers, the clanging of weapons, and the vicious heat of celestial flame—no longer a circle keeping everyone outside it at bay but an inferno devouring the space. Our only way out would be through the group of Dark Nephilim drawing closer with each passing second.

I glance over my shoulder, hyperaware of their increasing proximity. Why haven't they attacked yet? Then I remember the way Alexander glared at Hammurabi when he whacked Caleb on the head and it dawns on me that they aren't meant to. To the

Gray, Caleb and I are his possessions, and these Nephilim are wolves herding his prized sheep. They don't plan to harm us, but they definitely won't let us leave this place, either.

Frantic, I glance around for a way out of this mess, but around us, the throne room has devolved into chaos. The Nephilim not corralling us have jumped into the fight with my parents, and the fire lighting the space confines us in the citadel, spreading quickly and erasing the shadows for us to escape into. Dread creeps over my skin, making me shiver despite the encompassing heat. We're trapped.

Alexander has won.

Coming to this realization as well, Caleb takes me by the shoulders and spins me to face him, the fear like a living entity in his eyes.

"You can get out. You can take—"

Anger blisters my vision, and I push him off me when it dawns on me what he's about to say. He wants me to take the Blessed Road and escape, just like he told me to do at Babel. "Stop saying that. I'm not leaving without you!"

A looming face behind his shoulder snags my attention, and I shove Caleb to the floor just as Ishtar swipes at his back with one of her knives. I kick out a leg, tripping her, and she stumbles, laughing under her breath before quickly recovering. Turning, she grins at me.

"I'm so going to enjoy this, *little dove*." Her tone is derisive, her smile saccharine.

Shock tears through me as the Darks nearby all inch back, leaving us to the goddess's whims. They might be under orders not to harm us but Ishtar outranks them, and right now, I don't think she gives a damn about breaking Alexander's toys.

The goddess might not be able to wound me with her knives, but I'm sure she has more than one creative way to cause me pain, and she can definitely inflict far worse on a Nephilim. At that thought, I glance over my shoulder despite the immediate threat, remembering Hammurabi, worried about what's happened to him if Ishtar has turned her attention to us. Fear curdles in my stomach at the mental picture of the grouchy Nephilim injured, or worse, his life snuffed from this world.

To my relief, the Babylonian king is where we left him, engaged in battle with several Dark Nephilim—at least ten, much to my amazement—who he's managing to hold off, but just barely. Ishtar must've sent some of Alexander's other followers to distract him so she could come after us, seeking her pound of flesh. And I don't doubt for a moment that she would exact that vengeance on Caleb if doing so meant emotionally maiming me.

I snap my gaze back to the goddess as she launches herself at me, but Caleb jumps between us, grabbing her wrist and wrenching her arm behind her back. "Why don't you pick on someone your own size?" he taunts.

Ishtar twists out of his grip. "I knew you couldn't be trusted. The first sign of danger and you run with your tail between your legs. Your grandfather will be so disappointed."

A crooked smile hitches up the left side of his lips. "So, what? You going to kill me, Teach?"

"No," she seethes, twirling her knives again. "I'll leave that to the Great. But he did say I could punish you as I see fit should you get any ideas about leaving. Both of you," she adds, shifting her black-lined eyes to mine.

"Touch one hair on their heads and you die."

A gasp tears from my throat as a great golden figure slams into Ishtar, blasting the goddess and the other surrounding Nephilim several feet across the throne room in a blaze of light and flame. My heart buckles again at the sight of my mother, so close now—a terrifying, towering presence beside me. Meeting my gaze, she touches a warm hand to my face before averting her eyes back to Ishtar, who rolls across the floor a few times then flips, landing on her feet like a cat.

"You must go now," she warns. Then she's off like a shot, her sword in hand, her shimmering aura pulsating, threatening wrath and ruin.

"Go where?" I ask Caleb, on the verge of tears.

I glance around the room, taking in the mayhem, as panic squeezes my lungs, suffocating my every breath. A few Nephilim are on the floor, injured but healing, and any moment now, they'll return to battle, pushing the odds further in Alexander's favor. We need help, but Alaric is nowhere to be seen, nor Gilgamesh—not that my old teacher would help us, even if I begged him to. He's chosen his side. They still haven't returned from their errand to retrieve Lucifer, which likely means one of two things: Alaric couldn't tip off my parents before he and Gilgamesh tracked them down, and they had to prevent the Nephilim from racing back and warning Alexander about my mother. Or Alaric is stalling Gilgamesh in the Blessed Road so we have one less powerful first generation to contend with.

My gaze returns to Ishtar, watching as my mother exacts her vengeance on her, sword and knives clashing, resuming their unfinished fight from under the Serapeum. The thought of that day brings my focus back to my father, his golden hair slick with sweat, his chest heaving, as he crosses weapons with Alexander, batting away the odd Nephilim who dares approach. Lucifer might be far older than his opponent, but Alexander is a Gray. Having both the Dark and the Light at his disposal gives him an advantage, which he doesn't hesitate to use, slashing at my father with beams of light so sharp they appear tangible. Lucifer counters every attack with menacing whips of shadow, which slice at Alexander, catching him on the face and arms, pushing him back. But the fight is far from over, and every second we waste here could be the moment that turns the tide against us.

"Goldilocks—"

I glance at Caleb, but the helplessness on his face matches mine, and I can see in his expression that he wants to abandon our friends, our family, even less than I do. But what can we do? We're children compared to the Nephilim and angels here.

A strangled cry pulls my petrified gaze to my father, who clutches his chest as a thick line of red blossoms across his shirt and seeps between his fingers, dripping to the stone underfoot. Grimacing, he glowers at Alexander, who closes the distance between them when my father steps back, bloody dagger in hand. But he doesn't attack with his weapon this time, instead launching silver feathers of light at Lucifer, which pierce the Archdemon's limbs, pinning his body to the wall behind him like nails to a crucifix.

At my father's roar of pain, ruby fire blazes along my bare arms, and all the anger I've built up over the years—all the rage and loneliness I felt at having to grow up alone—consumes me as I direct the full extent of my strength at Alexander's back. A howling scream escapes my lips. I won't let him take my father from me.

Alexander's agonized yowl mirrors my own as his feathers burn from silver to black. Forgetting Lucifer, he turns to face me, a murderous fury alight in his gaze. His wings shudder, extinguishing the flames, and as he charges forward to attack me, I see it—the difference in his gaze when he looks at me now compared to how he did when we met. I glimpsed it the moment Lilith revealed the truth of the prophecy and have witnessed it growing in every moment between us since. Before he might've seen me as an asset, a soldier he could mold in his image, but now, he views me only as a threat.

Maybe, on some level, he always did.

When Alexander approaches, Caleb tries to shield me by putting himself in his grandfather's path. Gritting his teeth, he volleys a ball of purple and indigo fire at the Gray, who swats it away easily, as if it were a fly.

Alexander sneers. "What a disappointment you have turned out to be."

His eyes are wild as they lock on his grandson, diving into his mind, breaking him from the inside—I can feel the vibrations of his intent in the air, small ripples of power exuding from the angel in waves.

An inhuman cry rips from Caleb's lips as he drops to his knees, fingertips clawing at his skull, then his cheeks, carving bloody lines in his skin. Crimson dribbles from his nose and ears, and my heart concaves at the sight, terror paralyzing my body as I watch the person I love most in the world start to die.

"Stop! You're killing him!" I cry.

Alexander's frenzied gaze snaps to mine, breaking his connection on Caleb, who slumps to the floor. Tears slide down my cheeks as the angel steps toward me. I try to defend myself. I try to call on my fire, but the ruby flames igniting across my fingertips sputter out before they can fully form.

Time seems to slow as Alexander lifts his hand, raising his dagger. My eyes slide to my father, who throws himself forward, grunting as the silver feathers tear through his body, the blood drenching his clothes from where Alexander stabbed him in the chest, viscous and thick. Once free, he races toward us with little thought for his own injuries, his lips shaping my name. In my peripheral vision, I also glimpse my mother, who is now outnumbered at least twenty to one, the goddess joined by several other Dark Nephilim in their attempt to overwhelm the Archangel. While Gabriel manages the Nephilims' combined attacks with ease, her celestial flesh impervious to their weapons and her own sword in hand, my father's shouts distract her, giving the Nephilim an opening to strike. They all pounce on her, mounting one on top of the other like pigs on a pile, causing the Archangel to stumble.

It hurts my chest knowing that we're all going to die here in this fortress, casualties in Alexander's war. Well, maybe not my parents, unless they fall on the wrong end of Alexander's blade—the only enemy weapon here capable of killing either of them. But they have lethal weapons of their own, and the odds are with them, ensuring they'll survive. They're strong. They'll get out of this in one piece, even if Caleb and I won't.

My body trembles, but I can't seem to force myself to move. Terror more potent than anything I've ever felt has frozen my senses and limbs. And for the first time, despite the power thrumming under my skin, I feel weak.

My eyes lower to Caleb, and to my relief, his chest is rising and falling. He's breathing. He weakly lifts his head, looking up at me with a fear that makes his complexion clammy and pale.

I love you, I try to tell him, but I can't will my lips to utter the words.

I look back at Alexander, staring death in the face, as he brings down his hand, the dagger tip pointed directly over my heart. But when the blade plunges into flesh, tearing through muscle and sinew and bone, it isn't my chest it sinks into… but Alaric's, as he emerges from the Blessed Road in a flash of golden light, placing himself in front of Alexander and taking the killing blow meant for me.

A gurgle of blood parts the Nephilim's lips, but as he looks over his shoulder, he offers me that gentle smile I know so well now, relief flooding his kind amber eyes, even as the life within them fades. Alexander stumbles back, shock creasing his face, releasing his hold on the dagger as a mortified horror blows his pupils wide. He doesn't move. He doesn't try to come for me again. He just stares at Alaric as he falls to the floor between us, bleeding out across the stone.

A scream rips from my throat as I reach for Alaric, but someone restrains me, pulling me away from his body. Consumed by grief, I'm barely aware of my father as he scoops me up in one arm and Caleb in the other, holding us tight to his sides as Hammurabi comes up beside us, looking battered but unharmed.

My mother's voice is a deafening boom behind me as she screams for us to go, and I turn my head to see her swipe her sword, slicing one of the Nephilim clean in two. Ishtar makes her move when Gabriel's back is turned, but the Archangel dodges her incoming fist, grabbing the goddess by the throat and lifting her until her feet are dangling a foot off the floor. Ishtar tears at her fingers, but my mother is an angel. A mutinous glee spreads across Gabriel's face, and grinning, she slams Ishtar down to the floor, crushing her back into the ground with a bone-crunching crack, splitting the stone from the impact.

Ishtar groans, rolling onto her side, and I feel a momentary disappointment that the goddess is still alive and breathing. She spits blood out onto the floor, but doesn't move much more than that, her breaths haggard as her body slowly knits itself back together.

Around her, the remaining Nephilim all back away slowly, eyes wide, before turning tail and fleeing. Sheathing her sword, my mother watches them go before vanishing into a narrow slip of light, stepping into the safety of the Blessed Road.

Without looking back, Lucifer flaps his giant wings, smothering the lingering flames and gifting us liberation in the form of black shadows. He pulls us into the cool embrace of the darkness, and as the Shadow Road rises to swallow us whole, I feel Alexander's eyes on my back. In the weighted silence, they vow one thing.

Revenge.

TWENTY-NINE

CALEB

I FOLLOW LUCIFER OUT of the Shadow Road, clutching Luna's hand. She's refused to let go, not even taking the comfort offered by her father, clinging to me like ivy wrapping around brick. I don't think her dad likes it—I think he's even starting to resent me—but too damn bad. They can go to family therapy later. I need to take care of Goldilocks now, not just because I love her, but also because looking after her is the only thing keeping me stitched together. Dried blood crusts under my nose and ears, pulling on my skin, reminding me how Gramps almost pulverized my brain. The grooves I dug into my flesh with my own nails are healed, but the coppery stickiness remains. I barely recovered from the first assault. And now, I can add Alexander trying to kill Luna to my nightmares, only instead Alaric is the one who is dead. Calm, kind, ancient as fuck Alaric. Gone. Like dandelion seeds in the wind. Poof. Snuffed out. Someone as old and powerful as him shouldn't have been able to die so quickly. It isn't right.

His death broke Luna. I don't know if she'll recover. He wasn't her father, but she loved him like one. She never spoke about their relationship, but I'm not blind. I could see the affection they had for one another. I think he was the first adult she ever trusted, who stood in her corner. I didn't know him well but I liked him. Pain lances my chest as guilt bites into me with razor-sharp teeth. My grandfather murdered Alaric. If I hadn't met Luna, if I hadn't gotten her involved, maybe he'd still be alive. Or maybe we're all swept up in this fucking prophecy, helpless against the tide.

Shaking my head from those morbid thoughts, I blink, surprised to find us in Hampi, an ancient, abandoned city in India, which was once one of the richest trade cities in the world. I've never actually been here, but I'm a sucker for killer architecture, and Hampi has that in spades. Before transferring to the Serapeum, I planned to take Mom here on break. I have no idea why Lucifer has brought us here. I can't think of any Dark allies who occupy Hampi.

Gabriel appears in a shimmer of light near us, her raptor's gaze honing in on Luna, but Luna doesn't even glance her way, burying her face into my chest. Her tears soak my silk shirt. I bend, scooping one arm under her knees, and pick her up, cradling her against me. She's in no state to hurry, and even though the sun is setting, pink and orange staining the sky like a dreamsicle melting, this is a tourist attraction. The last thing we need is for Hammurabi to have to erase a bunch of mortal memories.

Gabriel and Lucifer both stare at us, and I can almost feel their need to snatch Luna from me. I ignore both of them, kissing Luna on the forehead. "It's okay, Goldilocks, I've got you," I murmur. And I do have her, I always will, but I don't know how to bring her back from this latest shock. Hell, I don't know how *I'll* come back. But she doesn't need to know that. I'll keep my shit together if it kills me. Shove all that trauma down until I choke on it. I feel Hammurabi's eyes on me, burning a hole through my flimsy veneer of competence. He'll corner me the moment we have a chance to breathe. He knows me well enough to know that I'm far from being okay. I don't think I can handle his gruff kindness. It'll be my undoing.

We pass by the famous stone chariot pulled by elephants, which forms a small palace, all columns and sculpted reliefs. A display of wealth and might this city once represented. I wish Luna and I could walk among the ruins and get swept up in their beauty and history and revel in just being with each other. But that feels like a dream that keeps slipping further and further away. Our future seems destined to be filled with pain and death.

"Come," Gabriel says, her voice almost a growl. Her fingers are clenched into fists as her eyes linger on Luna.

I know it sucks for Gabriel not to be able to hold her daughter now that she finally has her back, although I don't really take her for the warm and fuzzy type. But I'm honestly too soul weary to care about her precious feelings right now. She got herself into this mess as callous as that might sound, so she just needs to suck it up. My focus has to be on Luna and putting one foot in front of the other.

We trail Gabriel to Virupaksha Temple, the main structure resembling a croquembouche of stone, offering intricate carvings of the Hindu pantheon. A petite Indian woman descends the steps. Her kiwi-green eyes contain gold flecks, and her brown skin is flawless as is her curvy figure. She's a Nephilim, that's for sure, and a

Light. She's decided against traditional garb and instead rocks a black pair of skinny jeans and a scarlet T-shirt that slides off one brown shoulder. Her warm smile melts Gabriel's icy exterior.

"Welcome, Messenger," she says with a slight bow.

"Dearest Kali, thank you for allowing us to stay here," Gabriel says, kissing the woman on both cheeks.

The Nephilim's name pulls me out of my tormented stupor. Kali, the goddess of time and death, is a Light? There are paintings of her wearing a crown of human skulls as she defeats demons. The way humans depict her, I thought Kali would be Team Dark all the way. Well, I didn't even *know* she was a Nephilim, but that's beside the point. Kali catches my blatant gawking and smirks.

"You kill a few people and you get a bad reputation, but I'm also worshipped for being a mother figure, too, you know," she tells me.

I grin, grateful for her sarcasm. I didn't think I had it in me to smile today. Her eyes shift to Luna in my arms, and all amusement drains from her face. "Do you have a room where she can rest? She's had a shit day," I say. Luna doesn't even look up, just whimpers, and my heart cracks.

"Yes, *my* daughter needs somewhere quiet," Gabriel says, fixing me with another glare.

I just roll my eyes at her, too tired to offer witty banter, but Hammurabi steps next to me, placing a big hand on my shoulder. "We're all concerned about the flower," he says to Gabriel.

"Yes, let's not waste time quarreling over who cares for Luna more," Lucifer says, surprising me. He arches a brow at Gabriel, and she whirls away from him.

Kali's startled gaze flicks to Luna for a brief moment before she composes herself. Huh, guess she didn't know Gabriel had a kid, either. "Come, I have a room for her," she says, and we all follow her up the steps and into the cool, dim interior of the temple.

The inside is even more decadent, and suddenly my fingers itch to pick up a chisel and raw stone. I can do more than just make little clay spies, and the Creator knows it would take my mind off things. It's a shame mortal eyes aren't privy to what we see. We follow her down a corridor and up stone steps to the second tier of the building. Kali pushes open a door and ushers me inside. Heavy silk rugs in jewel tones overlap each other on the floor where a low bed rests, sporting pillows the color of peacock feathers.

I give the Light a grateful nod and enter, pausing for a moment to kick off my shoes. I do have manners, even in a crisis. Luna stirs, lifting up her face to mine. Her hazel eyes brim with a depth of agony I can't begin to fathom. Sinking to my knees, I carefully place her on the bed, smoothing her dress around her legs.

"You need to rest," I murmur, stroking her damp hair back from her face.

Her eyes are puffy, making her look mortal. Fragile. "Please stay with me," she begs, grasping onto my hand.

"Scoot," I say, and she wiggles over for me. I'm acutely aware of the two disapproving, scary-as-fuck presences hovering outside the door, but I can't focus on them right now. There's only Goldilocks and her bottomless grief. She rests her head on my shoulder, and I cradle her close. "Sleep," I whisper, knowing she needs to fall into oblivion for a while.

Minutes tick by and finally Luna goes limp against me, her breathing slow and even. I envy her, my mind like a hamster on a wheel. I wasn't even able to doze. I slowly disentangle my limbs from hers, my footsteps muffled on the thick rugs. Snatching my shoes, I pivot on one heel and give Luna one last glance. She's like a tragic princess in a fairy tale, waiting for a prince to wake her from slumber. Only there's no waking from this nightmare. I turn my back and glide across the threshold, finding Gabriel and Lucifer waiting.

Fury bubbles up inside me at their selfishness. Yeah, they want to see their kid, but don't they get that now is not the time for a family reunion? They're basically strangers. Hell, she's closer to Uncle Hammurabi at this point.

I don't give two shits that I'm facing an Archdemon and Archangel, the Messenger and the Morningstar. "Hey, leave Luna alone right now," I growl. "She needs to rest, and she can't deal with the two of you and your guilt. She's got her own shit to handle. Give her some space."

Lucifer's blue eyes narrow to slits, and Gabriel bares her teeth at me. I push past them and down the stairs, desperate for fresh air.

I stumble outside where the sun is now below the horizon, and the air is a little cooler. I rub my face, fingers stained rusty. Shit, I need a shower or at the very least a wet napkin. A damp white cloth is thrust into my face, and I jerk back. Goddamn Hammurabi. He's basically a cat waiting around a corner to jump you. But I am grateful for the cloth and rub it all over my face and ears until I don't feel the stickiness of blood anymore.

"If I was an enemy, I would have gutted you," Hammurabi remarks, crossing his arms over his chest. His eyes rove over the ruins.

"Being gutted sounds good right now. Fewer problems to deal with. Less…guilt."

I almost choke on that last word, and I chuck the rag away from me.

The Babylonian king turns to me, his face slack with surprise. "Guilt? What do you have to be guilty for, young one?"

"I took Alaric to Alexander," I say, my hands clenching into fists. "I brought him there and he's fucking dead now. He shouldn't be dead. It's not right." To my horror, my vision blurs, and I take a few steps away from him.

Hammurabi is suddenly in my face, gripping my chin, so I'm forced to look at him. "Caleb, Alaric was very old and very wise. He went with you of his own free will. He went with you because he wanted to protect the flower. You didn't coerce him. Your plan was the best plan, even if we didn't like it. This isn't your fault. Your grandfather killed Alaric. He nearly killed you, too."

I hear the logic in what he's saying, but guilt eats away at me. "It feels like my fault," I whisper. "I got Luna involved in this…" Something in my chest cracks open and tears break free, and I double over, unable to breathe.

Hammurabi tucks my head against his wide chest. "Let it all out, boy. That's it. Purge yourself of the poison. Go on."

I lean on him until the storm breaks, and I take great gulps of air. I lean on him until I wrestle myself under control once more. Then I straighten.

"I'm tired of being pawns in this game, this stupid prophecy," I say. "I'm tired of playing defense."

"Then no longer be a pawn, Caleb," Hammurabi urges, black eyes fervent.

Determination hardens my heart against my grief and terror. I nod. "Yes, now is the time to plan and fight back." For me, for Luna, hell, for the world.

EPILOGUE

A LEXANDER HAD ALARIC MOVED to his chambers. The Nephilim stretches across the bed, his lean, long frame elegant even in repose. Alexander admires his fair torso, highlighted by the candlelight, which lovingly caresses the dips and dents of muscle, sinew, and flesh. Alaric's rigid abdomen is once again flawless.

Alexander's jaw clenches as he recalls the image of Alaric shielding Luna, the fool. He could've been killed. If Luna hadn't been so much shorter, or his aim a few inches higher, he would've caught Alaric in the heart instead. But Alexander lost his lover to darkness once before. He won't lose him again. He is relieved he merely had to heal him and not resurrect him. He would've done it, but there was always a chance the mind would be too traumatized to go on. He didn't want that for beautiful, kind Alaric.

He had no such reservations about his son. But his son wasn't Alaric—he was a bitter disappointment.

Alaric was always too noble for his own good, and Alexander would have to be all but blind to see how the Nephilim looked at Luna like a daughter. Still, Alaric kept him from killing the only other Gray who could possibly herald his doom—if he actually believed fate could control his destiny. If he rid himself of the golden girl, there would be no one else to challenge his rightful rule, and his grandson would've fallen in line, his mind free of Luna's hold on him. Love turned many men into fools. As Alexander studies the long sweep of lashes kissing Alaric's cheekbones, he is aware he is not completely free of that affliction.

He forgets that the Nephilim is older than him at times. That he was the caregiver before the lover. Alaric was always content in his role, his only rebellion freeing Alexander's binding, which brought about the death of his father. Perhaps that cured him of ambition. Though he stayed by his side, Alaric never shared Alexander's vision to rule or to bridge the divide. Well, at least not to bridge the divide the way he preferred to, with ruling Earth.

A frown tugs down his lips. Before his capture, he sensed Alaric was growing discontent, uncomfortable with his march across the known world, of his conquering. He never spoke of the matter, and Alexander is certain Alaric didn't think he noticed his increasing withdrawal, but he had. Perhaps it was due to his wedding and bedding mortal women to provide heirs as was his duty to his mortal parents. But those relationships were meaningless compared to what he shared with the Nephilim. And before he could repair the rift and show Alaric he had nothing to fear, the Council entombed him.

Rage shivers over his body at the thought of his dark prison. If he weren't an angel, he would have gone blind with the lack of light. His enemies should have killed him. Now, they'll pay the price for their cowardice. He'll unite the Darks and the Lights and the Council will burn.

"Did I die?" Alaric's raspy voice scatters his thoughts, and his eyes clash with his former lover's.

Alexander hears the fear in the Nephilim's voice and shakes his head. "No, you didn't. I healed you before it came to that."

Alaric relaxes, his head flopping back against the pillow before he tenses again. "And Luna?"

Anger rises in Alexander, but he banks the fire. Luna is a problem he'll deal with later. "She's safe with her parents, you fool. For now. Do you love her because she reminds you of me when I was but a boy?"

Alaric's brows narrow over thoughtful eyes. "No, I love her for her. Other than being a Gray, you two are nothing alike. Even when you thought you were just a Nephilim, you always knew your place in life. You had security. She never had any of that, not even mortal parents to love her."

Absurdly, Alexander feels wounded by his words, having imagined Alaric took the girl under his wing because she is a Gray. Because she is like him. Because Alaric missed him.

"Although," Alaric says, "you are alike in one way. She, too, hates the divide. She hates anything that will keep her from Caleb. In that way, I suppose she does remind me of you."

Their eyes meet, a flicker of understanding passing between them, trapped words that don't need to be said aloud to be felt. A simmering heat stirs within Alexander, and he sees it reflected in the depths of Alaric's eyes before he turns his head. He's not indifferent then.

"Ah, yes. I would've cut down anyone who kept you from me," Alexander says.

"And you did," Alaric replies, his gaze darting to Alexander's again.

"You don't hold a grudge with me over Michael's death. That much I know."

Alaric shakes his head. "No, but I think I lost a piece of you that day." The sadness in his voice straightens Alexander's spine.

"Bound or free, I have always been what I am. You knew that. It's why you loved me. It's why you *still* love me." He reaches over and places a light hand on the Nephilim's knee, giving him time to pull away if he wishes. But he doesn't.

Alaric is quiet for a while, but Alexander is patient, refusing to move his hand.

"I may love you," Alaric finally says, "but I don't support what you're doing. I can't. I understand your love for mortals more than anyone just as I understand your disdain for angels." He holds up a hand when Alexander starts to protest. "Come, this is me. Part of your desire to rule the angels here on Earth is because of their rejection of you. You despise their superiority and their ridiculous clinging to their antiquated ideas of Dark and Light. You despise your true parents while you worshipped at the altar of your mortal ones. I know you actually *do* want to save the humans from themselves, but it won't end the way you think it will. They won't love you the way you'll want them to. They'll want to be free. It's in their nature."

Alexander's voice is gentle as he strokes his hand up over Alaric's thigh, the hitch in the other man's breath satisfying. "You are wrong, my love. And while you may not support me now, you will. You will stay by my side and see all the great things I'm going to accomplish. Now that I have you again, I won't ever let you go."

Alaric sighs, a resigned sound. "I know."

His melancholy grates on Alexander, and he slides into the bed next to Alaric, cupping his face and kissing him hard. He doesn't stop until Alaric clutches at him, his breathing feverish. When Alexander does draw back, he smiles at the glazed look in his lover's eyes. "As long as we understand each other."

He will rule with Alaric by his side as it was always meant to be.

END OF BOOK TWO

GRAYREIGN

BOOK THREE

"Never can true reconcilement grow where wounds
of deadly hate have pierced so deep…"

JOHN MILTON. *PARADISE LOST*

PROLOGUE

GABRIEL SITS ON A stone step outside Virupaksha Temple, in the ancient city of Hampi, elbows resting on her knees, hands dangling between her legs. Her head droops, as if all the ice that normally resides in her body keeping her rigid and upright is melting. Even her bones feel pliant. Her daughter began the thaw, and her time with Lucifer has completed it. All the love she has for both of them, lying frozen inside her in a deep icy well, is boiling up, burning her insides. The onslaught of feeling so much is a sweet pain. A terrible pain. She can no longer deny she loves something more than the Creator.

The guilt that usually comes with such blasphemous thoughts doesn't suffocate her this time. Gabriel sighs, weary to her marrow. She doesn't need sleep but she craves rest. The rising sun warms her face, and light invades her closed lids. A single treacherous tear slides down her cheek. A gentle, familiar touch wipes it away, making her ache, and she opens her eyes, blinking at the stunning beauty standing before her that rivals the sunrise. The budding illumination haloes the Morningstar's golden hair, marking him as a celestial being, despite his Fall. His bottomless blue eyes rove over her face, a much-missed tenderness blossoming in their depths.

"He's still guarding the gates?" Lucifer says before taking a seat beside her, long legs stretching out and pressing against her own. Gabriel's body heats further at the contact.

Frowning, she nods. She's being kept from her daughter by a cocky, young Dark Nephilim. One who has the audacity to stand between her and her only child. The same boy bold enough to stab her to save his teacher. The phantom ache in her gut deepens her frown, but she can't quite hold a grudge against Caleb. He succeeded where she failed. He took Luna from the Council and kept her safe. Safe enough until she and Lucifer could come for them, that is.

That doesn't mean she likes him. Or isn't hurt by how Luna turns to Caleb for comfort instead of her mother. Luna clung to the boy after they escaped Alexander, never even acknowledging her parents' presence. She only wanted Caleb. Gabriel knows she's responsible for the crater of distrust between them, but still, she'd like the little Dark Nephilim to kindly get out of her way so she can at least beg her daughter's forgiveness.

It's a shame she can't just cut him down, but Luna would never forgive her. The look in her eyes when she gazed at Caleb reminds Gabriel all too well of how she looked at Lucifer. How she still looks at him when he's not watching. She wants to warn Luna of the pain there but that is a fruitless endeavor. Besides, Luna is not a Light but a Gray. Her path will always be different.

"You're not thinking of smiting the poor boy?" Lucifer asks when the silence goes on too long.

Gabriel glances up, surprised to see amusement reflected in his eyes and a hint of violence. She gives a delicate snort. "No more than you are. I know you're ready to storm the proverbial gates as well, and you would be on your way if your daughter wouldn't hate you for all eternity for it."

His frown matches hers. "She does love him, doesn't she?"

"Quite desperately, I fear."

A long sigh escapes him. "I believe you're right. And though I'm loath to admit it, he's not wrong keeping us away. We'll…smother her with our love."

"And guilt," Gabriel adds, voice morose. Lucifer's hand clasps hers, and shock jolts through her at the contact. Her fingers curl reflexively around his. That's three times he's touched her today. Deliberate touches.

"Would it make you feel better to know I harbor guilt as well?" the Morningstar says, eyes fixed on the rising sun.

"Why in the Creator's name would you harbor guilt? I'm the one who kept you from Luna. I'm certain she won't bear you any ill will. I'll be the monster she despises." That last confession slips unaided past her lips, never meant to be spoken aloud.

Although he doesn't look at her, his hand tightens around hers. "You're not a monster."

Her laughter is brittle, mocking. "Seventeen years she's been gone and I didn't know. *Seventeen* years! I never felt my wards being breached, and I…the truth is I stopped going inside to see her." Her throat feels like a python has wrapped around her neck, coils squeezing. "It was too painful. And too tempting. I know I kept her from you, and I know you hate me for it, but you must understand I never really had her, either. The prophecy stole her from me, from us both."

Silence stretches like taffy between them, sticky with all the things unsaid and the wounds of the past.

Lucifer's chest heaves, another large puff of air escaping his lips. "I find I cannot hate you, much to my regret at times. It would've been much easier to hate you. And when I found out about Luna, there was a moment when I believed I could—a betrayal that would finally sever these ties that bind us." Fissures splinter across her heart at his words. His blue eyes trap hers, forcing her to hold his gaze. "But...I do understand. The divide was in place, and you were alone and fearful of the prophecy. And though you'll never admit it, fearful of the Creator and his retribution. While I'd like to believe I wouldn't have been petty enough to demand you fall to your knees and beg me for my help, I might have been. You destroyed me."

Pain lances her chest. "I destroyed me, too. You think it was my pride that kept me from you. Falling on my knees and begging wasn't beneath me to save our child. No, it was the certainty that even if you were to take her, the Council would've found her. The prophecy would find a way. Just as it has. Just as the Creator ordained. I was a fool to think I could stop it." She can't hold back the hot splash of tears scalding her skin. "Perhaps I should've given her to you. For however long you were able to shield her, she could've thrived. Instead, all she's known is abandonment and horror. Her pain is my eternal burden to bear."

His arms wrap around her, unexpected and undeserved, but the strong bands of iron surrounding her offer immeasurable comfort. Gabriel sobs against him, thousands of years of pain pouring from her into him. She knows he can withstand it. He can withstand anything. He's the mountain that will never break.

"The blame doesn't solely lay at your feet," Lucifer says against her hair. "Whoever released her into the world knew what she was and allowed her to go out unprepared, a danger to herself and others, uncaring of the damage she'd cause. They must shoulder some of the burden of her pain."

His kindness thaws the remaining frosty edges she uses to shield herself, and they fall away like bits of glacier breaking off into the sea. Gabriel sags against him, boneless, the love she still has for him dissolving all the jagged pieces she's been carrying around inside. Being steel is exhausting, and now she feels like she can bend for the first time in millennia. She twines her arms around him, and he allows it, hand sliding down her back in a caress that sends a delicious shiver through her.

"They remind me of us," he remarks, amusement and nostalgia coloring his voice.

She snorts again. "We were never that young."

Lucifer draws back to look at her. "Yes, we were," he chides. "We were that young when we discovered love, when we discovered passion. In that, we were completely new." His eyes heat as they travel over her face, and desire floods her at his expression.

And she, the Messenger, an Archangel and warrior of Heaven, blushes under his lustful perusal. His grin turns wicked as he observes her pink cheeks. She remembers their journey into pleasure all too well.

"Your memory hasn't failed you after all," Lucifer teases, blue eyes alight with mischief and desire.

"I remember everything," Gabriel admits, taking a precious moment from her consuming guilt to savor her former lover like this. Seductive and kind. Gentle. Then worry for her broken daughter wrenches her back to reality. "Let us hope they have a kinder ending than we did."

Lucifer sobers, his bright light guttered, and she feels the loss like a physical blow. "They *are* young, so perhaps they will outgrow their attachment."

Her brow arches in patent disbelief. "Have you seen the way she looks at him?"

His smile is grim. "Yes, she looks at him the way I looked at you. But he's…mortal. Not in the normal sense obviously, but eventually winter will come for him, and he'll wither on the vine."

Her fingers dig into his sides. "I don't want him to break her all over again."

"That won't happen for a thousand years at least."

"I want to protect her from heartbreak, the way I haven't before."

Censure fills his eyes. "That is not the battle to choose, Gabriel. She will neither welcome your intrusion, nor will she stand for it."

Her mouth tightens at his disapproval, and she glances away, though she knows he's right. Another weary sigh escapes her. "I know."

He tips her chin up to meet her eyes. "But I will have a talk with the boy. Not to separate them. I am not entitled to suppress their free will, but he needs to understand his situation, and I don't think he's quite grasped it." Lucifer runs a finger over her bottom lip, pressing lightly into the center. A faint gasp escapes her at the intimacy. "And Gabriel, we haven't had our ending yet."

LUNA

A FLASH OF GOLDEN light burns across my vision, and suddenly, Alaric stands before me, shielding my body from Alexander's wrath with his own. His arms spread out to the sides like great wings—as if, in this moment, he has finally Ascended—protecting me.

Always protecting me.

His name is a breath on my lips that's instantly stifled by silence as the disbelief and shock of what I'm seeing consume me. *This can't be happening. This isn't real. I'm imagining this.*

Please… Please, let this not be real.

Time seems to slow as Alaric glances over his shoulder and meets my gaze, the handle of Alexander's dagger protruding from his chest, a blossom of red blooming across his white shirt where the blade pierces his flesh, the gleaming steel buried to the hilt.

There's so much blood, and when he falls to the stone floor, the crimson seems to form a sea around him, engulfing his limp figure, much like the familiar tide of grief rises to swallow me. As it drags me, body and soul, down into its depths, I feel the water in my lungs, choking my breaths, filling me to the brim until I am only heartache and nothing else. And when I finally scream—the pain slamming against the dams of self-preservation that surround the fragments remaining of my sanity—something inside me cracks, letting the water burst through, flooding me completely.

I thought I knew what it felt like to be broken. I thought I had experienced the full extent of anguish.

But I was wrong. Only now, do I understand it.

Only now, do I feel its true and unrelenting hold.

I startle awake, my eyes bleary as the images of my nightmare linger for a moment before fading, granting me a much-needed reprieve. In their place, I struggle to make out my surroundings, and at first, all I can see is a hazy painting of blue, green, and purple tones smeared together and mixed with faint traces of gold. As I sit up, noting the shift of a soft mattress beneath me, the colors sharpen into definable shapes. A plush blanket. Pillows. A grand bed in the middle of an even more elegant bedroom.

My brow furrows as I scan the lavish space, taking in the exquisitely carved wooden furniture, ornate decor on the walls, and elaborately woven rugs, trying to figure out where I am. I don't recognize this place, which under normal circumstances would scare me. Beautiful or not, this could be just another cage someone has erected to confine me. And yet, where I should feel uncertainty or fear, I feel nothing.

Only a hollow ache in my chest that I'm not sure even time will be able to heal.

As the images of my dream return to haunt me and the familiar burn of tears creeps in, I fall back against the bedspread and bury my face in the nearest silken pillow, wishing I could claw the picture of Alaric in those final moments out of my head. The way he looked back at me with acceptance in his eyes, the subtle smile that turned up his lips knowing he had saved my life—that he hadn't failed me the way he told me he had failed Alexander…

The price for that sacrifice was too great. How many millennia had he walked this earth? How many years of his nearly immortal life were erased in the space of a heartbeat when that dagger tore through his flesh? He didn't owe me that.

No one owes me that.

I grip the pillow tighter. Who else will suffer because of what I am? Who else will I lose because of Alexander's mad lust for power?

Another face fills my thoughts, and I bolt upright again, shivering against the prickle of apprehension creeping over my skin.

"Caleb," I gasp.

What happened to him? What happened to my parents? I try to remember the events that brought me here, but there's a frustrating hole in my memory situated between our fight with Alexander and my waking up in this bed, as if the moments following Alaric's death have been completely erased from my mind. I remember watching as Gabriel and Lucifer faced off with Alexander and his cohort of faithful Nephilim. I remember the throne room erupting into chaos and fire. I remember watching as the Gray nearly killed Caleb in front of me, and I stood by, helpless to intervene or stop him—a victim to my own paralyzing terror. But I can't recall what became of them after…or if anyone else made it out of the fray alive.

Ironically, *cruelly*, the last thing I remember is the one thing I wish I could forget.

Panic courses through my veins like adrenaline. Whipping the blanket aside, I jump out of the bed, barely registering the golden gown from Alexander still hugging my body or that my wings are out and on full display, my feathertips brushing the lush rugs underfoot. I'm aware of nothing else except the resurfacing anxiety that Caleb and I have been separated again, and that my parents are gone from my life so soon after finding them, our reunion cut short. Perhaps for good this time.

That fear of never seeing them again pushes me across the room toward the door, and without a thought as to where I am or what danger might lurk on the other side, I throw it open, nearly tearing the wood off its hinges. The brass knob crumples beneath the strength of my grip, but I let it go almost at once, my hand snapping back as if the metal has burned me. I stop short just as quickly, pausing within inches of colliding with the familiar face blinking at me from across the threshold.

"Luna?" Caleb gapes at me, frozen in the doorway, seemingly as surprised to see me as I am to see him. An ornate silver tray laden with breakfast pastries and juice is held tight in his hands.

My heart jumps into my throat at the sight of him standing before me, every fear, every anxiety I've had since waking up forgotten at the tender caress of his eyes on my face. I can practically feel the tension leaving my muscles as I drink in his presence, and yet, there's a part of me that wonders if this is real—that remembers my time in my prison all too well, the tricks Mammon played to unhinge my mind teasing my every thought with doubt.

My fingers ache with the urge to reach out and touch him, to prove to myself that he's actually here. To take solace in the comfort of his arms, my one certain place in this world.

Sensing my distress, Caleb nods for me to let him into the room and carefully places the tray on the gilded table beside the door—the wood inlaid with what looks like real gemstones—only turning to face me again once his hands are free. For a moment, we stand in awkward silence, and I watch, transfixed, as his tongue darts out to wet his bottom lip, his eyes sweeping up and down the full length of my body. Then, as if some spell between us has broken, he pulls me into his arms, his hands slipping under my wings, his palms pressing flat to the exposed part of my back. I relish the delicious warmth of his fingers where they touch my skin, their heat intense and almost searing—not painful, but if it was, it would be a pain I crave. Addicted to the sensation, I burrow into his embrace and rest my cheek on his chest, listening for each thump of his racing heart, the repeated *ba-bums* a needed balm to my nerves.

As my hands clutch at the back of his T-shirt, my nails pinching the fabric in a talon-like grasp, Caleb presses his lips into my hair, pulling me close and yet, somehow, never close enough. Desire and a barely restrained need for comfort overwhelm me, forcing my hands to clasp tighter.

"Well, good morning to you, too, Sleeping Beauty," he murmurs with a breathy laugh.

My pulse thrums under my skin as he leans away just enough to raise his hand between us and tuck a lock of hair behind my ear. His palm then moves to my cheek, and when I lean into his touch, there's a moment where I almost smile before the pain of reality drives a wedge into my battered heart, reminding me what we've lost. What was *sacrificed* to get us here…

Wherever here even is.

"Where are we?" I lower my voice to a whisper, my eyes shifting between every visible nook and cranny, searching the rare pocket of shadow in the spacious room, nervous Alexander might step out of the darkness to gut me the moment I let my guard down. He already tried to kill me once. I have no doubt he'll try again.

"A safe place," Caleb assures me, squeezing my shoulder.

I blink up at him, frowning. "How long have we been here?"

"Two days." Although he grins down at me, there's an uneasy edge to his voice I don't like.

"Two days?" I blurt out. "I've been asleep that long?"

I search his eyes, but I don't find any trace of the apprehension I thought I heard in his tone. Maybe I imagined it. It wouldn't be the first time I saw or heard something that wasn't actually there.

As if determined to prove as much, he combs a hand through my hair, his smile turning mischievous as he tugs me toward him again. "Yup." He drags the finger of his other hand up my spine, coaxing a shiver over my skin. "I was beginning to worry you really were Sleeping Beauty and I'd have to wake you with a kiss—"

I snort and he pauses, his lips just shy of brushing mine. He immediately pulls away, a look of mock affront on his face.

"What exactly are you implying, Goldilocks? Are my kisses not magical enough for you?"

Another smile tempts my lips, but the ache in my chest obliterates any happiness in this moment, and all I manage instead is a weak grimace. Maybe I'm not even capable of smiling anymore.

With a faltering sigh, I step out of his embrace and rub my hands along my upper arms, my body struck by a sudden chill despite the warmth in the air.

"If it's been two days," I begin, shaking my head, "then my parents—"

"Are wearing holes in the floorboards waiting to speak with you," he finishes. "Kali would obviously never say as much to their faces, but you can tell she's getting aggravated with their constant pacing and lurking. I don't think she's used to having so many people crash here."

"Kali?" I ask, cocking a curious eyebrow. Just like this place, I don't recognize the name.

"Our host," Caleb clarifies.

A soft "Oh" is all I can think to say in response.

"Don't worry," he adds, closing the distance between us again and taking my fidgeting hands in his. "I'll take you to meet her later if you're feeling up to it. She's actually pretty cool. I think you'll like her."

I nod, but meeting yet another new celestial is the last thing I'm concerned about. My mind wanders, and my insides twist at the thought of seeing Gabriel, of meeting her again after everything that's happened. The image of her appearing behind Alexander in a blaze of golden light, her body adorned in her armor from the Great Battle of Heaven, sword held to his throat as she demanded he hand over her daughter is branded into my memory. I haven't had a chance to even process what occurred at the citadel, let alone examine that moment too closely, but one thought does find its way to the surface above all the other noise in my head.

She came for me.

Despite what I've learned about my birth, despite what she thought about me in regards to the prophecy, despite the danger of going to battle with Alexander—despite all that, Gabriel came. And when I heard her call me her daughter, it was like the entire world had turned upside down, and all the resentment and anger I felt toward her as I watched her fight for me was gone. Or at least, momentarily forgotten.

But now... Now, I remember it again, and I'm not sure how I should feel or if I'm ready to see her. With distrust and lies as the foundation of our relationship, where do we even begin to cross the chasm between us? Do I forgive her for locking me away for thousands of years, even if part of me can understand what drove her to do it?

Does she even want my forgiveness?

Or did she only intervene to lock me away again? To prevent the prophecy from coming to fruition, no matter the cost.

"Are you hungry?" Caleb asks, interrupting my thoughts. When I look up at him, blinking away the haze of my worries, he gestures toward the tray by the door.

"Not really," I mutter. If anything, I feel nauseated just thinking about everything I've been avoiding.

Things I know I can't put off any longer.

"So…" I hesitate, pausing to swallow around the sudden tightness in my throat. "You've seen my mother? How did that go, considering…" I trail off, wincing at the thought of Caleb coming face to face with the Archangel without me there to act as a buffer. The words of warning she spoke to me back at the Serapeum are still fresh in my head, and I can only imagine what she might have said to him in my absence.

"The divide exists for a reason, Luna."

"Keep your distance from that one."

After seeing her with my father, I can't help wondering if those were really her true feelings or if she was just speaking from a place of pain, irrespective of her responsibility to ensure the divide. After all, I saw how Lucifer reacted when he arrived to find her injured after Alexander escaped. There was an intimacy in their exchange that, even lost in the throes of agony as my wings pierced my skin, I would've been blind not to notice.

Whatever they once shared—the forbidden love that led to my birth—still lingers millennia later, even if they aren't together. I assume that's why she tried to warn me away from Caleb back at the Serapeum and why she'll probably try to do it again, especially now that she knows who I am to her. I wonder if she even cares that Caleb is the only reason I've survived this long. The only reason I didn't break sooner.

Then again, things are different now. Me being a Gray changes everything. And unlike her and my father, I don't fit on either side of the divide.

I straddle the line.

Caleb scoffs, snapping me out of my thoughts. "Oh, you mean considering I helped set a vengeful angel whose cuckoo for Cocoa Puffs free from imprisonment and then stabbed her with a dagger that could've ended her immortal life?" He considers for me a moment then shrugs, his expression unbothered, although his eyes say something else altogether. "Quite well, actually. She only *sometimes* looks like she wants to kill me."

A strangled breath parts my lips. "I should probably talk to her. And to my father."

My father. It still feels weird to say it aloud. After so many years as an orphan, alone in the world, part of me suspects it always will.

Caleb gently knocks me under the chin, tilting my face upward when my eyes drift from his. When I meet his gaze again, there's an intensity in the warm swirl of his irises that wasn't there a moment ago. "Don't let your parents or anyone else rush you if you aren't ready to talk. If you need more time to…process everything, I can tell them all to fuck off."

Everything meaning Alaric.

Tears threaten at the edge of my vision, but I blink them away. As much as the thought of the older Nephilim pains me, the guilt of his death a stain on my conscience, I know I can't stay in here forever. I need to come out at some point.

More than that, I need to face reality, even if it hurts.

"You can talk to me about it, you know," Caleb says softly.

I shake my head. "I don't think I'm ready for that."

"Well, whenever you are"—Caleb cups my face in his hand again, grazing his thumb across my cheekbone—"I'm here."

Forcing a watery smile, I nod. Then I curl into the comforting loop of his arms again, wishing time could stop and freeze us like this, just for a little while. I want to believe we really are safe here, but Alexander doesn't strike me as the patient type when it comes to exacting revenge—not after thousands of years waiting and plotting in his cell. Having witnessed his brutality and seen the madness in his eyes for myself, I can't help wondering how long this peaceful interlude will last. How long before he returns to finish what he nearly accomplished before Alaric stepped in to save us? How long before he tries to kill me again? Or Caleb?

How long before he succeeds?

Shuddering at the thought, I grind out, "We need to come up with a plan. Your grandfather will be out for blood after what happened." *Not to mention, there's still the threat of the Council to consider.*

I can't bring myself to voice that last part. Not when the threat of Alexander alone seems like an insurmountable hurdle.

Caleb exhales a strained breath, and I feel the hum of his words against my hair when he mutters, "I know. And we will. We'll figure something out. We have help, and now that your parents are with us, we have some serious muscle on our side. If anyone will know what to do, it's them."

I hope you're right.

And I wish I shared his confidence in that belief.

I offer a noncommittal "Mm" then reel back just enough to peek up at him. "First, though, I need to talk to them about what Lilith told me. I want their side of the story." Especially Gabriel's.

As if he was expecting me to say this, Caleb unlatches his arms from around my torso and holds out one hand for me to take before signaling toward the open door with the other. "Oh-kay, then. Let's go hunt them down. Not that we'll have to look very far." He mutters that last part under his breath.

My brow reaches for my hairline in question, but he says nothing else, instead interlacing our fingers when I take his proffered hand. Despite his silence, I can feel the tension radiating off his body like heat, and as he leads me over to the door, his aura whips and laps across his skin, more agitated than I've ever seen it.

Eager to know what's bothering him, I tug on his arm, stopping him just short of the threshold. He looks over his shoulder, his expression half bewildered and half something I can't quite put a name to.

"What's wrong?" I ask, unnerved by the strange apprehensive look flitting across his face.

He flashes me an uneasy smile and laughs once—a stilted, choked sound I've never heard him make before. "Uh, maybe, while you're speaking with your parents, you can slip in a few kind words on my behalf? You know, so they stop prowling around this place like two hungry lions who want to rip my guts out."

I stare at him for a moment, confusion lancing through me when I note the obvious tremor in his voice. It's almost like he's nervous. *No, that isn't quite right,* I realize the longer I look at him. He's not nervous.

He's afraid.

Surely, that can't be possible. Caleb is fearless. I've seen him outnumbered in a fight and still come out on top. I've witnessed him bravely take on Nephilim millennia older than him, not to mention he cut off Mammon's wing and double-crossed his own grandfather—an angel an entire band of ancient celestials together struggled to subdue—just to rescue me. He kept it together when we were at the citadel despite the horrors we both experienced there. Plus, he back-talks to Hammurabi so often I think he has a death wish.

I scan his face, assessing every detail, right down to the almost imperceptible twitch of his lips.

No, I say to myself again. *Caleb isn't frightened of anything.*

Is he?

"Are you…afraid of my parents?" I whisper.

I'm not sure how I would feel if he is. On the one hand, I can understand it. He's a Nephilim and they're full-blooded angels with the power and years to crush him like a grape. But I also don't ever want him to have a reason to feel uncomfortable in my presence. Because if there's anything I've learned from my time in the mortal world, it's that fear pushes people away.

Caleb averts his gaze, and the column of his throat shifts when he swallows, the sound audible in the abrupt silence between us. Even if his writhing aura wasn't a dead giveaway, I can practically smell how anxious he is. But why?

What happened while I was asleep?

"Caleb?" I hedge. Desperate for him to look at me, I touch a hand to his cheek, but his eyes still refuse to meet mine.

Finally, he says, "I'm not afraid of Gabriel or Lucifer. I've lived almost my whole life around Nephilim way older than me and Archdemons who could fold me into an origami swan with basically zero effort." He swallows again, more loudly this time.

My heart rate quickens. "Then what's wrong? Caleb, you're scaring me."

He lets out a raspy laugh devoid of humor. "Spending the last handful of months with my gramps made me realize that, in some respects, angels and demons are like animals. When it comes to their blood, they're territorial and violent, possessive in a way humans can never understand. They would cut down anything and anyone in their way—without thinking or remorse—to claim something they believe to be theirs." The *or someone* in his comment goes unsaid.

Panic is a bubble in my chest about to burst.

"Is this about Alexander—"

But before I can get the full thought out, he grabs me by the sides of my face and crushes his mouth to mine, kissing me long and deep like he's worried it will be the last time he ever will. My lips part on a shaky inhale, my knees buckling slightly, but despite the pain in my heart that threatens to pin me to the floor, the taste of him dulls the sharp edges of my grief as I sink into his touch. I feel it everywhere. In the smooth slide of his tongue across mine. Where his fingertips dig into my scalp as they wind around the strands of my hair, pulling me closer. In the heat building between us where his body presses against mine.

But, too soon, he lets me go.

"I'm not afraid of your parents," he says again, more fervently this time, his warm breath a kiss of its own against my lips. "But I *am* afraid they'll take you away from me. You haven't seen it—the way they resent that I've kept them from you. They want to stake their claim, and when they do, I'm terrified it will push me out of the picture. Hell"—he rakes a trembling hand through his hair—"I think part of me is waiting for it."

My eyes widen, my thoughts a confused jumble as my mind is violently torn one way then the other. On the one side, I hear those words again—"stake their claim"—and while I can picture my father feeling that way, it's hard to imagine my mother sharing such a sentiment. Of actually wanting me and viewing me as anything other than a burden. A mistake from her past that's finally caught up to her.

But before I can look at that thought too deeply, my mind is jerked in the opposite direction and I'm focused on Caleb again—and on the visceral fear of what he's saying. Of my parents actually trying to tear us apart, even after everything we've been through.

"That won't happen—" I begin to protest, but Caleb cuts me off.

"What if they make you choose?" True, unadulterated fear shines in the wells of his eyes, and my heart breaks at his words. That he could ever think I'd let that happen… That I would ever willingly let him go, especially after I came so close to losing him at the citadel…

"If they do, then they'll be disappointed," I retort. "Because I *will* choose you."

Caleb winces. "Luna—"

"No," I growl. I know what he's thinking. That this is my second chance to have the one thing I've been deprived of my whole life. But what he doesn't understand is that, as much as I crave that connection with my parents, I don't need it.

Not like I need him.

"You don't get to look at me like that and say these things and then act as if there's even a choice. There isn't. I don't care if they're my parents. They haven't been here. They weren't the ones who came for me when I was in that prison—" My voice breaks, and I draw in a ragged breath, shaking my head. "Gabriel gave up any claim to me when she locked me away. She doesn't get to dictate my life any longer or tell me who I can love."

His aura responds to that word—*love*—and I glimpse a flicker of hope in his eyes.

"What about Lucifer?" Caleb presses. "He never locked you away."

"Lucifer *fell* for love," I remind him. "He would never make me choose."

Caleb worries his lower lip between his teeth then whispers so softly I almost don't hear it, "Not even if he thinks I'm not good enough for you?" The confession is sour, tainting the air and plunging my heart into a tumultuous tempest of pain.

After everything he's done for me, how could he think that? No one will ever be right for me the way he is. We fit. And even if this world will never accept us together, I would rather waste a thousand lifetimes in a cage than spend even one without him.

Snaking my hands around the back of his neck, I yank him toward me and kiss him again. It's rough—a clash of teeth and lips—and hungry, with a raw desperation I've never let myself submit to before. When we pull apart, I finally say, my voice hoarse, "If he thinks that, then screw him. I love you, and I will never let anyone keep us apart. I promise."

For as long as we have together…even if it isn't forever.

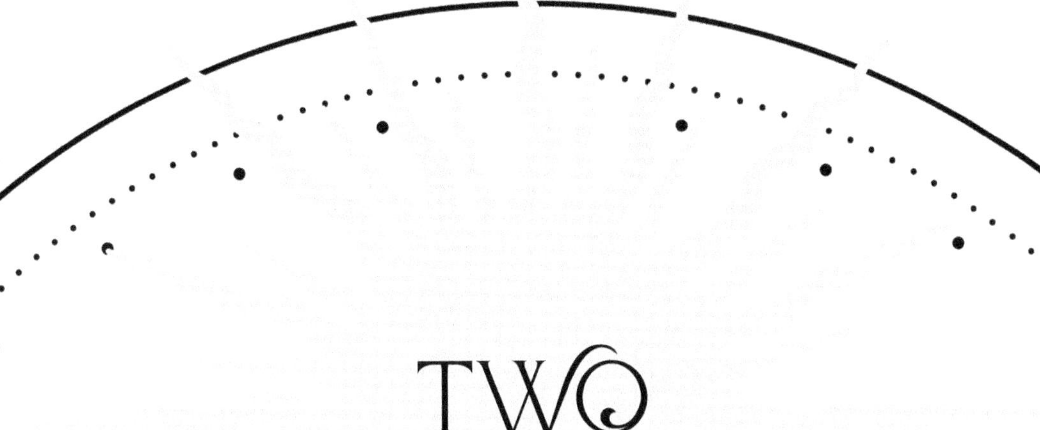

TWO

CALEB

LUNA'S FIERCE WORDS ECHO in my mind and her even fiercer kiss has left me in such a state that I'm not fit to be in front of polite company right now. I allow myself a moment to indulge in her wings, running my fingers down the satiny feathers until she jerks against me, and I groan. My forehead sags against hers, and we catch our breath for a moment.

"I love you, too," I tell her, voice raw. "And I trust you to choose me." Like I've chosen her. I know how much I mean to her. It's in every look, every touch she sends my way. "I shouldn't have laid all my shit on you about your parents. You've got enough to deal with." I can't deny I'm terrified they'll try to separate us, but Goldilocks didn't need to know that. She's dealing with Alaric's death. I should have swallowed my insecurities like a big boy.

Her full lips twist into a frown. "That's not how this works, Caleb. You always giving and me taking." Reproach lies heavy in her eyes. "I'm here for you, too, whatever you need. Always."

Guilt flushes through me at her words. "I know… It's just, I'm used to taking care of people. And with everything that's gone down lately, I want to make sure you're taken care of," I confess.

She pulls me close again with that supple angel strength. "Best we take care of each other, don't you think?"

Her earnestness wraps around my heart and squeezes. I kiss her again, pushing her up against the wall and she wraps one long leg around my hip. My tongue slips past her lips, and she tastes like strawberries and Champagne. Even when I thought she was just a Nephilim, she always tasted sweet, and the sweetness has grown richer since the bind on her was lifted. Despite sleeping for two days with nary a toothbrush or shower near, she's like decadent shortcake I want to devour. Little moans escape her, driving me crazy. I wrench myself away from her, holding her at arm's length. I have got to stop doing this.

"My timing is really the worst," I tell her. "At this rate, we're both going to have a permanent set of blue balls."

A surprised laugh escapes her, just like I wanted. And it's a real laugh, not a fake or brittle sound hiding pain. I chuck her under the chin with one finger, my eyes running down her lithe figure.

"As much as I love this dress on you, maybe you want to change into something more comfortable before dealing with your mom and pops?"

"Something to hide my blue balls?" she asks, smirking.

I roll my eyes. "You've been hanging around me too long. The Luna I met would blush at the word balls."

To my utter delight, a flush creeps over her cheekbones, staining her creamy skin. Then her eyes sober, and we're back in the ugly, uncertain present.

"You can put it off a little while longer," I tell her, knowing she's stalling as I hook a hand through hers. "I'll stand guard as long as you want. I don't think they'd outright murder me." Maybe. I do know Hammurabi would try to save me at least. That's something.

Her bottom lip trembles, and she catches it with her teeth. She gazes at me with huge hazel eyes. "No, I should go talk to them. It's better to rip off the Band-Aid and get it over with. Right?"

I shrug. "If that's what you want. But it's okay if you want to hide out. It's been an...intense week." I avoid directly mentioning Alaric. Or the fact that Gramps almost killed me. Or any of the other horrifying things bombarding my brain.

She grips my fingers, and I manage not to wince. She doesn't know her own strength yet.

Her chest heaves, and a huge sigh escapes her. "No, I can't hide anymore." She glances down at the gold gown, scowling. "You're right. I need to change. I don't need to go around looking like Alexander's prized pet anymore."

I nod. "I'll be waiting for you. There are some clean clothes in the chest over there. I'll just step outside."

Luna doesn't release my hand. "You don't have to do that," she says, her voice shy.

I grin. "I don't trust myself to be alone with you half-naked, Goldilocks. Let's not tempt fate."

She blushes again but dips her head, and I head for the door, letting myself out. As I wait for her to change, my anxiety ratchets up again. I meant what I said to Luna. I'm not afraid of her parents. No one is more terrifying than Grandfather. But what if Gabriel wants to hide her away again? Now that the Council and Alexander are hunting Goldilocks, what if Lucifer agrees with the Messenger, and they stash Luna where I can't find her? That's one way they can ensure they have their daughter to themselves. I also know Luna will fight them tooth and claw. She won't be caged again, even by them. *Especially* by them. I take a deep breath. I just have to trust that Luna can handle her parents.

She certainly has millennia of guilt to wield against them. I hope she's ruthless.

The door snicks open and Goldilocks steps out, clad in tight jeans, a fitted white T-shirt, and sneakers, her wings tucked out of sight. She gives me a rueful smile.

"Not exactly what I was expecting," she says with a shrug.

I chuckle. "Kali isn't exactly traditional. Then again, she predates tradition, so…"

She closes her eyes for a moment, her chest heaving. Then she looks at me. "Let's go now before I lose my nerve."

"You got it." I hold my hand out, and she clasps it.

"Um, where are they exactly?"

"Just down the hall. Their bedrooms share a common space," I say and note the way her brows arch.

Yeah, I was a little surprised the Morningstar wanted to be that close to the woman who betrayed him, too. But there's an unresolved tension between the two immortals that makes you very uncomfortable when you're around them for too long, which I try to avoid at all costs. They're either going to fuck or kill each other. I'm betting on them getting naked. Either way, I imagine it will be epic.

Half a corridor later and we arrive. Luna stares at the intricately carved door. She releases my hand, her fingers hovering over the doorknob. I hear her swallow.

"I was hoping it would take us longer to get here," she says, and I notice a fine tremor in her hand.

"We can go outside and come back if that'll help," I offer, mouth twisting into a lopsided smile.

"I don't think that will help," Luna says, then clasps the doorknob.

"Do you want me to stay?" I will if she wants me to. I'll stare down Gabriel the entire time.

"I'll be fine. Besides, I should probably do this alone."

"If that's what you want."

"I'll see you soon?" Her eyes snag mine, and the vulnerability I see there makes me want to wrap her in silk and run away with her. But that's not a way to live.

"I'll be in our room, waiting for you." I bend down and brush my lips over hers. "Don't let them give you any shit," I murmur. "You've faced down Alexander the Great. You can do anything."

She squares her shoulders. "Thank you." Turning from me, she twists the brass knob and the door nudges open.

I watch the room swallow Luna as the door shuts behind her, and I stare at the space she occupied just moments ago. I don't like her going in there alone but I get why she needs to fly solo here. Besides, if I'm with her, it'll just create more tension. As much as I want to be her shield, she has to establish boundaries with her parents herself. They won't respect her otherwise and think I'm the one influencing her decisions. Like I need to give Gabriel another reason to gut me.

My skin feels like it's too tight for my body—and not just because ten minutes ago I was making out with Luna. I'm not used to this restlessness. This uncertainty. This…fear. As a Nephilim, you get used to danger because you're around dangerous creatures who can kill you with their pinky finger. But there are rules, and though I bend them and let my mouth run away with me, I never felt truly unsafe. Sure, I got punished, a beating here and there, but nothing I couldn't handle. And those punishments ensured I understood what the line was and when not to cross it. But things are different now. I've been around angels and Fallen when they don't pump the brakes. They are terrifying. They are monsters.

Phantom talons rake at my mind and I shudder. I feel like Humpty Dumpty, all the king's horses and all the king's men couldn't put my brain back together again. It's like an egg that's been cracked, and all the pieces are glued back together, but you can still see the fissures. Gramps took two shots at me, and the last nearly killed me. Suddenly, I'm back in the throne room, the smell of smoke burning my nostrils, and Alexander is digging into my mind. Even though I know it's not possible, lancing pain pierces my skull and I bend over, panting. Taking a deep breath, I straighten with effort, blinking myself back into the present.

I turn away from Gabriel's room and amble down the hall, past the room I share with Luna. I need some fresh air, and I doubt her meeting with her parents will be over any time soon. I stumble out of the temple, breathing in lungfuls of humidity. I sink down on a step, the hard stone digging into my ass.

If it weren't for Alaric, Alexander would have killed me and Luna. I see him die in my nightmares. And I know Hammurabi says it's not my fault, that I'm not the reason he's dead, but guilt still haunts me like a ghost I can't shake. I liked Alaric, he was a good guy, and even though we weren't besties, I still miss his presence. He was soothing, even without his Calm. If his absence carves me up with grief, what does Luna feel? She loved him. She's been basically catatonic for two days over him. Other than me, I think he was the first person she connected to in a significant way.

My fingers curl into fists as the image of him bleeding out flickers in my brain. I give a violent shake of my head. The pain in my mind increases, and I grunt. Fuck Grandfather. I can't let him win. I deliberately relax my fingers one by one and stand. I have to keep it together for Luna. She doesn't need to know I wasn't ready to take a seat at the adult table. We're all eating there now.

I turn around and enter the cool dimness of the temple once more, blindly finding my way to our room. Kicking my shoes off at the threshold, I close the door behind me. A few quick steps and I'm at the bed. I flop down and close my eyes. Maybe I can sleep off some of my misery before Luna returns.

THREE

LUNA

WE SIT IN SILENCE for so long, I begin to think the figures on the cream-colored sofa before me are actually statues rather than my mother and father. Now that I take the time to look at them—to take them in and see them in a way I never had the chance to before, with the knowledge of who we are to each other in mind—I can accept how unnervingly beautiful they are, so much so they really could be carved from stone.

Lucifer is pure ethereal light despite being a Dark, earning every syllable of his nickname, and yet, between the two of them, my focus is drawn to the raven-haired angel beside him. Gabriel seems…different. I can still see the cold headmistress of the Serapeum in her dark eyes, but now, I see something else in her gaze as well.

Something almost like fear.

They sit side by side with their hands in their laps, their bodies frozen in anticipation as they stare at me, waiting for this uncomfortable silence to end. Their eyes are fixed on my face with an intensity I struggle not to recoil from, but there's no heat behind their rapt gazes, only curiosity and what my racing heart assures me is affection. Maybe even love.

Love. It's hard to believe I could have parents who love me after so long without family or anyone of consequence who mattered. When I think of love, I think only of Caleb, although I know there's room in my heart, however damaged it may be, for more. There already was room in my heart for another, but Alaric is gone now, snuffed out of existence as quickly and permanently as a flame doused by water. What's left after his loss is a gaping void, making me all the more starved for something to mend it, to take this gnawing pain away. Pain that makes me all the more afraid of losing anyone else close to me—even Hammurabi, who I haven't known for long, but whose loss would be a blow I can't take, shattering what's left of me like a hammer against glass.

Pushing aside these thoughts, I flick my eyes between the Archangel and Archdemon, noting the way their auras twitch with impatience—Gabriel's more so than Lucifer's, the golden tendrils lashing across her skin going rigid and forming a mountain range of stiff peaks, creating a spiky exterior that seems to fit her personality well. As I meet her gaze for the hundredth time since I entered the room, I wonder if this is as difficult for her as it is for me.

Swallowing the lump in my throat, I let out a timid sigh, and my parents shift in response, leaning in toward me, as if that one breath has freed them from the confinement of stillness.

Unable to hold her tongue any longer, Gabriel chokes out, "Luna, I—"

"Wait." I hold up a hand, and although her mouth snaps shut, her eyes flash, their depths simmering like water over heat. "Please," I beg. "I... I just want to say something first."

Lips pursing, Gabriel fists her hands in her lap. Without looking away from me, Lucifer wraps his fingers around hers, as if it's second nature to him to want to ease her distress. It doesn't escape my notice how she instantly relaxes at his touch, and although part of me is overjoyed to see them like this—to see them bridging the divide, even if only for a moment—the rest of me is angered by the inescapable thought of Gabriel's hypocrisy. By the realization that if she had only chosen love from the offset, so much pain and hurt could have been avoided.

But then, you wouldn't have Caleb, a voice says in the back of my head.

I bristle at the thought, unable and unwilling to imagine that scenario—to picture even a heartbeat of my life without him in it. I suppose, looking at it that way, I really should be thanking Gabriel for splitting up with my father and locking me away for thousands of years. If it weren't for her, if it weren't for my father's war against the Creator—hell, if it weren't for the prophecy that led to Alexander's imprisonment— Caleb and I might have never found each other.

Lucifer clears his throat, shaking me free of that grim train of thought. When I glance up at him, he nods for me to continue, a reassuring smile gracing his fair face that shines so bright despite the swath of darkness around him.

Licking my lips, I straighten then murmur, "Thank you, both of you, for coming for me. And for not killing Caleb," I add with a glance at Gabriel.

With a haughty look, she lifts her chin. "He might be a fool but I would never intentionally do anything to hurt you."

Now that you know who I am, you mean.

Although I know she was only doing her part to ensure the preservation of the divide, I can't forget the things she said to me at the Serapeum—the way she tried to deter me from a friendship with Caleb just because he's a Dark. My anger toward her during those months in Alexandria resurfaces at her use of that callous word *fool*, crushing any fleeting gratitude I felt a moment ago.

"Why is he a fool?" I snap, white-knuckling the hem of my T-shirt in my shaking hands. My fingers squeeze tightly around the bunched fabric. "For wanting a family? For being deceived by people he thought he could trust?" My indignation grows when I think of Ishtar. Although he's never outright said she was the teacher who sent him to the Serapeum to find Alexander, the full extent of the goddess's involvement was confirmed by her presence in Kandahār. Wherever she is now, I hope she gets exactly what's coming to her for dragging Caleb into this mess.

My insides curl in on themselves as I envision her whispering manipulative words in his ear, playing his own wants and vulnerabilities against him. Even if he blamed his own need for a father figure for why he ultimately went through with their mission, I know the truth. I know Ishtar was pulling his strings.

A harsh scoff breaches my lips. "I think it's safe to assume we've all experienced that kind of betrayal."

It's an unnecessary dig, but I can't stop myself. Unlike my mother, when faced with the decision between duty and love, Caleb chose me, even if by doing so, he sacrificed a monumental tie to his bloodline. Perhaps the only tie he has left. In that respect, he and Gabriel were faced with the same choice, but unlike when she chose the Creator over my father, Caleb chose me and he *keeps* choosing me, regardless of the danger that choice puts him in. If that isn't loyalty, if that isn't love, then I don't know what is.

Gabriel immediately opens her mouth to respond, but Lucifer shakes his head at her before she can speak. "From what I've heard," he interjects calmly, "Caleb is the one who set you free from the prison realm where the Council was holding you. For that, I'll be eternally grateful to him. As will your mother, I'm sure."

My gaze shifts to the Archangel, who clenches her jaw with such force, I hear the muscles pop. When I raise an eyebrow, she forces a thin smile and nods.

I let out a relieved breath. "Good. Because Caleb isn't going anywhere. I won't let him go, and if you have any intention of being in my life moving forward, you both need to accept that." My eyes narrow, flicking between them again. "Can you?" I ask, the words a low growl.

"Of course," Lucifer answers without hesitation, offering me a tender smile. The comforting undulation of the shadows encompassing his body make me believe him.

The light surrounding Gabriel, on the other hand, is so rigid it almost looks solid.

"Yes," Gabriel grumbles after a moment, her own expression tight-lipped.

The anxiety biting at me eases a little. "Good," I say again, softer this time.

A chuckle interrupts the abrupt swell of silence that follows, dragging my attention to Lucifer, who plants his chin in his hand, his elbow firmly propped on one knee. Cocking his head to the side, he appraises me with curious, cerulean eyes that are otherworldly in their vibrance. I don't think I've ever seen anything so blue before.

As I get lost in their depths, he asks, amusement heavy in his tone, "Do you have any other terms for us, Daughter?"

Heat spreads over my cheeks. Is that how he sees this? As some sort of negotiation? Or is he just teasing me, the way a father might had I actually grown up with that kind of bond in my life?

"Not presently," I mutter a little too stiffly then quickly add, "but I do want answers. I met Lilith, and she filled in some blanks, but there's still so much I don't understand."

I peer at Gabriel, who leans back into the sofa cushions, crossing her arms, her gaze hazy, as if lost to some faraway thought. "Where to start…"

"At the beginning." Her eyes snap to mine, and I stare at her, pleading. "I want to hear it from you."

With an encouraging nod from Lucifer, she sits up straight. Then, sweeping the curtain of her sable hair over her shoulder, she clears her throat. "Your father and I have known each other since we were brought into existence. We were children together, we grew up together, and it was in Heaven where your father and I—"

"Fell in love," Lucifer finishes, his voice a gentle purr.

He turns to look at her for only a second, but in that instant, a deep scarlet flushes the ivory of her cheeks, exposing the unresolved feelings I sense burning between them. The tension is pervasive, and the longing in their gazes makes me feel like I'm intruding on a personal moment. It also reminds me of something I'd rather not think about. Something that has haunted my thoughts since I spoke with Lilith.

What must it be like to love someone that intensely and that deeply even after millennia spent apart? For my mother and father, they have an eternity to reconnect— to make up for the time they lost together—if they choose to rekindle that flame. But for me and Caleb…we don't have that kind of time. One day, mortality will strike and he will die, and I will be left alone to harbor these feelings for him, possibly forever.

That thought is like a lead weight in my stomach. Desperate to change the subject and escape it—to push it away for as long as I possibly can—I rasp, "Was I conceived before or after the Fall?"

Gabriel's complexion returns to its usual color when she answers, though there's a darkness to her gaze that wasn't there before. "Just before." She stiffens, and there's a trace of what I think might be shame in her voice when she says, "Although, I didn't become aware of it until shortly after the Great Battle. In truth, I wasn't even aware angels *could* conceive as much as part of me secretly hoped for it. At the time, I believed it a blessing reserved only for humans."

I nod slowly then go still when another thought occurs to me.

When I was in the Council's prison, I spent a lot of time deliberating over the circumstances of my birth. When I was born. How old I actually am. These same questions, among others, tormented me constantly with no clues to elucidate the answers.

Even before my illuminating conversation with Lilith, I assumed I was born after the Fall. Mainly because Lucifer had no idea I even existed before we met at the Serapeum, and because Lilith had told me my parents weren't on speaking terms when the Creator delivered the prophecy and I was sealed away to prevent my fate as either Destroyer or Savior of this world. With what little I knew about the bloodlines of the Faithful and Fallen, that timeline made sense. After the Fall, my mother was a Light and my father a Dark, the perfect recipe for creating a Gray.

But what I never considered before now was my conception. If I was conceived before the Fall, before the angels' decisions were reflected in their bloodlines…

Before the chaos of war and strife split them into sides…

"Then how am I a Gray?" I whisper. At my parents' bewildered expressions, I add, "Before the Fall, all the angels were the same, right? So, when I was conceived, you weren't a Light and a Dark yet. You were both…something else."

Understanding dawns in Lucifer's gaze.

"If I had to wager a guess, I would say we had both already chosen our sides at the time of your conception. The physical change hadn't yet occurred but the psychological…" He trails off, peering at Gabriel, his brow lifting slightly. "Am I right?" he asks, though his tone holds no malice. Only the fleeting hint of what might be regret. "Did you know then that you would side with our Father?"

A long moment passes before the Archangel dips her head, offering a silent *yes* she can't seem to bring herself to voice.

"You weren't born until after the physical change was complete," she explains, avoiding Lucifer's piercing eyes. "The only logical answer is that the piece of your father inside me would have undergone that transformation as well. I can only assume that's why you are a Gray."

"So, short answer: because magic," I deadpan.

A smile tempts the edges of Gabriel's mouth. "You could say that."

I nod again, appeased with the resolution to that mystery, although there's something else I still don't understand. My brows draw together as I recall my lessons at the Serapeum and what I learned in *History of the Fall*. Gilgamesh said that before the Fall, all the angels were the same.

But *what* were they, exactly?

"Were you all Grays before the Fall, then?" I press. "Is that why you fear them so much? Because we symbolize a return to before?"

"To be a Gray is to be of both the darkness and the light." Lucifer's lilting voice draws my focus away from my mother, and I blink at him, captivated, as he says, "Before the Fall, we were the purest versions of ourselves as the Creator intended for us to be, molded for one purpose and made only of light. We were not Grays because that darkness, that desire for free will that led me to lead the revolt, and which triggered the biological change in our bloodlines, had not yet been born in our hearts." He reaches across the low table between us, brushing a hand across my right cheek. "You are a Gray, my darling daughter, because you have that darkness inside you as well, thriving alongside your light."

Goosebumps pimple my skin at his touch.

"So, before the Fall, you were all Lights."

Retracting his hand, he offers me a barely-there smile, but the only part of it that reaches his eyes is the pain and remorse I sense behind it. "Bound by our duty to the Creator. As the Lights remain to this day."

Gabriel bristles when he utters these words but says nothing, instead lowering her eyes as if conceding to the subtle accusation in Lucifer's voice. It isn't bitter so much as regretful. A sad truth about the wedge that lingers between them. That lingers between all the Lights and Darks.

And in the middle of it, there's me.

By their logic, I understand why I'm a Gray, but if they're right about the mechanics of how this all works…then why isn't Caleb one, too? Alexander is his grandfather by blood and was already unbound long before Caleb was even a twinkle in his father's eye. So, why is Caleb a Dark and not a combination of both factions, like me? Can

Grays even pass on their mixed DNA to their children, or is there some magical barrier in the very essence of who we are preventing us from continuing a bloodline so many view to be blasphemous? Maybe that's why we're so rare. Why Alexander and I seem to be the only two of our kind in existence.

Frowning, I peek up at Gabriel, figuring—of the two of them—she's more likely to know the answer to this particular mystery, having dealt with blood binds personally. After all, she put one on me. "At the Serapeum, when Alexander was speaking to me, he showed me some memories of when he was young."

Her eyes flash, her expression wary, as if she's not sure where I'm going with this.

Shifting uncomfortably under her scrutiny, I push on. "I know he was bound, like me, and I'm just wondering…could a blood bind affect what's passed on through the bloodline?"

Alexander seemed so young in those memories, but that means little when angels like my mother, who are hundreds of thousands of years old, remain trapped forever in immortal youth. For all I know, Alexander procreated before his blood bind was lifted. That's the only explanation that makes any sense.

Gabriel's lips pinch together in silent deliberation, and I can see the war raging behind her eyes as she considers what to tell me. "Blood binds are powerful but dangerous magic, and there are different kinds, some of which are more…permanent than others."

"Permanent?" I echo.

She nods. "If done correctly, certain binds are strong enough to completely sever the call between blood…" She places a hand over her heart, and I know she means that sweet song I hear even now, plucking at the strings in my heart, pulling me toward Lucifer, whispering in my ears that he's family. It's a song I don't hear with Gabriel, and now, I'm beginning to understand why. Because while Lilith might have helped her perform the bind to stifle my Dark side, there was another element to the magic they placed on me all those years ago. A more permanent aspect, as she stated, that would ease the burden of attachment she felt.

To make it easier to leave me entombed in infancy forever.

"Others," she continues, "can fully subdue one side of your essence."

"But it wasn't fully subdued," I counter. "Alexander and I both experienced our powers breaking through the binds on us long before that magic was lifted. Does that mean the spells weren't done correctly?"

Gabriel shakes her head. "Powerful doesn't mean invulnerable, and certain binds, however strong and restrictive, can still be immensely fragile. It can break under the slightest strain, as we have seen with the…complications you and the Conqueror both endured."

Complications like the red fire that instantly marked me as *other* to the Lights. Complications like possessing powers everyone told me I shouldn't. Complications like the madness Alexander and I have both struggled with. That I still struggle with, even being unbound.

"So, given the evidence we have, to answer your earlier question, yes," Gabriel says. "Had Alexander reproduced after the bind had been lifted, Caleb would also be a Gray."

I gape at her, and she offers me the first glimpse of a genuine smile.

"That is what you were wondering, isn't it? Why Caleb isn't a Gray, like you?"

Biting my lip, I bob my head. "Then for Caleb to be a Dark, that means his dad must've been conceived before Alexander was unbound…" My thoughts immediately turn to Alaric. They were together then. In love. Alaric told me as much and the memories Alexander showed me confirmed it.

So, where does Caleb's father factor into that timeline?

Sensing my confusion, Lucifer says, "It was a different time, Daughter. As a prince and then king, it was expected of Alexander that he produce heirs for his throne. Before learning what he really was, his sole duty was to his mortal parents, to ensure the longevity of their family's reign. That included taking a wife and having a child."

I balk, my jaw dropping. "Alexander was *married*?" While I knew he had a child with a woman at some point—hence the existence of Caleb and his father—the thought of him being married to one is a different matter entirely.

Once again, I contemplate how these events fit into the picture Alaric painted for me of his and Alexander's past. Does this mean Alexander was unfaithful to him?

Is that why he helped imprison the Gray?

"Three times," Gabriel answers. "To three mortal women who had no idea what he was."

"Did he have any other children?" I press. "Ones who could be Grays?"

I don't know why it matters so much. Maybe I'm hoping for someone else to shift the burden of the prophecy onto…or maybe I just want to believe a love like the one my mother and father once shared—like Caleb and I share—is more common than everyone in our world seems to think. That we can not only co-exist but co-habitat this planet without a wall built between us. And Grays are proof that such peace is possible. That we no longer need to be split into sides.

To my dismay, Lucifer shakes his head. "No. But that's likely due to Alexander's mindset once he discovered his true lineage. His preoccupations once he was unbound became…singular. By then, he cared for nothing other than his self-righteous campaign to declare himself Lord and Savior to the humans. By that point, he wasn't thinking of a future where he wouldn't be present."

"How can you be so sure?" I ask. "Maybe you just don't know about them."

Maybe they're in hiding, afraid of being imprisoned or worse. Afraid of being ostracized like I've been my whole life.

"This isn't like what happened with you, Luna," Gabriel says carefully. "We knew everything when it came to Alexander back then."

Understanding grips me at her words, and the realization rushes from my lips in a faltering breath.

"Because of Alaric. Because he told you," I whisper.

I knew the Nephilim had helped imprison Alexander—he admitted that to me on the mountaintop overlooking Kandahār—but I never knew how deep that betrayal ran or how long he was working against the Gray. Or why, other than his desire to atone for helping to unleash Alexander's wrath on the world by unbinding him.

But now, knowing what I know about Alexander's infidelity, I can't help wondering… was Alaric's fear of Alexander's ambitions really his only motivation for trapping the angel under the Serapeum, or was something else back then guiding his actions?

Something like a broken heart.

As if reading my thoughts, Gabriel murmurs, "He did what he thought was right."

What he thought was right…

Like taking a dagger in the heart meant for me.

Tears flood my eyes. "He loved Alexander. You know that, right? They were… friends." I trip over that last word, my conscious fumbling with the partial truth leaving my lips. Because I know they were so much more than that. But that isn't my story to tell and it matters little now that Alaric is dead.

I stare hard at the Archangel, her face slightly obscured by my grief.

"Sometimes," she begins, her voice more gentle than I've ever heard it, "to save the people we love from themselves, we try to stand in their way…even if it isn't the right decision." There's a weight to her words, as if she isn't talking about Alaric at all, but about herself. The surprised look my father gives her only confirms that I'm not the only one who heard it—the longing and regret in her voice. He gapes at her, a silent question in his probing gaze, and when her eyes finally meet his, an entire conversation seems to pass between them in the space of a breath.

As I glance between them, I can see that whatever once made her choose the

Creator over their love is no longer present. If faced with the same decision again, I have no doubt in my mind which way she'd choose.

A blush stains her fair cheeks again under the heat of my father's unwavering stare. It's so strange to see the Archangel this way—like a young, innocent schoolgirl experiencing her first love rather than an ancient celestial being capable of removing an enemy's head with a single determined swipe of her sword.

But as quickly as the redness flushes her skin, it fades and she looks at me again, her normally predatory gaze uncharacteristically consoling. "In Alaric's case, it was," she assures me.

"And in your case?" I retort. "Do you stand by what you did to me?" When she blinks in surprise, I add, "I know about the prophecy. That you entombed me because you thought I was the Destroyer." I allow a moment for this information to sink in before asking the only question that matters. The fear of the answer is a hand tightening around my throat, reducing the words to a whisper. "Do you still think that?"

"No," the Archangel declares with a fierce conviction that makes me want to believe her. Heaving a shuddering sigh, she mutters, "Truthfully, I haven't believed that since Alexander first made his mark on the world."

"What?" Lucifer and I say at the same moment, and we share a startled glance before fixing Gabriel with the joint heat of our stares.

"If that's the case, why did you keep her in stasis?" Behind the Archdemon's biting words, I can almost hear another question there that speaks to the darkest depths of my heart, plucking at the strings of loneliness I felt for far too many years. *Why did you keep her from me?*

"I was afraid," Gabriel explains, a trembling breath passing her lips. Her focus on me intensifies, the hard edge to her dark gaze pleading. "When you were born, I locked you away out of fear that you would become the blight on this world the Creator spoke of, as some sort of divine punishment for having the audacity to love anyone more than I loved the Creator. But I was also afraid that if you *weren't* the Destroyer, then that meant you would become the Savior. And as history would go on to prove, Saviors have a tendency to become martyrs." Her voice catches, and an unexpected whimper escapes. She then gives a morose shake of her head. "I knew from the moment I first saw Alexander that he was dangerous. Had I freed you then, you would've been defenseless against him."

"She would've had us to protect her." Lucifer's comment is little more than a snarl, and when Gabriel gives him a patronizing look, whatever heat and love I saw between them only a few moments ago seems to vanish again.

She raises an imperious brow. "Against the entire Council?" She scoffs. "We've had this discussion. Keeping the world ignorant about Luna's existence was the only way to keep her safe."

The ire behind my father's eyes fades. "Even if it meant never setting her free?"

His words are soft—barely audible, even—and yet, they seem to ring through the room like a death knell, unnervingly loud and clear. Gabriel's face contorts, her expression wounded, but once again, she says nothing. And although her silence is its own admission of guilt, I can't find it in me to be angry at her. Maybe it's that frustrating sense of loyalty I still seem to feel toward her, or maybe I'm just beginning to grasp how difficult the situation really was. How isolated and alone she must've felt in her decision.

Which brings me back to why she did it. What did the Creator say that scared her so much?

"Gabriel, what did the Creator warn you about?" I ask, immediately regretting the flash of hurt that crosses her face when I call her by her name. Although guilt nips at me for causing that look, I don't feel comfortable calling her anything else. Not yet. "What exactly *is* the prophecy?"

Gabriel lowers her gaze for a moment, and when she finally looks back up at me, her eyes are laser-focused but distant, as if she's recalling the details of a long-forgotten memory. Suddenly, her expression grows stormy, and when she speaks, her voice booms through the airy room, giving the impression that the Creator is speaking directly to us, using her as His mouthpiece.

"'A child born of the Dark and the Light will threaten the sanctity of the planet. They will leave a trail of bodies and red flame in their wake and none, immortal or otherwise, will be safe. Until another, also spawned of the Light and the Dark, steps forward to challenge the one who seeks to destroy. Should they embrace their strength, the Savior will reign victorious and return peace to the Faithful and Fallen, healing a rift believed to be irreversible. But should they fail, the Destroyer will emerge triumphant and the human and celestial worlds will be forfeit.'"

When the final word rolls off her tongue, understanding strikes me hard and fast like a slap to the face.

Heal the rift.

"That's why He let me out," I breathe.

"He?" Lucifer asks. Beside him, Gabriel goes rigid, as if she knows what I'm going to say. Maybe she does. Maybe she's suspected the truth from the moment she realized I'm her daughter.

"The Creator," I clarify then to Gabriel, I say, "No one else knew where I was entombed except for you and Lilith, right? But the Creator—"

"He is omniscient. He would've known," she finishes, sounding breathless.

Which means He also knew all this would happen. Hell, maybe He intended it to. Come to think of it, the Creator's involvement is also the only explanation for how I could've gone so long without drawing the attention of the academies, although, if I really am the Savior, I can't imagine why He'd want me so ill-prepared for the task. Wouldn't he want me trained and ready if I'm to take on Alexander? Unless—

My eyes widen as I recall Gabriel's conversation with Alaric when he first brought me to the Serapeum—how she had questioned why he didn't know of me sooner and how he had answered by saying my scent had been barely discernible, making it almost impossible to find me. Now, I can't help wondering if the Creator had a hand in that, too. If he hid me on purpose until the right moment. So that I would grow up far away from the ingrained prejudice of our world. So that when the time came and I crossed paths with Caleb, I would be drawn to him instead of repelled.

So that I would help him release Alexander since Gabriel never would.

The Creator wanted this to happen. He wanted Alexander free. He wanted my Dark side unbound. And He wants us to go to war—to see the prophecy to its completion, one way or another.

"What are you both trying to say?" Lucifer asks, a slight edge of irritation straining his tone.

It occurs to me that I've been silent too long, so I blurt out, "Lilith thinks the Creator is why I'm no longer entombed. That he purposely placed me in the mortal world and let me grow up believing I'm mortal—"

"Until He wanted you found," Gabriel cuts in, her voice the barest breath of a whisper.

The realization crossing my father's face sucks the warmth from his skin, and his expression hardens as he seethes through clenched teeth, "Which means He intended for all this to transpire."

Lucifer's rising fury is apparent, and I shrink back into the sofa, not wanting to anger him further, even though I know his outrage isn't directed at me. Still, I roll my lower lip between my teeth, hesitating a moment before finding the courage to speak again.

"I think the Creator... I think He *wanted* me to release Alexander." And although I know how much it will pain them to hear it, I add, "Had the circumstances of my childhood been different, I probably wouldn't have been willing to do that." Because it needs to be said. Because every step we've taken, every decision we've made, has been self-fulfilling, leading us down the very path the Creator seemingly wants us all on.

Had I grown up with parents who loved me, then Alexander wouldn't have been able to prey on my loneliness and deep-seated issues of abandonment and control me the way he did. Had I grown up knowing what I am, accepted in our world, he wouldn't have been able to use my feelings of isolation against me.

And then there's the matter of the divide. Had I grown up as a Light, exposed to such hate and divisiveness, I might have looked at Caleb the way the other students and teachers at the Serapeum all looked at him. Like he was beneath them. Like he wasn't worthy of a Light's love.

That thought turns my stomach.

Lucifer's brow furrows over eyes darkened with rage. "If you were the Destroyer the prophecy spoke of, I would understand why the Creator would want you to unleash Alexander. But if *he* is the Destroyer, then why—"

"You're forgetting one important part of the prophecy," Gabriel interrupts. Her face promptly falls. "The part where the Destroyer and Savior must meet in battle."

I nod. "And until we face off like the prophecy ordained, I can't do what it is the Creator really wants." When they both look at me in question, I sigh. "Remember what the prophecy said? About the Savior bringing peace to the Faithful and Fallen, healing the rift between them? That has to mean the divide."

Gabriel frowns. "I fear there are hidden meanings to the Creator's words that we are not grasping. Alexander is the Destroyer, I believe that, but he often spoke of erasing the divide—"

"Except he never wanted to heal the divide, he wanted to crush it," I counter. "He wants to remake the world as he believes it should be and rule over everyone in it."

Whereas I just want to walk this planet without anyone trying to shove me in a cage for being different. I want to love who I love without having to hide it. And I want peace between the Lights and the Darks. Real, lasting peace. No more bullshit fake truces. No more segregation. I want to bring our world back together…and heal it.

Even if I have no idea how I'm meant to do that.

"Lucifer?"

The unease in my mother's voice jerks me out of my thoughts, and following the direction of her panicked gaze, I glance at my father, startled by the sudden ruddiness of his cheeks. His hands are clenched into shaking fists on his knees and his eyes are pinned on a distant spot on the floor, unblinking but unfocused.

"The Creator waits millennia to try to make peace with his children and thinks He can use *my* daughter as some disposable pawn in his master plan?" With an ear-shattering roar, he jumps up from his seat, and his blue eyes blaze like twin flames seeking to burn and destroy. "If one hair on her golden head is harmed because of His scheming, I will storm the gates of Heaven and find a way to slay Him, consequences to all be damned."

"*Lucifer*," Gabriel barks, her tone no longer worried but sharp-edged with warning. He blinks, shaken from his rising temper, and stares blankly at her for a long moment before looking at me. I'm not sure what he sees on my face, but it's enough to extinguish the last of his rage.

"Forgive me, Daughter," he says gently, stepping around the table between us and kneeling in front of me. Raising a hand, he touches my cheek again. "I did not mean to frighten you."

"You didn't," I whisper, although the lump in my throat and the trembling of my fingers says otherwise. But the truth is, I'm not afraid of Lucifer. I'm afraid of what he's capable of.

Of what he might do if something were to happen to me.

I don't know how to respond to such an overwhelming exhibit of love. I gaze up at him, lost for words. Rising, he shifts his hand to the top of my head, patting the crown of my hair.

"I believe some fresh air is in order, so I will take my leave for the moment."

"Father..." The song in my blood bonding us pulls at my heartstrings, and only half-aware of what I'm doing, I reach for him, grabbing his hand. I don't want him to leave. Not because I can't face Gabriel alone, but because we've only just been reunited, and because I'm so afraid that anyone who leaves me won't come back again, however irrational that may be—especially here where we're actually safe for the time being.

That fear has been with me ever since I was a little girl and is part of why I always pushed people away. If I didn't let them close, I couldn't hurt them....and, in turn, they couldn't hurt me. But now, I have so much at stake—too many people I don't want to lose—and anything could rip them away, tearing them from my life like a page from a book at any moment. That apprehension is stronger than ever, like rot in my heart. Rot that's only festered since we lost Alaric.

A warm smile tugs at his lips. "You and I have plenty of time to better acquaint ourselves. But for now, you and your mother have much to discuss. Later, we will go for a walk through the gardens if you like."

I manage a weak nod, loosening my grip on his hand. Then without another word, he barrels from the room, leaving my mother and me staring after him in stunned silence. Several tense moments pass before either of us find the words to speak.

"Would he really try to kill the Creator?" I ask.

Is such a thing even possible?

Gabriel's answering expression is grim. "I doubt he could, even if he wanted to. But you must understand. You are the embodiment of everything your father fought and fell for. He gave up Heaven for the chance to have love. To have a family of his own. And now that he has it, he's fearful of losing you. Of the Creator stealing you away—"

"Like he feels the Creator stole you?"

"Perhaps," she murmurs, knitting her hands together, her expression contemplative.

Silence encroaches again, the air between us heavy with so many unasked questions and thoughts I'm not even sure how to begin to voice. So, I settle on the easiest one. The one that's been bugging me most these past months.

"How long have you known you're my mother?" When she doesn't immediately speak, I continue, determined to pry an answer out of her one way or another. "Although the Council tormented me about it and the others kept saying it, I honestly didn't know for sure until you came for me in Kandahār. When I actually *heard* you call me your daughter. But you knew long before then…didn't you?"

Looking down at her lap, the Archangel nods. "That day you were eavesdropping outside my office—" She flashes me a look when I try to protest. "Don't deny it. I know you were."

I wither under her stare. "And that somehow made you realize I'm your daughter?" Doubt laces my every word.

"No," she says, glancing down at her hands again. "But after I caught you, I did something I'm ashamed of…and it was that action that made me aware of the truth."

I think back to those initial moments following her conversation with Alaric, trying to puzzle out what she means, but the answer eludes me.

"I looked into your mind," she confesses, and my mouth pops open as all the air rushes from my lungs in a whoosh. "I never intended to harm you. I only wanted to see what you heard."

I shiver at the notion of such an unwanted invasion, imagining phantom claws in my mind, sinking in and ripping out thoughts I never invited her or anyone else to witness. For some reason, it feels so much more personal and invasive than what Alexander did to me at the Serapeum—all those months he spent in my head, poisoning my thoughts to use for his own gain. Perhaps because I know her motivation for breaking into my mind wasn't coming from a place of malice or a sadistic need to force my compliance, like Alexander's reasoning when he broke into Caleb's—the horror of which still haunts me, the assault fresh in my memory like a nightmare I can never escape. She knew better, as a Light she lives by a strict moral code, and she did it anyway.

Because of that, I can't help wondering what other lines Gabriel has crossed with me…or may yet cross if she deems it necessary.

"What did you see?" I press, half hopeful and half afraid the answer will make me despise her.

To my surprise, tears glisten in her dark eyes. "Your birthplace. It was just a glimpse—there were no other discernible thoughts I could sense. Just that image, which I could see as clearly as I see you here sitting before me."

Shock slams into me, knocking the air from my lungs. My birthplace? But I didn't even know where I was born until Lilith told me back at the citadel—months after the encounter Gabriel speaks of. So, how could I have been thinking about it?

"I don't understand," is all I can manage in my confusion.

"I didn't either at the time," she admits. "But with the prophecy and everything else that's transpired, it can't be a coincidence. That glimpse I saw in your head was surely a message."

"A message?" As these words leave me, I realize I know what she's going to say before she even says it. "From the Creator."

She nods. "I can only assume He wanted me to know who you were so I would offer you aid…and so you would have the strength of your parents behind you for the battle ahead. A strong indicator you are the Savior if there were any lingering doubts."

I consider her for a moment, her words dragging me back to those dire moments under the Serapeum when she and I both seemed so close to death. "Is that why you called Lucifer to you? Because you thought the Creator would want you to?"

A brusque huff escapes her, and she presses her fingers into her eyes, wiping away the tears collecting there. "I didn't know what I was thinking except that he was the only person in the world I felt I could turn to at that moment—who I trusted to guard you and fight for you with the same determination that I would've had I not been injured."

The sincerity in her voice steals my breath, and I gape at her, for once allowing myself to see her as who she really is instead of as the terrifying monster I've built her up to be in my head.

As a terrified mother, desperate and alone, who only wanted to save her child.

"Everything that has led us here has been my fault, no one else's," she proclaims. "Your father never knew, Luna. You know that, right? He wasn't even aware you existed until the day Alexander was freed. He only wants to protect you, so, please… don't bear him the same ill feelings I'm sure you must have toward me. He doesn't deserve them. He deserves only your love and to have the time with you that I robbed him of."

Time he might not actually have, goes unsaid.

"And what do you deserve?" I ask, cocking my head to examine her more closely.

Gabriel peeks at me through her fingers, clearly not expecting this question. "I…" A grimace contorts her face. "I deserve your hatred. And his."

"But that's not what you want."

She blanches, letting out a throaty, humorless laugh. "Of course not. But what I want doesn't matter. Not after what I've put you both through."

While there's a part of me—a very large part—that agrees with her, the child still residing within me who is desperate for maternal love disagrees. She screams for me to make amends, and as that tamped-down voice hums in my ears, reverberating in my bones and everywhere underneath my skin, I can't help wondering if maybe this is the call of our blood, finally speaking to each other after all this time—our connection not permanently severed despite what Gabriel said about the bind. Maybe the spell she put on me all those years ago to keep us apart is beginning to fray as the mutual yearning in our hearts begs it to. As we take the first step to heal the rift between mother and daughter.

Or maybe, it was there this whole time and we were both too deaf to hear it. Maybe that loyalty I feel toward her, even now, was the universe trying to tell me we are connected, even if our blood couldn't.

"I…understand why you did what you did," I say carefully, and as the words leave my lips, it sinks in just how much I mean them. What sacrifices would I make to keep Caleb safe? To keep him alive?

I would do anything, I muse, and as I stare into Gabriel's wide, surprised eyes, I recognize how much she was willing to do, how far she was willing to go to protect me.

How far she's *still* going.

"And I don't hate you, no matter how much you think you deserve it."

A strange air of discomfort overtakes the Archangel, as if she's not sure what to make of my admission. As if she's holding back the fleeting hope that I might actually find it in me to forgive her.

But the longer I look at her, the more I see the terror in the depths of her gaze, and it dawns on me that it isn't my forgiveness she needs.

It's her own.

"For what it's worth"—I keep my tone steady, even as my heart races a mile a minute—"I don't think it's my forgiveness you need, or even Lucifer's. I think you need to forgive yourself. Otherwise, how are we ever going to move past it?"

A skeptical breath fills the silence between us. "Is that what you want?" she asks. "To move past it?"

Do I want that?

Yes, a small voice in my head answers. The voice of that little girl still inside me who has waited her entire life for a mother.

"I'm willing to try." Then, with a delicate sniff, I add, "But *only* if you're nice to Caleb."

She lets out a stilted chuckle then sits up a bit straighter, lifting her chin with a dignified air. "*Nice* might be asking a bit much of me," she says, although an amused grin pulls at her lips.

The tension in the room melts away as I allow myself to envision the possible future before us. A future where I am her daughter and she is my mother and the loneliness, pain, and loss we've both suffered up until now no longer matter.

A future where I have the family and affection I've always wanted.

"Would you settle for civilized?" I counter, extending an olive branch.

To my immense relief, she takes it.

Her smile deepens. "I think I can do that."

FOUR

CALEB

I STRETCH OUT ON the colorful silks swathing our bed, my fingers laced behind my neck. Luna is still with her parents, and my anxiety ratchets up as I wait for her. She's been gone a long time. I didn't want to let her go. Not because I don't think she needs to have a come to Jesus moment with Mom and Pops—she totally does—but because purple smudges have taken permanent residence under her normally dazzling eyes, and her skin is still too wan. She's an angel; she should be immune from the physical effects of grief, but she's not. In her suffering, she remains all too human.

The old wood of my door rattles with the sharp sound of a knock. Three precise raps that tell me Hammurabi is on the other side of the door. I appreciate his manners. Other first generations think they can waltz right into my private space. Ishtar, anyone? I don't bother to get up, a mantle of bone-deep exhaustion cloaking me. While Luna has sought refuge in sleep—which she probably doesn't even need—I spend my nights restless, nightmares of blood and death all wearing my grandfather's face haunting me. It sucks ass. I hate being on this emotional see-saw from hell.

"Come in," I call, my eyes flicking toward the door.

It creaks open, and my teacher steps in, hovering in the doorway, which is unlike him. Normally, he strides into a room as if he has every right to own it. His eyes rove over my sprawling form, face torn between disapproval and worry.

"You're still in bed," he accuses and I stiffen, glaring at him.

"So?" I challenge. "We've been here all of two days, and I've been taking care of Luna. My grandfather tried to kill me. Again. Alaric is dead. I'm entitled to laze about and recover if I want to."

Hammurabi crosses his arms over his broad chest. "I thought you were tired of playing defense and wanted to give offense a try."

Arching an imperious brow at him, I shrug. "I can plot in bed just as easily." I neglect to say that after my brave words to Hammurabi, thoughts of Alexander and what we're up against have plagued me, rendering me frozen and useless. "Besides, I'm sticking around in case Luna needs me after her meet and greet with the parents."

The Babylonian king's face softens. "The flower finally decided to confront them. Brave girl. Let us hope they don't smother her."

"With love or guilt," I say, rolling my eyes. "Since Alaric…died, she's been talking in her sleep, blaming herself for his death. She's literally wallowing in guilt over him—it's not good. Anyway, she doesn't need their guilt as well."

Hammurabi frowns. "Alaric's death belongs to neither one of you. The sooner you accept that, the sooner you can start being productive. Moping doesn't become you, boy."

I send him a fierce scowl. "I'm not moping. My mind still doesn't—I'm not right in the head, okay?" I confess bitterly, turning my face toward the ceiling.

He snorts. "Who is?" He shakes his head, sighing. "You've gotten your first taste of real pain, one of many in your long life, especially in these times." He crosses the room and shoves my legs aside, sinking onto the bed next to me, his elbows on his knees. "We are nearly immortal. The things I've seen and experienced…" Hammurabi shakes his head again. "My soul has so many scars, boy, it's nothing but a white-striped lump of flesh, but I endure, as will you. You'll endure because you love this world, and you love the things in it. You love your beautiful mother." I scowl at the way his voice caresses the word beautiful. "You love the flower."

I wonder what Hammurabi has endured over the years. I've never given it much thought, other than knowing he is scary and powerful and has seen a lot of shit because he's practically a dinosaur. He's experienced blood and battle and death. Maybe he's loved some mortals along the way, too, and lost them. I remember Lucifer's remark at the citadel, that he hoped Hammurabi would soon be curled up at Asmodeus's feet once more. The mighty king honest-to-the-Creator blushed at those words, which makes me wonder if there's something more than friendship going on there? But Hammurabi would never admit he has the hots for the Archdemon, even under threat of death. And I know better than to ask, unless I want some broken bones to go along with my broken mind.

I swallow hard, meeting his eyes, those ebony depths swimming with uncharacteristic sympathy once more. Ugh, give me hard-ass Hammurabi any day. Mr. Nice Guy makes me want to snivel like I'm a baby again, and it's not that I think grown-ass men shouldn't cry, but I hate being vulnerable around such a powerful creature. I know Hammurabi won't use it against me or deliberately hurt me, but I guess my experience with Ishtar has left a deep scar on my soul. According to Hammurabi, just one of many that will mark me the longer I live. Yippee! Something to look forward to.

"I know I need to get my shit together," I admit. "For Luna and for my mom, if not for myself." I shoot him a warning look. "Luna doesn't know that I'm not Super Caleb right now, 'kay? And she doesn't need to. She can't handle my problems, too."

He rolls his eyes at me. "I'm certainly not going to discuss your feelings with the flower over a cup of tea like an old village gossip. That being said, it's important not to hide from your lover. She won't thank you for it. She might even feel you don't trust her enough to reveal your true self."

I scowl at him. "If she asks, I'll tell her. If not, it's not her worry."

He huffs out an exasperated breath. "Children," he mutters.

"The big question is, do we even have a plan? Kali is doing us a solid, but we can't stay hidden here forever. What's our next move?"

A worried look flits over Hammurabi's stern features. "We are caught between the Council and Alexander, and if we remain, we'll be ground to dust. It is not an enviable position, to say the least."

"So, in other words, you have no fucking clue," I growl and stare at the ceiling once more.

In one swift move, Hammurabi rises, grabs my legs, and dumps me on the floor. I land with a soft thud on the many carpets and prop myself on my elbows, glaring at my teacher. He towers over me, fists balled on his hips.

"If we want to survive this, we all must work together, boy. As much as I regret it, you can no longer hide behind my shield. You and the flower must leave childhood behind now, Caleb. You are young but clever. I know you don't believe this, but hiding with your grandfather was the right choice."

"Tell that to Alaric," I spit like a venomous snake.

Squatting on his haunches, Hammurabi grips my chin, giving it a firm shake. "Alaric would agree with me if he were here. You managed to get the flower to her parents and give us a fighting chance. We would not have survived much longer without the Messenger and the Morningstar. Your plan was unconventional, but it is that kind of thinking we need right now. You may not want it, but you must take a seat at the table."

My gut recoils at his words. I'm going to be dragged kicking and screaming into this war, whether I like it or not. And I don't like it. I hate it. Yeah, I told Hammurabi I was tired of playing defense all the time, but I didn't mean I wanted to lead the offensive charge. I just wanted to be a good soldier and do whatever the hell Lucifer told me to do. No matter what Hammurabi says, the last time I planned anything, someone ended up dead.

My teacher arches an annoyed brow. "Boy, your doubts are so loud in your mind, I can hear them. Mourn Alaric. Take a whip and flog yourself until your blood washes away your guilt. Then you—what is it the young ones say today?—you get over yourself."

I sputter with laughter at his phrasing, the words sounding so bizarre escaping from his mouth.

His eyes soften. "Toughen your skin and heart now, Caleb. It will make the next blow easier, the next scar bearable."

"Wise advice," a deep voice drawls.

Hammurabi and I both whip our heads toward the doorway where Lucifer himself lingers in the frame. I can't believe we didn't hear him. If I wasn't certain he'd kill me, I'd put a bell on him. His deep blue eyes find mine, the antique gold of his hair managing to shine even in this dim light. The Morningstar indeed. I wonder if Luna is still with Gabriel. I hope she's all right.

Though Lucifer wears a cloak of friendliness, when those ancient eyes meet mine, my gut clenches. I think I'm about to experience the "if you hurt my daughter" speech. Honestly, I'm surprised he's waited this long. Of course, I've been like a pit bull where Luna is concerned, so he hasn't had a whole lot of opportunities to threaten to cut off my dick.

I shoot him a faint smile. "Hammurabi is as wise as he is old," I say, rising from the floor and smirking at my teacher. Just like the predictable asshole he is, he cuffs me on the back of the head. I chuckle.

Hammurabi shrugs at Lucifer, exasperation written on his face. "Children," he says, his voice resigned.

"King, may I have a moment with the child?" Lucifer asks politely. It sounds like a request, but I'm not fooled, and neither is Hammurabi. That dinosaur knows an order when he hears it, even one coated in silk.

Hammurabi smiles. "Of course. Don't go too hard on Caleb. The flower does love him so."

My chest warms at his words. Despite his gruff, grouchy exterior, Uncle Hammurabi always has my back. "I'm sure he'll leave bruises in places no one will see," I say.

Lucifer's brows raise in surprise at my quip, and Hammurabi strides away from me, muttering, "Boy has a death wish."

I grin. As soon as Hammurabi exits, quietly snicking the door behind him, my lips droop into a frown. "How can I help you?" This time, my voice is deferential because despite Hammurabi's words, I don't have a death wish. I'm not stupid enough to keep baiting the Morningstar. Grandfather taught me too well what kind of pain an angel can inflict. "Is Luna okay?" This comes out more of a growl than I intended, and I flinch inwardly.

"My daughter is a beautiful miracle," he says, offering me a blinding smile. "Though I resented your interference…I want to thank you for being brave and protecting her from us." His lips twist. "You were right. We would have overwhelmed her."

I give a cautious nod. "So, you're saying it's all good now?"

His wide chest heaves as he sighs. "We've taken our first glorious step. Time will eventually heal our wounds, and should the war go our way, we have nothing but time." His blue eyes narrow on me, calculating, and it takes everything in me not to squirm. "Have you thought about time, Caleb?"

My mind spins at his abrupt change of subject. "Um, like we're running out of time to defeat my grandfather and the Council?"

Lucifer gives a dismissive shake of his head. "No, have you thought about your mortality."

My entire body goes on alert, alarm bells blazing in my head at his words, but I have no idea why. I just know there's something here I'm not going to like. "I'm only eighteen, and if Alexander doesn't cut my head off, I'll probably live a few thousand years or longer."

He takes a step closer to me, and I battle the urge to cower away. The thing is, I actually don't think Lucifer wants to hurt me, but Gramps has messed up my head good and proper. Our eyes meet, and goddamn, I see Luna clearly in his face. Their beauty is staggering. Seriously, how did Gabriel miss the resemblance?

"Yes, you'll live much longer than these fragile mortals who surround us. You'll remain ageless while they grow old, becoming husks of their former selves until their return back to the dust from which they came."

I suppress a shiver at his words. "Okay, I'm not trying to offend you here, but you're seriously starting to creep me out."

"Luna loves you. Greatly. I know this," the Morningstar says, affection in his gaze as he speaks of his daughter. Meanwhile, I'm getting whiplash from his constant change in direction. "I started a war over love and free will, Caleb." He slides his hands in the pockets of his black trousers. "I have no desire to subvert your will or your love. I would sooner cut off my wings than violate my daughter's ability to choose, but I want you to understand what choosing you means for her, for the both of you."

Suddenly, I have an anchor in my gut, slowly sinking. His words are like floating puzzle pieces finally linking into place, showing me a picture I don't want to see. Not that it hasn't been knocking around in the back of my mind, that dread, but Luna and I are both so *young*. Fuck, even if she's technically old, she's still a baby, still brand-spanking new. We have years ahead of us. Literally hundreds of years, maybe thousands. But I'll still…

"Because I'll die?" I push past a tight throat. "Depending on how this war turns out, I hope that won't be for a long, long time."

"A couple thousand years at least," he says, nodding. "And that sounds like an eternity, and to you, I'm sure it is, but to someone who is eternal…" He shakes his head, a sad smile flirting with his lips. "My daughter is like me, I'm afraid. There have been others besides Gabriel, but none who held my heart captive the way she did. Still does, despite our…differences. Luna feels that way about you, child. She'll love you with all her eternal heart. And when winter finally claims you, it will break her."

I'm struck by the abrupt urge to vomit. I clench my hands into fists to guard against the nausea consuming me. My head spins. I close my eyes briefly. *Get your fucking shit together, Caleb.* I find my center by the ends of my fingertips, clinging onto my manufactured calm. My eyes snap open, meeting the blazing blue of the Morningstar's. I detect pity there, and it makes me want to destroy mountains.

"I'll break her if I walk away, too," I counter, my voice hoarse. Clearing my throat, I say more firmly, "I love her, and I'm not going to abandon her like everyone else in her life has for her own good." Lucifer flinches. Direct hit. I want to crow in triumph. I want to pay him back a little for shredding my life apart, but this isn't about him. "Yeah, one day I'll die, and that fucking sucks, but that doesn't mean I can't love Luna the way she deserves. And I will love her until she no longer wants me."

The Morningstar's wings materialize on either side of him, ebony and menacing. Every fiber of my being tells me to curl into a ball so the predator doesn't notice me. But I hold my ground. I only wish I had badass wings to flare out, too, so we'd both be strutting peacocks, circling each other. Lucifer's face turns cold until he resembles the beautiful statues Nephilim like to sculpt of him and place around the academies. He studies me, searching for any weakness, anywhere in my armor he might slip an emotional blade and gut me. I don't waver. I don't bat a fucking eyelash. He tilts his head, a slow smile blooming over his face like a sunrise, warming his eyes and making him golden once more. He gives me a nod, and I know I've passed some sort of test.

"I may not like you diverting my daughter's attention, but I can't fault your loyalty," he says. "Love her the way she deserves or face my wrath. Do we understand each other?"

Nodding, I say, "Perfectly."

His wings vanish, the inky feathers leaving trails of darkness. "Good. Luna will return momentarily. She and Gabriel have many things to discuss. There are deep wounds that need to be healed between them."

I almost choke on a derisive snort. "Understatement of the year," I mutter.

Mr. Bat Ears raises an eyebrow, his blue eyes gone a few shades colder. "Gabriel is Luna's mother. She loves her. To be with Luna, you must accept that."

My smile is anorexic. "I do, and you have to accept that I want to protect Luna from everything that causes her pain—even her mother."

Lucifer observes me through hooded eyes, and I fight the urge to fidget. He doesn't like my answer, but it's the truth. Yeah, Gabriel had her reasons but Goldilocks got hurt. And I don't like that.

"The time for either of us causing her pain is over," Lucifer finally says. "You needn't worry on that score anymore, child."

I chuckle. I can't help it. For all his immortality, it's clear the Morningstar is new to this whole dad business. "You will, and you won't mean to, but it's all part of being a parent. You'll fight and make up and love each other even more. Don't try to be perfect. It's not possible. Just be there. That's what matters."

Anger flushes Lucifer's cheekbones at first, but then he laughs. "You're quite wise for an infant," he says and I smirk. "It gladdens my heart to know you have a sharp mind as we face the upcoming war. You'll be an asset."

That sobers me the hell up. "It looks like you and Hammurabi are on the same page." My stomach sours. I don't want the weight of that responsibility, but I'm going to be saddled with it whether I like it or not.

"The king is superb at spotting talent," Lucifer acknowledges. "And I know my daughter would never be attracted to an ignorant boy. She's too intelligent."

"She's smart and beautiful, a lethal combo," I agree, then I frown. "Look, I'll carry my weight, and I'll do what you tell me to do, but like you said, I'm an infant. Don't expect miracles."

"You have a brain and good instincts, which means I can mold you into an effective leader and warrior. That's enough. Miracles are not required."

Ugh, I don't want to lead anyone anywhere, but I know arguing with the

Morningstar is pointless. And stupid. Shoving my hands in my pockets, I rock back on my heels. "So, what's the plan now? We can't pretend to be Team Alexander anymore. Now, Gramps *and* the Council are after us. Hammurabi didn't give me much insight, which I won't lie kinda worries me."

Lucifer's smile is grim. "Now, I call upon my allies and all the favors owed to me. I am still the Morningstar, Caleb. I still command allegiance."

I believe him. I just hope it will be enough.

FIVE

LUNA

I LEAVE AFTER SPEAKING with Gabriel, feeling significantly lighter than when I first entered the room, the apprehension of facing my parents replaced with a budding, albeit tentative, hope for the future before us. I still carry wounds that will take time to heal from, but the thought of that future eases the sting. Because I know, moving forward, I'm no longer alone.

Whatever comes next, we'll face it together.

And yet, despite that hope, the heaviness soon returns to my chest, weighing my every step with dread, making it easy—too easy—for the fear to catch up with me. I quicken my pace, hurrying toward the bedroom I share with Caleb, eager to escape the dark thought nipping at my heels—the understanding that the future I keep envisioning depends on what happens next with Alexander...and even more so on the Council's stance on Grays. What if the impending war changes nothing and I have to spend the rest of my immortal life on the run, always looking over my shoulder in constant fear of being imprisoned again? I don't want to live that way, and I certainly don't want to force that kind of life on Caleb or my parents, either. So, where would that leave us if that's all that awaits me? Would they remain by my side if the only future we could have together is one in hiding?

The heavy wooden door slides into view, and it takes everything in me not to run just to escape the daunting silence of the corridor sooner. In the hush, I hear every single one of my fears reflected back at me as if someone is screaming them, the unspoken thoughts echoing off the walls, which seem to shrink, closing in around me as the anxiety in my chest tightens around my heart. The sensation only eases when I feel the cool brass knob to our bedroom beneath my fingertips.

Grasping the metal, I throw the door open to find Caleb sprawled on the bed on his back, staring up at the ceiling. Although the sight of him immediately calms the chaos inside me, something about the blank expression on his face and the unnatural stillness in his body gives me pause.

His eyes shift to mine when I stumble into the room. "Hey," he says, launching himself off the bed and crossing the distance to me in two long strides.

"Hi," I whisper, my momentary worry forgotten, grinning up at him as he takes hold of my hands, his thumbs brushing over the backs of my fingers in a soothing caress.

If fear of the future is a poison, then Caleb—being with him like this—is my antidote.

"You were gone a while," he mutters, unable to hide the frown dancing along the edge of his lips. "I was beginning to get worried. How'd it go?"

I consider my answer before finally settling on, "Good, I think. A little awkward, obviously, but…it was a good start." And with time, dedication, and hard work, maybe my relationship with my parents will almost feel normal.

Although relief shines in Caleb's eyes, the concerned expression on his face lingers. "Did Gabriel behave?"

An airy laugh springs from my lungs. "Yes," I assure him. "And she even promised she'd try to be nice from now on."

He raises a brow, fighting a grin. "Try, huh?"

I shrug. "It was the best I could get."

He nods, but the faint smile slips from his face, replaced again by that unwelcome frown. I wait for him to prod me about my father—to ask me if we have the Morningstar's approval—but the question never comes. Maybe he's not as concerned about Lucifer's opinion as he is my mother's. After all, they're both Darks. They share common beliefs and viewpoints. Or maybe it's for that very reason he seems so on edge. Like he has to live up to some grand expectation to be more, to make some all-important mark on the world, just because of who my father is.

Biting back a frown of my own at the thought, I tug one hand free of his and press it flat to his cheek. When he leans into my touch, I say, "You definitely don't need to worry about my father, you know. He told me he's eternally grateful to you. I daresay he might even like you."

But those words don't seem to bring him as much comfort as I hoped they would because he pulls away, averting his gaze. Clearing his throat, he lets go of my hand

and returns to the bed, plopping down on the mattress.

As I cross to the bed, I wonder what's bothering him—if Alaric's death is tearing him apart inside the way it suffocates me. Before, I was too wrapped up in my own grief to notice how exhausted he looks, like he hasn't slept in days. His face is drawn, as if something heavy weighs on his mind, although I can tell he's trying hard to hide it. He looks up at me and forces a roguish smile, acting like he's the same old Caleb when it's apparent he's anything but. I want to ask what's wrong, to encourage him to be open with me, but we've both been through so much—more than anyone else our age could possibly fathom—and it doesn't seem fair to goad him into talking when I'm not ready to talk about Alaric.

So instead, I sit down beside him and take his hand again, threading our fingers together. Whether it's the looming fear of his grandfather or Ishtar's betrayal or Alaric's death nagging at him, I'll be here when he's ready…just as he's always been there for me.

As if reading my mind, Caleb raises our joined hands to his lips and loosens his hold just enough to press a gentle kiss to the gold scar on my palm. I gaze at him over our fingers, and when our eyes meet, he lies back on the bed, pulling me with him until we're stretched out side by side on the blanket. A contented sigh brushes past my lips as he loops an arm around my waist and tugs me closer.

For a while, we stay like this. My cheek rests on his chest, his fingers grazing up and down the full length of my arm and occasionally skimming over my hip, sending small bursts of electricity arcing through me. It's soothing but dangerous, and I know if he keeps touching me like this, I won't be able to maintain control.

Suddenly, Caleb laughs under his breath, and it's only when I go still that I realize I've been fidgeting. Well, rubbing up against him more like. Not that I hear him complaining about it. He *did* say he always wants to have sex with me.

"So, what did you and your parents talk about?" he asks, to my disappointment, steering the conversation in a very unsexy direction.

I blow out a loud breath, feeling like I've been doused with ice water. Then flopping over onto my back, I tell him everything.

"Well, I guess it's good we're finally getting some answers," Caleb says once I've divulged the last detail, "especially where the prophecy is concerned."

His voice trails off at the end of that sentence, making me think there's more he wants to say. Propping myself up on my elbows, I look down at him, noting the way his attention is fixed intently on the ceiling again.

"But?" I prompt, my brows lifting.

He turns his head, his gaze drifting to mine, and for a long moment after, he just stares at me without saying a word, those beautiful dark eyes unblinking. I can practically see the wheels turning behind them.

"But I agree with your pops," he finally says, sitting up and swiping a lock of hair out of my face. "If the Creator really did set this all up, if we really are just pieces in some big cosmic game of chess and you end up hurt because of this shit with my gramps…" His jaw clicks when he clenches his teeth, his body stiffening as he lowers his hand, his eyes dipping down to the blanket beneath us. Shaking his head, he grinds out, "Then I'll be right there next to Lucifer, smashing down the gates of Heaven."

"Caleb—"

He shakes his head again, and his eyes snap back to mine, a stubborn pout contorting his lips. "Before you point out the obvious and say I can't fly, just know I will literally hitch a ride on your dad's back if I have to."

Biting back a laugh at that mental picture, I sit up and comb my hand through his hair. As my nails glide over his scalp, he sighs.

"It won't come to that," I murmur, trailing my fingertips down the back of his neck. "Why would the Creator have done any of this unless He wanted us to win?"

Exhaling, Caleb scrubs a hand over his face. "I have no clue, Goldilocks. But—and I can't believe I'm saying this—I agree with your mom. She locked you away so you wouldn't end up as a martyr, and I won't let you become one, either. Fuck fate. *Fuck the Creator's plans*," he growls. Cupping my face, he pulls me to him until I feel his hot breath on my lips. "We are going to win this war, and you are going to get the future you deserve."

The future I deserve…

And what kind of future is that? I'm tempted to say. But I don't because no good can come of that answer.

After all, it would depend on who we're asking.

Frowning, I whisper instead, "I wish I knew how we're going to do that."

Caleb plants a barely-there kiss on my lips then collapses backward onto the bed again. As the mattress settles beneath him, I hear him mutter, "I'm sure we'll find out soon enough."

✦

Fallen start arriving early the next day—half a dozen figures clad in rippling shadow, all claiming to be supporters of my father. As soon as the first one appears, Caleb and I are ushered into a large, open living space by a disgruntled Hammurabi, who it seems has once again been reduced to his role as our babysitter and herder. Despite his deep frown, I can tell he doesn't actually mind, his fondness for Caleb shining out in every interaction between them, even when he's smacking the younger Nephilim upside the head. And I can tell Caleb has a soft spot for the Babylonian king—hell, as intimidating as Hammurabi can be, even I find his presence comforting, which is much-needed these days given the frequent mayhem that seems to keep finding us. There's just something endearing about the old grouch.

My parents greet each of the new arrivals, although my mother doesn't receive the same warm reception from the Fallen as my father. They regard her like they might a snake, their eyes tracking her every move as if they fear she might attack as soon as they turn their backs. Still, they listen with rapt attention as my parents give a very brief—and vague—explanation as to why my father called them, and when Gabriel and Lucifer finally introduce me as their daughter, the Fallen stare at me not with the fear I expect, but with a thousand questions in their eyes. Despite admitting they heard rumors of Alexander's return, they seem less knowledgeable when it comes to Grays—as if they had no idea we exist. I wonder if this is the first time many of them have even heard of a Gray. Alaric said Alexander's followers all had their memories wiped, but what about those who didn't follow the Conqueror during his first conquest for power? Are their memories about what he is still intact, or was everyone—Light and Dark alike—given a clean slate in a desperate attempt to bury the past? Or maybe some never know the truth at all.

Either way, the newcomers don't turn tail and flee or threaten to turn us into the Council, which at this point, is really all we can ask for. Their respect and loyalty towards my father was all it took to guarantee their allegiance to our cause, though, I'm not sure how much help six Fallen will be when going up against Alexander, who has hundreds, possibly more, at his command...and the ability to resurrect any who are cut down on the field of battle.

I peer around the room, taking in the faces before me. To win the impending war against my fellow Gray, we need to be united, and yet, of our present group of allies, only two are Lights—my mother and Kali. Grief rises in my throat like bile when I think about how, if Alaric was alive, he would be here, too, standing with us, ready to fight by our sides. But he isn't, and it seems my mother doesn't command the same loyalty as my father. That, or she doesn't trust any Lights besides Kali to not run off and squeal to the Council should she attempt to involve them in our plan—assuming we ever actually come up with one. That thought only depresses me more. How am I supposed to heal the divide with so little trust between the two sides?

"Holy shit," Caleb whispers, and I follow his gaze from where he sits beside me in the middle of the U-shaped settee to the other side of the vast room where a towering figure steps out of the darkness drenching the distant corner in black.

A late arrival.

As the man emerges from the Shadow Road and steps into the light streaming in through the arched windows on my right, I notice his skin is a deep copper brown, and his eyes, which blaze orange, like glowing topaz, are decorated with black and gold paint, reminding me of ancient Egyptian paintings of royalty. Despite his modern clothing, he wears an elaborate choker made of what I suspect is real gold.

"Who is that?" I ask.

I glance back at Caleb, surprised to find him looking slightly star-struck.

"Abaddon," he answers, his tone almost reverent. "Headmaster of Machaerus Academy. Dude is a grade A badass, so having him on our side is a massive win. Plus"—he lowers his voice even more, leaning in to murmur in my ear—"the fact he's here means the Council isn't as united as we thought it was."

I pull back to meet his gaze. "That's good, right?"

He nods. "*Very* good. First, Asmodeus, then Beelzebub, and now Abaddon?" A smile spreads across his face as his eyes turn in the direction of the Archdemon again. "It means there's hope."

We watch, silent spectators to this reunion between Council members, as Abaddon approaches my father where he stands with my mother to the left of the sofa. "Lucifer," he says with a dutiful nod. His focus then shifts to my mother, and he looks her up and down with a contemptuous sneer. "Gabriel."

"Abaddon." The Archdemon's name rolls off her tongue like honey laced with venom. "Thank you for coming. I'd introduce you to our daughter, Luna"—she waves a hand toward me, and I instinctively shrink into the sofa, hoping to escape the latecomer's attention—"but of course, you already know all about her. You did, after all, aid in locking her in a cage."

"As did Asmodeus, who also helped to free her," Lucifer reminds my mother, placing a warning hand on her forearm. She stills at his touch except for her shoulders, which raise like hackles on a hissing cat, her brow furrowing over dark eyes. "Retract your claws, Gabriel. Abaddon is on our side."

Ignoring Gabriel's stormy glare, the Archdemon places a hand on his chest and once again inclines his head toward my father. "My allegiance is to *you*, Morningstar. I followed you into one battle, and I am prepared to do the same again. Give the order and I will take up my sword."

Lucifer grins, and his face is the very sun itself, momentarily dazzling everyone present. Especially me.

"Only words are needed today, Brother," he says, clapping Abaddon on the back. "Come. We have much to discuss."

"Is this everyone?" Abaddon asks as Lucifer steers him toward the sofa. "I fear you will need greater numbers than this if you are to take on the Conqueror's army. And where is Beele? I do not see him here."

"Beele?" I fail to stifle my shock at the nickname for the fearsome Archdemon. Beelzebub might resemble an adolescent on the cusp of teenagehood, but I have zero doubt he could take on anyone in this room and hold his own, if not come out on top. It's strange hearing him referred to in such an endearing tone, like someone might talk about their younger sibling. Or a puppy.

Caleb chuckles into his hand. "Well, that is just adorable. He must be the little guy's bestie."

I let out an unbidden giggle at that mental picture then immediately go silent when Hammurabi scowls at us from his perch at the far end of the sofa, giving a subtle shake of his head. If the others hear us, they don't comment on it, though I do catch my father watching me out of the corner of his eye from where he stands a few feet away, a grin tugging up one corner of his lips. Just past him, I notice my mother looks equally amused, though she's trying much harder to hide it.

Clearing his throat, Lucifer looks back at Abaddon, gesturing for him to take a seat before stepping past him and sinking onto the cushion beside me. "Beelzebub will show, of that I am certain. He has never failed me before."

Although Abaddon nods, he looks unconvinced, concern etched into his features as clearly as words printed on the page of a book.

"Do you come with any news of Asmodeus?" Hammurabi asks, drawing the focus of everyone in the room. "Forgive me for speaking out of turn," he adds, looking between my father and the other Archdemon, "but I have heard nothing of my mistress and fear for her safety."

My chest goes tight at the thought of the headmistress of Babel. The last time we saw her, she was preparing to confront the Council alone while Caleb, Hammurabi, and I fled to Hilla and escaped into the Shadow Road. While in Kandahār—as glorified prisoners at Alexander's base—we heard she was imprisoned but any other news about the Archdemon has been sorely lacking.

"Anything you can tell us, Abaddon," my father encourages, the pleading edge to his tone only eclipsed by the fury riding every word. "I, too, fear for Asmodeus. She has risked much for my sake, and I cannot let her suffer any longer on my behalf."

Beside me, Caleb straightens, and he grabs hold of my hand, his palm sweaty with anticipation and a worry that's almost palpable with how close he sits. I taste it in the air, I feel it in the trembling of his fingers, and I find myself praying to the Creator that Asmodeus is safe and unharmed. For Caleb's sake more than anyone's, even her own.

A dark shadow dims Abaddon's vibrant eyes. "I'm afraid I must disappoint you both," he says, casting a forlorn glance at my father and then at the Babylonian king, although there's a split second where his gaze catches mine. There's something there in the way he looks at me, however brief. Something my gut tells me is blame. "She is being held in an underground cavern on Thwaites Glacier, entangled in chains which are spelled to frost over and burn her exposed skin with her own ice should she struggle. Her punishment for aiding your daughter is not a pleasant one, Lucifer, and it is not due to expire anytime soon. I fear the glacier will melt long before her detainment there ends."

My stomach plummets, and I fight the overpowering urge to throw up. Asmodeus isn't only imprisoned because she helped me, she's being punished for it—and horribly from the sounds of it. I shiver at the thought of ice against naked skin, imagining the worst kind of frostbite—of burns inflicted by cold instead of fire, unsure which is worse. I wonder if whatever cage she's being held in is also preventing her from healing, much like that terrible egg hindered me.

"If we know where she is, surely we can go get her out?" I whip my head back and forth, swiveling between Lucifer and Abaddon, my voice hitched up an octave as an all-too-familiar panic sinks in.

Caleb tightens his grip on my hand, and when I look at him, the expression on his face only stokes the embers of my growing hysteria.

"We barely escaped in one piece from the Council's last prison," he says, his tone gentle, as if consoling a young child after a nightmare. "And honestly, Goldilocks, as much as I want to help Asmodeus, I don't want you within a hundred miles of those assholes again. It's too risky."

Tears well in my eyes. "But there are more of us now. And it's *my* fault she's in there—"

On my other side, Lucifer touches my shoulder, and when our eyes meet, he brushes my cheek with his knuckles. "The burden of guilt rests with me, Daughter, not with you. Do not let it trouble your mind."

I shake my head. "But—"

"Worry not," he says over me, offering a genial smile. "I will ensure she is freed. But first"—his expression darkens—"we must discuss Alexander."

There's the delicate sound of someone clearing their throat, then, "I hope you weren't planning to start the party without me."

My gaze is pulled over my shoulder where it locks on a woman standing in the doorway, her figure draped against the door frame like a sumptuous courtesan holding court. A devious smile curls ruby red lips as eyes of obsidian peer around the room.

"Lilith," I breathe.

"Who invited the traitor?" Abaddon growls, rising from the sofa.

"I did," Gabriel barks, stepping forward. She crosses the room to her friend, who hooks an arm around her, pulling her in for a hug. My mother returns the embrace—a lot less awkwardly than I would've expected given she isn't exactly renowned for warm, fuzzy displays of emotion—then pulls away, fixing Abaddon with a glower. "She isn't allied with the Conqueror. Not anymore."

Abaddon scoffs. "Since when?" Behind him, the other Fallen all gape at Lilith, expressions almost spellbound, as if this is the first time they've seen the ex-Archdemon in person. After siding with Alexander and then losing her wings, I can only imagine Lilith probably didn't make many public appearances. For all I know, this could be the first time many of them have seen her for thousands of years.

Lilith leaves Gabriel's side, prowling into the room like a panther on the hunt. Sneering at Abaddon, she bites out, "Since recent events made me realize I was wrong about the prophecy." She looks at me then, and her face instantly softens, a sincere smile curving her lips. "Hello again, Luna."

I blink at her, taken aback by the pleasant coo of her voice and the warm, almost fond way she regards me, even if I got a brief taste of it in those final moments of our last conversation. Still, it's a staggering contrast to the antagonism she displayed for the most part at the citadel, and the difference throws me for a loop.

Confused mutterings fill the room, mainly coming from the Fallen and Kali, who it seems had no idea there even was a prophecy, let alone that Gabriel had lied about the details.

Abaddon, on the other hand, merely arches a brow. "Wrong?" he echoes, bemused. "The prophecy has always been clear that a Gray will be the Destroyer of our world. Even before we knew of a second Gray, you were adamant Alexander was innocent." Now, he fixes my mother with a furious stare that would make any lesser creature cower. "So, I do wonder how our dear Lilith could have misinterpreted the prophecy to begin with unless there is something you failed to disclose to the rest of us when you first delivered the Creator's warning. We all know you have always held her ear."

Pinching the bridge of her nose between her thumb and forefinger, Gabriel lets out a long-suffering sigh. Then, with a blink-and-you-miss-it glance at my father, she says, "It's time you all knew the truth."

The Archangel repeats the full prophecy with the same possessed look she wore yesterday when she revealed it to me, her eyes hazy with distance and her voice thunderous in the encompassing hush. Everyone in the room watches her with unbroken focus until the last word leaves her lips.

Once Gabriel finishes speaking, Lilith takes it upon herself to fill in the rest of the blanks, explaining our suspicion about the Creator's involvement and what that means for the prophecy…

And for me.

"The Creator is playing a dangerous game," Abaddon mutters, rubbing a hand along his sharp jawline. "To what end? To see us all united in Heaven again? Forgive me, but I will not surrender my freedom on Earth to be His slave again."

"I think—" I hesitate, unsure if I'm supposed to speak or if anyone even cares what I think. I might be an angel—and possibly the Savior the prophecy spoke of—but I'm not a leader, and no one here ever asked for my opinion.

I swallow under the weight of every eye in the room.

"Go on, Daughter," Lucifer encourages, lightly touching my arm. "You are involved more than any of us, so if you have something on your mind, you should say it."

My teeth begin to worry my lower lip, but I catch the movement, not wanting to give the impression of weakness around such powerful beings—especially when the fate of the world rests on my shoulders.

Be brave, Luna, I chide myself.

"I think He just wants to see us all get along," I say, relieved my voice remains steady. "For the rift between our kind to be healed. Obviously, I don't know what He's *actually* thinking, but the Fall happened hundreds of thousands of years ago. Maybe He just wants to make amends."

Abaddon responds with a dubious laugh. "You are naive if you think such old wounds can be healed."

"Well, not with that attitude, they won't," Caleb mutters.

The Archdemon's orange eyes blaze like fire, and he glares at Caleb as if determined to burn him—to sear holes in his skin for his insolence. His mouth peels back in a snarl, and he rises, but his movements are halted by a fearless Hammurabi, who stands as well and crosses to Caleb, placing a protective hand on his shoulder, even though the Archdemon could destroy him if they came to blows.

Still, he remains by Caleb's side, protective and unmoving. Uncle Hammurabi, indeed.

"You speak of old wounds," the Nephilim retorts, "and yet, you have served on the Council with Lights for many long years now, Abaddon. You have worked together despite the divide. For the sake of the future and the welfare of our young, I think we can all stand to do the same. We are all capable of tolerance, at the very least."

"We are capable of more than that, King," my father agrees. "I, for one, am ready to put past hurts away." As he says this, he looks at Gabriel, his eyes on her face almost leering in their intensity, making no effort to hide the affection in his gaze. Although I witnessed glimpses of tenderness between them before—flickering remnants from the love they once shared—it shocks me to see him showing it so openly now, especially after how heated he got yesterday when we spoke of Gabriel's reasoning for keeping me locked away.

Then again, their rooms here are linked. Maybe they worked on their issues behind closed doors when I was no longer present.

"So, what's the plan?" Caleb presses, and when no one immediately answers, he lets out an exasperated huff. "I'm all for us holding hands and singing *Kum Ba Yuh* like some Whos on Christmas morning, but seriously, what's our strategy for dealing with my gramps? Because while we sit here clucking like a bunch of old hens, you can be sure as shit he's thinking about his next move."

"The Conqueror is past thinking," a familiar voice grunts, and my nose wrinkles at the sudden stink of smoke and sulfur flooding the space. Searching for the source of both, I shift on the sofa, my eyes widening when I catch sight of the small figure entering the room from the same dark patch of shadow Abaddon emerged from before.

Beelzebub hobbles into the light, one ice-blue eye swollen shut and blood oozing from a wound in his shoulder. A female Dark Nephilim with frosty white hair is beside him, and at first, I think she's helping him walk, until I realize it's his arm around her waist and not the other way around.

"The next move has been made," the Archdemon rasps, and I watch in stunned shock as my father and Abaddon both launch off the sofa. Caleb and I mimic the movement, jumping to our feet.

"Beelzebub!" my father shouts at the same moment Abaddon cries out, "Beele!"

Beelzebub stumbles, his fair skin black with soot stains, his clothes scorched and completely incinerated in places. The Nephilim beside him doesn't look to be in much better shape. If anything, she looks worse. Far worse.

"What happened?" Abaddon growls as Beelzebub moves the injured Nephilim to the sofa. Once she's deposited on the cushions, he straightens and looks up at my father.

"War is upon us, Lucifer." He grimaces then, and to my horror, a tear slides down his cheek, cutting through thick smears of blood and ash. "And Ashkelon…" he breathes, his youthful voice trembling. "Ashkelon burns."

SIX

CALEB

MY JAW TRIES TO connect with the floor as Beelzebub's words echo throughout the room. There's an honest-to-Creator tear running down his face. That freaks me out more than anything because Mighty B doesn't strike me as the emotional type. The Dark Nephilim tagging along with him reeks of smoke, and she's injured, her face wan, her breathing erratic. She clutches her chest and leans against the cushions, eyes shutting. I glance around, noticing everyone's face is a mask of shock. Considering I'm surrounded by beings who have seen some shit in their time, I know this is bad. Really bad. Ashkelon is gone. I can't believe Alexander would destroy a *school*. All that history gone. Ashkelon goes back to the time of Canaan. Did any of the other teachers get out? And what about the poor Nephilim kids? He wouldn't murder kids, would he? That goes against his whole savior MO.

"Even Gramps can't be that fucking crazy," I say aloud, drawing everyone's attention. "Why? What does this gain him? And what about the students? The teachers?"

The miniature Archdemon's darkness gathers around him like a cloud of wraiths, concealing the angelic blood dripping from his wounded shoulder. Rage practically lights his eyeballs up. "There is no line your grandfather won't cross, boy. He sent his followers and his loyal hound, that bitch, Ishtar, to take the students." Well, at least he didn't kill the kids.

Beelzebub's eyes land on Lilith, blue depths practically spitting fire when he registers her presence. Then he stills, as if he understands what her being here must mean. He shoots an accusing look at the ex-Archdemon. "*You*. This is your fault," he hisses. "Ashkelon used to belong to you. He's making a statement with its destruction. He's punishing you for your disloyalty.”

Lilith's posture stiffens, and she delivers a world-class fuck-you glare to the Archdemon forever locked in a pre-teen body. “You're a fool if you think this is the only school he'll destroy. Yes, he's making a statement. Nothing the Council has built is safe from him. He can and *will* conquer all. And he'll take our precious children and mold them in his image.”

“Let us not forget the weapons he's sure to have taken as well from the Fall,” Lucifer says darkly and I flinch.

“And it's not like we can make more,” I mutter, and Luna jerks her head toward me, her brow arched in question, bewilderment etched across her face. “The knowledge to make angel-killing steel and the armor to protect against it was lost after the Fall. No one has ever been able to replicate it. Who knows why? Maybe the Creator made us forget so we wouldn't fight anymore. Fuck all good that did since we're going to war. If Alexander gets those weapons, we are seriously fucked.”

Her eyes round with fear and she glances at her mother and father, as if waiting for confirmation of my words.

“He still has to find the bloodlines to match the weapons,” Gabriel points out, her voice surprisingly soothing as her gaze slides between Lucifer and her daughter. The Messenger's icy demeanor is thawing and I wonder who's responsible. Lucifer or Luna? “We have a little time.” Those last words are directed at the Morningstar, and his shoulders relax a little.

Beelzebub scoffs. “Not that much time, Messenger. Since when did you become an optimist? Has motherhood softened you?” A warning growl escapes Lucifer's mouth, but Beelzebub just offers a condescending smirk. “The Conqueror doesn't only have Nephilim on his side, but a fleet of Fallen who desire nothing more than to possess their weapons once again.”

Well, shit. This *is* really bad. Baddie, bad, bad. A gasp tears from Luna's mouth, wretched and terrified. The room freezes at that pain-filled wail. My head whips toward her, and she clutches my arm, horrified eyes clashing with mine. She shakes her head over and over again, the motion jerky, her eyes like those of a cornered animal. My heart sinks. We've been working on her stability and making progress, but I feel like all that effort just ran off a cliff. I mean, yeah, what's going on sucks, but why is it triggering Luna?

Out of the corner of my eye, I see Gabriel and Lucifer take a step toward us, uncertainty lining their faces. Hammurabi huddles closer to us, eyes narrowed on Luna, his body tense as if he wants to beat somebody up for upsetting his flower, but he doesn't know who to punch.

I keep my voice soft, soothing. "What's up, Goldilocks? Talk to me."

She glances over at Gabriel before her eyes land back on my face. Guilt buries itself in her hazel gaze. "I—at the Serapeum, when Alexander first started talking to me, he showed me a vision of buildings burning. The schools. And you. You were burning, too. He said he was going to burn down the divide, but I thought he was being... I didn't think he was being literal." She shakes her head again. "Caleb, if I had known, I would've told you, but he played with my mind so much... I'm so stupid. I didn't think. This is my fault." Tears drench her cheeks, and I pull her into my chest.

"This is definitely not your fault," I tell her, keeping my voice firm, steady. "Gramps was majorly messing with your mind back then to serve his own ends. Hell, you were so brand-spanking new you didn't have a clue what he was showing you. Alexander is good at spotting his enemy's weakness and using it against them. You know that. You know how ruthless he can be." I stroke my hand down her back in a soothing sweep. My eyes lock with Gabriel, and I see fury burning in her dark stare. I think she'd like a chance to smite my grandfather again.

"Alexander is a seasoned warrior, Luna. You stood no chance against him. You bear no blame," Gabriel says, taking those last steps toward us and placing a tentative hand on Luna's head.

"And after everything the Council put you through, Daughter, I'm surprised you've remembered what he showed you at all," Lucifer adds, coming to stand next to Gabriel. I start to feel a little claustrophobic.

Beelzebub gives a derisive snort that has me seeing red. "Is there anything else you've neglected to tell us?" he demands, upper lip curved in a nasty sneer. "Speak up before more schools burn."

I want to punch the little asshole in the face. Repeatedly. Hammurabi's angry hiss tells me he's right behind me in line.

Lucifer whirls on Beelzebub, wings flaring from his back, and the potential for violence sizzles along my skin. Luna burrows into my chest like she wants to disappear at the forever tween's scathing words while Gabriel turns fiery eyes on the Archdemon, and even stoic Abaddon appears surprised. The other six Fallen tense, eyes darting back and forth between the bigger players. Kali wisely backs up from the confrontation, maintaining a minimum safe distance.

Lilith just gives a venomous chuckle. "Careful, little one, or the Morningstar will finish the job Alexander started."

Inky darkness spills from Beelzebub. "Pardon me, wife of Adam, did you just have your school set aflame? Did you just witness loyal Nephilim getting cut down as your students were stolen by a madman? No? Then kindly fuck off."

"Don't you mean my school?" Lilith says, inspecting her nails.

Beelzebub's smile is vicious. "Oh, yes, *your* school. Before you betrayed us all and got your wings cut off for backing the wrong horse. Tell me, Lilith, are your wounds still tender?"

I barely have time to gasp before Lilith has her hands around Beelzebub's throat, and he coils his darkness around her neck, squeezing. She releases a hand and jabs her nails into his wounded shoulder. He gives a harsh grunt and backhands her, sending her flying away from him. I'm torn between disgust and awe at the display. These are our *allies*? It's so nice to see they're being grown-ups and getting along.

Lilith springs to her feet like a jungle cat, only this time Lucifer is there to restrain her. "Enough," he hisses at them.

Abaddon now leans over Beelzebub's shoulder, his orange eyes bright in the lingering darkness. He really does resemble the Nubian kings who used to rule Egypt.

"Warring amongst ourselves hardly serves our purpose," his deep voice rumbles.

Beelzebub pulls his power back, leaving the room brighter. He straightens. "Forgive my display of emotion. I've had a taxing day." His eyes flick to Luna, who now sobs quietly against my chest. "Though I may have been…harsh, Luna needs to tell us everything Alexander showed her, so we can save our schools."

"Hey, give her a minute. She's been through some shit," I growl, tightening my arms around Goldilocks.

"She'll answer our questions later when she's not so distraught," Gabriel says, narrowing her eyes at Beelzebub.

"The flower is delicate right now," Hammurabi interjects in a withering tone.

"We're all distraught, and coddling her now won't do any of you any good, especially her," Beelzebub counters. "If she can't contribute to our efforts, then hide her away again. For her sake and yours because she'll serve as a distraction that will get you killed."

That's about enough of that. "Okay, jackass—"

"Don't speak about my daughter that way," Lucifer booms, advancing on the mini Archdemon who, to his credit, holds his ground.

Luna pushes away from me, hard, the abrupt motion causing me to sway. She's a helluva lot stronger than she looks. All that angel strength.

"Stop!" Luna screams, wiping her cheeks with the backs of her hands. "Father, just stop. He's right."

Stunned amazement wipes the Morningstar's face clean of rage, and my jaw sways in the breeze for a moment before I find my voice. "Like hell he is," I snarl. "Goldilocks—"

She holds up a slender hand. "I know I'm not the poster child for stability right now, but I have to learn to be part of the team, or I *am* a distraction to you all. A liability. We can't do what we need to do to defeat Alexander if you're all constantly worried about me." Luna takes a deep breath, lips trembling. I want to bite her lips then kiss them better. "And I have to learn to…share more. I'm not used to having people to share with." Her chuckle holds bitterness, and I see Gabriel flinch out of the corner of my eye.

Lucifer is the very embodiment of pride as he stares at his daughter. "You're made of steel, Daughter. Never doubt it."

Luna gifts him with a soft smile stitched with love. If I thought he was pride personified before, he now wears a golden glow at his daughter's tender expression. I sneak a glance at Gabriel, whose mouth pulls down. I guess it sucks when your kid so obviously has a favorite.

"I wish I could give you more details, tell you what school he plans to attack next, but he wasn't that specific. He just showed me our world on fire," Luna says, chin up, eyes steady on Beelzebub. "He said the divide must be destroyed, and I guess that's what he thinks he's doing. And now, you know everything I do."

"Why would he show you your lover burning?" Beelzebub questions, his eyes tapered into dubious slits.

A blush creeps over her cheeks at the word "lover," and I suppress a grin. We're not lovers. Yet. "To manipulate me into helping him. He knew how much I cared about Caleb, even then," she replies.

Warmth fills my chest. Warmth with a shot of guilt. I know Goldilocks and I are cool now, but it doesn't mean I've forgotten how I lied to her. Her eyes drift to mine, and I let her see how much she means to me. It's uncomfortable being this vulnerable, but it's worth it, especially when I see my love reflected back at me.

Beelzebub rolls his eyes, snorting. "Save me from young love. Though, grandson of the Conqueror, he may want to burn you in truth now."

I shrug, not caring anymore that Gramps wants to kill me. "There's certainly no love lost between us. It's not like he hasn't tried to fry my brains before."

"Your family is more dysfunctional than most," the little Archdemon agrees, and I almost like him for the understatement.

"If Alexander plans to attack all the schools, we alone can't stop him," Abaddon says. "We don't have the numbers."

Lucifer gives a grim nod and looks at Gabriel, whose expression is equally dark. "No, we don't. And we can't allow Alexander to take more children. Or more weapons." He then turns to Lilith, mouth compressed in a thoughtful frown. "You do realize what must be done?" He sighs as she stiffens. "Come, Lilith, we all voted to take your wings in punishment, and yet you're here with us. You haven't tried to kill me—yet."

Beelzebub looks between them, his eyes widening. "Ahhh," he says. "Of course."

"Indeed," Gabriel replies.

I glance between them all as Abaddon and the other Fallen slowly nod. Hammurabi scowls, but looks resigned, and Kali just releases a weary sigh, like she knows what's coming, but thinks it's a terrible idea. Well, I wish they'd share with the rest of the class. I hate feeling like the only dumbass who doesn't get the joke. Luna snuggles next to me again and raises her eyes to mine in question. I just shake my head.

I wave my hand in the air. "Hey, the babies over here are clueless. Care to catch us up?"

"Yes, I thought we just agreed information must be shared," Luna says, and I'm proud of the bite in her voice.

Lilith pins me with her glare. "The Morningstar is suggesting we bring in the Council to help us deal with Alexander."

"The Council who just imprisoned me?" Luna protests, a tremor racking her frame, and I grasp her hand tightly.

"We can't fight both the Conqueror *and* the Council," Lucifer tells her. "Right now, our interests and the Council's align. We both want to stop Alexander, and we need each other to do it." He gently extracts Luna from me, and I reluctantly release her. He takes her into his arms. "And I promise you, Luna, they'll never put you in a cage again."

"So, the old 'the enemy of my enemy is now my friend' bullshit?" I ask, crossing my arms over my chest. I'm sure Mammon will just love seeing me again.

"We must deal with one problem at a time. This is the best way," Gabriel says, her eyes retreating from Luna and meeting Lilith's. "You know it is, dear friend."

"I agree," Beelzebub says. "The burning of the schools will spur the Council into action."

"So, are we all in agreement?" Abaddon asks, gazing around the room.

A chorus of "ayes" ripple across the space until only Lilith is left. "Yes, I agree," she finally says, her full lips twisting as if she's just ingested poison.

A hand lands on my shoulder. "Don't worry too much, boy. They can't be any worse than staying with your grandfather," Hammurabi says, but his words offer little comfort.

SEVEN

LUNA

WORRY BITES AT ME like teeth on my skin as I stare through the window at the gardens below, my eyes fixating on the bountiful plant life in desperate search for a distraction. Vines creep over stone, taking root in the foundation through even the smallest cracks they find, like the invasive thoughts in my head always seem to find the cracks in my sanity. Shuddering, I rub my hands along my upper arms and squeeze, hugging my torso to hold myself together—the panic in my chest inflating with every breath, a balloon about to burst.

The decision is made. We're going to approach the Council, which means facing my captors again…as well as the very real possibility of reimprisonment should our meeting with them go sideways. Sure, I'll have my parents with me this time, along with some powerful allies to protect me, but the Council outnumbers us in strength. Not to mention, certain members will undoubtedly be seeking their pound of flesh after what happened during my escape.

Another shudder rips through me at the memory of Mammon's eyes—shifting from the lie of Alexander's contrasting ones back into their true crimson hue—his howl of fury and pain a lingering echo in my ears, scratching at my composure like nails on a chalkboard. As terrified as I am for myself at the prospect of seeing the Council again, I'm frightened for Caleb even more. He didn't just help to release Alexander, he broke me out of the Council's prison and cut off an Archdemon's wing. As much as I keep telling myself my parents would shield him—would treat him as an extension of me—I know these actions will not be forgiven, and there will be little they can do should the Council insist he pay for his crimes. What if the

Council demands Caleb's life in return for asking for their aid? Regardless of their promise to accept him—to accept our love—would my parents hand him over for the chance to ensure a future for their daughter? I want to believe they wouldn't ever hurt me that way. But I also know the lengths Gabriel has gone to in the past and would go to yet again if it meant protecting me.

Swallowing past the rising lump in my throat, I shake that thought away. I wish we didn't have to go. I wish we could stay here forever, safe and undisturbed in this beautiful refuge. But I know that's not an option—not when Alexander continues to put other celestial lives at risk. It's only a matter of time before he finds us...or tears the world apart trying.

Ashkelon burning is an image in my head I can't escape. Although I've never seen the school—and can't pick it out from the images Alexander forced into my head—I imagine it as if I were actually there, my stomach twisting as guilt encroaches behind that ceaseless worry about meeting the Council. Back at the Serapeum, Alexander showed me his plan—he *showed* me he wanted to set fire to the academies and I...I did nothing about it. I didn't tell anyone. I didn't warn anyone.

And because of that, I'm as responsible for this chaos as he is, regardless of what my parents or Caleb think.

A hand brushes my shoulder, making me jump, and turning, I find Caleb standing behind me as if he somehow materialized from my thoughts, the liquid-like depths of his brown eyes scorching.

"You okay, Goldilocks? I didn't think it was possible to sneak up on an angel."

I force a small smile and shrug. "Just thinking."

"You're worried." Reaching up, he grazes a thumb over my cheek. "Your mouth gets all pinched whenever you're worried."

"Aren't you?" I breathe, trying not to let my voice wobble.

Exhaling, he retracts his hand from my face and redirects his fingers to his hair, brushing the thick locks back from his forehead. "Honestly? And I hope this doesn't tarnish my image too much as the coolest guy in the room, but I'm shitting bricks over here."

A smirk pulls at my lips. "Well, you're the only guy in the room, so..."

He huffs out a laugh but says nothing.

Silence swells between us like a physical force; if I were to extend a hand, I'm certain I'd be able to touch it. The claustrophobic sensation it stirs within me reminds me far too much of the Council's cage—of near invisible walls and an endless landscape on the other side, taunting freedom and eternal confinement simultaneously. Because beyond those walls, there was nowhere to go, and that's how I feel again now. Like we're stuck in one frozen moment when all I want is to go back to our usual banter and not have this constant terror hanging over our heads like a guillotine, the blade always one second from falling.

My eyes scan over Caleb's features, and although he's much better at hiding it than I am, I can read the fear on his face. I can sense what he's afraid of as clearly as if he said it in words.

Reaching up to cup his cheek, I say, "I won't let Mammon hurt you. I promise."

What good is being an angel if I can't use this strength and power to protect the person I love? Caleb has always been there for me, has risked the wrath of Alexander and the Council for my freedom, and now, it's my turn to be there for him—to ensure he makes it out of the coming war alive, even if it means sacrificing my immortal existence for his mortal one. I don't want to think of a future where we aren't together, but if the cost for him surviving is my life, then it's a price I will happily pay.

An unfamiliar pain I've never seen before flashes across his face, which contorts into an expression that's somewhere between a frown and a grimace. Grabbing my hand, he gently pulls it away. "That's not all I'm afraid of."

My pulse picks up speed at his casual dismissal of my touch, and I shake my head, confused. "If you're worried about the Council imprisoning me—"

"It's not just that," he interrupts, the words soft. There's a strange edge to his tone that knots my stomach.

A million questions race through my head when he doesn't elaborate, and as the silence stretches again, I'm overcome by the sickening temptation to break into his mind—to reach inside his skull and pull out whatever thoughts he's so reluctant to voice. But I don't. I couldn't.

I wouldn't, I vow. Because I am not Alexander, and I will not use force to get what I want.

Blowing out a strained breath through his nose, Caleb finally puts me out of my misery. "Yesterday, after you spoke with your parents, your dad came here to talk to me."

"Oh," I mutter, not quite sure what to make of that. "Why didn't you tell me before?"

A sheepish look crosses his face. "I've been processing what he said, but now, with us leaving soon to meet the Council and everything so up in the air..." His eyes bore into mine, piercing, and the words that follow are equally sharp. "We need to talk about it, Luna."

We need to talk. How many times have I heard those words in my life? How many times did they preface the decision to abandon me—to thrust me back into a system determined to see that I would remain alone? How many times have they made me feel like I'm not worth fighting for? Like I'm unworthy of love?

Is that what this is? Is Caleb giving me up?

Did I get my parents back only to lose him in the process?

I blanch, feeling suddenly unsteady, like the whole world might tip to the side and throw me off into space, gravity be damned.

"Are you…" My throat thickens. "Are you breaking up with me?"

"What?" Eyes going wide, he reaches for me, his fingertips searing into my skin as his hands flatten on both sides of my face. When he next speaks, his voice is a growl. "*No*, Goldilocks. Never—"

"Then what is it?" I demand, hysteria creeping into my voice. As much as I'm trying to keep it together, I'm on the brink of freaking out. "What did he say to you?"

His fingers tremble against my cheeks. "I love you, you hear me? And I want nothing more than to get through all this bullshit with Gramps and the Council and spend a million lifetimes with you. But…" My heart buckles at that word.

"We'd love to help you, but…"

"We can see how hard you're trying, but…"

"We know what we said, but…"

But…

How many times have I been fed false hope for that single word to then rip it away?

"But what?" I rasp when he doesn't continue.

Caleb winces. "But…as much as I wish that, we're temporary. One day, sooner or later, I'll die, and you…" He shakes his head. "You won't."

I suck in a startled breath, unprepared for this conversation and hating that our current circumstances are forcing us to have it. Caleb's mortality has crossed my mind a few times, but never like this—never as an immediate problem to be solved. I suppose I assumed it was something we'd talk about eventually, but not yet. Not so soon into our relationship when our time together is only beginning.

"You say that like it's something we need to worry about right now." I gesture vaguely toward the doorway. "Look at Hammurabi. Look at Alar—" My chest tightens, and I stop myself before his name can fully form on my lips. Pushing past the pain in my heart, I continue, unashamed of the pleading note to my tone. "Look at any of the Nephilim we know who have walked this earth for *thousands* of years. We have so much time."

Do you? that unwelcome voice of doubt taunts me. *The Council may kill one or both of you, and if they don't, Alexander will certainly try.*

"Maybe," Caleb mutters, averting his gaze. "But do you want to spend thousands of years with me only to spend thousands more mourning my death?" He looks back up at me and leans in, his voice low. "I will take however long I can get with you, Goldilocks. Ten years. Ten decades. Hell, I would take ten minutes with you if the alternative was nothing. Nothing will ever make me leave your side…unless you tell me to go."

"But I'm not telling you to go!" I shriek.

"I know," he says, nodding. "I know. But you need to understand what awaits us at the end of this. Because as much as I wish otherwise…we have an expiration date, baby. And as much as I want to be selfish and say fuck it, I can't knowing that it might hurt you. I would rather die now than leave you with that kind of grief because I know how much it would hurt me if the roles were reversed."

I claw at his hands, feeling the heat of his skin under my fingertips. "You say you'll take any time you can get with me… Can't you see I feel the same?"

Agony paints his face, his frown deepening. "I just don't want you to feel trapped. Talking with your dad made me realize it isn't about what I want. It's about what you need, and you need to know you have options. I need you to know you always have a choice."

A choice? As if I could ever envision a world where I wouldn't choose to be with Caleb.

"And you think us being together isn't my choice?"

He considers me for a moment then shrugs. "After everything you told me about the Creator, I started thinking… If Lilith is right and He *was* the one who placed you in the human world, then what else is He responsible for? You said it yourself—all signs point to Him wanting you to release Alexander and trigger the prophecy, which means He also planned for us to meet. And if that's the case, then chance didn't bring us together, fate did, and I…"

Hearing my own conclusions spewed back at me this way, from Caleb's perspective, is like a knife twisting in my gut. The realization forming in my head only sinks the blade deeper. "You're worried your feelings for me aren't down to free will?"

Free will means everything to Darks—to Caleb—and if he believes what we have is in direct contradiction to that, then where does that leave us? Could he continue to love me willingly if he thought he never had a choice in the matter?

A strained laugh parts his lips. "For the first time in my life, I don't actually care.

I'll take these feelings, regardless of where they came from, and I'll hold onto them for as long as I live. I meant it when I said I would take any time with you I could get. But you…Luna, you have forever. I just want you to be happy. *Always*. Even if that happiness isn't with me."

Anger tears through me, hot and fierce. Anger that Caleb could ever doubt my devotion to him. Anger that my father's words and the Creator's manipulations—however well-intentioned both might have been in the grand scheme of things—tangled together to poison him with such thoughts.

"Listen to me," I say slowly, "because I'm only going to say this once. The Creator might have drawn us together, but there isn't a single possible scenario where He could have *made* me love you. Don't you think if He had that kind of power, He would've stopped Lucifer from rebelling?"

Hope flickers behind Caleb's eyes, and I see his will to fight this—to be selfless when I would rather he be anything but—wavering just a little.

"I love you because of you," I persist. "Because I *want* to love you, not because fate or some deity neither of us have ever seen forced these feelings on me. And since what I said yesterday didn't convince you, let me say it again: regardless of what awaits at the end of this, I will always choose us…even if we don't have forever. I *love* you, and I would rather spend one Nephilim lifetime together than never be with you at all." I curl my fingers around his in a vise grip, willing him to hear me. To believe me. "I'm not afraid of your mortality, Caleb."

"Luna…" He exhales my name, muttering the word like a wish, and this time, when silence rises between us again, it's filled with a mutual desire and need that neither of us can ignore any longer. And understanding.

Understanding that we are meant to be together, and this love is our choice.

Stepping back, he tugs me away from the window, our eyes clashing as he brushes one hand against the side of my neck, his touch a kiss of skin on skin as it trails from the nape of my hairline to the dip in my collarbone, mere inches from my racing heart.

The caress of his fingertips sends a shiver rocketing through me, and it takes all the willpower I possess to not leap at him and attack his mouth with mine. To give into the animalistic urges inside me and take what I've wanted since the very first moment I saw him. His lips part, his tongue darting out to lick across the lower one, withering my restraint and tempting me closer.

An almost primal, base desperation pushes all inhibition and nervousness I might otherwise be feeling aside, leaving only the deep love and yearning I feel for him. I'm done wasting time not taking what I want, and I'm sure Caleb feels that way, too, especially when we have no idea what will happen moving forward. We might not get another chance if we don't seize this moment.

The column of his throat shifts when he swallows, and his dark eyes gaze down into mine, hooded and heady with the same lust rushing through me, overtaking every one of my senses. Lust we've both kept at bay for too long.

But no longer.

"I choose you," I murmur. Then rising onto my toes, I close the distance between us, slanting my lips over his. A perfect fit, as if we were put on this planet and molded to always come together. His arms snake around my torso, drawing me closer, and as his fingers travel upward, skimming under the straps of my tank top, I slide a hand under his shirt, teasing at the waist of his pants. His body buckles slightly and he lets out a strangled breath, pulling away just enough to look at me.

"We have time," he breathes, and I relish the sentiment, though I don't know if I believe it. I want to, but reality might have other ideas, as will Alexander. "We don't have to—"

I press a finger to his lips. "I want to."

His pupils blow wide as I slink backward, and hands shaking, I pull the tank top over my head before dropping it to the floor at my feet. Standing before him this way, I'm exposed, and as his attention falls to my chest, my cheeks flush, but I'm not embarrassed. I *want* him to look at me. To see me in this vulnerable way no one else has ever seen me before. To know that I want to give myself to him completely, now and for forever.

After appraising me for a moment, he reaches out and drags a knuckle along my side, a smile teasing the edges of his lips when I shudder. "You are so beautiful." The words are a throaty purr, and drawing me back into his embrace, he kisses me with fervor, every slide of his tongue against mine pitching me deeper into a euphoric haze I don't ever want to emerge from.

My hands reach out to grip the hem of his shirt, and when our lips break apart, I yank it over his head. I falter for a moment, appreciating the sight of his sleek muscles and the way the shadows of his aura dance across his bronzed skin in anticipation, begging me to touch him again. I comply, relishing the soft exhalation escaping him as I run my fingertips along his chest. Unable to contain myself any longer, I press a kiss to every single spot my fingers touch, eager to mark him. To claim him.

To make the world know he is mine.

Dragging his fingers through my hair, he lures my mouth back up to his, one big hand cupping my breast as his lips trail biting kisses along my jaw and throat. Then bending down, he hooks his arms under my legs and lifts me, pivoting until my back is facing the bed. Crossing the room in two great strides, he deposits me on the mattress, and I lie back against the blanket as he crawls over me on all fours, his black hair falling into his eyes as he once again looks down at me, taking in every inch of my naked torso. Bending down, he presses a feather-light kiss to the top of my stomach, and a sound that's half gasp and half giggle bursts from me unbidden.

Peeking up at me through thick lashes, he smirks. "Are you ticklish, Goldilocks?" I can't find the words to answer before he's kissing me in the same spot again, then lower, even more gently than before. Then lower again. With every kiss, my giggles lessen until the only sounds leaving me are near-silent and ragged.

When he reaches the waist of my jeans, he unfastens the button and hooks his thumbs into the belt loops before carefully tugging the denim down my legs, the scratch of the material against my skin an assault on my already overstimulated senses. I hear the low thud of the pants pooling on the floor after a moment, and I'm acutely aware of their absence as his lips graze my knees, my thighs, my hip bones, moving ever closer to where the heat building inside me is strongest.

"Caleb," I gasp, not even sure why I'm saying his name.

In the space of a breath, he's leaning over me again, his face close to mine and expression serious. All manner of teasing is gone from his tone when he asks, "Do you want me to stop?"

I jerk my head, too flustered to form a coherent thought.

He peers down at me for a moment, examining my face with intent as if checking to see if I'm really okay with us taking this next step. If only he knew how much I want this—want *him*. But I don't trust myself to say the right words, so instead, I press up onto my forearms and kiss him again, letting him know what I want with my actions instead of my voice.

He moans into my mouth when I raise a hand and brush it over his abdomen, dangerously close to his waistband, but the heat of his skin disappears all too quickly as he inches backward off the bed. I stare up at him where he looms over me, chest heaving, watching with wide-eyed wonder as he unfastens the button on his jeans.

As he frees himself, my gaze dips to his obvious arousal, and my cheeks heat further.

Climbing onto the bed again, he slides an arm under my back, pulling my chest flush to his. "We can stop at any time. Just say the word."

"What word?" I ask, breathless.

Caleb chuckles, dropping his forehead to my chest for a moment before peeking up at me, his own cheeks rosy. "I was thinking a simple no would suffice. But if you must know, my safe word is unicorn."

I snort. "Unicorn?"

"Mmhmm." He leans in, brushing the tip of his nose against mine before licking across the seam of my lips ever so gently, as if asking permission to kiss me again—to slip inside and claim me the same way my body is dying to claim his.

I open my mouth for him, and as I swallow his kiss, he slides a hand over my thigh, making my insides quiver. When he touches me, I gasp and he devours the sound, kissing me deeply. But soon, his touches alone aren't enough. I want more. I *need* more.

I want him more than I need air to breathe.

"I'm ready," I whisper against his lips.

He draws back to look at me. "I love you," he rumbles, his voice thick. He clears his throat. "More than anything."

I smile at him, unable to contain my elation knowing we've finally put all doubt behind us, and the next time he kisses me, we join in a way we haven't before, his movements slow and careful, part pleasure and part pain. It's the most overwhelming sensation I've ever experienced, and with every touch, I feel undone, like I might explode if I don't find a release. The feeling is both stifling and exhilarating, and the nerve endings in my body all scream in unison, begging for more. More stimulation. More heat.

More Caleb.

For the first time since finding myself in this world of celestial beings, I can picture what Heaven must be like and I know this is it for me. Here, lost in the warmth of his arms, where I am happy and loved. Nothing will ever be better than this. Nothing will ever compare. And in this moment, I know I would give up my wings if it meant never having to live a single day without him. If it meant I could live a mortal life with him rather than an immortal one where he won't always be with me.

Tears slip from between my closed lids. Everything Caleb said about the future has evoked a fear I wasn't quite ready to face and a dread that this thing we have together will be but a blink of an eye in the endless tides of my existence. I hate myself for thinking it, for ruining this perfect moment with such distant worries, especially after my own protestations about not caring about his mortality.

And yet, I can no longer ignore the reality that time will eventually tear us apart. That one day Caleb will die and this love—this sweet, beautiful bliss—will be gone.

Stifling a sniffle, I bury my face in his neck and rest a hand against his side, determined to savor every moment we have. However fleeting they might be.

"Am I hurting you?"

It takes me a moment to realize Caleb has stopped moving, and when I lean my head back to look at his face, apprehension floods the dark depths of his gaze.

"You're crying—"

I shake my head, squeezing my eyes shut. "I'm just…"

Scared. I'm just scared.

Scared of losing this.

Caleb grips my chin with his forefinger and thumb when I try to turn my face away, keeping me still. "Luna, look at me," he pleads, and at the trepidation in his voice, I open my eyes, glancing up at his worried face through my tears. The intensity of his gaze makes my stomach flip flop. "We can stop whenever you want—"

"No!" I nearly shout. "Please," I beg when he begins to pull away, my hands grasping at his back, holding his body to mine. "I don't want to stop. Really."

Brow furrowing, he sweeps an errant strand of sweaty hair behind my ear. His thumb lingers on my cheek, grazing the skin, then moves to my chin again, pressing firmly. "Then what is it?" he asks, his breath hot on my lips.

A tear dashes from the corner of my eye.

I love you so much I never want this to end, and my heart hurts knowing that one day it will. That I'm powerless to keep you with me.

That's not true, that small voice reminds me, and I shiver with revulsion at the picture forming in my thoughts of Caleb's father right after I killed him. At the memory of how Alexander then resurrected him as if it was nothing. Another image follows the first, reminding me what I'm capable of.

The moth in the Serapeum.

No. I shiver again. *I won't do that.*

Why not? the voice prods. *Then you won't have to lose him.*

But it wouldn't be him. Not really.

I don't dare utter these thoughts aloud, so instead, I say, "I love you. I just really, really love you."

A grin tugs at his cheeks. "You are the best thing that has ever happened to me, Goldilocks, you know that? And this…" With an airy laugh, he dips his head again, his sable hair brushing my chest. "You don't even know how fucking happy I am right now."

"Really?"

At my disbelieving tone, he raises his head, his eyes blazing with lust and love. "Yeah," he purrs, his grin widening. "You feel so good, I could seriously stay like this forever."

Forever.

That word knocks the air from my lungs and strips me bare of the pleasure I should be enjoying right now instead of this suffocating, premature grief. I don't want to feel this way. I don't want to mourn an eventuality so far in the future it's almost inconceivable. And yet, now that I've been forced to face it, I do.

I mourn it more than I mourn Alaric.

When my face falls, Caleb's smile disappears, as if he's realized his mistake. Shaking his head, he says, "I'm sorry. I didn't—"

"It's okay," I whisper. "I just got overwhelmed. I promise I'm not trying to ruin this."

"You aren't," he says. Then he leans down, pressing his mouth to my ear. "I love you. Nothing could ever ruin this." His next words are a tantalizing hum just loud enough for me to hear. "Now, let me show you how happy you make me."

He shifts his face, capturing my lips in a bruising kiss, then moves his hips again, setting every inch of my body on fire. Each slow, deliberate movement is ecstasy, driving me toward an unfamiliar brink. And as I lose myself to his touch, I let myself forget my fears, if only for a moment.

EIGHT

CALEB

GRITTING MY TEETH, I try to focus past how amazing Luna feels surrounding me. I always knew it would be good between us, but this torpedoes good. This is another level. I've never emotionally connected to someone like this before and certainly not during sex. I used to make fun of cheesy romance books going on about merging into one, sharing a soul, and all that horseshit. But I can feel her heartbeat, her every breath, every gasp. The fine tremor that ripples over her every time I move. And I can feel her pain mixed in with the pleasure. Not physical pain, but raw grief that's pushing through this moment. She's trying to process losing me, and I'm right here. That's not how our first time should be.

I want her to forget her own name until *my* name is all she remembers. I want her to exist in just this moment. And I think I know how to do that. I grip her hips and roll, placing her on top of me.

The sudden move lands her firmly in the present. She blinks wide eyes at me. I squeeze her delicious butt and grin.

"What are you—"

"Do you trust me?" I say, even though I know the answer.

"Of course, I do. You know that," she says, biting her lower lip as her eyes track down my chest.

"Then take what you want from me," I tell her, sliding my hands down her thighs and back up again. "Take control."

That's what this is about. Luna feels like everything in her life is beyond her control. She's caught up in some bullshit prophecy, designated to be a savior, and she didn't

HAVE YOUR WICKED WAY WITH ME.

ask for any of it. Now, with my mortality messing with her head, there's another element to add to the list of things she has no say over.

A blush stains her cheeks and streaks downward until it paints her beautiful breasts a pale cherry. Mmm. My eyes dash up to meet hers, and I let her see how much I want her.

"I don't know how to," Luna whispers.

"Yes, you do. You've imagined it a thousand times. I know you have because I think about you like this all the time." I smirk. "Have your wicked way with me."

It's as if my words free something inside her. Her wings burst from her back, swooping around us. I shudder as the velvety feathers brush my skin. She clenches my wrists and bends over me, placing my hands by my head. Her mouth fuses with mine as she begins to move her hips. Experimentally at first, then faster, her movements frantic. I groan inside her mouth. She feels too fucking amazing.

She releases my lips and falls back, her pupils swallowing the hazel of her irises.

Panting, she says, "Help me, Caleb."

I know exactly what she wants. I sit up and tangle one hand in her hair and kiss her again, the other hand sliding between us. She grinds against me as I move my mouth to run my tongue along her neck, her chest, and back to her lips while my fingers dance. Her moans are the sweetest music. She's not quite there yet, and I grit my teeth to hold on. No way am I coming before her.

My eyes open, snagging on her wings. I slide my hand up her stomach, causing her to whimper in dismay. My other hand slides from her neck and she cries out when my fingers sink into the luxurious feathers of her wings and caress the upper curve of muscle. My touch is firm, and she arches against me, crying out again as tremors rack her entire body. Her wings unfurl to their full span, pewter feathers glistening. A soft, golden glow encases her entire body, like the beginning of a sunrise. I growl and finally let go, my vision washing white. Honest to fuck ringing fills my ears as all my senses are wiped out by the best orgasm of my life.

I fall back and she sinks against me, her feathers splayed over us like a blanket. I'm trying to catch my breath, and I feel her chest rise and fall rapidly against mine. "Jesus, baby, you killed me," I say, grinning when her head pops up and her eyes meet mine.

"You killed *me*," she gasps as a flush colors her cheeks.

I shut my eyes against temptation and squeeze her against me. "We killed each other," I amend and feel her shift, her lips brushing mine in a tender caress.

"Thank you," she whispers, and my eyes pop open once more. She's so goddamn sexy when she's satisfied, her body all loose and pliant. Her eyes are clear and tender, missing the darkness that so often haunts her.

"For what?" I say, cupping her cheek.

"For making this perfect," she answers, delivering a kiss into my palm. "For getting me out of my head."

"Goldilocks, it was never going to be anything but perfect between us," I say. "I was always going to make sure of that." The way we felt together…perfect doesn't cover it.

Then it hits me like a sledgehammer. I just came inside Luna without a fucking condom. Me, Mr. Safe Sex. Fuck. Noticing my frown, Luna tenses, and I smooth my thumb against her cheek, soothing her.

"What's wrong?" she asks, her eyes locked on mine.

"With the sex? Like I said before, perfect. You own my dick," I say, and a shocked giggle escapes her. I smile at the sound then sober. "I just realized that we didn't use protection," I admit, watching her face. Her eyes widen and she sits up, stunned, pulling away from me.

Luna shakes her head, her skin paling. "I didn't even…oh, my God, I…we can't…"

I sit up, too, and take her into my arms. "Good news is I doubt I knocked you up—I don't think. I mean, from what I've learned, Nephilim don't procreate easily with each other. That's why there are more human/Nephilim offspring. But we don't have a real big population, as you know. I'm not sure about angels, but I think the principle would hold. Anyway, best to ask your auntie Lilith. Whatever you do, don't ask Gabriel." My muscles tense as I imagine that conversation. "Though, she probably heard us and is plotting my death," I mutter and Luna turns red.

Then she relaxes a little and nods. "I'll ask Lilith about it as soon as I can." She blushes then at her eagerness, and I chuckle, chucking her under the chin.

"I knew it. I've created a sex fiend. I even made you glow," I tease, and her eyes go wide at that. Brushing a quick kiss across her lips, I say, "We just have to be careful, not celibate. But first, I need to be a gentleman." I gently untangle myself from her limbs as she looks at me with a questioning gaze.

Like all these ancient places, there's no shower, but I find a water basin and a clean cloth. I wring the cloth dry and return to bed. When Luna realizes what I'm about to do, her cheeks turn fiery.

"No, Caleb, I can do that myself," she shrieks in protest, hands trying to ward me off.

"You're cute when you're embarrassed, which considering what we just did, is hilarious," I say. "Stop that and let me take care of you."

I clean us both up, and my eyes assess her naked body with a predatory gleam. She's flawless. I legit wish she'd never put clothes on again. She stills at the hunger in my gaze, her chest rising and falling rapidly once more. Grabbing her ankles, I pull her toward the edge of the bed and sink to my knees.

"Caleb, what are you—" she gasps, clenching my shoulders.

I glance up at her. "I said we just have to be careful, not celibate. And I want to make you feel good again. Are you okay with that?" She didn't let me spend nearly enough time here before. At her shy nod, I growl, "Sit up a little so I can touch your wings."

Her pupils blown, she obeys, trembling. I lower my head as my hands snake up, my fingers burying themselves in silky softness. "Fuck," she says, moaning, and I grin against her skin.

NINE

LUNA

MY STOMACH IS A tangle of nerves as we walk along a dusty path lined with low-cut shrubbery, approaching a simple-looking rectangular building. Although somewhat unimpressive on the outside, the Queen's Bath in Hampi is exquisite and ornate on the inside. Covered walkways surround the four sides of a large sunken bath, decorated with beautiful arches and alcoves that form balconies over the empty space in the middle. It's now little more than a ruin turned tourist attraction, but once the structure would have been filled with water and used as a bathing spot for royalty.

Kali suggested the bathhouse as a neutral spot for our meeting with the Council due to its proximity to her home at Virupaksha Temple, should we need to make a quick escape back to our temporary hideout. We're too vulnerable on the Roads, which provide little cover were we to end up in another lengthy pursuit like what happened after Caleb broke me out of my prison and Mammon chased us across the globe. This way, in the event our gathering doesn't go as planned, we're close enough to flee on foot. Unlike the Roads, the real world has plenty of nooks and crannies to hide in.

The downside is that this meant Kali couldn't join us to avoid compromising our refuge since the Council keeps tabs on all the Fallen and Nephilim and where they reside in the world—a countermeasure in case they ever need to do any damage control and alter human minds, my mother explained. While the logic behind the decision made sense, I can't help wondering if the ancient Light was relieved to be sidelined from our impending confrontation. Even with my parents, Caleb, and a frowning Hammurabi accompanying me, I know I'd sit this one out if I could. But I can't. They're all involved because of me, and this war is only occurring at all because of my misguided actions. Because I let Alexander out of his tomb without really understanding what I was about to unleash on the world.

Granted, the Creator intended for that to happen, so I can't help feeling He should shoulder some of the blame, but He's not the one down here on Earth who needs to clean up the mess.

Swallowing, I step through one of the archways lining the cloister forming the outer perimeter of the building and proceed down the narrow stone stairs into the spacious empty bath below. Overhead, the morning sun is blazing despite not even being at its highest point in the sky yet, and sweat prickles my skin, though I'm not sure if that's down to the oppressive heat or the fear gripping me—likely the latter since the other angels and Fallen present seem unaffected by the sky-rocketing temperature. Come to think of it, I don't think I've seen my mother look so much as dewy. Perhaps, unlike certain other mortal needs that confinement in the Council's cage forced me to abandon, I'm stuck with this one lingering habit. Physical proof of the terror I can never quite shake.

Even now, that terror coils around my lungs like a snake as my eyes dart in every possible direction, searching the ruin for any sight of the Council, but there's no one here apart from our small party of five—not even mortals. Then again, it is the off-season for tourism and the humidity is atrocious.

Although Beelzebub and Abaddon are on our side, along with at least a handful of other Fallen, my father stressed that it was vital we don't give the Council any reason to think we're calling them here to declare war. This meeting is meant to result in a truce, not give them further reason to hunt us, and the best way to achieve the desired result is for Abaddon and Beelzebub to partake in this exchange from the side of the Council and speak up for us when the timing is right to turn the remaining members in our favor. As for Lilith and the six Fallen who arrived yesterday to declare their support, they're lingering somewhere nearby out of sight, just in case we need them. I hope it won't come to that.

"Are we ready?"

Lucifer's lilting voice draws my gaze, and I glance between him and my mother, who dips her chin, her expression and golden aura unwavering and resolute.

Behind me, Hammurabi grunts. "No time like the present and all that," he grumbles.

"Daughter?" Lucifer presses, his blue eyes burning with fatherly affection and concern. The shadows surrounding him writhe and dance, reaching out to me as much as the limits of their movements allow.

I try to swallow again, but my throat is almost painfully dry, the insides of my mouth gritty. It feels like I've been gargling sand, and I struggle to form a response as the snake around my lungs squeezes tighter.

Stepping in front of me, Caleb cups my face and bends down until his gaze is level with mine. When our eyes meet, I'm reminded of what we did last night, and the memory gets wrapped up in my panic until my body is a tempest of chaos and longing and heat, the emotions and sensations within me at war. "It'll be all right, Goldilocks," he murmurs. "I'm here. *We're* here. No one is going to take you again, I promise." His thumbs rub soothing circles on my cheeks, pushing down the inflating anxiety in my chest.

I drag in one deep breath then another, and on the third exhalation—the air pushing past trembling lips—I manage a weak but hopefully convincing nod. I turn my focus to my father, but he's no longer looking at me; he's looking at Caleb, envy written into the perfect contours of his face. There's approval there, too, but the jealousy is what I notice most, though it isn't malicious or resentful so much as sad, as if seeing Caleb comfort me is just another reminder of all the time and bonding we've missed out on as father and daughter. I wish I could find the words to tell him that he's important, too—that I *need* him, too. That while he might not be the prime pillar of support I lean on, he is becoming a vital part of my foundation—the base the rest of me relies upon to stay standing. If anything were to happen to him, stealing away that beautiful song connecting us, surely everything that makes me what I am would crumble to the ground in ruin. I already lost one father figure. I can't bear to lose another.

And the truth is, that's what frightens me most, not just about meeting with the Council, but about this whole ordeal with Alexander. The Gray already stole Alaric from me. Who else am I inevitably going to lose before this war is over?

Pushing that thought aside before it can cripple me, I clear my throat and say, "I'm ready."

Lucifer, shaken free from his own silent musings, rolls up one sleeve of his charcoal button-up shirt then gestures for us to stand behind him before pressing a fingertip to a pale white symbol branded into his forearm just beneath the crook of his elbow. Low mutterings breach his lips, and déjà vu ripples through me as I recall a similar moment under the Serapeum when my mother, wounded and bleeding out on the stone in front of Alexander's tomb, called out to my father the very same way. Even their tattoos are identical—thin crescent moons, barely visible against their fair flesh. Just like then, apprehension pools in my unsettled stomach like curdling milk.

And just like then, the Council is sure to come.

We don't have to wait long. A couple of minutes later, a burst of bright light floods the sunken bath and the first angel steps from the radiant depths of the Blessed Road into the scorching Indian sun. When the blinding light fades and the figure's features slide into focus, it takes all my self-restraint not to recoil.

"Uriel," my father purrs with a respectful bow of his head.

The Archangel's golden aura brims with contempt as he locks eyes with Lucifer, but he says nothing, instead redirecting his gaze over his shoulder when the entrance to the Blessed Road once again opens and five other Archangels emerge from its glowing maw. Behind them, I sense movement in the shadows of the cloister and note dark, looming shapes filling the archways above us, surrounding the empty bath on three sides. My eyes jump between the Archdemons, catching and hanging on Mammon as I search the faces above us for Abaddon and Beelzebub. The fear sweeping through me hardens like ice in my veins when I notice Mammon's crimson gaze is locked intently on Caleb, his upper lip curling back in a snarl. He looks furious and I shudder, consumed by the thought of what danger I've put Caleb in by bringing him here. He didn't have to come. He could've stayed behind with Kali or waited out in the wings like Lilith. He didn't need to be here, front and center, a target to the Archdemon's wrath.

But it isn't in Caleb's nature to cower in fear, and I know I couldn't have made him stay behind even if I tried. Not that it would've changed anything. Regardless of Caleb's presence here today, he stole something precious from Mammon, and I doubt a truce with the Council will stop the Archdemon from leaping at the first opportunity to make him pay for it. My wings bristle under my skin at the thought, thrumming with restrained power.

When that time comes, I'll make sure I'm ready.

Tilting my chin up, I inch closer to Caleb until I'm also in Mammon's line of sight, meeting his furious gaze with a scowl and glaring at him until he breaks our battle of stares with a disinterested scoff. Relief floods my system—as temporary as I fear it may be—and remembering the task at hand, I peer through the shadows once more, finally glimpsing Abaddon among the Council, his poker face firmly in place. Beelzebub, on the other hand, is nowhere to be seen—a fact that hasn't gone unnoticed by the others on the Council who raise curious eyebrows and mutter his name softly under their breath in question to each other. If I wasn't so certain of his loyalty to my father, I might wonder if his absence is a sign he intends to stab us in the back.

"Brothers, sisters, thank you for coming," my father says, tugging me away from such thoughts, his soothing voice echoing through the empty space.

The tapping of shoes against stone draws my gaze, and my stomach turns as I force myself to look at the angel who orchestrated my mental torture in the Council's prison. Mammon might've been the one in my head, tricking me with his many false faces, but it was Uriel who held his leash. He and he alone tried to use my worst fears against me as a bargaining chip.

Hands clamped loosely behind his waist, the Archangel steps toward my father. "I assume, Morningstar, that you have not called us here to surrender yourselves or your daughter?"

Lucifer lets loose a soft, breathy chuckle. "Wishful thinking on your part, I'm afraid." Although I can't see his face, I can picture the easy smile he must be wearing. The calm, collected poise and confidence of someone who isn't afraid.

Which, of course, only infuriates Uriel.

The Archangel's own expression darkens, but before he can say another word, one of the other Faithful steps forward. The man's skin and hair are a stark lily white—made brighter by his simmering golden aura—and his blue eyes are so pale in color they look almost gray, closer in hue to ice than the sea. His hands are fisted at his sides, and two red patches spread across his cheeks like blooming roses, staining his features with the evidence of his anger.

"Then tell us, Brother, why have you summoned us if not to surrender? Are you declaring war?"

"Of course not, Amenadiel," my father assures him. "My intention is to bring us all together, not drive us further apart."

"Together?" Amenadiel retorts. His upper lip quivers as he spits, "You have *betrayed* us. You have consorted with Gabriel—a *Light*—and actively worked to undermine our authority." His eyes cut to my mother then. "And *you*...the bearer of the prophecy. How righteous you have acted all these years when in reality you harbored such a filthy secret."

My mother reels back as if she's been slapped but Lucifer just snorts, raising his face to the sky, and whispers, "Consorted..." so softly I'm not sure the others hear it. But I hear it, along with the blatant disbelief constricting his tone. It squeezes the word with a sorrow and heartache that are reflected in the wavering darkness around him, which sags as if pulled down by a heavy weight, making the shadows almost look like they're weeping.

Chest rising and falling with a sigh, he looks back down at the other celestials. "Tell me, were we not all Lights once?" he asks. "Were we not, at one point, all the same?

This senseless division between our kind needs to end."

"Careful, Morningstar," Uriel warns, clicking his tongue. "You're beginning to sound an awful lot like Alexander."

"He is *nothing* like the Conqueror," Gabriel hisses. When she speaks, flashes of light crackle around her like bolts of electricity, and her irises glow an otherworldly orange I've never seen before. She marches forward, trying to push past my father toward Uriel, but Lucifer holds out an arm, stopping her.

She looks up at him, fury etched into her face like a chisel to stone, but he just shakes his head.

"Unlike Alexander, I desire peace, not war." There's a hard edge to Lucifer's voice that begs anyone listening to disagree. "And despite what I'm sure many of you might think, I do not wish to see another Fall. I only want the freedom we Fallen fell for all those long years ago…and the freedom to live that peace how I choose." He takes Gabriel's hand then, eliciting a number of shocked gasps from the Council, though no one looks quite as stunned as my mother, who blinks up at my father, confused. Her expression is an eddy of disbelief, terror, and doubt.

"With *whom* I choose," he adds, interlacing their fingers, and I can't suppress a smile as the fear in her face gives way to hope.

A hope that is quickly shattered when a dark-haired Archangel—*Serathiel,* I remember, recognizing her from that fateful day under the Serapeum—barks out, "Your blasphemous words are a mockery of everything we have worked toward for thousands of years. Need I remind you, Gabriel is not Fallen, Lucifer. She does not possess these freedoms you speak of—"

"Which is why our laws need to change," he bites back, his knuckles whitening as his grip on my mother's hand tightens.

A sudden movement to my left draws my attention, and a lean Archdemon with freckled, tan skin and inky black hair jumps down into the bath from the shadows of one of the archways above. His face is all hard planes and sharp angles, like those of high-fashion runway models, and his deep green eyes are hooded by thick sable brows. "Have you not already sullied this world enough with the one offspring you share?" He sneers, his eyes darting between my parents. "Or will you keep testing the limits of the divide and put us all in further peril? The prophecy—"

"The prophecy is why we are here, you ignorant fool!" My mother's outrage booms through the bath, and I can feel the tingle of the electricity that swirls around her again like static in the air. It presses against my skin, a pressure filling the space that threatens to shatter the stone underfoot and bring the whole bathhouse toppling down.

Caleb loops an arm around my waist, pulling me close to his side, and I'm certain he can feel it, too.

"If I am ignorant, it is only because you have made us so with your half-truths and deception," the Archdemon snarls.

"Enough!" Lucifer bellows, and a sudden chill clings to the air, banishing the overwhelming heat and making me shiver. Above us, the clear sky grows dark, and shadows stretch across the stone, laid atop the ruins like a blanket. It only lasts for a moment, but it's long enough to silence everyone present. "Neither I nor my daughter are the real threat you fear," he continues once the sky brightens again. "And we did not summon you to waste time slinging insults at one another. Though"—he stalks toward the Archdemon who last spoke, and this time, when the shadows descend, they congregate around where he pauses with only a few feet between them, lending menace to his tall form—"I will warn you, Belphegor, say one more negative word about my daughter, and it *will* be the last thing you say. She is a blessing to this world, and we are here to prove it."

"A *blessing*…" The Archdemon stares at Lucifer, mouth agape. "Have you lost your mind?"

"My goodness, I do *not* miss this," trills a familiar voice, and I glance up in the direction it came from, shielding my eyes from the sun—more out of reflex than necessity. My stomach flips when I spot Lilith sitting perched on the crumbling balustrade on the low open roof overhead, her legs encased in skin-tight black leather, dangling over the edge, crossed at the knee. A cunning smile twists her scarlet red lips.

"What is she doing?" I mutter under my breath.

I peer up at Caleb, catching his eye, but he just shrugs. "Fuck if I know," he whispers back.

Considering who Lilith sided with the last time Alexander started a war, her presence before the Council could endanger our chances of actually getting them to agree to a truce. That's why she was supposed to stay out of sight until *after* this meeting. Until *after* we convinced them Alexander is the real enemy to our kind, not me. Until *after* we had a chance to tell them the ex-Archdemon has switched sides.

"Lilith?"

I recognize the Archangel who speaks, noting the strawberry blonde tones of her hair and the way her delicate brow is furrowed as she stares up at the roof in disbelief. She was also there the day I released Alexander, but I can't recall her name.

Pursing her lips, she cuts her eyes to my father. "What is the *traitor* doing here, Morningstar?"

Lilith jumps down into the bath, landing with the steadiness and grace of a cat despite wearing dangerously thin stiletto heels. To my amazement, she doesn't even wobble.

Rising like a phoenix reborn from its ashes, she struts forward, waving an indifferent hand. "I could hear your senseless bickering from miles away. It's a wonder you haven't attracted the attention of every creature in the country."

A glower contorts the female Archangel's face. "Why don't you go back to whatever hole you crawled out of—"

"Sticks and stones, Raphael," Lilith simpers. Then, with a tinkling, mischievous laugh, she says, "Oh, don't look so put out. I promise, your words have positively *wounded* me."

"Remove yourself from this congregation, Lilith," Uriel warns, "or we will—"

"You'll what?" she challenges, pausing mid-step. "You'll take my wings?" When he says nothing, she rolls her eyes and crosses her arms. "I see nothing has changed. The lot of you are still sanctimonious bores. Seriously, Lucifer," she throws over her shoulder, "at this rate, the war will be over before you've even negotiated the damn truce."

"Truce?" The word leaves Uriel in a skeptical huff. "Is that why you called us here? Desperation has driven you to delusion, Morningstar."

"This is a trick," a deep voice growls, and my eyes snap toward the archway just above the Archangel's left shoulder. Toward Mammon, who has been unnervingly silent until now. An ominous shadow darkens the bloody hue of his gaze.

"I assure you, Brother, it is not a trick," my father says. "Nor delusion," he tosses at Uriel, unable to keep the frustrated bite from his words, "as I am hoping you will come to agree that a truce is in all our best interests."

Incredulity paints the Archangel's face. "How can there be a truce when you have broken our most sacred law? When you stand against the Council you swore to uphold?" His dark eyes flash behind Lucifer then, to where Caleb and I stand back with Hammurabi, not yet daring to utter a word. "The boy with you…he is of the Conqueror's blood, is he not? The one who aided your daughter in his liberation? Not to mention the *traitor* in your midst," he adds with a derisive sneer at Lilith, "who so loyally stood by the Conqueror the last time we were faced with such madness. So, tell me, Morningstar, how can you seek a truce with us when your allies of choosing have aided the enemy? Unless you, too, have joined Alexander and this is merely a ruse?"

"I have not joined Alexander, Uriel," my father snaps, losing his patience, the shadows around him vibrating. "I called this meeting because we must stand against him. *Together.* As for young Caleb, he is here for the same reason we are—to unite and overcome this threat to our world and our kind. And while it's true he helped to free Alexander, his only crime was being easily led. He was not alone in his actions, and he did not know what he was unleashing."

"So that excuses it?" Raphael asks through clenched teeth.

"No, but how can we punish ignorance?" Lucifer counters. "We neglect to teach our young of these dangers and then punish them when they break laws they knew nothing about. How is that just or right? Besides, thanks to both the boy and Lilith, we know where Alexander is hiding and have a better understanding as to his numbers. I am certain, as the Council, you are eager to possess such knowledge. Knowledge I am willing to share, should we reach an…understanding."

Mammon lets out a sharp laugh, the sound abrasive and cruel. "Or use to lead us all into a trap."

Whispers echo throughout the large space and my pulse hitches, racing under my skin until my heartbeat is everywhere at once. I clench my jaw, frustrated. The angels and Fallen argue like I imagined immortals would—like they have all the time in the world when time is the one thing we don't have. Lilith was right. This is getting us nowhere, and at this rate, Alexander will make his next move long before we make any progress with the Council. I glance toward the shadows of the cloister again, meeting Abaddon's watchful gaze. If there was an ideal moment for the Archdemon to intervene and put in a good word for us, it would be now.

With a barely perceptible nod in my direction, he jumps down from the ledge and crosses the empty bath to stand beside Uriel, drawing everyone's bewildered attention. "You are all willfully choosing to ignore the one question we should be asking," he says, looking at my mother. "You said you're here because of the prophecy, Messenger. So, what of it? What tidings from the Creator do you bring to us now?"

She hesitates, and I watch her side profile as she looks up at my father, noting how she licks her lips and the way her throat shifts when she swallows. Is she nervous? The thought is almost laughable, but then, I suppose unearthing a several-thousand-year-old lie that has affected the lives of literally all of our kind is bound to rile up some nerves.

With an encouraging nod, my father squeezes her hand and she nods back, letting out a deep breath. "I do not come with new tidings…but old ones." At the confused mutterings of the Council, she says, somewhat louder, "I have not been forthright with the full extent of the Creator's warning. When I told you of the prophecy those long years ago, I only delivered half of His words. The truth is, He spoke not of one Gray but two. A Destroyer and a Savior…destined to meet in battle, which will ultimately decide the fate of our world."

Everyone is silent for an uncomfortable moment, and I follow the glances shared between a handful of the Council members, searching for any sign of intrigue or the barest hint that they're open to the possibility presented before them. To my dismay, a sharp laugh breaks the tense hush.

"And you expect us to believe your daughter is this Savior?" Amenadiel asks with a dismissive titter. "Why should we accept your words as truth when you have just admitted to *lying* about the prophecy—a deception you have kept up for nearly as long as we have been on Earth?"

"I lied to *protect* our kind," Gabriel seethes, a flush of indignation sweeping up the back of her neck. "I was pregnant when the Creator first delivered the prophecy, and the timing of it made me believe it was His way of punishing me for faltering in my faithfulness to Him." There's a fleeting pain in her tone that clenches my heart—that makes me worry she will never be able forgive herself, not only for her actions with me but with Lucifer—but she forces it behind her usual icy persona. "I knew my daughter wouldn't be born a Light, that she would be different, having the blood of both factions, and as such, I feared she would grow to become the Destroyer the Creator spoke of. So, I did what was necessary and I locked her away where she wouldn't be a danger to us."

To my horror, there isn't a single sympathetic face in the bathhouse. To think, these unfeeling angels are the ones responsible for shaping so many young lives.

Gabriel continues, undeterred. "Then, millennia later, Alexander appeared…and I began to have doubts. But even then," she growls, "I did not release her."

"Then who did?" Serathiel presses, arching a dubious brow. "If the child was locked away as you say, then how is it she stands before us now if you did not release her?"

Every eye turns and settles on me, and I still under the combined weight of the Council's inscrutable gazes. I know I'm supposed to be strong—that I need to prove I'm a force to be reckoned with, on equal footing with the immortals before me—but I can't seem to force myself to speak. To stand up for myself, even though I want to.

To my surprise, Lilith is the one to speak for me. She crosses the bath and stands to my left, throwing her arm around my shoulders like we've known each other forever. I suppose, on some level, that's true.

"Because the Creator did," she explains. "Can't you see? He wanted all this to happen. He released Luna without anyone knowing and made it damn near impossible for anyone to find her in the mortal world…until the moment came when He wanted us to."

"Like a Dark transfer entering the Serapeum on a mission to find and free his grandfather," Gabriel adds.

Uriel balks. "You are implying the Creator *intended* for these children to meet and release Alexander?"

"I had assumed that was obvious, yes," Lilith answers, a sweet, mocking smile upturning her lips.

"But why?" Raphael asks, exchanging panicked glances with Serathiel. "Surely, He would desire another war between our kind even less than we do."

"He doesn't. But a war between the Destroyer and Savior is the only way to unite our kind again...and we believe that is His intention," my father grinds out, the words rife with the same bitterness I heard in his voice when he swore he would go to war with the Creator should anything happen to me.

"Unite..." Uriel rolls the word on his tongue for a few seconds before understanding dawns, and a harsh, accusatory scowl mars his features. "You mean destroy the divide."

"No, not destroy. *Heal* it," I blurt out, finding my voice. Panic strips my senses raw, but I persist, and closing my eyes, I recite the one part I remember verbatim from the prophecy. The one part that haunts my every thought with a daunting purpose I feel too small to live up to. "'Should they embrace their strength, the Savior will reign victorious and return peace to the Faithful and Fallen, healing a rift believed to be irreversible. But should they fail, the Destroyer will emerge triumphant and the human and celestial worlds will be forfeit.'"

Lids fluttering open, I lock eyes with Uriel, who stares at me, his expression unreadable. His dark eyes scan my face with keen perusal before fixing on my parents again. "How convenient that would be for you all, wouldn't it? Tell me, Messenger, why should we believe your words now when the tidings you deliver, claiming to be gospel, would serve to benefit only you and those you hold dear? And if what you speak of is, in fact, true, then how do we know your daughter is the Savior and not the Destroyer the Creator spoke of?"

"For fuck's sake, haven't you already been through this once?" Caleb groans, pushing sweat-slicked hair back off his forehead. "My grandfather wishes to rule us, not free us. Does that sound like a Savior to you?"

Belphegor snorts. "And we're supposed to believe this *girl* is the Savior? You'll forgive me for having my doubts as to this measly whelp's ability to go to arms with Alexander."

"Which is why we called this meeting," Lucifer states, his calm, level tone completely at odds with the violent, murderous thrashing of his aura. If such a thing were possible, I'm certain the black and violet tendrils of shadow would lash out and choke Belphegor into silence. "Not just to beg for a truce…but your help."

Uriel narrows his eyes at my father. "And if you're mistaken about the girl? If we offer you aid and neutralize Alexander only to discover she is the real threat? If you are wrong and she is the Destroyer, you will have doomed us all."

Terror trickles down my spine, and I shiver as I'm finally forced to acknowledge the one fear I can't bring myself to face. That it isn't only this war, or imprisonment, or Caleb's mortality that frighten me, but that everyone I care about is wrong about who I am. *What* I am. Caleb. Alaric. My parents. Even Hammurabi, who had no reason to fight at my side but has stood by as a loyal protector, even at the risk of his own safety. I never wanted or asked for any of this, but at least by being the Savior, there was a glimmer of hope. A shred of peace in believing I am good and not the monster I spent seventeen years believing myself to be. But if I'm not…

If I *am* the Destroyer…

Then I deserve every second of eternal punishment Caleb rescued me from.

Out of the corner of my eye, I track Gabriel's movements as she pulls free of my father's grip and crosses to where Uriel stands a short distance away, silent judgment rolling off the Archangel in waves. Reaching over her shoulder, she pulls her sword free from the invisible scabbard on her back but makes no move to attack the Archangel. Instead, she slowly drags the sharp edge of the blade along her palm, opening the skin until blood drips onto the cream-colored stone.

Then, lifting her chin, she holds out her hand.

"If that proves to be true, you can have her…and we will no longer stand in your way."

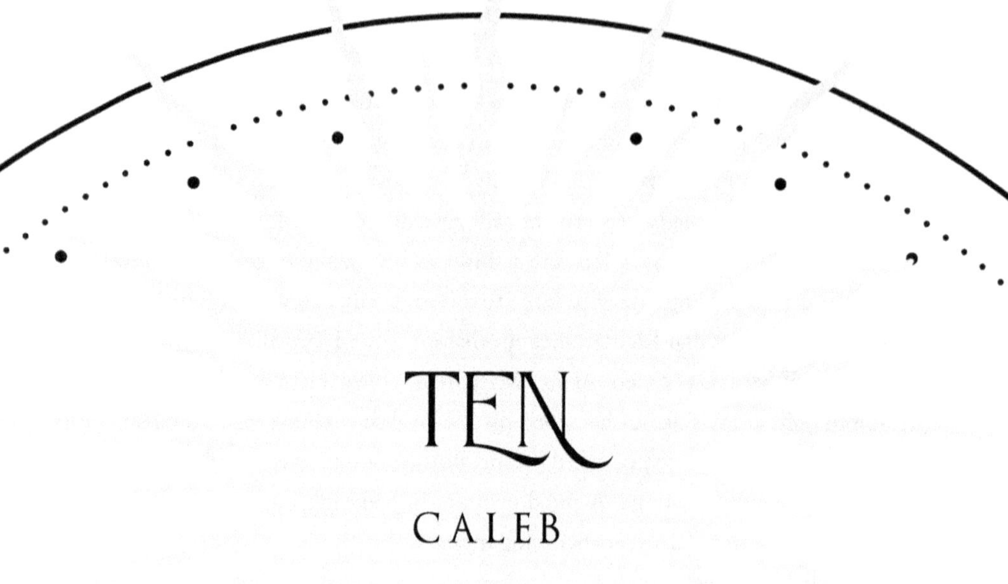

TEN

CALEB

GABRIEL'S WORDS HANG IN the air along with the scent of her blood, and rage fogs my brain. What the actual fuck? She did not just offer up Luna on a silver platter to the Council. A rabid wolf has better maternal instincts than she does. Goldilocks stills next to me, her muscles locked tight, and I hurt for her.

"Are you out of your goddamned mind?" I snarl at Gabriel, anger pounding through me as I take a step forward. I don't give a shit that she's an Archangel and I'm just a lowly Nephilim. Or that the entire Council is witness to my anger. You don't offer your kid up to your enemies. That's just *Parenting 101*.

Luna places a delicate hand on my forearm, stopping me. "It's okay, Caleb," she says, giving me a faint smile.

A chiding huff escapes Hammurabi's lips. "Boy, calm yourself. No one is taking the flower anywhere because she's not the Destroyer, and we all know that, especially her mother."

My eyes clash with Gabriel's, and she gives me a grim nod. Okay, maybe she has to say that bullshit for the Council to take her seriously. I still don't like it, but I snap my mouth shut. United front and all that. Reaching out to Luna, I squeeze her hand, but she's already relaxed. Guess she has more confidence in her mom than I do.

My gaze shifts to Uriel, and I scowl. The Archangel was a big player in Luna's psychological torture, so I hate him on sight. He sneers as he regards Gabriel's sword. "I find it ironic that for all your insistence that you're not here to declare war, you've certainly arrived armed for one."

Gabriel releases a scornful laugh. "As if you didn't arrive armed as well. Stop with your useless stalling. Are you going to accept my offer or not? I won't make it again."

Uriel pulls a blade out of thin air—or maybe his ass. Something has to be wedged up there to account for his shitty attitude. He cuts open his palm and holds it out to Gabriel. His eyes hold a hint of malice. When she clasps his hand, he says, "Betrayal is no longer an option now, Messenger."

Ah, now, I get Gabriel's oath and some of my anger loosens. Her eye-roll is epic as she draws her hand away. "It's just like you to state the obvious."

Raphael's eyes flick to me for a moment, then she glances at Gabriel. "Now that the dramatics are out of the way, I'm curious. Do you always allow little Darks to speak to you in such a disrespectful manner?" Her lips curve into a condescending smile.

"This little Dark managed to cut off the mighty Mammon's wing," Gabriel purrs. "Why don't you think on that before you speak about matters you don't understand."

Raphael's eyes widen, and her head whips around to meet Mammon's now blazing red gaze. The hulking Archdemon is framed by one of the bathhouse's delicate pointed arches, but there's nothing delicate about him. The heat of his fury is blistering, and it takes everything in me not to step back. The lanky Archangel pivots to study me.

"Well, I guess you really are the Conqueror's blood, although Alexander would've taken his head as well as his wing. Lucky for Mammon, you're not Alexander," Raphael says to me, then her smile turns poisonous. "But I think being unable to fly is worse than death, so maybe he's not so lucky after all."

I blink. Wow, the Council is so full of love and sunshine for one another. I'm really getting the warm and fuzzies just being around them.

Lilith tosses her hair and gives Raphael a bored look. "Oh, it's so good to be back amongst you again. How I've missed the malice and backstabbing all in the name of world order."

"Enough," Lucifer hisses, arms crossed over his broad chest. His shoulders stiffen, and I'm sure he'd like to bust a few heads. "To stop Alexander, we must work together, unless all of you relish being under the yoke of the Conqueror. No? Then let's play nice, shall we, like the good little angels we all used to be." His head jerks toward Mammon. "And don't get any ideas, old friend, about killing the boy. He's under *my* protection."

"And mine," Gabriel says, shocking me. After my outburst, I wasn't expecting the back up. I give her an apologetic smile when she looks over her shoulder.

"And mine," Luna declares, twining her fingers through mine. Damn, I didn't think she could get any hotter, but protective Luna just proved me wrong. Man, do I love this woman.

Mammon's lip curls as his eyes peruse Luna, but he tilts his head in deference to the Messenger and the Morningstar. "As long as we have a truce, he's safe enough from me."

I don't believe him, but Lucifer just gives him a nod. Hell, they've known each other since the beginning of time, so I guess the Morningstar can tell when Mammon is lying. I hope. But then again, even if he's lying, would it matter? We still have to work together.

Hammurabi mutters out of the side of his mouth, "Keep eyes in the back of your head, boy."

Sweat trickles down my neck, and it's not just from the oppressive heat. Well, that confirms it. Mammon is lying, and I have to make sure I'm never alone with the murderous asshole.

"Now that we've all decided to play nice, perhaps we should wait for Alexander to make a move," Raphael suggests and Uriel nods.

Out of the corner of the bathhouse, where the shadows are thickest, darkness pools out like an inky puddle spreading across the stone. The liquid puddle rises, swirling, and out steps Beelzebub. I grin. Man, that is the second dramatic entrance that little dude has made in as many days. "My, my, I suppose your intel isn't up to date," Beelzebub says. "I thought your spy network was better than that, Raphael. How disappointing. The Conqueror *has* made his first move. Ashkelon lies in ruins at Alexander's hands, and he's taken the children *and* the weapons." Stunned murmurs ripple around the open space, but the ancient tween ignores them. "I was lucky to escape with one of my loyal Nephilim after we were ambushed. We must act now and swiftly to protect the other academies before he targets them, too. I think even we can all agree that Alexander amassing weapons from the Fall is quite terrifying."

Uriel frowns. "Why didn't you report this to us immediately?"

Beelzebub sneers at the Archangel. "I went back to look for survivors and to see if any children had managed to hide. I don't know how you Lights run your schools, but Darks don't leave their people behind."

Uriel growls at him, baring his teeth, and the Archangels visibly bristle at little B's words. Here we go again, but to my surprise, sanity prevails as Uriel manages to overcome his anger and ask, "Why destroy the schools? Why not just take the weapons and the children? That kind of destruction can draw unwanted attention from mortal eyes."

Luna lifts her chin and stares her tormentor down, and pride puffs my chest out. Lucifer is right: she's solid steel. "He wants to burn the divide. Literally. He wants our kind united again, but not in a true alliance—not as equals, at least not to him. He just wants us united enough so he can rule over all, regardless of if we're Light or Dark. If we're all banded together in fear, he doesn't have to worry about an uprising from either side. Considering this isn't the first time he's tried this, I thought that would be obvious," she says, mimicking Lilith's earlier statement.

I hide my smirk at her snark. Go, Goldilocks.

Uriel gets his panties in a twist at her mocking tone. "Perhaps it's obvious to you, Gray, because you think like the Conqueror."

"Or maybe because she exhibits intelligence," Lilith shoots back with a saccharine smile.

I can't help it. I hold my other hand out, making a fist and presenting it to the saucy ex-Archdemon, but she just gives me a blank stare. I sigh. But Luna gives my knuckles a tap, grinning. Lilith rolls her eyes at both of us.

"Just so you know, you were equally awesome," I tell Goldilocks in case she doubted.

"Oh, I know," she says pertly, which makes me want to strip her naked again as soon as possible.

Uriel opens his mouth, his lips twisted into a snarl, but Gabriel interjects smoothly, "Whether he's bothered by unwanted attention from mortals or not, our children are in danger—as are we once those weapons are dispersed. We need to evacuate the schools and empty the armories and museums."

Serathiel, clad in a fitted suit, black hair clipped short, scowls at Gabriel. "Yes, we must act swiftly. This is a potential disaster for us and the world."

Beelzebub barks out a laugh. "Way to state the obvious, Sister."

Lucifer ignores the pissy tween and says, "Yes, we must act now and form teams to evacuate the schools. You must return Asmodeus to the fold. We need her."

Leviathan, a massive Archdemon who is the size and breadth of a sumo wrestler without the fat, chuckles at Lucifer's demand. His blue-black hair is pulled into a half ponytail, highlighting his inky eyes, which are so dark and liquid they border on creepy. "I don't think so, Morningstar, not until you prove that this isn't some elaborate ruse to save your daughter. We need something from you to cement our alliance."

My jaw drops as I regard the overgrown Archdemon. I guess Gabriel bleeding and swearing a fucking oath wasn't enough. I glance at Luna who rolls her eyes. "Of course they do," she mutters, and I suppress a laugh.

For the first time since we've begun these negotiations, I see Hammurabi get pissed. He delivers a death stare to Leviathan, and I can almost spot steam curling from his ears.

"Asmodeus is one of you," he spits. "She does not deserve to be imprisoned because she had the wisdom to see what Luna really is."

Wow, he actually said Luna's name. He's furious.

The angel of death, Azrael, who's been silent this whole time, cuts in. "I always had a touch of envy for Asmodeus for possessing such a loyal hound," he says, and Hammurabi stiffens at the insult. Asshole. Too bad Azrael didn't keep his trap shut. "But we don't trust you. Your motives are suspect at best and selfish at worst." His dark eyes focus on Luna, his reddish-brown skin gleaming. I think the Native American tribes based their pantheons on him. "Evacuate your respective schools and Babel and bring us the Nephilim and the weaponry. Then we'll release sweet Asmodeus." He sits back, eyes darting to meet those of the other Council members.

"Agreed," Uriel says, "and that means you return your swords to us, too." His last words are directed at Lucifer and Gabriel.

"How shall we fight Alexander then? With harsh language?" Lucifer retorts. "We can't evacuate our schools with our power alone. We need angel-killing steel."

I almost laugh at how the Council members collectively flinch. Mammon, however, just stares at me, hatred and menace emanating off him like cheap cologne.

"Having just battled Alexander, I know we can't go into the academies unarmed. Perhaps a compromise? One of you can travel with us, sword in hand, and aid with the evacuation. That way you can witness for yourself what's happening and keep us in check, as you so love to do," Gabriel offers with an icy smile.

Raphael's grin holds razor blades. "As you so loved to do as well, Messenger. Don't be a hypocrite. It doesn't suit you, and you did more than keep us in check. I thought deception was more your lover's forte, but you wear it well." Gabriel's face darkens, and I straight up think she's going to slap a bitch when Raphael adds, "But that is acceptable to me. I'll accompany you."

Mammon's ruby gaze latches onto mine. "And I'll accompany you, Lucifer."

Beelzebub bares his teeth at the larger Archdemon. "That's not necessary. I'll accompany the Morningstar. It's my right to seek vengeance."

I wonder if the Council has any idea about little B's real loyalties, but as my eyes pass over their faces, I realize they don't have a clue about Beelzebub's alliance with Lucifer. Damn, the spymaster is good. Luna catches my eye, and I know she's thinking the same thing. I'm glad no one is questioning B's real motives to go with Lucifer because I plan to hitch a ride with them to help with Babel's evacuation—I've got friends there—and I'd rather be with the pissy tween than the murderous Mammon.

"Not to point out the obvious," Luna says, drawing the eyes of everyone. She swallows bravely before continuing. "But shouldn't you begin the evacuation of your own schools, too? We don't know where Alexander is going to strike next." Her eyes dart to Raphael. "How are you going to do that if you're with my mother?"

"Well, I suppose I shall have to persuade Gabriel to stop by Mount Sinai and aid me in escorting my little flock to safety. I would certainly remember such generosity," Raphael says, her message clear.

Gabriel scratches her back and Raphael might be more hesitant about locking Luna away again. Whatever, we have to take what we can get from this group of assholes. We need them to defeat Alexander, but no matter what happens or what Gabriel promised, no one is locking up Luna again.

ELEVEN

LUNA

SILENCE ENGULFS THE SUNKEN bath as the Archangels and Archdemons exchange sullen nods. The Council might not be fond of this new peace between us, but reluctant or not, it's a truce, and I take some comfort in the safety this ceasefire will bring. Now, at least for the moment, we only have one enemy to worry about instead of two. And maybe, with the Council's help, we can eliminate the threat hanging over all our heads before too much damage is done.

"What of the Gray?" Mammon calls out, his voice grating, cutting into the hush like a serrated saw through bone. I shudder as every eye swings toward where he hangs back in the shadows above, thick brows drawn low over that gleaming red gaze. "Where will she be while her parents are preoccupied with the evacuations?"

"With me," my mother announces before I even have the chance to consider that question. I've been so worried about this meeting, I didn't spare a thought for what would come after it. Or what part I'd play beyond my fated role as the prophecy's Savior—and that's what the Council will expect me to be or I'll find myself with a one-way ticket back to an eternity in that glass egg. Either that or they'll just kill me to avoid me becoming a second Alexander. Gabriel might have bought us some time—and allies—with her promise to Uriel, but that time will mean little if I don't figure out what I'm meant to be doing. Regardless of what anyone expects of me, the real trouble is, I don't know *how* to be a Savior, and I certainly don't know how I'm going to save anyone, let alone the entire world. I can't even seem to save myself. Hell, at this point, I'm little more than a piece on a chessboard, being moved around by one side or another with no apparent free will of my own.

Mammon's gaze narrows on my mother. "You expect us to trust—"

"I gave you a blood oath," Gabriel interrupts. Though her words are a growl, her voice is clear. "That should be proof enough I won't go back on my word." A soft, humorless laugh parts her lips as she peers down at her hand, the sliced skin already stitched back together. "I couldn't now, even if I wanted to."

"Worry not, Brother," Raphael says, giving the Archdemon an impatient look. She slinks across the space toward my mother, and her slow steps remind me of the orderlies back at the hospital who would always hover nearby in case one of the patients needed restraining. Pausing an arm's reach from Gabriel, Raphael snaps her eyes over her shoulder, locking me in the heat of her stare, as her lips twist into an unnerving smile. "I will keep an eye on the little bird."

"Then it is agreed," Uriel barks, his commanding tone putting an end to any further objections. He turns in a circle, taking in each Council member's face. "Depart to your respective schools and evacuate the children and retrieve the weapons at all costs. Once the task is completed, we will reconvene." His eyes cut to Lucifer. "Your next actions will determine the veracity of your claims here today."

I blink, glancing between the glowering Archangel and my father, feeling like I'm missing something. Beside me, Caleb clears his throat.

"Reconvene where, exactly?" he asks, sounding just as confused as I am.

Gabriel scoffs, flipping her raven hair over her shoulder. "A location that will be disclosed, I assume, once the Council is adequately convinced this has not all been some elaborate ruse."

"Indeed," Uriel says, plastering on a forced smile that raises the hairs on my arms. "For your sake, let us hope that is not the case, Messenger. And that, this time, your warning has not come too late."

There's a beat of silence, then a flurry of movement erupts around us as the Archangels and Archdemons vanish into their respective Roads. Of those not accompanying us, Uriel and Mammon are the last two to leave, and as the Archangel steps into the blinding glow of the Blessed Road, he shoots one final warning glare at my mother before his dour countenance is swallowed by light, and the opening seals behind him like a zipper. Mammon lingers a moment longer, his eyes burning like flames in the shadows. They dart between my face and Caleb's as he steps back into the embrace of the darkness.

A breath whooshes out of my lungs once the Council is gone until I remember Raphael is still here, her watchful gaze looming over our party, and my heart rate escalates once again. Licking my lips, I look at Gabriel out of the corner of my eye then back at the other Archangel, waiting to see who will make the first move.

Raphael spares a split-second glance in my direction, giving a delicate sniff of disdain, before pinning the full weight of her gaze on my mother. "Time waits for no one, Messenger. Let us be off." Turning slightly, she trails a hand through the air, as if feeling for that invisible zipper. At the touch of her fingers, radiant light pours across the sand-colored stone, opening the Blessed Road.

Smirking, the Archangel steps back from the entrance and gestures with a dramatic sweep of her arm for Gabriel and me to enter.

I shake my head as understanding sinks in. "But Caleb—" I begin to protest, finally registering that by going with my mother and Raphael, Caleb and I will be separated. As a Dark, he can't travel the Blessed Road, and I know Gabriel would never let me go with him on the Shadow Road. Nor would Raphael, who is looking for any reason to distrust us. The only alternative is Caleb meets us at the Serapeum, but there's no way in hell I'll let him take the Shadow Road alone—not when Alexander's minions could be out there lying in wait. Which leaves only one option.

He doesn't come at all.

Crossing the distance between us, Gabriel brings her mouth to my ear, lowering her voice to a barely audible whisper. "I cannot shield him on a Road I'm unable to travel," she murmurs, echoing my thoughts. "*You* are my concern, Daughter." Then, slightly louder so Caleb can hear, she adds, "Caleb will be safer with his fellow Darks." I don't ask if that's because she would leave him behind in a heartbeat if doing so meant protecting me.

Swallowing, I follow her piercing gaze to my father, who nods, as if he can sense my concern. But although I trust him—trust the song humming between us—the thought of leaving Caleb behind with him doesn't bring me any peace.

Tears blur my vision. "We said we'd go together," I whisper, turning to look up at Caleb, remembering the night at Babel after he rescued me and how he said we wouldn't be separated again.

With a frown, he brushes his knuckles against my cheek, stroking me gently. I sigh at the touch of his fingers on my skin as he leans in, touching his forehead to mine. "I know, and I wish we could, but..." He trails off, tensing his jaw, as if he wants to say something else but thought better of it. He remains this way for a moment then says, "Don't worry about me, Goldilocks. I'll be fine. Just...stick to your mom like glue, you hear me?" I don't miss the warning edge to his tone, which only makes the snake around my heart coil even tighter.

"Worry not, little Dark," Lilith coos, stroking a hand through my hair. I almost forgot the ex-Archdemon still stood beside me. "I will keep an eye out for our dear Luna," she says, winking at me when I look over at her.

Gabriel arches a dubious brow at that, and Lilith gapes at her, affronted.

"Oh, you didn't think I would stay behind, did you?" Nostrils flaring, she hisses under her breath, "Someone will need to watch both your backs, and I don't trust Raphael as far as I can throw her." As she says this, she directs her dark eyes to where Raphael lurks by the Blessed Road entrance, watching us.

My mother lets out a resigned sigh and nods. "I'll be glad to have the help."

Lilith's lips peel back into a mischievous grin. "Nothing will scare the little Lights into the Blessed Road faster than a Fallen on their doorstep."

Heart racing, I glance at my mother then Caleb. "If Lilith is coming, then Caleb wouldn't be alone on the Shadow Road. He could come with us," I plead.

My eyes flash to Lilith, whose mouth splits into a simpering smile. "I suppose he could tag along if he likes. Don't worry, boy. I don't bite. Much."

"As fun as *that* sounds," Caleb begins, shooting a finger gun at Lilith, "I'm going to follow G's suggestion and go with your dad, Goldilocks. I have friends at Babel, and I need to make sure they're okay."

"You don't have to go at all, you know," I breathe, desperation forcing the words out in a rush. "You could go back and wait with Kali." *Where it's safe.* I don't say that last part aloud.

Caleb's mouth pinches into an even deeper frown until the look he gives me borders on a scowl. "Is that really something you think I'd do?" He cocks a wry eyebrow, and I feel myself flush.

"No," I say quickly. "...no. But if Alexander is there—"

"He'll what? Kill me?" Caleb snorts. "Tell me something new." He rolls his eyes, but I wince at his words—at the fear they instill in me with every breath and with every moment that takes us closer to crossing paths with his grandfather again.

Caleb must notice my expression because his hands are on my face again in a heartbeat, and he's bending down until our eyes are on the same level.

"Hey, look at me," he murmurs, brushing the warm pad of his thumb over my lower lip. "I'll be okay, I promise. Besides, good ol' Hammurabi will be with me, won't you?" He flashes a look to his left, and I follow his expectant gaze to the Babylonian king, who crosses his arms over his broad chest and nods.

"I will watch out for the boy," he rumbles.

"As will I," Lucifer seconds, stepping forward.

Caleb moves back as my father approaches, surrendering his place before me—

perhaps out of respect for the Archdemon or to give us some space to say a proper goodbye. Tears prick my eyes at the thought. We've had so little time together, and I can't help fearing it's all we'll have. That this will be the last time we see each other, the song in our hearts destined to go silent.

As if sensing my fears, Lucifer draws me into his arms, pulling me into the comforting warmth of his chest. "We will be together again soon, I swear it," he whispers in my ear.

I want to believe him. I *need* to believe him.

Otherwise, the terror might consume me.

"This is all very touching," Beelzebub grinds out in a growl, "but can we leave now?"

"As much as I hate to agree with you on anything, Brother," Raphael drawls, examining her nails with a bored expression plastered on her face, "waiting for you all to finish mooning over each other and say your farewells is getting tedious. Let's get on with business, shall we?"

Lucifer breaks our embrace, and I glance at Raphael before looking over at the tiny Archdemon, who glares at us like a sulking child on the verge of a temper tantrum. If he wasn't so frightening, I might find it funny.

Sighing, Lucifer meets my gaze again and presses his palm to my cheek. I rest my hand on top of his. "Be safe," I whisper back, squeezing his fingers.

Nodding, he turns toward my mother. "Look out for her," he pleads. "And look after yourself." A strange energy passes between them like heat, and I watch—torn between happiness and discomfort at the lust in their gazes—as the sparks of their distant past reignite.

Gabriel tilts her chin up, her gaze fierce. "You know I will."

They stare at each other for another long moment, then Lucifer retreats, making for the nearest stairs leading up into the cloister and the thick shadows within. Beelzebub tags along behind him, barking for the others to follow.

A heavy weight presses down on my chest as the reality of the moment fully sinks in, and heart racing, I glance at Caleb, who gravitates toward me again and clutches my hands.

"You better come back to me," I rasp, my voice hoarse. It's a command and a plea rolled into one.

An easy smirk lifts the edges of his lips. "Like anything could ever stop me."

But despite his playful tone, I can tell by the way his aura squirms, pressing tight to his frame, that he's just as uneasy about being apart from me as I am from him.

Tugging free of his grasp, I rise onto my toes and fist my hands in his velvet-soft hair, yanking him toward me until our lips are touching. The move is a bit rougher than I intend but I can't control the panic swelling in my chest. I just need to hold him close for a moment—to brand him on every inch of my soul so I never forget what he smells and tastes like. So I can carry at least that much of him with me.

Not caring that we have an audience, I deepen the kiss and breathe in, letting Caleb's nearness, his touch, flood every last one of my senses. And for this fleeting moment, it's as if we're the only two people in the world. As if nothing and no one could ever tear us apart, even though I know that's not true.

Behind me, my mother clears her throat. "Come now, Luna," she says gently, placing a hand on my shoulder.

I don't even realize tears curve down my face until we pull apart, and Caleb brushes the moisture from my cheeks. "See you soon," he murmurs, and there's a promise in his voice that comforts me, even if my trepidation still lingers far too close to the surface.

He pivots, turning to follow my father, and I watch his retreating figure for a moment before shifting my focus to the ancient Nephilim falling into stride beside him.

"You be safe, too, Hammurabi," I call out, my throat thick.

The Babylonian king looks back and gives me a curt nod. "You, too, little flower," he says, and I swear he offers me the smallest glimpse of a smile.

I watch, my fear like a lead weight in my stomach, as the pair ascend the stone stairs and vanish into the Shadow Road behind my father and Beelzebub.

"Caleb will be all right," my mother assures me, her voice caught somewhere between a consoling croon and the hard-edged reservation she always wears like armor. "Your father will make sure of that."

Nodding, I let her guide me away, and together, we approach the Blessed Road entrance where Raphael waits for us, tapping her foot. Lilith flanks me on my other side but pulls back before we get too close to the light.

"I suppose that's my cue," the ex-Archdemon says, and with a salute to my mother, she saunters away in the opposite direction, tracing the other Darks' steps toward the stairs. "See you at Mount Sinai," she calls over her shoulder, then she, too, disappears into the shadows.

A shudder races through me at how alone I feel now with only Gabriel beside me, all our other allies departed. Apprehension hardens in my gut as my eyes turn to Raphael, not exactly a friend or a foe, but certainly not someone either of us can trust.

Lips pursed, the Archangel glowers at us. "Took you long enough," she grumbles when we finally step over the threshold of light into the Blessed Road.

Immediately, I'm consumed by warmth, and the touch of the Road's radiance on my skin as we walk, passing marker after marker, takes my mind back to the last time I traveled this path…and forces me to picture the person who was there at my side. The crushing memory of Alaric's face is a weight on my chest I can't take on right now. Not when the anxiety building under my skin already threatens to pin me to the ground.

"What's Mount Sinai like?" I ask, eager for a distraction from the thoughts that seem determined to keep me confined in my panic.

Although Raphael is the headmistress of Sinai and best positioned to answer my question, I look to my mother, my brow raised in question.

Behind us, keeping several paces back to make sure we don't attempt an escape, I hear Raphael jeer, "Yes, Gabriel, do tell us what *my* academy is like."

Gabriel shoots a scathing look over her shoulder then mutters, "Far more isolated than the Serapeum."

Raphael snorts. Clearly, that answer wasn't sufficient.

Rolling her eyes, Gabriel expands, "There is a human monastery at the base of the mountain… Sinai resembles that but is much larger in scale and far grander. It truly is a sight to behold," she finishes, her voice mockingly reverent.

"You sound envious, Gabriel," Raphael coos. "Or perhaps you're just feeling the loss of your own academy?"

That stops my mother in her tracks.

"Loss?" I echo, pausing beside her.

My eyes shift to Raphael, who practically purrs as she says, "Your mother has broken the law, little bird. As has your father. And neither have been present to oversee their academies since you freed Alexander." Her lips curve into a menacing grin that's all teeth. "The Council obviously had no choice but to fill those positions with more *worthy* candidates."

Malice drips from every syllable uttered, and my heartbeat thunders in my ears as I contemplate the severity of what Raphael is saying. Of course, I knew my parents were on hiatus from their academies—how could they run their schools when they were physically on the run from the Council? But I never really took the time to consider the bigger picture of what their absence would mean. How could I? Since the moment Caleb cut me out of my prison, everything has happened so fast. I've barely had time to process most of it.

"Does that mean you're not on the Council anymore?" I ask, the words nearly choking me as I gape at my mother, though her eyes—always so sharp and alert—

avoid mine. Her silence only compounds my fears, and dread sinks into my bones when Raphael lets out a low, cold laugh.

"That remains to be seen, doesn't it? The situation is rather…*gray*…at the moment. Not as black and white as it was," she taunts, roughly pushing between us. Stumbling, I whip around, glaring holes into the Archangel's back as she continues a few steps ahead—just far enough to encourage us onward but not enough to risk giving us space to flee. Not that we could…or would. The blood oath my mother made with Uriel would likely backfire on us if we tried, and besides, we need the Council's help. Running from them now would be counterproductive. "Come," she crows when Gabriel and I don't resume our forward march. "Sinai draws near."

Still, neither of us move, my feet rooted to the soft, airy ground underfoot despite the required urgency of our mission. Chest heaving, I snap my eyes to Gabriel, watching her blank, stony face with a growing alarm that rings deep in my bones.

Only Council members preside over the academies, which means if someone has taken Gabriel's place as headmistress…that same person will also inevitably supplant her on the Council, just like Beelzebub replaced Lilith all those years ago when Alexander was imprisoned. While part of me has recognized that my parents' rebellion against the other Archangels and Archdemons has put a strain on their positions, I never considered just what it would mean if they were no longer part of the Council. Or the consequences that would come from their expulsion. Those effects might not impact my father too greatly, but my mother…

"If you're off the Council, does that mean you'll have to go back to Heaven?" My voice is reedy, my tone hollow, and my airways tremble with the returning threat of tears. The only Faithful allowed to remain on Earth are those in charge of the Light academies. If that no longer includes Gabriel, then what's stopping the Creator from calling her back?

It would be almost karmic, I suppose, to have my mother ripped away from me when I'm just finally coming around to the idea of embracing her in my life.

"No," she bites out, the protestation gruff. Glancing up at me, she reaches out, grabbing my hands, and her fingers are cold around me despite the warmth of the light engulfing us. "Even if it's what the Creator demands, I won't make the same mistake. Not again."

I gape at her, taken aback by the vehemence in her voice…and by the sheer sincerity of her words. She couldn't have made her meaning clearer if she had outright declared her intentions to stay. Hell, she just practically said she's choosing me over the Creator. If there was ever a moment when I sensed Gabriel's affection for me, this is it. And it's enough to make me weep, my eyes pricking with tears of joy. But the moment of honesty and feelings bared passes quickly, and before I know it, Raphael clears her throat and we're trudging forward, progressing the rest of the way to Mount Sinai in total and unnerving silence.

It takes far less time than I imagined it would to return to Egypt—this time to the mountains southeast of Alexandria, not far from the border to Israel—and as we step out of the Blessed Road, exchanging one expanse of bright light for another, I breathe out, the air all but torn from my lungs at the sight of the immense palace before us. There's no other way to describe the grandiose structure built into the mountain face. My mother was right—it does resemble a monastery, but it's so much more than that. And as my eyes trail over the golden roof tiles glinting in the late morning sun, there's a moment when I could swear the Creator is here with us, His presence reflected in the imposing and otherworldly facade of this place, as if we're in Heaven itself.

"Wow." That one word escapes me in a gasp as I step through the freestanding archway preceding the steep stairway leading up to the entrance.

"Impressive, isn't it?" Raphael asks, a satisfied smirk on her lips. But she doesn't wait for me to answer before continuing onward toward the towering doors up above. Although I'm a good distance away from them still, they give me déjà vu, and I'm struck with a momentary flashback to the first time I approached the Serapeum. Even if everything else looks different, this one aspect—and the uncertainty writhing within me—is the same.

Except…Alaric isn't here.

Swallowing the returning thickness in my throat, I move to follow her, then pause when I hear Gabriel hiss, "Any trouble on the Road?"

I shift my gaze over my shoulder, confused why she would be asking me this when we were together on the Road the whole time, only to find Lilith walking beside her a few feet behind me. I'm not sure how long the ex-Archdemon has been here or if she arrived at the mountain before us, but I'm relieved to see her all the same. My nerves settle a little knowing Gabriel and I have at least one ally here at Sinai.

"None at all," Lilith responds with a sigh, sounding almost disappointed. Her eyes flash between us as we ascend the stone steps. "You?"

Gabriel shrugs. "A little. That is if you count Raphael's incessant chatter," she says dryly.

The ex-Archdemon chokes out a coarse laugh. "I think I'd rather cross blades with every member of the Council at once than fall victim to that."

Silence sweeps over us, and my attention jerks back to the top of the stairs when the doors boom open, the sound a deep rumble echoing through the mountains, the glinting gold parting before us like the Red Sea. Given this mountaintop is said to have been where Moses received the Ten Commandments from the Creator, I can't help wondering if he really existed…or, perhaps, *still* exists. Maybe he's a Nephilim like Hammurabi and Gilgamesh and the others I've met over the last several months. Figures that once existed to me only in history books and myths.

I'm about to ask Gabriel when a woman with bronzed skin and a chin-length obsidian bob emerges from the doorway, her steps clip-clopping across the stone like hooves as she hurries forward to greet Raphael. She falters when she sees us, her brown eyes taking in each of our faces before settling on the Archangel.

"Headmistress, you have returned…with guests," she says once we reach the top of the stairs. The woman's tone is droll and her upper lip curls back in disgust as her gaze settles on Lilith.

Raphael waves away her unspoken concerns. "Unfortunately, we come with bitter tidings, Hatshepsut. We must evacuate the school."

This seems to get the Nephilim's attention. "Evacuate? Why?"

"The potential danger I confided in you about, that I told you to prepare yourself for…it is here. The Conqueror is free again and he has declared war," Raphael says in a low voice filled with warning, and my brows lift at her words. Considering Alexander has been amassing an army for months, it's surprising so many still don't know he's on the loose. Even the Fallen we met with in India said they only heard rumors about Alexander's return, nothing more. I guess the Gray has been covering his tracks well. "We must escort the children to safety and empty the museum at once. The weapons cannot be left behind."

Hatshepsut's lips press into a taut line, and she peers over her shoulder back into the school, staring into its quiet depths for a moment. When she finally looks back to question Raphael further, her voice is equally hushed. "War? You know this for certain?"

"If you require proof, why not visit Ashkelon?" my mother suggests, the words snide. "It's little more than ash and cinders now thanks to the Conqueror."

The Nephilim stumbles back a step, disbelief seeping into the features of her face like spilled ink on paper. She looks to Raphael, her pupils blown wide, and in her stricken expression, I glimpse the one question she's too afraid to ask aloud: *Is this true?*

The Archangel can only nod. "Quickly, Hatshepsut," she commands, placing a hand on the Nephilim's upper arm.

Her touch seems to jerk Hatshepsut out of her shock. She startles, dipping her head, before turning and hurrying back inside the school.

"She's another first generation, I take it?" I whisper to Lilith as we watch the Nephilim's retreating figure. There's something majestic about the way Hatshepsut carries herself, making me all the more certain she's played a larger role in history than whatever her current position is here.

An unexpected smile touches the ex-Archdemon's lips. "And she was the first woman to rule over Egypt. I quite admire her for that."

A flood of respect fills my chest alongside the internal groan trying to quash it. "So, a pharaoh. Why am I not surprised?" Seriously, are all first generations royalty of some kind?

Except Alaric, a small, melancholic voice in the back of my head reminds me.

Stamping it out, I glance at my mother. "What now?"

She shrugs. "This is Raphael's school. I am sure she will give us our orders and tell us where we can all best be put to use." She offers the Archangel a sardonic smile.

Raphael's mouth pinches at the corners. "Messenger, you are to remain in the entrance hall to oversee the children. Hatshepsut will see to it that the other teachers are alerted and the students are sent down here to be organized for immediate evacuation." The Archangel's gaze cuts to Lilith, and she looks her up and down as if she isn't quite sure what to do with the ex-Archdemon. "Lilith...I don't really care. Just don't get in anyone's way. As for Luna, she will come with me to the museum to secure the weapons."

Gabriel's ire erupts with the fury and rage of Mount Vesuvius. "If you think I'm going to let you go anywhere alone with my daughter—"

"We are short on time," Raphael interrupts, "and I do not trust that you won't spirit her away at the first opportunity should I leave you two alone. Nor do I trust Lilith with the students. At least, not unsupervised."

My mother can only bare her teeth before Lilith plants a hand on her shoulder. "Worry not, Gabriel. I will accompany Raphael and Luna to the museum in your stead. Ensure she doesn't traumatize the poor dear." She gives Gabriel a pointed look, which brings whatever reaction that was boiling inside my mother to a less violent simmer.

Clenching her jaw, my mother stares at her friend for a moment before sucking in a breath through her nose. "Two eyes, Lilith," she growls.

"If we are quite finished here," Raphael snaps, "we have work to do and little time to do it."

The Archangel beckons for me to follow, and I share a fleeting glance with Gabriel before tailing Raphael into the school, Lilith following closely at my heels. As we proceed into the palace that is Mount Sinai Academy, I examine the gilded doors in passing, but up close, I can see that the gold and size are the only two things they have in common with the entrance at the Serapeum. Instead of a depiction of the Fall like in Alexandria, here the surface is carved with intricate patterns that I can't make out at first, the lines too tied up in one another to form a clear, discernible picture. It's only once I'm in the entrance hall and I peer over my shoulder, taking them in from a distance on the other side where the pattern is repeated, that it dawns on me what I'm looking at. The lines seem to come together before me, forming…not exactly a shape—especially with the doors still standing open, cutting the completed image in half—but a concept. A feeling of utter beauty.

I don't know how I know it…but something in my gut tells me I'm right.

Maybe because I've seen it, I muse. Nearly eighteen years ago, when I was let out of the tomb my mother locked me in.

"Is that…?"

"The Creator," Raphael answers without slowing her pace, her tone reverent. "As He is perceived by our eyes."

I'm not sure what to say to that, so I say nothing at all as Raphael leads us through wide passageways with high-vaulted ceilings and broad, multi-colored windows, which look out over the mountains. This academy is beautiful—more so than the Serapeum—and there's a heightened feel to the very air we breathe, though that may just be the elevation. I'm not used to being so high up. I don't have much time to appreciate its splendor, however, as the Archangel beckons us to move quickly.

Every hallway we hurry through is empty, and I wonder if the students are all in class at the moment—or on their way now to the entry hall, if Hatshepsut has begun the evacuation. I haven't heard any sounds that would suggest she has, but then she might be trying to avoid a panic. Or outright chaos. That would surely only complicate things. I haven't given much thought to what it will be like leading so many people through the Blessed Road, most of them children, and all of them likely to be scared and very, very confused.

My mother's words to Lilith when we arrived reverberate in my ears, and a sickly dread pools in my stomach. I can only hope we don't run into any trouble, either here or on the Road.

Raphael slows her gait as we approach a set of glass doors, and past the transparent panes, I glimpse white stone bookcases and rows of marble tables run through with veins of glimmering silver and gold. Though it takes my breath away, the library pales in comparison to the sky-scraping grandeur of the one in Alexandria. The thought of my one safe haven at the Serapeum brings me back to a less complicated time when I would spend late nights in a hidden nook between the bookcases with Caleb. Then, my only real worry was that my powers were manifesting in a manner unbefitting a Light.

Now, however, the weight of the world seems to rest solely on my shoulders.

The handful of students present scatter at Raphael's scolding command, leaving the library empty for us to explore. As expected, the main room leads through to the museum, and like in Alexandria, this space is dark, lit by low-hanging hurricane lamps to avoid degradation of the treasures within. Curiosity pulls my gaze to each of the display cases standing in tidy rows, but I don't glimpse any moths inside, or any monuments to the Nephilims' history. Only weapons.

The same weapons we've been tasked to secure.

I startle at a loud *thud*, my heart jumping up into my throat as I look down at the open trunk by my feet, then up at Raphael, who glowers at me.

"You're rather jumpy for a supposed Savior," she scoffs.

Lilith emits a low, threatening snarl, but Raphael just rolls her eyes.

"This will unlock the exhibits," she says, gesturing to the cases around us with one hand while pressing a dull brass key into my palm with the other. "Remove the weapons and put them in these trunks. That shouldn't be too hard for you. And do be quick about it. We're short on time." She points to a second trunk at the edge of the room before stomping off toward another door in the corner. "Oh, and Lilith?" she calls, pausing at the threshold to glare at us. "I'm aware of everything that happens in this room, so I'd think twice before you try anything, or you'll find yourself missing another appendage."

Lilith mutters something unintelligible under her breath. The only word I make out is "Bitch."

We set to work, moving quickly, unlocking each case and removing the weapons to be secured someplace safe—or at least out of reach of Alexander, which is better than nothing. The task is easy, and although I know these blades can't actually cut me except when branded by their owners, it's unnerving to hold them, to be near them. To know, in the hands of the right person, the steel could cut through my skin when no mortal weapon has that power. The thought sends a violent shudder up my spine. The Council might not wish me dead at the moment, but who knows how the other Lights and Darks who haven't sided with Alexander will feel once the truth of what we are is revealed and my existence becomes public knowledge. All it would take to get rid of me is a single one of these weapons and the right bloodline to wield it.

My eyes drift to the door in the corner, watching the shadows for movement, as I inch a bit closer to Lilith. I don't know when I began finding comfort in the ex-Archdemon's presence. It's insane given how little I know her, but she really does feel like family now—like what I imagine an eccentric aunt would be like if I had any experience to draw from. Or, if not family, then at least someone I know I can depend on, even if some of the others on our side still view her as a traitor.

Traitor… That word feels so hateful, so demeaning, like *crazy* always has for me. Does it pain her to know what the Council thinks of her? To know even other Darks see her that way? As someone not to be trusted for a single error in judgment made millennia ago?

I frown. The ostracism I've witnessed her facing reminds me far too much of what I experienced myself back at the Serapeum…and at every other school before it. Except, she has to bear the added burden of being without her wings. Surely, that alone was punishment enough.

My hands still at that thought, and I suddenly find myself thinking back to our meeting with my father's allies, hearing Beelzebub's voice in my head, of all people. What was it he said about Lilith's wings?

My stomach drops as the memory sharpens.

"Lilith," I prompt, and she looks up at me, arching a brow. "Something Beelzebub said yesterday is bothering me."

"Oh?" She sounds mildly intrigued but only just.

I chew on my lower lip for a moment, not wanting to dredge up bad memories, but needing to understand. To make the pieces in my head fit together. To make the questions burning inside me make sense. "About…" I hesitate, swallowing around the lump in my throat. "About how the Council voted to take your wings." When her expression doesn't so much as flicker, I croak, "Surely, that would've included my mother?"

Lilith nods, though she doesn't look as upset as I imagined she would.

"So, why help her then?" I press when she doesn't speak. "Why don't you hate her, too, like the rest of them? Like you hate my father?"

While the ex-Archdemon has never come straight out and said she hates Lucifer, her meaning was clear enough when we first spoke at length back in Kandahār, and she told me of my origins. But my mother is just as much—or was, at least—a part of the Council. If being stripped of her wings is why Lilith has no love for my father, surely, the same feelings should apply to my mother, regardless of any pre-existing friendship.

"I don't hate her," Lilith begins, speaking slowly, "because she didn't *want* to do it. Hell, she didn't even want to vote. She planned to abstain, but I wouldn't allow it."

"Why?" I ask, jarred by this revelation. Not because I believe Gabriel to be cruel, but because everything I'm learning about her is making me realize she's the opposite. That the cold demeanor she wears like a layer of ice is just to hide her pain. To push people away. But not to hurt them.

To protect herself.

Lilith shrugs. "Because Council decisions must always be unanimous, and I knew no good would come of her refusal to participate. Her abstaining certainly wouldn't have changed my fate. If anything, it might've very well led to her being placed on the chopping block beside me. You know, guilty by association and all that." Clicking her tongue, she looks down at the trunk and carefully wedges in a bronze-hilted broadsword. "I believe that's part of why she volunteered to be Alexander's warden, you know. I think she felt responsible for what happened to me. Yet another burden she carried." She murmurs this last part under her breath.

"She wasn't mad you supported Alexander?" I ask, my voice rife with disbelief as I shove another sword into the trunk. I struggle to envision Gabriel not feeling at least somewhat betrayed about that decision.

Lilith lets out a sharp laugh. "Oh, she was irate. And she attempted, on countless occasions, to make me see reason. I almost relented once or twice, but I couldn't let go of my certainty that Alexander was the Savior from the prophecy, a belief I very much regret now. Fortunately for me, just as she never stopped loving your father despite him choosing free will over Heaven, Gabriel never stopped loving me despite my decision to side with Alexander. She was quick to forgive me."

"And my father?" I press. "When we first spoke in Kandahār, you didn't seem to think much of him. I guess I'm just trying to understand why when it was his side you chose during the Fall."

Lilith purses her lips. "To be clear, I did not choose Lucifer, though I can admit our motivations at the time aligned. I told you about Adam. *He* was my choice. And I live with the outcome of that decision to this day." She shakes her head, letting out a soft sigh. "As for my feelings toward your father, any bad blood between us arose after the Fall. I didn't actually dislike him at first, though—and I'm loath to admit this—I was jealous of the bond he shared with your mother as it reminded me of what I so desperately wished to have with Adam. When Lucifer's rebellion offered me that possibility, I took it, but despite our different allegiances, I *never* abandoned Gabriel. Not like he did. Once she discovered she was with child…although I knew he wasn't aware of you, part of me resented Lucifer for leaving Gabriel in that position. For forcing her to go through her pregnancy alone. For leaving *me* to pick up the pieces of her shattered heart. And it was shattered. Gabriel might have ended things between them when she chose to side with the Creator, but I think part of her always hoped Lucifer would find his way back to her, regardless of the divide, the same way I did. In her eyes, as unlikely as she knew it would be, having him only as a friend was better than not having him at all, but he shut the door on that option." Her eyes darken with sadness, and she averts her gaze as she layers two more swords into the trunk. "Then there was the matter of my wings. While the Council agreed that I should be punished for supporting Alexander, it was the Fallen who would determine how that punishment would be enacted. Darks decide on Dark business, Lights on Light. That has always been the way." A long beat passes before she adds, "The Darks agreed my wings would be forfeit and your father was the executor of their will, though in hindsight, I suppose it was the more merciful retribution when the alternative was rotting for eternity in a tomb. At least, I still had my freedom."

Although I suspected Lucifer might have had something to do with Lilith losing her wings, hearing her confirm it only floods my chest with an aching sense of remorse.

"I'm sorry," I whisper, not sure what else to say.

Lilith snorts. "What for? You did not steal them from me. And in truth, I find myself unable to hate your father as I once did. Not now that I can see how blind I was in my choices. I was foolish, and I have only myself to blame for the consequences of my actions."

"Um…speaking of consequences…" A flush heats my skin, circling around to the back of my neck. If there was ever the perfect segue to ask about unprotected sex, this is it. "How easy is it for angels to get pregnant?"

Lilith's outstretched hand freezes mid-motion, and she looks up again, staring hard at my burning face. I'm about to dive behind the nearest display case to escape her unfaltering scrutiny when a wide grin splits her lips.

"You are smart to come to me about this and not your mother," she says through a chuckle, returning to the task at hand. "She may very well kill the poor boy."

My heart trips on the terror surging to the surface, the panic behind it squeezing the air from my lungs. The twin daggers in my grasp clatter to the floor at the thought of Caleb at my mother's mercy, a victim to her maternal wrath.

"You won't tell her?" I squeak, not quite sure if I'm asking or begging for the ex-Archdemon's silence.

Lilith arches a brow. "And risk finding myself in her warpath? No, thank you. Even

I am not immune to your mother's temper."

I nod then tentatively pick up the weapons I dropped, carefully lowering them into the trunk, before moving on to the next display and doing the same again. Lilith mimics my movements until both trunks are full to the brim and the surrounding cases are empty.

"Is that everything?" I ask.

"Seems like it," she mutters with a glance around the cavernous room. An exasperated sigh parts her lips. "Let's go inform Raphael we've finished."

"Okay."

Closing the lid, I lock the clasps on the second trunk then follow Lilith across the dimly-lit space toward the door in the corner where we last saw Raphael. As we move, neither one of us utters a word, and in the tense hush, my thoughts drift to Caleb. The sooner we finish here, the sooner we can move on to the Serapeum. And the sooner we evacuate everyone there, the sooner he and I can be reunited. As concerned as I am about the innocent students at the academies, that's all I want—for today to be over and to find myself in the comforting warmth and safety of his arms.

"Um, Lilith?" The ex-Archdemon looks down at me with a hooked brow. "You never answered my question. You know, about…" I trail off, feeling the returning heat flood my cheeks.

An amused titter escapes her. "You needn't worry. Female angels can…self-actualize, so to speak, which is why our kind doesn't procreate very often. Think of it as natural birth control. The males will spread their seed, but the women, well, unless they want it—"

My heart seizes at her words, and I falter, stumbling to a standstill.

Lilith continues, oblivious that my perception of my birth has been torn to shreds by that one simple statement. "Nephilim and humans don't have that option, of course, which is why there are far more of them than there are us. Their procreation lies in the hands of Mother Nature and luck. But angels?" She shakes her head. "The Fallen are more inclined to parenthood, but you'd be hard-pressed to find a single mother among the Faithful besides Gabriel. Come to think of it, it's actually quite rare for two angels to produce an offspring. I can count on one hand how many times I've actually seen it happen."

She only now notices I'm no longer beside her, and she pauses, glancing back at me with a worried crease to her brow.

"Luna?"

My heart drums so loudly in my ears I barely hear her say my name. Genuine concern twists her features, and she crosses back to me, placing her hands on my shoulders.

At her touch, I peer up through a thick haze of tears. "So, you're saying…my mother *wanted* me?" My voice breaks, and Lilith lets out a strangled breath as understanding dawns in her gaze.

Pain and remorse go to war on her face, and for a horrible moment that feels like an eternity, she doesn't answer. Then, when I don't think I can bear her silence any longer, she smiles—not in a sarcastic or devilish way, but with an honesty and affection that touches my soul.

Her smile spreads to her eyes as she lightly grips my chin between her thumb and forefinger. "I'm *saying* if she didn't…you wouldn't be here, Luna."

TWELVE

CALEB

ADRENALINE PUMPS THROUGH MY veins and not just from Luna's desperate goodbye kiss, her lips a hot brand upon mine. Though that kiss keeps me warm on the cold Shadow Road. That and all the memories of everything we did last night until early morning. My skin flushes hot, then my eyes hit Lucifer in front of me, and I feel the icy sting of the Road once more. I hope he's not reading my mind because he'll definitely smite me, and he's got his sword out and ready. Hammurabi walks directly behind me, and Beelzebub brings up the rear. Soon, we approach the marker to Babel. My heart pounds in my chest and my skin feels clammy. Shivering, I thumb the dagger resting in a leather sheath strapped around my leg. Hammurabi gave it to me before we left. It won't kill an angel, but it'll provide me some protection.

Lucifer turns to me then, blue eyes stormy. "Young Caleb, you and Hammurabi will have to direct us once we get inside. Though I've been a guest at Babel, she was never mine, so I don't know her the way you two do."

I raise a brow, my heart suddenly thudding in my ears. It sounds like he's asking us to look for survivors, not prepare for battle. "Do you think…do you think Alexander has already hit Babel?"

The Morningstar's face has all the softness of chiseled stone. "The Great has a way of being one step ahead of us, and unfortunately until the Council fully commits to our cause, he has greater numbers. Babel was your home, and I understand how much you care for the people there. I want you to be prepared for the worst."

"Your friends will be safe, boy," Beelzebub cuts in. "Your teachers on the other hand… Most of my Nephilim didn't make it out alive."

I glance back at the slight Archdemon, who wears lines of grief etched into his youthful face. I know all his Nephilim were like Hammurabi, ancient and powerful and wise. To lose such beings leaves a permanent scar on the world. They are irreplaceable. Hammurabi looks disturbed by Beelzebub's words, and I wonder how many friends he's lost that he's not talking about. He's not exactly Mr. Feelings. Oh, he can dish out solace and sympathy, but I don't think he's comfortable taking it. Giving him a manly pat on the back seems lame and inadequate, so I just shove my hands in my pockets and keep my mouth shut. Maybe sparing him from my sputtering platitudes is comfort enough.

"If Babel burns, the boy and I will lead the way," Hammurabi says to Lucifer, his expression stony. "We must save as many of our brethren as we can."

I give a grim nod. Even if Alexander managed to take Shalina and Rafe, they'll be fine. Well, maybe fine isn't the right word. They'll be safe enough until the brainwashing begins. But Gramps will try to charm them first before he resorts to breaking their minds to get what he wants.

As Lucifer reaches the marker for Babel and steps off the Road, I steel myself for what is to come and follow him…into bright sunshine and cerulean skies. The scent of citrus trees and jasmine curls around my nose, and I breathe in the paradise that is the Hanging Gardens. The scent of home. The Tower rises before us, flawless. I spot students trudging up the stairs toward the entrance, oblivious to the danger set to fall upon them like a hammer. But…there is *no* danger right now. I can't sense anything. Granted, I'm a second generation Nephilim, so I could be missing something, but I'm pretty damn sharp. My eyes dart to Lucifer and Beelzebub, who stand still as statues, sampling the air. I meet Hammurabi's gaze and he shakes his head. He doesn't feel anything, either.

"They're not here," Lucifer says, eyes finding Beelzebub.

The mini Archdemon nods. "No, they're not. Let's make haste. Just because they're not lurking in the shadows at the moment doesn't mean they won't pop out of one soon."

"Come," Lucifer says, and we make our way toward Babel, the Morningstar masking our presence until we reach the stone steps.

Two first-years gasp as we appear in front of them, Lucifer allowing his massive ebony wings to swing on either side of him. The girls stare at him, rather dazed, like they've just spotted their favorite celebrity, and he lives up to all the hype. One of them looks positively punch-drunk. Yeah, yeah, the Morningstar is a golden god.

We get it.

But I can't say I blame them for their infatuation. He *is* the original rebel after all. And it's not like he goes around touring schools so Nephilim can fawn over him.

"Children," he says to them, his voice a velvet rumble. "I have a task for you. Don't ask questions, just obey me. Do you understand?"

Dark Nephilim generally would balk at such demands, but when you're faced with the Morningstar, you shut the fuck up and do what you're told. The young girls nod at him, their expressions dazzled.

"What do you need us to do?" one of them asks, stepping forward. "We're your servants."

I roll my eyes and barely restrain myself from making a gagging gesture.

"I need you to round up your first-year classmates and evacuate them from Babel. Take them to the Hanging Gardens and wait for me there." Lucifer's eyes land on mine. "Caleb, go with them and help. Hammurabi, seek out your Nephilim teachers and explain the situation and aid Caleb in the evacuation effort. Beelzebub and I will find whomever the Council put in charge of the school and place defensive wards. Babel will not burn on our watch."

At the word "burn," the two girls manage to roll their tongues back in their mouths, a touch of fear now brimming in their eyes.

"B-Burn?" one of them repeats, and I shoot her a confident smile, trying to project calm.

"Hey, didn't you just hear the Morningstar? He's not gonna let that happen. You heard the man—let's start rounding up the students. I'm Cal—"

The other one focuses on me and pipes up, "We know who you are." I blink, staring at her. Her entire face flushes. "You're at the top of your class and…" She trails off lamely, and I smother a laugh.

Huh, I guess my reputation must precede me seeing as I haven't been a student here since the beginning of the school year when these girls would have only just been starting at Babel. That will definitely make everything easier. "Good, you can tell me your names on the way." I give the two Archdemons and Hammurabi a brief salute and then hurry up the steps, the two girls practically tripping on my heels.

Dahlia and Inma prove to be good little helpers, rounding up the first-years with all the skill of cowboys lassoing cattle. It doesn't hurt that I'm there, a final-year student barking orders when kids get a little mouthy. It also doesn't hurt that rumors about Lucifer and Beelzebub being in the building have already spread like wildfire, lending credence to our story. But then again, they did experience a Council invasion two weeks ago, even if they weren't directly involved. Those war horns are fucking loud. Asmodeus is gone, and I know that raised all kinds of questions, and while things appear normal on the outside, there's a ripple of unease in the air I can feel.

Darks are naturally curious, but I guarantee no one's answering any of their questions about their headmistress's disappearance. I don't know the Fallen who's taken Asmodeus's place, but whoever they are, they have massive shoes to fill, as the Archdemon is beloved by the student body. Sure, she's terrifying, but that doesn't detract from her popularity.

Once we've pretty much emptied out the first-year dormitory and classes, I turn to the girls. "Go wait outside with the others. I can take it from here."

Inma shakes her head, her curly hair a cloud around her face. "No, Caleb. You can't evacuate everyone by yourself."

I sigh, deciding not to put up a fight. I'm not too proud to admit when I need help—most of the time. "Fine, start getting out the second-years, but I'm heading to the final-year dorm by myself. Those lazy asses will still be in bed. I'll meet you on the third year floor in fifteen with some help," I promise.

At their nods, I bound up the stairs and into the familiar corridors of my dorm. Final-year students have the privilege of starting class later in the day, so most of them sleep in or do the walk of shame from being out all night. We have a curfew, but that doesn't mean we abide by it. I head straight for Rafe's door. Not bothering to knock, I thrust the door open.

Big mistake. I see Rafe…well, thrusting, and the face that stares over his shoulder in horror and shock looks familiar. Shit. It's Shalina. Ugh, someone blind me right now. I've seen Rafe's ass. Who doesn't lock the door while getting busy? I spin around, staring out the now open door, wishing I could bleach my mind clean.

"*Caleb?*" Rafe's incredulous voice says behind me. "What the fuck are you doing here?"

"Knock much?" Shalina growls. "I didn't think voyeurism was your thing, pervert!"

I make a gagging noise, debating on whether to get Hammurabi to wipe my memories right now. "So much for you two hating each other. Guess you had to work out all the negative energy somehow." I smirk at Shalina's outraged hiss.

"What are you even doing here? Aren't you supposed to be with the stuck-up Lights stroking harps or some shit?" she demands.

"Yeah, about that… You two need to get dressed. Now. We have to leave Babel," I say, cautiously peeking over one shoulder. Thank the Morningstar the sheet is now covering all the important bits.

Rafe stares at me like I've started spouting Enochian, then he laughs. "Okay, what's really going on, Caleb? Did you mess with some Light's mind, and you've pissed off Gabriel, so now you're on the run?"

Wow, I guess everyone really is clueless about what's going on. The Council locked that down tight. I pick up his discarded pants off the floor and hit him in the chest with them. "Listen, I haven't been at the Serapeum for months. I've been with—I'll tell you all about that later," I say, shaking my head. "I'm here with the Morningstar himself, and we've got to leave. *Now.*"

Shalina and Rafe exchange a look. "The Morningstar?" Shalina says. "Does this have anything to do with Asmodeus being taken away?"

There's a reason she and I compete for the top spot in school. "Yes, it does. Schools are under attack, so I'm here with Lucifer, Hammurabi, and Beelzebub, trying to get your asses out of here before that happens."

"Hammurabi is with you?" Shalina asks, her eyes round. "He just disappeared around the same time as Asmodeus, and no one is saying a damn thing. Ishtar has been gone for months, too."

"Who the hell is attacking schools?" Rafe demands. "Caleb, you're not making any sense."

I sigh, rubbing the bridge of my nose. "Okay, short-short version. I released my grandfather, Alexander the Great, from his tomb in the Serapeum with Ishtar's help. Turns out, he's actually a Gray angel, and now he's on the warpath. He's burning schools and taking students for his army. I've been with him most of the time until Luna… Yeah, no time for that. Anyway, he might be on his way here, so we need to get the fuck out, okay?"

Both their jaws literally drop as they stare at me like I've gone insane. Rafe recovers first.

"Is that why you were chosen as the exchange student? Because of Alexander?" he asks, proving why he's also a fierce competitor for best in show.

"What is a *Gray* angel?" Shalina asks, her normally glowing brown skin pale. "Is it…what I think it is?"

I hold a hand up, staving off more questions. "Ishtar played me pretty hard," I admit bitterly to Rafe then shake my head. "And yes, Shalina, a Gray angel is exactly what you're thinking, both of the Dark and Light. I swear I'll give you all the details the minute we're out of the danger zone. Unfortunately, Babel isn't safe for us anymore."

As I say those words, sourness churns in my gut. Babel has always been the epitome of *safety*. It's our home. And my grandfather wants to burn it to make a point.

Shalina edges off the bed, taking the sheet with her, and for the second time that day, I'm seeing way too much of my best friend. Rafe growls at her as he stabs his legs through his pants, and I give them my back once more.

"You sound like a stark raving lunatic," Shalina says, and I hear her shrug on her clothes. "But I believe you."

"Me too," Rafe says, "but as soon as we're out of here, you're going to spill every last little detail, including who Luna is."

So, he caught that. I nod. "You'll be meeting Luna soon enough. And she'll blow your mind," I promise.

✸

Rafe and Shalina help me drag all the final-year and third-year kids outside. We might have had a real struggle on our hands, but good ol' Uncle Hammurabi showed up and threatened to bust heads if asses didn't get on the move. I love that sourpuss. Plus, once everyone got a load of Lucifer and Beelzebub, they stopped grumbling real quick. I don't recognize the Fallen with them—the one who took Asmodeus's place. He's tall and rangy, towering over Beelzebub and managing to look Lucifer in the eye. He doesn't look too happy to be between the two Archdemons, but he's outgunned.

I recognize some of my other teachers like Blue Jay, who shows up in Salish mythology as a trickster god. Along with Ishtar, he's a master at mind manipulation and illusion, and he earns his reputation. His black eyes find Hammurabi, and I see relief flit across his face.

I push my way to the front with the Babylonian king, Shalina and Rafe trailing in my wake. Lucifer watches us approach, turning away from the Fallen. The stranger looks at me and Hammurabi, lips pursed with displeasure. I guess Lights aren't the only ones who have sticks up their asses. I ignore him, focusing on Lucifer.

"We've gotten out all the students," I report, resisting the urge to salute.

"There is no one left," Hammurabi confirms, eyes mournful. "Babel is now a shell, empty and alone."

I shiver at his words as I look back at the ancient tower standing proudly in the sun, defiant, just like its former inhabitants. My chest tightens at the thought of those lively halls gone silent.

"She won't be that way forever, my friend," Lucifer soothes, but Beelzebub gives a derisive snort.

"Unless we stop Alexander, she will be. Let us hope he doesn't burn the school down out of spite. I do believe he's just that petty," Beelzebub says, and I see rage reflected in his eyes. I know without a doubt if he gets the chance, he'll take off my grandfather's head himself. We just might need to find him a box.

"If that is true," the Fallen says with an arrogant tilt of his head, silver hair gleaming in the sun, "then shouldn't we be going? We present a rather large target out here." His condescending tone raises my hackles, even if I happen to agree with him.

"Sagar," the mini Archdemon says with a cutting smile. "Just because you've been temporarily promoted, it doesn't mean you have a seat at the table. Asmodeus will be with us soon enough. Remember your place."

Damn, the tween is starting to grow on me. I smirk at the Fallen—Sagar. Lucifer wears a long-suffering expression on his face as he listens to the biting exchange. Come to think of it, despite the Morningstar being the original Archdemon, I've never really heard him get into the petty politics of the Council. Yeah, he's all about it now because they threaten Luna, but he doesn't go on and on about hierarchy. Even when he confronted Alexander, it was more about scolding Gramps for having the audacity to think he could make Lucifer a puppet in his war. I guess when you've led the Great Rebellion, you don't have to prove shit to anyone anymore.

"You two are like Egyptian street cats fighting over scraps, puffing yourselves up to look bigger," Lucifer says, and I stifle a laugh. "Let us forget the power games for a brief moment and focus on safely removing these children from harm's way, shall we?" He gives Beelzebub and Sagar both a withering glare before turning to address the Nephilim strewn across the steps of Babel in clumps like patches of weeds.

"Dear children," he begins, projecting his voice until his smooth baritone rings out around us. Then his eyes snag on a few of the teachers, and he smirks. "Well, no matter your age, you're all children to me."

I see Hammurabi roll his eyes, and I have to say, I've never met someone less child-like.

Lucifer's face hardens. "I apologize for tearing you away from the shelter of your home, but Babel no longer represents a safe haven for you. None of our academies, Dark or Light, are safe anymore. An old threat to our world has emerged, and I refuse to allow you to be pawns in his war."

Murmurs ripple over the crowd, and I know everyone is dying to start peppering Lucifer with questions, and they only abstain because he's the Morningstar. And he's scary. They're afraid, too. Their orderly word has been turned upside down. We Darks might bend the rules but we rely on them to keep us secure.

"We first go to Megiddo, and then we'll take you somewhere safe." Lucifer's eyes soften as he takes in all the young faces before him. "Look at all of you, dying to drown me in your curiosity, but I'm afraid it will have to wait." His battle mask slides back on.

We all trail behind Lucifer like ants in a nursery rhyme. Once we're back on the Shadow Road, paranoia settles under my skin again. We're traveling with close to four hundred kids to Megiddo, and as fast as Nephilim can move, I still feel like we're a herd of tortoises shuffling along. I'm in the middle of the pack with Hammurabi, Lucifer leads, and Beelzebub and Sagar guard our backs. I think Lucifer put them together as punishment for their earlier sniping. Teachers are strewn throughout, offering protection. It doesn't feel like enough, and I hate this vulnerability chafing at my skin.

It's not like the Nephilim kids are delicate butterflies who'll be forever maimed if something brushes against their wings. Hell, the third and final-year students will put up a decent fight, especially if they have strong bloodlines. But they're just kids. They fight simulated battles in a carefully controlled environment. They're not worried about dying.

I know because until a handful of months ago, I was just like them. Now, I've wounded two angels and was in the middle of a major brawl and barely survived.

Shalina's slim hand on my shoulder shakes me from my somber mood. I meet her green eyes and suppress a groan. The interrogation is about to begin. Well, I was expecting it, and I owe them an explanation.

I glance at Rafe, who looks like he's been biting his tongue this whole time. I roll my eyes and wave a hand. "Ask."

But before Rafe can open his mouth, Shalina holds up her hand. "Start at the beginning, with Ishtar."

I give her a bitter smile, well aware that the two of them love Ishtar, too. So, I spill about Ishtar's plan and how she convinced me—quite easily, fool that I am—to release my grandfather.

"She's obsessed with him," I tell them, "at the cost to all others around her. Her first loyalty is to him, and if you're not prepared to bow before the king, you're her enemy. She had no problem throwing me away."

Rafe and Shalina look deeply troubled by my words. "Is Alexander really bad news?" Rafe asks.

"Well, he's a Gray angel. How can he be good news?" Shalina says with all the prejudiced contempt she can muster.

"Cut that bullshit out right now," I hiss, taking her by surprise. "Being a Gray has fuck all to do with it. Gramps has a Messiah complex. He thinks being a Gray makes him the rightful ruler of us all, and that he can smash down the divide between us. Problem is, he doesn't care how much destruction or death he causes to reach that goal. Get me? Luna is a Gray, and she's as sweet as pie. She doesn't care about power and just wants us to stop being assholes to each other. She's the best of both worlds."

Shalina's brows rise at my venomous tone, and Rafe cocks his head to the side. "You mentioned Luna before. Who is she?"

"There's *another* Gray," Shalina says at the same time.

I glower at Shalina as I say, "Luna is my…girlfriend." I hesitate over the word, not because I'm commitment phobic, but because calling an angel your girlfriend seems so lame. Like it's not an adequate enough word to describe what Goldilocks means to me. "We met at the Serapeum."

"There was another Gray just wandering around in the *Serapeum?*" Shalina asks, voice shrill.

"You have a *girlfriend?*" Rafe demands.

Well, it's clear where both their priorities lie. Hammurabi hears our voices and shoots me a warning glance across the body of Nephilim crowded on the Road. I give him a sheepish shrug and glare at my best friends.

"Cut the dramatics," I say. "Luna just thought she was a Light Nephilim—she didn't know she was a Gray, not until later. Her Dark side had been repressed. Anyway, we became friends, and it turns out she's a Gray. And an angel."

"You're banging an angel?" Rafe asks, glee and admiration in his eyes.

"I'm going to punch you in the face," I threaten, and I'm not joking.

"I'll join you," Shalina says, giving her lover a poisonous glare.

He throws his hands up. "Sorry, but this is just too good. Plus, you liked her when you thought she was a *Light.* That's some Romeo and Juliet shit right there."

I roll my eyes and give them a brief rundown on what happened at the Serapeum, finishing up with who Luna's real parents are. That leaves them both speechless and I chuckle, enjoying a nice moment of quiet. It doesn't last long.

Shalina's eyes narrow on the front of the crowd, as if she can see through them to get to Lucifer. Nephilim can see well, but we don't have X-ray vision. "The Morningstar…and Gabriel?" She looks like she's about to be sick. "How…*what?*"

"Hey, Ishtar and Gilgamesh have been sleeping together for years," I say. "He defected to Alexander for her, so it does happen." I mean, it rarely ever happens—at least that we know of.

"Ew," Shalina gasps, and Rafe gives her an irritated glance.

"Baby, I didn't realize you were such a prejudiced little prick," he says, frowning, and she glowers at him. "We're Darks. We're meant to break rules, and Lucifer is the original rule breaker. And Gabriel is hot, even for an ice queen."

"And this happened before the Fall," I point out. "But Rafe is right. When did you become so narrow-minded, Shalina?"

"I'm sorry, Caleb, but I don't remember you being all Team Light before you left," Shalina counters. "You sure weren't advocating for us all to just get along."

Point scored. "You're right. Meeting Luna changed a lot for me. I never realized how…petty we all are to each other. I don't agree with my grandfather's methods, but he's right about one thing. We gotta bridge this divide between us. All this hatred, what good is it doing us? What are we so scared of? And with Alexander going all Conqueror, we're going to have to somehow get along, or we're not going to survive."

Shalina frowns, rubbing her hands up and down her arms. "I never thought of it like that. Coming together to defeat a common enemy. I guess…we have to, don't we?"

Rafe slings an arm around Shalina, looking more relaxed. "Besides, Luna is half Dark so that makes her one of us."

Warmth soothes my tension at his words. It's not like I'd give up Luna for them, and I'd straight out kick their asses if they disrespected her, but it's a relief to know I don't have to lose my friends.

A small smile tugs on Shalina's lips. "You're right. She *is* half Dark and Lucifer's kid. How bad could she be?"

I grin at them both as we edge closer to the marker for Megiddo. As the kids ahead of me go through, my eyes wander to Hammurabi, and he nods, letting me know to keep my guard up. Babel was a cakewalk, so I choose to be optimistic about Lucifer's school.

The acrid smell of smoke assaults me when I step from the Road, dashing my hopes for an easy evacuation. Screams echo around us, and I look at where the school is supposed to be. Megiddo belches black smoke and scarlet flames. My heart sinks as I take in the destruction.

"Caleb, look," Rafe breathes, pointing.

My eyes round as I see soldiers in black Kevlar armor herding the Nephilim kids into the streets. A battle cry rents the air, and my head snaps toward that enraged bellow. Lucifer has his wings out and his sword drawn. He soars up the hill, Beelzebub following.

Oh, shit. It's on.

THIRTEEN

LUNA

THE EVACUATION FROM MOUNT Sinai goes smoothly. Shortly after securing the weapons, we return to the entrance hall along with Raphael, where we find Gabriel, directing the students with the help of Hatshepsut and a few other of the academy's teachers. When the first generation Nephilim catch sight of the trunks in our hands, they relieve us of the responsibility, leaving Lilith and me empty-handed and with little else to do but part ways and return to our respective Roads. As Mount Sinai is a secondary academy, most of the students have experience with the Blessed Road, which streamlines the process. But it doesn't quell the obvious panic looming among the hundreds of Nephilim whispering in hushed voices to each other, their questions and murmurs of dread carrying to my ears where I walk at the front of the crowd with Raphael and my mother.

I can understand their unease. Uncertainty plagues our every step, and there is no answer any of us can give—no reassurance—that will assuage their fears. If only we knew something of the war to come or what to anticipate next from Alexander.

If only I knew what the Creator expects from me.

Once again, a sense of helplessness gnaws at my thoughts. *No…not helplessness,* I realize. Because I'm not. What I am is powerless. Powerless to act beyond the role and path decided for me by fate.

A scornful breath escapes me. I wish I knew what the hell I'm meant to be doing.

I peer at Gabriel out of the corner of my eye, exchanging one weighted thought for another. We haven't said a single word to each other since we reconvened at Sinai. While things have always been awkward between us, now the tension is exacerbated, and what's worse, it's completely my fault. I'm acting weird and I'm sure she can sense it. That's the only explanation for why she avoids my gaze, even though I know she can feel my eyes on her face.

I frown at the croon of Lilith's voice in my head again, and though it's not loud enough to drown out the terror clawing at me, it's persistent enough that I can't ignore it any longer.

I was wanted. I wasn't some unplanned accident—a burden Gabriel got saddled with—like I assumed. I was *wanted.*

And for some reason, knowing that breaks my heart.

It's not that I ever thought Gabriel didn't care for me. After all, she wouldn't have gone to the lengths she did to protect me from the prophecy if she didn't. But to hear that I wasn't some unwelcome mistake, that she actually *wanted* me, that I wouldn't exist at all if she hadn't, on some subconscious level, desired a child with Lucifer…

I shake my head at the thought, unable to imagine the pain she must have endured when she chose to lock me away. For so long, I've battled my own anger and resentment about what she did to me, but now…now, I'm struck with a heartache and sympathy that fills every inch of me like water rushing into my lungs.

My mother wanted me. She wanted me and she lost me, just like she lost my father. And though she vowed she would defy the Creator before being separated from us again, I can understand now why she seems so terrified to embrace our reunion, embrace *us.* She hides behind her guilt, but the reality is, she's afraid. Afraid of having her happiness snatched away.

I part my lips to say something—*anything*—but no words rise to the surface. I can't bring myself to tell her I know. To tell her I also wanted her, more than any child could ever want a mother. I want to say it, but I don't. I can't.

Because the truth is, I'm afraid, too, and saying those words only makes it all the more likely I'll eventually lose her. It's too late to push away my father or Caleb, but Gabriel…I can keep her at a safe distance. I can shield my heart from this one potential loss.

For now, at least.

The journey from Mount Sinai to the Serapeum takes only minutes using the Blessed Road, and before I know it, I'm stepping out of the encompassing light of the celestial path back into the warm Egyptian sunshine of the mortal world. Raphael and my mother emerge with me—followed by the students and teachers from Sinai, who remain by the entrance to the Road, awaiting our return from a distance just in case the academy isn't safe—and together, we approach the Serapeum, sharing the unspoken hope that Alexander hasn't already been here.

Unlike the last time I stood in front of the academy like this, I don't need to look past its glamor to see the structure's true magnificence. Now, with the bind lifted, I see it more clearly than ever.

My stomach twists. I'm not sure how I feel about being back here. This place has served as the setting of so many of my worst memories, but at the same time, it's also home to some of my fondest. Like meeting Caleb. And growing close with Alaric. Plus, if I hadn't ever come to the Serapeum, who's to say I would've ever found out what I am? If I had remained in Maine in the hospital, or even attended a different academy, I likely still wouldn't know what a Gray is…or who my parents are, for that matter. Looking at it that way, the good that came out of my attendance at the Serapeum far outweighs the bad. And yet…

"It's strange to be back," I mutter, placing my foot on the bottom-most stair as Raphael and my mother ascend on each side of me. Above us, I glimpse the familiar golden doors carved with a depiction of the Fall. Although I can't see the image fully from here, the details are carved into my memory, although some are sharper than others. Like the face of my father. Looking back at when I arrived in Alexandria, the moment I walked through these doors was the first time I felt something between us—not the song of our blood, but a connection. I just didn't realize what that connection was.

"It is for me as well," Gabriel admits. "Especially now that I can see how blind I was to what was right before me."

"Blind?" While I know she's talking about me, I don't entirely know what she means. I don't hold it against her that she didn't realize I'm her daughter when I was a student here. How could she have? The song between us was severed—*is* severed, even if I swear I can feel the tingle of it trying to return.

Her eyes shift to mine, and the barest smile quirks the edges of her lips. "You look so much like your father. Only a fool wouldn't have noticed."

A malicious chuckle escapes Raphael. "She's his reflection. You were a fool, indeed, to fail to notice the resemblance."

"Or in deep denial," Lilith mutters, trudging up the stairs on my mother's right side where a moment ago there was nothing but air. The ex-Archdemon is beginning to make a habit of popping up out of nowhere.

Raphael gives a dramatic eye-roll, but Gabriel ignores her, scowling at Lilith, who laughs. "Don't give me that look. You know I'm right."

My mother grumbles under her breath, but she doesn't protest as we continue to the top of the stairs. Like at Mount Sinai, the doors open at our approach, but unlike at Mount Sinai, no Nephilim or angel steps out of the school's depths to meet us. Whoever's in charge here must not know we're coming.

"No welcoming party this time, I see," Lilith comments, arching an imperious brow.

"Are we supposed to be welcomed?" I ask. No one came to greet us when Alaric brought me here. Then again, it was his job to escort new students to the academy, and if any of those other arrivals were anything like me, meeting another Nephilim or even Gabriel within moments of stepping foot in this place would've been one mind-blowing interaction too many. Especially when I was already grappling with the bombshell he tossed into my lap that I wasn't actually human. Given Alaric's kind nature, he probably didn't want the experience to be any more overwhelming or confusing for me than it already was. The focus had to be on calming me, not overstimulating my already fragile mind.

"Not if we were entering a Dark school," Lilith says, "but the Lights *thrive* on pomp and circumstance. After Sinai, I merely assumed we would receive the same warm welcome here." Her tone drips with sarcasm.

Raphael crosses her arms, tapping a forefinger against the crook of her opposite elbow, a glower darkening her fair face. "It is *not* pomp and circumstance," she retorts, glaring at the ex-Archdemon. "It is good conduct to send someone to greet important arrivals, just as it is considered good conduct to not enter another Council member's academy without their permission. At least, not unless they're expecting you."

Her words make me think of Caleb and my father. I'm not sure who the Council put in charge of Babel in Asmodeus's absence, but I doubt the unknown Fallen is expecting their arrival either, though I can't exactly see that stopping Lucifer. I only hope they don't encounter any problems—from Alexander or otherwise.

"The Lights here clearly have to work on their manners then," Lilith scoffs before strutting forward, sauntering through the open doors without a care in the world.

"What are you doing?" Raphael snaps.

Lilith waves a dismissive hand over her shoulder but continues walking. "Whichever of your trained dogs you put in dear Gabriel's stead isn't officially on the Council yet, are they? Besides, we do not have the leisure of time to care about manners."

Raphael gives a haughty sniff. "I...concede you have a point," she grinds out before reluctantly tailing Lilith over the threshold.

My mother and I follow closely behind, and as we take the path from the entrance hall to the administration office, my eyes scan the details of the school as if this is the first time I've seen them. It's all so familiar and yet somehow foreign—or maybe it all just feels so different because of how much I've changed since I last stepped foot in these halls over half a year ago. Either way, I feel out of place, like I don't belong.

Then again, I never really did.

"How is it Hatshepsut knew we were coming at Sinai but no one was aware of our arrival here?" I muse aloud as we pass through the cloister into the long hallway of classrooms. I keep my voice low so as not to interrupt the muted din of lectures on the other side of each door. At least if the students are all in class, the evacuation should move quickly.

"Think of the academies as living entities of sorts," Raphael says, a surprisingly patient drawl to her words. "Each one is attuned to the angel or Fallen who oversees it. They know when we are there. They know when we are gone. And they know when we return, as will those who we trust to help run them. I suppose you could say they speak to us, in a way."

"Interesting, then, that no one came to greet us, wouldn't you agree?" Lilith sneers. "It's almost like the Serapeum doesn't approve of Gabriel's replacement."

Raphael bares her teeth in a growl, but before she can utter a scathing word in response, my mother cuts in, "That's enough, both of you. We have more pressing matters at hand."

Picking up her pace, Gabriel charges ahead, leading the way into the administration office at the end of the corridor, never once faltering in her determined advance as she pushes through the set of glass doors. I race to keep up, brushing past Raphael and Lilith, who are locked in a battle of glares.

As I near the office, I hear a familiar voice squeak, "Headmistress!" and I peer through the glass to see Evangeline jumping up from her desk. Remembering herself, she clears her throat and amends, "Gabriel. You're back." Relief glistens in the blue pools of her eyes, which snap to me as I step into the office. "I hope—" she begins before gasping out, "Luna! I…" She shakes her head, glancing between us, visibly rattled. "What—"

Gabriel holds up a hand. "Your questions will have to wait, Evangeline. We need to speak with Zerachiel immediately."

Zerachiel?

I didn't think my mother knew who took her place as headmistress. Then again, she entered the Serapeum once before, uninvited and unannounced, to retrieve her armor and sword before coming to my rescue at the citadel. She could've easily discovered who is running this establishment in her stead at that time. Either that or the school somehow told her, if the academies really do speak to their caretakers and the Serapeum still sees Gabriel in that role.

"O-Of course," Evangeline says, her cobalt eyes darting between Gabriel's face and the black door in the corner. "I'll just—"

"I'm afraid we don't have time for pleasantries or polite conduct," Gabriel interrupts with an apologetic smile at the Nephilim, crossing the room to her old office. She hesitates for a moment before grasping the handle, giving a soft snort at the large silver Z imprinted into the wood in place of her own sigil. Then, with a dignified lift of her chin, she throws open the door.

"What is the meaning of—" The booming male voice falters mid-sentence, and I pause behind Gabriel, peering over her shoulder into the spacious office at the angel I presume to be Zerachiel. Violet eyes stare, dumbfounded, at my mother. "Messenger," he breathes, rising from his seat, long chestnut hair brushing his shoulders. "I'll admit, I didn't expect you to show your face here, but then, you were always a bold one. I assume it was you who purloined your sword and armor from the museum?"

She shrugs. "It is not theft if they are rightfully mine."

His aura contorts as he leans forward, placing his hands on the desk that once belonged to her. "Give me one good reason why I shouldn't contact the Council and turn you over."

Although I can't see her face, I can easily imagine the icy smile forming. "Because the Council is here with me," she retorts, her tone somehow both frigid and scalding.

As if on cue, Lilith and Raphael appear at my side, and I watch the contempt on Zerachiel's face transform into unease as the latter steps past me and Gabriel into the office.

"Hello, Zerac," Raphael purrs. "Enjoying your time on Earth, I take it?"

Straightening, he glances between the two Archangels and Lilith, confusion written into the furrowed crease of his brow. "I...don't understand," is all he says.

"And we're short on time," my mother huffs. "So, here's the abridged version."

The shock that Hatshepsut displayed when she learned about Ashkelon pales in comparison to the horror stripping the color from Zerachiel's face. Learning about the fate of the Dark academy is all the convincing he needs, and over the course of the next twenty minutes, we split off into groups—my mother, Evangeline, and Zerachiel scouring the library and securing the weapons in the museum, while Raphael, Lilith, and I knock on dorm room doors and visit every classroom, urging students to proceed to the entrance hall of the school for immediate evacuation. The Nephilim all react to our presence with audible confusion, though it's Lilith who bears the brunt of their poorly concealed shock the most. They gape at her with the same question in each of their nervous gazes—why is a Fallen in a school strictly for Lights?—but they seem to know better than to question her and obey without hesitation when she tells them to move. Fear of the unknown is a powerful motivator and outweighs whatever distaste they have toward Darks.

Once every last room has been checked, we join the rest of the school, preparing to re-enter the Blessed Road and finally make our way to the Council's rendezvous location. The teachers—some of whom I recognize, like Vesta, and some I don't, like Gilgamesh's replacement for *History of the Fall*—corral the students alongside my mother and Raphael, herding them into manageable lines.

I watch them work, standing off to the side of the entrance hall with Lilith—ever the outcasts—beside the white marble statues of the seven Archangels, counting every second with building unease. Curious eyes keep looking my way, and I spot recognition in some of those glances, though it seems uncertain, as if the onlookers aren't quite sure they know who I am.

"Is that...?" I hear someone say in a thick, Southern accent, and goosebumps pimple my skin as a shiver of dread rolls through my body.

I know that voice. It tormented me for months. And sure enough, I spot Lisbeth and a gaggle of girls walking past us, gaping at me like I've taken the form of a hydra and I just sprouted several heads.

My eyes sweep over the crowd, looking anywhere but at the girls who bullied me mercilessly when I was a student here. The last thing I want is to give them the satisfaction of knowing I can hear them. Still, I can't stop myself from watching them in my peripheral vision, clinging to every word.

"Holy shit, it is," Ellie mutters before shaking Lisbeth's shoulder and pointing to the front of the crowd where my mother is overseeing the students. "And look, Gabriel is back, too."

Lisbeth doesn't take her eyes off me—I can feel them burning into the side of my face—or lower her voice when she says, "Hey, does Lunatic look kinda different to you?"

Different?

Without meaning to, I glance at them, and Ellie recoils.

"C-Come on," she stammers, a genuine terror in her voice. She tugs on Lisbeth's arm. "Let's go."

As she pulls the other girl away, Lilith whispers in my ear, "They can sense it."

"Sense what?" I ask, finally tearing my gaze from the group as they hurry to join the shifting lines now proceeding through the open doors. When I peer up at her, she places a hand on my shoulder.

"That you aren't like them. Not anymore."

She jerks her chin, gesturing for us to follow the crowd, and as we make our way back out of the school and down the steps into the afternoon sunshine, I mull over her words. I know I'm not like them—I never have been—but I never realized how different I am now until I saw that fear in Ellie's eyes. I used to think Gabriel was terrifying—before I knew who she was to me and, if I'm honest with myself, even after—but it's what Caleb once said to me that sticks in my head now. That angels are beautiful and terrible and can frighten the wits out of even first generation Nephilim.

Is that why Ellie was so scared? Because I give off a sense of otherness that I didn't possess when I was bound? If so, I wonder if Caleb senses it, too. If I seem different at all in his eyes to the meek, bullied girl he met at the Serapeum.

Would it matter? I ask myself. Angel or not, immortal or not, Caleb loves me. So long as I have that, I suppose I don't really care.

My eyes drift to the bottom of the stairs where the students are ushered into the Blessed Road by their Nephilim teachers before they, too, vanish into its radiant depths. I hurry down the steps toward my mother, who waits by the entrance with Zerachiel and Raphael.

"That's the last of them. Now, where are we going?" Gabriel asks in a hushed voice, her heated glare on Raphael. When the Archangel doesn't immediately respond, Gabriel growls, "We've proven our sincerity, Raphael. Surely, you can see that."

"And if the threat really is as great as you say, we shouldn't dally," Zerachiel says.

Raphael's eyes flash with annoyance at the other angel's words, but after a moment, she nods. "Indeed," she agrees, sounding somewhat begrudging. Then, clearing her throat, she adds, "Of course."

Closing her eyes, the Archangel draws in a deep breath and tugs her blouse sleeve down over her shoulder, pressing her forefinger to the white Enochian symbol branded into her now-exposed upper arm—similar to the one my mother possesses on her forearm, though the character isn't exactly the same. Her eyes flutter beneath their lids for a moment before they slide open again.

"We're to reconvene in Derinkuyu," she says in a careful voice, keeping the words just a breath above silent. Her stern gaze snaps between us then fleetingly across our surroundings and back.

My mother exchanges a quick glance with Lilith, who touches a hand to my shoulder before retreating toward a half-broken pillar nearby and the slip of darkness puddled underneath it. She vanishes into the Shadow Road without a word.

With our mission completed, we don't delay our departure, and my mother, Raphael, Zerachiel, and I hasten to join the Lights in the Blessed Road. Once again, Gabriel and I head to the front of the crowd—the combined student body now a staggering eight hundred, plus a few dozen teachers—while Zerachiel heads to the back, stating his intention to keep an eye on his pupils. Unlike when we traveled to the Serapeum, Raphael doesn't join us this time, either, instead opting to check in with her teachers from Sinai. I hope the fact that she's no longer hovering over us like a vulture means she trusts our intentions and plans to join our cause against Alexander. Or, at the very least, stop trying to force me back into a cage.

Once Gabriel and I are out of the Archangel's earshot, I turn to her, lifting a questioning brow. "Derinkuyu?"

"An ancient underground city in Turkey," she answers. Then, with a nod of approval, she adds, "A sensible place to hide so many innocent souls."

I'll have to take her word on that.

"And she knew that's where the Council wants everyone to meet just by touching her tattoo?" After Caleb freed me from the Council's prison, I stood witness as Asmodeus gifted Alaric one of these sigils, and while I remember what she said about how they work, I still don't fully understand the process—even if the thought of a celestial cell phone is probably the least bewildering thing I've witnessed since the day Alaric brought me to the Serapeum.

Gabriel tugs on the collar of her shirt, pulling it down over her shoulder and revealing an Enochian symbol on her upper arm, identical to Raphael's. I knew about the crescent moon on her forearm—the symbol she used to call my father to her side shortly after I released Alexander—but I never knew she had more than one of these brands.

"With these, we can call each other to our locations. This sigil is for everyone on the Council, though I haven't dared to use it in months, and I doubt anyone would answer me now if I tried."

"Like how you called Lucifer to you under the Serapeum?" At her surprised expression, I say, "I saw the Enochian symbol on your arm."

Her mouth hardens into a grim line, and her eyes cloud with the memory of that day. She probably didn't think I was coherent enough in my pain to notice. "Yes," she murmurs after a moment. "Though that sigil isn't true Enochian. None of the ones we use to commune are."

I blink at her, confused. "They aren't?"

She shakes her head. "This"—she tugs up her shirt sleeve, revealing the thin, crescent moon tattoo—"is a sigil your father and I created for our personal use. And this"—she repeats the gesture with the other arm, exposing a symbol a few inches above her wrist that resembles an X—"is mine and Lilith's. Many of us do that, you know—come up with our own sigils when we desire private communication— otherwise anyone, Fallen or Faithful alike, could brand themselves with the same symbols and…eavesdrop on the connection in a sense. Even the Council's sigil is an altered form of an existing Enochian letter." She points now to the E-shaped brand on her upper arm. Then righting her shirt, she glances at me. "Think of these variations like angelic slang. They're all based in the pure language but you won't find them in any alphabet."

I snort. "I wouldn't be able to find them regardless. Enochian isn't taught anymore, remember?"

Gabriel gives me a pointed look. "Not in the schools, no. But I could always teach you. Or your father could," she amends when I just stare at her, rendered speechless by the offer. "I'm sure he'd be happy to."

I mull over that notion, imagining myself learning the language of my lineage, one piece closer to being whole. To becoming who I was always truly meant to be. It warms my chest, and yet, the idea quickly sours, turning my stomach.

"You don't think the Council would have something to say about that?"

My mother's responding expression is defiant. "They can say whatever they want. Despite what they think, you are not Alexander."

Tears prick behind my eyes and I nod, desperately hoping she's right. That my actions in the war to come will prove that we haven't made a huge mistake and misinterpreted the prophecy. That I really am the Savior and not the monster destined to destroy this world. That I'm a force for good, even if I don't quite believe it. Otherwise, Gabriel will have no choice but to follow through on her bluff and help the Council lock me away again.

Shaking that thought away, I change the subject. "Asmodeus gave Alaric a sigil."

"An…unheard of gift for a Nephilim," Gabriel says, but I notice she doesn't sound surprised. I suppose she wouldn't be. She was with my father when Alaric met up with him while I was at Babel with Caleb—before we found out about the tracker in my head, and everything went to hell.

"So he said." I clear my throat, swallowing the rising lump of emotion that always grips me when I think of the Nephilim. "When Asmodeus was telling him how to use it, she called the connection an echo, but I don't really understand what she meant. How exactly does it work?"

Gabriel considers that for a moment. "Well, when Raphael touched her sigil, the others branded with that same symbol would've felt it. Through that connection, she could've either informed them of her location or discerned theirs, if they were open to it, which, clearly, someone on the Council was, or she wouldn't have received an answer. The communication…" She falters, searching for the right way to explain it. "Well, it comes to us in pictures, so yes, I suppose you could call them echoes, as it's quite similar to echolocation."

"So…we're basically human-shaped bats?" I peer over my shoulder, imagining my outstretched wings, and immediately begin to wonder if Alexander had it all wrong when he called me a dove.

Gabriel chuckles, drawing my gaze again. "Hardly. Many creatures use echolocation, and last I checked, neither one of us resembles a whale."

"Raphael kind of looks like a shrew," I mutter. "In certain lights."

An amused smile tugs at Gabriel's lips. "I don't think that's the insult you intend it to be." When I arch a bemused brow at her, she shrugs. "What? Shrews are…cute."

Cute? Did Gabriel really just call something *cute?* A shocked gasp escapes me. "That might be the nicest thing I've ever heard you say."

Her grin widens. "Don't tell Raphael. Our entire relationship is built on mutual loathing."

A smile of my own forms at that, and I revel in the comfortable silence that falls between us, relishing how normal this feels. Well, not the whole escorting nearly one thousand scared Nephilim to a safe haven part, but the mother part. The being someone's daughter part.

Turning to face her, I open my mouth to say something—to finally tell her everything that's been floating around in my head over the last few hours, to cross the final chasm between us despite the risk to my heart and sanity should I lose her—when a shrill cry in the distance chills me down to the bone and all but freezes the blood in my veins. Gabriel and I whip around at the same moment, scanning the mass of Nephilim for the source of the scream. Panic rises through the crowd, the students' terror a mirror image of my own.

"What's happening?" Fear is a hand around my windpipe, choking the words to a rasping breath, and its grasp only tightens when flames of the deepest blood red erupt along the Road, scorching across the full breadth of the path behind us.

The screams become widespread now, and the terrified Nephilim try to run—to flee the unknown danger and reach the nearest marker, regardless of where it might throw them out in the world—but the fire seems to sense their movements, blocking their every attempt at escape and building around the large group like a fiery pen intended to trap us like sheep. The only route of escape is ahead, but the flames are moving quickly, and it won't be long until that path is blocked.

It's just like in my nightmares and like in the visions Alexander tormented me with at the Serapeum. Angry crimson flames roar around us, hungry and ready to devour the world.

Gabriel's hand flies to my wrist as I whisper, "He found us," and before another coherent thought can form, she grabs my shoulders and roughly turns me to face her.

"Listen to me," she hisses, her gaze piercing. "Run ahead now while you can, leave this Road, *hide*, and once the coast is clear, contact Lilith." As she speaks, she shoves up my shirt sleeve and clamps her hand around my forearm, her grasp like a vise. I wince at the slight burning sensation that follows then stare at my skin, amazed, when she pulls her fingers away to reveal the same X-shaped Enochian brand she showed me on her own arm only moments ago.

"What?" I shake my head, glancing between her fierce face—a resolute devastation burning deep in her eyes—and over my shoulder toward the flames, which grow bolder and larger as screams ring out around us. The Nephilim scramble toward us, trying to reach that sole available route of escape, their fear of this unfamiliar threat palpable, like the scent of rot in the air. Any moment now, they'll trample us in their terror, but I don't move despite my mother's plea. I glance around, my eyes alert, searching for Alexander. He must be here. Only a Gray can create red fire and I sure as hell didn't start this inferno. But in a sea of nearly one thousand Nephilim, he is a needle in a haystack, and I see nothing but chaos.

Past the screaming, I catch the grating sound of swords clashing, and I wonder who else is here on behalf of Alexander—how many Lights he's managed to sway to his side since we left Kandahār and are now attacking their own kind. *No, this isn't just an attack, it's an ambush,* I realize. He knew we would come this way. Maybe he even planned for us to and attacking Ashkelon was just the catalyst to corner a larger herd on the Road.

I look back at my mother as the horror of another realization sinks in. She wants me to run—to leave her and everyone else here to die. Or worse, leave them to become chained puppets in Alexander's conquest for power.

"No—" I begin to protest as she shouts over me, "This isn't a debate! Go *now!*"

The seconds slow to a standstill, and all the blood rushes to my ears, drowning out the screams and fighting. My eyes track a movement over Gabriel's shoulder, and I let out a gasp as flames rise up like a wall ahead of us, cutting off our only path of escape. That's when I finally see him: Alexander emerging from the fiery depths, descending on Gabriel from behind, his dagger upraised to smite her.

"Mom!" The warning tears from my lungs with the force of a thunder strike, and I only have a split-second to embrace the blood song between us, finally freed from the cage of our hearts as that one all-important word leaves my lips, as if saying it aloud has somehow broken the spell cast over us. No, not a spell. A *bind*.

A fleeting happiness spreads across Gabriel's face as this realization hits her as well, but it's instantly dampened by the understanding that something isn't right—that I didn't call for her out of affection but fear. Noting the direction of my petrified gaze, she begins to turn to face our enemy, but her movements come too late. Alexander's blade already descends and she'll never react to the threat and reach her own weapon in time to stop him from cutting her down.

But I can.

Swallowing my fear, I hurl myself forward, reaching for the pommel of Gabriel's sword where it sits in the invisible scabbard on her back. I can't see it, but I can sense the steel as it rings out like the tings of a tuning fork, calling to me, just like it did the first time I saw it in the museum at the Serapeum, even if I didn't understand why at the time. Sensing my desperation, it guides my hand until my fingers wrap around the cool metal, and as I pull it free—pushing Gabriel out of the way—the bronze hilt and steel blade reveal themselves, gleaming in the light of the Road. The sword vibrates under my touch, and as I lunge toward Alexander, meeting his dagger in a clash of metal on metal, it yields to me even as I feel the full force of his blow reverberating all the way down to my bones, the steel holding steady despite my inexperience in battle…and despite Alexander's clear intention to kill. His strength is formidable, and if I was a Nephilim, I have no doubt he would've cut right through me. But, as I'm learning, I have strength of my own, and with the sword in my hand, I feel stronger than ever. This sword is the power of my bloodline, and like Gabriel before me, this weapon is mine to wield. Because I am not just a Morningstar.

I am my mother's daughter.

"Hello again, little dove," Alexander purrs before jumping back several steps, out of reach of my weapon. I lunge forward again, but he just clicks his tongue, retreating farther. "There will be time for that yet," he says, flashing me a bone-chilling smile, which he then directs with pure venom at my mother. He dips into a low, mocking bow. "Until next time, Messenger."

He thrusts out a hand, extinguishing the flames ahead, then vanishes from the Road.

Shell-shocked, I stare at the spot where he stood only seconds ago, trying to piece together what just happened. Beside me, Gabriel climbs to her feet.

"I'm sor—" I begin to say, expecting her to berate me for stealing her sword—or at least for endangering myself—but she just pulls me into her arms, hugging me so tightly I can't finish the sentence. The song in our hearts rings like a church bell, tolling in my ears, making me feel complete in a way I never expected or imagined, and I know she hears it, too, because she hugs me tighter. Her aura blazes around us like she is the sun itself, swallowing me whole, and my fingers slacken, dropping the blade to the ground, before curling around her back.

We stay that way for a moment, and when we finally part, I notice the flames that barricaded the path behind us have been extinguished as well, returning the Road to normal again. The screaming and clang of battle have both ceased, and as far as I can tell, no one seems to be injured or any worse for wear—a fact we confirm with Raphael, Zerachiel, and the Nephilim teachers from Sinai and the Serapeum after we gather and do a head count. To my dismay, I was right. Lights have joined Alexander and a dozen or so first generations attacked the students. But what's strange is that no one is missing, no one is hurt, and most peculiar of all, none of the weapons were taken.

So, what was the point of that ambush other than to terrify us?

"What the hell was that about?" I growl in a low voice to my mother when we resume our forward march to Derinkuyu a short while later. Her sword has been returned to its rightful place on her back, though my fingers tingle, mourning the loss. Or maybe I'm just realizing now how important it is that I learn to defend myself, not only against those who would seek to do me harm, but most importantly, against Alexander. "Why didn't he fight back?" I find myself asking, confusion leaching into my tone. Not because I wanted him to—he would've killed me if he had—but because his inaction doesn't make any sense.

Gabriel shakes her head. "I don't know. But whatever the Conqueror's reasoning, it doesn't bode well for us."

FOURTEEN

CALEB

THE GREAT TEMPLE IS halfway gone. I mean, archeologists and tourists already think it *is* gone, but now it actually resembles the ruins people come to gawk at in wonder. Made out of mud bricks, it's much more vulnerable than other ancient sites that have the fortune to be hewn of stone. The tall gates with their sentry towers writhe in orange and scarlet. I can't tell how many of the palaces are on fire, but they couldn't have escaped unscathed—not with this much smoke.

My throat burns and I cough, eyes watering, but I still manage to spot a few bodies lying on the steps in front of the temple like broken dolls. I know in my heart they aren't students but brave teachers who tried to protect their charges. How old were those Nephilim? How many gaping holes are left in the world now that can never be filled? I can't imagine how many treasures were inside Megiddo that we have lost.

Treasures and weapons.

"Boy," Hammurabi hisses in my ear, and I whirl to face him, startled out of my immediate horror. "Draw your dagger and follow me. We join the Morningstar in battle."

I glance back at Rafe and Shalina whose eyes brim with terror. I try to give them a reassuring smile, but it comes out more like a grimace. Hammurabi barks orders to the Babel teachers, and they herd their charges together, going for safety in numbers. I notice Sagar stays with them, instead of joining Lucifer and Beelzebub. But I guess they are *his* responsibility now, and he has to protect them. Besides, it's not like he can take them anywhere—those assholes on the Council have made sure of that, holding the location of the safe house hostage until we finish with the evacuations.

Steeling myself, I leave my friends and sprint toward my grandfather's troops, heart pounding in my chest like a battering ram.

Hammurabi and I run past the burning gates and straight into the chaos. Smoke surrounds us, and my eagle eyesight tries to punch through the wall of gray. The bright light of the Morningstar can't be denied, and I see Lucifer in all his golden glory swing his silver sword in a vicious arc. A moment later, a head rolls down the stone-paved street, stopping when it meets the toe of my boot. The face of the Nephilim is forever frozen in a state of shock.

Some of Alexander's Nephilim yank kids into the Shadow Road as fast as they can while others face the fury of Lucifer and Beelzebub. But once the students see the Morningstar, they begin to fight back. Hammurabi flashes me a savage grin and wades into the melee, blades flashing. I follow him into the scuffle, but I'm not trying to cross swords with more experienced soldiers. I'm just trying to snag as many kids as I can. While the Babylonian king attempts to relieve an enemy Nephilim of his guts, I swipe two young first-year students—a boy and a girl—and shove them toward the gates.

"Run!" I scream. "Teachers from Babel are outside and can help you. Go to them." They look at me, expressions shell-shocked. "Move!" I order, voice like a whip, and they turn from me and flee into the haze.

I whirl around, trying to find other students I can help. One of Alexander's Nephilim recognizes me, and her aquamarine eyes fill with hatred. She abandons the group of kids she was herding along and comes at me. I feel her power. She's a second generation like me, but she's older. Much older. And shit, she has a sword. I dodge her first strike, coming in close and kissing my blade to the underside of her ribs. She roars, and I dance out of the way, keeping my distance and looking for an opening, but it's hard in all this smoke. I cough, keeping my eye on her as she fades in and out of sight.

Then she's suddenly on my right side, sword heading straight for my shoulder in a diagonal slash. I raise my knife in defense, but tendrils of inky blackness whip past me and wrap around the Nephilim. She's lifted in the air and slammed into the burning walls over and over again until her broken, bloody body goes limp. The tendrils release her and she slides to the ground. The whole thing was over within a matter of seconds. My terrified eyes find Beelzebub, who gives me a bored nod.

"You were taking too long," the Archdemon drawls. "Go help the children."

That is one seriously scary forever tween.

I pivot, eyes darting around for any other stragglers I can poach from Gramps. Two charred bodies rest near Lucifer's feet as he gently pushes a group of students toward the gates. The kids rush past me, alarm plastered onto their faces. In the distance, near one of the ravaged palaces, I see a tall figure standing motionless, staring at me. I still and gaze back. He's an old Nephilim. Really old. I can sense his power from here. A gust of wind momentarily clears the murkiness, and my raptor's vision picks out the details of the man's face. High cheekbones, amber eyes.

My head rings like it's been hit with a sledgehammer. I blink and blink again. Is that…Alaric? But he's dead. I mean, we saw him straight up get murdered. Sourness settles in my gut. Unless…did Grandfather resurrect him? Could someone as old as Alaric even survive that with his mind intact? I start toward him, and he breaks eye contact, vanishing in a mushroom cloud of smoke. When it clears, he's gone.

Is this some sort of trick? Was some shape-shifting Nephilim imitating Alaric? I shake my head because that's not possible. Only Mammon has that ability. And what would be the purpose of imitating Alaric if I'm the only one who saw him?

A flaming beam cracks and swings toward me. Shaking myself from my daze, I leap out the way, barely avoiding being crushed. The intense heat and screams tearing through the air bump me back hard into the present. I want to give chase and hunt the Nephilim down until I'm certain he's really Alaric, but I'm here to save kids. The mystery of Alaric will have to wait, no matter how painful that is. I spot another small cluster of teens who have managed to escape their abductors. I take a step forward, only to stagger back, one hand going over my heart.

No, this can't be happening. I didn't think it was possible, but…I hear it. In my blood, in my mind, sweet notes of family like a saxophone solo in a Blues piece. I focus on the group of young Nephilim until my eyes zero in on a petite girl with straight black hair and huge brown eyes. I can't see much of my dad in her, and if I had to bet, I'd say she's of Japanese descent. She stops running and stares at me, too. She's about fourteen, and a swell of protectiveness crests within me, which seems ridiculous because we haven't even officially met yet, but she's family. *Family.*

She's also a huge target. Alexander would love to get his dictator hands on his granddaughter. Prime clay for molding. I again shake myself out of my stupor and hurry toward the kids.

"Hey!" I call as I run. "I'm with Lucifer. I'm here to help." My eyes snag on my sister once more. My *sister*. She's looking at me, too, her large eyes practically popping out of her head like a deranged cartoon character. I feel you, kid.

"You're my brother," she blurts out, and I wince as the other students stop and stare at me.

"It sure looks that way, Sis," I say smoothly, "and as I'm trying to rescue you from being kidnapped by the big bad, let's save the family reunion for later."

Hammurabi clips me on the back of the head, and I turn around, glaring at him. Blood paints his face, but I don't see any wounds, so it's not his blood. "Move it, boy. The Morningstar says we're done here."

I glance behind me, spotting Lucifer and Beelzebub strolling toward us. Scarlet stains Lucifer's blade, and a few bodies litter the ground in his wake. Rage glows in the Morningstar's eyes, and I shiver at the violence there. He's still craving blood. Not that I blame him. By my count, we've managed to save some of his students, but not all of them. I turn back to the kids and make a shooing motion.

Hammurabi barks, "*Move*," and they hurry their asses down the hill, me trailing behind.

My sister keeps darting glances at me over her shoulder, and I wonder if she's trying to figure out if I look like our dad. It's not like she's ever met him. Unfortunately, yes, I do look like my pathetic father, but I wear his features better than him, if I do say so myself.

A bigger crowd awaits us, and I'm happy to see that our numbers have increased substantially. We haven't exactly doubled in size, but we're close. Fuck you very much, Gramps. I find my way to Shalina and Rafe, my sister practically tripping over my heels. I gently reach back and tug her to my side. My friends study her with open curiosity.

"Who the hell is this?" Rafe asks, eyeing the younger girl up. "Don't tell me you picked up another fangirl."

The girl twists her mouth in disgust. "Ew, this is my brother, dick," she grits out, and I snort.

Shalina's brows raise in surprise, but she grins. "Yep, she's your sister all right."

I glance at the girl and chuckle. Just what I need, a sarcastic mini-me to torment me. "I'm Caleb," I say to her. "You wanna tell me your name? It'll make things easier."

"You think?" She tosses back her hair. "Aya," she says. "Do you know if you're my only brother?"

Whelp, she didn't wait to open that can of worms. "Not even close. Dear Dad spread his seed a lot from what I've heard." Her eyes widen at my words. "But you're the first sibling I've ever met."

"He's a manwhore then. So, are there enough of us to make a baseball team?" she asks, crossing her arms over her chest.

I nod. "It's definitely a possibility. He's like the Bob Marley of Nephilim."

Her brow crinkles, and she gives me a questioning look. Right, kid doesn't know who Bob Marley is.

The tall presence of Hammurabi looms over us. "This is hardly the time or place to speak about your father's breeding habits." He delivers a ferocious glare to me and Aya. "Or did the burning buildings and dead bodies not offer you clues that we're in danger?"

Aya flushes. "I was just asking—"

"Did I give you permission to speak, girl?" Hammurabi hisses, and my sister's jaw snaps shut. I swallow my protest at the Babylonian king's harsh words because he's right. Now's not the time or place for twenty questions. "We're at war. Gossip later. Fall in line. We're crossing into the Shadow Road now."

I look ahead and see Lucifer vanish, and kids start entering the Road in pairs. Sagar is near us in the middle of the pack, and scary-ass Beelzebub remains at the rear of the train, bleeding darkness. It's creepy as fuck, and I'm not sure what the inky spill does, but I wager it's something horrible and painful.

"He's cranky," Aya whispers to me, and I grin when Hammurabi throws over his shoulder, "I can hear you, small child. And this is me being perfectly reasonable. Ask young Caleb what it looks like when I lose my temper."

I flinch. "He's fond of the whip when you really piss him off. You do know that's Hammurabi, right?"

My sister shrinks behind me a little, and I muffle a laugh, meeting Shalina's amused eyes over Aya's head. Hammurabi only believes in physical punishment when you've really fucked up and decided to meddle with the mind of a human or something. But my sister doesn't know that. Best for her to treat the king like the scary asshole he is.

After a few minutes, it's our turn to jump into the shadows. I breathe a little easier when we land back in the cold, charcoal-gray world of the Shadow Road. Well, we're not really safe here, but Alexander's minions burned Megiddo to the ground and looted what kids and weapons they could. It's not exactly a victory, as we have a sizable chunk of the student body with us, but the weapons from the Fall alone will make it worth their effort. Gramps can lure even more Lights and Fallen with the promise of glory and slaughter.

Aya slides up to me again, keeping her voice low. "Are we allowed to talk now?"

"Sure, as long as we don't attract too much attention to ourselves," I say. "What do you want to know, kid?"

Rolling her eyes, she digs into my ribs with a bony elbow. "What the hell is going on, obviously. I mean, our school is attacked, and this Light finds me and tells me to run, that I can't let them take me. He singled me out. Why? And since when do

Lights help Darks?"

I stare at my sister, unable to comprehend her words for a moment. I feel like my head has been shoved underwater and everything sounds muffled and distant. Sniffing out bloodlines is a rare talent, and the only one I know who possessed such a skill was Alaric. I replay seeing that powerful Nephilim through the smoke. Those familiar amber eyes. In that moment, I thought it was impossible. That my mind was messing with me—or that someone else was playing a cruel trick. Or maybe my psyche conjured up the kind, patient Light to assuage my guilt.

I was wrong on all counts. He's not some mirage or trick, and even if Gramps raised him from the dead, he's alive with his sanity seemingly in check. But what will Alexander do when he finds out Alaric isn't exactly Team Conqueror and is carrying out his own agenda? Obviously, he's not blatantly giving Grandfather the middle finger, as he was there with Alexander's forces, but I'm terrified of what will happen to Alaric if Alexander discovers the Light is helping his blood to escape him. The memory of phantom fingers ripping my mind open washes over me, and I shudder.

Nephilim can take a lot of punishment, but that doesn't mean we don't suffer under the brutality of the pain, and I know firsthand how brutal Gramps can be. Maybe that's the reason why Alaric hasn't contacted us yet, because he's afraid of the agony Alexander can and will inflict. That's the only explanation I can think of because he'd never willingly turn his back on Luna, and he's got that nifty Bat Signal. Then again, maybe he's tried and Grandfather found out.

"Caleb!" Aya's loud hiss interrupts my frantic thoughts.

I glance at her, noticing her scowl. "What?" I say, my tone unintentionally harsh, and she shies away from me. I can't bother to apologize, though, because knowing Alaric is alive and trapped with my grandfather has left me shaken. In my gut, I know if he could've, he would've returned to us. He loves Luna too much to abandon her.

I watch Aya square her shoulders. "Do you know the Light who helped me?" she whispers.

"Yes, I saw him die," I say, and her mouth forms an O of surprise. "Or I thought I did. He's one of the best people I've ever known. And now he's…" I shake my head, bitter at my helplessness. Oh, God, this will kill Luna. She'll be happy he's alive of course. She loves Alaric. But the thought of him with my grandfather might send her spiraling. She understands all too well what Alexander is capable of.

"He's what?" Aya persists, fingers clamping my wrist with surprising strength. Fourteen-year-old girl or not, she's still a second generation Nephilim.

I give her a bleak smile. "He's at the mercy of our grandfather."

She cocks her head at me. "We have a grandfather? Who?"

"Alexander the Great. Ever heard of him? I wouldn't get too excited," I say when I see the expression of awe on her face. "He's responsible for burning down your school and killing your teachers. He was looking for you. He wants all those of his blood gathered to help him in his great war."

She shakes her head. "Great war? But he's a *Nephilim*. How is he going to fight angels?"

My laugh holds no humor. "Because he's not a Nephilim and your blood is a little purer than you thought."

"He's an *angel?*" she breathes, and I resent the sparkles in her eyes. I guess she skipped over the whole great war and burning down your school bits.

"A *Gray* angel," I say. "And again, don't get too excited. The whole burning and pillaging thing."

"What's a Gray angel?" she demands.

I never have the chance to answer as two Nephilim pop onto the Shadow Road and snatch two Babel kids in front of Rafe and Shalina and vanish. Shalina screams and I grab Aya's wrist, plastering her against me. I draw my dagger with my free hand, terror pounding through me.

"Stick close to me!" I shout to Rafe and Shalina as more screams echo on the cold Road. "Whatever you have to do, don't let them take you!"

Hammurabi's battle cry cuts across the mayhem like a cleaver, sending icy ripples over my skin. The teachers react to that sound like a call to arms. They form a perimeter around the kids, clashing with enemy Nephilim. But they're outnumbered and more students disappear off the Road.

A first generation Nephilim pops up next to me. He's a big brute, with neon blue eyes and a shaved head. I don't recognize him from my time at Alexander's citadel, but his eyes light up with triumph when he sees me. Like he's just won the lottery. A malicious smile curves his lips, and I know he's going to kill me. There is no dragging me back before Gramps. I've crossed Alexander one too many times. The Nephilim draws a blade and strikes. I barely manage to raise my own dagger in time to avoid having my carotid artery severed.

I shove Aya away from me so I can have space to maneuver. The battle around me quiets until it's nothing more than a dull roar, and it's just me and him. And then we dance. But he's better than me. And fast. So fast he's a blur. I dodge and parry, but in seconds, I'm bleeding from slashes across my chest and arms. He ducks under a strike and tries to bury his knife in my armpit, but I slide back at the last minute, earning a deep wound across my deltoid. Fuck. I won't last long at this rate.

He knows it, too. A vicious smirk spreads across his lips. I gasp for breath, my thoughts full of Luna. I can't die here on the Shadow Road like this, not when my Goldilocks needs me. Life can't be that cruel. But I'm slowing down, despite my supernatural healing abilities, and I take another slice across my opposite side. I pant and the Nephilim laughs, and I think I hate him more in that moment than I have ever hated anyone. He's going to take me away from Luna.

Then the Nephilim topples over, and I shake my head, trying to clear my mind. I look down. Rafe has tackled him from behind, trying to pin him to the ground. But he's stronger than Rafe and manages to rise to his knees only to meet Shalina's fist as she punches him in the face. Once, twice, three times, and his nose cracks. Then my *sister* delivers a bone-crunching kick to his ribs. Still, the asshole doesn't go down, bucking against Rafe's hold. A savage scream rips from his lips. If he gets his knife hand free, someone is going to die.

I have to get my shit together and end this. My gut roils as I take a step forward. I stabbed Gabriel, and I cut off Mammon's wing, but I've never killed anyone. But Hammurabi is busy, and Lucifer and Beelzebub aren't coming to save me. Alexander's soldier won't hesitate to murder me or possibly my friends. Not after what they've done to him. I shut my guilt down, lock it away tight. There'll be time to mourn my innocence later but not if I'm dead.

I straighten, the pain in my body already dulling. Two determined steps bring me right in front of the struggling Nephilim. His eyes meet mine, and his movements become bestial as he reads my intent. He manages to get one leg under him, dragging Rafe up. I don't hesitate. I don't falter. My long fingers clamp onto his bald head in a ruthless grip, and I draw my blade across his throat until the metal meets bone. He can't heal from this. Blood sprays, saturating my face and clothing. I know I'll never forget the shock in his eyes for the rest of my long life.

Rafe lets go and the body thuds to the ground. I sink to my knees. The taste of copper coats my tongue like a slimy film, and I vomit, heaving and heaving until there's nothing left. Shalina's hand grips my shoulder while Aya kneels next to me, running a soothing hand over my back. Rafe stands in front of me, quiet.

I spit out one last time and rise. My ears pop as the sounds of battle roar back in. There are patches of kids missing, creating gaps in the line. We have to get off the Road to wherever the hell the Council is. We're sitting ducks out here.

Darkness spills from the back of the line, encroaching on us like a nightmarish tidal wave. Aya screams but I don't even flinch. Beelzebub has unleashed the beast. Within seconds, I'm blind. This isn't natural darkness. There isn't a sliver of light. I feel like I've been dropped in a vat of tar, and it's drowned my senses.

Just as I adjust to the suffocating blackness, bright liquid gold bursts across my irises, burning them. Momentarily blind, I tighten my grip on Aya's hand, clenching it. She gropes my arm, molding herself against my side, trembling.

I hear another roar—from Lucifer this time—then silence. Tears stream down my face, and I blink rapidly. Shapes form in my vision and finally color returns. Well, what little color that is found on the Road. My jaw drops when I take in the scene before me.

Alexander's soldiers whittled about a third of our numbers. But with Lucifer and Beelzebub's shocking display of power, the last of the Conqueror's warriors who attacked us lie dead around us, their bodies mangled.

A blood-coated Hammurabi finds me, his countenance grimmer than usual. "We're safe for now, boy. Let's not tempt fate by lingering." He turns from me, shouting, "Move!"

I gently nudge a shell-shocked Aya, and we shuffle along behind the thinned crowd, Rafe and Shalina trailing us.

FIFTEEN

LUNA

WE EMERGE FROM THE Blessed Road into a subterranean labyrinth of volcanic rock. Tunnels branch off all around me, leading into nooks, other passages, and down, deeper into the bowels of the Earth for nearly three-hundred feet and at least eighteen levels. In terms of space, it's definitely fit for purpose, and considering the underground city was created to protect its past inhabitants from war, I suppose my mother was right: it *is* a sensible place to serve as a safe haven for the thousands of Nephilim crowding its depths.

I had never heard of Derinkuyu before today, so I absorbed whatever information I could glean from Gabriel on the Road. That way I would know what to expect once we got here and actually be prepared for once. Still, despite her descriptions, I didn't anticipate how truly ancient the site is, or how I would almost be able to *feel* all the years of history in the rock underfoot, as if the memories of the people who once walked through these caverns linger to this day, like ripples in water from a stone thrown a long time ago. The ghostly hum in the air makes me wonder if, in thousands of years, this moment will also be remembered. If our kind will look back on this day and see the one bright spot in the darkness or if they'll only recollect our fear. I desperately hope it's the former—that they all remember what transpired here the way I see it now.

As a turning point.

I'm not sure I could've ever envisioned it—what it would look like to see so many Lights and Darks together in one space. Bodies flood the tunnels, the students from the other academies spilling over into every available side room, and as Gabriel ushers me forward toward a wider cavern up ahead, I notice how the opposing auras around me form a checkered pattern of black and gold. In every other respect, the Nephilim are the same, united not only in their celestial blood, but against a common foe. Not that the students know that yet. I glance behind me at the horde of Lights we brought with us from Sinai and the Serapeum, taking in so many confused faces as they all shuffle forward through the passage behind us, uncertainty and a clear disdain for their new living situation stamped onto their features. They mutter in terrified whispers to each other much like they did on the Road, voicing questions I don't know how to answer. My mother doesn't attempt to answer them, either.

"Gabriel!"

The sound of my mother's name grabs my attention, and I look ahead, spotting Lilith cutting her way through the crowd, hurrying toward us and barking at any Nephilim who dares to get in her way. When she reaches us, she throws her arms around Gabriel, pulling the Archangel into a fierce hug.

"You're late," she growls. She then takes a step back to look at both of us, her dark eyes scanning our faces. "Did something happen on the Road?"

"Alexander," is all Gabriel says.

The ex-Archdemon's expression turns hostile. "What happened?" she asks again, this time through clenched teeth. The muscles in her jaw pop with each word.

"Nothing," I mutter, shivering at the recollection of crossing blades with the Gray. Of how close I came to certain death…had Alexander actually been inclined to fight me. "That's what's so weird about it. He blocked the Road, spent all of five seconds attacking us, and then he just vanished. He didn't even *try* to steal the weapons."

Lilith's eyes swing to mine and hang there, uncertainty burning in the dark pits like black flames. Then, brows raised, she shoots a questioning look at my mother, who scrubs a hand over her face.

"Has Lucifer returned?" Gabriel asks.

My stomach flips at the thought of seeing Caleb—of imminently being in his arms again—but my rising excitement is quashed when Lilith shakes her head. "Not yet. But the others have."

Gabriel doesn't quite manage to hide her own disappointment, giving a jerky nod. "Then let's find them and, together, maybe we can figure out what Alexander is planning."

"Yes, let's," a familiar voice coos, and we turn to find Raphael standing behind us, her thin arms crossed over her chest. "Don't mistake this to mean I trust you. I *don't*," she adds with a steely glance at me. "But neither am I foolish enough to ignore the obvious threat the Conqueror poses. He did not harm any of my students today… but next time might be a different story."

To my surprise, my mother places a consoling hand on the Archangel's shoulder. "We stopped him once. We can do it again."

"For good this time," Raphael asserts, and I shudder at the insinuation behind those words—not because I want to spare Alexander or believe he deserves it, but because I know that one misstep, and I'll be treated with the same disregard.

After all, the Council won't make the same mistake twice.

My father, Caleb, Hammurabi, and Beelzebub still haven't returned by the time we find the other Council members and recount our run-in with Alexander on the Blessed Road. Raphael and Zerachiel testify to the truth of our words, adding their own accounts—although Uriel could have just as easily asked any of the eight-hundred-plus Nephilim who were there if he did have any doubts. To my increasing unease, no one has any explanation for the ominous encounter, and the lack of insight only makes me more anxious about where Caleb and the others could be. Why aren't they back yet? Are they okay?

Are they alive?

Tears burn the backs of my eyes as I shake that unwanted thought away, and swallowing, I focus only on the passing stone as a first generation Light Nephilim I don't know leads me, Lilith, and a group of young, terrified students from the primary academy at Mount Nebo down several levels, deeper into Derinkuyu, to the rooms we've been randomly assigned during our stay here—however long that may be. The ancient city will serve as a makeshift dormitory for the foreseeable future, but I hate being so far underground. It's claustrophobic and reminds me of how it felt to be encaged in that egg.

I wanted to stay as close to the surface as possible where the air is fresher—at least until Caleb is back and can find creative ways to distract me—but my mother wasn't having it. She told me to go with Lilith and get some rest, as if I could while this worry eats at me. Meanwhile, she stayed behind with the Council and the Nephilim who serve as teachers and staff at the academies to aid with organizing the students until the others return—though not before verbally sparring with Uriel and demanding he release Asmodeus, reminding them of their agreement. I was stunned by my mother's insistence regarding the Archdemon, but then Asmodeus is important to Lucifer, and I know Gabriel was sticking her neck out for his sake. To get his friend back in one piece. If my father was present to witness her dressing down the Archangel, he probably would've swept her off her feet and kissed her then and there.

A few of the other Council members made the point that the deal wasn't considered upheld until Lucifer returned, but Gabriel wasn't having any of that, either. Though I could see it pained her to say it, she asked them what they would do if my father and Beelzebub didn't return at all. Would they leave Asmodeus in her prison and willingly choose to be down three allies instead of two? No one had a response for that. Except for Uriel, who, in a clipped tone, told one of the Archangels—Azrael, if I remember correctly—to go "attend" to the Archdemon. Code, no doubt, for *bring her back.*

Relief scorches my insides at the thought of seeing Asmodeus again, burning away some of the guilt I carry from leaving her behind at Babel. I've barely been able to escape the mental picture of her in that frozen prison—a prison I'm responsible for putting her in—but knowing she'll be free and reunited with us soon helps chase it away, just a little. I can only imagine how my father and Caleb will feel when they see her again. And Hammurabi, who I suspect harbors something a bit stronger than just respect for the Archdemon. My gut tells me he'll be the happiest of them all.

Our group thins as we deliver the students to their rooms until it's only me, Lilith, and the Nephilim leading us, who keeps casting wary glances at the ex-Archdemon out of the corner of his pale eyes. As a Light, I imagine he's only heard stories of Lilith, and not complimentary ones I'd wager. But if his behavior bothers her, she doesn't show it. Instead, a diabolical amusement shines in her black gaze, and a jaunty whistle leaves her lips as we descend into the bowels of the city.

While Derinkuyu isn't masked by a glamor like the academies, appearing to my eyes as the old world ruin it is, the cave system has been updated since its last known human use thousands of years ago—the Council's handiwork, I assume, in the event of a scenario just like this one. While not lavish, the rooms are each fitted with a bed and wash basin as well as a door that locks, ensuring the privacy and comfort the students will undoubtedly need during this time of upheaval. Not only to make them feel safe from Alexander...but also from each other.

Because, as united as we are in our terror, it's going to take much more than forced proximity to bring the Lights and Darks together. To make them accept one another and finally put this ancient feud behind them. But this animosity didn't originate with the Nephilim—they just inherited it from the Faithful and Fallen. The rest of us have a chance for a clean slate if we just make the choice to leave the past in the past.

I only hope the students here will come to see that.

"Your rooms," the Nephilim leading us says, pausing before one door and gesturing across the passage to another. He throws one last nervous look at Lilith then departs with a hasty nod at me, scurrying back the way we came.

"I better not have a roommate," Lilith calls after him as we watch the Nephilim flee like a dog with its tail between its legs. Then, with a devious smile, she says to me, "Not unless they give me one as handsome as yours."

My nose wrinkles. "Hands off, cougar," I grumble.

As Lilith barks out a laugh, I push open the door and, with an uninterested glance at the sparse furnishings, I cross the small space and drop face first on the bed. The mattress is hard but I don't care. I couldn't sleep even if I wanted to.

Rolling over onto my back, I stare up at the low ceiling. The creamy stone is pockmarked with thousands of dips in its surface, each one representing a moment I fear I'll spend here waiting for Caleb to return.

Nerves prickle under my skin, and I fidget against the soft blankets, so close to coming undone now that the adrenaline of my encounter with Alexander is wearing off. I hate this. I hate not knowing what's going to happen. I hate not knowing where my father and Caleb are or if they're okay. And above all, I hate how helpless I feel. How, despite fate's plan for me, I still seem like little more than a child, wrapped up in a battle intended for adults.

"Your thoughts are so loud, I can hear them from here," Lilith trills.

I lift my head and glare at the ex-Archdemon where she lounges in the doorway, her feet crossed at the ankle and one shoulder propped against the stone frame.

"Does it bother you?" I ask through my teeth, sitting upright.

She arches a barely interested brow. "What?"

My eyes dip to the ground, and I cross my arms, hugging them tightly around my chest. "That you've gone from being a valued member of Alexander's army to being my babysitter. I'm sure this wasn't what you had in mind." I don't mean to take my sudden bad mood out on Lilith, but she's here, and I need something to distract me. Plus, this question has been eating at me, and as much as I want to trust her, I can't really see what she's getting out of being here. Choosing our side won't get her wings back. Not that choosing Alexander's would, either.

Lilith snorts. "Am I not valued here?"

I look up at her, stunned. "That's not what I—"

"I know." Sighing, she walks over to the bed and plops down on the mattress beside me. Her hands knot in her lap. "I wouldn't blame you, you know. For thinking me fickle.”

I shake my head. “I don’t think that. But…I don’t want you to feel indebted to me, either.” I hesitate, rolling my teeth over my lower lip. Lilith blames herself for misinterpreting the prophecy and aligning herself with Alexander, but I don’t want guilt or some unspoken need for repentance to be why she’s helping us. “I don’t want you to be here because you feel like you have to be or because my mother asked you to.”

Lilith flashes me a humorless grin. “No one forces me to do anything, child, and if Gabriel had that much sway over me, I wouldn’t have joined Alexander in the first place.”

I open my mouth then promptly close it again as her words sink in. She has a point.

“I’m here with you because I *want* to be, Luna,” she says. “That might not mean much given my past alliance with Alexander, but I am still capable of thinking for myself, and this is where my heart is telling me I should be. As for your other comment, you hardly need a minder, but your parents and I don’t trust the Council, and we agreed that it’s best you aren’t left by yourself, just in case. Your parents are expected to aid the Council in their current endeavors, which means they can’t be with you at all times, whereas my absence will hardly be noted. Around others, you have the protection of visibility, but we’d rather not take any chances when you’re alone.”

My breath catches. “Do you think they’d try anything?”

Lilith shrugs. “Hard to say. I would hope not, seeing as Alexander’s recent penchant for arson only supports our claims about the prophecy.” She looks at me with a supercilious hook of her brow. “Snatching children and burning down schools isn’t very Savior-like of him, is it?”

A frown tugs at the edges of my lips. “There’s nothing very Savior-like about me, either.”

“That’s not true.” When I try to look away, Lilith grabs my chin, and although I try to avoid her gaze, her eyes are like magnets, drawing the focus of mine. “I have known your parents for a very, *very* long time, dear girl. So, believe me when I tell you that you possess the best of both of them. There isn’t a malevolent bone in your body, and I know I’m not the only one who can see that.” She snorts. “Even Uriel and those other tight-asses on the Council would be hard-pressed to deny it.”

Although her confidence in my moral virtue is reassuring, it doesn’t change how frightened I am of the unknown path before me. A path I’d be leading who knows how many innocent people down toward their potential demise.

“What am I supposed to do, Lilith?” I ask, my eyes filling with tears. “How can I possibly fight him and win?”

"With help," she breathes, taking my face in both hands. "You are *not* alone."

A small, hiccuping sob escapes me. "I don't know how to fight with a sword. I can barely control my flame! Not to mention, Alexander's numbers are greater. And he'll—" I wince at the memory of Caleb's father, his screams silenced, his body unmoving on the floor of the citadel…and of how easily he rose again. "He'll just bring them back if they fall."

This notion doesn't seem to worry her nearly as much as I think it should. Her expression remains unchanged as she counters in a level voice, "Battles have been won with worse odds."

Worse odds? I choke back the urge to laugh. Our odds are about as bad as they can get, especially if the future of our kind and the preservation of the entire world is dependent on me.

"That's not very comforting," I grumble.

She shrugs again, lowering her hands from my face. "If it's comfort you're after, I'm certain that lover of yours would be all too happy to oblige." An impish grin slides across her features, and she chuckles at the rising heat on my cheeks.

I groan. "You're going to give me shit about our sex talk literally forever, aren't you?"

"What else are aunts for?" Lilith smirks then stands, ruffling my hair. "Have faith, sweetling. When the time comes, we will prevail. Of that, I have no doubt. And in the meantime, I can teach you a thing or two about wielding a blade."

I sober at her words and nod. That's definitely one offer I'll be taking her up on. Because someday soon, I'll have to fight Alexander, and while I doubt I'd ever be able to outmatch him in physical combat, I want to make sure I'm capable enough with a weapon to not be helpless against him, either.

"Ow." I gasp, my eyes snapping down to my forearm when a strange burning sensation sears into my skin, as if I've accidentally pressed against something hot. Pushing my sleeve up, I gape at the Enochian sigil my mother branded into my arm, the edges of the white symbol shimmering like a fresh coating of snow reflecting the light. "It's…*glowing*," I whisper, bringing my arm up to my face to get a closer look. The burning has subsided—either that or I just fail to notice it anymore past my awe.

"Gabriel is calling us to her," Lilith murmurs, and I look up to find the ex-Archdemon staring down at her own sigil, identical to mine in every way, from the shape of the tattoo to its location on her forearm. Her brow creases. "Something must be happening upstairs."

"My father? Caleb?" I choke out, bolting upright, my pulse leaping under my skin.

Lilith tugs down the sleeve of her silk crimson blouse. "Let us hope," she says, but there's an apprehensive edge to her tone that only feeds my unease.

Neither of us says another word as we retrace our steps to the top level of the city. Lilith doesn't even question how I got the sigil—not that it would take a genius to work out why Gabriel gave it to me—nor does she seem bothered by sharing a connection previously reserved for only her and my mother. I don't anticipate the rush of emotion that follows this thought or how her unspoken acceptance makes me feel.

Loved, I realize. It makes me feel loved, like I matter to the ex-Archdemon as something more than just an instrument in a prophecy.

The top level of Derinkuyu is packed with fresh bodies, replacing the horde of students already funneled into the lower depths of the city. My eyes dart between the faces before me, but it's hard to pick out any features I recognize in the overwhelming mass, the Dark auras of the Nephilim combining into one solid blanket of shadow.

Spotting my mother's golden light through a break in the crowd, I push forward into one of the larger caverns, Lilith close at my heel, and as we squeeze past the students, my nose wrinkles at the distinct burning smell filling the space. I stumble, fear freezing my steps as my gaze catches on the scorch marks on some of the Nephilims' clothing.

My stomach plunges into my feet. Was another academy attacked?

Was Babel attacked?

It's strange to think I was only just there—that a place I took shelter at only a few weeks ago might no longer exist on this planet. But what troubles me more is that Babel was Caleb's home and he might have had yet another thing he loves—or wanted to love—stolen from him. First Ishtar, then his grandfather, or rather, the dream of a father figure, since he never really had him.

Still, how many more losses must Caleb endure? How many more can he take?

"Students from Babel and Megiddo," Lilith says in my ear, as if reading my thoughts, and placing a hand on my shoulder, she urges me ahead until we're standing side by side with my mother.

The troubled expression on Gabriel's face does little to comfort my nerves.

"Any sign of them?" I manage in a meek whisper.

"Not yet." Her lips press into a hard line, and I can tell she's trying to keep it together—to mask the fear I know she's feeling. But I see it, simmering deep in her eyes, just like I glimpsed it that day under the Serapeum. Except this time, it isn't me she's afraid for.

It's my father.

"He'll be here," Lilith assures her.

My gaze hangs on my mother, and the longer I watch her, the more it sinks in how much we have in common in this moment—both of us waiting here, silently worrying for the safety of the men we love…even if Gabriel's too proud to admit her lingering feelings for my father aloud.

Suddenly, the muttering around us falls silent, and beside me, I hear my mother's breath falter when a familiar crown of golden hair appears over the crowd. Bodies part before us as Lucifer steps into the room, and my attention snaps away from my mother as I find myself caught up in my own relief, which plows into me like a tidal wave.

"Father—"

I'm nearly to him before I'm even aware my legs are moving. Bemused Nephilim step out of my way, and whispers of surprise pass through the watching crowd as I leap into his arms, throwing mine around his neck. As he hugs me back, the song of our blood shouting out in glee at our reunion, the bewildered whispers around us grow louder, and it occurs to me—somewhere in the back of my head where I can still think clearly—that it must not be common knowledge yet that the Morningstar has a child.

My hold on him tightens as tears streak my cheeks.

"Luna." He lets out a strained breath, hugging me tighter. "Are you all right?"

With a strangled laugh, I pull away, taking him in. He looks like he's been to Hell and back, and while he doesn't appear to be hurt, I can't ignore the smattering of blood painting his clothes. Whose blood is it? "I'm fine," I promise. "Are *you* okay? What happened? Babel—"

"Still stands unscathed, thankfully."

A heavy weight lifts off my chest at his words, and I exhale, thankful they got there in time—that Caleb's home remains intact. Surely, with the students and weapons removed, Alexander has no reason to destroy it—

My breath catches at that thought. If Babel is fine, then the students whose clothes were burnt had to have come from somewhere else.

"And Megiddo?" I dare to ask, glancing at the scorch marks and ash staining his shirt. My eyes flick up to his face, and although his jaw is tight, his expression stoic, his gaze is grief-stricken.

"Not as fortunate, I'm afraid," he murmurs.

Tears swim across my vision. "I'm so sorry."

I can't even begin to imagine how he feels or what it must be like to see thousands of years of love and devotion destroyed in one day of violence. As powerful as angels and Nephilim are, it makes me far too aware of how fragile some of us are, too. Of how easily our world can change in a moment. Of how much hangs on the prophecy…

And of what we all stand to lose should I fail.

"We will rebuild," Lucifer vows.

Sniffing, I dab at my eyes with my shirt sleeve. What happened to Ashkelon and Megiddo is my fault. They would still be standing if I hadn't—

I bite my tongue, trying to curtail that thought. I can't go down this road. I can't think about the lives that were lost or how the blood of innocent Nephilim is on my hands because I was foolish enough to release Alexander. I can't let the guilt consume me or I'll never find the strength to fight. To be the Savior we need to stop him.

"Where's Caleb?" I rasp. I need to see him. I need to wrap myself in his arms and hide away in our room for however many hours it takes for him to make me forget everything.

I glance past Lucifer's shoulder, but I don't see any familiar faces in the crowd behind him. Caleb *is* okay, isn't he? Surely, my father would've said if something happened to him.

Lucifer touches my arm, drawing my gaze again. "He's here. Or will be any moment now. Students are still entering from the Road. But he's *safe*, I assure you of that," he says, his voice soothing my frazzled nerves. "And probably looking for you as we speak."

Another wave of relief washes over me as the same three thoughts circle through my head on a loop—*Caleb's okay. He's here, somewhere. He's alive*—only pausing in their endless merry-go-round in my skull when I notice Lucifer's attention drift over my shoulder, and it dawns on me that Caleb isn't the only one here searching for someone. Lucifer is looking for Gabriel—*at* Gabriel. I can sense it, and the unabashed longing in his gaze only confirms my suspicion. A knowing smile curves my lips, and I step back farther, moving out of his path. We've had our moment and I'm not the only person in his life.

Nor am I the only one he loves.

"Like you were looking for Mom?" I say softly.

His brows reach for his hairline. "Mom?" he echoes, spluttering slightly. His eyes snap back to mine, and I don't miss the shock I glimpse in them. Or the overwhelming pleasure behind it.

The smile slips from my face, and I glare at him. "Don't change the subject," I warn. "And don't even *think* about making fun of me. This is all weird enough as it is."

Chuckling, he holds up his hands in surrender. "I wouldn't dare. Though…am I correct in assuming you two have reconciled your differences?"

I consider that for a moment then nod, and the way his face lights up in response makes every second of my discomfort worth it.

"She'll probably never admit it," I whisper, following his gaze, which has once again inched toward Gabriel, "but she was worried about you."

"Oh?" He cocks a golden brow. "She told you this?"

I snort. "Of course not."

"Then how do you know?" There's an uncertain pang in his tone that hits me straight in the heart. But in it, I also hear hope.

"Well, for one, she told me she wouldn't 'make the same mistake again.'" I draw out these last words, hooking my fingers into air-quotes for emphasis. Caleb is definitely rubbing off on me, and not just in the bedroom. Lowering my hands, I shrug. "But aside from that, I guess I can tell because I know how it feels to love someone the way I know she loves you."

Lucifer gapes at me, as if he's not entirely sure he heard me correctly, but the moment of hesitation passes quickly, and standing a little bit taller, he straightens his shirt. "Go. Find Caleb," he says with a wink. "I have some unfinished business with your mother."

He turns, making a beeline for Gabriel, and all around, I notice the way the Dark Nephilim stand in silence, watching the scene unfold like an audience in a movie theater. All that's missing is the popcorn. Their palpable confusion and shock makes me bold, and fighting back a grin, I call out, "Hey, Dad?"

Lucifer turns at the sound of my voice, his blue eyes blazing bright, and I wonder if he relishes the startled gasps filling the room nearly as much as I do. A smile, brighter than any I've ever seen, lights up his face. "Yes, Starlight?" he asks.

I warm at the endearment, returning his smile.

"Thank you. For keeping Caleb safe." And I mean it more than I could ever mean anything.

My father frowns. "I'll admit," he begins, his tone unnervingly hesitant, "with everything that transpired at Megiddo, I did not keep as close an eye on him as perhaps I should have." My heart jackhammers against my ribs at those words, and I feel a strange mixture of sympathy and fear—of sorrow for everything my father lost today and an overpowering unease as my mind spins in circles, trying to comprehend what he's saying. I'm about to ask what he means when he quickly adds, "You needn't worry. Beelzebub tells me Caleb held his own." A contented grin shapes his lips and he beams again, my own personal sun. "That boy is strong. You've chosen well."

My heart swells at the pride in his voice, and with a nod, he turns again toward my mother, his long stride crossing the space to her in only a few steps. Although I could easily hear what they say, I choose to tune them out, stepping back and immersing myself into the throng of students to give them privacy—or as much as they can get with so many spectators.

I weave through the crowd, searching the faces around me for Caleb, pausing only once to look back at my parents. I choose the right moment. Gabriel flushes as Lucifer takes her into his arms, and when he kisses her, she kisses him back, the divide—and past hurts—between them finally healed.

SIXTEEN

CALEB

I'VE NEVER BEEN SO happy to be underground before. Blinking, awe fills me at the sight of my surroundings. Although I haven't gotten around to visiting yet, I recognize Derinkuyu from photos I diligently studied in art history. This isn't exactly how I imagined ticking the place off my bucket list one day—on the run from a megalomaniac—but I take comfort that this ancient city has provided refuge for those in need for thousands of years.

Ironically, we jump into one of the Christian chapels where a fresco of vengeful angels draw swords and point at the demons writhing in the pit below. I think one of the gray, leathery-looking beasts is supposed to be Lucifer himself. I snicker. The Morningstar has gone ahead and Beelzebub leads our procession out of the chapel. I think of Lucifer's golden curls and smirk. Grotesque demon, my ass.

I wonder if Luna is back with Gabriel and Raphael. Does Alexander have enough Lights on his side to attack them on the Blessed Road? I don't think he'd venture out of his fortress yet, not until he's at full strength, but Gramps isn't exactly predictable or sane. My heart thunders in my chest, and I want to push past everyone to get to Beelzebub, but it's not like he has any more information than I do at this point. By the speed in which he's leading us into the maze of corridors, I know he's just as anxious as I am for more information.

I need to see Luna, kiss the hell out of her, then disappear to our room for a few days or a couple of hours at the very least. She's an angel, I know that she's almost impossible to kill, but she's not a match for Alexander, and I need to see with my own two eyes that she's okay.

Aya clings to me, her nails digging into my biceps and yanking me back to the here and now. Her eyes round as she takes everything in. "Where are we?" she demands.

Shoving down my worry, I smile at her. "Derinkuyu, ancient city in Turkey. Don't let the Christian art fool you. This place has been around since the Hittites."

"The who?" She smirks at me. "You're such a nerd."

"No, little sis, I'm just smart. Maybe you should try it sometime," I counter, chuckling as she scowls. "Besides, this is all part of Nephilim history, and I know firsthand that our history can and will come back and bite us in the ass." Especially when you let your daddy complex persuade you to release a monster into the world.

"He is a nerd," Rafe says, coming up beside me, "but he's not wrong. Damn, I've always wanted to visit this place. Not while running for my life, obviously."

As we file into a wide corridor, Shalina gazes around in wonder. "Me too. If I wasn't so terrified, I'd go exploring."

"I'm surrounded by nerds," Aya mutters.

Shalina glances at Aya. "Children are best seen and not heard."

I snort. "Give her a break, Lina. She's just a kid." Aya gives me side-eye, which makes me laugh harder. This is just the distraction I need to keep my head from exploding worrying about Goldilocks. "What? You're a baby."

"I helped you kill that guy," Aya points out. "I'm not a baby."

That sobers me the hell up again. And I'm reminded that my skin is tacky with dried blood that pulls at my flesh every time I move. Rafe and Shalina both fall silent, looking everywhere but at me. They helped, sure, but I'm the one who took his life. My intestines knot themselves into one giant ball.

Aya bites at her lip. "I'm sorry, Caleb."

"That's okay. Kids say stupid things." My voice is sharper than I intended and she flinches. I turn my attention to Rafe and Shalina. "This place can hold up to twenty thousand people, so we'll have plenty of room. But, um, fair warning. You'll be staying next to Lights."

"Excuse me?" Shalina says, almost tripping over the uneven stone floor. "We're going to room with *Lights*?"

"I got no problems with Grays," Rafe says, "but I don't know about Lights, man."

"You'll conduct yourself as a student of Babel and follow the rules," Hammurabi interjects, bumping into Rafe's shoulder. "The Conqueror is after us all. There is no Light or Dark to him, just potential pawns for his war. I understand it's a bitter pill to swallow, but swallow it we must."

Shalina pouts but one look at Hammurabi's hard face has her giving a hasty nod.

Rafe dips his head, too.

"I still have my whips, and I don't mind making an example of children who are foolish enough to step out of line in a time of war," Hammurabi rumbles.

"Yes, sir," Shalina and Rafe say, straightening.

"Yes, sir," Aya squeaks, pressing herself against me.

"I'm cool with everyone these days," I tell him, and he rolls his eyes.

"I'm aware, boy. The lovesick looks you exchange with the flower are enough to make me ill." He strides ahead of us as I narrow my eyes at his retreating back. He pauses and looks over his shoulder. "I'm sure the flower is well. She's proven she's not so easily bruised."

I give a curt nod, swallowing hard. I hope he's right. I watch as he barks orders at students to move along.

"Big bro's in lurv," Aya taunts, grinning at me. Rafe and Shalina laugh. "As your sister, you have to let me meet her, so I can decide whether to give my approval."

"The only person whose approval I give a damn about is my mom's and she loves Luna," I tell Aya. "But nice try."

"She met your mom, bro?" Rafe asks in surprise while Aya says, "You know your mom?"

And for the second time, an uncomfortable silence descends on us. Shit, that means Aya's mom just dumped her at Nephilim daycare and never came back. I always knew I was lucky Mom didn't do that to me. That she stuck it out, even though she had a half-immortal kid with superpowers. Aya literally has no family in her life but...me. No pressure there.

"We're going to catch up with Hammurabi," Shalina says, eyes darting between Aya and me. "Come on, Rafe."

"I've missed that old asshole," Rafe says, and he and Shalina speed up, leaving me alone with Aya.

Well, not alone, as we have scared students milling around us. I wince, feeling bad for them. Their entire world has been ripped to shreds in a matter of hours. At least I had slightly more time to adjust. I sigh and focus on Aya.

"You don't remember your mom at all?" I ask cautiously. Sometimes, human mothers keep their Nephilim children for a little while before giving them up. I don't know what's worse, for Aya to have no memory of her mom or to have bits and pieces stuck in her brain, tormenting her.

She shakes her head. "Nothing, not even a feeling of her being there. A smell. For a long time, I hoped my dad would come at least." Her laugh is bitter. "Clearly, that never happened."

"Dad's a piece of shit," I tell her. "He doesn't care about any of us. I wish I had better news for you."

"You've met him?" she demands, big eyes hard on mine.

The memory of me bringing the whip down on my father's back is seared into my brain. I give a reluctant nod. "Yeah, I did, and I wish I never had. It didn't give me the closure I thought it would."

Her eyes go bleak, as if she held out some small thread of hope, no matter how thin, of our father coming into her life and filling the enormous void there. "And Alexander?"

I grimace. "Grandfather cares, but not in a way you want. He wants to build a dynasty and use his blood to further his glory. We're all just tools to him. Pampered, well-cared for tools if we obey him, but tools nonetheless." She still looks skeptical, like maybe that doesn't sound that bad as long as she gets a grandpa out of the deal. "I didn't exactly get in line and go along with his 'take-over-the-world plan,' and he almost killed me for it. And Luna." And I thought Alaric. But it doesn't seem like that's true...

"So, basically our whole family sucks?" she says, resentment lacing her words.

"Hey, I'll have you know most people consider me fucking amazing," I tell her, pleased when a small smirk twists her lips. "And I'm totally willing to share my mom with you, but be prepared to be spoiled and fed really, really well. And don't even think of saying no when she tries to ply you with seconds."

Tilting her head to the side, Aya studies me for a moment. "You mean that? You'd let me meet your mom?"

I nod. "Yep. Not right now, obviously, with a war on and all, but the moment it calms down, we'll take a road trip to New York. I promise."

She blinks shiny eyes at me, her brash attitude gone, making her look like the young girl she is. "Thank you, Caleb. That's...thank you." She frowns again. "Are there really more of us? Other brothers and sisters out there?"

I huff out a laugh. "I guarantee it. I'm pretty sure we'll be meeting them sooner rather than later, though I can't promise they'll be as amazing as I am. Few are."

She rolls her eyes. "Maybe they'll be more modest."

It's my turn to roll my eyes. "Nephilim? Modest? You *are* young." I loop her arm through mine once more. "Come on, kid. I need to see my girl and make sure she's all right."

Now that I've taken care of Aya the best way I can for now, my whole focus—and worry—returns to Luna. I mean, she was with her badass mother and the eternally annoying Raphael so odds are she's perfectly fine. Not to mention scary Lilith treats Goldilocks like her new favorite niece and will no doubt crush anyone who tries to harm her. But Gramps wasn't considered a military genius for nothing. No matter your arsenal, you'd be a fool to underestimate him.

We wind our way through the tunnels until we come into a larger room, which appears to be a shared communal space. There, her golden mane shining, is my Goldilocks, not a hair out of place, weaving through the crowd. A panicked expression has taken residence on her beautiful face, quickening my steps. As if she can sense me, her head swivels my way and our eyes clash. My steps falter as I take her in. Relief flashes in the depths of her gaze, and her eyes sweep over me from head to toe, searching for injuries. I know my mortality worries her, but I haven't got a scratch on me. Physically. My soul is a little worse for wear.

Then her relief vanishes and panic floods her expression again. I glance down at myself and frown. Fuck, she's freaking out because I'm covered in that dead Nephilim's blood, and she thinks it's mine. I desperately need a shower. I stride toward her, long legs eating up the distance. I can hear Aya scurry along behind me.

Luna meets me, reaching for my hands and clenching them, but holding herself back, as if she's afraid she might hurt me. "Caleb, what happened? Where are you hurt—"

I drag her against me, folding my arms around her back. "Shh, baby, I'm fine," I croon. "This isn't my blood."

She gazes up at me, tears glistening in her eyes. "Are you sure you're okay?"

I want to banish the worry and doubt in her voice, so I sweep her up, one arm hooked under her ass. Her legs wrap around me as our mouths clash in a desperate kiss, tongues dueling. She's okay. We're okay. I feel her tremble, and I try to control my own shaking. A whoosh sounds as her wings spring free, and I stroke one thumb over the beginning arch of a wing as I break our kiss and bite her where her slender neck meets her shoulder. She shudders, and I want nothing more than to carry her to our room and stroke her wings until she comes.

"Caleb," Luna admonishes me, breathing ragged. "People are staring at us."

I glance up to see a delightful ruby flush stain her cheeks. I smirk. "I haven't given them anything to stare at. Yet. Embarrassed of me?" I tease and she frowns at me.

"Of course not. I just…" She blushes again. "I can't control myself when you touch me like that," she whispers, burying her face in the crook of my neck.

My body tightens at her words, and at this rate, I'll embarrass myself in front of all the gawking Nephilim. Not that I have anything to be ashamed of, thank you very much.

"Yeah, well, I can't control myself when you touch me, either, baby, so we're even," I murmur into her hair before gently unwrapping her legs and placing her on her feet, smooth as butter. "Has Lucifer seen you already?" I ask. Mentioning Luna's father douses my lust just as well as ice water.

She nods. "Yes, right before you. He's with my mom now."

I raise a brow at the ease with which she calls Gabriel "mom." Something good must have happened on the trip between the two of them. I stroke her cheek, happy for her.

A wolf whistle pierces the charged air, slicing through our tender moment. I jerk my head around to see Rafe standing behind us, grinning at me and giving me a slow clap. "Damn, that was quite a show. Now, all we need is dinner."

Shalina is next to him. She rolls her eyes at Rafe, but mischief glimmers in her gaze when she turns to me. "Caleb was always one to put on a good show."

I slide my arm around Luna's shoulders, taking care with her wings. "Um, considering the show you two put on for me this morning, you owe me dinner for the next year."

Shalina glowers at me. "Voyeurs don't get free meals."

Luna arches a brow at me. "Voyeur?" Her eyes dart back and forth between us, clearly lost.

"Voyeur?" I choke out. "I'm lucky my eyes didn't melt out of my sockets. And who doesn't lock the door, for fuck's sake?"

A body wriggles under my free arm, and I look to see Aya staring at Luna, an awestruck expression on her face. "Your wings are beautiful," she breathes. "They're *gray*. I didn't know angels could have gray wings."

She's not the only one staring at Luna's silver feathers, but Goldilocks is too intent on Aya to notice. Her eyes narrow as she studies my little sister, Rafe, and Shalina, then she turns a questioning gaze on me.

"I'm his sister," Aya says before I can give a proper introduction. "But don't get pissed that he's never introduced us before. We just met." She smiles at Luna, clearly already won over. "I can't believe my big bro landed an angel! You better hope you're good enough for her," she adds, her dark eyes sliding to mine.

I glare at the suddenly annoying presence by my side. "Pipe down, little sis. Didn't we just have a conversation about how awesome I am?" She knows me for five whole seconds, and already she's butting into my love life. I think I took being an only child for granted. "This annoying child is Aya, and those two hypocrites are Rafe and Shalina."

"Sister?" Luna breathes, stunned amazement in her face. "But how? I thought…" She winces, her face darkening.

I know what she's thinking. She's remembering killing my father. My theory is when she killed my dad, the deal he made with the Darks became null and void, and now all his kiddos can find each other.

I nudge Aya with my elbow harder than necessary and give Luna a bright, teasing smile. She doesn't need any more dark thoughts. "I'm sure I'll meet many more brats who make my life difficult soon."

"I'm not a brat," Aya protests, scowling at me.

"If it walks like a brat, and talks like a brat—"

"Caleb," Luna scolds but she's grinning, and my heart feels like it's made of helium. "It's so nice to meet you, Aya," she says, turning toward my sister, and her warmth reminds me so much of Lucifer. Aya practically melts under the beauty of her smile. "It's nice to meet you, too, Rafe and Shalina. I just wish it was under better circumstances."

Before Rafe can open his mouth and bust my balls, an excited ripple rolls over the front of the crowd. Hammurabi is suddenly behind me, gripping my shoulder. I glance back at him, noticing his intense expression.

"I'm so glad you're safe," Luna says to him.

"Thank you, little flower," he replies, and I grin at his affectionate nickname.

"What's going on?" I say as I feel Luna huddle closer to me. Aya presses against my other side. I think Hammurabi scares the shit out of her. Rightfully so, the old grouch.

"I'm afraid to hope," he breathes, which has Goldilocks shooting me a look of concern.

"Hope for what?" she asks him, one small hand reaching over me to cover the Babylonian king's.

It's a testament to how far their relationship has come that he doesn't throw off her hand or even flinch at her touch. He gives her an indulgent smile. "Asmodeus, child."

Shock reverberates through me, but Luna doesn't look surprised, and I see a mixture of hope and guilt reflected on her face. I know she blames herself for Asmodeus being taken, even though it wasn't her fault. Aya just gazes at me with round, confused eyes, poor kid. I honestly didn't expect the Council to return the Archdemon so soon. I see the Babel students swarm around a figure, which just shows how scared they are, because Asmodeus isn't the give-you-a-hug-and-cookies type. Yes, she loves us, and we love her, but she's still terrifying. Rafe and Shalina rush forward, but I hold back because Hammurabi isn't moving. I don't understand why. I know for a fact he's happier to see the mistress of Babel than anyone if I've been reading the room right. Maybe he's just giving the kids their moment.

A small crack in the crowd appears, and I see Asmodeus's hair, otherworldly in its garnet sheen. Her green eyes meet mine for the briefest of moments before they latch onto Hammurabi. Her lips curve at the sight of him—a warm, relieved smile—then she's swallowed by the mass of bodies once more. What does he mean to her exactly? Does the Babylonian king now occupy the place Ishtar used to hold? Or is their relationship different? There's no doubt a deep affection lies between them.

"I never understood why she let Ishtar live," I mutter to myself, but of course, Hammurabi and Luna hear me. Luna's brows raise at my odd question, which literally landed out of nowhere.

"Ishtar? Like *the* Ishtar?" Aya pipes in, but I ignore her.

Hammurabi just gives a sad shake of his head, expression grave. "When you have lived as long as Asmodeus, there are few things that you treasure, that you love. Ishtar was one of those things."

My heart clenches at his words for a moment. I know I will be one of those things for Luna. The same way she'll be for me—if I'm lucky to live a long life and Alexander doesn't kill us all first.

Asmodeus breaks away from the students and strides toward us, her steps so light I can't even hear them. She eyes Luna's hand, still offering comfort to Hammurabi, and Goldilocks snatches it away, as if she's been caught touching something that isn't hers. I smother a laugh because I don't see jealous possession in Asmodeus's eyes, only a pleased expression that grumpy old Hammurabi finally got with the program.

Hammurabi steps forward and offers a deep bow. "It's so good to see you again, Mistress." His rich baritone rings with unnamed emotion, and I fidget a little, feeling like I'm interrupting a private moment. Luna's hand finds mine and squeezes. Aya has practically burrowed into my side at the sight of Asmodeus. Smart girl.

Asmodeus flicks long ivory fingers. "None of that, old friend," she says. "It brings me joy to see you safe." Reaching out, she clasps his shoulder. Their eyes meet, and then she acknowledges Luna and me. "All of you. I knew, King, you would not fail me. You never do." Her gaze lands on Aya who squeaks. "It seems you've made a new friend, Caleb."

"Sister," I say, and the Archdemon's eyebrow arches. I grin at her. "We're damn happy to have you back." I was worried about her, especially considering how vicious the Council is.

"I failed to keep you safe," Hammurabi says and her eyes narrow.

"Nonsense," Asmodeus scolds him. "I'm the mistress of Babel. It's my job to keep *you* safe."

"I'm so sorry. I should've stayed to help," Luna blurts out, and I hear her guilt. "I could have—"

Asmodeus holds up a hand, silencing her. "Child, you couldn't have." Her voice is surprisingly gentle. "You would've just been captured again. I knew the three of you would end up exactly where you needed to be."

I snort. "I'm glad you were so confident."

Hammurabi growls at me in warning, but Asmodeus chuckles. "Haven't I always said Babel students are superior? Clever Caleb, of course, I was confident in your ability to survive."

Luna shivers. "Let's hope we can survive the upcoming war."

Asmodeus nods. "Yes, child, let us hope we can all come together and defeat the Conqueror once and for all."

SEVENTEEN

LUNA

"WE NEED TO TALK. Alone," Caleb whispers in my ear once Asmodeus departs a few moments later, spouting an excuse about wanting to find my father, with Hammurabi following at her heels. Although the Archdemon seemed no different than the last time I saw her, I can't help wondering if her imprisonment affected her as much as mine impacted me. Then again, I was in that hell for four months whereas Asmodeus only had to endure the Council's torture for a matter of weeks. To an angel who's walked the Earth since the Fall, that length of time must have seemed like a heartbeat.

"What about your sister?" I whisper back, glancing down at the girl practically nestled into his other side. At the sound of my voice, she blinks up at me with starstruck eyes, and I offer her a shy smile.

Caleb follows my gaze and shrugs. "She can hang out here with Rafe and Lina." Raising his voice for the others to hear, he says, "You guys don't mind watching over Aya for a bit while I catch up with Luna, do you?"

Aya reels back, visibly appalled by the suggestion. "I'm fourteen, not four," she grumbles. "I don't need a babysitter."

Before Caleb can comment, Rafe huffs out, "I see how it is. Stick the friends with babysitting duty so you can ditch us to go bone your girlfriend." With a dramatic sigh, he drapes a languid arm across Shalina's shoulders. "And here I was hoping we could find a dark corner to finish what we started earlier." A salacious grin forms on his lips as he waggles a brow at her, but she just rolls her eyes and sighs.

Caleb lets out an affronted gasp and slams his hands over Aya's ears. "Children are present!"

"Shove off, you big idiot," the younger girl growls, slapping his hands away. Her dark eyes then shoot daggers at Rafe and Shalina, who both chuckle under their breath. "Again, for those who need the reminder, I am *not* a child. And I know what sex is, thank you very much."

I watch with quiet amusement as Caleb wrinkles his nose.

"You do *not* know what sex is, and as far as I'm concerned, you're going to die a virgin," he tells her. Then shaking his head, he clears his throat and says, his tone almost comically authoritative, "Aya, stay here. And don't you dare sass me about it. You're my responsibility now. You two"—he jabs his pointer and middle fingers at his own narrowed eyes then shifts his hand, directing them at Rafe and Shalina—"behave yourselves. I'll be back soon."

Grabbing my hand, he tugs me away from the group, and as I stumble after him, I give his sister a small goodbye wave, somewhat unnerved by the devious smile curving her lips. We barely make it five feet before Aya's voice projects through the busy cavern behind us.

"Don't be upset if he doesn't last long, Luna. Boys his age never do," she calls after us. "I'm sure he'll get better."

Caleb falters, throwing a glare over his shoulder, and I swear I hear him grumble, "The audacity," before he trudges ahead, once again pulling me after him, even though he has no idea where he's going. "If this is what having siblings is like, I want to be an only child again."

I glance at him, biting back a laugh, though my cheeks are unbearably warm—not from embarrassment but from the thought of having sex with Caleb. We've only just taken that step in our relationship, and it's only happened once, but at least I can safely say he has nothing to worry about in that department.

I grip his hand tighter, grinning to myself, and since he has no idea where to go, I quicken my pace to get in front of him then pull him toward the archway up ahead, which leads through into the adjacent passage. We weave through the Nephilim in our path, and we're about to step out of this room into the next one when—

"Going somewhere?"

I instantly recognize the voice that coos from the shadows, and a second later, Lilith steps into our path, a sly obsidian brow hooked upward.

Beside me, Caleb growls, "Damn, Lilith. Lurk much?"

He rakes a trembling hand through his hair—the sable strands filthy with ash and blood—and as I watch him out of the corner of my eye, I focus on the low thud of his racing pulse as it slows back to normal. Although he would never admit it, whatever happened at Megiddo has made him jumpy.

I clear my throat, drawing the ex-Archdemon's attention. "I was just taking Caleb down to our room so we can talk in private. Where are my parents?"

I peer past her shoulder, squinting my eyes with intent, as if my parents will manifest in the passage behind her if I look hard enough.

A grin tugs up the corners of her lips. "Having a reunion of their own."

I grimace at the insinuation in her tone. The last thing I want to think about is what my parents get up to together behind closed doors.

"Nice job, by the way," she adds with a wink. "I don't know what you said to your father about Gabriel, but it clearly worked. How very *Parent Trap* of you."

I blink at her, confused. "I don't know what you mean—"

"Wait, you know what *movies* are?" Caleb cuts in. He shakes his head, his mouth agape. "And here I thought all angels were technologically challenged."

The ex-Archdemon crosses her arms. "I have been in exile for thousands of years. I had to spend that time doing *something*." She looks us both up and down and shrugs. "Well, what are you waiting for? Come along."

She turns her back toward us, beckoning over her shoulder for us to follow, but Caleb doesn't move.

"You aren't coming with us," he asserts, though the comment comes out more like a question.

Lilith glances back at him and snorts. "Wipe that scandalized look off your face, child. I am merely walking you to your room. I have no intention of staying to watch." She flashes a teasing smile, though it takes a moment for me to grasp her meaning.

"W-We aren't—" I stammer, but I fumble the words, a blush burning its way across my cheeks again. Well, we aren't going to our room explicitly for *that*, though I certainly won't complain if it happens again while we're there.

Lilith clicks her tongue. "Methinks you doth protest too much, Luna," she says, wagging a scolding finger. "Just remember what I said. Now, let us be off."

"I don't—" Caleb begins to say, but she cuts him off with a warning glare.

"And save your questions," she growls.

I can feel Caleb's eyes on my face, his confusion almost palpable, but I can't bring myself to look at him. The heat in my blood has reached boiling point, and if I meet his gaze, I might erupt.

Thankfully, the walk through the many levels of Derinkuyu gives me time to cool off, and by the time Caleb breaks the silence again, my thoughts have shifted elsewhere, my anxiety ratcheting higher as I wonder what he'll tell me about Megiddo once we're alone.

"So…we need you to escort us, why?" he asks once we're several levels down.

"My parents and Lilith don't trust the Council," I murmur, taking care to keep my voice low, my eyes darting between the many wooden doors lining the passage. Although I don't hear anything on the other side of them, I can't say for certain if the rooms beyond are actually empty…or if anyone inside might be listening. "They think it's best if I'm not left alone…just in case."

To Caleb's credit, he doesn't puff his chest out and try to act like he could protect me from the Council. He's not a fool, and he knows even a seasoned Nephilim like Hammurabi would struggle in a fight against someone like Mammon. Hell, it took four of us to hold the Archdemon off when Caleb sprung me from the Council's cage and I'm an angel. Lilith, on the other hand…

"If those smug shits try anything on my watch, they'll live to regret it," she vows.

Caleb raises a brow at me. "I don't doubt it," he mutters.

We walk the rest of the way without saying a word, and upon reaching our room, I grab the handle, pushing the door open without delay. I jerk my head for Caleb to enter then hurry in after him, relieved we'll finally be alone in a moment. I've missed him, and I need him to hold me without a hundred eyes watching us.

"I'll wait for you in my room," Lilith says from the doorway, glancing across the hall at an identical door less than five feet away. "Let me know when you wish to rejoin the others. I have little doubt the Council will be calling a meeting again now that everyone has returned, so keep in mind, you may not have long."

I nod.

"Oh, and Luna?" she calls just as I'm about to close the door. "Because of the stone, these rooms are well-insulated. It also makes them virtually soundproof, so you needn't worry about being too loud." A wicked grin forms on her lips. "Just thought you'd like to know."

Caleb laughs under his breath as I slam the door shut with more force than necessary. "Lilith has really settled into protective aunt mode, hasn't she?" he asks as I slump against the wood. His lips tug into a lopsided grin.

I heave a sigh, pressing a hand to my forehead. "Who knew having a family could be so exhausting?"

He snorts. "Try exasperating." But as he says this, his smile lingers, and I can sense happiness behind his false veneer of annoyance.

Caleb, who has spent his entire life disconnected from the Nephilim side of his family, finally has someone he's tied to through his angelic blood—someone not only outside Alexander's influence but who, from the brief encounter I witnessed between them at least, seems just as eager to accept him as her brother as he is her as his sister. The one silver lining to come out of the evacuations.

That thought sobers me, and pushing away from the door, I cross to him, gently taking his hand. "Was it bad?" His warm brown eyes search mine, and bracing myself, I whisper, "Megiddo."

The smile finally slips from his face, and he nods. "Yeah," he says, and for the first time, I notice the trembling in his fingers and the lack of color in his cheeks. Unless, of course, you count the dried blood, which still stains his skin.

Releasing his hand, I cross to the brass wash basin a few steps from the foot of the bed—the only means of washing we've been provided in this ancient place—and dunk the small cloth hanging over the side into the tepid water.

"May I?" I ask, turning to face him and raising my hand, the sodden fabric clenched tight in my fingers.

His gaze darts to my hands, and he snorts. "So much for modern plumbing," he grumbles. When I arch a brow, he nods, his eyes shuttering.

Returning to his side, I carefully drag the damp cloth across his left cheek. The blood flakes off at my touch, but there's a pain in his expression that surfaces. That I can't wipe away.

"Caleb?" I hedge when he doesn't speak. He swallows loudly then swipes his tongue across his lower lip. It wobbles slightly.

"I…" he begins, his eyes opening slowly, and there's a dreary emptiness in his gaze that tells me everything I need to know about the horrors he encountered today.

I move the cloth to his other cheek, but his hand flies up, touching mine, and I freeze.

I can't stop myself from asking—from needing to know what's troubling him so I can do whatever it takes to banish it from his thoughts. "Caleb…what's wrong?" I breathe, my heart racing.

And then, to my heart-wrenching horror, he breaks.

"I killed someone." A single tear cuts down the cheek I just cleaned, which he hurriedly brushes away. "They deserved it," he adds before I can respond, as if he feels the need to justify it. "He would've killed us if I hadn't, and I—"

"You did what you had to," I protest, lowering my hand and the cloth from his face. With my free hand, I twist my palm, threading our fingers. "All that matters is that you're okay. When we saw Alexander—"

"Wait, what?" His eyes blow wide, and he gapes at me, his expression dancing between horror and disbelief. "What do you mean you saw Alexander?"

His voice is breathy, his tone saturated with panic, and I berate myself for not breaking the news more gently, especially considering the hell he's already been through today. The shock on his face is apparent, and I wish I could take it all back—erase that fear—but I can't. Just as I can't take away the trauma he'll carry for taking a life. A trauma I know all too well.

"On the Blessed Road," I explain. "On the way here after evacuating the Serapeum. He and some first generation Lights intercepted us."

A shadow crosses the planes of his face. "I was afraid of that. I guess that means Gilgamesh has been recruiting," he muses.

My answering frown is bleak. "It seems so."

"Was anyone injured?"

I shake my head. "Well, Alexander *tried* to kill Gabriel," I correct myself, "but I stopped him—"

"Wait," Caleb says, interrupting me for the second time. I blink up at him, taken aback by the unexpected anger I glimpse in his gaze. "What do you mean, you *stopped* him?"

I spend the next few minutes recounting what happened on the Blessed Road. The whole time, Caleb stares at me with stunned incredulity, saying nothing.

When I finish, he takes my face in his hands and leans in. "As badass as that sounds, Goldilocks, you could've *died*," he breathes, the words hot on my lips.

"I know." I keep replaying that moment, and the realization of how close I came to death sits just under the surface of my skin at all times now, like an itch I can't scratch. And yet, I'd do it all over again to avoid the alternative outcome I'd be faced with if I hadn't acted. "But he was going to kill Gabriel. If it was your mom, what would you have done?"

He opens his mouth and then immediately snaps it shut. He can't argue with that. After all, we both know he wouldn't hesitate to defend his mother if her life were in jeopardy. Hell, he didn't hesitate to protect her from a thirsty Hammurabi.

The worry creasing his brow only deepens. "I don't like this. Alexander wouldn't attack for no reason—everything he does is calculated and deliberate." He pulls away from me and begins pacing the room, scrubbing a hand over his face, one cheek clean and one still dirty, almost like he's wearing war paint. "He's a military strategist, for fuck's sake."

"Maybe it was a distraction," I consider. "To delay us and stop us from helping at

Megiddo." I know I'm grasping at straws, especially since the Darks didn't ask for our aid, but I can't figure out what other motivations Alexander might have had for intercepting us.

Caleb pauses mid-step and throws a dubious look over his shoulder. "I mean, yeah, assuming the Roads follow a similar path, you would've passed through Israel to get here from Egypt, but it still doesn't really add up. Like, how would you even know Megiddo was being attacked from inside the Blessed Road?"

"The sigils?" I suggest. "Gabriel told me the Council has one they all use to commune with each other, and she also has one just to contact my father. Maybe Alexander knows that."

"Maybe." Caleb looks only slightly more convinced than he did a moment ago. Plopping down on the edge of the bed, he bends forward, resting his head in his hands. "I don't know. Something about all this doesn't feel right."

A sinking feeling twists my gut at those words, and I find myself hoping Caleb is wrong—that the ambush on the Blessed Road really was just a diversion and not a sign of something worse. Because if he isn't, then that means Alexander's appearance today was an omen, a warning of what's yet to come. And I can't help fearing that— whatever that something is—we won't be ready for it.

"Luna." Caleb's voice shakes me free of my thoughts, and I glance at him, not realizing my concentration drifted. He sits straight now, his face no longer obscured by his hands, but when our eyes meet, the sensation in my gut only worsens.

"There's something else," he says, a slight, unnerving tremor distorting his tone. "Aya said a Light was at Megiddo, that he warned her to run before Alexander's followers could take her. Just her…like he knew who she was."

My brow furrows as I try to make sense of what he's trying to tell me. *A Light?* Why would a Light be at Megiddo?

He jerks his head, wincing, one of his eyes fluttering closed for a moment as if he's in pain. "I saw him when we arrived at the school, but it was chaos, and I thought I was seeing things—"

"Saw who?" I cut in, an all-too-familiar panic swelling inside me. "What are you talking ab—"

"Alaric," he whispers. The misery in his voice when he says that one word is reflected on his face. He licks his lips, staring at me with wide eyes. "Luna…I saw Alaric."

I freeze, and for a long moment, I'm not even sure if I remember to breathe. It's not possible. I *saw* Alaric die. I watched Alexander plunge his knife in his chest, and I saw the light of life leave his eyes. It's not possible.

Alaric is dead.

"But he's…" I trail off, barely able to form a coherent thought in my shock. If Alaric is dead, Caleb couldn't have seen him at Megiddo. Not unless—

My knees buckle, and I stumble forward a step, as if I'm the one who's been stabbed in the heart. Caleb jumps up from the bed and launches forward to catch me, his warm arms forming the safety net I need to keep me afloat as the waters of grief rise again to drown me.

As he pulls me close to his chest, I manage through a sob, "Did Alexander…" But I'm unable to bring myself to finish voicing that thought, even if I hear it on repeat like a constant scream ringing in my skull.

Did Alexander resurrect Alaric?

"No," Caleb says, but his answer struggles to penetrate the haze of my mind as the memory of our brief time at the citadel comes rushing back. In my head, I see his father again and as I watch him die—and then relive how easy it was for Alexander to raise him, it takes every ounce of self-control I possess to keep myself from retching… or weeping.

Although I didn't stick around to see what became of Caleb's father after his resurrection, I do remember the eerie emptiness in his gaze—how when he rose from the stone floor, he looked at me with zero recognition, even though I had just killed him.

I didn't want to admit it then, but I understand now why resurrection is forbidden among both the Lights and the Darks. It *is* unnatural, and I want to cry picturing Alaric that way, like an empty vessel for Alexander to manipulate and control. And on the off chance he did come back as himself, what was stopping Alexander from wiping his memories—or at least any recollections he had of me?

What if Alaric no longer knows who I am?

"No," Caleb says again, firmly this time, tilting my chin up with his finger. "I mean, it crossed my mind for a hot second, but if that was the case, why would he help Aya? I don't know all the ins and outs of resurrection, but it can't be that different to how we Darks give life to inanimate objects. It's all based in the same root premise, and I feel like Alaric would be beholden to Alexander or something, like those objects are to us. It *is* magic at the end of the day, and Alexander would be his tie to the living world."

Although my head is foggy with shock and grief, Caleb's reasoning makes enough sense to reach me. He has a point. In Kandahār, Alexander made it perfectly clear he planned to use Alaric's talent to track down his other grandchildren and bring the rest of their bloodline into the fold. If Alaric *was* under Alexander's command, he would be hunting Caleb's siblings down, not warning them to run.

As if we share one mind, Caleb adds, "If Alaric was in any way being controlled by my gramps, he wouldn't have just let her go."

My mouth puckers into a grimace, the words sour on my tongue as I choke out the only other explanation for how Caleb could've possibly seen Alaric if he wasn't resurrected. Because if Alexander didn't bring him back from the dead, then that can only mean…

"So, you think he's been alive this whole time?" That thought is a sledgehammer to my lungs, and I gasp around tears, "That we left him…"

That *I* left him.

My knees go weak again, and slipping out of Caleb's arms, I sink to the floor in a near catatonic heap, my mind a whirlwind of unwanted memories, which assault me with merciless abandon. Again, I see Alexander's dagger, buried to the hilt in Alaric's chest. Again, I see the Nephilim glance at me with a devastating relief in his eyes—relief that I was physically unhurt, even though my heart was breaking.

"We didn't know," Caleb whispers when a strangled sob escapes me. Crouching to the floor, he plants his hands on my shoulders. "We didn't know, Goldilocks. This isn't our fault."

You're right. It isn't our fault. It's mine.

Hot tears burn my cheeks, and a full-body shudder wracks me down to my marrow. Alaric took that dagger to the chest to save *me*. He sacrificed his life for *me*. And although logic keeps screaming at me that we couldn't have saved him—that Caleb is right, that we didn't know—I still can't help blaming myself for this outcome.

My fingers snake into my hair, gripping my skull, as I jerk my head side to side. Everything bad that keeps happening is my fault. Alexander's freedom. Alaric almost getting stabbed to death. The destruction of Ashkelon and Megiddo.

How can I possibly be the Savior when the blame for all of these terrible occurrences rests on my shoulders?

"No," I persist, the word like broken glass in my mouth, cutting me. "No, he can't be alive. If he was, why would he stay with Alexander? Why wouldn't he come find us?"

Why wouldn't he come find me?

"Maybe he can't." Caleb's tone is unnervingly gentle, like every word is an egg he's taking care not to drop. "I doubt my gramps let him hang onto his phone."

I sink my teeth into the inside of my cheek, biting back the influx of emotion I feel rising in my throat. "But he has the sigil, remember? He could contact my father." Hell, he could have contacted him at least a hundred times by now. And yet, he hasn't.

Frowning, Caleb touches a hand to my cheek, sweeping his thumb across my wet cheekbone. "Something must be stopping him. Trust me, Alaric is not Team Alexander. If he's in his right mind, then he has his reasons for not leaving."

I nod. Caleb's right. The trouble is, Alaric *has* a good reason to stay. Because even after everything, he loves Alexander…

And if he isn't careful, that love will get him killed. For good, this time.

As Lilith predicted, the Council does call a meeting, and less than an hour later, I, along with thirty-three other angels, demons, and Nephilim, sit cramped together in one of Derinkuyu's more secluded caverns, perched in a ring of wooden chairs that seem to have materialized out of nowhere. I have no idea who found the time to furnish the place before our arrival at the underground city, but they seem to have thought of everything—including how many chairs we would need to host the extra guests.

Aside from the fourteen Archangels and Archdemons in charge of the academies—still including my mother and father—Zerachiel and a Fallen I don't know are here, along with one chosen Nephilim per each member of the Council, with the exception of my mother, who chose to bring two. In addition to Evangeline, she also invited Kali to the meeting, and after everything she did to help us in India, it's a relief to see her here—a familiar, kind face among so many that still look at me as if I can't be trusted just because I'm a Gray.

I regard the unfamiliar faces with curiosity. I can only assume the unknown Fallen is the one who temporarily stepped in for Asmodeus at Babel. I peer around the room, taking in the many faces around me, recognizing some of the first generation Nephilim joining our meeting. On Caleb's right side, Hammurabi sits tall and stiff beside Asmodeus while Evangeline grins at me between my father and Kali, who sits next to Gabriel, my mother a beacon radiating stern silence on my left. Hatshepsut is here as well, accompanying Raphael, and the tall woman beside Beelzebub is the same injured Nephilim he brought with him when he escaped from Ashkelon, though I can't remember learning her name. Aside from those five, I only recognize one other Nephilim in the room. She watches me from the other side of the oblong circle, her dark eyes swinging back and forth between my face and Asmodeus, as if waiting to see which of us will come at her first.

Nzingha.

I tense in my chair, my fingers wrapping around the edge of the wooden seat, which begins to splinter beneath the force of my grip. Because of her, we had to go to Alexander for help to get the Council's tracker out of my head. Because of her, Alaric—

Drawing in a deep, cleansing breath, I chase that thought away before it can form. I need to focus. I can't let her get to me, even if I would love to rip her to shreds for betraying us.

We're all allies now, I remind myself, but even as this thought crosses my mind, I find myself glancing at the glowering hulk of a man beside Nzingha. Mammon's aura is a menacing shroud of hate, his burly arms crossed over his chest, those red eyes staring daggers at Caleb, who sits impressively still under the Archdemon's scrutiny in the seat beside me on my right.

I have zero doubt Mammon would ignore the truce and attack Caleb if given the chance. If there weren't at least two Archdemons, one Archangel, a Gray, and a grumpy Nephilim who would stand in his way, I have no doubt he would try right now. But Caleb won't always have this much protection around him, and that's the time I worry about most—about what awaits once this truce is over.

I'll be there, I vow, releasing my grip on the seat of the chair and reaching for Caleb's hand. He grips mine back when I squeeze his fingers. *And I won't let anything happen to you.*

Someone clears their throat and I glance to the left as Uriel rises to his feet. "Two academies have fallen," he announces, his tone crestfallen. A beat of silence follows these words, then when the moment has passed, he adds, "I suppose it could've been worse."

"Of course *you* think that," Beelzebub seethes, his small hands balled into shaking fists in his lap. He looks about as restrained as I feel, which doesn't say much for our shared lack of composure. "It wasn't Light schools that have been burned to the ground."

Uriel's upper lip peels back in a snarl, and he opens his mouth to fire back what I'm sure is a scathing retort lacking any form of compassion for the Archdemon's loss. Fortunately, my father's voice booms through the space, silencing the Archangel before he can utter a word.

"For once, can we conduct a meeting without resorting to petty squabbles? Two schools lost is two too many, regardless of if they are Light or Dark."

"Lucifer is right," Abaddon says with a respectful nod toward my father as Uriel sinks back into his chair. "And if the Conqueror is willing to raze our academies, what else is he prepared to do? What extremes is he willing to go to? The danger to our students aside, the glamors would have been destroyed when Ashkelon and Megiddo burned. It will not be long before the mortals take notice, assuming they haven't already."

Caleb lets out a harsh, humorless laugh, unafraid in this company of more powerful beings. "I was there when he turned Gilgamesh, and Alexander's whole speech persuading him to 'come to the Dark side' was about how we won't have to hide anymore once he's running the show. He *wants* the humans to know we exist. For all we know, the attack on the schools was just the prelude to our big coming out party."

An unsettled murmur spreads through the room as the Faithful, Fallen, and Nephilim all exchange worried glances. I don't like that look or how afraid they all seem by the prospect of our kind being revealed to the humans. Then again, while our species is superior in strength, mortals vastly upstage us in number, and the last thing the angels and Fallen want is a repeat of the early days of the Nephilim when many were lost to prosecution and terror. There are only so many places left on Earth where our kind can hide. Blind ignorance is what keeps us safe.

"No one is asking the obvious question," Mammon interjects, and beside me, Caleb tenses as those crimson eyes rove over his face before shifting between the others in the room. "Why Ashkelon and Megiddo? Why those two schools of all the academies?"

To my surprise, Caleb is the one who answers, though his voice is soft, barely a whisper, and he only says one word. "Aya." When everyone looks at him, he clears his throat and adds, louder now, "My sister is a student at Megiddo. The Darks attacking the school tried to take her."

"Then it isn't just *any* student the Conqueror is after," Uriel muses, and his gaze turns stormy as he looks at my father. "Did you know about this?"

I watch Lucifer with bated breath as my mind turns over the same question. Caleb once told me the Archdemons made a deal with his father to hide his kids from each other so they wouldn't unite and hunt him down—a deal that came in the form of a blood bind, similar to what Gabriel did to me. A bind that I can only assume broke the moment Caleb's father died at the citadel, however brief that death may have been. When *I* broke into his mind and killed him.

Caleb and I have barely had time to talk since we got back from evacuating the schools, so we haven't even been able to really broach the topic of him having a sister—or that my father would've known about her. The whole "Alaric is still alive" bombshell dominated the little time we've had together.

"About the Conqueror's grandchildren?" Lucifer asks, his lilting voice yanking me from my thoughts. "Yes, though it would be foolish of any of us to think that was Alexander's only motive. He may wish to locate his descendants and broaden his dynasty, but we all know his real priority is building an army, and for that, he needs bodies and weapons. Weapons that can actually harm us."

He's right. Alexander might want to unite his family, but he's not sentimental enough to actually care whether they live or die. What he truly cares about is gaining devoted followers, and he probably figures blood relatives are the easiest Nephilim to persuade to join his side. It's like dominoes—turn one and others will follow. The vast numbers he already commands are proof enough of that.

I glance at Caleb. He doesn't look angry or accuse my father of withholding the information about his sister from him. After all, he knew he must have siblings out there in the world, and he knew the Archdemons had put a bind on them—though how they detected them to begin with is a mystery to me unless the Darks have someone in their ranks with a gift like Alaric's.

I quickly dismiss that thought. If there *was* someone else out there who could sniff out bloodlines, Alexander wouldn't be sending Alaric to the academies to track down his grandkids. Surely, he wouldn't trust him not to attempt an escape. No, I have a feeling that's a one-of-a-kind talent, which means the Archdemons have another way of recognizing Caleb's bloodline. A detection ward, perhaps, built into every Dark school?

Filing that question away in the back of my mind to ask my father about after this meeting, I direct my focus back to Caleb. I can't imagine how he must be feeling, how something that was so distant and untouchable for so long can suddenly be so present and real. And while anger doesn't illuminate his gaze, he does look afraid, like he now has so much more to lose.

"How would the Conqueror even know where to find his grandchildren?" Abaddon asks. His deep, rumbling timbre draws my attention. "From what you have told us, Gabriel, the only Nephilim we know of with the ability to detect bloodlines is dead. And even if Alaric *were* alive, the bind on their line should prevent such detection."

A lump forms in my throat at these words, and I flash a quick glance at Caleb only to find him already looking at me, his eyes wide with the same fear I'm certain he sees reflected in mine. He hasn't told anyone else what he told me about Alaric, and this is why. Too many questions would be raised. Questions about Alaric's allegiance. And given that Alaric was the one who removed the bind on Alexander in the first place, the Council would have justification to wonder where his loyalties lie, even if in the end he helped them imprison the Gray. I have no doubt someone like Uriel would suggest Alaric might regret that decision.

I swallow, turning my eyes back to Abaddon, trying to keep my face calm and composed. Even though I want to shout it from the rooftops, the Council can't know about Alaric. Not yet. Not until we have tangible proof he's alive…

And that he isn't willingly helping Alexander.

"Unless the bind has been broken," Belphegor considers. "How else would the boy know of his sister?"

All eyes focus on Caleb, then on my father, as if searching for an explanation. But before either can speak, Leviathan asks, "What about the boy's father? It is he, after all, who makes us aware of his spawn."

I blink, taken aback by the Archdemon's cavalier statement. Could it really be that simple? No detection wards at the schools? No complex magic? The Archdemons know about Caleb and his siblings because his father told them?

Well, that's one mystery solved, I muse. My jaw clenches and my free hand once again grips the edge of the chair seat so hard it cracks. Caleb once told me his dad never sticks around to raise his kids. But this—this agreement his father has with the Archdemons—implies he at least sticks around long enough to confirm if whoever he's sleeping with at the time has a bun in the oven. Like Caleb's mom. Caleb's wonderful mom whom he left to deal with pregnancy all alone.

Asmodeus snorts, rolling her eyes at Leviathan. "Yes, right before he frolics off to make another sperm deposit elsewhere."

Beside me, Caleb is unnervingly silent, and as the Archdemons discuss the matter, I watch him out of the corner of my eye, searching for a reaction. Aside from a slight tightening of his lips, there is none.

"I highly doubt the boy's father is aiding the Conqueror on this matter," Abaddon drawls. "Have we forgotten why he bargained for the bind in the first place? His children nearly killed him once. He wouldn't risk facing their wrath again, especially now that their numbers could almost certainly populate a large village. No," he mutters, shaking his head. "If the bind has somehow been broken, it's far more likely he would make himself scarce."

"But he was at the citadel, wasn't he?" Gabriel asks. She's the only Light to enter the conversation while the others all glance between the Darks as if they're watching a game of tennis. "Hammurabi, you told us as much when recounting your time there."

The Babylonian king crosses his arms. "As a prisoner," he clarifies. "I do not believe

Alexander had any intention of bringing him into the fold."

"It wouldn't matter if Alexander's controlling him," Caleb says.

My brows draw together and I blink at him, confused. Caleb and I both know his father has nothing to do with how Alexander is finding his siblings. Alexander made his intentions clear when we were at the citadel, and Caleb spotting Alaric at Megiddo only confirmed it. So, why…

The answer crosses my mind as Caleb's eyes cut to mine, and I realize he's giving the Council a scapegoat, something to draw their focus—and blame—away from Alaric. I give a quick nod, urging him to continue.

He clears his throat. "The bind on our line is definitely broken because I *felt* my sister at Megiddo and—"

Leviathan holds up a hand, cutting him off. "For the bind to be broken, your father would have to be—"

"Dead. Yeah," Caleb says in a blunt monotone, interrupting him right back. I'm grateful he purposely leaves out the part about me being the one who killed him. "But he didn't stay dead for long. Alexander resurrected him, and, like a true villain, is now probably pulling his strings like an evil puppeteer."

"And sending him to hunt down his bloodline," Lucifer mutters. He hums softly under his breath then nods to himself before exchanging a grim look with the others. "I believe Caleb may be right. When our paths last crossed, Alexander was quite insistent he would not hesitate to resurrect any who follow him. He has always been obsessed with establishing an empire, and it is very likely he would kill his own son just to raise him again if doing so could help him achieve his goals."

"Resurrection?" Amenadiel says, aghast. "Surely, he wouldn't dare use such a power. It is unnatural!"

"We should not presume to know what the Conqueror is willing to do," Gabriel growls. "Nor should we underestimate him or his attachment, however shallow, to his bloodline. Clearly, there are many elements at play here."

"Are there others, then?" Serathiel chirps. Her attention turns to Beelzebub. "Did the Conqueror have any kin studying at Ashkelon?"

My stomach dips at the question, and Caleb's hand tightens around mine when Beelzebub nods.

"A boy of sixteen. Though he was not found among the wreckage, so we assumed he was taken by the Conqueror's allies to add to his ranks like so many others. Or he's…" He trails off, and his shining blue eyes shift to Caleb.

Dead, they seem to scream in the silence.

The hand wrapped around mine goes slack, and I risk a concerned glance at Caleb, noting the haunted look in his eyes and the waxy, wan tone to his skin.

"Does it even matter?" Azrael scoffs. "We are speaking of adolescent Nephilim. They hardly pose a threat to us."

A mortified laugh rips from Serathiel's throat. "I certainly hope you aren't suggesting that you would take up arms against children?" She balks, and I know she must be thinking of her own young students at the primary academy at Petra.

"Age matters little in war," Belphegor snarls. "And if they join the Conqueror, then they *are* the enemy. Besides, our softness toward the Nephilim may be precisely what Alexander is hoping for. They are a weakness he will use against us."

"He's right," Lucifer says, his tone stiff. I glance over at him to find him already looking at me, and I can't help wondering if he sees *me* as his weakness—the one vulnerability in his armor that Alexander will try to exploit. "It's likely Alexander knows we will do everything in our power to avoid going to war with our students, and he may even present them as a bargaining chip to force us to submit to his rule. Though, I doubt there are many who would side with him willingly. These are scared children we speak of, not seasoned warriors. We must take that into consideration and not judge too harshly those who may act under coercion."

Uriel frowns and rubs his large hand over his chin. "War with our students should be avoided at all costs, but we must also consider the greater good. We cannot let the safety of a few sway us from defeating this threat."

Serathiel flinches. "Our students *are* the greater good, otherwise what have we been working toward all these long years? Why construct the academies if we do not do everything in our power to protect those we have dedicated our lives to? We cannot let the Conqueror make a mockery of our legacies any longer. We must make the safety of the children a priority…until doing so is no longer a viable option."

"We do not have time for this," Gabriel says, her expression hard. "Whatever Alexander's intentions are for the children, the more immediate risk is our exposure. The preservation and secrecy of our kind has always been paramount to this Council. We must act before Alexander reveals us to the world or worse."

"What then do you propose, Messenger?" Uriel asks, his words patronizing and snide. He sneers. "What course of action would *you* have us take?"

Her jaw clenches, and I can practically hear her teeth grinding together with derision. Her dark eyes flit around the room, jumping between the many faces around us. "We must rally those loyal to us and strike first before Alexander can enact whatever other devious plans he has for us. We cannot sit idly by any longer, not when another devastating attack could be imminent."

"We have the advantage of knowing where he is," my father agrees. "This may be our only opportunity to get the drop on him."

"And with us on the defensive, surely the Conqueror will not expect our swift retaliation," Asmodeus adds. "Plus, we can take this opportunity to try to get the children out safely and perhaps retrieve some of our lost weapons while we're at it. Given what they mean to us and the strides Alexander took to steal them, it's likely he will keep both very close."

I peer between my parents and Asmodeus, gauging the mutual agreement stretching across each of their faces, but I'm unable to ignore the uneasy weight forming in the pit of my stomach. They're right—this may be our only opportunity to turn the tables on Alexander—but all I can think about is that smug look he gave me and my mother on the Blessed Road. He's up to something, I know it…

And once again, I can't help fearing the worst is yet to come.

"Or maybe that's exactly what he expects." Everyone looks at me, but I hold steady, refusing to flinch and refusing to blindly agree with this plan just because it was my parents' idea. Or maybe I'm just speaking out of fear—out of my terror of returning to the citadel, which serves as the setting in many of my nightmares. That and that awful egg I wasted away in for months. I swallow the rising lump in my throat. "Alexander *knows* we know where he is," I point out. "And that's assuming he's even still in Kandahār."

"She's right," Lilith says from where she sits beside Asmodeus. "We could be walking into a trap. We need to consider the risk."

"Do not make the mistake of believing you have a voice on this Council, Lilith," Uriel growls, spitting her name like a curse. "You lost that right when you chose to side with Alexander the last time we were in this predicament."

A cruel, mocking laugh parts her lips. "And yet, I know Alexander better than any of you. I would think you'd want to use what information I possess about him to your advantage."

"That's assuming we can trust anything you say, *snake*," he bites back.

"Enough," Gabriel hisses, glaring at Uriel before offering an apologetic look at Lilith. "The reality is, the risk is just as great if we choose to do nothing. And if his next move exposes our kind? What other option do we have but to act?"

She holds Lilith's gaze for a moment, and in the silence between them, I sense an unspoken conversation—some deeper meaning to my mother's words. It isn't just exposure she's worried about but something else…and I realize that deeper meaning is me. Because every moment this war is drawn out is another moment that leads me closer to becoming a victim of the prophecy my mother has feared since the days of the Fall. A fear that led her to lock me away as a baby so she wouldn't have to lose me. A fear she's faced with again now and had to experience firsthand on the Blessed Road when Alexander had the chance to kill me in front of her.

As much as I don't like it, I accept that she's right. The scales are already tipped in Alexander's favor, and by doing nothing, we would only be giving him more time to unbalance them further. I don't like it, but what other choice is there?

I bite my lip, holding back the sudden burn of tears, as another thought strikes without warning.

If we go to Kandahār, we might find Alaric.

If nothing else, surely the risk is worth that?

"Let us not forget that taking up residence here was always a temporary measure," Beelzebub says, his youthful voice echoing through the cavern. "We cannot remain in Derinkuyu forever, so let us take advantage of this opportunity and be done with all this."

"We would be foolish to squander what might be our only chance to take the Conqueror by surprise. We know Alexander's location when he does not know ours. It is not often we have been able to say that," Raphael agrees, her tone lacking its usual acidity. I'm shocked she's managed to stay silent so long. Usually, she injects her opinion at the first available opening.

"And if the Conqueror *has* left Kandahār?" Mammon presses. "What do the traitors here suggest we do then?" His upper lip curls back in a contemptuous snarl as he glares across the cramped space at my parents.

But before either of them can answer, Caleb blurts out, "Then we figure out where he's relocated by searching the citadel." My eyes dart to his face, and I'm relieved to find the anguish in his gaze replaced with a fierce determination, which he directs at the scowling Archdemon, as if to say, *I'm not afraid of you*, even if I see the truth in the jerky movements of his aura. After a moment, he looks at me, and when he squeezes my hand again, I know we're thinking the same thing. That if Alexander and his forces aren't in Afghanistan any longer, then maybe we can at least find some clue about Alaric. Some confirmation he really *is* alive...

And if so, where we might be able to find him.

"Either way, we need to end this. Quickly," my father stresses. "Before any further damage is done." There's a pain in his voice as he says these last words, and my chest tightens when it dawns on me he's talking about Megiddo.

Once again, his eyes find mine, and as I stare into their shining depths, it occurs to me that he and my mother are driven by fear as much as I seem constantly hindered by it. They want this over because dealing with Alexander and removing the threat hanging over our heads is the only way to ensure not only my survival, but the safety of the Nephilim they've been charged with the task of caring for—a role that has consumed their lives for hundreds of thousands of years.

"Then our decision is made." Uriel stands, and the others all follow suit, as if sensing the impending conclusion of our meeting. "Send out messengers and call on your allies," the Archangel urges, and the angels and Fallen exchange weighted glances with their Nephilim companions as he says, "We leave at dawn."

EIGHTEEN

CALEB

I STARE DOWN AT the last place on Earth I want to be. Alexander's fortress rests below, as harsh and forbidding as I remember. The sun beats down on us, warming the cool mountain air. Pain slices my skull as I remember Gramps cracking my mind like a nut—something that might happen again if we meet today. I shake it off. Now is not the time to lose my shit.

Luna crouches next to me, and we wait for Uriel—I still hate that asshole—to give the signal. Gabriel and Lucifer should be in charge. Hell, put Hammurabi as general, even if he's just a Nephilim, but Creator forbid the Council take orders from someone who isn't an angel. The three of them have actually been inside Alexander's lair. But nope, before we left Derinkuyu, that dick Uriel insisted he lead because he's still unsure of our loyalties, thinking Lucifer and Gabriel will just run off with Luna if shit heads south. I hope when this is over, the Morningstar and the Messenger beat his ass. They have lots of scores to settle with him. I'll lend a hand.

Hammurabi flanks my other side, and Lilith remains behind Luna. I glance over my shoulder, seeing the Council—including Gabriel, Lucifer, and Asmodeus—perch on the sharp cliffs like birds of prey, along with other Fallen allies. They're unnaturally still, and it reminds me of just how *other* they are. I mean, I have celestial blood, but sometimes angels seem so alien to me. I know Luna is an angel, too, but she's so young that she hasn't evolved into what they are. At her core, she remains human. Her wings are tucked under her skin, as she's not adept at flying yet, though her parents have promised to teach her.

I wonder how much Lilith hates being down here with us, not because we're

Nephilim, minus Luna, but because she must really miss her wings. An evil grin paints my face. Mammon is down here, too. Somewhere. He's keeping his distance, being watched by both Hammurabi and Lilith. He can kill Hammurabi but Lilith is a different story. Every once in a while, I feel ice slide down my spine, and I know he's watching me. I might make it out of this war alive only to be murdered by that shape-shifting psycho.

Luna is restless beside me, practically bursting with unease. She can't be easily hurt physically, but mentally she's vulnerable, and facing Alexander isn't good for either of our sanities. Lucifer and Gabriel don't like that Luna's on this mission. They didn't come right out and say it, but I know they wanted her to stay behind where she'll be safe, but they can't exactly suggest that. They have to convince the Council Luna is the Savior, so whether they like it or not, she has to come along to give truth to their claims. The Council will turn on her in a heartbeat if they think they're being played, and her parents know that.

Nephilim surround us, waiting on Uriel's signal. The angels and Fallen are the cavalry and we're the infantry. Once our scout reports back to Uriel about Alexander's numbers and the locations of his guards, we'll slip into the Roads and pop out and attack.

"This is wrong," Hammurabi murmurs beside me, his eyes fixed on the citadel.

"What about this fucked-up situation is right?" I whisper back and he elbows me. Hard.

"Where are the Conqueror's sentries? It's too quiet," he says, and my eyes dart around.

"We're still waiting for our scout to come back. Let's not panic just yet," I counter, frowning. "Gramps probably doesn't think we have the balls to attack him in his secret headquarters. Even if he knows we're with the Council, he's probably banking on the fact that they can barely agree on lunch, let alone battle plans." As those words leave my lips, I really hope they're true, but doubt gnaws on my gut. I understand why the Council chose to make this move, but I don't like this plan, not that I would ever say that aloud—I don't want to call attention to the universe and give us more bad luck.

Hammurabi shakes his head. "Boy, you know better than anyone that Alexander is never unprepared. We should have killed at least a couple of his soldiers by now. He wouldn't let the mountains go unwatched."

Luna gazes at me with worried eyes. "But with everyone the Council has called in to help, we have the larger force now. We can counter him, right?"

"We hope," Hammurabi says, and I wish for once Mr. Sunshine could try to be positive, although I secretly agree with him. Gramps is too fucking smart to get caught with his pants down.

"Creator be, King, you're full of optimism as always." Lilith's tart voice echoes behind us. "But in this, I fear you may be right. It is too quiet for my liking as well."

Terror blossoms inside me, and I see my trepidation reflected in Luna's hazel eyes. Like a jab to the face, it hits me again how *young* we both are. Two babies on a battlefield. Well, no matter what Alexander has up his sleeve, we'll be forged in battle today. And we're potentially not the only kids here. I have a younger brother who might be down there somewhere, but I can't let myself linger on that too much. It's a distraction I can't afford.

My eyes flick back to the fortress. With my Superman eyesight, I can pick out a few figures moving along the top of the outer wall, like two tiny dots creeping along.

"Ha!" I crow to Hammurabi, who immediately growls at me to shut up. "I see two sentries on the wall right now, so someone is keeping watch. Maybe we got lucky and missed their rotation in the mountains." Even to my ears, that sounds lame, but anything is possible. I hope.

"That proves nothing, child," he chides me. "And you can't possibly be that naive."

Luna, voice hesitant and unsure, asks quietly, "If he suspects we're coming, what do you think he has planned?"

The Babylonian king shakes his head. "That I don't know, little flower, but I am certain that whatever the Gray plans, you are his top priority. And the boy."

A shudder runs over me. By priority, I think Hammurabi means we're first on Alexander's kill list—Luna for interfering with his savior status and me for betraying my blood.

A Nephilim pops out of the Blessed Road and scurries up the cliffside like a mountain goat, whispering into Uriel's ear. I tense, watching the Archangel's expression closely, but his features remain flat. Man, that prick has a good poker face. He nods at the Light Nephilim and calls to us, "We go."

My balls shrivel at those two words, and I can feel bile creeping up my throat. Fuck me, I don't want to go down there. I'm no coward, but this is the big leagues, and I'm not ready to come up from the minors. I glance at Luna, and her creamy skin has gone wan with fear. *Be brave for her, Caleb.* My lips crash onto hers as I give her a desperate kiss, then we let the Shadow Road swallow us.

A few moments later, we emerge inside of the outer wall framing the main courtyard. The plan was to split our forces and subdue the Nephilim in each section of the citadel, securing the students we find, if any, and killing the enemy until we reach Alexander. Hammurabi and Lilith are in charge of the first layer of defense while babysitting Luna and me, though there is no doubt that Goldilocks and I are here to slaughter as well. I'm not comfortable with that part, and I know Luna isn't, but Uriel and the Council insisted anyone helping my grandfather is to be killed and anyone showing his people mercy might suffer the same fate. There are no second chances, and in some cases third, I guess. Gilgamesh's face flashes across my vision for a moment, and I swallow. He's a self-righteous dick, but I can't say I want him to die. Ishtar led me astray, too, but I guess that's not entirely fair. I was there when Alexander persuaded Gilgamesh to the dark side but still. He's the King of Uruk. When he's dead, all that history and knowledge will die with him.

"Caleb, come on!" Luna's urgent tone hooks me back into the present.

Hammurabi and Lilith lead the charge up the wall, and we follow. I draw my dagger, but as I look at the Nephilim guards we're about to clash with, my heart thunders in my chest. Grandfather's Nephilim—all first generations—don't draw their swords. They don't react at all to the incoming threat of an ex-Archdemon and her band of warriors barreling their way.

A tall woman with blue hair marks our progress. Her eyes find mine, and a grin slashes her face, like she's a funhouse clown luring kids to their doom. It's creepy as hell. "The Conqueror sends his regards," she says, and she jumps off the wall, her comrades following.

I rush to peer over the wall, Luna at my side. The Nephilim all vanish into the Shadow Road. The foreboding presence of Hammurabi hovers next to me. I glance at his grim face, mouth pulled into a scowl.

"I hate that you were right," I tell him through gritted teeth—I hate that I was right, too—my eyes sweeping around the walls. Nothing. We're alone here. My stomach clenches. Even if Gramps suspected we were coming, how did he know we were coming today of all days? Does he know the Council better than I think and expected a swift retaliation, or do we have another Nzingha situation on our hands? My gut roils.

"I hate it as well," Hammurabi replies, staring at the ground.

"Now what?" Luna says, an edge of hysteria coloring her voice. "We're back to square one. What will the Council do if we don't find any clues and can't figure out where they went? If we don't know where Alexander is, will the truce be void? Will they try to take me again?"

"That's never going to happen," I tell her, clenching her hand. I'll fight to the death to keep her from being locked away again. And so will her parents.

"No, it won't," Lilith chimes in, placing a hand on Luna's shoulder. "Now, we secure the perimeter and find your mother and father." She points back to the courtyard. "Children, wait there."

I scoff at her command but take Luna's hand and jump off the wall. We both land as nimble as cats. Lilith, Hammurabi, and a handful of Nephilim comb the walls, only meeting us once the outside is clear. Then, together, we head inside, the interior cool after being out in the blazing sun.

Eerie silence permeates the corridors. It's not just the absence of sound that's unsettling, it's the fact everything is gone. All the creature comforts and civilized touches Alexander added have disappeared. It's like no one has been living here for several months.

Beelzebub steps from the shadows, a frown painted on his lips.

"It appears as if we've missed the party," he says, and his eyes briefly clash with Lilith's. "It's almost as if a little bird whispered in Alexander's ears that we were coming. A poor, flightless bird with a proverbial ax to grind."

I don't even fight my epic eye-roll. Here we go again, but to my surprise and utter pride, Luna speaks before an obviously pissed-off Lilith can.

"Stop," she hisses. "Lilith wouldn't betray my mother. She wouldn't betray *me*. I understand you're angry—we all are—but this is why Alexander is one step ahead of us. We can't stop fighting with each other."

Lilith gifts Luna a smile ripe with affection before rounding on Beelzebub. "Indeed. Perhaps if some of us would remove our heads from our asses, we wouldn't be so blind to the truth."

I choke on air and even Hammurabi's mouth twitches. The other Nephilim have taken a few steps back from the scary duo, but I'm over this dumbass fighting.

"Hey, can we get our shit together and focus on the big picture here?" I demand, managing not to piss myself as Beelzebub and Lilith turn their rage toward me. "You two don't like each other. I get it. There's history I can't possibly understand, but my gramps is now out there in the world, planning and plotting, and we have no idea where he is. Luna and I can't be the goddamned grownups in the room." My eyes skip to Hammurabi who growls, "Stupid boy," under his breath.

When I turn my back on the two predators, Asmodeus is there, garnet hair shimmering. I manage not to scream, retaining my street cred, and from the amusement glinting in her eyes, I'm pretty sure she heard my last comment. I give a slight bow of my head to the mistress of Babel, positive she's there for Hammurabi. Those two don't stray far from each other since she's returned. I still haven't quite been brave enough to give him shit about it.

"Let's go find your parents, Goldilocks," I say, tucking her hand closer to me as I step around Asmodeus and walk away.

She and I agreed before we left Turkey that we'd try to sneak away to find clues about where Alaric is when we had the opportunity. We haven't told anyone he's alive—a lone Nephilim being held against his will isn't exactly on the Council's priority list—and now that the superpowers in the room are in a bitch fight, it seems as good a time as any to make ourselves scarce.

Luna leans against me and whispers, "That deserves a standing ovation."

I snort. "Just don't let them kill me, okay? And speaking of standing ovations, I enjoyed your smackdown of Baby B."

Goldilocks shoots me a horrified look. "Shhh, he might be able to hear you." Her head swivels, and her eyes dart over her shoulder.

"Like I said, don't let them kill me." And that pissy tween just might be spiteful enough to do it.

A giggle squeaks from Luna but abruptly dies as we travel deeper into the building. I expect to find at least traces of the kids Alexander stole because kids are messy, but there's nothing. Not even a stray sneaker.

"Should we go to Alaric's room first?" Luna asks, and I hear the catch in her voice. The tears she's trying to swallow.

I nod, caressing her fingers with my thumb. "Yeah, let's hope he's left us some clue."

My hope fades when I push open the door to his old room, ushering Luna in before me, and see just an empty chamber. No traces of Alaric remain, but we dutifully search the walls and crevices for anything. Some sign that he left behind.

"There's nothing here," Luna says, and this time she doesn't bother to hide her tears. They pool in the corners of her lovely eyes.

I pull her into my arms, and she sags against me, as if she can no longer bear her weight. "Hey, this doesn't mean we won't find anything, okay? We've got more rooms to search. Don't give up just yet." My words come out confident, though I'm anything but. I fear Alaric is lost to us for now, but I can't say that to Goldilocks.

Her sigh is heavy against my chest. "Okay, let's keep looking."

"Did the little mice think they could escape the cat so easily?" Lilith purrs from the door, startling us both.

Heart hammering in my chest, I glare at the ex-Archdemon. "We're basically on the set of a horror movie. Was sneaking up on us really necessary?"

Her smile holds a hint of malice. "Just as necessary as you taking it upon yourself to scold Beelzebub and me. You should remember to respect your elders."

Score one for her, but I choke back a laugh when Luna retorts, "Not if they don't act like elders."

Lilith arches one perfect brow at Luna then snorts. "Point taken. Why are you children here?"

"We're searching for clues as to where Alexander might have gone," Luna interjects quickly. "That way the Council can't accuse me of not helping."

"Then I'm happy to aid you. Shall we continue?"

We move on to my room, and Lilith checks out a different room across the hall. My chamber is stripped bare. It's like my time here—our time here—was a bizarre dream or nightmare. Goldilocks squeezes my hand tightly but doesn't speak. I don't, either, although I'm having a screaming freak-out in my head. How did they manage to evacuate so quickly? When did they decide to blow town?

And the million dollar question: how did they know when we would come?

Hammurabi was right. We underestimated Alexander the Great, military genius. Well, it's not that I don't know what Gramps is capable of, I just wanted this to be over. I wanted it over so badly that I was willing to go along with the Council's plan, even if I never really believed we could take the Conqueror by surprise. Besides, it's not like we had any better ideas. This was the only plan that made sense. The best option in a sea of shitty scenarios.

And I don't really think the Council—the Light side—really understand, despite Gilgamesh's defection, that it's not just Darks willing to pledge their allegiance to the Great. Lights are, too. For fuck's sake, they make it a point not to talk about Gilgamesh, like burying their heads in the sand will make the Lights switching sides to Team Conqueror go away. Maybe there are other Lights sick of the divide, too. Or hell, maybe they're tired of Darks having all the fun and want a little free will of their own. The honest truth is we can't see one another as we really are. We're stumbling around looking for the forest but the damn trees keep getting in our way.

I sigh as I look around my barren room. "Let's give it a thorough once-over just to be sure," I say and Goldilocks nods.

She takes the left side of the room, and I take the right, my eyes scanning over the walls and along the floor. I'm about to call it a day when my eyes snag on something folded on the stone. It looks like a piece of light-colored leather, but it's irregular, the edges jagged in places. Crouching down, I rest on my heels and reach for the leather, unfolding it. There's a marking on it, and my brows kiss my nose as I frown.

"What do you have?" Luna calls and I shrug.

"I'm not quite sure..." My voice dies as my stomach lurches, and I taste bile as I drop the piece of leather like it's on fire. No, not leather. Skin. Alaric's *skin*. That marking was the sigil Asmodeus gave him to call Lucifer.

Horrified, I take a step back. What the fuck is Alaric's skin doing in my room? And who cut it off of him? Did Alexander see the sigil and carve it from Alaric in a fit of rage? But that can't be right because the skin was deliberately planted in my room. There's no other explanation for why it would be here. Maybe Alaric sliced it off himself and left it for us to find, to let us know why he hasn't contacted us. But why cut off your only means of communication? My head spins.

Luna's small hand slips into mine. "Caleb, are you okay? What's going on?"

I point at the dried patch of skin on the floor. "Alaric left us a clue," I whisper, wincing at the way my voice shakes.

Our gazes clash and alarm is written on her face. She releases my hand and takes a step forward.

"No!" I yell, yanking her back. "You don't need to see that."

"Why? Alaric left it behind for us. We have to take it with us," Luna says, jerking out of my hold.

"For fuck's sake, Goldilocks, don't. It's his—"

But she's so desperate for news of Alaric, she moves with angel speed, stunning me, and picks up the skin. Her brows furrow in confusion before her eyes round in terror, and a cry of pure horror escapes her lips.

"What is *this?*" she demands, clutching the skin. Tears stream down her cheeks, and my heart aches for her.

"You know what it is, baby," I say, shoving my own fear in a box marked "shit I have to deal with later with a qualified therapist." I do my best to keep my voice calm, soothing.

"Alexander *cut* it off him?" she snarls, rage overtaking her dread. She shoves the skin toward me, and I fight the urge to recoil.

I shake my head. "I honestly don't know, Goldilocks. But if he did, I can't imagine he would want us to find it, which means Alaric must've left it here. For us. For *you* to find."

Footsteps echo and I whirl around as Lilith rushes into the room, face battle ready. She slows when she doesn't see any obvious danger, but her body tenses when she sees Luna's expression. "What's happened?"

Luna holds up that gruesome slice of Alaric. "This is Alaric's *skin*. It has the sigil Asmodeus gave him on it. He left it in our room for me to find."

For a moment, the ex-Archdemon's jaw slackens and she blinks. I've never seen the glib Lilith at a loss for words. This might be funny if it wasn't so goddamn tragic.

"Luna, Alaric is dead," Lilith says gently.

"Um, yeah, about that," I say, shoving my hands in my pockets. "I saw him at Megiddo. He found my sister and sent her away before she could be taken."

"And now, we know why he hasn't contacted us," Luna growls. "Because Alexander cut this off him!" Her enraged screech makes me flinch.

Lilith's eyes dart to Luna's folded fingers. A myriad of emotion flicks across her face too fast for me to follow. Maybe when you're as old as she is, nothing surprises you much anymore. "I see. Hmm, perhaps we should tell your mother and father about this?"

I don't know what they can do about it but Luna nods. "Okay," she says.

I expect her to drop Alaric's skin, but she slips it in her pocket, and I shudder. I don't tell her to put it back, though. Even if it repulses me, I get why she's taking it.

As we make our way to the makeshift throne room in silence—Lilith said Lucifer and Gabriel were headed there—Hammurabi catches up with us, but Asmodeus isn't with him. If possible, his grim visage has gotten grimmer. He doesn't even lecture me about my bad behavior with little B so I know he's just as spooked about this place as I am. And he doesn't even know about the little gift we found.

I spot Lucifer outside the doorway the moment we turn into the corridor leading to the throne room. The enormous doors are thrown open, resembling a sinister maw waiting to devour us. The Morningstar's mouth is a slim slash and his expression is troubled. His eyes find Luna's and the worry—the fear there—makes my heart clench.

"Starlight," he calls. "Halt. I don't want you to come in here." Gabriel slides in by his side, and the two of them create a formidable blockade.

What the fuck is in there? How many horrible surprises are we going to face today? If the two of them are scared enough not to let us pass, then it must be really bad. I tuck Luna against me as I stare at the space between Lucifer's and Gabriel's bodies.

"What's in there?" Luna asks, and I can hear the slight tremor vibrating her voice. Then she straightens, pulling away from me slightly. "If it has to do with me, I want to see it." Her shoulders square, and I'm damn proud of her. She's being braver than me right now. I don't want to see anything that can possibly hurt my Goldilocks.

Gabriel frowns. "Luna—"

Luna gives a violent shake of her head, golden hair swinging. "No, I'm part of this war now." Her eyes dart to me. "*We're* part of this war. How do you expect me to go up against Alexander if I can't even face a possibly upsetting thing in a room? I can't be that fragile. I won't be."

I can't help it. I give her a slow clap. And I admonish myself for being a chicken shit in this moment. She's right. We have to start handling things.

"Well said, flower," Hammurabi says, his praise making Luna's cheeks pinken. She gives him a shy smile. I do believe she's quite fond of Uncle Hammurabi.

"We can't clip her wings when she needs to fly," Lilith points out, and the irony of her wing comment isn't lost on me.

Her parents, however, attempt to shoot lasers out of their eyes, as if they'd like to burn the Babylonian king and Lilith to ash. Hammurabi doesn't even flinch, taking his role as our de facto guardian seriously. Plus, I know Asmodeus would inflict serious damage to anyone who dared to hurt him. Lilith just shrugs, giving them a bored look.

"Dad," Luna says, her voice uncharacteristically sharp. "Let us pass."

Lucifer searches her face as if testing her resolve. Sighing, he steps aside. Gabriel's eyes narrow at him, but she moves as well, albeit reluctantly.

Goldilocks takes my hand, and we stride through the door, the Morningstar, the Messenger, Lilith, and Hammurabi following at our heels. Like the other rooms in the citadel, this, too, is empty, the open space amplifying every sound. The absence of the large stone bull might as well shout out that the seat of power has been moved. Well, it's empty except for that asshat Uriel, Raphael, and villain-of-the-week Mammon. Three of my least favorite people. They hover around the dais, murmuring to each other. As the rest of the great chamber is bare, whatever upset Gabriel and Lucifer must be there.

Mammon pivots toward us, his red gaze latching onto Luna. For a moment, I see pure malice glint in his eyes, then the emotion smooths over into indifference. Uriel and Raphael turn as well, but unlike the terrifying shape-shifter, I don't see any ill will when they regard Luna. Their expressions are a mix of concern and puzzlement. Their movement has opened a straight path to the dais, and I see Gramps has left something behind.

Luna's first golden gown Alexander forced her to wear to dinner during our time here drapes across his throne, a sword skewering the fabric where her heart would be, pinning the silk to the marble. My own heart thunders in my chest until I can hear its frantic dashes in my ears. I clutch Luna's hand in a crushing grip, my other hand curling into a fist.

This is a dire warning. Luna threatens the Great's power, and he doesn't tolerate threats. It's also a clear message. The time for taking Luna into the fold is over. He's no longer interested in having her as an ally. The next time we see Alexander, he'll kill her.

He didn't threaten the Council—he threatened *Luna,* establishing just how important she is. And how shaken he is by the prophecy. He will crush fate and anyone else standing in his way.

I feel Luna trembling next to me, and I fight the urge to take her in my arms. But I can't do that here, not with three predators in the room, watching our every move. I have to take my cue from her, but my heart aches for her. She doesn't deserve to be caught up in this prophecy bullshit, tasked to take on Alexander the fucking Great. It isn't fair. She can't die. I won't let her. The Creator didn't release her from stasis just to let her be killed by the Conqueror. I have to believe that. I clutch to that thought like a life raft in the middle of a stormy ocean.

I hear her swallow in the silent room. Then she gently frees her hand from mine. I raise a brow at her as our eyes meet. Determination and courage radiate from her gaze and I nod, willing to follow her lead. She walks toward the dais, stopping a few feet from the handle of the sword. She grasps the pommel, knuckles white from the force of her grip.

"No!" Uriel shouts as she yanks the sword free.

White-hot heat sears my brain, and agony screams along my nerve endings, setting them on fire. The last thing I hear is Luna crying out my name in panic before I fall head first into the abyss.

NINETEEN

LUNA

A RUSH OF WHITE noise floods my ears as the sword slips from my fingers, clattering to the floor by my feet. The echo of the blade as it strikes the stone is like a siren on the edge of hearing. I'm aware of it, but it's so far away, almost imperceptible past the panic assaulting my brain.

I snap my horrified gaze between the faces of these people—some family—I recognize so well, now reduced to mere writhing bodies on the floor before me, their expressions stricken, stretched into silent screams, and complexions drained of color. Their auras thrash wildly, the tendrils of shadow and light lashing out, as if attempting to detach from the bodies they surround.

I don't understand. All I did was wrench the sword from Alexander's throne. Ignoring it wasn't an option—not once I noticed the way the blade had been purposely positioned to stab through the heart of the first golden dress Alexander made me wear during the brief but horrible time we spent in this place. When I saw it, red washed across my vision—a blinding rage swaddled in an even more crippling fear, both born of how helpless this entire situation keeps making me feel—and it was all I could do to grab the pommel and yank the sword free. If I hadn't, my fire would have surely erupted and burned through the entire room along with everyone in it. If I hadn't, something terrible might have happened—like what I did to Caleb's father—and I would have been unable to stop it.

And yet, something terrible happened anyway. Because of me. Because I grabbed hold of that sword. *I don't understand.* It took little effort to free the blade despite the steel being firmly rooted in the marble, but then, I'm a full-blooded angel and I often forget I'm stronger than the mortal I once believed myself to be. With one tug, it lifted easily from the crack, which ran along the full length of the seat, the damage to the throne obscured by the golden fabric until the moment my arm jerked back and the dress, now freed as well, slipped from the stone. I don't know who the weapon belongs to. None of our bloodlines or else Alexander wouldn't have left it here—and that's assuming it's even a weapon from the Fall. I didn't notice any Enochian symbols etched into the steel but then I didn't take the time to look. The details didn't matter in my anger. Nothing mattered except grabbing that pommel.

I heard Uriel's alarmed protest as my fingers wrapped around the grip, but it was as if I wasn't in charge of my body—as if I was being controlled by the anger and fear I've spent so much of my life victim to. As if I was back at the group home when I was five, and then at the Serapeum, and in every other awful memory where I couldn't stop the evil inside me from being unleashed. Except this time, it wasn't my fire I set loose but a promise.

A silent vow to stop Alexander, no matter what it takes.

The anger that overtook me has since disappeared but the fear remains, joined now by confusion, which rises like a wall around me until I'm trapped by it, unable to move. My airways tighten. I can still feel Caleb's name on my lips, though I can no longer find my voice to scream it again.

I don't understand. That's the only thought I can manage. It spins through my head on a loop, surges through my body like a poison in my bloodstream, robbing me of sense. This shouldn't be happening. How is this happening? These are celestial beings before me, angels and Fallen and Nephilim more powerful than anyone or anything I've ever encountered.

Except Alexander, I find myself thinking.

And if my exclusion from this nightmare is any indication…

Except me.

That comprehension is the needed jolt to my heart to set me free from my terror, and stumbling forward, I reach out a hand to nothing and no one in particular, unsure what the hell I should do. The seconds tick by one after another, and my heart pounds in my ears as I attempt to process what I'm seeing. Caleb, my parents, Lilith, Hammurabi, the Council members…no one in the room is unaffected.

Except me, I consider again.

But why? Because I was the one who pulled the sword free, setting off the trap Alexander laid for us? Or because I'm a Gray? It can't be because I'm an angel as the Faithful and Fallen in the room aren't immune to whatever is happening—to whatever cruel magic is attacking their bodies and minds from within.

I clamp a trembling hand around my mouth, choking back a sob. Knowing Alexander, he intended for this scene to play out exactly the way it has, with me as the sole survivor of this attack, cripplingly aware of my own helplessness. I'm no match for him—this proves that. Just as it proves I'm sure as hell not the Savior. I can't be. Not when everything I do only leads to chaos and pain.

The worst part is I only have myself to blame. The sword was the powder keg but I was the spark. *I* set this off. *I* caused this…

And I have no idea how to stop it.

Tears cut lines down my cheeks as I drop to my knees, my hands curling into fists on the stone. This is just like what happened to my foster parents and to Caleb's father when I tore their minds open, the memory of their convulsing bodies a mirror image of the violent seizures now gripping the others. Out of the corner of my eye, I glimpse my mother, her back ramrod straight even as she thrashes against the hard floor, but my gaze quickly turns away, my focus drawn to one more than the others. Because as much as I doubt this attack could actually kill an angel—it will likely just keep them in a never-ending cycle of torment, effectively removing them from this conflict—I know it can kill *him*.

A strangled cry escapes me when I spot blood dripping from Caleb's nose. I shake my head as the tears come faster, harder. I can't let him die.

Not like this.

"I won't let you!" I cry, scrambling across the ground toward him. His head is limp when I pull it into my lap, his eyes shifting back and forth beneath their closed lids, and his skin is cold—so cold—almost as if he's already dead. "I-I don't know how to help you," I stammer, but as those words leave my lips, my eyes spring wide, and I realize that's not entirely true.

I witnessed this exact pain on Caleb's face two other times—both of which were here at the citadel—when his grandfather broke into his mind. First, to teach Caleb a lesson, and then, with the intention to kill.

But Alexander isn't here now and I can't fight the invisible hold he left behind. Not unless I attack it at its source.

A horrified gasp fills my throat, and as I stare down at Caleb, understanding dawns. This is why Alexander laid this trap—because he knew I won't be able to do the one thing that needs to be done to stop it. I don't have the control. I can't do it without destroying the person completely. And yet, there's no other way.

Sweat rises across my palms, and my pulse jumps under my skin, ratcheting higher, as I peer at the others, trying not to freak out over the wasted seconds as I assess each of their faces in turn. The effects of the spell are working more slowly on the angels than they are on the Nephilim. Hammurabi doesn't look to be in a much better state than Caleb, despite being several millennia older, while the angels haven't even started to bleed yet, though their expressions are agonized, revealing their pain.

Swallowing, I force my eyes back to Caleb, my fingers twitching against his cheeks. If I break into his mind, he might die, but he'll die for certain if I choose to do nothing. Tensing, I flatten my hands to the sides of his head and close my eyes. If there was time, I would try this first on Uriel or Mammon—someone I don't care about just to be sure I can do it—but there isn't. And their lives aren't in jeopardy. Not the same way Caleb's is.

My lips push out a shaking breath, and then I inhale again, concentrating as much as I can in my growing hysteria.

Be calm, I tell myself. *Focus on Caleb.*

My temples throb as I extend my thoughts outward, mentally reaching past the confines of Caleb's skull and breaching the boundaries of his mind, which relent to me easily, like a door opening. I expected more resistance but there is none, and suddenly, it doesn't feel like I'm breaking in at all but like he's welcoming me. Like he's okay with me being in here. Like he trusts me not to break him. And I won't. Unlike with his father, my focus is singular. I don't think about the past. I don't think about what I might do if I mess this up. I don't think about anything else except Caleb, and as I dig deeper, I smile at the memories unfolding before me. Everywhere I look, I glimpse my face—I see *me* the way Caleb sees me, and as I take in each memory, it dawns on me just how much he loves me. How much I consume his entire soul the same way he consumes mine.

"Caleb," I whisper, and I feel a tear drip from my chin as the memory of our first kiss plays before me as if it's happening all over again. I didn't notice it at the time— his happiness in that moment—but I sense it now…just as I sense his fear and worry that he'll never get to kiss me again. That he'll die here, trapped in the horrors of this malicious spell cast by a man who claims to want to see our world united when, in reality, he is doing everything possible to tear it apart.

I won't let that happen, I promise, pushing deeper into Caleb's subconscious, trailing that fear like a path of breadcrumbs. But as I descend, it occurs to me that what I'm sensing isn't breadcrumbs at all but a string—an invisible thread connecting one thought to another.

That thread leads me into a place of darkness, of sorrow and twisted recollections where nothing is clear, and all I'm aware of is pain. It's a strange, murky place, and the images around me are fuzzy and distorted, almost shapeless in the encompassing gloom. This isn't what I imagined Caleb's mind to look like, and dread squeezes my heart as I try to separate the tumultuous thoughts—as I try to figure out how to help him.

Panic shoots through my veins like adrenaline, and I can feel sweat beading along my hairline and dripping down the back of my neck, my body still convinced it's mortal in the throngs of terror. I'm running out of time—I can sense that in Caleb's increasing convulsions, can *smell* it in his blood, which flows faster and surely from more than one orifice now, draining him of life.

"Come on," I hiss, forcing myself even deeper. It feels like hours have passed in his head when it can't have been more than a minute or two, but even so, that's a minute or two too long.

Desperation claws at every inch of my skin. Why can't I find it? The source of Alexander's spell should be in here somewhere…shouldn't it? Shouldn't I be able to see what's causing this distress inside Caleb—see what's physically tearing him apart? Because this isn't the true state of his mind; this dark, cold place isn't the Caleb I know. No, this is Alexander's doing and whatever magic he cast is responsible for this pain. I just can't separate the chaos around me enough to see where it is and stop it.

Something catches my attention then, like a glint of light in the corner of my eye, and again, I notice the pull of that thread—that peculiar string tying Caleb's thoughts together.

My stomach swoops, and I feel the thrum of magic so close now I can taste it. I sense both Dark and Light at work here—Gray magic. Alexander's magic.

That's it. Heart racing, I feel for the string and tug on it with all the strength I can muster, trying to undo the spell, to free Caleb from this mental anguish. But the thread is tangled and for every pull, another section of string seems to take its place.

A scream of frustration rises in my throat. How am I supposed to save him if I can't even unravel the spell?

Because Alexander doesn't want you to save him, a voice says in the back of my head.

I do scream then, yanking as hard as I can on the thread. This time, it snaps, but my momentary relief is overshadowed by the comprehension that whatever magic is in here still lingers. The connection hasn't been severed…but why?

And that's when I realize…it isn't a string. It's a web.

"A spider's web," I breathe, horrified.

As these words leave my lips, several threads manifest before me, shooting off in different directions, and as I follow each one like a branch in a tree, I finally grasp why this spell is so cruel.

They're all tied together. Everyone who was in the vicinity when Alexander's trap went off is linked, their minds connected by the threads in the web. I can feel them at the end of each string, and so long as they're joined, I will never free Caleb from this misery…or anyone else.

Violent sobs rack my chest. I can't do it. I can't save them because saving one means saving them all, and I can't be in eight minds at once—

A gasp rips from my lungs, and suddenly, I find myself…standing? I blink, confusion throwing off my center of balance. I'm in the middle of the throne room, staring down at my family and the Council members, who remain on the floor, trapped in the nightmare of Alexander's magic snare.

My gaze shifts. *I don't understand.* A moment ago, I was on the floor next to Caleb. A moment ago, I was in his head, but now…

The air rushes out of my lungs, and I stumble back a step. There, not far from the dais, I spot Caleb, blood seeping from his closed eyes and ears now as well as his nose…and beside him, I see me, kneeling with his head in my lap just like I was only seconds before.

I stagger forward, my heart a stampede of confusion and horror, and unsure what else to do, I reach out a hand, then quickly wrench it back with a small, alarmed cry. I peer down, my mouth popping open in shock. I turn my hand over, gaping at the flagstone floor, which is clearly visible through my palm, as if I'm an incorporeal being. As if I'm nothing more than a ghost.

I glance up again, focusing on Caleb and the other me—the physical me—noting the strain on my face and the sweat dripping down my temples and neck as my hands tremble against his head. How is this possible? How could I be over there but also here, outside my body?

My eyes spring wide, and I let out a gasp as the answer hits me like a wrecking ball to the chest. Swallowing my fear, I turn on my heel and dash across the floor to my mother. I don't feel the stone against my legs as I drop to my knees, nor do I feel the silky touch of her hair as I press my hands to her head, but that doesn't matter. All that matters is that I can do what needs to be done to save her.

To save everyone.

Breathing out, I close my eyes, and just before the lids slide closed, I see myself, repeating this same exact gesture with the others in the room. My fingers catch in the sweaty strands of Caleb's hair, my awareness abruptly shoved back into my physical body, but now, I also feel myself with my parents, with Hammurabi and Lilith, and even with Uriel, Raphael, and Mammon, my focus and mind split eight different ways—a piece of my soul cast out to each one of them like a lifeline at sea.

As I work, I feel a sense of control I've never known before. I don't question how I'm able to do this or if it's something the others are capable of. I don't question or think about anything except finding the threads tying them all to one another.

One by one, I find those threads—reaching out and working together with the projections of myself to untangle the knots—until finally, the web comes undone, slipping through my fingers as if it never even existed at all. When the last string falls away, I blink my eyes open, retreating from all minds until I'm only in mine, and with bated breath, I watch the now still faces around me, silently begging for them to wake up.

The first to rouse is my father, who sits up with a look of bewildered dismay on his face. Shaking his head as if to clear it, he crawls across the floor to my mother, who wakes a few seconds later. Her dark eyes immediately seek out mine.

"How?" she breathes, clambering to her feet. "How did you do that?"

Her question stuns me because it implies that she knew I was there in her head… and in the others' minds.

"I…" I trail off, unsure how to answer. Before I can form a coherent thought to explain what I did, the others begin to wake until the angels and Fallen and Hammurabi are all standing around me in silence, exchanging strange, perceptive glances. All except Caleb, whose eyes remain closed, though the erratic movement behind his lids has ceased.

I lick my lips and touch my hands to his shoulders, shaking him slightly, but he doesn't stir.

"Why isn't he waking up?" I croak, snapping my eyes to my mother. Her gaze is uncertain, and to my increasing dread, she says nothing. "Why is he still asleep?" I press, looking now at my father then Lilith.

In the space of a heartbeat, Hammurabi is beside me, touching a finger to Caleb's pulse. "He's alive…but he's young compared to us, flower. And the tie to his ancestral blood is weaker. Whatever devious spell we just walked into has taken a tremendous toll."

What does that mean? I nearly shout, but I can't find the words.

"He'll be all right, Starlight," my father assures me, stepping forward and crouching on the other side of Caleb, where he lies unnervingly still on the floor. "Look, he's already beginning to heal."

A quiet, hiccuping sob escapes me as I follow my father's gaze to Caleb's face.

Sure enough, the bleeding at his nose and ears has stopped. Still, that brings me little comfort.

"We should leave this place," my mother murmurs, looking the perfect picture of health despite the hell her body experienced only moments ago.

To my surprise, Lilith, Uriel, Mammon, and Raphael remain completely silent. They say nothing, though the weighted looks they keep throwing at me speak volumes in the tense hush.

"Come," my father urges, and rising, he scoops Caleb off the floor as if he weighs nothing. With his body limp in Lucifer's arms, Caleb looks like an oversized, sleeping child. "We will find nothing else of use here."

"I will reconvene with the others and direct everyone back to Derinkuyu," Uriel says, his expression unsettled. "Raphael and Mammon will accompany you back to the city."

I blink stupidly at him as the Archangel departs the room. That's it? I just saved his life and I don't get so much as a thank you?

I half-expected Uriel to berate me for touching the sword—for setting the trap off in the first place—since it's clear to me now there was magic encasing the weapon, the tingle of which I feel still on my hands, like the touch of static electricity. But he didn't. He said nothing. He *did* nothing except look at me as if my actions here were somehow sacrilege. Maybe they were. Maybe breaking into another angel's mind is the worst sort of crime, and by doing it, I unwittingly added to the list of reasons the Council already distrusts me.

Hammurabi glances at the doorway Uriel just left through and frowns—probably at the thought of leaving without Asmodeus. But then his eyes shift to Caleb, limp and so pale in my father's arms, and the worry stretching across his face pulls him after Lucifer into the Shadow Road without further hesitation.

"Come, flower," Hammurabi croons over his shoulder, his gruff voice a needed tether to sanity.

Neither my mother, nor Raphael protest when I stumble into the Shadow Road after my father and Hammurabi, Lilith tagging closely at my heels. No one is separating me from Caleb right now and I know my mother understands that feeling better than anyone, her desire to stay by my side etched into her face at all times. As for Raphael, the Archangel has reason enough to believe we wouldn't try anything at this point, and we have Mammon tailing us to ensure it. We need the Council's help more than ever, and besides, where else can we go except back to Derinkuyu?

I walk between my father and Hammurabi, occasionally reaching out a hand to brush my fingers through Caleb's hair, hoping my touch will be enough to wake him. It isn't.

"He will wake up, Luna," my father says, and tears blur my vision when I meet his gaze.

"How do you know?" I breathe, my voicing breaking. "What if I took too long to stop it? What if—"

"Don't do this to yourself, little flower," Hammurabi cuts in. "What you did…" He shakes his head, scrubbing a hand over his beard. "If it wasn't for you, we would be dead. Well, the boy and I would be, at least."

"And we would be trapped in that nightmare until Alexander draws his final breath, severing the spell's connection," my father mutters, a slight pinch to his lips. "Which, given the fact he is immortal, may have been a very long time."

"I think I scared Uriel and the others," I whisper, risking a nervous glance over my shoulder at Mammon, who follows like a skulking, hungry dog in our wake. He keeps his distance, tracking my movements with those ominous eyes, his focus shifting between watching me and staring hard at my father's back—at Caleb, who lies helpless in his arms. If there was ever a moment for Mammon to strike, to seize his chance at revenge, this would be it.

A shudder rolls through me at the thought, and I inch that little bit closer to Caleb, ready to protect him here and now should it come to that. I didn't just dive into the deepest recesses of his mind and pull him free from his grandfather's sadistic booby trap only to lose him moments later to Mammon.

"Perhaps," my father considers, and it's only when I meet his gaze again that he adds, "None of us have seen that kind of power before."

That stops me in my tracks. "No one?"

Lucifer pauses only long enough to look over his shoulder then gestures with a tilt of his head for me to keep walking. "No one," he echoes. "Breaking into the mind of one angel or first generation Nephilim would be a tremendous feat for any unskilled in the art, but to break into several simultaneously?" His expression darkens. "The Council has a tendency to fear what it does not understand."

Like Grays, I almost say aloud then stop myself. After all, where Alexander is concerned, the Council's fear is more than justified.

"Surely, this is proof," Lilith murmurs, walking on the other side of my father. Until now, she has been unusually contemplative since stirring from the effects of the trap.

"Proof of what?" I ask, glancing at her.

Her eyes find mine in the grayness of the Road. "That you *are* the Savior…and you have the power to challenge Alexander and defeat him."

Those words are a weight on my shoulders I don't know how to carry, and silence grips us the rest of our journey, none of us daring to utter a word. Upon reaching the marker for Derinkuyu, we step out of the Shadow Road into the city. It's quiet within, disconcertingly so, and empty, as if we're stumbling into the premises late at night rather than in the middle of the day.

I glance around, narrowing my eyes, searching for any sign of the Nephilim we left behind. Bowls and plates lay across every available surface, as if abandoned mid-meal, but the students they belonged to are nowhere to be seen. My eyes shift, and I spot a small discarded shoe in the middle of the floor, forgotten by its owner.

"Where is everyone?" My voice wavers, and a shiver of trepidation spreads under my skin.

To my left, Gabriel and Raphael appear, stepping out of the shining golden light of the Blessed Road. They immediately sense that something isn't right, and my mother is beside me in seconds, signaling for silence with a long finger to her lips. When she grabs my hand, I glance back at my father—at Caleb still lying limp in his arms—and to my relief, he follows me as I trudge after Gabriel, trying and failing to swallow the lump in my throat. She leads me through the passages until we reach the large cavernous space where we reunited with Lucifer only yesterday. That moment the three of us experienced here, of happiness and pure bliss…

It will be forever tarnished by the horror that now paints this room.

"Evangeline," my mother gasps, and I watch, outraged, distressed, disgusted—more emotions than I can even count racing through me—as Gabriel releases my hand and runs forward, dropping to her knees beside one of at least a dozen unmoving bodies strewn across the stone floor. Tears spring to my eyes as she rolls the Nephilim onto her back, but it's clear, even at a distance, she's dead, her face and blue shirt spattered in blood.

Hammurabi, Lilith, Raphael, and Mammon rush past me, checking the other victims, but the outcome is the same with every last one.

"They're all dead," I breathe, staring at the terrible scene of bloodshed before us. The first generation Nephilim—teachers and other staff from the academies—who volunteered to stay behind to watch the children while the rest of us went to Kandahār have been brutally slaughtered, but how? By whom? Most of them I don't know, but some…

I stifle a sob when I glimpse familiar copper hair, noticing one of my teachers from the Serapeum—Vesta—among the casualties. I didn't even know Vesta was here, and now, she's gone, snuffed from this world like a flame in the wind. We might have had a rocky relationship but I never wanted her to die.

"How…" At my father's strangled breath, I turn, no longer able to hold in my tears. "How did they know where to find us?" he whispers.

I don't have to ask whom he means because only one person we know could have committed such a barbaric atrocity. Only one person could've given the order for such needless death.

But how did Alexander find us? I thought we were safe here. I thought we were hidden. I thought—

And that's when I see it. The symbols painted in blood on the wall.

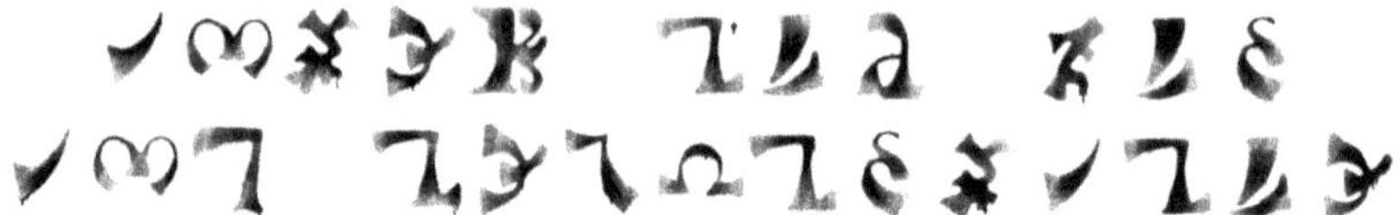

It's written in Enochian, that much is clear, but I can't read it and part of me—a very large part—is certain I don't want to know what it means.

"Luna?" a small voice squeaks, and my heart jumps into my throat when I catch sight of Aya in the distant doorway, her head of dark hair poking around the stone arch. Seeing her releases me from the spell of my shock, and I sprint across the room, taking her in my arms.

"Are you hurt? Where is everyone?" I ask, cupping her face in my hands.

There are sticky streaks on her skin from tears that have fallen and dried, and at my question, fresh ones follow the tracks, carving new lines down her cheeks. Her face crumples. "They took them," she sobs, burying her snotty nose in my chest. "They killed the teachers and took them."

"Who?" My tone is pleading, but when she lifts her head, her eyes catch on something behind me, and I know at once she's seen her brother, who remains asleep in my father's arms.

"Caleb!" she shouts then lets out a heart-wrenching cry when she tries to run to him only to find a dozen dead bodies in her way.

Grabbing her by the shoulders, I pull her out of the room. "He's fine," I say quickly, though the words come out weak and unconvincing, even to my own ears. Maybe because I still struggle to believe it myself and probably won't until he wakes up. "He just needs rest. Is there anyone else here or is it only you?"

She takes a long moment to process my words, and in the seconds I wait for a response,

I pray she isn't the only one here. That she hasn't been left to face this horror alone.

"Aya?" I press, and she jolts at my voice, shaking her head.

"T-There are others," she manages, her voice weak. "On the next level down. Rafe and Shalina and a few other kids I don't know. A teacher from Babel found us and we hid. His gift is illusion and he…he used it to hide us so they wouldn't see where we were."

I let out a shaking breath. At least Aya, Rafe, and Shalina are safe. I don't know how I would've broken that news to Caleb if they weren't.

"That would be Blue Jay," a familiar voice says, and I turn to find Hammurabi standing behind me. A troubled look crosses his face. "Where is he now, young one?"

Aya trembles. "Down—down a level. With the others."

My brows lift at that, and my voice comes out harsher than I intend when I snap, "Then why are you up here all on your own?"

Aya flinches, and I mentally berate myself, pulling her in for another hug. "I'm sorry," I whisper into her hair. "But you shouldn't take risks like that. What if, when you came up here, it wasn't us but whoever took the others? What if they had come back for you?"

Alexander's forces already tried to kidnap Aya once, and even if they didn't come here specifically for her, I have little doubt they would try again if they knew she was here.

"I felt him," Aya mutters, a sheepish look crossing her face when she peeks up at me with tear-filled eyes. "I felt Caleb and so I snuck away. I needed to find him. I needed to know he was okay."

I stare at her for a moment, confused. "You…felt him? You mean your blood song?"

Aya nods, and I glance at Hammurabi, somewhat baffled by this revelation. I remember the first time I felt that song connecting me to each of my parents, and I can feel the melody even now despite being a room away from them, the chords a thunderous choir in my heart. But as the space between us grows, the song gets softer, duller, until I can't hear it at all. So, how did Aya feel Caleb from a whole level below us?

But as I ask myself this, I remember the look on Caleb's face when we talked about Aya and how readily he embraced her as his sister. Embracing my family hasn't been as straightforward for me, and although we've already made huge strides, we still have a long way to go to put the past behind us. Maybe our blood is aware of that. Maybe the song is more sensitive for Caleb and Aya because there's nothing hindering their connection—no guilt or traumatic separation. Just a fearless and willing acceptance.

Aya sniffs, wiping her nose on her sleeve. "Are you mad?"

The whimpering way she asks me that breaks my heart, and shaking my head, I pull her in even tighter. "Never," I promise. "I'm just glad you're safe and I know Caleb will be, too."

"Come, child," Hammurabi interrupts, extending a large hand to Aya. "I need to speak with Blue Jay. Perhaps you can take me to him and the others."

I blink at the hulking Babylonian king, taken aback by the unexpected gentleness in his tone. I've seen glimpses of this side of him before but never like this. But then, he is a teacher, and this is a traumatic thing for a child to see. It's no wonder he would want to do anything to lead her away.

"Thank you," I whisper as he walks past, and he gives me a curt nod before trailing Aya down the nearby steps to the next level down.

Curling my quivering fingers into tight fists, I turn back into the room to find my parents, Lilith, Raphael, and Mammon gathered together, staring up at the bloody message on the wall.

"What's it say?" I try to keep my voice steady as I cross the space to my father, who—to my immense relief—hasn't relinquished his hold on Caleb.

Lilith's brow furrows in bemused consternation. "More or less, it says, 'Thank you,'" she begins, hesitating a moment before adding, "'for the inspiration.'"

"What is *that* supposed to mean?" Raphael asks, her pert nose wrinkling in frustration.

I stare hard at the Enochian symbols, repeating Lilith's words in my head. "*Thank you for the inspiration.*"

The inspiration? What inspiration? And how the hell did they track us here—

My breath catches in my chest, and I go completely still until even my heart seems to cease its thundering rampage. Suddenly, I'm transported back to the Blessed Road, my memories a slideshow of horror as I relive the moment Alexander intercepted us. I didn't know what he was up to then. I assumed it was a diversion, and my gut tells me I was right about that, but only now do I realize how wrong I was about what he was distracting us from.

"He tracked us here," I whisper, and once again, I hear the clashing of swords on the Blessed Road. There were first generation Lights there who had joined Alexander, and at the time, neither I, nor my mother, nor anyone on the Council could understand why they made such an effort to corner us. Why they would attack without actually harming anyone.

But now, I know exactly why they did it, and what's worse is we gave Alexander the idea. The *Council* gave him the idea.

"Thank you for the inspiration."

"Luna?" my mother prompts me, and a tear slides down my cheek as I turn to her.

"It's all our fault," I choke out, and she shakes her head, clearly not understanding the message the same way that I have. She wouldn't—she wasn't there when we went to Alexander for help.

She wouldn't know we gave him the weapon he needed to hit us where it would hurt most.

I swallow then force out the words, "He put trackers in the students' heads." I want to lay the full blame on the Council for this and shed myself of any guilt or culpability. I want to blame them for ordering Nzingha to put a tracker in my head back at Babel. And I do blame them. I blame Uriel and Mammon and their malicious vendetta against Grays. I blame them for being so caught up in their prejudices and allowing their fear to escalate this conflict. But although they were the perpetrators of this nightmare, I can't escape the blame I carry for presenting the idea to Alexander. For offering myself—and a tool he could use against us—on a silver platter. And I can't escape how foolish we all were to think evacuating the schools would be enough to keep everyone safe.

Turning my eyes back to the Enochian symbols, I reveal the devastating truth. "We did this. *We* led Alexander here." *We're all to blame for this.*

And now, the children and weapons are gone.

TWENTY

CALEB

I BLINK MY EYES open, shocked I haven't crossed the River Styx into the afterlife. My whole body feels like a bruised piece of meat, and I just lie there for a minute, happy to be alive. My angelic blood worked overtime to heal me, but I welcome the pain because that means I get to see *her* again. My Goldilocks.

Tilting my head, I seek her out, drawn to the glowing light in the otherwise dim room. She's slumped in a chair near the bed, palm open, ruby flame dancing above her pale skin. The flame hovers for a moment before splitting, forming complex patterns and motions. I prop myself on my elbows, astonished by Luna's newfound control. The fire then bounces from palm to palm, the small fireballs arcing back and forth as if Goldilocks is a master juggler giving a performance. The globules speed faster and faster until all I can track is a ring of scarlet. Then Luna folds her fingers and the fire vanishes. My eyes squint as they adjust to the sudden absence of bright light. A weary sigh spills from her lips. I know she's not tired from that display, as spectacular as it was. For us, that's just parlor tricks.

Then I realize she hasn't noticed I'm awake and is probably worried about me. Giving myself a swift mental jab, I say, "Damn, baby, that was amazing. How are you doing that?" Her head snaps up, stunning eyes widening when she sees I'm vertical. Kind of.

"Caleb!" She rises from the chair and collapses on the bed next to me, her arms sliding around my waist, her nose burying itself in my chest. She holds me for a moment, inhaling my scent, then says, "I don't know how I'm doing it. It just feels… easier now. Like things are clicking into place. What happened in Kandahār must've unlocked something inside me."

I stifle a flinch and wrap my arms around her. She smells like sunshine and wildflowers. She smells like home. "I was scared shitless there for a moment, Goldilocks," I confess into her silken hair. "I didn't know if I'd get to come back to you. But I felt you there in my mind, trying to help. I was grateful you were there, even if it was my end." I don't mean for those words to pop out, but that dance with death was too close for my liking. That old bastard can find another partner.

A tremor ripples over her slender frame, telling me just how terrified she was of that prospect, too. "I thought for a moment that I'd lost you, and that Alexander had finally won," she says, her own confession stark with pain and fear. She lifts her face from my chest, tears pooling in her eyes. "It wasn't just you. It was everyone."

I blink, confused. "What do you mean?"

"When I removed that sword, I triggered some sort of magical…bomb that hit *everyone*. Angels, Fallen, Nephilim. Alexander wanted to wipe out his enemies in one fell swoop, and I walked right into his trap." Anger and bitterness paint her words. I run a soothing hand through her hair. Then she grins, surprising me. "He used both his Dark and Light powers against us, and he didn't think I could figure out how to undo it. Stupid little girl who knows nothing about her powers. But I did, Caleb, I did figure it out. I saved *you*." She kisses me then, an eager clash of lips and teeth and tongue.

When we finally part, we're both gasping for breath.

"I couldn't let you die. I wouldn't let you. You have no idea how terrified I was—you had blood coming out of your mouth and nose and eyes. And I remembered how Alexander had almost killed you before…" A full-on shudder racks her frame. Her hands cup my face. "I knew my parents were in trouble, too, and I was worried of course, but I…I love you more than anything in the world. I refused to lose you. Alexander wasn't going to take you from me."

My lips seal over hers again, tongue delving into her mouth. I tear away from her, my breathing erratic, but manage to say, "You saved me, baby. You're my fucking hero. Thank you. I'm so proud of you. How did you do it?"

Her mouth drags down in a pensive frown as she explains how all our minds were ensnared in a magical web. "I could see you all lying on the floor, and I—I don't know how—but I somehow slipped out of my body. It was like I instinctively knew what to do, and when I realized the threads had to be severed at the same time, I…duplicated pieces of myself."

I reel back, stunned. "You *what*?" I've never heard of that before, and if the Faithful and Fallen can do that, they never talk about it, that's for damn sure.

She hurries on. "I know that sounds crazy, but it's the best way to describe it. I cut the threads connecting you, and you all woke up. Well, you didn't, but the rest of them did. If I were mortal, you would've taken a decade off my life."

I digest what she's just revealed. "Do your parents know how you did that?"

Luna shakes her head. "No. They seemed pretty shocked actually. *Everyone* seemed pretty shocked. I'm guessing it must be a Gray thing. Only I—and maybe Alexander—can do it."

She finally mastered her power all on her own and beat the Conqueror at his own game and saved all those assholes on the Council. If that doesn't show beyond a doubt she's on their side, nothing will. "You've just proven that you're a force to be reckoned with. You broke the *Conqueror's* spell. Do you understand how amazing you are?"

Her cheeks flush a pretty rose, and I want to strip her bare and celebrate life in the most primal way possible. But I still see that impossible weight of melancholy dragging her down. I tip her chin up with a finger. "Hey, you're officially Wonder Woman. What's wrong?"

Grief floods her eyes. "Remember when I told you I saw Alexander on the Road, and I couldn't understand why he was there? He could've killed me but didn't. I crossed swords with him, and he let me walk away..." Luna shivers, and I rub my hands down her arms. Her gaze latches onto mine, and dread fills me at the desolation I see there. "We underestimated him. Again. And now...the kids are gone. He *stole* them," she whispers.

For a moment, my heart stops, and I can't comprehend her words. "Stole them?" I parrot, shaking my head. "What do you mean? How? He doesn't even know where our base is." Against my will, my voice rises, booming across the small room. "*Aya.* Did they take my sister? What about Rafe and Shalina? All the teachers?"

My heart seizes as tears track down her face. "Aya is fine," she says, and relief is like a dam, bursting inside me. I've barely had a minute with my sister, but I care about her. She's family. "Rafe and Shalina and Blue Jay managed to hide, along with a handful of others, but..."

"But?" I prod, desperate for more information. Maybe this is all an illusion, and I'm not really here with Luna right now. Maybe I haven't woken up yet, and I'm still lost in the nightmarish confinement of my own mind.

"But Alexander managed to take most of the kids and slaughtered the teachers." Her voice is low, scratchy, as more tears roll over her smooth cheeks.

Her words are a gut punch. Rafe and Shalina weren't the only friends I had at

Babel. And my teachers…those powerful first generation Nephilim…some of them are now gone. They were a bunch of hard-asses, sure, but wonderful hard-asses who loved their students. And I loved them. I want to throw up. I want to kill someone. Preferably Gramps. But this still doesn't make any fucking sense. How did Alexander know we were here? But then again, how did he know when we were going to sneak into his base? Who's the serpent in our midst?

"Who the fuck is selling us out?" I growl, fury bubbling through my blood.

Luna gives me a sad smile. "No one, not in the way you think. I have no idea how he knew we'd try to ambush his base—I don't think anyone does—but as for the rest… Well, we gave Alexander the perfect way to find us," she says, and I recoil from her, horrified. Her hands slide to my wrists, cuffing them. "Remember my tracker?" I give a slow nod. "On the Blessed Road, Alexander didn't fight me because that wasn't what he went there to do. It was all just one big distraction so the Lights he had with him could slip trackers in some of the students' heads. That's how he knew where we are."

"How do you know that for sure?" I demand, shaken.

"Because he left a message in blood, thanking us for the inspiration."

"You mean he sent Ishtar to do his dirty work? She's the only one he'd trust with this big of a job, and she'd enjoy the slaughter." Guilt swamps me, drowning my rage. "Oh, fuck, this is *my* fault. If I hadn't taken you to Alexander…" If I hadn't brought her to my grandfather to remove that tracker, he wouldn't have Pied Piper'd our asses.

Luna releases one of my wrists and places a finger over my lips. "It's not your fault, and trust me, I've been blaming myself, too, but you did the right thing by taking me there. We had no other option. But now…the problem is that we don't know Alexander well enough to stay one step ahead of him."

She's right. I know she's right, and I'd do it all over again despite what just happened. Because if I hadn't, there's a good chance she'd be back in a cage somewhere, and I'd rather die than let that happen. I had to bring her to Alexander. This isn't my fault, but it sure as hell feels like it is. But anger sprouts in me again. Luna and I are the kids in this scenario. Why in hell aren't the adults behind the damn eight ball? Alexander almost conquered the world before. The Council—hell, even Lucifer and Gabriel—need to start thinking like him. Either they've gotten arrogant in their old age or they still can't wrap their heads around such a young angel running laps around them.

"You're right," I tell Luna. "This isn't our fault. We just made the best possible choice in a shitty scenario, but I really hope this is the thing that finally makes the Council—the Lights and Darks—remove their heads from their asses and start acting like a team. We won't win if they don't."

Luna shifts her hands and braids her fingers through mine. "I know. I hope with my mother and father together again, and with us, obviously, that the others will see that unification *is* possible."

I give her a bitter smile. "They have to for our survival. But hey, if that old dinosaur, Hammurabi, can come around to liking a Gray, then I have to hope that others can change, too. Little flower," I tease and she blushes. Then I sober. "And I think you and I have to stop playing Follow the Leader."

"What do you mean?" Goldilocks asks, brows knitting together in confusion.

I swallow, my mouth suddenly sand-paper dry. "Hammurabi, your dad, they both want me to take a seat at the table, and I thought that's what I was doing. I listen, I do as I'm told, but I gotta do more. You and me, we're not bogged down by ancient history and bullshit. We've spent a lot of time with my grandfather lately. More time than the Council, that's for damn sure. We have to start thinking like him. He has no limits, and we need to start really believing that." Gripping her hands tightly, I say, "You've just proven how powerful you are. And I don't want to say it, and I know you don't want to hear it, but you *are* the fucking Savior, baby. But that doesn't mean some prophecy controls you. Free will exists, so you can guide your own destiny here. You started back at the citadel, telling your parents to back off, and you need to keep doing that. We both do."

Her luscious mouth presses into a flat line, and her lids lower, shielding me from her thoughts. I tense, hoping I didn't press too hard. I've never outright called her the Savior before because I hate this prophecy with my entire being, and I don't believe fate is fixed. I don't want to spook her, but her power has blossomed, and it is glorious.

"I am the Savior, aren't I?" she whispers, and I lean down, giving her a chaste kiss.

"I'm afraid so," I say, "and that really sucks, but I believe in you, Goldilocks. With every fiber of my being, I believe in you, in my gut and in my balls. I'll be with you to the end, whatever end that is."

Our stares lock and tears glisten again in her luminous eyes. "I love you," she says, "and you're right. We have to start taking control of our own destiny."

I draw her flush against me. "There's my girl." I kiss her again, and this time, there's nothing chaste about it. This time, I throw away the chains of my self-restraint and strip her to her bare skin, wanting to celebrate being alive and desperate to be close to her in a time of such great fear and uncertainty.

TWENTY-ONE

LUNA

I SIT HUNCHED ON the edge of the mattress, staring down at the leathery patch of skin Caleb found in Kandahār as I turn it over in my hands. Behind me, Caleb snores softly, his breaths light and soothing in the silence. I long for sleep, but it evades me, and since I no longer need it to survive or function, I'm wide awake, plagued by the buzzing relentlessness of my thoughts.

We're still in Derinkuyu despite the city being compromised by the enemy, but the Council have erected extra protection wards for the time being, and we'll be leaving soon enough once they establish a new refuge for us. *Before* Alexander can return, I hope. The Council doesn't seem as worried about that possibility as I am—as far as they're concerned, he has no reason to come back. I hope they're right, and I'm overestimating his interest in his grandchildren, and he'll leave Aya alone.

And Caleb. Though, the time for bringing him into the fold has passed.

My stomach turns. If Alexander finds Caleb now, he'll kill him. He already nearly succeeded twice—first, just before we escaped the citadel when my parents came to rescue us, then again with the trap I set off. The memory of the pain Caleb suffered stokes the fires of guilt burning inside me, and the dark and terrible feeling stirring in my gut tells me Alexander will succeed if given another chance. Third time's the charm, as they say.

I frown, my fingers clenching tightly around the skin. I wish this could all be over. I wish we knew where Alexander is hiding so we can finally end this madness.

I wish I knew for sure if Alaric is alive.

Dragging in a deep, shaking breath, I shutter my eyes and scrub a hand over my face as the same four words circle through my head on a loop.

Where are you, Alaric?

I don't know what I expect. Some kind of answer from the universe, I suppose, but the universe frustrates me with its silence.

With a disheartened sigh, I force open my eyes, then pause, glancing around the dark space, my pulse an erratic rhythm reflecting my panic as my disorientation builds to a crescendo. My surroundings are different than they were only seconds before, and my breath immediately catches when I register the similarities to what happened to me back at the citadel. I glance behind me to be sure, and not only am I not in my room in Derinkuyu with Caleb anymore, but like then—when I somehow left my body to free the others from the spider web of Alexander's insidious magic—I'm standing when a moment ago, I was sitting. And, just like then, I can see through my hand as I raise it in front of me, my fingers still clutching the patch of skin, which now possesses the same translucent quality.

Unlike then, however, my physical body is nowhere in sight. This time, I am completely detached from my corporeal form, and I can barely contain the hysteria bubbling inside me at the thought of being separated from my body for good. What if I can't get back to it? What if I'm stuck like this forever?

Calm down, Luna. Take a breath.

My lips tremble around my slow exhalation, and swallowing, I feel for that tie to my body like how I felt for that thread connecting Caleb to the others when we walked into Alexander's trap. It takes me a moment, but that link is there in the back of my head, and as I wrap the threads of my power around it, I know that if I just follow it, I'll find my way back to my body. Back to Caleb.

But not yet.

I narrow my eyes, trying to work out where I am and why my mind—or soul, or whatever I am at this moment—has drifted here, wherever here is. But just as I take a step forward, I freeze. A bed seems to rise out of the darkness in front of me, and there, with one leg thrown over the blanket, I glimpse the defined outline of a body. Of a man—wearing a T-shirt and boxers—sitting up in the bed, his face, cast in shadow, tilted up toward the ceiling. I could be looking at anyone on the planet right now—friend, foe, or stranger—and yet, I recognize something in the reserved way the man holds himself. Just as I sense something deeply familiar about his aura.

"Alaric?" I whisper, breathless.

There's a brief moment—in the space of time between me saying his name and his amber eyes snapping to mine—when I'm convinced this is a trick. When I fear I'm still trapped in the Council's glass egg where everything I want and love is nothing more than a memory, out of reach. But then the moment passes and our eyes lock, and I see him as clearly as I can see the sun on a cloudless day. I *know* there's no way this isn't real because life can't possibly be that cruel. It's him. Alaric's really here. He's really alive.

I can't bring myself to believe anything else.

I swallow the lump in my throat, suddenly glad I had the sense to put my clothes back on after my latest tumble with Caleb or else Alaric would be seeing a whole lot more of me than either of us would ever be comfortable with.

Scrubbing that thought from my mind, I smile—my lips peeled so wide it almost hurts—but Alaric just stares at me, those warm, comforting eyes pinned wide in disbelief.

Luna? he mouths. He doesn't say my name aloud, and when I take a step toward him, he thrusts out a hand, warning me not to come any closer.

I'm about to ask him what's wrong—to ask him why he won't speak to me—when he casts a nervous look over his shoulder. Unease ripples through me as I follow his gaze...

And that's when I notice the other body in the bed.

The sleeping figure stirs, letting out a soft moan, but, to my immense relief, doesn't wake. Alaric shifts slightly, revealing the blond hair cascading across the pillow beside him, but seeing it doesn't spark any feelings of horror or anger or disturbed recognition like it might for anyone else were they to find themselves in my position. Because I already know who it is. I know it as irrevocably as I know that I'm in love with Caleb.

Alaric's focus drifts away from Alexander and settles back on me, then holding up a finger to his lips, he nods toward the door. I nod back, clamping my mouth shut, watching as the Nephilim carefully untangles himself from the bed sheets and slides from the mattress with the grace and finesse of a prima ballerina. In the time we've spent apart, I almost forgot how tall and lithe he is, and yet, instead of awe, I watch his every movement with terror and unease as he pads across the floor toward where I wait by the door. Terror because I'm anxious I could be ripped back into my body at any moment without finding out where he is. Without getting the chance to speak with him and find out if he really stayed away because he had no other choice or if something else was keeping him here. Something like his feelings for Alexander. And then, behind the terror, there's that sense of unease because he's always seemed so normal to me—or, at least, more so than the other Nephilim and angels I met—

but now, with his hair mussed and deep purple bags under his eyes, he looks more vulnerable and human than I've ever seen him.

There's a strange intimacy to seeing him like this. Not romantic—never romantic—but like seeing someone who always seemed impervious to pain crying over a cut.

I watch him closely, never daring to blink in case it breaks the connection between us. I want to hug him so badly. I want to touch his face, to prove to myself that he's real, but I can't. Not like this. He must feel the same because he reaches for my wrist as soon as he's beside me, but his fingers pass through my arm, touching nothing but air.

Recoiling as if he's been burned, he looks down at his empty palm for a moment before gaping at me, a dozen different questions written into his features. He only mouths one.

How?

I don't know how to answer that question—I'm still not entirely sure how I'm doing this. So, instead, I lift the hand still holding the skin patch as my lips soundlessly shape the words, *We need to talk.*

Alaric stares at my upraised hand for a moment then composes himself, wiping the shock from his face. Nodding again, he creaks the door open—slowly, so slowly—and slips out of the room, beckoning for me to follow. The corridor beyond is equally dark, but I can make out the buttery stone surrounding us easily, every crack and crevice visible to my eyes. Alaric still doesn't dare utter a word, and as several long moments pass with me just following blindly, I wonder where he's taking me. Is there even a safe place here for us to talk?

As we progress through the long hallways, I take stock of my surroundings, hoping they'll provide me with an obvious clue as to where we are, but I'm not a history buff like Caleb and, to my dismay, I recognize nothing. Whatever this place is, though, it's exquisite, with tall pillars and rich colors lining the floors and ceilings and tapestries on the walls depicting an ancient world I can't even begin to imagine.

"What is this place?" I whisper to Alaric, but he just shakes his head and presses a long finger to his lips again.

My building anxiety ratchets higher the longer we spend in silence. While I don't feel any particular strain being this far from my body—aside from a burgeoning anxiety at how freaky this whole thing is—I don't know how long I can hold onto this connection. I need to speak with Alaric now, before this chance is lost to us.

"Alar—" I begin, but his name dies on my tongue when he disappears through a door on my left, and I follow him without hesitation into…a bathroom?

At least, that's what I think the room is. There's a chair made of stone with a hole in the seat that resembles a toilet and a large wash basin on the floor that reminds me a bit of a bird bath, although both look so old I'd be afraid to use them. Like Kandahār, this place isn't exactly rife with modern amenities.

"I'm sorry," he says in a rush, turning to face me. "It wasn't safe to speak with you so close to Alexander. At least if he wakes and finds me here, it won't rouse any suspicion."

I blink at him, then give a slow nod, but when I open my mouth to speak, I find I'm suddenly at a loss for words.

"How are you here, Luna?" Alaric asks before I can manage my thoughts. "Are you even here?" He reaches out a hand to touch my shoulder, but like before, his fingers pass through me. "Am I dreaming?" he whispers.

"This isn't a dream," I rasp, and as tears puddle in my eyes and his, I consider how bittersweet this reunion must be for both of us. This is the first time we're together again and we can't even hug or touch hands. Hell, we might as well be on different planets. The pain growing inside my heart at that realization—at this unwanted distance between us—could crush me.

"How are you here?" he asks again, his voice thick.

I shrug, wishing I could give him a better answer than the only one I have. "I don't entirely know. I…can leave my body somehow? I only just figured out I can do it. Must be a Gray thing," I mutter as a lame aside, shrugging one shoulder again.

"More like it's a you thing," he murmurs contemplatively, then he gifts me a smile, wiping his wet eyes on his forearm.

"A me thing?" I echo.

He nods. "Whatever you're doing…I have *never* seen that power before. Not even in Alexander. But then, you are the child of two of the most powerful angels to ever exist, not to mention you are a Gray. It is unsurprising you would possess such a unique talent."

I let that sink in for a few seconds then say, "Are you sure? I mean, maybe he just doesn't flaunt it."

Alaric arches a brow at me. "This is Alexander we're talking about. If he had such a power, he would not only flaunt it, he would most certainly use it. It would be perhaps the greatest weapon in his arsenal…" He trails off, shaking his head, then in a softer voice adds, "He cannot do this, I promise you that. I know because…I know everything there is to know about him." Shame kisses every word leaving his lips. Heaving a discontented sigh, he scrubs a hand over his face. "He hasn't changed."

Averting his eyes, Alaric combs back his bedraggled hair as an intolerable hush descends between us. It swallows the cramped space—it swallows me—and I wish I knew what to say to erase it, to ease his remorse and let him know I don't judge him, not for his feelings. Not for anything.

"I'm sorry, Luna," Alaric breathes after a long moment, finally breaking the unbearable silence. "I'm sorry you had to see me like that. I'm…sorry I succumbed to my weakness."

My chest tightens, and I realize he means how I found him together with Alexander. In bed.

"You don't need to apologize for that," I assure him and it's true. If I were in his shoes, and Caleb turned into a psychotic dictator, I still don't think I'd have the strength to stay away from him. I would choose him over everyone and everything, even if it went against every moral fiber in my being.

Besides, I've known about his past with Alexander for a while now, since I was at the Serapeum, and Alaric never lied to me about the extent of his feelings for the Gray. I knew he was in love with him, just as I know how painful it was for him to see Alexander again after so many years apart, especially after millennia of carrying the guilt of having helped the Council entomb him.

Does Alexander know Alaric betrayed him? I quickly push that thought aside. If he does, then the Gray is far more forgiving than I gave him credit for. And if he doesn't…

Then all the more reason to find out where Alaric is and get him to safety as soon as possible.

"I don't?" Alaric says, his tone doubtful. "But I'm literally sleeping with the enemy. How can you ever forgive me for that?"

"Have you switched sides?" I ask.

He balks. "I…what?"

"Have. You. Switched. Sides?" I say again, more slowly this time. "Are you helping Alexander of your own free will or would you rather come back to Team Savior?"

A smile quirks the edges of his lips. "I see Caleb is rubbing off on you."

Heat creeps up the back of my neck. Caleb is definitely rubbing off on me every chance he gets, just not always in the way Alaric is thinking.

I cross my arms and give him an impatient look. "Answer the question, Alaric."

The smile slips from his face, and he sighs. "Of course, I'm on your side, Luna. I love Alexander, and part of me always will, but this—" He gestures vaguely toward the door, his expression defeated. "I can't condone what he's doing."

"Then tell me where you are," I plead, reaching for his hand before remembering I won't be able to touch him."

He stares at me for a few seconds, uncertain. "It isn't safe for you to come here. Besides, I can't leave."

"Why?" I counter. "Why can't you leave?" And then, all the questions I've been holding in tumble out of me, one after another. "If you're on my side, why didn't you come back? Why leave me *this* if you didn't want me to find you?" I hold up the skin patch, wagging it in his face. "You did leave this for me, didn't you?"

His mouth drops open then gradually closes again before he says, "Yes. I did. But only to let you know I was alive. I didn't want you to live with the burden of believing me to be dead, or worse, thinking my death was somehow your fault. Especially after Caleb spotted me at Megiddo. I knew he would tell you he saw me, and I hoped, by leaving that, you would know I wasn't helping Alexander because I wanted to. I...I didn't want you to think less of me."

"I could never think less of you!" I practically shout then draw in a breath to control my rising temper. Exhaling through my nose, I continue, "I'm just trying to understand. You already risked your life for me once, and I can't let you do it again. I can't let you stay with him because if you do, you *will* end up dead, and I couldn't bear that."

"Luna..." Alaric whispers, and there's a tremor of misery in his tone.

"Tell me." I stare up at him, feeling the tears on my cheeks now, even though my body is miles away. "Tell me why you didn't come back."

A dejected expression crosses his face. "The same reason he found out about Derinkuyu."

"I—" I wrinkle my nose, confused. Then it hits me. "You have a tracker, too, don't you?"

He nods, and although darkness swathes us, I see his jaw clench. "Despite how it might look, despite what he's having me do, I'm a prisoner here. Alexander doesn't trust me not to abandon him, so he's taken that option away, treating me like a possession instead of a person. And I...I hate myself for still loving him after he's done this to me." As he says this, his eyes lose their usual luster, their depths haunted. Exhaling, he presses the tips of his fingers into his eyes. "We both know the Council won't come for me, even if you beg them to. There's too much history there to question, and I'm just one Nephilim—"

"They will if it will hurt Alexander."

Alaric just looks at me, his brow deeply furrowed, as if he's not following what I'm suggesting. "What?"

Ignoring him, I glance over my shoulder, looking around the small room, as if by doing so I'll be able to assess the full interior of this place. "Where are the children and weapons he stole? Are they here with you?"

Comprehension softens his features. "Yes, but—"

"Then that's what we tell them," I say, interrupting him again, more forcefully this time. "We tell them we know how to blindside Alexander and take back what he took from us. If he no longer holds their students, the Council will have nothing to fear from him. Together, we can level the playing field."

A flicker of...*something* crosses Alaric's face. Something, I realize, that looks almost like hope. But it fades before it can fully take hold, and once again, he stares at me with that crestfallen expression.

"And what about my tracker?" he presses. "Alexander created his own. It's a Gray device. The Council won't be able to remove it."

This version of Alaric, downtrodden and despairing...I don't recognize him, and it hurts my heart to see him this way. To see what Alexander has reduced him to. Well, I refuse to abandon him like this.

I refuse to let Alexander win.

"Then *I'll* remove it. Along with any others that might be planted in the students he kidnapped." Every word has weight to it, like a sworn vow. I just have to hope Alaric believes me.

But the resignation in his eyes tells me he doesn't. "Luna..." he begins, my name unfurling slowly on his tongue. I just shake my head.

"I can do it, Alaric. I *know* I can." I'm not sure who I'm trying to convince—me or him. Either way, I can't stop the words from coming, and with every last one that transitions from thought into sound, I feel more certain of myself. And of what I can do. "Really, I should thank Alexander. Because of that trap he left for us in Kandahār, I've finally figured out how to control my power. He doesn't even realize he almost single-handedly turned me into the Savior. But I'm going to make sure he finds out."

I've been fighting the notion of me being the Savior since Lilith first put the idea in my head, but after saving lives instead of being responsible for taking them for once, I can finally feel my perspective changing. I felt the beginnings of acceptance on the Shadow Road after I unweaved Alexander's spell then more firmly when Caleb and I spoke of it just a few hours ago. And now, I know my role in this war for certain.

I am the Savior. And I will overcome the Destroyer, no matter what it takes.

Alaric looks at me, those amber eyes wide, but not in disbelief—not this time. Now, he looks at me in astonishment, as if he's seeing me for the first time. Really seeing me.

"We're in Persepolis," he blurts out. "In one of the palaces here—the Tachara. It looks like ruins to the mortal eye, but its true form is hidden by a glamor."

Rolling my teeth along the curve of my lower lip, I nod. "Okay. I'll tell the others."

"You should wait," Alaric says, and when I give him a bewildered look, he shakes his head as if to clear it of some wayward thought. "To strike when Alexander isn't here, I mean," he clarifies. "To defeat him, you first need to beat him at his own game. Don't just level the playing field, tip the scales." Those words hang in the air between us, and when I nod again, Alaric adds, "I need a little time to come up with a plan. Come back tomorrow night. Same time. I'll be right here, waiting for you."

"In the bathroom," I deadpan, cocking an amused brow.

He grins. "It's the safest place. I can always blame my absence from Alexander's bed on indigestion."

I stifle a laugh at that, turning to leave before remembering I'm not really here. Unlike Alaric, who is in danger every passing moment he remains in this place.

"Alaric?" I whisper, facing him again and holding up the patch of flesh. "I need to know… Did Alexander do this to you? Is that why you didn't contact my father?"

A shadow crosses his face, and he lowers his eyes, staring at the skin in my hand. "I was unconscious for a while after he stabbed me, and when I awoke again, the sigil was gone. I was already healed at that point, so I didn't notice he'd cut it off at first, but then…I found *that* in a drawer in his chambers and put two and two together." He swallows, the sound gunshot loud in the cramped silence of the minuscule room. "Creator knows why he was holding onto it. Perhaps he knew I'd find some way to escape him, and he wanted something of me to keep. Whatever his reasoning, I took it and hid it in Caleb's room just before we left the citadel. I knew, if the two of you came, you would find it."

And we did.

I smile, feeling truly optimistic for the first time in months, but the sensation is fleeting. My lips immediately pull down at the corners as a dark thought crosses my mind.

"Wait, if Alexander was holding onto this like some kind of trophy"—I wag the skin patch in my hand again—"then does that mean he knows it's gone?" My heart rate skyrockets and I let out a tiny gasp. "Do you think he suspects anything?"

Like the Nephilim leaving it behind at the citadel to lead us to them…not that Alexander, or even Alaric, could have ever predicted I'd be able to find him.

"Oh, he knows. In fact, I made sure of it. Just as I made sure to let him know how repulsed I was that he'd kept it," Alaric says through clenched teeth. At my startled expression, he clears his throat. "*But* we don't need to worry," he assures me. "As far as Alexander is concerned, I destroyed it."

I arch a dubious brow. "And you're sure he believed you?"

A wry smile curls Alaric's lips and he lifts one hand, his golden fire erupting across his palm. "I was very convincing. After all, nothing I said was a lie. Other than the part about burning his little trophy, of course." He waves a hand then, extinguishing the flames. "At any rate, you should be going now. I don't want to risk him noticing my absence."

I nod, albeit reluctantly. "Tomorrow," I murmur. It comes out more like a question. "Tomorrow," he says.

There's a promise behind that one word, and yet, I can't suppress the sudden fear rising within me. Fear that I've found him now only to never see him again, promises to each other be damned.

Driven by that fear, my hand shoots out, reaching for his, as if he is the cliff edge that will keep me from plunging to my death. Although my fingers pass through his, there's a fleeting moment of resistance when I swear I can feel the warmth of Alaric's skin—when I sensed some tangible proof of his hand instead of air. And as the room around me begins to fade, I can tell by the widening of his eyes that he felt me, too.

Returning to my body feels strangely like waking up from a dream. One minute, I'm standing with Alaric in that small closet of a room in Persepolis. The next, I'm opening my eyes to find myself firmly back in Derinkuyu. Except, unlike before, when Caleb was asleep in the bed beside me, now he's kneeling in front of me, hands on my face, his dark eyes wide in panic.

"Luna!" He takes me into his arms, all but collapsing when I mutter his name in confusion. "Thank the Creator," he breathes in my ear, his relief almost tangible in the way he holds me against him. Placing his hands on my shoulders, he pulls back to look at me. "Are you okay, Goldilocks? I've been trying to wake you up for the last five minutes. I was literally about to go grab Auntie Lilith and your parents and have someone call a damn priest. What the hell happened?"

A priest?

I jerk my head, glancing around the unlit room, feeling somewhat drained from the effort of leaving my body. Can Caleb see that on my face? It never occurred to me to wonder what I must look like when I do…whatever it is I can do now. Do I look possessed? Did I look like a zombie? Curiosity scratches at every inch of my brain, and I consider asking Caleb to take a picture next time.

With a startled laugh, I mumble, "I left my body again."

Caleb gapes at me like I've lost my mind. "What? W-Where did you go?" Rising from his knees, he settles himself on the bed beside me, taking my hands in his. "Listen, Goldilocks, until we know more about this newfound talent of yours, I don't know if you should be—"

I free one hand from his and press my fingertip to his lips. "Caleb, it's okay," I assure him.

His narrowing gaze is skeptical, but I shake my head when he tries to speak. Drawing in a breath, I lower my hand.

"I know where Alaric is."

TWENTY-TWO

CALEB

After I meet with Aya, Rafe, and Shalina to reassure them I'm okay and back in the land of the living, we crowd in Gabriel's and Lucifer's room—me and Luna, Lilith, and Hammurabi with Asmodeus, completing our secret circle. Despite them being the Messenger and the Morningstar, they only scored a slightly bigger room than Luna and me, and it's positively claustrophobic in here. Luna's parents hover on one side of her, Lilith and I on the other, and Asmodeus and the grumpy Babylonian king both lean against the opposite wall. The power enclosed in this one tiny room staggers me.

After Luna's out-of-body experience gave me premature gray hair, we decided to tell her parents and our most-trusted allies about her ability to project her soul from her body and go on walkabout. The image of her sitting there, open eyes resembling milky marbles, is tattooed onto my brain. On the scale of freaky, it was at *Exorcist* level. Even though the sight of her like that terrified me, pride buoys my chest that my Goldilocks has unlocked this badass ability. That she's gained so much control in such a short period of time. She practically glows with the new confidence and determination she has. She finally believes she's the Savior and it shows.

And of course, Gramps is at Persepolis. That city is a mark of pride for him, where he burned the structures Xerxes helped build, taking revenge for the Persian king destroying the temples of Athens. Ending the Achaemenid Empire. Well, he burned most of the city, but the ruins of Tachara—the Palace of Darius I—still stand. We only *believed* they were ruins. That's a classic Alexander move, and I'm not surprised by it. It was clever of him to glamor a palace everyone thought was the beautiful remains of a faded empire so he had a refuge to escape to. And if we weren't going to war with him—and he wasn't such a murderous asshole—I'd beg him to let me play tourist.

Lucifer clears his throat, drawing me from my musings. His blue eyes focus on Luna, worry written there. "We're all here now, Starlight. Why did you call this meeting? What's happened?"

Gabriel interjects, "Has anyone on the Council threatened you because of what you did in Kandahār? You saved them, those thankless monsters."

"If they did, let's devise a way to put them all in their own personal prisons for a few months after we win the war so they can suffer as we did in our cages," Asmodeus says to Luna, venom dripping from her every word. Hammurabi snorts his agreement.

Luna shakes her head so fast her hair catches on her lips. Brushing the golden strands away, she says, "No, nothing like that, but something did happen last night. Something similar to what happened at the citadel."

Her eyes turn to me, and I nod, encouraging her to go on. Yes, she's confident about her new ability, but that doesn't mean she's not still frightened of how other people will react to it—especially those she loves. And we still haven't dropped the Alaric bomb.

Her fingers braid together, twisting, and I watch as she deliberately relaxes them. Her gaze is steady as she looks around the room. "Certain...recent events have led Caleb and I to suspect that Alaric is still alive," she begins, and I hear a startled grunt escape Hammurabi. "And we found a piece of his skin with your sigil, the one Asmodeus gave him"—she inclines her head toward Lucifer then Asmodeus—"at the citadel in Caleb's old room."

Gabriel's voice is uncharacteristically gentle as she says, "Luna, that doesn't mean he's—"

"I saw him at Megiddo," I interrupt, startling them all once again. "It was from a distance, and I wasn't quite sure, but Aya—my sister—mentioned that a Light Nephilim showed up in the chaos and told her to run. So, when we went to Kandahār, Luna and I decided to see if Alaric left something behind for us to find, something to let us know he was alive."

Luna reaches into her pocket and pulls out the withered piece of skin. My first instinct is to shrink back from it, but the older players in the room don't even flinch. I guess when you've witnessed—and participated in—bloody wars, a little piece of hacked-off flesh doesn't bother you. I hope to the Creator it always bothers me.

"I contacted Alaric last night using this," Luna explains.

"How?" Lilith demands.

"And what do you mean it was similar to what you did at the citadel?" Lucifer presses, taking a step forward as if to snatch the skin from her.

Luna lowers her hand, making a fist over the one piece of Alaric she has within her reach. "I was holding this last night, trying to figure out where Alaric is and why he hasn't contacted me, because I know if he were able to, he would have." Damn straight he would've. Alaric loves my girl. "And just like before, I…stepped out of my body somehow. Suddenly, I was with Alaric, just by focusing on *this*." She shakes her clenched fist.

"You were able to travel to Alaric?" Gabriel asks, shock rippling over her face. She, too, focuses on the dried skin, hidden within the confines of Luna's hand, as if it's a poisonous snake, waiting to strike.

"I've never heard of this kind of power before," Hammurabi rumbles, his black eyes darting between the angels and Fallen present.

Lilith gives a slow shake of her head, regarding Luna with awe. "Neither have I," she murmurs. "I have never heard of an angel being able to loosen their soul from their body, using their shell as a tether."

Asmodeus's liquid green gaze roves over Luna. "Nor I. What a power to have."

Focusing on Lilith, I ask, "So, Gramps can't do this?" I mean, Alaric told Luna he can't, but if anyone has knowledge of what Alexander can do, it's the ex-Archdemon, Alexander's former teacher and fan girl.

Her glossy curls bounce with the force of her denial. "No, he does not possess this gift. If he did, he certainly would have employed it by now."

"Yes, he wouldn't have need to attack us on the Road, planting trackers into the children," Gabriel says. "If he had a power like Luna's, based on what she's told us about finding Alaric, he could've used anything the two of you left behind at the citadel to find you. Or just his blood connection with you, Caleb."

Well, isn't that thought enough to give me nightmares for days. "So, this is definitely a special Goldilocks power then," I say.

Luna's gaze darts between her parents. "Mine and not just a Gray thing, right?"

Lucifer inclines his head. "It appears so, but in all my long years, I've never witnessed anything like it. I don't even know what to name it."

I raise my hand. "Ugh, I'm not being a smartass here, but it sounds like astral projection to me."

Hammurabi scoffs. "Ridiculous," he mutters.

"You've been reading too much mortal fiction," Lilith says to me, and Luna scowls at her.

"Astral projection?" Gabriel repeats, raising an eyebrow at Lucifer, who shrugs, a bewildered expression on his face.

Luna looks at me and nods. "It does, doesn't it?" She shoots Lilith major shade. "And don't all angel powers sound like mortal fiction?"

A loud burst of laughter escapes me. "She's got a solid point," I tell the ex-Archdemon, who glowers at me before a grin curves her full lips.

"I suppose she does. So until we find a better name, shall we refer to your new talent as astral projection?" Lilith says.

Asmodeus's laugh cuts like glass. "Although you know when the rest of the Council gets wind of this, they'll insist they have the right to name it."

"The flower shall tell them politely where to stick their suggestions," Hammurabi rumbles. He smiles at Luna. "Isn't that right, flower?"

His kindness always makes her blush. "If they don't try to lock me up again, I promise I will." She sobers. "Do you think my being able to…astral project will make them suspicious of me again? More than they already are after what happened."

Lucifer and Gabriel exchange a look laced with a thousand meanings before the Morningstar says, "You were able to enter their minds when they were under duress, which is more than enough to frighten them, and now that you can find someone just by focusing on an object that belongs to them, they'll fear their secrets aren't safe." A deep sigh puffs past his lips. "But if we present this to them as an opportunity, as a way to win the war against Alexander, they'll be less likely to revert to their base instincts, which is to imprison first, ask questions later."

"Yes, we must present your new ability as an asset—one we can't win without," Asmodeus chimes in.

"But how do we get them to that conclusion? Unless Luna can use Caleb's blood tie to locate Alexander," Gabriel says.

"We don't need to use Caleb for anything. I found Alaric, remember?" Luna says, her voice tart. Gabriel has the grace to look a little embarrassed about volunteering me without my permission. "Alaric can tell us where Alexander is. In fact, he already has."

Once again, she's managed to stun these old fossils who have seen it all.

"Perhaps you should have led with that," Lilith grumbles, crossing her arms over her chest. "What is it mortals say? Way to bury the lead."

Lucifer stares at his daughter. "So, you didn't just see him, you were able to make contact? Communicate with him?"

"He could see you?" Gabriel questions. "When I felt you in my mind, I knew it was your presence, but I didn't see you."

"Yes, he could see me. I startled him pretty badly," Luna admits. "He wasn't… alone." I blink at that bit of information, and she holds a hand up to stave off my and her parents' frantic questions. "Don't worry, no one else saw me. He led me away somewhere private. It was just like Caleb and I suspected—he's being held against his will. Being used to track down Alexander's bloodline. He told me they're in Persepolis."

"In Darius I's palace," I clarify.

"Clever bastard," Hammurabi says, begrudging admiration in his voice. "Even *we* believed that palace was ruins."

"It's fitting he chose Persepolis," Lucifer muses, taking his chin between forefinger and thumb. "Considering there are so many places he left his mark on, it would have been difficult to search them all. This certainly is information we—and the Council—need if we're to win the war."

"Who was he with?" Hammurabi inquires, and despite the curiosity in his tone, the fine hairs on my neck stand on end. I'm suddenly afraid of the answer.

"I'm curious to know that as well," Lilith croons, an unfriendly smirk hitching up one side of her mouth.

Dread fills me. I'm surprised Luna didn't mention Alaric's companion to me. She's gotten better at opening up, at sharing her fears and secrets, but I know she still struggles with being forthcoming. But why keep this specific bit of info from me?

Luna tenses, her eyes darting around the space but somehow managing to avoid looking at anyone. "Um, he was with Alexander…in bed," she admits, her voice barely more than a whisper.

My head jerks back, but no one else in the room looks surprised. Gabriel and Lilith look resigned, Asmodeus sighs, Lucifer just nods to himself, and Hammurabi frowns in disapproval. Once again, I'm the odd man out.

"It's not what you think," Luna rushes on. "I mean, it is. I'm guessing from the looks on your faces you all know they used to be involved, but it isn't like that now. Alaric isn't staying with Alexander of his own free will, I swear it."

I stare at her. "How long have *you* known they were involved? This can't be a recent development." It suddenly all makes sense—the weird tension I sensed between the Nephilim and Alexander. The current between them that I could never quite define.

Giving me a pleading look, Goldilocks says, "They were together before Alexander tried to conquer the world the first time. I've known for a while, but I never said anything because it felt…wrong. This wasn't like the vision Alexander showed me of the academies. I *know* I should've said something about that. But this? It wasn't my secret to share. The only person getting hurt by Alaric's feelings was himself. But now that he's trapped with Alexander again…"

"Proximity took over," I mutter. "I get it, kind of. I mean, I guess he still loves Gramps?" That seems impossible, as Alaric is such a kind, gentle soul, but then again, he knew Alexander before he was the Conqueror, so maybe that's the man he's still in love with. Maybe this Alexander still pretends to be that man for him.

"If he does, can he be trusted?" Hammurabi asks, focusing on Luna. "I like Alaric. I always have despite him being a Light. But now that he's with Alexander again, it does call his loyalties into question, does it not? Love blinds even the most far-seeing people."

"Yes, he still loves Alexander, but he hasn't switched to Team Conqueror," Luna retorts. I can't help but grin at her phrasing. She's been hanging out with me too much. "This is another reason why I never said anything, not even to you." Her eyes flick to mine, apologetic, but I'm not angry with her. Outing someone is never cool, and Alaric's feelings really weren't anyone's business until now. "I didn't want anyone questioning his allegiance. You didn't see him. He looks awful. And lingering feelings aside, he *wants* to leave. The only reason he hasn't is because he has a tracker inside him. Even Alexander knows Alaric doesn't want to stay," she says and I blink, horrified. Gramps sure knows how to treat the people he loves. She whirls on Gabriel. "And he's turned on Alexander before. Right, Mom?"

Gabriel tilts her head. "Yes, he has. He was instrumental in bringing Alexander to heel the first time. He fed the Council information, and we were able to imprison the Conqueror. I convinced the Council to let Alaric retain his memories and work for me because of his loyalty. It wasn't easy for Alaric to betray Alexander. Although I always wondered about the true depth of his feelings, it was well-known to many that they were dear friends, and I know he suffered greatly for turning on him. But he didn't believe Earth needed an emperor. He knew it was wrong." Weariness weighs on the Archangel's face. Her gaze falls on Lucifer. "I have great empathy for Alaric. To betray the person you love most leaves a gaping wound that never manages to scar over."

Lucifer takes one of her hands, entwining their fingers. These little displays of affection between them have grown bolder since we returned from Megiddo. It's nice to see. It gives me hope.

"I hadn't realized it was Alaric who betrayed Alexander," Lilith says softly. "I suppose that changes things."

"As does the tracker," Hammurabi adds.

Asmodeus tosses garnet hair over her shoulder. "I've always been fond of Alaric. My trust in him has never been misplaced. I prefer to give him the benefit of the doubt."

"Let us keep this information about Alaric's glorious return to ourselves right now until he gives Luna something useful we can bring to the Council," Lucifer says, tucking Gabriel into his side.

"Indeed. As Luna said, we don't want anyone questioning his allegiance," Lilith agrees. Her heeled boot taps a steady rhythm on the floor. "And Creator knows we're all guilty of jumping to conclusions."

Hammurabi snorts as I say, "Wait? You guys? No way."

Gabriel's eyes meet Luna's before turning to me. "For now, this goes no further than this room."

I roll my eyes. "Who are we going to run and tell? We avoid the Council like they have the plague or a rampant venereal disease."

A shocked giggle escapes Luna, then she composes herself. "We may have more information to present to the Council sooner than you think. Alaric wants me to meet with him tonight."

"Tonight?" Lucifer echoes. "Are you sure that's safe?"

"Safe as in Alexander might be with him again?" I ask, confused.

"She's just begun to learn to use this talent. Is it safe for her to…astral project so soon?" the Morningstar clarifies. His eyes scan his daughter as if searching for invisible damage. His love for her is obvious, but he has to watch that he doesn't smother Luna with it.

"As long as you keep her physical form safe, she should be fine, in theory. Little birds must learn to fly eventually," Lilith says to Lucifer, a sharp edge to her smile. He frowns at her.

In our cramped space, Luna just has to reach out to clasp her father's free hand. "I'll be fine. I have control over this, I promise you, Dad. Besides, you'll be with me when I do it again, so you can watch over me."

Luna offers these words of comfort as a kindness to her father, but I know she has no idea what will happen if shit goes south when she astral projects again. No one does, and as much as I want to keep her safe, she and I both know our current situation only grows more desperate. Whether I like it or not, Luna has to contact Alaric again. This could be our ace in the hole.

Luna reclines on some pillows on our bed, clasped hands holding Alaric's skin. It's the best seat in the house. Only her parents are with us now, as Lilith, Asmodeus, and Hammurabi decided to give her some space in case Goldilocks gets stage fright. I think she'll be just fine, but I do appreciate having more leg room. Plus, all that power in one room feels loud, like a drum solo that never stops.

I sit on the chair next to the bed and smooth back a golden thread of her hair. My eyes snag on Luna's, and she smiles at me, soft and reassuring. I didn't expect to be more nervous than she is. Although, that could be due to the hovering forms of the Messenger and the Morningstar standing above me.

"Are you ready?" I ask her, doing my best to douse the urge to elbow the two scary angels behind me so they give us some breathing room.

She nods. "Yes, I'm ready to see Alaric again." There's a fragile hope in her voice, and I know how much she wants him back with her, safe and sound.

"Tell him hi from me and thank him for finding Aya," I say.

"I will. Let's do this." Her eyes close, and she tips her head back, settling into the pillow.

For a few moments, all I observe is her beautiful face, serene and peaceful. Then, just like when I woke up the night before, her eyes pop open wide, milky white covering the entire surface, as if the sclera has swallowed the iris and pupil whole. Her body turns rigid, tension rippling through her muscle, despite the fact that she remains lying on the bed, signaling her soul has left her body. It's scary as fuck to look at my Goldilocks and know she's not really in there anymore. I'm staring at an exquisite shell. My heartbeat explodes in my chest, and I reach out, placing a hand over her clasped ones. I trust her. I do. I know she's got this, but I can't help my rush of fear.

I hear a gasp behind me, then Gabriel is leaning over my left shoulder. "Is that what she looked like before?" she demands.

I see the edge of Lucifer's jaw over my right shoulder. "Is she all right?" he barks, voice guttural, and I shiver at the suppressed violence there. He wants to smite someone if she's not, and I'm uncomfortably aware I'm the only target in the room.

These two are doing nothing to help my nerves, and I want to snap at them both to back the fuck off. But I don't have a death wish, no matter how tolerant they are of me. "Yes, this is exactly like before. It looks scarier than it is. She's in complete control," I say, proud of the confidence ringing in my voice. They don't need to know I'm scared. The calmer I am, the calmer I hope they'll be. "She'll be back soon."

The Morningstar grunts and Gabriel says nothing. A few minutes pass and the tension steadily ratchets up in the room. Sweat beads on the back of my neck and slicks my palms.

"How do we get her to return if she's in danger?" Gabriel asks Lucifer.

"I do not know. How does one call a soul home?" he replies, not bothering to hide his worry.

"She's fine," I grit out. "Have faith in your kid. She's strong—you two should know that."

I feel both their eyes on my back like twin lasers ready to burn through my skin when the cloudiness dissipates from Luna's eyes, and she blinks up at me. Relief is like a flood, rushing to fill all the corners of my body.

"Baby, I'm so glad to have you back," I say, squeezing her hands.

She sits up, staring at me, then her gaze jumps to her parents. "Alaric says he knows how we can draw Alexander out to rescue the children."

TWENTY-THREE

LUNA

IF I WASN'T IMMORTAL, I might fear a one-way ticket to Hell for what we're about to do. Then again, even immortals can die by the right blade, so maybe eternal damnation is still a possibility, depending on how this all pans out.

A shiver ripples over my skin as I follow the straight path of the Blessed Road beside my mother, mentally recounting the events of the last twenty-four hours. As promised, Alaric had a strategy for how we could turn the tide of this war against Alexander. A questionable, borderline morally-reprehensible strategy, but a strategy that he swears will work.

Despite the losses we've suffered, the one upper hand we still have is that Alexander isn't aware we know where he is. Although that gives us the element of surprise, Alaric was right—we need to tip the scales before we can beat him, and storming the gates when the Gray and his army are there in Persepolis would only result in needless casualties and a potential, unfavorable early end to this conflict. We need to weaken the snake before we can cut off its head, and to do that, we need to hit him where it will actually hurt.

Alexander might be a narcissist, but even he has a weakness, and from what Alaric told me, that weakness is his mortal parents. They might both be long dead, little more than particles of dust and bone now, but Alexander is apparently sentimental about them—a strange thought given how quick he was to turn on Caleb, his actual flesh and blood. According to Alaric, the Gray even went so far as to place protection wards on his parents' tombs in Greece. Whether that's because Alexander anticipated us attacking the sites or because he does actually intend to eventually raise them from the dead as he offhandedly proclaimed when we were captive at the citadel, one thing is certain: if we ransack one of the tombs, he will come, leaving his new base unguarded for us to then slip in and rescue Alaric and the children.

Between his parents, Alexander holds a greater fondness for his deceased mother, and so, at Alaric's suggestion, that's where I head now with Gabriel, Raphael, and Uriel—to the queen of Macedonia's resting place in the town of Korinos where a handful of the Archdemons, including my father, will meet us. The plan is for us to break into the tomb, then split up, with half of us making our way to Persepolis once we're certain Alexander has abandoned the city while the other half leads him on a wild goose chase on the Roads. The remaining Council members, along with Caleb, Lilith, Hammurabi, and the other Fallen and Nephilim at our disposal, are on standby in the mountains above the ancient Persian city, keeping an eye on any movement below and ready to act once we give the order. Lilith wanted to accompany me and my mother to Korinos, but I begged her to stay with Caleb—to protect him, should the need arise, even if he wasn't happy about it. The ex-Archdemon makes him uncomfortable, not that he would ever admit it. Still, while I knew Asmodeus would watch over him, as would Hammurabi, I felt better knowing Lilith would be there with him, too.

Getting the Council to agree to this plan was actually far easier than I anticipated it would be—especially considering it was coming from me. Then again, they want to humble the Conqueror and make him realize he's not as invincible as he thinks. Immortals can hold a grudge better than humans, and they want to pay Alexander back for all the trouble he's caused them, both in the past and now. If what Alaric said about him still rings true, there's only one way to do that—by exhuming his mother's remains. The thought makes me queasy, but there's no telling how many wards the Gray put on the tomb, and he might not come at all unless he truly believes his mother's resting place is in jeopardy. Plus, we need something to lead him away from our true aim, which is to raid his base.

"What will we do with it?" I whisper to my mother. "The queen's remains, I mean."

Gabriel's mouth hardens into a line. "Alexander might be a brilliant strategist, but even he is not immune to anger…or slight. Heightened emotions make even the best of us careless, and I am certain he will view our actions in Korinos as a grave personal insult. His reaction today will be his downfall."

My brow furrows, and I turn my head, looking at her more closely. "You didn't answer my question."

Raphael sidles up on my right before Gabriel can answer, interjecting, "We will be respectful, don't you worry your pretty little head. Something of such great import to the Conqueror may come in handy as a bargaining chip, should we need it."

My mother scoffs. "Bait is the more likely alternative. The time for bargaining is long past."

We step out of the Blessed Road at one of the markers in Greece into the dying light of a setting sun. When my feet touch asphalt, I glance around, thrown by the modernity of our surroundings. We're on an empty road in the middle of what I think might be farmland, the mostly flat earth interrupted only by a highway visible to my left through some trees and a gas station and rest stop not far off straight ahead. I'm not sure what I expected to find here, but nothing about this place screams ancient burial site.

A short distance away, there's a large mound covered in trees, under which I notice three Archdemons emerging from a cluster of shadows. Situated between Mammon and Beelzebub, I spot my father, but instead of coming over to meet us, they head for a small structure to the left of the hill, which looks like little more than a wooden roof propped up by a handful of steel beams for cover. The Archangels cross the field to the building without hesitation, but despite my mother nodding at me to follow, I find myself frozen in place, my fingers curling into tight, trembling fists. So much depends on this part of the plan going right. Since Alexander was the one who put the ward on the tomb, it stands to reason only another Gray will be able to break it—assuming Gray wards work anything like Light and Dark ones. But what if I can't? Or worse, what if he's laid another trap in wait for us? One I won't be able to overcome?

Don't think like that, I chide myself. *This has to work.*

This is the only way to rescue Alaric.

Holding onto that thought like a lifeline, I draw in a breath and launch into a run, only stopping once I've joined the others, and we're all gathered together just outside the lean-to, my father and Beelzebub silently assessing the dark opening ahead. Surprisingly, there's no fence surrounding the site, or any sort of deterrent to stop us—or mortal grave robbers—from entering the premises, assuming there's anything left inside to steal. The building doesn't even have a door. It's open to the elements, with the entrance to the tomb on full display.

"I do not sense a ward here," Uriel grumbles, crossing the stretch of wooden planks that form a footpath from the edge of the structure to the tomb opening.

"Some may yet lie ahead," my mother warns, her dark eyes shifting to mine. "Alaric said there is at least one, and he would not lead us astray."

"Perhaps," Uriel retorts, noncommittal, before stepping into the passage beyond.

I scowl at the Archangel's back. He was the last person I wanted to accompany us on this mission—even more so than Mammon, who I'm actually glad is with us rather than in Persepolis with the others, waiting for our signal to begin the rescue. At least while he's here, I know he can't hurt Caleb. But Uriel on the other hand… his presence is a constant thorn in my side, and I know he came with us to keep a watchful eye on me as much as he did for the chance to spurn Alexander.

"How do the wards work when it comes to humans?" I ask, glancing between my parents, who stick close to my sides as we make our way along the unlit stone path, the floor underfoot sloping in a steady decline. The ceiling above us is low and rounded, and we pass two large marble slabs propped against the walls, which I can only assume were once doors used to close off the approaching end of this passage. "I mean, this is an excavation site, right?"

"Different wards serve different purposes," my mother answers vaguely as we reach the end of the corridor and step through the open doorway ahead into a small antechamber. Unlike the plain earthy whites and beiges of the stone blocks in the passage behind us, the top half of the wall intersecting the path directly before us is red. While I'm sure the color was probably vibrant once, now it's the same hue as rust, aged by many long years and decay, though there's a certain grandness to the partition that remains despite the passage of time. It rises in a pointed triangle at the top where the peak meets with the barrel-vaulted roof, seeming to serve as some sort of grand arch.

The official entry to the tomb.

As I take in the details, I think of Caleb, not only because he would be fascinated by the architecture, but because the tomb was erected for a woman who is essentially his great-grandmother. The history-lover side of him would be elated.

"Some wards block entrance entirely while others merely…deter," Gabriel continues after a moment, dragging my attention away from the engraved markings at the top of the facade.

"Think of it like bug spray for humans," Beelzebub grumbles, rolling his eyes, which are bright, like polished sapphires, even in the darkness.

"That would explain why this place isn't locked up or guarded," my father says, crossing the space and stopping abruptly in front of the doorway leading into the next chamber. "Something about this edifice is keeping the mortals away."

"And now us," Raphael adds, sidestepping my father. Raising a hand to the opening, she flattens her palm against what I can only assume is an invisible wall, not unlike the wards I encountered with Caleb and Ishtar under the Serapeum what feels like a lifetime ago.

"Is something there?" I glance between the faces of the angels and Fallen around me, but whatever they're sensing here, I don't feel it. Then again, I didn't feel the wards back in Alexandria, either.

My mother's brow wrinkles in consternation. "A ward, just like we expected. It's blocking our way deeper into the tomb, but…it's unlike any I've ever encountered."

"Of course, it is." Mammon sneers at her. "This ward was created by a Gray, remember? Did you believe it would resemble anything we can create?"

"It matters not," Uriel chides, gesturing to me with an indifferent wave of his hand. "We have another Gray here who can break it. After what occurred at the citadel, the Morningstar's daughter will make quick work of it, I'm sure."

I don't miss the skepticism and distrust in his tone—or the obvious exclusion of my mother from his comment, as if he still can't believe the Messenger could have committed the blasphemous act of helping to bring a Gray into the world. He arches a thick black brow, and my jaw tenses as I suppress the violent urge to break something other than the ward. Like his teeth.

"Come, Starlight," my father murmurs. "Ignore these old cynics and tell me what you sense."

I nod, but the trouble is, I sense nothing.

Exhaling, I position myself before the unobstructed doorway then take a step forward into the next chamber, testing the ward to see if it's anything like the ones I encountered in Alexandria. Like then, I proceed without issue. Nothing stops me and I don't feel myself passing through anything, but then, my exposure to wards—and our world in general—has been limited. Maybe I just don't know what to look for.

Focus, Luna, the voice in my head snaps. *Focus and you'll feel it. You have to.*

Turning to face the others, I draw in a shaking breath, and when I raise my hands—mimicking what Raphael did, pressing them flat to the ward—I close my eyes and force my thoughts outward, searching for any sign of Alexander's magic, just like I searched for the threads linking their minds at the citadel. It takes me a moment but I find it, much to my relief, and exhaling again, I open my eyes, holding the picture of it close in my consciousness. Now, aware of what I'm looking for, I can see it—the wall separating me from the others. But this time, it doesn't take the shape of threads at all or anything I can snap or cut.

It's glass and I just need to shatter it.

Summoning a strength I wasn't even aware I possessed, I throw everything I feel toward Alexander at the barrier. Anger for all the hurt and pain he's caused Caleb.

Rage for what he's doing to Alaric. And an irrepressible contempt for how he's forced me into a role that threatens to crush me at every turn. But I won't let it crush me. I can't.

Because I am the Savior and I'm destined to stop him.

A strange energy I've never felt or seen before suddenly explodes out of my palms in a blinding light, cracking the wall beneath my touch and illuminating the tomb and passage behind the angels in white. It heats every inch of me down to my marrow until I'm burning as bright as the hottest fire. No, not like fire. Like a star.

A Morningstar. I smile at the thought.

The light fades after a few seconds, and I blink, my eyes quickly adjusting to the returning darkness of the tomb. I curl my fingers, feeling for the ward before me, but I don't sense anything there. The glasslike barrier hasn't only been broken, it's been obliterated—wiped from existence, with no indication it was ever there at all to begin with. I don't know why that surprises me. I guess I supposed that kind of magic would leave a permanent mark, like a stain that I would still see or sense. Or maybe I just wasn't entirely convinced I had what it takes to break it.

But I did. I overcame yet another obstacle Alexander threw in my path. And now, with the ward destroyed, we're one step closer to turning the tables against him.

We move quickly. We don't have time to waste, and if the Gray ward is anything like the wards the Council placed at the Serapeum to guard his prison, Alexander will already know we're here. He'll know what we've done—what *I've* done, which is exactly what we're banking on.

The middle chamber in the tomb is empty, but the last room, the burial chamber, has what we came for. Two white funerary beds sit positioned in an L-shaped arrangement. Uriel pushes past everyone, making a beeline for the smaller of the two, which has a snake relief on the front of the stone.

"Is that it?" I ask.

"See, the child *is* useful," Raphael practically purrs, planting herself on the untouched coffin and picking at her nails.

Uriel flashes her a scornful look over his shoulder but stays silent as he lifts the marble box from the floor as if it weighs nothing. Although I've experienced my own angel strength many times now, it's still so strange to witness just how different we are from humans. We really are a separate species, and the more aware I become of that fact, the less I know how to feel about it. Maybe because it reminds me that half of Caleb is human—that he's mortal, and every moment this war carries on is another potential moment the fire of his life could be snuffed out.

"Luna?" my father prompts and I jolt, scrubbing all thoughts of Caleb from my mind.

Blinking up at Lucifer, I nod. "I'm ready."

"Make haste," my mother says, her tone brusque. "We don't have long."

I swallow, distressed by the thought of projecting with several members of the Council watching—of leaving my body vulnerable to their whims—but I know we don't have time for nerves, so I try to take comfort in knowing my parents are with me. That they'll watch over me. Steeling myself, I nod again, then pulling the leathery patch of flesh from my pocket, I think of Alaric. Projecting my soul is even easier now than it was the last two times I did it, and before I know it, I'm back at the Tachara, standing in the cramped bathroom again. Alaric isn't here, but I didn't expect him to be, nor do I expect him to come. Because as much as I can't wait to see him again, my friend isn't what I need right now.

What I need is a sign.

I spot it within seconds. There, on the wall above the doorway, is the sigil Asmodeus gifted Alaric scrawled on the stone near the ceiling in chalk—the signal we agreed upon for him to use to let me know our plan is working. My heart buckles, smashing into my ribcage with enough force to thrust me back into my body, and wrenching my eyes open, I gasp out the words the Archangels and Archdemons are waiting for.

"He's coming."

With a curt nod, my mother rolls up the sleeve of her blouse—my lips twitch at the realization that she still dresses like the headmistress of the Serapeum, even when we're robbing a dusty, old tomb. Once her wrist is exposed, she presses her fingertip to the sigil I share with her and Lilith, and I feel the burn of her call, my eyes dropping to the glowing white lines in my skin as my pulse gallops at the thought of the others in Persepolis.

This is it—the signal they're waiting for.

"Let's move," my mother growls. Grabbing my hand, she yanks me through the chambers, retracing our steps toward the path that will lead us back to the light. Raphael and Uriel follow our lead, the latter still tightly clutching the marble box. I look over my shoulder, glancing past them at the Archdemons, who remain in the shadows, preparing for the role in this heist they still have to play.

"One word of this to anyone, and I swear—" Mammon threatens, but my father waves him off with a smile.

"My lips are sealed," Lucifer promises. Beside him, Beelzebub snorts.

The youthful Archdemon's sudden laughter follows our steps up the incline. "I think I prefer you this way, Mammon," he says through hysterics.

This time, when I look back again, I swear I see two Fallen in the shadows of the tomb instead of the three we left behind. And between them on the floor is the same box Uriel carries, except this one emits a low growl of contempt.

Seeing the Tachara in person is strange, like visiting a place I've only ever seen in my dreams. At first glance, it looks like little more than well-preserved ruins, but upon further inspection—beyond the ripple of the glamor encasing it—I see the truth of the palace's real form. The vibrant exterior colors—the reds, greens, and yellows— along with the intricate carvings into nearly every pillar and available surface, mimic the beauty I briefly saw within the first time I astral projected my soul here. Before, the details were dulled somewhat by the monochromatic darkness of night, but now, in the sunlight, I glimpse every mark left behind by the artists who built this place, and I'm mesmerized by the otherworldliness of it all, of how it makes me feel like I'm stepping out of time and into a once-distant past.

My mother, Raphael, and I skirt around a handful of dead Nephilim as we climb the steps up to the palace. We don't bother to sneak in through a back or side entrance. We don't have to. The skeleton crew Alexander left here has already been overwhelmed by our forces, leaving a clear path for us into the Tachara. Just as Gabriel predicted he would, Alexander reacted rashly to our assault on his mother's tomb, and just as Alaric predicted, he took most of his army with him to hunt us down, leaving this place vulnerable and exposed. Just like when he invited my father to the citadel, expecting him to bend the knee, Alexander has let his overconfidence get the better of his judgment. He was wrong to assume we wouldn't ever find out about his base here in Persepolis.

He was wrong to underestimate me. And Alaric.

Inside the dwelling, the Archangels, Archdemons, and Nephilim who were waiting for our signal are already hard at work, gathering the students who were abducted and the weapons from the Fall that were stolen, herding them all into the main foyer. To buy us time, my father, Beelzebub, and Mammon are leading Alexander astray in the opposite direction from the Persian city, making him believe they have his mother's remains when, in reality, the real funerary box is with Uriel at our new hideout in Cambodia, where we'll meet him once we finish here. At the time we discussed this plan with the Council, the Archangels and Archdemons didn't go into specific detail as to how they would trick Alexander—just that they would use a believable decoy to distract him. Looking back, I suppose I should've paid more attention to the amused looks everyone kept flashing at Mammon.

I bite back a chuckle at the memory of Beelzebub's laughter and my growing comprehension of what I saw just before I left Korinos. Once, Mammon was the star in almost all of my nightmares, his shape-shifting ability tormenting me even in sleep. But now, picturing him in my father's arms, taking the form of a harmless stone box, leaches away some of the terror I feel when I think of him. If only Caleb had been there to see it, then maybe he wouldn't be so scared of him, either.

Thinking of Caleb pulls me back to reality, and my eyes snap between the surrounding faces, looking for him in the crowd. Worry spreads through me, coating my skin like sweat—not only because I don't see him here, but because I can't stop thinking of my father on the Shadow Road, pursued by Alexander and his army. The thought gives me flashbacks to his fight with the Gray at the citadel, when Alexander pierced his body with feathers of silver light, shot through his limbs like arrows. Although I know Lucifer can hold his own in a fight, I'm glad Beelzebub is with him to back him up if needed. If anyone can help my father stave off Alexander, it's the feisty Archdemon.

Pushing my apprehension aside, I tell myself to calm down—that my father will be fine and that Caleb is here somewhere, and we'll be together again soon. But as always, my attempts at self-soothing are fruitless, and I breathe out a shaky breath as I trail my mother's steps through the large, crowded hall—the grand black-tiled floor lined with tall pillars—my stomach clenching at the sight of the frightened children filling the space.

Much like with the evacuations at Sinai and the Serapeum, the angels and Fallen have organized the students, except the lines they form here serve a different purpose to the ones they were separated into at the academies. Now, every student is checked for a tracker—not just the Lights who were ambushed on the Blessed Road but everyone, in case Alexander decided to mark his new property. Then, once they're cleared, the students are ushered into two growing groups by the doors—one for Darks and one for Lights—where they then wait to be escorted into their respective Roads and spirited away to safety. Again.

The progression moves quickly and efficiently, with an undercurrent of urgency I can physically feel in the air. It clings to my hair and clothes like static electricity, and the longer I watch the Lights and Darks work, the more I recognize the sick feeling inside me and why I can't seem to shake my discomfort. The angels and Fallen seem to be having no issue removing the trackers in the students, which means Alexander wasn't the one who planted them—he left that job to his lackeys. But Alaric...he told me himself the tracker inside his head is a Gray one, and I want to vomit at the thought of Alexander violating him that way. Clearly, that was one tether Alexander wasn't going to risk letting the Council remove. Or maybe Alexander is sending me a message. That Alaric belongs to him and not me.

As the Nephilim's tortured face fills my head, my eyes catch on an amber-haired head in the crowd.

"Alaric!"

His name bursts from my lungs in a shriek, and as he turns at the sound of my voice, I lunge forward, crossing the space between us as fast as my legs will carry me.

"Lu—" he begins, grunting when I slam into his chest before he can get the full word out. My arms wrap around his back, and I hug him so tightly he would break if he were fully human, but I can't bring myself to let him go or ease my hold on him even a little. Despite speaking to him previously, despite seeing him with my own two eyes and knowing he was alive, getting this glimpse of him here in the flesh gives me a sense of confirmation and consolation I desperately needed. It's as if part of me didn't truly believe he was actually alive until this moment. As if I needed tangible evidence I could touch to convince my senses of what my heart kept wishing to be true.

Alaric lets out a breathy chuckle and curls his arms around me as well. A contented sigh parts my lips, and pulling away, I grin up at him. "It worked."

"Yes," he murmurs, but the tentative smile he offers me wavers. "For now. But we don't have much time. We don't know when Alexander will return."

I nod, stepping free of his embrace. He's right. There's so much to do here, and we need to ensure we're all miles away before Alexander suspects what we're up to. My father will contact my mother through their shared sigil to give us a heads up if Alexander backs off his trail, but we don't want to take any chances. The sooner we finish here, the better for everyone, especially Alaric.

My smile slips when I think of the tracker still in his head, and more than ever, I'm determined to release him from Alexander's sadistic hold. Alaric doesn't deserve this—to be treated this way by someone who claims to love him. He, more than anyone, deserves to be free.

My mouth sets in a scowl as that returning rush of guilt weighs on my chest. Alexander got this idea because of me...which means I'm partly to blame for any suffering Alaric endured since he stepped in front of Alexander's dagger and took the killing blow meant for me. Hell, even before that, since I let Alexander loose from his cage. But I'm also the only one who can relieve Alaric of this burden, even if that means mimicking the person who did this to him in the first place.

Swallowing, I raise my hand to his ear just like Alexander did to me. "First thing's first—"

"That can wait," he protests, his voice hoarse. I blink up at him, my gaze shifting between his stony expression and the way his fingers clamp around my wrist, holding my hand away from his ear. Clearing his throat, he relaxes his grasp on me, adding, "We have more important problems to deal with right now."

My heart drops into my stomach at the mention of "problems," but before I can organize my thoughts enough to ask what he means, another voice joins the conversation.

"What kind of problems?"

I turn, finding Gabriel standing behind me with one delicate obsidian brow raised at Alaric.

"Gabriel," he mutters, inclining his head at her.

She steps forward, placing a hand on his shoulder, and there's a tender kindness in her gaze when she looks at the Nephilim that's so at odds with the last interaction I witnessed between them. But then, their argument that I eavesdropped on back at the Serapeum was about Alexander. About *me*. In the mountains above Kandahār— before everything went to hell—Alaric told me about Alexander's first conquest for power…and the aftermath. Considering Gabriel was the one who spoke up for him, who fought against the Council to ensure the Nephilim would retain his memories, I can't help wondering if her hostility toward him that day in Alexandria was merely her way of trying to protect him again. That time, from himself.

"I'm glad to see you again, old friend." Although there's a careful distance in the Archangel's voice that I've grown to expect from her, there's also a sincerity to her words that tells me she's as relieved to see him again as I am. In typical Gabriel fashion, however, her tone shifts back to its usual collective coolness almost immediately. "Now, tell me—and be quick—what problems do you speak of?"

"Is it Caleb and the others?" I cut in before he can answer. "Have you seen them? Where are—"

"They're fine," he promises, holding up both hands, palms out, to placate me. "They're here. But"—his honey gaze swings to my mother—"there have been some… complications."

"What *kind* of complications?" There's a razor-sharp edge to my mother's voice now, but all I feel in this moment is panic. What else could possibly go wrong?

Why can't we just catch a damn break already?

Alaric lowers his own voice to a whisper. "Some of the children are choosing to stay. They won't leave."

"Wait…*what*?" I sputter, choking on the words. Alaric can't be serious, can he? I've lived under the same roof as Alexander, and it was the most stressful week of my life, which is saying *a lot,* considering I spent the four months before that trapped in a literal glass egg. Even Caleb, who lived with his grandfather for far longer than I did, got the hell out of dodge, and that was *after* Alexander offered him a seat ruling at his side. But Caleb is his grandson, and these Nephilim are nothing to the Gray—just more numbers for his army. So, what could he be offering them that would make them want to stay?

The same impossible lie he's offered to all the others who have chosen his side in this war, I suppose.

As if reading my mind, Alaric says, "They believe Alexander will protect them. That they're safer with him than with the Council."

"I wonder what lies he fed them to make them believe that," my mother hisses, crossing her arms.

A tired sigh parts the Nephilim's lips, and again, I notice how…*off* he looks. I can only imagine what Alexander has put him through, both emotional and otherwise.

"They're frightened, Gabriel," Alaric reminds her. "They were abducted under the Council's watch and then thrust into a world of perceived safety and riches. And… Alexander has been preaching about the prophecy, proclaiming himself as their Savior. You all don't know Alexander like I do. You don't know how charismatic and convincing he can be. Can we really blame them for wanting to stay?"

My mouth pops open at that, but no sound comes out. I can't seem to find my voice.

I didn't even think about the fact that Alexander might be using the prophecy to sway followers to his cause, and while I doubt that's been his only tactic of recruitment, I can't help wondering if that was how he got those Lights we encountered on the Blessed Road to join him. I've heard the prophecy and often doubted its vague words myself, and while I can say which role I think I fall into, the only being who knows our roles for certain is the Creator. If anyone were to question the prophecy's meaning, it would come down to Alexander's word against mine and which of the two of us they're inclined to believe. Thinking about it that way, I'd be willing to bet those who follow Alexander are convinced I'm the Destroyer just as much as those who stand by me think I'm the Savior.

My stomach ties in knots at that notion. The prophecy doesn't say who will prevail in this war, just that the fate of the world will be decided by the outcome. So, even if we win, we still fail because how can we ever unite our people without proof? Without some way to *show* them I'm the Savior—that I'm meant to heal the rift between our kind and not tear us further apart?

"The fools," Gabriel growls, but she's wrong. These terrified children aren't fools—they're just misguided. And the Council only has themselves to blame. For fanning the fires of division for so long and for allowing the divide to grow so vast that the kids now caught in the crossfire can't believe we'd ever want to mend it.

Assuming that's what anyone following Alexander actually wants. I'm sure there are many who don't care about the divide at all and have only joined the Gray because they're tired of hiding. Because they want to be free to be who they are without fear… or because they just want to lord their superiority and power over humans. In which case, if we do win this war, we have our work cut out for us. Because freedom for us isn't the same as freedom for humans, and to co-exist, we need a middle ground. A way for us to live life how we want without impeding on the safety and liberty of others.

But that's a problem for another day. For now, we need to think about the students whom the Council has a sworn responsibility to protect.

"What about your Calm?" I ask, focusing on Alaric. "Could you do anything to… persuade them?"

The words taste sour in my mouth as I say them. Not that long ago, I resented Alaric using his power on me, and here I am, now suggesting he do the same to others. But I don't know what else we can do. I don't know what other option there is available to us.

As I feared he would, he shakes his head. "I'm only one Nephilim, Luna. To hold that many under at once would require a strength even I do not possess, and the second I let go, even a little—"

"They might run back to him," Gabriel finishes, her mouth pinched at the corners.

"What about the Council?" I propose, looking between them. "Maybe they could do something?" Like take away the memory of the students' time here and any inclination they might have to side with Alexander. It wouldn't be the first time the Archangels and Archdemons intervened in such a way.

Alaric gives me a hard stare. "What you're suggesting…" A grimace crosses his face and he shakes his head again. "Taking them by force would make us no better than Alexander. I think you both know this, and I think I know you both well enough to be certain that's not what you want."

A shudder rolls over my skin at his words. I do know that and it isn't what I want. But hearing the disapproval in his voice only makes it that much harder to admit.

Instead, my eyes dip to the floor in shame, and my hands curl into clenched fists in frustration. Even now, even finding a way to one-up him, Alexander still found a way to defeat us. It isn't right. It isn't fair. If I'm truly the Savior, it shouldn't be this freaking hard to save everyone.

"Then let any who wish to stay remain."

My eyes snap up, and I gape at my mother, wondering if I heard her correctly. Her gaze is blistering when it meets mine.

"Will the Council agree to that?" I ask. Azrael and Belphegor already made it perfectly clear they're both willing to harm any who side with Alexander, even if that means their own students. And there are others on the Council who are probably of a similar opinion. Like Mammon. I'm sure even Uriel would stoop to that level.

"They won't like it," Gabriel answers, her voice almost a hiss when she adds, "but I will make them agree. I will not stand by and watch as frightened, unarmed children are slaughtered, nor will I partake in such sacrilege."

"And how exactly do you plan to convince them?" Alaric presses. "We do not have time to make the Council see reason. They may decide to cut their losses and run."

Gabriel's gaze darkens like the sky before a storm. "We cannot coerce the resistant students and we do not have the time to convince them, so this is our only option to avoid any further, immediate bloodshed. Besides, those who choose to stay may yet change their minds. We need to allow them that chance, otherwise, we really are no better than Alexander. And if they don't...if they *do* choose to fight beside the Conqueror and for all he stands for..." She doesn't finish that sentence but her unspoken words ring loudly in the silence that follows.

Then we'll meet them on the battlefield, and their fates will be decided there.

"That might be harder for some to hear than others," Alaric interjects. "Caleb—"

Panic lances through me as my focus shifts to the Nephilim's face. "What about Caleb? Where is he?" The words come out in a half-strangled shout.

Alaric is silent, his expression dejected, and it takes all my self-restraint to not grab him by the shoulders and shake him until he answers.

"Alaric?" I press, my tone bordering on hysterical.

"With his brother," a familiar voice says behind him.

My eyes drift over Alaric's shoulder to Lilith, who stands with her arms crossed and dark brow creased in annoyance. She offers me and my mother each a cursory nod. "I've been *trying* to convince him the effort is futile but, of course, no one ever listens to me."

"His…brother?" I repeat, dragging out the word.

I can practically feel all the color drain from my skin as I recall our meeting with the Council before we went back to Kandahār. The Archangels and Archdemons talked then about Alexander's grandchildren, and Beelzebub mentioned a child at Ashkelon—a boy. A boy who was missing…or dead.

A worse realization takes hold of me then. What Alaric said about students refusing to leave and the way Lilith mentioned Caleb's brother…

He's one of those children.

My agonized thoughts must be written all over my face because Gabriel gently squeezes my fingers. "Go. Find him," she encourages. "Caleb will listen to you. But don't dally," she immediately adds in a stern but not unkind tone. "The sooner we can leave this place, the better."

My eyes burn as I return the comforting grip on her hand. Not that long ago, Gabriel wouldn't have cared one bit about Caleb or dared to let me out of her sight in enemy territory. But now, since that moment on the Blessed Road when I grabbed her sword, there's a level of trust building between us that wasn't there before. I'm thankful for it, just as I'm thankful she seems to be coming around to my relationship with Caleb. "What about you?"

She waves a hand in the direction of the Archangels nearby. "I will aid with removing the trackers. Those afflicted won't be going anywhere with us so long as they remain intact. And"—she lowers her voice to a whisper—"I still have a Council to persuade."

That's true, and us standing here talking about all these bleak things certainly won't move things along.

"Lilith?" my mother prompts and the ex-Archdemon nods, trailing her steps as Gabriel throws one last curt "Be quick" over her shoulder before hastily strutting away.

"Come." Alaric's warm palm grazes my shoulder. "I'll take you to Caleb."

Alaric leads me through the elaborately decorated corridors of the palace, my senses assaulted by broad sweeps of red and yellow, past a communal sleeping area where I glimpse a few dozen students sitting on unfurled mats on the floor—the ones refusing to leave, I'd wager—to a bedroom a short distance farther down the hallway that reminds me of Caleb's room back at his grandfather's original base. It's much grander than the large chamber where the other students are gathered but, like the rest of this building, marked by the time period in which this city flourished. There isn't a single modern detail to be seen aside from the clothes worn by the pair of arguing teens in the room.

It's immediately evident the two take after their father. Despite having different mothers, they look so similar, there's a moment when I almost mistake the younger Nephilim for Caleb. It's the eyes that stop me in my tracks and make me realize my mistake. Eyes—one brown and one a pale, haunting blue—that are identical to Alexander's.

I stand frozen in the doorway—Alaric hovering closely behind my right shoulder—my gaze fixed on the sulking boy sitting on the ornately carved wooden bed with his arms crossed, his Dark aura a bramble-like tangle of fury and resentment as he glares up at his older brother, who keeps his back to us. It's eerie, like someone took Caleb's face and his grandfather's and mashed their features together, creating this new person who is so familiar in looks and yet, at the same time, a stranger.

"Listen to me," Caleb pleads, his attention firmly set on his brother. I'm certain the boys must've heard us arrive, but if they did, neither one of them spares us a glance or shows it in any noticeable way. Or maybe they're too caught up in their disagreement to care about having an audience. "You *can't* stay here," Caleb continues, his voice tight. "I know better than anyone what he—"

"You know nothing!" the other Nephilim roars, anger turning his bronzed cheeks ruddy. His English is clear but his accent is thick—Spanish, I think. Or Portuguese, maybe. "And you do not know me. We might share blood but we are not family."

"And Alexander is?" Caleb counters.

I glance between them, suddenly feeling a bit like a voyeur—like I shouldn't be watching this—but I can't bring myself to move, transfixed by the scene unfolding before me. It doesn't feel like my place to intervene, but I will if I have to if it means saving Caleb from what I fear is a losing battle. The time we have left to evacuate the Tachara is dwindling, and I refuse to let him risk capture and death at the hands of Alexander or one of his followers trying to persuade someone who obviously doesn't want to be persuaded.

A hostile expression crosses the younger boy's face. "Alexander is our grandfather and a legend. He is the only family I need."

A shiver runs over my skin at his words. Words that sound very much like something Ishtar would say. My jaw clenches, and I can't help wondering if she was the one who put these dangerous thoughts in his head.

Caleb's entire body goes rigid. I can only imagine what he must be feeling—the sense of responsibility that must be eating at him, telling him to rescue his younger sibling and save him from repeating his own past mistakes. "I thought that way once, too," he says. "But the second you fall out of line, he'll disown you. He'll kill you if you cross him, Marcos."

"Why would I cross him?" his brother—Marcos—asks, rising from the bed. When standing, he's almost as tall as Caleb despite being a few years younger. "He is offering me everything I have ever wanted. Obedience is a small price to pay."

I step forward when Caleb grabs his brother roughly by the shirt, but Alaric stills me with a hand on my shoulder. "This is between them," he whispers in my ear at the same time Caleb shouts, "It's not that simple! Can't you see what he's doing is wrong? I'm trying to save your life, man."

"I never asked you to," Marcos growls. His cheeks are an even deeper red now, his ire rising to the surface like a flush of heat.

"No," Caleb agrees, relaxing his grip a little but not fully releasing his hold on the fabric, "but that's what family does. And I am your family, whether you like it or not."

Marcos bats Caleb's hand away, then shoves him back, unswayed. "You are not family," he retorts, then to my horror, he spits on the floor at Caleb's feet. "You are a stranger. And I do not trust you. I do *not* choose you."

Enough.

For a split second, I think I must have said this aloud because Marcos's eyes—which are so like Alexander's—dart to mine and lock on me like a missile homes in on its target. I stiffen at the derisive look he gives me. I don't know if he recognizes me—if Alexander or Ishtar told him about me, though I wouldn't put it past either of them to tell this boy all about the disappointment of a grandson and the angel who betrayed them—but I don't care enough to ask. I have more important things to deal with, and I need to get Caleb out of here before it's too late. He might feel some sense of responsibility toward his brother, but *my* responsibility—and my loyalty—will always be to him.

"Caleb," I breathe, fixing my eyes on his back.

The tension in his shoulders eases at the sound of my voice, and turning, he flashes a heartbreaking smile before crossing the room and pulling me into his arms.

He hugs me for a long moment before stepping back and gently cupping my face in his hands. "You have no idea how glad I am to see you. Did everything go okay?"

I nod. "Yeah, but..." My gaze drifts over his shoulder, landing on Marcos again. "We don't have much time..." I fall silent because the rest is far too hard to say. It's too hard to tell him we need to leave his brother behind if he won't willingly come with us.

"I hear you, Goldilocks," Caleb murmurs, angling his face to glance over his shoulder, as if he's afraid his brother might run off if he dares to look away for too long. "But I can't leave. Not until I've convinced my dumbass brother to come back from the Dark side."

But he won't. I can see it in the boy's mismatched eyes that nothing Caleb or anyone has to say on the matter will convince him to leave—to abandon the foolishness of siding with Alexander. He'll make the same mistakes Caleb made or worse in his naivety. And he will suffer for them.

"We have no choice," Alaric says from the doorway, echoing my thoughts. Caleb's gaze slides from my face to Alaric's as the Nephilim steps forward until we're standing shoulder to shoulder. "If we take him against his will, think of the danger he may pose," he continues, keeping his voice just shy of a whisper. "Your location was already compromised once. Can you be certain he wouldn't betray us?" Then, even softer, he adds, "And is it a risk you're willing to take?"

"Think of Aya," I plead, grabbing Caleb's hand and desperately interlacing our fingers. "If we force him to come with us, it could backfire on her." A lump rises in my throat, which I struggle to swallow. It distorts my next words with the threat of tears. "I...I don't want to lose anyone else."

Especially you.

And I fear that will happen the longer we linger in this place.

Something in Caleb seems to deflate at my words, and for a long moment, he doesn't say anything, his dark eyes staring blankly at the floor. Finally, after what feels like an eternity, he walks over to his younger brother, grabbing him once more by the front of his shirt.

"Listen to me, you little punk. If you stay here, he *will* make you fight. And if I meet you on the battlefield, I won't go easy on you. I don't want to have to kill you, dude."

The responding smile that stretches across Marcos's face raises goosebumps on my skin.

"The Savior will prevail," he says with adamant certainty, though I definitely don't think he's referring to me. Pushing Caleb away again, he grinds out, "See you on the battlefield, Caleb."

Caleb doesn't spare his brother another glance as he storms out of the room...or me, his eyes dodging mine as he shoves between me and Alaric to reach the doorway. Unease grips my gut as I follow him out into the hallway.

A frown twists my lips as I consider that he might be mad at me, but my worries are eased by a familiar rush of Calm abruptly flooding my senses. I turn my head, glancing up at Alaric, who offers me a consoling smile.

"He isn't upset with you," he says under his breath so only I can hear.

I nod once. I know he's right—that Caleb's just mad he couldn't convince his brother to leave with us. Still, I change the subject. "Your tracker," I prompt, raising a hand to his ear just like I attempted to earlier. "We should remove it now—"

But he grabs my wrist again, stopping me before I can even get the full thought out.

I go still at his almost crushing touch, gaping at his expressionless face in equal parts horror and bemusement. "Why?" I ask, clearing my throat when the words come out raspy. "Why are you so reluctant for me to remove it?"

Alaric's face crumples as his fingers relax their grip. "Because…" Shame paints his face red, and with a sigh, he retracts his hand and scrubs it over his face. "Because, once the tracker is gone, there will be nothing left holding me to Alexander. It will be finished…and knowing that makes me more sad than relieved, as twisted as it is."

Sorrow and pain emanate from him like heat, his aura wavering under the weight of both. I can't even begin to comprehend what this must be like for him—what it must be like to see someone he loves so much corrupted and blinded by power. I wish I could take this pain from him, but I don't know how to do that. I can only give him a choice—the same one we're giving the students. To let him choose which side he fights on moving forward, the way I would want that choice for myself. Or he could decide to sit out of this conflict altogether…not that I truly believe Alexander would give him that option.

"You can choose to stay, too, you know." Out of the corner of my eye, I notice Caleb waiting for us just down the hall, and I ignore the searing look he gives me as I carefully pull Alaric's hand away from his face. The Nephilim stares at me with wide, startled eyes. "If you want," I amend, giving him the same comforting smile he offered me just moments ago. "It's your choice. I won't take that from you."

"No," he says, a little too quickly, then bowing his head, he takes my hand between both of his. "Thank you, Luna, for always understanding. But no. I have to end this toxic thing between us. It's time." He says this last part with a conviction that threatens to steal my breath.

Blinking up at him, I whisper, "If you're sure."

When he nods, I raise my hand to his ear, and this time, he doesn't push me away.

It's easy to remove the tracker—easier than I expected it would be—but then, a lot has changed recently, and I have a firm grasp on my powers now that I didn't possess when I first went to the citadel, seeking out Alexander's help. Just like when he removed the tracker Nzingha implanted in my head on behalf of the Council, it takes only seconds for me to locate Alaric's. Like the pull of a magnet, I sense its presence, and using that same pull, I beckon it to me, watching in wonder as it slides free from his ear canal at my silent call. I clench the silver beetle-like device between my fingertips, but Alaric doesn't ask to see it or react with revulsion like I did with mine. Instead, he keeps his gaze averted the whole time, even once the tracker is removed.

Without saying a word, I crush the device in my fist.

"Ready to go—" I begin to ask, but Alaric cuts me off.

"I want him to know it was me," he chokes out.

I'm about to drop the broken shell of the tracker when the Nephilim's words stall my movements, my fingers outstretched and hand half-tilted toward the floor, as if frozen mid-motion.

"What?"

His amber eyes burn with resolve, and though his voice is a growl, I can sense the tears behind it when he says, "I might love Alexander, and I know I'm probably giving you whiplash"—he shoots me an apologetic look—"but I can't condone what he's doing. I never have. I know I helped imprison him before, but he never knew of my involvement, and I...I don't want to hide behind the Council any longer. I can't. Not this time." He draws in a deep, steadying breath then blows it out slowly before finally adding, "His mother's tomb...the children...the weapons...I want him to know I orchestrated it all. I need him to if I'm going to end this for good."

"One last grandiose fuck you." Caleb grunts in approval, crossing his arms as he ambles back in our direction, his eyes momentarily shifting to the doorway to Marco's room behind us before settling on Alaric's face. "It's as much as the asshole deserves."

I peer between them—between these two people I love so dearly who have been hurt by Alexander. Who wouldn't have been hurt at all if I had never opened that tomb at the Serapeum in the first place.

But I can't take back what's been done. All I can do now is try to help them move forward.

Reaching into my pocket, I pull out the patch of skin Alaric left for us and lay it beside the tracker on my other hand. Extending both to the older Nephilim, I give a firm nod.

"Then let's make sure he knows."

I walk beside Caleb on the Shadow Road a short while later, trailing Hammurabi and Asmodeus as we lead the rescued Dark students away from Persepolis. Thankfully, the majority of those who were abducted chose to leave; only a small percentage opted to stay in the end, and they were left unharmed as my mother managed to persuade the Council to leave them to fight another day. I don't know what she said to convince them, and I didn't ask—I can only assume enough of the Council shared my mother's distaste for murdering their own students. And since the children aren't *technically* helping Alexander at present—unless you count cowering in fear in his palace as aid—they can't be treated as disloyal. Still, I fear for those children. The Council will not show them mercy if they go to war.

As we walk, I mourn Alaric's absence at my side. I hated separating so soon after getting him back, but I was torn between accompanying him or Caleb, and I got the impression Alaric wanted to be alone with his thoughts. After everything he's been through and sacrificed, I owed him that privacy.

Just before leaving the Tachara, we stopped by the bedroom Alaric shared with Alexander, where he placed the broken tracker and the dried patch of skin deliberately on his pillow for the Gray to find when he returns. It was a stronger message than any he could've penned in words, but that doesn't mean it came without great personal cost. I could see the heartache on his face as clearly as I sense the uncomfortable tension radiating from Caleb, his aura an ebbing wave of agitation, the shadows lashing across his skin like small whips committing self-flagellation.

I glance at him, my fingers flexing and curling again with the urge to reach out and grab his hand. He hasn't said a word to me since his argument with Marcos, and while I know it isn't really me he's upset with, that voice of doubt always living in the back of my brain has a way of reminding me that the things I love most can still be torn away. That he can still leave, even if my heart tells me he wouldn't. All my many years of abandonment issues rise to the surface at once, and I shudder, unable to stand the thought that he might be angry because I told him we should leave, or worse, that his failure with Marcos might make him push me away. It's a ridiculous fear—deep down I know he wouldn't—but still, that fear persists. It's happened to me too many times before for it not to.

"Are you mad at me?" I ask in a clumsy rush, unable to keep the thought at bay any longer. "Because I said we should leave your brother behind?"

Caleb exhales a long-suffering sigh. "No," he answers without hesitation, and relief slams into my chest like a wrecking ball. "I know you're right, Goldilocks. It just sucks. I guess I had hoped..."

"That he'd be more like Aya?" I finish when he trails off.

He shrugs, staring off into the distance ahead.

"Well, if it makes you feel any better"—I knot my hands behind my back, trying to keep my tone airy—"I saw Mammon shape-shift into the stone coffin holding your kind-of-great-grandmother's ashes."

That stops him in his tracks. "I'm sorry, *what*?"

Now a few steps ahead, I glance back at him, giggling. "It was weird hearing Beelzebub laugh."

Caleb lets out a long, whooshing breath. "Damn. I wish I could've seen that."

Crossing the space between us, Caleb leans in for a kiss, taking my hand and knitting our fingers together as we continue our forward march. As we approach the marker that will take us to our new hideout in Cambodia, he barks out a sudden laugh.

"What?" I reel back to look up at him, but he just shakes his head, laughing again behind his hand.

"Nothing," he assures me. "It just dawned on me that little B finally has a box."

TWENTY-FOUR

CALEB

AYA SITS NEXT TO me, her eyes round with wonder as her gaze skitters around our luscious surroundings. We're in the middle of the jungle in Cambodia, and the ancient, abandoned city of Angkor Wat stretches out before us, the largest religious complex in the world, and our new base. Four times as big as Vatican City, this former capital of the Khemer Empire stands as a testament of faith to Hinduism and its gods, Shiva, Brahma, and Vishnu—especially Vishnu. Though later taken over and still maintained by Buddhist monks, the five towers of the central temples were built to represent the dwelling place of the Hindu gods. The architecture is like a rich feast for the senses, each course more delicious than the last.

The conical towers are carved with precision and intricate detail to resemble lotus buds. Unlike what tourists—or even the monks see when they look at the temple—a riot of color greets my eyes. Splashes of gold, scarlet, and blue decorate the building, just as it did when the edifice was created. Bas-reliefs fill the walls of the sandstone temple, illustrating tales of the most famous Hindi epics. The pathways of Buddhist sculptures are a delight. Even the large trees that have meshed with the structure until they are now one with the stone add charm and beauty to this stunning display of human creativity. I can't help but think of how much my grandfather would love this place. How he would covet it for his own. But he never touched this part of the world, and he's not modern enough to Google it.

"I have to head back in," I tell my little sis, standing. Sweat beads at my hairline and rolls down my cheek. The humidity is oppressive, and it's been raining hard on and off since we arrived a few days ago. Birds and insects play a constant symphony that fills the silence, as tourists avoid Angkor Wat in the summer because of the overbearing heat and rain.

Aya and I observe the complex from the wall of the moat, enjoying the break in the weather. After my baby brother chose to stay with Team Conqueror, I decided to spend a little time with her before I have to inevitably leave again to fight Alexander. I don't tell her she has another brother, though. Aya doesn't need that burden, too. She's young and shaken and it's not fair. "We're having a big meeting inside." I ruffle her hair, and she grips my hand. My brow raises in question.

"Can you tell me anything? Are you leaving again?" she asks, fear threaded through her voice.

My large hand enfolds her smaller, delicate one. "No, I can't because I don't know anything concrete. But now that we have the kids back, we have to plan our next move. We can't let Gramps get the upper hand again." I squeeze her fingers and say as gently as I can, "Yeah, I'll probably be going away again. I'm too useful not to be used. And I won't let Luna go anywhere without me."

Her large eyes blink at me. "You mean to fight Alexander?" She shivers when I nod.

And to fight our brother. My gut clenches. Can I kill him? I don't know. I don't want to. "Yeah, to fight Grandfather. I'm not looking forward to it, believe me, but he has to be stopped." I lightly pull her to her feet. "I'll do my best to come back to you, kid. I have a promise to keep."

Her eyes narrow for a moment in thought, then she says, "To meet your mom, you mean?"

"To meet *our* mom," I tell her. "I told her all about you on our weekly call. She's already adopted you. Be prepared to be bossed around." I wink.

Aya punches me in the arm. "You better come back then," she says fiercely.

Rubbing my upper bicep in mock pain, I say, "Ouch, brat. Is that any way to treat family?"

She wraps her arms around me, burying her nose in my chest. Surprised, I hug her back tightly. I know we've only just met, but I've become an anchor for her in this chaotic world she's been thrust into, all the order in her life banished into uncertainty and fear.

"Let's go," I murmur into her hair. "You can walk back with me."

We're silent as we enter the city. I decide to take the eastern entrance of the temple so we can pass by the scene of the Churning Sea. This is one of my favorite bas-reliefs in the entire construction, and I want to sit here and nerd out, but the Council waits for no one. I spot Rafe and Shalina ahead, studying the wall with awe written on their faces. Of course, they'd be nerding out, too. They don't have the weight of the world on their shoulders. Yet.

Before I can call out to them, Aya says, "Let me guess? You're giving them babysitting duty again?" Bitterness edges her voice.

I cross my arms over my chest. "As you keep pointing out, you're not a baby. I just thought you'd like company. If you don't want to hang with them, just say so. Go find your friends from Megiddo. Besides, I thought you like Rafe and Lina."

She shrugs. "I do, but I hate being the third wheel. I don't want them to feel like they have to be my friends just because you're my brother."

Spare me from teenage dramatics. "You're basically just the female version of me, okay? I'm sure they appreciate you for your wit and sarcasm. Look, I don't really like you being alone. Not after…" I shut up when I see alarm flood her eyes.

"You don't think he can find us here, do you?" She can't hide the tremor in her voice, and I curse myself for opening my big mouth.

I shake my head and loop an arm around her shoulders. "No, he can't. I'm just being paranoid as fuck. You're safe here, I swear." Sighing, I add, "Just do your big bro a favor and ease my mind. Go with Rafe and Shalina, okay?"

Aya nods. "Fine, I will. Unless they give each other 'fuck me' eyes, then I'm outta there."

Chuckling, I say, "That's fair."

Shalina spots us and gives a little wave, and we make our way over to the duo.

"Hey, I gotta meet with the Council, and Aya desperately needs some lessons in art history. Can you two fill the gaps in her poor education?" I ask.

Rafe offers a fist bump. "Sure thing, man. And you will tell us what's going on at some point, right?" Ever since Alexander's people attacked us in Turkey, Rafe has been on edge. Not that I blame him.

"Yeah, Caleb, don't leave us out here blind," Shalina says, tapping a foot on the stone.

"I'll do what I can," I promise. "Now if you'll excuse me, I've left Goldilocks alone too long." It's ridiculous that I miss Luna when we've only been apart for a few hours, but we are all fools when it comes to love, and I am one big damn fool for that girl. And I wouldn't have it any other way.

Rafe rolls his eyes. "I never thought I'd see you so whipped," he teases, and I grin at him, unperturbed by his words.

"I don't mind being saddled," I shoot back, and Shalina giggles while Aya makes a face like she's just sucked on a whole basket of lemons.

"Ugh, any reference to my brother's sex life will *not* be tolerated," she says.

"Back at you, kiddo," I call over my shoulder as I walk away. I climb the steps and enter the temple proper. The air is immediately cooler as I move deeper into the interior. The rooms begin as grandiose and grow smaller and more intimate the higher you climb.

Vishnu stands outside the entryway to the top level of the temple. Built like a warrior born to swing a sword, his nose is a blade and his cheekbones knife points. Teal-green eyes gleam against the polished teak of his skin. I'm not fooled by his bored expression. We invaded his territory, and he desperately wants to be in the inner circle. Having mortals think of you as a god lends ancient Nephilim a staggering sense of arrogance and entitlement. Ishtar, anyone? I wonder if he was pissed when the Buddhists moved in.

His eyes narrow on me as I push past the silk curtain.

"Where are you going, young one?" he drawls. "This isn't a place for children."

My smile has teeth. I'm so over these inflated egos. "Vish, you're looking a little blue. Haven't you gotten the memo? I'm more important than you. Maybe if you really had four arms, the Council would find you useful." By the rage in his eyes, I think I just heard a big pop.

He takes an aggressive step toward me, the promise of violence in his eyes, when a tall figure built like a prize fighter steps between us.

"The boy is under my protection," Hammurabi rumbles. "And while I can certainly appreciate your desire for retribution, as the child's mouth tends to run away with him, I cannot allow that."

I take a step back, barely managing not to jump like a spooked cat. Where the hell did he come from? A dude that big should not be able to move so silently. This Christmas, I'm getting everyone silver bells. Still, his words lift me up. Ain't no one better to have on my side than Uncle Hammurabi.

Vishnu's sneer drips with derision. "You cannot allow it? Who are you to allow me anything, Dark?"

Oh, for fuck's sake. Hammurabi's shoulders tense, and I brace myself for a brawl—one that I'm responsible for and feel shitty about—when a slender ivory hand curls over my shoulder, and I nearly leap out of my skin. Bells, goddamn bells for everyone.

Asmodeus's husky voice croons, "While I have utter faith that my Babylonian king can hold his own against you, Light, *I* won't allow you to attack the child. He's *mine* as well, and I always protect my students."

Vishnu goes rigid, wary eyes latched onto the Archdemon. I know he resents her for intervening, for having to obey her. But she's the great white shark here and he's just a barracuda, waiting to get snapped up.

Asmodeus stuns me by ruffling my hair. "Even when they behave badly, but the poor lamb has had a terrible few months, so you'll have to excuse him, Vishnu. Being the grandson of the Great carries heavy burdens. And you know the rules—no infighting. We are at war. Don't make me report you to Uriel."

"That won't be necessary," the Hindu god pushes out through clenched teeth.

The Archdemon gives him a feline smile. "Run along now"—she flicks her fingers at him as if he's an annoying fly buzzing around her—"Uriel will call you if you're needed."

The Nephilim's cheeks flush a deep red before he stalks off down the corridor. Hammurabi chuckles before turning and delivering a hard stare at me.

"You need to curb that tongue, boy. I won't always be around to save you."

I rub the back of my neck. "He was a dick first," I protest, guilt trickling through me.

"Caleb." Asmodeus's tone is bland but I flinch.

"I'm sorry and super grateful you saved my ass from a beating—not that I wouldn't have fought back," I say.

Hammurabi actually rolls his eyes at me. "Of course, you would. I trained you. I trust you would have inflicted some damage of your own."

"I'm sorry about your brother's defection," the Archdemon says, looping an arm through mine and leading me inside where some of the Council await. I guess they heard our little scuffle as I'm met with disapproving looks.

Acid churns in my gut. "Yeah, me too," I bite out, suddenly full of bitterness. I just found him and now we're on opposite sides. At least I'm not attached to him like Aya. That's a small blessing.

My gaze snags on the ossuary vessel in the middle of the room, pulling me out of my depressing thoughts. A shiver ripples over my skin, chasing away the last remnants of heat. Olympia's ashes reside in there. That's my kinda great-grandmother. Robbing graves doesn't exactly sit well with me, but it's not like we had much of a choice. Ever since Ishtar concocted the scheme to release Alexander, my whole life has been a series of pick the least shitty option. The only good choice I got to make was saving Luna. That's one choice I'll never regret.

Speaking of Goldilocks, she enters the small chamber with Alaric. Her eyes sweep the room until they meet mine. She leads Alaric to where I stand, holding up the wall, with Hammurabi and Asmodeus. I grin at her, letting my tension melt away, as she wraps her arms around me. She's worried about me—about what happened with my brother—and I appreciate her support, though the role reversal makes me a little uncomfortable. I'm used to taking care of her. I bury my face in her hair and inhale her sweet scent. The others greet each other with quiet murmurs, and when I surface, I see Alaric watching us with an indulgent smile.

He hasn't been out of Luna's company much since we arrived at Angkor Wat. When he's not with her—or the two of us—he's with Hammurabi and Asmodeus or Gabriel and Lucifer. Hammurabi has been especially kind to the other Nephilim, who still appears fragile. Someone as old and strong as Alaric shouldn't look that vulnerable, and my gut clenches at the haunted expression in his eyes.

He left the love of his life—gave Gramps the big middle finger. And despite the fact that I know he wants to be here—that he doesn't want Alexander to take over the world—that shit has to hurt. Even if Luna had turned out to be the Destroyer, I don't think I would have been strong enough to abandon her. Alaric is pure titanium.

"Hey, man, you look rested," I lie, smiling at him. "Happy to have you at these meetings. You can bring in some much-needed warm and fuzzies."

A chuckle bursts from his lips, and he looks surprised, like he didn't realize he could still laugh. "Never change, Caleb. I missed your roguish charm."

I smirk. "I don't plan to."

Hammurabi sighs. "Don't encourage him," he mutters.

"I like you just the way you are," Luna tells me, hazel eyes sparkling. My lips cling to hers for a moment.

"Oh, the fallacies of young love," Asmodeus says, and I break away from Luna to grin at her. I appreciate this banter between my family. It feels normal in a time where absolutely nothing is.

Then Gabriel and Lucifer walk in accompanied by Lilith and the rest of the Council with a few higher-ranking Nephilim trailing behind, and the levity is broken.

As always, I track Mammon's movements, and his ruby eyes find mine for a brief moment. The hatred there burns so hot I force myself not to cower and hide. Instead, I avert my gaze as if he's not important enough for me to worry about. I know my dismissal of his threat will piss him off even more. Luna whirls around, her back to my front, and glares at the Archdemon, as if daring him to try anything. Her fierceness no longer surprises me, and I rest a hand on her hip and squeeze, letting her know I'm okay.

The one-winged chicken ignores us both and settles next to Uriel. For two beings who warred with each other, they're surprisingly chummy. But I guess it's all the enemy of my enemy and shit.

Lucifer and Gabriel settle on the other side of me and Luna with Beelzebub slipping in next to them. This chamber isn't very large, and with the ossuary taking up space, it's a bit claustrophobic.

"We have taken something precious from the Conqueror, and now is the time to draw him out," Uriel begins, then he nods to Alaric. "Son of Michael, you have our endless gratitude for not only giving us a means to retrieve our children, but to lure Alexander to a place of our choosing to end his threat once and for all. You're forgiven any and all past transgressions and will be greatly rewarded."

What past transgressions is that dick referring to? Loving Alexander or helping free Luna from her cage? Although the Council now believes she's the Savior, I know they're petty enough to hold Alaric's actions against him, even if they were the ones in the wrong.

Alaric just bows his head and says, "I'm grateful for the Council's generosity. I am here to serve."

I smother a derisive snort, as always ever impressed by his grace, even if the Council doesn't deserve it.

"Do you truly believe Alexander will surrender in exchange for his mother's remains?" Azrael asks from his seat in a corner. His mouth is a moue of distaste. "That's very sentimental for an angel bent on ruling."

I want to punch that guy in the face. Lilith rolls her eyes so hard it's almost audible. For the first time, anger stirs on Alaric's face.

"Of course not, but he will come for her," he hisses at the angel of death. "Did he not leave his palace to pursue her grave robbers? His mother meant more to him than anything in this world. Most of you weren't raised with a parent, so you cannot hope to understand, unless you have a child of your own," Alaric says, his voice a blade of contempt. "He will go to any lengths to retrieve her—and punish us for her theft. No, he won't surrender, but we can draw him out."

I guess Alaric doesn't think the Creator was much of a parent. I can't say that I disagree with him. Azrael stiffens at Alaric's tone, but Raphael steps forward and stares down her fellow angel.

"Alaric is right," she says. "We all know Alexander values humans more than his celestial brethren. He especially held his mother dear. Didn't you say, Lucifer, that he would have raised her if he could?" The Morningstar nods. "So you see, Azrael, you can stop with your bothersome doubts. I'm sure you'll attain much glory in battle, which is what you really want anyway."

I bite my lip at her scathing tone. Even on the eve of battle, the angels still squabble like a bunch of back-stabbing teenagers. It hardly inspires confidence.

"Enough," Uriel barks. "Stop yipping at one another like stray dogs. It's beneath you." Raphael and Azrael glower at Uriel, but he ignores them. "We'll need to send a messenger to Alexander with terms for his surrender. We'll tell him to meet us in the Arabian Desert, far from humans. There, we will end this."

There are nods and murmurs of assent rippling around the room. I just want this over and done with. I'm tired of balancing on a knife's edge, waiting to see if I'll get cut, so I raise a hand, waving my fingers.

Uriel's brows form a vee of surprise as his eyes connect with mine. For a moment, I don't think he'll acknowledge me, then he says, begrudgingly, "Yes, little Dark?"

"I volunteer as tribute," I tell him, lowering my hand, and I hear Luna gasp. Winking at her, I say to Uriel, "I'll text Ishtar with the conditions of returning my kinda great-grandmother, and she can give them to Alexander." As the Archangel's jaw slackens in shock, I chuckle. "What? You thought I was volunteering to meet Gramps's people in person? I'm not that crazy." Slipping my cell phone from my pocket, I hold it up. "I have Ishtar's number. Just tell me what to text, and I'll make sure she gets the memo. Easy peasy lemon squeezy."

Stunned silence meets me for a moment as all these beings who are basically primordial sludge—with the exception of Luna—stare at me in bafflement. Goldilocks wears a huge grin, and I bite my inner cheek hard to keep from laughing. At this point, I fully expect the angels and Fallen to take drummers into battle, announcing our arrival.

Lucifer does laugh. "Yes, that makes sense, Caleb."

"My students always show brilliant initiative," Asmodeus purrs.

Uriel gives a slow nod. "Yes, I suppose that will do. I shall dictate what you need to say after the meeting. Well done," he says, his expression turning sour as those last two words leave his lips.

"No problem," I say, smirking at him. Man, will Ishtar be pissed that I'm the one sending demands for Grandfather's surrender—just another reason she'll want to kill me.

Ignoring me, he continues, "Though we are fighting as one, Darks and Lights know their forces best, and we shall lead our own units. Lucifer, as you led the great rebellion, it's only fitting you lead the Darks in this fight." Mammon's mouth thins at his words, and I smother a grin. "You inspire loyalty, not only with our beloved first generation Nephilim, but with your students—of all Dark academies." Huh, the Archangel got all that out without choking. And he sounded sincere. Miracles do happen.

Lucifer inclines his head. "It would be my honor."

Uriel's eyes suddenly narrow on me, and I resist the urge to flinch at his focus. Luna moves a little in front of me, offering protection from the Archangel. I want to kiss her, but Uriel's dour expression cools the urge.

"Students will have to fight, too," the Archangel says, and my stomach sours. Yes, I know I'll fight, but I hoped the student body would be left out. "The loss of our teachers in Derinkuyu has left a dent in our forces. Final year students are capable and trained. We would be foolish not to use this resource. And as Caleb has proven, young Nephilim can be very resourceful indeed. Only a babe and he managed to wound the Messenger and maim the Shapeshifter."

Mammon almost purples with fury at Uriel's words, and I'd like to sink into the stone behind me as his scarlet gaze locks onto mine. The promise of death lies in those red depths. It must be humiliating for him to be reminded in front of the Council that a lowly second generation Nephilim cut his wing off.

"I agree that our students are well trained," Abaddon says, drawing my attention away from the psychotic Archdemon. His arms are crossed over his broad chest. "But they are untried in a real battle. Are they more of a liability than an asset? Will they fight or run? Young Caleb has demonstrated much fortitude in situations even older Nephilim would struggle with, and he should step out on the battlefield with us. But the rest of them..."

"If they run, Alexander's troops will chase them, drawing them away from the battle, and they'll still be an asset. Even if it is as fodder," Mammon says, gaze still on me, his voice so cold I almost have frostbite.

Asmodeus stiffens beside me. "Our students are not fodder, Brother," she hisses, and the air around me loses its tropical warmth as ice crackles along all the surfaces. Mamma bear is turning this place into the Fortress of Solitude.

"Apparently losing your wing made you lose your mind as well," Beelzebub growls, his darkness lashing around him like whips.

"We're at war. This is a reality we have to face if we want to save the world," Mammon counters. "You put unbloodied soldiers into battle, and some will die. This is reality."

I really think he means he hopes I die, but I swallow that thought. "The fodder comment is some cold shit," I say, drawing the attention of everyone in the room. "But kids dying, yeah, that's true. I get why you want to put us out there, and I'll do my best to help the students get ready for what's coming if you do decide to use us." I direct my gaze at Uriel. "I don't like it, but I understand the necessity. That being said, it should be on a volunteer basis. We shouldn't force anyone who is too scared to fight." That's what Alexander would do and I don't want to be anything like my gramps. Still, I should do my best to rally the troops and give us as much of an advantage as we can get. I know the Dark students will step up and listen to me if I tell them the real deal, but I don't know if the Lights will. Guess I have my work cut out for me.

"I agree. Thank you, Caleb," Asmodeus says. "As I've always said, Babel students are exceptional."

Blushing at her praise, my eyes meet Luna's, and I shrug at her stunned expression. She's stepped up into her Savior role. Now, I have to step up, too.

Uriel's eyes dart around the room. "Shall we vote on it?"

Although there is some reluctance, everyone raises their hand in confirmation, and just like that, kids are going to war. A knot forms in my stomach, tightening like a fist.

Uriel nods, a look of grim determination on his face. "It's decided then. Let us send Alexander our invitation and start moving out the troops."

TWENTY-FIVE

LUNA

THE ARABIAN DESERT STRETCHES out before me like a barren sea, the large outcroppings of rock marking the horizon like violent waves frozen in time. According to my parents, this part of the desert was a lake thousands of years ago, but now, the earth beneath our feet is cracked and scorched—devoid of human life and, today, all life in general, as the animals residing here hide out of sight, aware a threat has descended on their home. As my eyes scan the flat, dusty ground, I can't escape the thought that this all feels somewhat apocalyptic, like an omen. That thought is sobering and reminds me of how much is at stake should we lose.

I peer at my parents and Lilith, who stand to my left side, then up at Caleb, who stands close on my right, his sweaty palm clamped tight to my own. Although I can hear the thunderous clash of his heart against his ribcage, he appears calm, like a duck, perfectly at ease on the water while its legs kick madly under the surface. He looks determined. No...not exactly determined, I suppose, but resigned. Like he's accepted his role in this battle and the inevitability of it all.

Just as I have.

I breathe out through my nose, squeezing his fingers, my nerves a constant, anxious flutter under my skin. The text he sent Ishtar after our meeting with the Council two days ago read like a ransom letter, and I have no doubt it would've only thrown fuel on the fire of Alexander's rage. While that was the point—a necessary evil to draw the Gray here while those heightened emotions make him vulnerable and put an end to this conflict between us, to fulfill the prophecy, whichever way fate intends it to go—I wish we had more time to prepare. That *I* had more time to prepare.

Once again, my eyes slide to my parents and Lilith, my gaze catching on my mother, who stands tall in her golden armor, her bronze-hilted sword strapped to her back. The other Archangels and Archdemons are all dressed similarly, resembling mighty warriors from Heaven. This is the first time I've ever seen my father in his armor from the Fall, and he looks like a gleaming god, his blond curls reflecting the sunlight. The Fallen wear their armor, too, but the Nephilim and people like me who weren't alive to fight during the Fall don't have such a luxury to rely on, and there wasn't time to figure out an alternative. Not when we were sequestered away, just trying to stay off Alexander's radar until the final battle. It was a risk just sending out small teams to the academies—now emptied of angel-killing steel and children, the schools would no longer be a draw to Alexander in theory—to retrieve the training weapons stored at each to at least arm the Nephilim on our side for the battle. But they weren't stocked with any armor other than what was in the museums from the Fall. As such, with nothing to use for additional protection, we remain in modern clothes—jeans, T-shirts, and even one or two business suits among the crowd of checkered gold and shadowed auras behind us, though nothing too loose to be a hindrance when fighting. It's a strange contrast to the almost majestic appearance of the angels and Fallen, as if the past has collided with the present.

One Fall merging with what may well be another.

Like armor, our supply of weapons from the Fall—weapons that can actually kill angels and Fallen—is scant. Although we managed to reclaim most of what Alexander's forces stole, too many on our side are equipped with ordinary swords and daggers that might be able to kill Nephilim but will be useless against the Fallen we're about to go to arms with. Even I face this battle empty-handed. The weapons of our bloodlines are in limited supply, and the two I *am* capable of wielding will be far more deadly in my parents' hands than they would be in mine. With everything that's been going on, there's only been time for a few—somewhat disastrous—sparring lessons with Lilith, and I'm nowhere near proficient enough with a physical weapon to rely on one to keep me alive. But I can't sit this battle out, and I wouldn't, even if that was an option. Fate has dictated that I need to be here, perhaps more than anyone aside from Alexander.

So, the plan is to stay close to my parents and Lilith and to use the innate talents I have to fight. I just hope that will be enough to keep me alive—at least long enough to end this.

"Don't worry, Goldilocks. Everything will go our way. It has to," Caleb whispers, nudging my shoulder with his. "After all, you're the Savior. We're meant to win."

I grin at him, though the expression is forced.

"Caleb's right," a familiar timbre says in my ear, and I glance over my shoulder to find Alaric behind me standing close to Hammurabi, who looms over Caleb like a helicopter parent keeping a close eye on their toddler. A warm smile curls the corners of the Nephilim's lips as his honey eyes lock on mine. "Plus, I'll be with you the whole time, I promise."

Relief flushes through me like a strong rush of heat, and I nod, comforted by the notion of having Alaric by my side through this. I'm going to need him to ground me, to keep me calm, because once the battle begins, Caleb won't be able to—as much as I hate the idea of separating, especially with Mammon out here on the battlefield with us, we'd be too big of a distraction to each other, and I have enough people protecting me as it is. Besides, Alexander's sights will be set on me, and I want Caleb as far away from his grandfather as possible. It's the only way I can keep him safe—the farther he is from me, the more likely he'll make it out of this alive, even if I don't. And Caleb also has skills that can be put to better use elsewhere, not only as a warrior but as a leader. The Archangels and Archdemons have their own forces to lead, and Caleb is someone the students who volunteered to fight can trust—who even the Lights would be persuaded to follow into battle, knowing he rushed into it first, not wanting to seem like cowards next to a Dark. They might not be so willing with an angel or Fallen, who don't need to fear death the way Nephilim do. And that is the role we both know he needs to play, even if it means we won't be at each other's sides through this fight. Even if it means that, if everything goes very wrong, this moment now is the last one we'll have together.

My stomach curdles at that thought as a building panic rises up through my body and settles in my throat, trying to choke me. Immediately, I feel Calm sweep through my senses, putting me at ease. Without it, I'm not sure I'll stay sane.

Breathing out, I offer Alaric a small smile. "No regrets?" I ask.

I don't mean choosing to fight by my side, but choosing to fight in this war at all. While I have no doubt in my mind that Alaric will go to blows with Alexander if it comes to that, that he'll protect me no matter the cost, I need to make sure the events of today won't break him when it's finally over.

"No regrets," Alaric echoes. Then bowing his head, he reaches over his shoulder, producing a short, copper-hilted sword from a leather sheath on his back. The blade gleams in the sunlight, which highlights the swooping symbols etched cleanly into the steel.

"Is that...?" I trail off, my eyes going wide.

"Enochian," Caleb murmurs beside me. "Yeah. That is definitely a weapon from the Fall. I didn't know you had one, Alaric."

"My father's," Alaric says nonchalantly as he stares down at the sword in his hand. "It was found among Alexander's possessions in Persepolis with the other purloined weapons from the academies."

My lips purse. "Do you think Alexander knew it was there?"

If he did, then he's either incredibly confident in his hold over Alaric, or he just enjoys toying with death. Maybe he even got a thrill from knowing Alaric could've ended his immortal life had he any inclination to.

Alaric nods, his gaze growing distant, though there's a tightness to his jaw that wasn't there a moment ago. "I imagine so."

Caleb sneers. "The bastard probably didn't even try to hide it."

"No," Alaric agrees. "Had I thought to search for it, I would've easily found it with the others."

"Kind of brazen of him," I mutter. "How did he know you wouldn't go looking for it?"

"He didn't," Alaric admits, his teeth gritted. "He likely just assumed I would never dare use it against him."

His fingers clench around the hilt, and I frown at the burning intensity of his aura, which pulsates around him like a beating heart. I can only imagine the complexity of emotions Alaric must be working through right now. He probably never wanted to lay eyes on his father's sword, let alone use it, and now, he's faced with fighting the very person he once protected from his father with the weapon Michael would have likely used to kill Alexander. That's a betrayal Alaric can never come back from. The final nail in the coffin of the love he shared with the Gray.

I open my mouth, hoping to say something reassuring, but I can't find the words, and a sudden shout distracts me from any further attempts.

"Forces sighted!" a Fallen scout who had been hovering a half mile above us bellows as he descends, retaking his place among our army.

"Looks like shit's about to get real," Caleb says, and his hand tightens around mine as I narrow my eyes on the rocky horizon, waiting for whatever the Fallen saw to appear. I don't have to wait long. Within seconds, a dark silhouetted herd emerges from the hazy distance like a mirage in the desert heat. I can sense Caleb's fear in the way his pulse flutters rapidly under the skin in his hand, the movements reflected in his aura, and in the muttered string of curses slipping past his lips. My own heart trips at the size of Alexander's force, my only consolation being that ours is bigger—

though not by much from the looks of it. Still, unease grips me because too many on our side are unseasoned in battle. Like me. So much is riding on my shoulders, and I'm about as competent at fighting as I am at flying. Quality over quantity, as they say, and experience will win this battle over numbers.

I turn my head side to side, my gaze drifting over my shoulders, searching for the familiar faces of the Archangels and Archdemons scattered tactically among our forces.

We have the Council, I remind myself. *We have the most powerful angels on our side.*

My eyes stray to the Light and Dark to my left, standing side by side, hands tightly clasped.

We have my parents.

That alone has to count for something.

I swallow, forcing myself to focus on the incoming threat—to have faith that we can and *will* succeed—but apprehension drowns out what little confidence I manage to find among my darkening thoughts when it dawns on me that Alexander is nowhere to be seen. A solitary figure emerges from the enemy force, their face sliding into sharp focus as they draw closer, but that figure is not the Gray I'm destined to battle here.

It's Ishtar.

Caleb tenses beside me, and I cling even tighter to his hand for support, though I don't know if I intend it for me or for him.

I spare him a glance, noting the hard lines of his face, and a scowl hardens my own as my mother calls out, "Goddess of love and war, where is your master?"

Ishtar pauses her advance twenty or so yards away—close enough to converse with us while keeping a safe distance from the angry flock of angels who would all happily tear her to shreds. She's wearing a black armored vest over her clothes, modern in look, like a human soldier heading to battle—just like the armor Alexander's soldiers donned that first day in Kandahār when we were escorted to the citadel like prisoners of war. It's human-made—nothing that will protect her from a blade from the Fall—but protection enough against our mortal weapons. And more than our own Nephilim have to protect them.

Caleb goes even more rigid as Ishtar approaches, his hand a vise now, strangling mine.

Shrugging, the goddess gives a lazy wave of one hand, fluttering her fingers. "Around," she coos, her tone flippant and taunting. "He's sent me as his emissary to oversee our...negotiations."

"This isn't a negotiation," Uriel snaps. The Archangel steps forward, moving to the front of the crowd to stand near my parents and Lilith, and for once, they appear as a united front instead of as reluctant allies. "If the Conqueror wishes to see his mother's remains returned intact, he *must* surrender. If not, he will die. As will you. Those are our terms."

"Just fucking accept, damn you," Caleb whispers, as if he's trying to will the thought into existence, even if we both know that will never happen. My eyes peruse his face again, and my heart breaks for him in this moment—for how much he mourns the teacher he once loved and looked up to.

But that woman, whoever she was before all this, is gone.

Ishtar crosses her arms and taps a long finger against her chin, her dark eyes skimming the ground as she paces, as if she's genuinely considering the Archangel's offer. But I know better. I can tell by the ease of her steps and by the glint in those eyes, which she turns on Caleb as a wicked smile curls the corners of her lips. He flinches under the heat of her stare when she hisses, "Not if we kill you first."

Then, in a movement that's almost too fast for even my eyes to track, she lifts her hand, and all I see is the concealed blade leaving her fingers before I have the chance to fully register her words. It's not a large dagger, but, like any blade, it's large enough to kill should it hit the right target.

Especially if that target is mortal.

I barely have time to think as the knife sails toward Caleb, and with more force than necessary, I yank on his hand, pulling him down to the ground. I shift then, taking his place in our line-up so no one behind us takes the hit in his stead. I don't hesitate. After all, I'm an angel. This dagger can't hurt me like it can hurt Caleb or any of the other Nephilim—

A surprised grunt escapes my lips as the sharp sting of metal pierces my skin, then terror unlike anything I've ever felt burns through me as fire spreads across my shoulder and the blade sinks deeper, cutting through sinew and bone.

"Luna!" several voices shout, though the one that rings the loudest is Caleb's. He scrambles to his feet, but I'm barely aware of him or the others swarming me, my thoughts focused solely on the dagger embedded in my right shoulder.

Wincing, I wrap my fingers around the silver handle and pull, and as the blade slides free of my flesh, I glimpse the Enochian symbols etched into the blood-coated metal.

My eyes widen. From a distance, this looked like a normal blade, the symbols masked by Ishtar's grip. But it's not. It's a weapon from the Fall—belonging to one of Ishtar's parents, wherever they may be. I don't understand. When we were in Kandahār, I never once saw Ishtar with one of these blades. Was this why? So she could take us by surprise? But by throwing this dagger at Caleb, she all but tossed it away, like trash to be discarded. There's no way we'll return it to her, so what's her plan for defending herself when the battle begins and my parents go after her? And they *will* go after her for this. They'll be out for her blood.

I find Ishtar through a gap in the worried faces around me, and she smirks as if reading my mind before turning and sprinting away, retreating to rejoin the waiting army in the distance.

"Is that…?" Caleb begins, trailing off when I toss the bloodied dagger to the ground with a sneer.

"Angel-killing steel," my father says grimly, hovering over my injured shoulder.

"Why waste an Enochian blade on a Nephilim?" my mother asks, giving voice to the same thoughts plaguing me. She glances between my face and Caleb's, her brow creased with the fear of what—for a fleeting moment—she might have thought she lost.

"She didn't," I whisper as the realization hits me. The angels and Nephilim crowded around me—my parents, Lilith, Uriel, Alaric, Hammurabi, and Caleb—all look at me, not comprehending what I just have. I clear my throat, holding in every urge I have to weep at the pain, and press my hand to my shoulder, which bleeds as if I'm human again. Blood, warm and sticky, seeps between my fingers. "He wasn't her target. I was."

Because she knew I wouldn't let Caleb die. That I would make the exact idiotic assumption I made and step in front of any weapon thrown his way. That I would mistake my immortality for invulnerability. Had I been standing a few inches to the right, she could've ended this battle before it even began. And then, the Conqueror—the Destroyer—would've won.

And I would have cost us everything.

For Ishtar, that chance was worth losing such a weapon.

"That bitch is even more sadistic than I am," Lilith seethes, the tendrils of her aura snapping like a tattered cape in the wind.

"And she will die here today," my mother vows. Fury gleams in her orange-ringed eyes as she turns her sights on Alexander's army, drawing her sword.

I nod, biting back the searing pain in my shoulder and pushing it behind my anger. It won't heal quickly—I know from the wound my mother received under the Serapeum—so I just have to hope the distraction of battle and literally fighting for my life will keep me going. "Just like Alexander," I promise.

"He was given a chance," Uriel growls, and exchanging a meaningful look with my father, he spreads his wings, taking his weapon in hand. A shadow darkens Lucifer's gaze as he nods at the Archangel and pulls his own sword free of its sheath. Ebony feathers cut through the air with a whoosh as he extends his wings, and then, with one final, worried glance at me, he raises his hand, giving the signal to attack.

Chaos ensues as angels and Fallen sprint forward at my father's unspoken command, their bodies racing past where I stand in a blur. I follow their movements, my heart a symphony of hurried notes, a needed rush of adrenaline spiking through my blood that helps stave off the pain.

Curling my hands into fists, I once again glance at the army in the distance, only to find Alexander's forces have grown closer and grow nearer yet with every passing second.

This is it, I realize.

The battle is beginning.

My eyes cut to Caleb's when he frantically grabs hold of my uninjured arm. "Luna." His gaze wanders to my wound, his expression conflicted, his lips pinched tight in concern. Concern neither of us have time for now.

"I'll be okay. *Go!*" I urge him.

"Stick to the plan, boy!" Hammurabi shouts, roughly grasping his shoulder. "The flower will be fine."

Caleb hesitates for only a second before taking my face in his hands and pressing his lips to mine in a bruising kiss. "I love you," he says. But behind those three precious words, I hear two others.

Be careful.

"I love you, too," I whisper.

Grimacing, he lowers his hands and runs in the opposite direction of the awaiting fray toward the other Dark and Light students who agreed to fight alongside us. Like me, Hammurabi watches his retreating figure for a moment before he races off to join Asmodeus's forces as planned. They have their own task to deal with today. And I have mine.

My mother's dark eyes dart over her shoulder, locking on mine, and I give her a nod. I'm ready. Or as much as I'll ever be.

Lilith and Alaric flank me on each side while my parents position themselves in front of me, leading the charge as we move forward together, the dirt and sand kicking up around our feet as we shift across the cracked earth. Every impact of my feet against the ground sends a shock wave of pain through my shoulder, but I clench my jaw and keep going, refusing to let this injury slow me down or stop me from what we came here to do. I don't want my parents, Lilith, and Alaric to worry about me anymore than they already are, either.

As we run, closing the distance to what may very well end up being my demise, Alaric says under his breath, "Don't show it."

I risk a questioning glance at him before turning my gaze back to the approaching army, which rolls toward us like a violent wave. We're mere moments from colliding, and I only hope I won't be drowned by the force of it. "What?" I ask him, unable to hide the tremble in my voice.

"Your astral projection," he answers, and I don't miss the warning in his tone. "Don't show it until the last moment. It's one of the only elements of surprise we have."

I choke out a doubtful laugh. "We have others?"

"Just one," he whispers, the words so low I almost don't even hear them.

A frown tugs at my lips. "I'm a little short on other party tricks, Alaric," I retort, feeling more unprepared than ever. "I don't think my fire on its own is enough."

"That's why you have us!" Lilith crows from my right, and I notice she looks almost excited by the prospect of fighting. "Just watch your back and stay close."

"We will protect you, no matter the cost to us," my father vows, almost shouting the words. He runs a few steps ahead of me, his large sword clutched tight in his right hand, which he raises now, lobbing off the head of a Fallen who foolishly believed they could take on the Morningstar.

"And no matter who has to die," my mother growls, side-swiping a duo of Nephilim with lethal precision, spilling their guts onto the desert floor.

There's no more talking after that, only the somewhat maniacal laughter that keeps coming from Lilith. Uriel has vanished among the horde, and I only catch passing glimpses of the other Council members, on missions of their own to downsize Alexander's forces. Around me, I hear battle cries and the clash of metal on metal, but so much of the noise is drowned out by my thundering pulse as a near debilitating terror courses through my veins like a drug. My feet are in a constant shuffle, my brain screaming at me over and over again to turn my back so I don't leave myself exposed. Flames erupt across my palms like lava, but when I'm not busy hurling fire at anyone who comes too close or floundering at the brink of a panic attack, I find myself watching Alaric, his figure as graceful in combat as it is in all other manners of life. He wields his father's sword with deadly accuracy, which surprises me given his kind and gentle demeanor that makes it hard to envision him even hurting a fly, let alone another person.

Like Alaric, Lilith is a force to be reckoned with. She brandishes her own weapon from the Fall—returned to her by the Council after our last meeting to aid us in this fight—a long, curved dagger of devastating consequence that resembles a farming sickle. Her death of choice is the throat slit, which she executes at least a dozen times in the span of only a minute. I'm both in awe of and terrified of her, perhaps because, in a lot of ways, her fighting style reminds me of Nzingha and Ishtar—graceful like Alaric but almost catlike, as if she's playing with her food before eating it.

Maybe that's just the Dark way of fighting, I consider, or maybe Lilith, Nzingha, and Ishtar are just a bit more twisted than the rest of us.

A blood-curdling scream has me whipping around as shadows submerge the battlefield, and from their midst, I glimpse Beelzebub, walking forward without a care in the world, his youthful face murderous with intent as he rips one Nephilim after another apart from within using his terrifying power. Abaddon lurks beside him, cutting down any strays, his vigilance around the other Archdemon reminding me of a sworn knight watching over a child prince.

Beelzebub's eyes find mine in the disarray, and he touches his pointer finger to his right temple, giving me a little salute before concentrating his wrath on his next victim.

My chest heaves as I search for other familiar faces in the throng. I spot a few— Nzingha taking out several Nephilim with her kunai, Uriel slashing at Lights, possibly even the ones who attacked us on the Blessed Road, Asmodeus encasing her victims in ice and then shattering them into frozen pieces with a swipe of her sword— but aside from them, there are too many bodies—both standing and slain—on the battlefield, and after a few moments, I recognize nothing except a deep, crippling sense of danger.

Briefly, I let my harrowed thoughts drift to Caleb, but I push them away as soon as they form. I can't think about him right now or else the worry will eat me alive.

The minutes stretch uncomfortably long, and I do my best to keep up with the others and ignore the ceaseless pain in my shoulder. Around me, my parents, Lilith, and Alaric move in tandem with me always at the center, guarded by them on all sides. But I know this shield of protection can't last. Eventually, I'll have to face Alexander. And when that time comes, I have a feeling fate intends for me to do it alone.

Movement in the corner of my eye grabs my attention, my gaze catching on a Fallen approaching Lilith from behind as she fights off two Dark Nephilim.

"Lilith!" I shout.

She spins, cutting through her two attackers with the curved side of her sickle, then snaps her head toward me as fire blazes across my palms, my shoulder protesting when I raise my hands. With all the force I can muster, I then push my power outward, directing it at the Fallen, who shrieks as the flames lick over her wings.

Lilith whips around, blade raised and ready, but the Fallen writhes on the ground now, trying to put out the hungry inferno, all thought of killing the ex-Archdemon forgotten. Lilith doesn't hesitate. She drops to one knee and brings her arm down with brutal force, dragging her blade across the Dark's throat.

"Cheers, doll," she calls, shooting me a grateful look.

I let out a relieved breath and straighten slightly, shaking out my arm and carefully rotating my injured shoulder. The wound from where Ishtar stabbed me hurts like hell—a burning agony that screams every time my skin stretches and moves. The pain is only made worse when an unseen force knocks me off my feet, slamming my back into the ground. The impact itself doesn't hurt—not like my once mortal mind trained me to expect—but the vibration running through my shoulder is a different kind of pain altogether.

Clenching my jaw, I force myself into a sitting position and clamber to my feet, coughing as I breathe in what feels like a lungful of sand. The air around me is suddenly thick, my vision obscured by a swirling storm of beige, and my teeth are gritty with dust, which hovers over the desert floor like fog. I peer through the haze, apprehensive of the oppressive surge of power crackling through the atmosphere—like lightning on the cusp of striking—trying to pinpoint the source of it, even if my gut already knows that answer.

As I scour my surroundings for Alexander, I note the angels, Fallen, and Nephilim struggling to rise up from the ground. They must've been pushed down to the desert floor, just like I was, and yet, there's something…prohibitive about their movements as they climb to their feet. Worry eats at me as I try and fail to find Alaric and Lilith. I scream their names—I scream Caleb's name—but no one answers me, not even my parents. Desperation is a physical force crushing my chest, my focus shifting between the faces around me so fast it makes me dizzy. When I finally locate Gabriel and Lucifer through the now-blustering winds, my eyes snag on my mother. Even from a distance and through the dust storm still raging around us, I can see her reaching out to me, just like that day under the Serapeum when the Dark ward stood between us. But this time, I can't hear a single word she's saying, although I can read my name on her lips.

My father's face is equally agonized, and it's only when I take a step toward them that I see it—the wall of energy separating us. The glasslike barrier just like the one I destroyed in Olympias's tomb.

A Gray ward, I realize, a surge of bile rushing up my throat.

The relief that chased away my fear at the sight of my parents disappears as quickly as it surfaced. How the hell did Alexander erect a ward around me and separate me from the others so easily? I snap my head side to side, taking in the full scale of the ward, my dread growing in size to match its breadth. It's *big*—significantly larger than the one I destroyed in the tomb in Korinos. I'm not even sure I can break it and I'm nowhere close enough to its boundary to try. Swallowing, I take another step toward my parents, my heart a lead weight in my chest, then falter when the howling winds suddenly die—the dust and sand that was swirling through the air now falling to the ground like rain.

A strange sensation prickles my skin, and I whip around, searching for those mismatched eyes amidst the thousands of others watching me. I can feel him, just as I feel like a sheep that's been corralled exactly where the lion wants me to go, my movements growing increasingly frantic as I search for his face in the surrounding crowd.

I hear his chuckle before I see him, and when I spin on my heel, our gazes finally clash. Alexander walks toward me, his pace leisurely and dagger in hand, dressed like a king in a white tunic and red chlamys that scream of his intention to rule over all, a golden crown of leaves on his head. His aura is a swirl of razor sharp glass that I half expect to lash out and slice me to ribbons.

I glance around again, desperation and terror rocking my core, searching for help I know won't come, and that's when I see it—the bodies twisting on the sand that now climb to their feet like revenants rising from the grave. Horror spreads through me, hot and fast.

He's resurrecting them. A sick feeling twists my stomach in knots. *Just like he said he would.*

I try to swallow the lump lodged in my windpipe, but my mouth and throat are sandpaper dry. Flop sweat beads at my hairline, even as I tell myself to be brave, but how can I be brave when Alexander is resurrecting his soldiers, leaving us with no true way to defeat them unless we kill their master and sever that connection? When the death of said master now hinges solely on me, and I don't have the means to put him down without help? My fire might hurt him for a few moments, but on my own, I'm powerless to kill Alexander, whereas one plunge from his dagger will snuff out my immortal life.

I take a step back, stalling for time. I'm so far out of my depth. I was foolish to think we could ever possibly prevail. I'm completely defenseless, I'm injured, and I'm going to die here on this battlefield, just like everyone else I care about.

My thoughts flip through their faces like the pages of a photo album, but most of all, they linger on Caleb, and my heart aches thinking of everything we won't ever have. I wish I could see him one last time before I die, but I have no clue where he is or where Alaric or Lilith got thrown when Alexander erected the ward.

But I do know where my parents are, and once again, my eyes slide in their direction—to Gabriel, who bangs her fist on the invisible wall, while my father screams at me to run. But run where? There's nowhere to go. I could sprint to the edge of the ward and try to break it before Alexander reaches me, but I know there isn't time to even attempt to, not with him steadily closing the distance between us. There's nothing for me to do now except face the prophecy head on and try to achieve the one thing fate led me here to do.

Even if, in the end, I lose.

Resolve hardens my quivering insides as I narrow my eyes on Alexander, and a menacing smile curls the corners of his lips when I widen my stance and raise my hands, blood-red fire exploding across my palms.

"Are you so eager to fight me, little dove?" he asks, amused. He saunters closer, the inches between us quickly dwindling with those steps, prowling toward me like the predator we both know he is. "So certain are you that you will prevail? The Council must have you quite convinced that you are their Savior."

My upper lip curls back in a sneer. "They didn't have to convince me of anything. I *know* I am."

I might not have always believed it, but as I stand here facing Alexander, I know that anyone willing to plunge the world into the kind of chaos he has planned for it can't possibly be the Savior.

Because he isn't.

My heart trips in my chest at this thought because it isn't coming from me, but from a distant voice outside myself that's somehow foreign and familiar at once, as if I've heard it somewhere before. Long, long ago—perhaps as a baby when some powerful force spirited me away from that tomb on Easter Island. It doesn't even speak in words exactly so much as in a strong, overwhelming conviction that spreads through me like a comforting warmth before settling with certainty in my gut. And as it speaks, I feel a tingling in my shoulder that steals away my pain, the skin knitting itself back together, as well as a sudden weight at my back—an offering of strength when I need it most.

I recognize the tinny echo of angel-killing steel ringing in my ears before I register the strap around my chest connecting the scabbard to my back, hidden from all eyes, even mine. I don't hesitate, reaching my hand over my now healed shoulder with intent as Alexander scoffs at the audacity of my words. As my fingers curl around the hilt, pulling the blade free of its sheath, the calming voice of the Creator speaks again, encouraging my use of this gift. He tells me that I *am* the Savior the prophecy spoke of.

And He tells me I will win.

TWENTY-SIX

CALEB

THE LATE AFTERNOON SUN brushes the sky gold and pink in the west of the Arabian Desert, but the heat remains obnoxiously oppressive. Fighting for my life certainly hasn't helped me cool down, either. Not for the first time, I'm jealous of the angels and Fallen because the scorching air doesn't bother them. Sweat isn't making it hard for *them* to hold onto their weapons.

The plan was to attack in waves—angels, Fallen, and first generations upfront, second wave, students and everyone else. But now we are all in the fight, and carnage reigns.

Copper coats my tongue and my skin, and I feel like I'll never rid myself of the taste of blood. Rafe, Shalina, and I fight back-to-back, moving as one unit, ducking, slashing, and parrying. The once hard-packed, rose-colored sand now resembles raw brick, squelching under my feet and threatening to throw me off balance at a time when I can't afford to make any mistakes. I spot Hammurabi through a gap in the mayhem, whirling like a dervish, a creature of grace, delivering death like it's an art.

The Nephilim I battle smashes a punishing overhead blow against my sword, and I grit my teeth as my muscles scream in protest. My back foot sinks into the now-muddy sand, and Alexander's lackey grins as I stumble backward a step, knocking into Shalina. I hear a startled grunt before I use her body to right myself, snarling at the Mohawked motherfucker in front of me. He's about my height and weight, and we're on the same power level, which sounds good on paper, but he's older than me. Everyone I've fought today is *so* much older than me.

Mohawk presses his blade into mine, throwing his whole weight into it, but I hold steady against him. Something has to give. We can't stay in a clutch forever, and he's better with the sword than me. Fuck it. Jerking to the side, I fall back, taking him with me. I thrust my feet out, catching his hip bones, and use all that forward momentum to toss him over my head. Springing to my feet before he hits the ground, I spin around and watch as he lands on the flat of his back. Two seconds later and I'm above him, my blade thrust into his chest. Bottle-green eyes regard me in shock, and he manages to bring up his sword and push my own away. I slice across the back of his hand, and his sword loosens from his grip, then I slash his throat open, adding to the gore soaking into the ground.

A heavy weight slams into my back, and I'm kissing bloody sand, the air whooshing from my lungs. I blink the grit out of my eyes, my brain momentarily stunned, but my survival instincts claw their way to the surface, screaming at me to get the fuck up. Before it's too late. I manage to get my hands under my chest to push this asshole off me when the crushing load pressing down on me goes limp. I wriggle free of the body and stand, meeting the fearful eyes of Rafe. His sword is out in front of him, wetted with fresh blood. Glancing at the ground, I see the body of a Nephilim with dark blond hair. I roll the corpse over, meeting the lifeless eyes of my father.

My throat tightens as I stare at his face. Gramps sent him to murder me. My own father. Then I snort at that. He was never a father, just a sperm donor. But still, it's not like he had a choice. Alexander resurrected him, so I doubt he had much free will left. I wish I could say I feel sad, but mostly, I'm relieved.

My gaze catches Rafe's, and I give him a grateful nod. Rafe dips his head then turns, jumping right back into the melee. I go to follow when I catch sight of my baby brother, and I still. He's staring at our father, and my heart clenches at the thought that I might have to fight him—kill him. Marcos's eyes lock on mine, and I study his expression, trying to anticipate his next move. Suddenly, he stiffens, his mismatched eyes—our grandfather's eyes—round with fear, and he scurries away like a rabbit in front of a bigger predator.

My body hair stands on end as I catch the sound of a metallic whine careening toward me. I duck and roll, my shoulder hitting the sludgy sand. Popping into a crouch, my eyes dart up, my sword ready. Terror renders me momentarily frozen as I meet Ishtar's pleased gaze, her teeth bared in a feral smile. It's shocking she can look so regal with blood streaked across her face like war paint. She's come to kill me then.

I can't say I haven't been expecting it. In her eyes, I betrayed her—and more importantly, I betrayed Alexander. I guess I did, but she betrayed me first, manipulating my need for family—for a father—to play me. Feeding me bullshit that Luna wouldn't get hurt. It's not like I don't accept my part in freeing Alexander. I do. I'm guilty as shit, but Ishtar, the woman I thought loved me like a son or at least a favorite nephew, twisted my feelings to get what she wanted and then turned her back on me the moment I decided not to be a good little sheep and fall in line. And the sad thing—the thing that pisses me off the most—is that a part of me still loves her. A part of me still wants her to love me like she used to, or like I *thought* she used to. And I hate that. I hate her for disappointing me so badly. I hate her for injuring Luna. Fuck, she could have killed her, and for one horrifying moment when I saw Goldilocks's blood, I thought she had.

Rage fires me up and I straighten, never breaking eye contact as I sheathe my sword. Ishtar's brows arch in surprise. The familiar handles of the knives we used to train at Babel slide over my palms, offering comfort like an old friend as I grip them. I can't best her with a sword, but I have a chance—albeit a slim one—with my daggers. I don't know if I can kill her, but I might be able to damage her enough to escape. Though her body armor is going to pose a bit of a problem, it can be penetrated with enough force, especially if it's not made to defend against blades. The last time we had a mock fight at Alexander's citadel, I was out of practice, but Hammurabi has whipped me into shape since then. For all his bulk, he moves like lightning.

Ishtar's full lips curve as she also sheathes her sword, fingers curling around the hilts of her own daggers. "Good choice, young one. I don't want to kill you too easily. There's no pleasure in that. Now, I can whittle you away one cut at a time."

She lunges at me, steel flashing. I get my blades up, catching her attack. She's like an adder, viciously striking at me again and again. I know only a couple of minutes have passed, but time no longer has any meaning, stretching into infinity. For a while, I keep up with my former teacher, muscle memory kicking in, and I deliver just as many blows as she does. My knife catches her in the bicep, penetrates her side through the Kevlar, and slashes along her forearm. Fresh blood wets her black clothing, causing it to cling to her tall figure.

But slices decorate my torso like stripes, slowing me down. My angelic blood is working overtime to heal me, but I'm not as close to Heaven as she is. She heals faster. She *is* faster. I don't move my arm down quickly enough, and she manages to stab me under the armpit. Lucky for me, the strike is too low and glances off a rib instead of sinking into vulnerable flesh, sparing my life. It still hurts like a bitch, and the terror I've managed to hold off rushes to the forefront of my mind.

I can't beat her. I'm good but she's better. I'm going to die.

Panic seizes my chest, stopping my heart. Immediately, my eyes seek out Luna amongst the brawling celestials, but I can't find her. I want to see her one more time before Ishtar puts me in the ground. My neck tingles, and I slide out of the way as metal kisses the air where my throat just was, but I'm off balance. I fall to one knee, and the goddess of love and war looms over me, a triumphant smile turning the corners of her mouth.

"You shouldn't have betrayed Alexander," she spits at me. "You never turn your back on blood."

I know this is the end, and all I can think about is Luna and how I'm leaving her. How she'll have to face Alexander without me. How I'll never get to tell her I love her one more time. How life is so un-fucking-fair.

I meet Ishtar's black, pitiless gaze, and suddenly, my heart stutters back to life, clinging to hope. Ice crystals form lacy patterns over her brown skin like frost hardening grass. Her ruby lips fade to blue, and fear creeps into her gaze. Maybe I'm an asshole, but it's gratifying to see that fear. She has no problem dishing out terror.

And in the middle of the clamoring chaos, I spot Asmodeus, striding over to us as if she doesn't have a care in the world. Hammurabi trails behind her, alert and tense, gaze sweeping the area for any threats that get too close to his mistress. I rise to my feet, mouth agape. The Archdemon stops behind Ishtar, slipping one arm around the Nephilim's waist and the other around her neck, like a lover. She's shorter than Ishtar, but far more terrifying. Everywhere she touches, the ice blooms, crystals growing into solid sheets of bluish white. I'm cold just looking at my ex-teacher.

Asmodeus slides her fingers into Ishtar's braided locks and tilts her former friend's head down so she can whisper in her ear. Her garnet hair shimmers like a beacon in the desert.

"Young Caleb isn't the one who chose wrongly, dear friend," she croons, her voice honeyed venom. "He's not the one with dreams and ambitions that far exceed his station. He was wise enough to recognize Alexander for what he really is. A wisdom that you sorely lack, though your years are much more advanced. *You* betrayed *me* after I spared your life. Because I loved you. Because you were my friend."

Ishtar's skin loses its warm color, turning pale as the crystals thicken. Her eyes round with horror, and I know she realizes this is the end. There are no do overs and Gramps ain't around to save her.

"Know this, traitor, that Alexander will die, and the world you envisioned—the world where you had your own little kingdom to rule with the King of Uruk beside you, lording over mortals the way you believe you deserve—will die along with him. There are no second chances this time, and I won't mourn for you."

Ishtar is frozen solid except for her eyes, darting back and forth rapidly in their sockets, as if seeking help. It's disturbing as hell. Asmodeus moves both hands to rest under the Nephilim's jaw. My stomach clenches and I glance away as the Archdemon says, "Goodbye, dear one."

I hear a sickening crack followed by a thud and shudder as something hits my foot. Against my will, my gaze pulls down, and I see Ishtar's head resting against my boot. I really wish people would stop rolling heads at my feet. You'd think with as much blood and death that I've witnessed today, that nothing would bother me, but this makes my stomach churn and bile creep up my throat. I step away from the decapitated head, my eyes finding Asmodeus's.

"Thank you," I say, my voice hoarse. Clearing my throat, I repeat, "Thank you for saving my life." For giving me a chance to see Luna again.

She inclines her head. "You're welcome, child. Judgment had to be passed upon her, and it was my responsibility to dole out punishment."

A roar cuts across the fray, somehow drowning out the sounds of battle, of screams, of the dying. I whip around to see Gilgamesh charge toward us, anguish and rage twisting his features into a mask of pure fury. I scramble out of his way, but he doesn't even see me. His whole focus is on the Archdemon who just slayed his lover. I grimace at his suicidal actions, knowing Asmodeus will end him as surely as she did Ishtar, but when he brings the weapon down, I see bright scarlet swell on the Archdemon's shoulder. Her shock mirrors my own.

Gasping, I pivot toward Hammurabi, screaming, "He's got a weapon from the Fall!"

But Hammurabi is already on the move. He slams into Gilgamesh like an enraged rhino hitting a tourist jeep. He lands on the King of Uruk's chest, holding guard position, and wrenches the angel-killing weapon from his hand before smashing his head into the Light Nephilim's. Bones crunch. Gilgamesh screams. He manages to get an arm free and punches Hammurabi in the face, rocking him back. But the Babylonian king is in a frenzy of his own, steadying himself and delivering a matching staggering blow. He then hits Gilgamesh over and over and over again. I glance away from the other Nephilim's mangled face.

My eyes land on Asmodeus, whose bleeding has slowed, as G only managed a shallow cut. She meets my gaze, and I don't bother to hide my horror.

"That's enough, King," she calls. "Finish him."

Her eyes remain locked on mine as I hear a strangled cry then a gurgle. Then nothing. Grief seizes me. No matter that they were my enemies, Ishtar and Gilgamesh were two bright flames that just got guttered. They can never be replaced.

It's so goddamn tragic. This whole fucking situation is tragic. Asmodeus's smile holds sorrow and sympathy.

Then her face is swallowed by dust as a sandstorm rushes toward me, whipping around me, rendering me momentarily blind. What the fuck is happening? I know in my bones this storm isn't from Mother Nature. Magic saturates the air, causing me to shiver despite the heat. I recognize that magic. It's left scars on my mind.

Alexander.

I feel a ripple of energy, a mere warning, before I'm blasted off my feet, eating sand for the second time. Shaking my head, I struggle to stand, as if my feet are encased in drying cement, blinking as the haze clears. My mouth slackens as shock punches through me. Bodies rise, including Gilgamesh and a headless Ishtar. For a moment, the sight is too gruesome for me to process. Fuck me. Gramps actually did it—he resurrected the dead. As I stare at the King of Uruk, his eyes eerily empty, I hear someone screaming my name.

"Caleb, where are you?" Rafe's panicked voice pops the little balloon of silence surrounding me, and I wince. I forgot all about him and Shalina as soon as my former teacher decided to kill me, and I left them vulnerable to attack. What a shit friend I am. And with Alexander raising his own zombie army, we're even more fucked.

Pivoting, I search for him, as we got separated when I squared off with Ishtar. I spot him and Lina, and they're bloody but alive, thank the Creator. Rafe is waving his arms frantically and pointing. Fear reflects on his face, and dread seeps into me. I follow the direction of his finger, and my fucking heart nearly stops in my chest.

Luna—my precious Goldilocks—faces my grandfather, with a sword drawn. Where the hell did she get a sword? And her shoulder's not mended yet. I know she's powerful now in her own right—she's the *Savior*—but she can't beat Alexander the Great with a blade, especially wounded. She's all alone, too, and my eyes search for her parents. I spot Gabriel screaming and pounding on air. It takes a few precious seconds for my brain to catch up. The Conqueror has erected a ward around them.

I'm sprinting before I'm aware my brain has given my legs the command to run. My eyes remain trained on the two combatants, and I shove bodies out of my way, ducking blows as I clamor to reach Luna. I'm not going to make it in time—I can't even help if I do. I don't have the power to break a ward, but I have to get to Goldilocks. She needs to know I'm there for her. My mind urges me on once more, and I race over the sand.

I dodge and weave until I reach the barrier, my fists banging on the now-solid air, hardened like resin. My throat scrapes raw as I scream over and over again for what feels like hours, but I know is only seconds. Unsheathing my sword, I hack at the ward, even though I know it's useless. Even though I know I'm wasting precious energy. Luna doesn't hear me, the entirety of her attention focused on her enemy.

My breath stutters in my chest when I see Gramps lunge for her, dagger arcing in a precise strike. But then Luna's wings unfurl in a snap, and she takes flight for the first time, soaring over Alexander's head. My steps falter as she climbs higher as if reaching for the clouds, wings booming in a steady beat, sword raised like an avenging angel in a Renaissance painting. Determination slides over what I can see of her face like a battle mask, the breadth of her wings bolstering her slender form, the silver feathers a symbol of hope in all this death. Despite my terror, I can't help but admire the glow radiating from her being. In this moment, she manages to outshine the Morningstar. Then Alexander rises in the air after her, his own metallic feathers glinting in the sun.

Luna must sense him because she turns, raising her blade in defense, and my own sword sags as it finally dawns on me that *her* sword has Enochian etched into the steel. That sword doesn't belong to either of her parents, which means… Fuck me, which means the *Creator* gave her that sword. That's the only explanation.

Though my chest aches with fear and the thought of watching, helpless, as my grandfather cuts down the love of my life, hope manages to break through my crippling panic. If the Creator gave her that sword, that means He is present right now. He intends for her to win.

I hold onto that thought like a lifeline in a tempestuous sea. She's the Savior. I have to believe she will prevail because I can't live with the alternative.

I can't live if she dies.

TWENTY-SEVEN

LUNA

WHEN I WAS TRAPPED in the Council's glass egg, there were many times when I would just sit there and wonder what it would feel like to fly. I would stretch my wings out as much as the cramped space of my prison allowed and try to imagine the feel of the wind in my feathers—of a weightlessness I found myself desperate for after so many years crushed by the burden of my trauma and guilt.

Now, I realize even my most detailed daydreams didn't come close. The breeze runs over my wingtips in a gentle caress that only comes second to the feel of Caleb's fingers brushing against my skin, sending a thrum of exhilaration through my system. Or maybe that's just the adrenaline in my blood—the fight or flight reflex that launched me off the ground when Alexander swung his dagger. I didn't even mean to fly— didn't even think I *could* yet—but in that moment, it was a natural impulse, as if my wings knew what they needed to do, taking the thought process away.

Now, as they carry me high above the ground, my eyes drawn away from the desert below to the blazing sun overhead, I'm reminded of the story of Icarus—of what happened when he dared to drift too close to that light. For the first time, I fathom the true extent of temptation. Of grasping for something just out of our reach. And suddenly, I understand why my father fell—not only for the right to love without restraint, but for this exhilarating sense of uninhibited freedom.

For the chance for each of us to live how we choose.

A choice. That's all I ever wanted. And as I consider what losing that would mean to angels like my father—to the Fallen who fell for the right to choose—I realize just how much Alexander threatens not only the liberation of those who stand against him, but also those who fight at his side. Promising to bring our kind out of obscurity isn't the same thing as freedom, and if he succeeds here, he will inevitably shackle us all just like the Darks once felt shackled by the Creator.

Well, I won't be shackled. Not again. Not by humans, not by the Council, and sure as hell not by some megalomaniac on a power trip. Or even by fear. I've wasted too many years terrified of what I am and what I'm capable of, and I'm *done* being afraid. I might not be as skilled or as smart as Alexander, but I am far from weak, and I will use what strength I have to fight for the same choice my father once did. For the chance at a life not confined to a cage. For a life, however brief, with Caleb.

Savior or not, victorious or not, what I do now is for me.

My fingers tighten around the hilt of my sword, reaffirming my grip, as a loud gust drags my gaze down just in time to glimpse Alexander taking off from the ground, his body rocketing toward me faster than I can dodge him.

I raise my blade, and sparks fly as metal strikes metal, Alexander's dagger meeting my sword with enough force to push me back several feet, my legs flailing in my panic, searching for purchase where there is none to catch me. My stomach flips, and for a heart-racing moment, I think I'm going to fall. But I don't. I remain airborne, my wings holding me aloft and steady, once again doing exactly what I need them to do, even if I'm not entirely sure how they're doing it.

Invisible hands seem to push at my back then, and I wonder if it's the Creator, offering me support, or if I really am somehow doing this on my own. Either way, my wings flap with fervor, launching me toward Alexander, who sneers, batting my sword away with ease. I swing it again, probably a bit more overzealous in my attempt than is wise, and he cackles, stoking the flames of the fury rising inside me. I'm no match for him and he knows it, but I can't afford to go on the defensive because as soon as I give him the opening to turn the tables and he comes at me full strength, I know what the outcome will be.

Alexander's victory here will only come at the cost of my death, and though I was willing to fight to that point if that was the required price for defeating him, I can't afford to die. I have too much to live for. Caleb's face flashes through my head, and fueled by my desperation to see him again—to live out his mortal days together—I grit my teeth and lunge forward, aiming the blade tip for Alexander's heart. Like the Nephilim below who weren't alive during the Fall, he isn't donning armor—not even the modern variety his own soldiers are wearing. Maybe he doesn't want to tarnish his appearance as an ancient king of legend, though I'd wager the lack of protection is down to his pride and the misguided belief that he'll triumph here today. That he doesn't need armor if it's his destiny to win. Even if he's right—even if I'm not meant to survive this—I take advantage of the opening his overconfidence has given me, allowing myself the small and dangerous hope that I might not only make it through this, but come out as the victor.

To my bemusement, instead of trying to block me, Alexander sheathes his dagger as I close the distance between us, as if he has no intention to fight me. Alarm bells ring through my skull because I know he isn't willing to die, but everything happens too quickly. When he makes his move—shooting out an arm and grabbing me by the throat—that hope inside me burns out like the last embers in a hearth.

"You fool," he hisses, his fingertips squeezing my windpipe as his other hand grabs my wrist, stopping my advance before my blade even comes close to piercing his flesh. I let out a cry as he twists my arm back, but I clench my fingers tighter despite this new, excruciating pain in my arm, doing everything in my power to keep my grip on the pommel.

A deranged chuckle parts the Gray's lips as he sneers at me—our faces so close I can smell honey and wine on his breath—and horror floods my body as it dawns on me that he gave me that opening, luring me in with the intention of catching me like a fly drawn to sugar. I could've struck out at him a hundred times, and it wouldn't have mattered.

I never would've gotten close to landing the blow needed to stop him.

"You should have joined me when you had the chance," he seethes, his eyes creeping over my face with contempt. His gaze then dips to the sword still clenched in my hand. "Your strength of will is admirable, little dove, I will give you that. But *I* am the one who shall prevail here. It is my birthright to be great—to save this planet from its constant chaos and strife." His lips peel back into a smile that sends a chill through my bloodstream, and pulling me closer until his breath touches my ear, he says, "There is only room in this world for one Savior, and though you all fight it, it is *I* who will cleanse the Earth of its savagery, not you."

The blood rushes to my head as his fingers grip tighter, and although I know he can't suffocate me, my life flashes before my eyes as if I'm standing at the brink of death, facing down my final moments. Maybe because I am. Any second now, he'll reach for his dagger and run me through and that will be it.

I'll have failed and the Destroyer will have won.

"You're wrong." The words spring from my throat in a gasp, though I'm not entirely sure if I'm talking to Alexander or myself. All I know for certain is there's a fire inside me—that hope I thought extinguished now a raging inferno, refusing to accept that this is the end.

"Don't show it until the end."

Alaric's voice echoes in my memory as I play the only card I have left in my hand and focus all my power outside of myself—one final attempt to outmaneuver death before it comes to claim me. As my eyes slide shut in acceptance of whatever comes next, my fingers loosen their grip on my sword. Time seems to slow as the pommel slips from my grasp, and as it drops, my mind slips fully free of my body and I reach out—not with my physical form, but with my astral one. I channel every thought and hope I possess, willing my intangible fingers to catch the hilt…

And when I feel the metal graze my palm, I seize it.

Taking the sword in both hands, I thrust my arms upward, only catching the barest glimpse of my face—of Alexander's fingers still taut around my throat—as the blade sweeps up behind the Gray, slicing through the flesh and bone of his wings. The roar that expels from his lungs is inhuman, rippling through the air around us like a shockwave, and as he tumbles to the ground far below like a giant bird whose wings have been clipped, I watch my immobilized body plummet alongside him, as if we're experiencing a Fall of our own.

Darkness washes over my vision, blotting out the sky and the desert beneath me, as I will my current form back into my physical one. As the two slam together, rejoining, I open my eyes with a strangled cry. They water from the air whipping at my face as I free fall, my body a tangle of thrashing limbs. My wings flap wildly, attempting to slow me, but the desert floor is rushing upward too quickly to stop the impact I know is coming. I've fallen too far already and the speed of my descent is too great.

I hit the ground only moments after Alexander. He crashes into the earth, now sludgy with blood, like a meteor, leaving a small crater in his wake—as destructive even when bested as he's been in his conquests. I don't see where my sword or his dagger fall, but I do hear his wings as they flop, one after the other, against the dirt with grotesque *thuds* that would turn my stomach if the world wasn't blurring and spinning out of control. The force of my collision rattles my bones and punches the air from my lungs, robbing me of breath, as I skid and roll across the ground, tricking my once-mortal mind into believing I might actually be dead. Thankfully, it doesn't take long to regain my senses—to remember I'm immortal—and realize I'm not actually injured, even if, for a moment, my mind thinks I've broken every bone in my body. The pain of the impact is fleeting, but the phantom touch of Alexander's fingers around my throat remains, and coughing, I raise my head, searching for something to ground me—to assure me I didn't just imagine all this, and he isn't still strangling me up in the clouds.

Blinking away the bleariness of tears, my eyes immediately lock on Alaric, who stands only inches away from me, pounding on the glass-like barrier between us. Behind him, the battle rages again, more furiously than before, as if everyone can sense that this moment is the apex, and that what happens now will dictate what happens to us all moving forward.

My movements are sluggish, my arms shaking as the adrenaline coursing through me wears off. Like how I felt after my first soul journey to Persepolis, my body is drained of energy—this time, completely, likely from the power I exerted to force my projection to interact with the physical plane. Exhaustion cripples my senses and limbs, but I push myself upright enough to thrust out a hand toward the ward, my fingertips brushing the surface, willing it to break—or, at least, to crack enough to let Alaric through.

Alexander doesn't try to stop me. My eyes trawl over my shoulder toward the last place I saw him, where he kneels in the center of the crater, his hands limp in his lap, blood oozing from the wounds in his back as he stares down at the sand, his eyes unfocused. His hair is askew and the crown that previously adorned his head is gone, lost during the fall back to Earth. He doesn't look up even when a funnel of sound comes rushing back to our isolated pocket of the battlefield.

A hand brushes my shoulder and I snap my head up, only catching the side profile of Alaric's face as he slips through the narrow hole I created in the ward and walks past me, his stride slow and steady. Determined. A soothing wave of Calm funnels through me, almost disorienting in strength, as if he's trying to smother me, but it's not enough to tamp down the building ache in my chest or the knowledge of what he's going to do—of what he's sparing *me* from doing.

The prophecy might have foretold this battle, but it never explicitly stated that one Gray had to die by the other's hand to fulfill it. Only that the Savior had to draw on their strength to defeat the Destroyer, and I have. The people willing to fight by my side have been my greatest strength. Even now, I feel them here with me, especially Alaric. And as I watch him walk toward Alexander, all I can think is that maybe things were always meant to play out this way, with the Gray's story coming full circle, beginning and concluding with the one person who was there through it all.

The crunch of sand beneath Alaric's feet is almost deafening, his proximity pushing all other sounds into the background, like I'm hearing them from underwater. Alexander, shaken from his stupor, lifts his gaze, finally noticing the Nephilim's presence, and when their eyes meet, he utters Alaric's name with a gentleness I didn't

think him capable of.

"Alaric…"

Shushing him, Alaric steps into the crater and slowly drops to one knee, close enough now to Alexander he could lean in and kiss him. "I wish this time could have ended differently." Although his back is toward me and I can't see his face, the pain in Alaric's voice rings like a death knell above the chorus of war leaking in through the hole in the ward.

Alexander's mismatched eyes spring wide, just visible over Alaric's shoulder, as if whatever daze consumed him in his pain is now fading in response to the Nephilim's words, jerking him back to this moment. But the realization gripping him comes too late. Alaric curls one hand around the back of the Gray's head and pulls it close to his chest, while his other reaches for his sword. And as the blade slides free of its sheath on the Nephilim's back, Alexander chokes out his lover's name once more, that single word escaping his lips like a plea. Alaric doesn't give him the chance to finish.

Around us, the bodies that were resurrected collapse to the ground, the strings holding them to their puppeteer snapped as their connection is severed by death. For a long moment after, Alexander and Alaric remain frozen in their final embrace— Alaric with his head bowed, his forehead resting against Alexander's golden hair, while the Gray stays on his knees, slumped over the long blade impaling his torso.

I don't know whether Alaric killed Alexander so I wouldn't have to or because he felt it was his duty to put an end to the monster he helped unleash on this world. Maybe it was a combination of both. Either way, my fated role in all this is complete. The Destroyer is dead.

And this madness can finally be over.

Familiar voices shout my name, and I glance up to see my parents and Lilith calling to me through the barrier, searching for the invisible hole where Alaric came through. It's only when I feel the heavy blanket of Calm lift off my senses and I find the strength to climb to my feet that I notice the rest of the desert is eerily silent on the other side of the ward. The fighting has come to a standstill, as if Alexander's death has broken a spell that's been cast over us all, freeing everyone here from the desire to spill anymore of each other's blood.

I glance away from all of them, my attention focused solely on Alaric, who stands now, his movements languid. Carefully removing the sword from Alexander's chest, he lays him back against the flat earth, lingering for a moment in a squat beside the Gray's unmoving body before leaning forward and brushing his lips gently against his forehead.

"I will remember you…as you used to be," I hear him murmur, then he straightens and takes a step back, abandoning his sword on the ground beside Alexander.

"Is it over?" I ask when Alaric looks over at me, and he hesitates for only a moment to scan the sea of faces around us before nodding.

"Yes," he says. Closing his eyes, he lets out a sigh as if to shed the heavy weight that's been tormenting him for millennia. "I believe it is."

But there's a melancholic note to his tone, and as I trail my gaze across the ominous stillness of the battlefield, noting how many have fallen today, it dawns on me that we might have won this battle, but there was never any winning this war. Not truly. This really is like the Fall all over again, with too many deaths on both sides to see this whole ordeal as anything other than tragic. Our victory here was always going to be hollow at best.

But tragic or not, it's still a victory we need to grasp, and I can only hope, now that it's over, we'll finally find it in us to overcome our division. That this time will be different. That the prophecy, now that it's come to fruition, will ensure that war among our kind can finally be put to rest and that we no longer need to endure such pointless devastation moving forward.

That we *can* heal the rift, the way fate and the Creator intended.

Heaving a sigh of my own, I scour the herd of angels, Fallen, and Nephilim on the other side of the ward again, this time searching for Caleb. With Alexander gone, we can do what we wish. No more running. No more fearing imprisonment. Hell, the Council will have no choice but to acknowledge me as the Savior and dismiss their whole anti-Gray agenda now that the real threat is eradicated, which means we'll be free to be together without any obstacles or the divide standing between us.

Buoyed by that thought, I continue my search, and to my immense elation, I find Caleb within seconds, as if some unseen magnetic force is drawing us to each other. Relief slams into me like a brick wall at the sight of him standing at the opposite side of the circular stretch of desert still encased by the barrier, his mouth shaping one word, silently shouting my name.

A smile tugs at my cheeks, and as I feel the shock of this battle wear off and my energy return to full strength, I begin to walk toward him, drawing on my power and readying myself mentally to demolish the rest of the ward, which had begun to dissipate with Alexander's death, the magical connection destroyed, though not enough for anyone to step through yet.

But I don't get anywhere near it before I find myself stopping abruptly, my heart jumping into my throat when I spot the red eyes gleaming behind Caleb's shoulder.

Mammon's movements are lightning quick, and the words to warn Caleb die on my lips before I even get the chance to say them.

Caleb's expression contorts, and although I can't hear him, I can imagine the sound he makes from the look of surprise flitting across his face. He looks down, his eyes locking on the Archdemon's hand as it punches through his chest. And then he's gone, collapsing in a lifeless heap to the ground, taking my sanity with him.

TWENTY-EIGHT

CALEB

I CLUTCH MY CHEST where my heart used to be, but to my utter astonishment, there's no longer a ragged hole there. My agony vanishes, my pain disappearing in an instant. All that remains now is warmth spreading through my body... But I don't think I *have* a body. Not in the physical sense anymore. I hold my hands up before my eyes, but they seem translucent, as if I'm only a spirit now, no longer tied to earthly things.

Grief gutters out that warmth for a brief moment—an icy douse on a hot summer day. A keening ache arrows through me. I know I'm leaving someone I love behind. Someone who means more to me than anything. Then the heat wraps around me again with comforting arms, and whispers surround me, assuring me that everyone I love is okay. That I'm complete.

That I can let go.

But I don't want to let go. She—Luna, Goldilocks—needs me, but drowsiness overwhelms me, and the whispers urge me to rest. That I've earned it. That I've been brave and true. That I deserve this reward.

I want to laugh. I'm a Dark, and the Creator doesn't reward Darks. But the voice tells me I'm more than just a Dark, and the Creator rewards those He sees fit. Languidness overwhelms me and I give into the voice, slipping away into the vast velvet pool of darkness.

TWENTY-NINE

LUNA

MY BREATHS ARE DEAFENING in my ears, blocking out all sound aside from the rapid burst of my pulse. It pounds through the entire length of my body with furious denial, from my feet—rooted to the earth in shock—to my trembling fingertips, which now raise, reaching out, although I don't really know to what. My eyes burn, locked on the bloody lump in Mammon's hand...

On the still beating heart in his fist, which might as well be my own.

"Ca..." I begin to say, stumbling forward an uneasy step, but his name catches in my throat. This can't be happening. We can't have made it this far—through all the pain we've both experienced and separation and near-death encounters—for our story to come to a grinding halt here. This isn't how this was supposed to go. Alexander is dead. We *won*. This was supposed to be over. And we were supposed to live and spend however many long years together Caleb's mortality was willing to give us. His fire wasn't supposed to extinguish. Not yet. It was supposed to burn fiercely, the way I've burned for him since the very first moment we met. Our love was supposed to keep us together. Not forever—I'd already accepted we didn't have that long—but we were at least supposed to have longer than this.

I inch forward another step, the lump in my throat growing as my gaze drops to the unmoving body at Mammon's feet. The shell *looks* like Caleb, but that's all it is now. A shell. I give a jerky shake of my head, and the sob building in my chest transforms into a deranged scream that tears through the air with rage and abandon.

After so long fearing I was a monster...after so long wishing and praying I wasn't... for the first time, I actually wish I *was* the Destroyer because if this is the price of being the Savior, I don't want it. This wasn't his burden. Alexander might have been his grandfather but this battle was mine.

If anyone was going to die here, it should have been me.

Please, take me instead. Just let him live, I silently pray, but if the Creator is listening, He does nothing to show it.

The grief rising to drown me is short-lived, overwhelmed by an anger so visceral and all-consuming that it makes me want to destroy the world, not save it. I can't hold it in—the energy and loathing and pain lancing through me that all climb to the surface at once—and it dawns on me I don't want to.

Not until I make Mammon pay.

Voices shout at me from the other side of the ward, but I don't listen. I don't spare them a glance. My focus is only on Mammon. Hands clenching into fists, I latch my eyes onto the Archdemon, my hatred for him boiling the blood in my veins until every single inch of my insides are on fire. The inferno spreads outward, blasting through what remains of the barrier—throwing the Nephilim and angels surrounding me back. Only Mammon is untouched by my outburst of power, left isolated without potential allies so I can kill him. Flames the same ruby as the Archdemon's eyes ignite along the skin on my arms as I begin to walk toward him, burning the fabric of my short sleeves away. My wings fan out, spreading the flames farther.

Mammon's lips twitch with amusement. "Haven't you learned anything, little girl? You can burn me all you like, but just like the last time, I will heal. I will *always* heal." He waves an indifferent hand. "Be glad it was his life I took and not yours," he adds with an indignant sneer at Caleb's body. "Now, we can consider the debt of my lost wing repaid."

A life for a wing. It's not a fair trade.

None of this is fair.

What am I supposed to tell Aya? When we said our goodbyes before leaving Cambodia, I promised her Caleb would be okay. That her brother would come back to her in one piece.

What am I supposed to tell his mother?

These thoughts only stoke the fire of my fury as I draw in a shaking breath through flared nostrils, ignoring the overwhelming wash of Calm suddenly crashing into me, once again attempting to penetrate my senses and bring me back to sanity—the only thing managing to reach me in my blind rage. In my peripheral vision, I glimpse Alaric's familiar outline, his eyes watching me with a terror and worry I can practically taste. Other eyes watch me, too, yet I don't turn to look at any of them, though in the crowd of faces tracking my movements, I'm aware of my parents and Lilith. But they don't attempt to interrupt my advance. No one does, not even Alaric despite how hard he's working to subdue me—even harder than he was when he first stepped through the crack in the ward, though I cast it off with ease this time as a strange new power thrums under my skin. Maybe because they're all horrified by what Mammon has done—by this horrific betrayal of our truce with the Council. Or maybe because my power is holding them back, keeping them out of the way of my wrath—a sort of ward of its own.

A darkness I've never felt before—not even in my worst moments when I was so close to tumbling over the edge—swamps my entire being alongside the inferno until every negative feeling eating at me begins to ooze out of my pores, taking the form of shadows pouring out of my fingertips and palms like sentient tendrils of ink. The humor and conceit drains from Mammon's expression, and all the Nephilim and angels around us—already pushed back by my power—retreat even farther when I raise my arms, the fire and the shadows fusing into tangible whips of wrath, which lash out with intent at my silent command. They wrap around his wrists and throat like hands determined to suffocate him, dragging him down with a force that reverberates through the earth as his knees strike the now clay-like sand. He grunts from the impact, and as I hold him down like prey pinned in a trap, he stares up at me with an emotion flickering in his gaze that I sincerely hope is terror.

Exhaling loud, quick breaths through his nose, the Archdemon strains against the pulsating darkness, which squeezes around his windpipe. I might not be able to suffocate him or kill him like this, but I can still make every second hurt. The flames lick across his skin, hungry in their outrage, charring his nose and cheeks a deep black. "This won't kill me," he wheezes, the stench of his burning flesh pungent.

"No," I agree, somewhat surprised I'm able to find the word in my fury.

I stand before Mammon now, only separated by the body lying prostrate on the ground between us, using every last ounce of control I possess to stop my eyes from once again dipping to that broken shell of the person I love the most. Grinding my teeth, I focus on the Archdemon's right hand, outstretched before him as if he's offering the organ clamped in his fist to me, his arm held aloft by the tendril, which constricts until his fingers go slack on reflex. My own hand shoots out, and I catch the heart when it drops from his grip as my other hand curls in beckoning, using the darkness pouring out of me to find my sword. A thick blackness pools over the sand, flooding the area, as if returning this patch of desert to some semblance of the lake it used to be.

"But this will," I promise as the searching tendrils retract back into my body, and the hilt of my sword collides with my palm. Grasping it, I thrust the weapon forward, the gleaming tip piercing the center of the Archdemon's face, cutting through the cartilage of his nose. A discomforting gurgle escapes him as the blade slides through his skull like butter, and for a moment, I just stand like this, staring at the point where the steel meets his skin, my hand trembling around the golden hilt of this gift from the Creator.

My lower lip wobbles, and finally, I can't hold the growing pain in my chest at bay any longer. It fills my lungs like water, drowning me from within, and as a primal scream tears free of my lips once more—that part of me that remembers what it's like to be human gasping for air, for relief from this agony—the shadows and flames pouring out of me seem to explode, pulling the Archdemon's head and limbs in different directions. Hot specks of blood splash my face and arms, and gasps ripple around me from the watching crowd, but I barely notice any of it. I feel like I'm trapped in a soundproof box, or worse…like I'm back in that egg where everything I can see is just there to torment me. To remind me of what I can no longer have and can never have again.

Like his shell.

I tilt my head, and slowly, my eyes drop to my feet. Up close like this, with Caleb's face turned to the side, one cheek pressed into the dirt, I can count every lash lining his closed eyes and glimpse every year in his features—eighteen years, which is so much less than what I hoped for and yet so long compared to the less than one we shared. I try to stop myself from looking away from his beautiful face, but I can't help it. My gaze inevitably strays to the gaping hole in his back, to this horrific proof of his mortality. To the wound that not even his angelic blood can heal.

Tears scald my cheeks, burning thick lines into my skin and pooling at the corners of my lips, assaulting my mouth with the tang of salt and a grief I know I will never overcome. Not in this lifetime or any.

"I can't," I gasp, dropping to my knees, my wings going limp around me as I fight for air through the pain. The power surrounding me fades to a fizzle as the sword pommel slips from my fingers, the blade falling flat to the ground as my hands clumsily flip Caleb over and paw mindlessly at his face, his features blurring through my tears. "I can't do this without you," I breathe. "I can't. I *won't.*"

Then don't, a voice says in the back of my head. *My* voice.

The voice of what used to be my conscience, now as warped by this loss as I am.

"Then don't," I echo, the words a whisper, my eyes widening as understanding sinks in. I reel back, my attention shifting to his mangled chest then to the heart still in my hand—to the missing piece of the broken puzzle he's become.

A puzzle I can fix.

I only considered this once—the first time I was forced to acknowledge Caleb's mortality, and at the time, I vowed I would never do it. I would never resurrect him. But now that I'm faced with actually living without him, I see no other option. I nearly lost him once when that bomb went off at the citadel. I can't lose him again.

Without thinking of the consequences—without thinking of anything other than my desperation to have him here with me, alive—I shove his heart back in the hole in his torso and clamp my hands over the open wound. Blood seeps through my fingers as I think of the moth back at the Serapeum, of that fateful day when I first heard Alexander's voice in my head, and I sink into myself, picturing those fluttering wings and how they represented a return to life, not that unlike a pulse. *I did that.* I brought that moth back from whatever lies beyond mortality. *I did it*…and I can do it again. I don't care if it goes against nature. I don't care if it's a power meant only for the Creator. I don't even care if Caleb comes back different.

I just need him to come back.

"Wake up," I plead, my breathing ragged.

Warmth flashes through me as I push every thought and all the power I know I'm capable of into the picture forming in my head and the silent words encircling it like a prayer. I imagine Caleb's body stitching itself back together and his heart, still beating in my hands, reattaching itself to the places it needs to in order to bring him back to me. More than anything, I imagine him waking up. Of this all being nothing more than a nightmare.

"*Please*, Caleb, come back to me."

My fingers curl, attempting to push the cavity closed, but if the damage, inside or out, is healing, I can't see any sign of it.

"Please!" I say again, screaming this time.

Fingers wrap around my forearms and tug as something familiar and powerful invades my senses like a sudden blast of heat from a furnace.

Calm, I realize somewhere in the back of my mind, but the thought is hazy and fleeting.

"Luna, stop," Alaric pleads, his soothing baritone so close and yet so far away. He's next to me now, the barrier of my power no longer keeping him and the others at bay. His grasp on me tightens, but I shrug him off, shutting out his voice and his gift as he tries, yet again, to restrain me.

"Starlight, please," another voice begs. My father's voice.

I shake my head, muttering the same word over and over, all logic and reason gone. "No, no, no, no, no…" *Wake up!*

"Luna."

My mother kneels beside me and sliding one hand across my back, she rests the other on top of mine where it lingers over Caleb's exposed heart. At first, I think she's going to stop me, but she doesn't even try to pry my fingers away. She just leans in, whispering soft words in my ear.

Words that wrench my own heart in two.

"Caleb wouldn't want this."

My anger and grief collide then, forming a cyclone of agony that rips me to shreds from within.

"You don't know what he would want!" Using my wings to shove her and Alaric away, I glare at them and then at my father and Lilith, who stand a short distance from us, their gazes shiny with pity and unspoken remorse. "*None* of you know!" I shriek.

Because no one, human or otherwise, knew Caleb like I did. To the world, he was cocky and confident but I got to see the hidden sweetness inside. I got to see his vulnerability, even in the moments when he tried so hard to hide it. I shake my head again, firm in my certainty. No one else saw those sides to him. No one except maybe…

I turn my head, searching the crowd for Hammurabi. As if sensing my need for him, the Babylonian king emerges from the sea of bodies with Asmodeus beside him, pushing through the barricade of Nephilim and Fallen, snarling at those in their way to move. He stumbles to a standstill at the sight of Caleb, his pupils blowing wide, his large chest catching on a breath. He stays that way for a moment, shock written into his features, then he looks at me with those dark, silvered eyes, and I'm suddenly not sure what he mourns more. The dead boy on the ground I'm certain he loved or me, the broken girl he gave the rare gift of his kindness who we both know will never recover from this.

"He wouldn't want to leave me. He wouldn't," I mutter, speaking only to the ancient Nephilim. The one person here who might actually be on my side and want Caleb back as much as I do. "*Please*, Hammurabi, you know him. Tell them he wouldn't want to leave me."

Everyone—my parents, Alaric, Lilith, Asmodeus, and the thousands of others around me—all watch as Hammurabi closes the distance between us. No one dares to utter a word in the silence.

Crouching beside me, the Babylonian king plants his large hand on my head. "He loved you, flower," he begins, then clears his throat, his fingers sliding over my hair. As his arm drops and he stands again, a tear slides down his cheek, disappearing into the thick hair of his beard. "But your mother is right. Caleb wouldn't want this."

"No," I breathe, the pain in my chest like a festering wound turning septic. "No, I won't let him go." My hands move away from the hole now, gripping frantically at the collar of Caleb's shirt. "Caleb, wake up," I bark, shaking him roughly. His head lolls lifelessly against the ground, which only makes me shake him harder. "Wake up, damn you!"

I reach for his heart again, silently pleading to the Creator or fate or whatever or whoever is dictating our roles in this world to listen to me, to bring him back. But again, if anyone is listening, they don't respond, and gradually, the beats pulsating against my hands slow to a standstill.

"No, no, no." Unsure what else to do, I push against his heart with my flattened palms, repeating the movement and praying that if I can't save him as an angel, then maybe human methods can do it. But no matter how hard I push, no matter how much I wish for it, no matter how hard I search for the power inside me to reverse this—to turn back the clock and save him—I can't. Time is immovable, a barrier I can't seem to cross.

Even the Savior doesn't have that kind of power.

A choked breath catches in my throat. "Why?" I breathe, glancing at my mother, who's standing now, her face a smear of cream framed by black through my tears. I blink, and her features sharpen for a moment. "Why isn't it working?"

It worked for Alexander. He raised his soldiers, even ones who had been cut limb from limb, so why can't I raise Caleb? Why can't I fix him? This is a repeat of what happened in Kandahār all over again but with the worst possible outcome.

Gabriel frowns, her hands balled into trembling fists at her sides, as if she's fighting back the urge to reach for me. To console me. She says nothing, but then, I don't think I really expected her to have the answer.

I think I knew from the moment I saw his heart leave his body that I wouldn't be able to bring him back. He's too broken, his shell too damaged, and I don't have the experience or power Alexander possessed. Or maybe that's just an excuse I tell myself now to assuage the guilt of my failure. To shift the burden of Caleb's death off my shoulders because I already carry too many others. There isn't space. And my own heart can't take it.

Or maybe it's none of that, and my mother was right. Maybe Caleb doesn't want this and that's why he's not coming back.

The tears come more quickly with that thought, my breaths panicked and harrowed as I try to breathe through the hysteria clawing at me from the inside. I grab at the dirt to ground myself, to find an anchor in the darkness, but the world suddenly feels too big, and I am hopelessly lost in it. Like I've drifted from the marked path in a dense forest, and I'll never find my way back again.

Caleb was always that anchor for me, the one who managed to make me feel safe and like I belonged in a world that was determined to make me feel neither…and now, he's gone. I might have Alaric again and my parents, but the hole of Caleb's loss is too great. I can already feel it beginning to swallow me.

Drawn to him even in the cold stillness of death, I reach for his face—to touch him for what might be the final time—but something stops me, and lured by the vibrating hum in the air, I glance down at my sword where it lies abandoned in the dirt. As if in a trance, I wrap my fingers around the pommel, testing the weight, the gleaming blade sharp enough to pierce even rock. It's angel-killing steel, which means it could end this pain. It could end everything so long as I'm the one to wield it.

No, Luna.

I shutter my eyes, and a shaky breath escapes me as I relax my grip, letting the sword fall to the ground. If I could carve this pain from my heart, I would. I'd bear the scars so long as it meant no longer feeling like this. But not wanting to live without Caleb isn't the same as wanting to die. And I don't. I *want* to live. I *want* to experience life and everything this vast world has to offer. I want another taste of that freedom I felt up in the sky. After so long trapped in one cage after another, I deserve that much.

But Caleb deserved it, too. *We* deserved the acceptance we fought for. We deserved our chance at a life together, free from the opinions and prejudices of others. Hell, we never should have had to fight for it in the first place.

"Are you all happy now?" I rasp, prying my eyes open and trailing my heated gaze across the drawn faces around me. Lights and Darks with me in the middle, the sole Gray in a world that should be vibrant with our shared existence, not divided by such pointless disdain. My eyes narrow, taking them all in—the angels, Fallen, and Nephilim—and somewhere inside me where I can still feel something other than this terrible agony, I'm pleased to find they all look ashamed. "Are you *satisfied* with what your hate has accomplished?"

I slap a hand over my mouth as a wracking cry grips my lungs, and buckling, I bend forward, pressing my forehead to Caleb's chest. What a cruel twist of fate that we would fight to heal the divide only to be separated in such a permanent way before that could happen. I just wanted the freedom to love him, but I never would have let myself love him at all if I knew this was where the road would end.

"Come back…" I whisper this again and again until the words become lost on my tongue, and the only sounds escaping me are sobs.

Come back.

A hand grazes my back, offering comfort, but I shy away from it, sitting up slightly. The only touch I want is Caleb's and if I can't have his, I don't want anyone's. Undeterred by my rebuff, fingers creep along my spine, and a warm palm flattens against my lower back, applying just enough pressure to push me back down a little. It feels like an embrace, but that can't be right. Because the only person this is bringing me closer to is Caleb, and I know there's no one left inside the empty vessel beneath me.

"Stop," I beg, my eyes clamped shut as if to escape this nightmare, but the word has barely passed my lips when a low, husky voice whispers, "I hate it when you cry, Goldilocks."

I lurch back, snapping open my eyes again, a tremor that's part horror and part disbelief racing through me. The feel of that hand slips away, making me all the more certain I must've imagined it. No, I know I did. It was just a hallucination—a desperate wish manifested in my mind, nothing more. I've clearly reached my breaking point and maybe I've finally taken that long-awaited step off the cliff edge into insanity. But even if that's the case, there's a part of me that doesn't care—that would take even a figment of him over nothing. And deeper than that, there's a part of me that still hopes.

That knows a love like ours can overcome anything, even something like death.

"C-Ca…?" I stammer, my mouth and brain at odds with each other, unable to form his name in my shock.

I stare down at his face, hastily blinking the tears from my vision. His eyes remain closed, his features as unmoving as they were moments ago when I last looked upon them, his stillness destroying the flicker of hope igniting in my broken heart. But then I see it—a subtle twitch to the lips.

"Caleb?" I force out in a strangled breath, certain I didn't imagine that movement. My fingertips shift, my nails digging into the torn fabric of his T-shirt.

At the sound of his name, he opens his eyes. "Didn't think you'd be rid of me that easily, did you?"

His mouth tilts with a crooked smile that steals the breath from my lungs, and as he raises a hand to my cheek, his thumb brushing the tears from my lips, a million thoughts and feelings race through me at once. Elation. Confusion. A deep-seated doubt.

Because as much as I want this, I don't trust it.

"But you were dead," I manage to say after a moment. "And I tried..." I trail off as my gaze returns to his chest, and it takes a full minute for my brain to comprehend what I'm seeing. Although his shirt remains torn, the exposed torso underneath it is healed, his bronzed skin gleaming in the afternoon sun. There are no marks or scars to be seen. No proof at all that Mammon ever laid a finger on him, let alone ripped his heart from his body.

Speechless, I stare at his chest in a daze. With a grunt, Caleb sits upright, and looping his arms around my back, he pulls me close without a word, hugging me tightly as if I'm the one who just departed this world and not him.

Stunned whispers erupt from the onlookers around us, and above it all, I hear my father's voice saying, "So, it worked? She resurrected him?"

I don't turn to look at him, so I'm not entirely sure who he's asking or if he's merely thinking aloud, as gobsmacked by this turn of events as the rest of us.

"This shouldn't have been possible," Hammurabi says, dropping to his knees and yanking Caleb away from me enough to take him by the shoulders, his dark eyes scanning him up and down for injuries that no longer exist. "Your heart was *outside* of your chest, boy."

I wince at the thought, but Caleb just shrugs, that lazy smile unwavering. "And now it's back *inside* my chest where it belongs. All's well that ends well and all that, Uncle H."

I glance at Hammurabi, tears still streaming down my cheeks, and he looks nearly as bemused as I feel. His eyes shift to mine as he stands, and as he inches back—presumably to give us space—I don't miss the weighted look he shoots at Asmodeus, who watches Caleb with a concerned yet observant expression, her head cocked to the side like the doctors at the hospital used to look at me. One long finger taps her chin.

Caleb inhales a deep breath, pulling the warm air into his lungs as if for the very first time. The sound draws my gaze, and as I watch him, I can't stop one single thought from escaping.

"Are you still you?" I ask, my voice trembling.

"I don't know if when you resurrect someone...they come back right."

The words he spoke in Kandahār after Alexander resurrected his father still haunt me, and although I didn't care when he was lying here dead and the alternative was not having him at all, now I grapple with the very real fear that this isn't really my Caleb but a mere shadow of him. A fabrication that's just saying the things I want to hear because the magic I used to bring him back is forcing him to say them.

But I don't want the lie. Unlike Alexander, who was willing to use resurrection as another means of control, I don't want to pull Caleb's strings. I would rather not have him at all than have a poor imitation of the real thing.

He blinks a few times then runs a hand through his hair, pushing the thick strands back off his forehead as his face melts into an even deeper smile. His gaze isn't void like his father's was after Alexander resurrected him. If anything, it shines with a newfound light, and I don't think I've ever seen him look so happy or content, which only makes the feelings building inside me that much more conflicted. Tears glisten in the corners of his eyes as he lets out a small laugh. "I'm sorry if I'm scaring you, Goldilocks, I'm just processing. But yeah, I'm still me in here, I promise. Plus a little more…thanks to the Creator."

I blink, unable to mask my surprise.

The Creator?

Before I can ask Caleb what he means, large appendages unfurl from his shoulder blades covered in sleek black feathers. They're massive, at least double the span of mine, but there's no mistaking what they are.

"Wings," Lilith gasps, stealing the word right out of my mouth.

It can't really be possible, can it? For all the Lights' preaching about Ascension, no one has actually achieved it before. Besides, Caleb is a Dark. Darks don't Ascend because to Ascend is to be selfless and to love the Creator more than anything or anyone on Earth. Caleb might be able to tick the selfless box but as for the rest of it…

Unless that's not how it works.

My eyes widen. Perhaps Ascension *is* a reward, just not in the way the Lights have always believed. Ascension isn't something you can earn through piety and certainly not through the continued enforcement of the divide. Hell, if the prophecy has made me realize anything, it's that the Creator *wants* us to be united again, and that unification is something Caleb literally gave his life for.

My own wings shudder as I reach out a hand and graze my fingertips through his smooth ebony feathers. Caleb shivers as a sound that's half laugh and half sob escapes me. "You've Ascended. You're—"

"Like you now, yeah." Clearing his throat, he threads his fingers through mine and tugs me forward until our foreheads are touching. "I guess the big guy upstairs felt I deserved a bit more time here on Earth."

"I didn't bring you back. The Creator did." I let out a shaky breath, feeling somewhat foolish for believing I had and at the same time so incredibly relieved I didn't. That the Caleb I see before me is completely, entirely him and not some warped recreation I created in my grief.

Caleb nods. "And He sent me back with a message."

His tone is mirrored in the look in his eye as he pulls away to meet my gaze, both somehow reassuring and unnerving at once.

"What kind of message?" my mother asks, beating me to it.

Using his wings for balance, Caleb stands, dragging me to my feet alongside him. He's only been an angel for all of five minutes, but his movements are incredibly graceful—as if he was born into the world like this. I guess, in a way, he was. Because he wasn't just resurrected. He was reborn.

My knees wobble and I feel light-headed, like I might pass out from shock. Or maybe it's happiness that threatens to plunge me into the depths of oblivion.

As if sensing my need for support, Caleb wraps an arm around my waist, holding me close.

"It was more of an edict," he clarifies, raising his voice loud enough for everyone on the battlefield to hear. "One final command for his children." His gaze strays to my parents as he says this part, and I watch as my father's hands tighten around my mother's shoulders where he now stands behind her, his mouth contorting into a deep frown as he bristles at the word "command." As for my mother, she wrings her own hands nervously in front of her waist, her expression far more dismayed than my father's. Before today, she was the only celestial being the Creator ever tasked with imparting His words, and yet, Caleb stands before us all now with who-knows-what kind of message from the Heavens.

He clears his throat. "The Creator says the fighting ends here. That it's time for a blank slate...for all of us." He turns his head then, sweeping his eyes across the desert, taking in the carnage, the corpses interspersed among the living. There's something strange about his expression—as if he's aware of something the rest of us aren't yet or as if he's not entirely himself. As if, perhaps, the Creator is in there somewhere, looking out through his eyes just for this moment.

Suddenly, the sunlight seems to grow brighter, and as one, all the angels, Fallen, and Nephilim lift their heads, looking up at the sky. Caleb taps my waist, drawing my gaze, and when our eyes meet, he jerks his chin toward the ground—toward the bodies and the blood soaked into the sand, which now illuminate with the same blinding intensity as the sun, glowing a vibrant gold. Startled gasps echo around us like a ripple effect as all evidence of the death that occurred here gradually dissolves into particles of light before floating away, wiping the desert clean.

A clean slate, I realize.

Just like the Creator wanted.

Even Mammon's scattered remains disappear, though the last victim of this war to fade is Alexander. Alaric stumbles forward an uncertain step toward his body as it's engulfed by that warm golden light—as it's lifted high into the sky where it breaks apart into what looks like a cluster of stars before blinking into nonexistence, never to do us harm again. I frown at the Nephilim's stiffening back and the way he raises a hand and then lowers it, as if he's had to forcefully hold himself back. Even now, he's so conflicted in his feelings—torn between his love for the Gray and the ever-present need to put it behind him. I wish I could take those feelings away, to cleanse him of his pain the way the Creator cleansed this battlefield of our blood.

When the last of the glowing light has vanished, everyone turns to look at Caleb, their expressions equally eager and wary, waiting to hear what he has to say next. I look up at him as well, my heart racing with anticipation, every beat sitting too close to the surface, making my entire body vibrate. Sensing my gaze, he glances down at me, gifting me another crooked smile. Whatever I saw in his eyes before is gone now. This person standing beside me is entirely Caleb but with an added weight to his existence that seems to elevate him above us all in this moment. And as he lifts his chin, his voice cuts through the silence not like a knife, but like a bolt cutter through chains, setting us free.

"From now on, the past must stay in the past. Set aside your differences and go live your best lives, however, wherever…and *with* whomever you wish." He grins at my mother as if this last part is intended specifically for her, and who knows, maybe it is. Maybe the Creator was listening that day we met with the Council in India when my father said almost these exact words, and this is His way of honoring that desire. After everything they both sacrificed—Gabriel especially—the Creator owes them that much.

A tentative elation bubbles in my chest, but I can't find the words to express it. My parents gape at Caleb, but neither one of them says anything, either. In fact, everyone in the vicinity—immediate or otherwise—seems just as tongue-tied, each expression as visibly taken aback as the last. Everyone is quiet except for Asmodeus, who chuckles under her breath.

"I'd say a Dark being the first known Nephilim to Ascend would have been message enough, but I think we can all appreciate the clarity these past moments have afforded us. This gives us much to consider, I'd say. Wouldn't you all agree?" She arches an imperious brow at the other Council members, who have found their way toward us and stand dotted in a loose circle around me and Caleb. They all nod in agreement, including Uriel, who stares at Caleb, his dark eyes unblinking.

As if shaken from a daze, he murmurs, "Yes, this certainly changes things. For all of us." His gaze strays to my face, and in the split-second our eyes lock, I know I don't have to worry about the Council locking me away again. His attention then shifts to my parents, and he watches Gabriel and Lucifer for a long, thoughtful moment. "We might have our differences, but the Creator's intentions could not be any clearer. We would be unwise to ignore His wishes for us."

In an oddly unified motion, everyone relaxes their grip on their weapons, dropping their swords and daggers to the dirt—not sheathing them for a later time but discarding them altogether. A promise to end the fighting for good.

"Thank the Creator," Beelzebub says, rolling his neck on his shoulders as he tosses his own blade to the ground. "This whole ordeal was beginning to bore me." Beside him, Abaddon hums his agreement, a satisfied grin playing at the edge of his lips.

"Indeed," Asmodeus trills, bobbing her head. "Though, now the true test of our mettle begins." With a satisfied sigh, she shutters her eyes for a moment before glancing back at Hammurabi. "There is much work to be done. Let us be gone from this place, King."

Hammurabi bows his head then steps toward us again, placing one hand on my shoulder and the other on Caleb's, his face scrunching as if he's searching for the right words to say something sentimental or endearing to sum up everything we've been through together and what we mean to each other.

To my surprise, he ends up saying nothing, instead tugging us both into a tight hug that threatens to squeeze the air from my lungs. I don't expect it—Uncle Hammurabi never struck me as the physically affectionate type—and it soothes me in a way I don't expect, either. My free arm winds around his back, returning his embrace, and in this moment, I know that if my heart could break from happiness, it would.

When we part, he spares us each a fond glance then grunts out, "Boy. Flower," before tailing his mistress, who flashes a smirk at Caleb over her shoulder as they strut away, her emerald eyes beaming with pride.

"I've always said Babel students are extraordinary," she murmurs, and the mischievous twinkle in her gaze tells me she can't wait to go around bragging about how one of her own students was the first Nephilim to Ascend. It certainly seems like the type of thing she would do. And I have zero doubt Hammurabi will boast about it as well. Except his pride comes from a deeper place. Not just as a teacher, but as Caleb's family.

Beelzebub and Abaddon mimic Asmodeus's lead, and one by one, the remaining Council members follow suit, which encourages the angels, Fallen, and Nephilim alike, who all leave this place and their hatred behind. The Lights step through pockets of light, disappearing into the depths of the Blessed Road, while the Darks shuffle off to search for the nearest patch of shadow. Everyone is eager to return to their lives, whatever that may look like moving forward, and within moments, the only ones left on the battlefield aside from me and Caleb are my parents, Lilith, and Alaric.

The latter heaves a trembling breath. "Finally," he murmurs.

Relief paints his face, and though I'm eager to bask in it—to experience such contentment for myself—I can't ignore the niggling unease poking at the back of my mind. It's strange—and almost hard to believe—that Alexander's reign of terror is over and that, by working together to overcome the chaos he wrought on our kind, we've begun the process of demolishing the divide. We might actually be experiencing the first taste of real, lasting peace, and yet, I can't escape the thought of how that peace was hard won. And how, for some, healing from this conflict will take a lot longer than it will for others.

"Will you…" I hesitate, rolling my teeth over my bottom lip. "Will you be okay?" I ask.

Alaric's eyes flutter shut then open again, and he gives a tentative nod. "With time."

He moves toward me then, and I meet him halfway, stepping into the warmth of his arms. "Thank you," I whisper, pressing my face into his shoulder. There are a thousand things I could say to follow these words.

Thank you for finding me.

Thank you for getting me out of that hospital.

Thank you for bringing me into this world where I belong. For being a friend when I had no one else.

Thank you for helping Caleb break me out of the Council's prison. For always choosing to rise above the divide.

Above all, thank you for doing what you knew was right, even though I know it caused you immeasurable pain.

Thank you…for everything.

His swallow is audible, and as he hugs me tighter, he whispers back, "You deserve all the happiness in the world."

A long moment passes before we part, and when I finally pull away, I wipe a tear from my cheek. "What will you do now?"

He shrugs. "Back to work, I imagine. As Asmodeus said, there is much to do now. Though, a brief respite is needed, I think." His gaze strays to my mother, as if seeking her permission, and she nods, offering the Nephilim a small, consoling smile of understanding.

"Seconded," Lilith drawls, flicking at some dried blood on her sleeve. "I would *kill* for a bath right about now." Looking up, she struts toward me, planting herself in the space that's been created in front of me now that I'm no longer hugging Alaric, and takes my chin between her fingers. "You take care of yourself, sweetling. I expect to see you very soon. Don't think you can just abandon Auntie Lilith now that no one is trying to kill you."

Beside me, Caleb snorts and I bite back a grin. "I wouldn't dream of it," I assure her.

Pursing her lips, she glances between us with a haughty brow raised, then blows me a kiss and turns, throwing her arms around my mother.

"Take care of my Gabriel, Lucy," Lilith commands when the two friends break their embrace. Her voice is lilting and friendly enough, though her eyes shoot daggers at my father. "I might have found it in the goodness of my heart to forgive you for taking my wings, but I won't be so benevolent if you hurt my friend."

Lucifer holds up his hands in surrender then drapes one arm around my mother, pulling her close to his side. "Duly noted," he says, and Gabriel's cheeks burn as they share a swift glance. "But I don't think that will be a problem for either of us. Not this time."

A smirk shapes the ex-Archdemon's lips. "Good." She lets out an airy sigh and puts her hands on her hips. "Well, I'm off. I have a date with a bathtub and a bottle of red. Be seeing you, darlings."

I can't help the surprised laugh that escapes me when she walks away, sauntering toward the mountains in the distance. It's crazy to think the terrifying woman I encountered in Kandahār would end up becoming my family. Just goes to show first impressions aren't everything.

I suddenly find myself reminiscing about another first meeting—the day I met Caleb. What would my life look like now if he had let his initial impression of me and his past distrust of Lights keep us apart?

I immediately shove that thought away when I feel the familiar warmth of his hand on mine, meeting his gaze when he takes his place by my side. Because a life without Caleb is a life I don't want. And now that he's immortal, I don't even need to consider it.

A throat clears, and my cheeks flush as I look away, meeting Alaric's gaze. He winks.

"I shall take this as my cue," the Nephilim says with a respectful bow of his head toward my parents. "I'm sure you all have much you wish to say to each other without any spectators present." He looks at me then, and panic twists my insides when it dawns on me he's leaving.

Don't go, I want to say, but those words sit heavy and thick in my throat. I don't want him to leave me, not yet. I only just got him back. But I also know demanding he stay for my own selfish needs would be no different than what Alexander did to him, and he deserves better than that. He deserves a true friend, someone who cares about his feelings more than their own, not a leash.

"I'll still see you…right?" I ask instead, my voice wavering.

"Of course," he answers, his tone a low, calming croon that soothes the jagged edges of my nerves. "With the Roads, no one is ever really as far as we think. And in the meantime, I'm only a phone call away."

A smile as radiant as his aura lights up his face, and then, before I can say another word, he's gone, swallowed by the blinding glow of the Blessed Road.

For a long moment after Alaric departs, Caleb, my parents, and I stand in awkward silence, uncertain what to do or say next—the lone presence in the now eerily quiet desert. I don't think any of us allowed ourselves to really think about what would come after the battle. A sort of self-preservation in case things didn't go our way. I know that, for as much as I wished for the future—for real freedom—I never let myself dream about it in detail. The thought of it was always hazy, as if I was looking at it through clouded glass and all I had to do was step around it to see that future clearly. Even now, I struggle to see it—not because I don't want to, but because there's a lingering fear under my skin that I can't seem to shake telling me this is all too good to be true.

"W-What now?" I stammer, glancing between the three faces staring back at me, hoping one of them will have an answer that will quiet that deep-seated sense of foreboding.

"Well," my father begins, a faint smile tugging at his cheeks. He looks at Caleb and holds out his hand. "I suppose we should officially welcome you to the family. Especially now that you aren't going anywhere anytime soon."

A chisel seems to chip away at some of my residual fear as I peer at Caleb, watching the surprise flit across his face. A grin quickly rises in its place as he eagerly shakes my father's hand. "I hope you don't mind me sticking around for a while."

Gabriel lifts her chin at his words, giving a delicate sniff. "Just don't keep Luna away from us for too long. Remind her she has parents who will miss her if we don't see her often enough."

My brows raise as she risks a glance at me, looking more vulnerable than I've ever seen her—even more so than when she was bleeding out under the Serapeum after Caleb stabbed her. I didn't expect her to let go of me so easily after everything that's happened—to do anything other than smother me with attention and love to make up for lost time...in whatever form that would take coming from someone as emotionally distant as the Archangel.

She offers me a tender smile, and fresh tears prick my eyes as comprehension sinks in. Now that we're safe, she would sacrifice seeing me—not forever since we have all the time in the world, but she would give up the foreseeable future together so I can experience real freedom in a form I choose for myself. It's selfless in a way I didn't know she could be, and more than that, it shows her acceptance of Caleb, even if she won't dare say it aloud.

Steered by emotions I didn't think I was ready to feel, I step forward and wrap my mother in my arms, crushing her to me as that blood song rages between us, escalating into a beautiful sympathy. Gabriel lets out a surprised huff, but then I feel her hands on my back, and I clutch her tighter.

"I love you, Mom." The words slip out unintended, but in this moment, I realize I mean them. I *do* love her, and that love guides me around that clouded glass wall in my head, allowing me a peek at the other side. At the never-ending future awaiting us all.

She doesn't say it back, but she doesn't need to. I can see it in her eyes and in the glistening streaks of moisture decorating her cheeks when she pulls away. I see an eternity of love in those tears.

"Come," my father says after a moment, taking my mother's hand. When she looks up at him, he brushes the tears from her cheeks. "Let's leave the children alone to process, shall we?"

Gabriel beams at him, and with one more glance at me, she nods.

Leaning in, my father kisses me on the top of my head, and then, with my mother's hand in his, they amble away like two people who don't have a single care in the world, their auras a tangle of shadow and golden wisps in the late afternoon light.

As I watch them walk away, Caleb slings his arm around my shoulders. "It's crazy to think back to how all of this started, and now look," he says, jerking his chin toward my parents. "Didn't I tell you we might start a trend?"

He nudges me and I muster a smile, hoping he's right. Hoping beyond all hope that the angels and Fallen will really put aside their differences—not just long enough to face a common enemy, but for good.

"By the way," Caleb says, his airy tone a balm to my inescapable worries, "I'm starting to think your mom might actually like me."

I narrow my eyes, feigning deep thought, and then shrug. "Maybe. She at least seems to have moved past wanting to murder you."

A thoughtful expression crosses his face. "While it's definitely an improvement, we should probably make sure her sword is out of reach during family dinners. Just in case." He winks at me, and though I know he's joking—that my mother's sword lies abandoned in the sand just like the other weapons from the Fall, a gesture of peace and promise to end the fighting between us—his comment raises a curious question.

"Speaking of…what do you think will happen to them?" I ask, trailing my gaze across the barren desert, the ground spotted with blades of all shapes and sizes like a patterned blanket beneath the sun.

"I don't know," Caleb admits. "But I imagine the Creator has a plan for them."

"Just like He does for everything else," I say softly.

The Creator set this war into motion by delivering the prophecy to my mother. And in doing so, he brought me and Caleb together. But despite Caleb swearing he doesn't care about free will when it comes to loving me, I can't silence the voice of doubt in the back of my head. It grows stronger in the presence of that gnawing fear.

"Hey, what is it?" Caleb cups my face in his hands, brushing his thumb across my lower lip. It trembles beneath his touch.

"Is this what you want?" I manage past the threat of fresh tears, that terror inside me like a hand choking me.

Caleb's brow furrows and he pulls back a little. "What do you mean?"

I shake my head. "You…like *this*…" I wave one hand, gesturing to the still staggering sight of his wings. "We never talked about you being immortal because neither of us thought it was a possibility." I hesitate, hating how self-conscious I sound. I don't want to doubt this, but the part of me that's so used to disappointment can't help it. "I know what you said back in India about taking whatever time with me you could get, but now you have all the time in the world, and it wasn't exactly your choice, and I just—"

"You're wrong."

His tone is firm, his mouth set in a serious line. I balk under the intensity of his gaze, his molten eyes piercing, as if they can see every thought and feeling writhing inside me.

I blink, unable to mask my surprise. "What?"

He readjusts his grip on my face, pulling me closer. "About this not being my choice," he says, his breath hot on my cheeks. His brow creases as he licks his lips, and for a moment, it looks as if he might cry. "When I had my 'come into the light' moment, all I wanted was to be back here with you. To *never* leave you. And the Creator gave me exactly what I wished for." With a breathy laugh, he leans forward, once again touching his forehead to mine. "Honestly, Goldilocks, I wouldn't have cared how He brought me back. Shit, he could've brought me back as a human. A few decades, several thousands years, an eternity, I'd take any of them so long as I get to spend them with you."

The last of my fear withers and dies at these words, that terrible voice of doubt silenced as a happiness unlike anything I ever dared let myself believe I could have fills me up until I am bursting to the seams with it. It makes me feel weightless, and suddenly, I'm not just looking around that clouded glass wall but over it. And up here, I can see everything. The future, beautiful and vast before us.

Flinging my arms around Caleb's neck, I bury my face in the space where his chin meets his shoulder. He hugs me back, his wings folding around mine, and we stay like this for what feels like an eternity until he's touching my face again, pulling me away enough to kiss me.

A shiver tears through me and I sigh. I might be an angel, but I don't need Heaven.

Not when I have this.

"I love you. More than anything," I breathe against his lips, repeating the exact words he said to me the first time we made love.

Smirking, Caleb tilts his head back to appraise me. "Good. Because I meant what I said to your parents. I fully intend on sticking around for a while." He scrunches his face in consideration then adds, "How does forever sound?"

A soft laugh escapes me, and for the first time in my life, I feel truly happy—unburdened by fear or dread of what might come after this blissful moment.

Now, for the first time, I truly feel free.

Smiling, I rise onto my toes and press another kiss to his lips.

"Forever sounds perfect."

EPILOGUE

A LARIC STANDS AT THE base of the Sacré-Coeur in Montmartre. The interior of the church isn't all that impressive, but that's not why tourists flock here in droves. It's not even its majestic white domes reaching for the heavens, offering a testament of faith. As stunning as this architectural display is, it doesn't compare to the panoramic view of Paris seen from the church's steps. The wonders of the city to be discovered on both sides of the river greet him, painted with a bold brush of color and curving lines. That special blend of art and culture and food found only in Paris.

His eyes rove over the narrow, winding streets below him paved with cobblestones, crowded with shops, patisseries, restaurants, and cafes. Alaric can still taste the bold espresso he had minutes earlier at a tiny cafe bar, the scruffy interior still charming with its classic chairs and tables and vintage rock posters. The heavy scent of good butter and dark chocolate caresses his nose, and he yearns for a pain au chocolat. Yes, he's in Paris on business, but one can't visit the city without indulging in its pleasures as well.

Alaric pauses in his casual perusal, breath trapped in his chest as he spots a familiar golden head. Luna. She leans over a tiny cafe table, a sable-haired handsome young man beside her, his body bent to meet hers. Caleb. The two are scarcely apart, and where one is, the other will surely be. Their fingers are braided together, their foreheads almost touching. A spark of pure joy shoots through Alaric as he observes their utter happiness. The intimacy and freedom they're enjoying just being two young people reveling in that special magic Montmartre brings to the world.

A shadow dims his elation as images of the final battle assail him. Even though a year has passed, as much as Alaric would wish it, he can't banish the vivid image of him slipping the sword into Alexander's heart. The stunned expression on the angel's face. The betrayal. He can't banish his love for the Conqueror, either, only that love is now wrapped in nostalgia. Of his dreams for what could have been had there not been the divide. Had Alexander not been obsessed with power. When he was younger, he clung to the naive hope that one day he and Alexander would be like Luna and Caleb. Free of cares and in love. He mourns the loss of that dream, lets the last embers flicker and die until nothing but ashes remain.

His dream never came to fruition, but Luna—the daughter of his heart—is building her dreams on those ashes, like a phoenix reborn. When Caleb Ascended and received his wings—his immortality—the divide was well and truly destroyed. Or maybe mended is the right word. The fact that the Creator gifted Caleb, a Dark, with angelic status finally proved once and for all that the hurts and betrayals Darks and Lights harbored for each other could be placed firmly in the past. The Creator no longer holds onto his grudge from the Fall. There is no room now for grudges and petty grievances. There is no more Light and Dark, just Nephilim. Just angels. Just a beautiful girl and boy loving one another so deeply they defied death to be together.

Some angels have even descended from Heaven to help integrate the academies. Free from their rigid allegiance, they can walk among mortals and take pleasure within this world if they so choose. A soft smile curves Alaric's lips. Peace is a wondrous thing.

Gazing at Luna, he slides his phone from his pocket, his thumbs swiftly typing out a message.

**How are you enjoying Paris? Is it everything
you hoped it would be? -A**

He watches as Luna's head jerks away from Caleb, and she reaches into her jacket pocket, bringing out her phone. He sees her delighted grin, and his heart swells with love. She shows Caleb the message and he smiles. Alaric loves the boy, too. He treats Luna like the treasure that she is, and one can't help but like Caleb and his roguish charm.

His phone pings and he looks down at the screen.

**It's better than I imagined and everything you said it would be. I'm
in awe. I can't stop eating! I never want to leave. Where are you?**

Alaric considers that for a moment. He wants to see Luna, but he doesn't want to interrupt this moment she's having with Caleb. He wants to give them a little time just to breathe. They earned it.

Out scouting for Nephilim children with Hammurabi. Despite being a rather terrifying presence, children adore him. -A

He watches Luna and Caleb exchange words and grin, then his phone pings again.

Caleb wants to know how Hammurabi is doing. Actually, what he really said is, "How's that old dinosaur? Still a grumpy asshole?"

Alaric chokes back a laugh. Caleb has such a way with words.

Hammurabi took Alaric by surprise when he decided to leave Babel to help him find and shepherd Nephilim children. Alaric knows just how attached Hammurabi is to Babel. And its mistress. Though the Babylonian king would never admit to his feelings for Asmodeus, even under the threat of death.

He's well. He's actually shopping, believe it or not. -A

LOL. Caleb says he's not that surprised.
He uses shopping as a way to pick up women.

Alaric's brow raises at that because he knows Hammurabi is buying Asmodeus a gift. Apparently, the ex-Archdemon loves ridiculous tourist trinkets. He can't imagine a creature as terrifying as Asmodeus being amused by human knick-knacks. That knowledge somehow humanizes her.

Hammurabi materializes next to him then, a delicate cotton-candy pink paper bag clenched in his large first. Alaric suppresses a grin at the image.

"Did you find something worthy of her?" he teases the stoic king, unable to resist a bit of ribbing.

"Nothing is ever worthy of her, but I found something that will amuse her." Hammurabi scowls, growling, "I should have never revealed her indulgence to you."

"It makes me admire her more," Alaric says, earning a genuine smile from the other Nephilim.

"How are the children?" he asks, nodding toward Alaric's phone where Luna's name glows. "Freedom has made the little flower bloom."

"They send their regards," Alaric says, warmed by the affection in the king's voice. He watches Luna take a sip from her coffee cup, her eyes clinging to Caleb's face as he speaks to her. Yes, freedom has indeed made her blossom into the strong, capable woman he always knew she was meant to be. Freedom and love.

Hammurabi releases a skeptical snort. "I doubt the boy was that restrained. He's become even worse since gaining his wings. There will be no living with him now."

Alaric grins, not fooled by Hammurabi's gruff words. He knows just how much the Babylonian king loves Caleb, knows how relieved he was when Caleb cheated death and Ascended. And Alaric knows, that like him, Hammurabi is especially proud of the example Caleb sets for others in overcoming all boundaries between Darks and Lights, going so far as to embrace the younger brother who fought against him. The last Alaric heard, Caleb even introduced the boy to his mother.

Alaric's phone chimes and he glances at it.

Will I see you soon? I miss you.

Tenderness envelops him at Luna's words. His thumbs quickly move over the keyboard.

Sooner than you think. -A

He slips the phone back into his pocket and focuses on Hammurabi. "Shall we go meet the child we've come to find?"

Hammurabi nods, still clenching his ridiculously frilly bag. "Yes, it's time."

As they turn to walk away, Alaric gazes over his shoulder. Luna and Caleb share a kiss in the warm Parisian sun, their beauty so stunning his breath catches—not just their physical beauty, but the beauty of their love. A love that was strong enough to heal an ancient divide and give the world hope. A love that gave him a world he's grateful to be alive in.

He blinks back tears as he faces forward again and follows Hammurabi. Now, endless possibilities await him—and all their kind—as they step into this new world together, released from the shackles of their past. Truly…finally…free.

THE END

ABOUT THE AUTHORS

M. A. PHIPPS and **REBECCA JAYCOX** met while working together at a small publishing house in the United Kingdom as a cover designer and editor respectively. Having forged a strong friendship, and sharing similar interests, they decided to co-author.

THE ORIGIN PROPHECY is their first series together, but it will not be their last.

Find them online at:
WWW.BOOKISHDEN.COM
IG & TikTok: @the.bookish.den
Facebook: @thebookishden